Praise for Sharon Kay Penman and *Falls the Shadow*

"Penman brilliantly evokes the medieval world. . . . As usual, she illuminates the events of individual lives as well as the political and cultural forces that characterized this tumultuous era, in a thoroughly engrossing book." —*Publishers Weekly*

"*Falls the Shadow* has that rare ability to simultaneously entertain and instruct. . . . While most history books only scratch the surface of this time period, Ms. Penman does justice with her vivid and realistic novel." —*Richmond Times-Dispatch*

"A wonderfully constructed story . . . sure to please fans of Penman and those unfamiliar with her work . . . as fine a love story as any set in modern times." —*Denver Post*

"Penman is a superb storyteller. . . . One of the many pleasures of Penman's novel is that while she shows how different and difficult life was then, it is still, in its fundamentals, recognizable to us today. . . . Good historical novels—and good histories, too—do not isolate the past. They give warning or cheer to the present. In this mission, Penman has succeeded admirably." —*The Miami Herald*

"Penman . . . takes real people and real events, and she creates a book that is as compelling as a bestseller. . . . You many judge for yourself her consummate skill in storytelling and her ability to re-create an era in a way that makes the thirteenth century seem as immediate as the twentieth century." —*The Knoxville News Sentinel*

"Like a splendid medieval tapestry, rich with intertwining threads in brilliant colors, Sharon Kay Penman's latest book, *Falls the Shadow*, brings the world of thirteenth-century England and Wales alive to the modern reader." —*Press-Telegram* (Long Beach)

"Few can match and none can surpass Sharon Kay Penman when it comes to writing great historical fiction. . . . Readers can almost see, feel, taste, and smell the people and places in this turbulent tale." —*Pasadena Star-News*

FALLS THE SHADOW

SHARON KAY PENMAN

 St. Martin's Griffin ☷ New York

To Marian Wood

FALLS THE SHADOW. Copyright © 1988 by Sharon Kay Penman. All rights reserved. Printed in the United States of America. For information, address St. Martin's Press, 175 Fifth Avenue, New York, N.Y. 10010.

www.stmartins.com

Maps by Anita Karl and James Kemp

Library of Congress Cataloging-in-Publication Data

Penman, Sharon Kay.
    Falls the shadow / Sharon Kay Penman.—1st St. Martin's Griffin ed.
      p. cm.
    ISBN-13: 978-0-312-38246-9
    ISBN-10: 0-312-38246-4
    1. Great Britain—History—Henry III, 1216–1272—Fiction. I. Title.

PS3566.E474 F35 2008
813'.54—dc22

2008023607

First published in the United States by arrangement with Henry Holt and Company, Inc., by Ballantine Books, a division of The Random House Publishing Group

10 9 8 7 6 5 4

Between the idea
And the reality
Between the motion
And the act
Falls the Shadow

T. S. Eliot, "The Hollow Men"

Royal House of ENGLAND
(as of 1237)

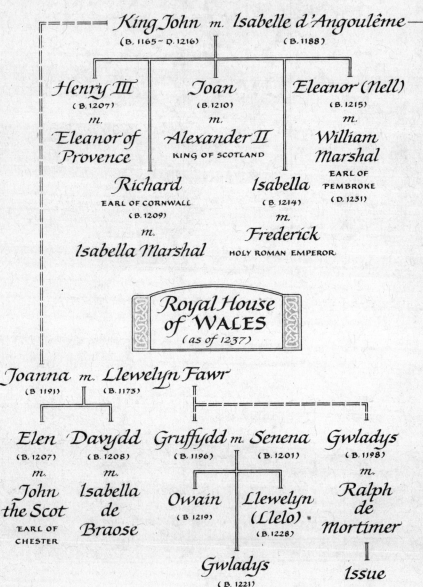

King John m. **Isabelle d'Angoulême**
(B. 1165 – D. 1216)   (B. 1188)

Henry III
(B. 1207)
m.
Eleanor of Provence

Joan
(B. 1210)
m.
Alexander II
KING OF SCOTLAND

Eleanor (Nell)
(B. 1215)
m.
William Marshal
EARL OF PEMBROKE
(D. 1231)

Richard
EARL OF CORNWALL
(B. 1209)
m.
Isabella Marshal

Isabella
(B. 1214)
m.
Frederick
HOLY ROMAN EMPEROR

Royal House of WALES
(as of 1237)

Joanna m. **Llewelyn Fawr**
(B. 1191)   (B. 1173)

Elen
(B. 1207)
m.
John the Scot
EARL OF CHESTER

Davydd
(B. 1208)
m.
Isabella de Braose

Gruffydd m. **Senena**
(B. 1196)   (B. 1201)

Gwladys
(B. 1198)
m.
Ralph de Mortimer

Owain
(B. 1219)

Llewelyn (Llelo)
(B. 1228)

Gwladys
(B. 1221)

Issue

House of LUSIGNAN
(as of 1237)

— m. 1220 **Hugh de Lusignan**
COUNT OF LA MARCHE

Hugh — Geoffrey — Aymer — Alice — Agatha

Guy — William — Isabella — Margaret

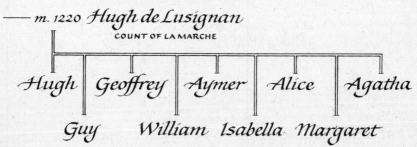

House of MONTFORT
(as of 1237)

Robert
EARL OF LEICESTER

Robert — Amicia m. **Simon de Montfort** — Margaret
m.
Saer de Quincy
EARL OF WINCHESTER

Simon de Montfort m. **Alice de Montmorency** — Bertrade m. **Hugh**
(D. 1218) — (D. 1221) — EARL OF CHESTER

Amaury — Robert — Simon — Ranulf
(B. 1208) — EARL OF CHESTER (D. 1232)

Guy — Amicia

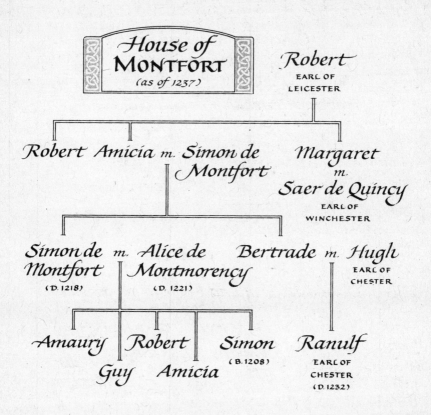

════ denotes illegitimacy

© 1988 A. Karl/J. Kemp

Prologue

Castle of St Jacques-de-Beuvron, Brittany

February 1231

They crossed the border into Brittany at noon, soon afterward found themselves in an eerily silent landscape, shrouded in dense, spectral fog. Simon showed neither unease nor surprise, merely commented that they must be nearing the sea. But his squire was not so sanguine. Geoffrey fumbled within his mantle, seeking his crucifix. Bretagne, he whispered, as if the ancient name of this ominous realm might prove a talisman, protecting him and his young lord. It was a land steeped in dark legend, a land in which the people spun firelit tales of Merlin and the Celtic King, Arthur, a land with its own myths, its own arcane tongue, not a land to welcome strangers—Bretagne.

Geoffrey did not fear Breton bandits, for he'd never seen a better swordsman than Simon. But he wondered how they'd fare against shadows, against the demon spirits that were said to haunt these dark, foreboding forests. Once he broached the subject; Simon only laughed. Geoffrey was very much in awe of his lord, but understanding so far eluded him. How was it that Simon seemed so blessedly free of the fears that plagued other men? How could he believe this mad quest of his might succeed?

So thick and enveloping was the fog that they were upon the castle before they realized it. They drew rein while Simon studied the fortress, almost as if he were planning an assault. And indeed, Geoffrey thought, he was! It was a formidable edifice of Caen stone, erected by the most ruthless of Normandy's dukes, William the Bastard, who—against all odds—had won the crown of the island kingdom of England. Geoffrey wondered if Simon was thinking of that now, if he was daunted by the odds he himself faced. But Simon's face revealed nothing. Urging his stallion forward, he emerged from the swirling, smoke-colored mist, his sudden, sorcerer-like appearance before the gatehouse drawing an immediate challenge from the startled guards.

Simon raised a hand. "I am Sir Simon de Montfort," he said, "of

Montfort l'Amaury in France. I am here to see my cousin, the Earl of Chester."

THE chamber was as dimly lit as if it were dusk, for all the windows were shuttered against the fog, the damp, chill air. A sputtering oil lamp at Simon's elbow cast flickering shadows, occasionally flared up to illuminate the face of the man across the table. As brown and sun-weathered as any crusader's, it was a face that attested to every one of his sixty years, attested to a lifetime spent in the saddle, on distant battlefields in the service of his King. He shared with Simon the dark coloring of their kindred, but his hair was scanty, well-silvered, and the narrow black eyes were oblique and wary, utterly lacking Simon's hope, his eager zeal. They were first cousins, but strangers, and some of Simon's confidence began to falter; his dream seemed suddenly as elusive as the Holy Grail, as fanciful as tales told of unicorns and winged griffins. Why would Chester ever agree?

"You're your father's son for true," Chester said at last. "Do you remember him?"

Simon shook his head. "My memories are blurred. I was only ten when he was slain." Chester had provided mulled wine, and Simon started to drink, then stopped. Why delay? Better to plunge ahead, to gamble all on one quick throw of the dice. "I am here, my lord, to talk to you of the English earldom that was once my father's."

If Chester was surprised, he didn't show it. But then, Simon suspected, it had been many years since Chester had allowed an unruly emotion to break free. "The earldom of Leicester," he said, and in his voice, too, there was nothing.

"It was my lord father's by right, unjustly taken from him by King John of evil fame, and then bestowed upon you, our kinsman. I have come to St Jacques-de-Beuvron to ask you to restore the earldom to me."

Chester leaned back in his chair. "Now why," he said, "would I want to do that?"

"Because you need it not, my lord, because you hold far more lucrative earldoms, those of Chester and Lincoln, whilst your nephew and heir, John the Scot, also holds the earldom of Huntingdon in his own right. Because you are said to be a man of honor and my claim is a just one. Because the greatest attributes of knighthood are prowess on the battlefield and generosity." Simon paused for breath, then grinned. "And to give away an earldom would be an act of the most extraordinary generosity imaginable—or else an act of utter madness. In either case, my lord, you'd pass into legend for certes!"

Chester's mouth twitched; he gave an abrupt cough of a laugh.

"Most men would vote for madness," he said dryly, and then, "How old are you, lad?"

"Twenty and two." Simon had rehearsed his plea until it was memory-perfect, but now instinct kept him silent. He watched the older man intently, sought in vain to read the expression in those slanting dark eyes. "The earldom means little to you, my lord," he said softly. "To me, it would be a rebirth."

Chester nodded. "It is no easy thing," he said, "to be a younger son. And you were the youngest of four, if my memory serves. There'd be little left for you, I expect." Another thin smile, another hoarse laugh. "But if you lack for lands, by God you do not lack for gall!"

Simon took heart; laughter was in itself a bond. But at that moment a servant entered the chamber, leaning over to whisper a message in the Earl's ear. Chester pushed back his chair. "A royal courier has just arrived from England. You must wait upon the King, Cousin, as must we all. I'll send a servant to tend to your needs."

Soon the table was laden with food, kept warm by silver chafing dishes. But Simon could not eat a morsel, so keen was his disappointment. He'd besieged enough castles, fought in enough battle skirmishes to know the strategic importance of momentum. Now that his initial foray had been checked, how likely was it that he could rally his forces, regain this lost ground?

"Love, I have the most wondrous news—Oh!" The girl was already in the room before she realized she had the wrong man. She came to an abrupt halt, staring at Simon.

She was very young; Simon judged her age to be fifteen, sixteen at most. She had the vibrant prettiness of extreme youth, but there was a hint in her bone structure of more, of the possibilities that maturity would bring. Although her hair was hidden by veil and wimple, she had the fair skin, the blue eyes that their society so prized, and a gown of soft sapphire wool revealed to Simon both that she was well-born and that she had her full share of womanly curves.

"I'm sorry," she said. "I thought my lord husband would be here." But she made no move to depart, appraising Simon no less unabashedly than he was studying her.

Moving to the table, he poured a second cup of wine, held it out toward her. "Good news," he said, "is meant to be shared, even with strangers."

She had the longest lashes he'd ever seen; they fluttered like fans, cast deceptively demure shadows upon those elegantly hollowed cheekbones. And then she smiled, displaying a sudden dimple. "Why not?" she said, and reached for the wine cup.

"This letter is from my sister Joanna. Well, my half-sister, actually, although no less dear to me for that. Joanna is wife to a Welsh Prince, Llewelyn of Gwynedd, and for the past year, they have been estranged. All thought the marriage was doomed, and I grieved for Joanna, for she loves her husband well. But there was naught to be done. Yet now . . . she writes that she and Llewelyn have reconciled, that he has . . . that she is back at his court, in full favor! Is that not miraculous?"

"Indeed," Simon agreed politely. He suspected there was much more to this story than she was willing to reveal. Those telling pauses of hers hinted at scandal; so did that incautious phrase, "in full favor." An elusive memory flitted just beyond the boundaries of recall, half-forgotten gossip of a Welsh lord and an unfaithful wife, a lover caught in her bed, a sin shocking enough to reach even the French court. Could this lass's sister and that adulterous wife be one and the same? No, not likely; what man could forgive a betrayal so great?

He shifted in his seat, and as the light fell upon his face, she exclaimed, "Why, your eyes are grey! Your hair is so dark that I assumed your eyes would be dark, too." A blatant bit of flirting, yet so obviously innocent that Simon was touched when she then blushed. It occurred to him now that, as youths must be schooled in the use of arms, so must pretty girls learn to wield their weapons, too; this one, he'd wager, was just becoming aware of the formidable arsenal at her disposal.

Picking up his wine cup, he clinked it playfully to hers. "Let's drink then," he suggested, "to your sister's miracle. A pity they are in such short supply, for I could use one myself."

"Ah," she said, quick to comprehend, "so you seek a boon from the Earl of Chester? I think you'll find him to be generous. Lords are expected, after all, to be open-handed. Within limits, of course; I'd not suggest you ask him for his favorite roan destrier!"

Simon joined in her laughter. "No," he said, "I'd never ask a man for his best horse. I ask only for an earldom."

Her eyes widened. "You are jesting . . . are you not?"

He shook his head, and then, caught by the wonderment in those rapt blue eyes, he heard himself say, "My claim is a just one. My name is Simon de Montfort. My lord father was Count of Montfort and Evreux, Viscount of Beziers and Carcassonne." But he got no further. If up until now the girl's interest was sparked by his smile, he'd just fully engaged her curiosity.

"I've heard of your father," she cried. "Who in Christendom has not? He led a crusade against the French heretics in Languedoc, and won great renown for his daring, although men did say he was utterly without mercy—" Too late, she clasped her hand to her mouth. "I'm sorry, in truth! When will I ever learn to bridle my tongue?"

Had that comment come from a man, Simon would have taken

quick offense. With her, though, he was prepared to be more tolerant, and he was amused rather than irked by her injudicious candor, mollified by her contrition. "My father's mother was heiress to the earldom of Leicester," he explained, "and the title passed to him in turn, but then it was seized by your English King, John, and eventually given over to my cousin of Chester. I have just asked him to restore it to me."

"Indeed, you do need a miracle. The young knight come to seek his fortune—what a marvelous tale your quest would make, just like Sir Lancelot's arrival at Camelot!"

Simon was heartened by her enthusiasm. "But how does my quest end? Even if I get my miracle and the Earl agrees, I must then convince the English King, and that—"

"—will be right easy," she assured him. "Henry is truly kind-hearted, too kind-hearted for a king, I sometimes fear. I think he'd willingly grant your petition, and I will certainly speak to him on your behalf."

Simon brought up his cup to hide a smile. "Few, indeed, have the ear of the King. May I know your secret?"

As much as she enjoyed teasing others, she'd been little teased herself; her husband was fondly indulgent, gravely tender, and always protective, but the one virtue he lacked was humor. For a moment, she studied Simon, while deciding if her pride demanded that she resent his banter. And then that beguiling dimple flashed again.

"My secret?" she murmured. "Well, it might be that the King thinks so highly of my husband. Or Henry's aforementioned kind heart. It could even be because I am Henry's favorite sister."

Much to her delight, she more than got her own back; Simon almost choked on his wine. "You are the English King's sister?"

"I am the Lady Eleanor, Countess of Pembroke," she said serenely, holding out her hand for him to kiss. He brought it to his lips, but as soon as their eyes met, they burst out laughing, rollicking, spontaneous laughter that continued even after they'd forgotten the reason for their merriment. And it was at just that unpropitious moment that her husband strolled into the solar.

"Nell? You were looking for me?"

Simon tensed, for he knew many a man might have bristled at the sight meeting Pembroke's eyes, might have misread the innocent intimacy of their laughter. But Nell was utterly unconcerned by her husband's sudden appearance, rising to greet him with an eager smile.

Pembroke acknowledged her introductions with the aloof benevolence, the disinterested courtesy due an unknown, impoverished knight. Although he was much older than Nell, he'd not yet reached that age when his young wife's beauty might no longer be cause for pride, but rather for unquiet dreams, fevered suspicions, and when she confided the story of the de Montfort lost earldom, he politely concealed his skepticism, wished Simon well.

Now that Pembroke was here, Nell was impatient to share with him the news of her sister's deliverance, and Simon soon found himself alone in the solar. His pride had been rankled by Pembroke's condescension, and the waiting seemed suddenly intolerable. Crossing to a window, he fumbled with the shutter. The fog still held the castle in a state of siege, blotting out all traces of the sun; the air was cold, carried the scent of the sea. He stood there until he'd begun to shiver, not turning away until he heard the door opening.

"You did not eat?" Chester strode toward the table, seated himself, and gestured for Simon to pour them wine. "Your brother Amaury is the firstborn," he said briskly, as if their conversation had never been interrupted. "As I recall, there were two other brothers, now dead. Which leaves you and Amaury, Amaury with your father's titles, his estates, and you with . . . what? Assuming for the sake of argument, that I would entertain this mad proposal of yours, what of Amaury? Should I relinquish the earldom of Leicester, would it not then pass by rights to him?"

"No, my lord." Simon leaned across the table. "My brother has agreed to renounce all claims to the English earldom."

For the first time, he saw surprise flicker in Chester's eyes. "And how," he asked, "did you ever manage that, lad?"

"Amaury is Constable of France, sworn liegeman of the French King. He well knows that the King of England would never permit an English earldom to pass to a French Count. So my chances, however meagre, are still better than his." After a moment, Simon grinned. "And in all honesty, I do not think he expects me to succeed. It is always easier to make a generous gesture when it is likely to remain just that—a gesture."

Chester's brows had drawn together, yet there was an amused quirk to his mouth; Simon did not know which signal to heed. "Tell me, Simon, have you not considered that Amaury might have regrets? Should you gain your earldom, what is to keep him from renouncing his renunciation, from laying claim to it himself?"

Simon's smile vanished. "My brother would never forswear his oath," he said coldly. "No man of honor would."

This time Chester's black brows shot upward. "I doubt that you'd have prospered at King John's court," he said sardonically. And then, "But it remains to be seen how you'll fare at Henry's."

Simon set his wine cup down, very carefully. "My lord?"

"You know, of course, that there is no logical reason under Heaven why a man would willingly yield up an earldom. Men will conclude that you must have ensorcelled me somehow, beguiled me with the Black Arts. Either that or I'm in my dotage."

Simon's breath stopped. "You mean to do it," he said in wonderment. "You mean to recognize my claim!"

Chester nodded. "But do not ask me why, lad, for I'm damned if I know!"

He'd never seen any man's eyes take the light like Simon's. He'd never seen such joy, and for just a moment he allowed himself to share in it, to revel in his young kinsman's jubilation.

"I will never forget this, my lord, never. It is a debt of honor I shall be proud to owe, although I know it is one I can never repay."

"Speaking of debts . . ." It was a relief to Chester to recognize the habitual tones of irony, to hear echoes of the mordant wit that for so long had served as his shield. Back on familiar ground, he said, "Between my momentary madness and Henry's good will, we might make you an Earl, Simon, but a rich man you'll not be. The Leicester lands are heavily mortgaged, the woods despoiled . . ."

"But they'll be mine," Simon pointed out, and Chester abandoned the attempt to anchor Simon's dream in reality, accepted the younger man's euphoric expressions of gratitude, and secretly marveled at what he'd done.

He was still in the solar, sitting alone at the table, when Pembroke entered.

"I just encountered de Montfort," he said. "The last time I saw a man looking so elated, he'd been reprieved on the very steps of the gallows. Jesú, Ranulf, you did not agree, did you?"

Chester nodded, and Pembroke could not suppress a startled oath. "Sweet bleeding Christ, man, why?"

"The truth, Will? I'm not sure. Mayhap because I remember what it is like to be afire with ambition, with the sort of hunger that burns clean through to the bone. Mayhap to liven up Henry's court. I suspect that my cousin Simon is not one to pass unnoticed; I'll wager he hits England like one of those Saracen windstorms!"

He grinned; Pembroke did not. He looked so perplexed that Chester sighed, then shrugged. "All I did, Will, was to give the lad a chance. But it will be right interesting to see what he makes of it."

1

Nefyn, North Wales

December 1236

Just before midnight on the eve of Christmas, the storm swept in off the Irish Sea, struck the little hamlet that had grown up around the manor house of Gruffydd ap Llewelyn, Lord of the cantref of Llŷn. The village herring boats were battered and broken by the surging tide, thatched roofs were ripped away, and lightning blazed across the dark December sky, setting afire a venerable oak in the priory garth, an oak that had survived two hundred winters, Norse raids, searing summer droughts, and the invasion of the Norman-French adventurers who'd followed William the Bastard to England in God's year 1066. With the coming of light, the Welsh villagers would look upon the blackened, splintered tree and mourn its loss. Now they huddled for shelter in shuddering cottages, fretted for their livestock, and prayed for Christ's mercy.

As thunder echoed overhead, Llelo jerked upright on his pallet. Slowly his eyes adjusted to the darkness; the foreboding shadows took on familiar forms. His dream had been of his grandfather's court, where he'd lived for most of his eight years, where he'd been happy. It took him a moment to remember that this was Nefyn, his father's manor.

A section of the great hall had been screened off for their sleeping quarters, but he was alone; his brother Owain's pallet was empty. The storm was seeking entry at every shutter. Llelo was not a timid child, accepted nature's fury as unthinkingly as he did its softer favors. But the violence of this Christmas tempest was too awesome to be ignored. He pulled his blanket up to his chin, sought refuge in sleep. Too late. He was wide awake now, unable to shut out the eerie keening of the wind, the relentless pelting of the rain.

So uneasy had Llelo become that he even found himself wishing for Owain's return, and he usually looked upon Owain's company as a penance, for there lay between the brothers the formidable gap of nine discordant years. Finally he reached for his tunic, hunted in the floor rushes for his shoes. There was sure to be leftover food somewhere in the kitchen, and even if he awakened the cooks, they'd turn a blind eye, for he was Lord Gruffydd's son, grandson to their Prince, the man known to enemies and allies alike as Llewelyn Fawr—Llewelyn the Great.

But as he made ready to slip around the screen into the hall, a meagre glow caught his attention. In the center of the hearth, flames fed upon dried peat. Smoke spiraled upward; no matter how much whitewash was lathered upon the walls, they still showed the smudged proof of past fires. It was not the flickering firelight that brought Llelo to an abupt halt; it was the oil lamp that illuminated the dais, the intent faces of his mother and brother.

Llelo shrank back, for to make his presence known would be to invite two sharp scoldings. Balked but by no means deterred, he pondered strategy, and then remembered that wine and bread were always set out in his father's bedchamber for night hungers. And the stairwell lay to his left, hidden from his mother's view by the shielding screen.

The door to Gruffydd's bedchamber was ajar. It creaked as Llelo pushed it inward, and an imposing shape loomed before him, barring the way. Unfazed by the growl, he whispered, "Gwlach, down," and the wolfhound quieted. Fire still smoldered in the hearth, and by its light, Llelo was able to reach the table, keeping a wary eye upon the bed all the while. He had torn off a large chunk of bread, was turning toward the door when his father cried out.

Llelo spun about, and the bread fell to the floor, to be pounced upon by the wolfhound. His heart pounding, the boy braced himself for the reprimand. But none came. His father lay back against the pillow; his words were slurred, unintelligible. Llelo let his breath out slowly. His relief was considerable, for he dreaded his father's disapproval, never more so than when he seemed most bound and determined to provoke it.

He'd begun to sidle toward the door when his father cried out again, gave a low moan. Llelo froze, until another moan drew him reluctantly to the bed. His father was twisting from side to side, as if seeking escape. Llelo was close enough now to see the sweat streaking his face and throat; one hand was entangled in the sheets, clutching at . . . at what? Llelo did not know. Unable to move, he stared, mesmerized, at the man on the bed. A troubled sleeper must not be abruptly awakened. But he knew, too, that demons came in the night to claim the unwary, to steal away men's souls, and he shivered. His father turned his head into the pillow, groaned. Llelo could bear no more. He leaned forward. "Papa?" he said softly, and touched Gruffydd's shoulder.

Gruffydd gasped, lashed out wildly. His outstretched arm caught Llelo across the chest, sent the boy reeling. Flung backward, he crashed into the table; the trestle boards buckled, plates and flagon and food thudding to the floor. The dog scrambled for safety, began to bark, and Gruffydd's favorite falcon snapped its tether, soared off its perch and swooped about the chamber with the wolfhound now in frenzied pursuit. Gruffydd sat up abruptly, blinking in dazed dismay at the chaotic scene that met his eyes. He swore, snarled a command that dropped the dog down in a submissive crouch. The falcon circled and then alighted upon the bed canopy. Gruffydd rubbed his eyes, swore again. And only then did he see his son sprawled amidst the wreckage upon the floor.

"Llelo? What are you doing here? What—" He broke off, seeing the blood trickling down the boy's chin. "How did you hurt yourself? Did I . . . did I hit you, Llelo?"

Llelo shook his head, got unsteadily to his feet. "No, Papa." He swallowed. "You cried out in your sleep and I . . . I sought to wake you. When I fell, I bit my lip."

For a long moment, they regarded each other in silence. They were very unlike. Gruffydd's hair was almost as red as the hearth flames, his eyes a clear cat-green, while Llelo's coloring was dark. He had begun to assess the damage done, and now turned wide brown eyes upon Gruffydd's face, eyes that showed sudden alarm. How could he have caused so much havoc with such good intentions?

"Come here, lad," Gruffydd said, and Llelo swallowed again, wiped his mouth on the sleeve of his tunic, then sat cautiously on the edge of the bed. To Gruffydd, he seemed like a wild bird poised for flight; he flinched as Gruffydd touched his arm.

"Well, I'll grant you this, Llelo. When you set out to wake a man, you take no half-measures."

Llelo's eyes widened even farther. Still not fully convinced that he was to escape unscathed, he could not help grinning, nonetheless. "I am sorry about the broken flagon, Papa," he said, and Gruffydd shrugged.

"I expect it can be mended. But what of you? You took quite a tumble. Are you sure that you need no mending yourself?"

Now, it was Llelo's turn to shrug; he'd taken much sharper buffets from Owain. "Papa . . . do you remember your dream?"

Gruffydd's mouth tightened so noticeably that he'd have called the question back if only he could. He tensed, but then his father's shoulders slumped. "Yes, I remember," he said, so low that Llelo had to strain to catch his words. "But I'd rather not talk of it, Llelo. And I'd not have you talk of it, either. I want you to keep this night to yourself, lad. Will you do that for me?"

Llelo stared at him, mouth ajar, eyes full of wonder that his father would ask when his was the right to command. For most of his life, Gruffydd had been a remote and forbidding figure, quick-tempered, not easy to please. And now, Llelo marveled, he needs my help! Now they shared a secret, a secret somehow shameful, one his father did not want known. "I'll not tell a living soul, Papa! I swear by all the saints," he vowed, and spat on the floor to seal the bargain.

Gruffydd laughed, was surprised to find he could. Most often he was shaken for hours after one of the dreams, despairing of what he saw as base weakness, dreading the nightmare's recurrence. "Good lad," he said, and for the first time, he found he could look into his son's dark eyes and see no ghosts, see beyond the boy's disquieting resemblance to the man whose name he bore, the man who had given Gruffydd life and then taken away six years of it.

"We ought to sweep up the chamber, Papa, ere Mama comes back," Llelo suggested, an eager accomplice in this complicity of silence. But even as he spoke, they heard the footsteps upon the stairs.

The door was shoved back; Senena and Owain burst into the room. "Gruffydd? A servant said he heard a fearful crash! Are you all right? Did you—Llelo?"

Senena's voice registered more than surprise, it registered disapproval. Owain was even more outspoken, saying accusingly, "What are you doing here, Llelo?"

Llelo was accustomed to finding himself in the wrong. He said nothing, retreated into the stubborn silence that his parents and brother found so infuriating. But this night was to be different; he was to have a defender. As Senena frowned, started to speak, Gruffydd said, "He heard me cry out in my sleep, deserves no rebuke."

Owain's face was easily read; his surprise was all too apparent. Senena's eyes flew to her husband's face, and Llelo was forgotten.

"Was it your dream again, beloved?" She was meticulous in the keeping of her house, prized her possessions. But now she never even glanced at the broken crockery strewn about the floor, hastening toward the bed. "I should have been here for you! But that accursed storm, I could not sleep . . ." As she spoke, she was fluffing the pillow, smoothing the sheets, stroking her husband's tousled hair. Llelo could not look away; he'd not known that his mother's hands, so sure and so capable, could be so tender, too.

Gruffydd seemed content to be ministered to, and he raised no objection when Senena insisted he lie back in bed. "I know what you need, love, a cup of hot mulled wine, well sweetened with honey. Owain, go to the kitchen, see that a servant fetches it straightaway. Llelo, go to bed."

She was not a woman to repeat herself; both boys obeyed at once. But just before they reached the bottom step in the stairwell, Owain stopped abruptly, shoved Llelo back against the wall. "You keep your mouth shut about this, you understand? Not a word to a single soul!"

Unable to free himself, Llelo glared at his brother. "I take no orders from you!"

Owain had the proverbial temper of the flaming redhead, and reacted with rage, cuffing the younger boy across the ear. "Curse you, this is no game! I'm warning you in earnest!"

"Owain!" Senena was standing at the top of the stairs. "Let him be!" They retreated before her wrath, into the hall. She swiftly followed, but to Llelo's gratified surprise, this time the object of her anger was Owain, her favorite, her confederate.

"I'd expect no better from Llelo, but you're nigh on eighteen. Would you add to your father's cares? This is no time for a foolish squabble, and yet you—"

"But . . . but Mama!" Owain had inherited his father's uncommon height, towered over his diminutive mother. There was no defiance in his protest, though, only the indignation of one who'd been done an unjust injury. "I was not squabbling with Llelo! I was seeking to make sure he does not spread the story of Papa's bad dream all over Llewelyn's court."

Senena had compelling eyes, a dark sea-grey; they focused now on her younger son with sudden and unnerving intensity. "Why should you fear that, Owain?"

"Jesú, Mama, you do not know? Llelo thinks the sun itself does rise and set at Llewelyn's whim!"

Llelo gasped, and Owain swung around to face him. "Dare you deny it? I've seen him, Mama, seen him trailing after Llewelyn like a starveling puppy, begging for a smile, a pat on the head. He seeks to please Llewelyn as a pagan seeks to appease an infidel god, and this would be a rare offering, indeed, a tale to give Llewelyn great amusement."

Llelo did not think his grandfather would be amused at all, but he knew better than to venture a defense of Llewelyn. And there was more at stake. His pride stung by Owain's jeer, he said hotly, "He lies, Mama! I'd never tell on Papa, never!"

"I would to God I could believe that," Owain snapped, but subsided when Senena held up a hand for silence.

"Owain, your father waits for the wine."

He nodded, gave Llelo one last warning look, and Llelo silently mouthed the word "churl," that being the worst insult he knew.

If Senena noticed, she gave no sign. As soon as they were alone behind the screen, she said, "I think we must talk, Llelo. Come closer, so we do not disturb the others sleeping in the hall."

"Mama, I would not tell, truly I would not."

"I want to believe you," she said quietly. Although she was looking directly into his face, it seemed to Llelo that she was not truly seeing him, and he shifted nervously. At last, she said, "I know you have no memories of your father's confinement at Deganwy Castle. You were too young, a babe when his imprisonment began, only six when it ended. It was very difficult for your father; he of all men could never abide being caged. Owain was old enough to understand. But you and your sister were too young. Like all children, you would play your games, shriek and squabble, ask awkward questions . . ." She stopped, appeared to sigh.

"It seemed best to send you and Gwladys to Llewelyn's court, rather than to keep you with us at Deganwy. Better for Gruffydd, and for you. I hoped, too, that it might help, having you serve as a constant reminder to Llewelyn of the evil he'd done. I thought, Let him look upon his son's child and remember that son, mayhap relent. Well, two years ago he did, set Gruffydd free. We took you back then . . . or so I thought."

"Mama . . ."

"Hush, child, listen. I can understand, Llelo. Your grandfather is a man of uncommon talents, and he has ever been able to bedazzle when he so chooses. Over the hearth fires of our people, they talk of his exploits and the legends take wing. The bards sing his praises, call him the Lion of Gwynedd, Llewelyn the Great. What youngster would not take pride in such a celebrated kinsman?"

She reached out suddenly, grasped the boy by the shoulders. "But it must not be, Llelo. Under Welsh law, a man's lands are divided amongst all his sons. That Gruffydd was base-born matters for naught in Wales. When Llewelyn dies, Gruffydd has a blood right to his share of Gwynedd."

Her grip had tightened; she was unknowingly hurting her son. "But Llewelyn scorned the ancient laws of our countrymen, adopted the alien customs of our enemies. He decreed that Gwynedd should pass to Davydd, his younger son, his half-English son. He raised Davydd up over Gruffydd, and when Gruffydd protested the loss of his birthright, Llewelyn cast him into Deganwy Castle."

"But he did free Papa, and gave him Llŷn, part of Lower Powys . . ." Llelo's words trailed off, a broken breath atremble with swallowed tears.

"Llŷn, Powys!" Senena spat out the words. "What are they but crumbs from his table? He has cheated Gruffydd of a crown, has cursed his nights with dreams of Deganwy, and there can be no forgiveness for him. Not from Gruffydd, not from me, and not from you. To give love to Llewelyn is to betray your father." She stepped back. "You're

old enough now to understand that," she said, and turned away without
another word, left him alone.

GRUFFYDD, his wife, and children reached Llewelyn's palace at Aber soon
after dusk on Monday, Epiphany Eve. As they entered the great hall,
an expectant hush fell. Gruffydd moved toward the dais, greeted his
father with brittle courtesy. If Gruffydd's grievance lay open and bleeding, Llewelyn's was an internal wound. His voice was even, his face
impassive as he said, "You and your family are ever welcome at my
court."

As Llelo started forward, Owain grabbed his arm, murmured against
his ear, "Remember, not a word to Llewelyn or his Norman-French slut
about Papa's bad dreams!"

Llelo jerked his arm away, and then turned at the sound of his
name, turned with reluctance for he'd recognized her voice. The Lady
Joanna, his grandfather's consort. Sister to the English King Henry,
daughter to King John of evil fame, the mother of Davydd. The woman
Owain called the "Norman-French slut." She was smiling at Llelo, making him welcome. She'd never been anything but kind to him, but he
could not respond to her kindness; he dare not. She was his father's
enemy, the foreign witch who'd cast a sexual spell upon his grandfather,
brought about Gruffydd's ruin. Llelo knew the litany of his House by
heart. That the witch herself was soft-spoken, friendly, and fair to look
upon only made him fear her all the more, for he suspected that he,
too, could fall prey to her alien charms.

"Ah, there is my namesake." His grandfather had left the dais, was
moving toward him. "Tell me, Llelo, do you want your New Year's gift
now? Of course if you'd rather, we can wait till the morrow?" Llewelyn
grinned at the boy, and Llelo grinned back.

"Now," he said, while trying to ignore Owain's accusing grey eyes,
eyes that brought a hot flush to his face, shame for a sin he could not
disavow.

IN England, dinner was the main meal of the day, served between ten
and eleven in the forenoon. In Wales, however, there was but one meal,
eaten in the evening, and Gruffydd and his family had arrived just in
time for the festive repast: roast goose with Spanish rice, porpoise frumenty, stewed apples, venison pasty, a rissole of beef marrow and
lamprey, sugared plums, wafers, even an elaborate English-style subtlety, a dramatic marzipan sculpture of a storm-tossed galley. When
Llewelyn suggested, tongue-in-cheek, that this might depict the English

ship of state, the best proof of the eased tensions between the two peoples was that his English guests laughed in unfeigned amusement, and afterward, Llelo overheard some of the Marcher border lords agreeing that England was indeed a ship without a firm hand at the helm, for King Henry was a good Christian, a loving husband, but a weak King.

After the trestle tables were cleared away, Davydd Benfras, Llewelyn's court bard, entertained for his Prince's guests, and then there was dancing. Having succeeded in eluding Owain's watchful eye, Llelo was wandering about the hall, admiring the bright silks and velvets, enjoying the cheerful chaos. At his father's manor, the English were not welcome; Gruffydd did not dine with his enemies. But Aber on Epiphany Eve was a crucible in which the Welsh and their Norman-French neighbors could meet as friends, at least for the evening.

Llewelyn's daughters had married into the English nobility, and three of them were at Aber this night: Marared and her husband, Walter Clifford; Gwladys, Gruffydd's favorite sister, and her Marcher lord, Ralph de Mortimer; Elen, Countess of Chester, and John the Scot, Earl of Chester, Llewelyn's most powerful English ally. Although she'd been wed to John the Scot for fourteen years, Elen's marriage was still barren, and she'd been forced to gratify her maternal instincts by lavishing love and attention upon her young nieces and nephews. Llelo adored Elen, but his affections were tainted by guilt, for he feared that this allegiance, too, was suspect; Elen was the Lady Joanna's daughter, Davydd's sister.

Someone had brought in a tame monkey, and Llelo was so captivated by its antics that he bumped into a man threading his way amidst the dancers. He recoiled, staring tongue-tied at his uncle Davydd, mortified to see he'd spilled Davydd's drink. But Davydd took the mishap in good humor, smiled, and moved on. Llelo had never seen Davydd in a rage. The contrast between his turbulent father and his self-contained uncle could not have been greater. At age forty, Gruffydd was no longer young, but he was tall, big-boned, with all the force and vibrant color of a fire in full blaze, a man to turn heads. Llelo thought he utterly overshadowed Davydd, who was twelve years younger, six inches shorter, as dark as Gruffydd was fair, with pitch-black hair and slanting hazel eyes that revealed little, missed even less.

Davydd had stopped to talk to his mother's English kin, come from the King's Christmas court at Winchester. Llelo knew them both, Richard Fitz Roy, Joanna's half-brother, and her half-sister, the Lady Nell, Countess of Pembroke, youngest of King John's legitimate offspring. Nell was just twenty-one to Joanna's five and forty, and like her brother, the English King, she'd turned to Joanna for the mothering they'd never gotten from John's Queen.

Llelo thought the Lady Nell was as lovely as a wood nymph, but he'd often heard his mother call her a harlot. Nell had been wed in childhood to the powerful Earl of Pembroke, and when she'd been widowed in her sixteenth year, she'd impulsively taken a holy oath of chastity. Although she'd never repudiated the oath, she'd soon abandoned her homespun for soft wools and Alexandrine velvets, soon returned to her brother's royal court, where she'd earned herself a reputation as a flirt. Llelo was old enough to know what a whore was, a bad woman, but he still could not help liking Nell's fragrant perfumes, her lilting laugh.

Across the hall, he saw his father, surrounded by Welsh admirers. The Marcher lords might look at Gruffydd askance, but he was popular with his own; there were many among the Welsh who thought he'd been wronged. Llelo would have gone to him, had he not noticed Owain hovering at his father's elbow. Instead, Llelo found himself gravitating toward the dais, where his grandfather was, as always, the center of attention.

"Say that again, John," Llewelyn instructed, "but more slowly."

His son-in-law smiled, obligingly repeated, "Nu bisiche ich thee."

Although Llewelyn spoke Welsh and Norman-French and Latin, he had never learned English. "And that means?"

"Now beseech I thee," John the Scot translated, adding, accurately if immodestly, "I have always had a gift for languages. In addition to my native French, I speak my father's Gaelic, Latin, a smattering of your Welsh, and I've picked up some English. It does come in handy at times; English is still the tongue of the peasants, the villeins on my Cheshire manors. Shall I lesson you in English, my lord Llewelyn? What would you fancy learning?"

"Mayhap some blood-chilling English oaths?" Llewelyn suggested, and the men laughed. So did Llelo, until he saw that Owain had joined them. He flushed, edged away from his grandfather, from his brother's suspicious stare.

Pausing only to retrieve his mantle, he slipped through a side door, out into the bailey. There he tilted his head back, dazzled by so many stars. His grandfather had once offered to teach him how to find his way by making use of the stars, but had never found the time. Llelo fumbled at his belt, drew forth his grandfather's gift. The handle was ivory; the slender blade caught glints of moonlight. He'd had an eating knife, of course, but this knife was longer, sharper; with a little imagination, he could pretend it was a real dagger. Ahead lay the stables, where his true New Year's gift awaited him, for his grandfather's favorite alaunt bitch had whelped, and tonight he'd promised Llelo the pick of the litter, as soon as they were weaned.

The stables were dark, quiet. Mulling over names for his new pet, Llelo did not at once realize he wasn't alone. He was almost upon them before he saw the man and woman standing together in the shadows of an empty box stall. Instinctively, he drew back, would have retreated. But they'd whirled, moved apart.

"Llelo?" Although the voice was low, breathless, he still recognized it as Elen's.

"Yes," he said, and she came toward him. The man followed her into the moonlight. He, too, was known to Llelo, and it took him but a moment to recollect the name: Robert de Quincy, a cousin of Elen's husband.

"I vow, Llelo, but you'd put a ferret to shame, padding about on silent cat-feet! You're like to scare the wits out of me, God's truth," Elen said and laughed. Her laughter sounded strange to Llelo, high-pitched and uneven.

"I am sorry," he said, and she reached out, ruffled his hair.

"No matter. But I was talking with Sir Robert on a private matter, so I'd be beholden to you, love, if you'd not mention that you saw us out here together." She gave him a crooked smile. "It will be our secret, Llelo . . . agreed?"

He nodded, hesitated, and then turned, began to retrace his steps toward the great hall. They watched him go, not daring to speak until they were sure he was safely out of earshot. Then Robert said softly, "Can he be trusted?"

She bit her lip. "Yes. But Jesú, how I hated to do that to him!"

He forced a smile. "You need not fret, sweetheart. What youngling does not like to be entrusted with a secret?"

Elen still frowned. "Mayhap," she whispered. "Mayhap . . ."

Llelo had lost all interest in viewing the puppies. He did not know why he felt so uneasy, knew only that he did. He'd been proud to share his father's secret. But he sensed that Elen's secret was different. He loved his aunt Elen, worried that she was somehow in peril, worried, too, that he might inadvertently give her secret away. He'd never been good at keeping secrets before, but he would have to learn. He had two now that he must not betray, Papa's and Aunt Elen's.

Llelo's father had joined those gathered around Llewelyn, so Llelo could in good conscience do likewise. Llewelyn noticed his approach, welcomed him into the circle with a smile, but did not interrupt himself, having just revealed his plans to meet with Gruffydd Maelor, the new Prince of the neighboring realm of Upper Powys.

"His father, Madog, was my cousin, a steadfast ally." This said for the benefit of his English listeners. "He died at Martinmas, may God assoil him, and was buried at Llyn Eglwystl, the abbey you English know as Valle Crucis. That is where Ednyved and I have agreed to meet his son."

"And I daresay you'll find the time to do some hunting along the way," Joanna murmured, with the indulgent smile of a longtime wife, and Llewelyn laughed.

"And would it not be a deed of Christian charity to feed my own men, rather than to have the poor monks empty their larders on our behalf?" Llewelyn accepted a wine cup from a servant, and his eyes strayed from Joanna, came to rest upon his eldest son. He drank, watching Gruffydd, and then said, "You have ever loved the hunt, Gruffydd. Should you like to accompany us?"

For the span of an indrawn breath, Gruffydd looked startled, vulnerable. "No!" he said, too vehemently. "That would not be possible."

"As you will." Llewelyn drank again, then felt his wife's hand upon his arm. "What say you, breila? Should you like to come?"

Joanna smiled, shook her head. "Alas, I've never shared your peculiar passion for hunting in the dead of winter!" Llelo was standing beside her, close enough to touch. She recognized the look of wistful yearning on his face; she, too, had been a solitary child. "Llewelyn . . . why not take Llelo in my stead?"

Llewelyn glanced at his grandson, surprised but not at all unwilling. "Well . . . think you that you're old enough for a hunt, Llelo?"

"I'm nigh on nine, Grandpapa," Llelo pleaded, and Llewelyn no longer teased, seeing the nakedness of the boy's need.

"I can think of no better companion, lad, will take you right gladly . . . if your lord father has no objection."

All eyes were now on Gruffydd. He looked at his son. The boy's heartbreaking eagerness was painfully apparent, his mute entreaty far more poignant than begging or cajoling would have been. From the corner of his eye, Gruffydd saw his wife, knew she was silently willing him to say no.

"I often took you hunting when you were Llelo's age." Llewelyn's voice was very quiet. "You remember, Gruffydd?"

"Yes . . . I remember." Gruffydd bit back a harsh, humorless laugh. As if he could forget! "I'll not forbid you, Llelo. The decision is yours."

Llelo drew a sharp, dismayed breath, for he knew that his father wanted him to refuse. Yet he knew, too, that he could not do it.

THE ten days that Llelo passed with his grandfather at the Cistercian abbey of Llyn Eglwystl were touched with magic. His grandfather had never had much time for him before; now they shared a chamber in the abbey guest house, and at night, Llelo would listen, enthralled, as Llewelyn and Ednyved reminisced, related stories of their boyhood, of a lifetime of wars with the English. Best of all, his grandfather kept his promise, took the boy hunting with him. On a cloudy, cold day in late January, a day Llelo would long remember, his had been one of the arrows that brought down a young hind, and when venison was served that night in the abbey guest hall and the infirmary, Llewelyn had announced to one and all that they were eating Llelo's kill.

Only one shadow marred the utter perfection of the day, Llelo's awareness that their time together was coming to an end; there were just four days remaining until they returned to Aber. But he soon forgot all else when Ednyved began to spin a tale of Saracens, hot desert sands, and queer humped beasts called camels. Ednyved was his grandfather's Seneschal, a lifetime companion and confidant, and one of the few Welshmen who'd seen the Holy Land. He'd returned that year from a pilgrimage to Palestine, and Llelo was spellbound by the stories he had to tell; the only bedtime tales he enjoyed more were those accounts of Llewelyn's rise to power. He'd begun a rebellion at fourteen, had eventually wrested control of Gwynedd from his uncles in a bloody battle at the mouth of the River Conwy, and Llelo never tired of hearing about it.

Propping himself up on his elbow, he glanced across at his grandfather's pallet. The Cistercians were an austere order, and the Abbot did not have lavish private quarters to offer his Prince, as a Benedictine abbot could have done. Llewelyn had reassured his apologetic hosts that he was quite comfortable. He had, after all, done his share of sleeping around campfires, he'd laughed, and Llelo felt a sharp twinge of envy, yearning for the day when he, too, could sleep under the stars with a naked sword at his side. It had been some moments now since either Llewelyn or Ednyved had spoken, and he hastily sought for a conversational gambit, one that would keep sleep at bay for a while longer.

"Did you never want to go on crusade like Lord Ednyved, Grandpapa?"

"I thought about it, lad. But our English neighbors covet Wales too much; I never felt I could risk it."

"My father hates the English."

"He has reason, lad. He spent four years in English prisons."

"He did? I did not know that! When? How?"

"I've told you how King John led an army into Gwynedd, how I had to send Joanna to his camp, seeking peace. When I yielded to him at Aberconwy, he compelled me to give up thirty hostages. He insisted that one of them be Gruffydd." Llewelyn was staring into the hearth flames. After a time, he said, "He was just fifteen, and he suffered greatly at John's hands."

"Do you hate the English, too, Grandpapa?"

"I hated John. But no, I do not hate all the English. I'd hardly have found English husbands for my daughters if I did. Davydd's wife is English, too. Of course they were marriages of policy, done for Gwynedd's good."

"Was your marriage done for Gwynedd, too, Grandpapa?"

"Indeed, lad. Joanna was the English King's bastard daughter, just fourteen when we wed." Llewelyn laughed suddenly. "An appealing little lass she was, too, but so very young. I can scarce believe we've been wed for more than thirty years."

Llelo sat up on the pallet. He knew, of course, of the great scandal that had scarred his grandfather's marriage; he'd heard his parents discuss it often enough. Six years ago the Lady Joanna had taken an English lover, and Llewelyn had caught them in his bedchamber. He'd hanged the lover, sent Joanna away in disgrace. But in time, he'd forgiven her, had created another scandal by taking her back. Llelo yearned now to ask why, did not dare.

"Grandpapa, may I ask you a question? I do not want to vex you . . ."

Llewelyn turned on his side, toward the boy. "Ask," he said, and Llelo blurted it out in one great, breathless gulp.

"Grandpapa, why did you choose Davydd over my father? Why did you keep him in Deganwy? Do you hate him so much?"

"Hate him? No, Llelo."

A silence settled over the room. Llelo shivered, drew his blanket close. "Are you angry?"

"No, lad. I was but thinking how best to answer you, how to make you understand. Do you see our hunting gear in yon corner? Fetch me a quiver of arrows."

Mystified, Llelo did. Llewelyn sat up, spilled arrows onto the bed. "Think of these arrows as the separate Welsh principalities. This first arrow is for Gwynedd. These two shall be for Upper and Lower Powys. And this one for South Wales, for Deheubarth. Now add these others for the lesser lords, those who stand by their princes." Holding them up, he said, "Watch, lad, whilst I try to break them. There . . . you see? It cannot easily be done, can it? But take Gwynedd alone, take a lone arrow . . ." He gripped a single shaft in his fists; there was a loud crack as the wood splintered, broke in two.

Llelo was intrigued, but uncomprehending. "I do not fully understand," he admitted, with such obvious reluctance that Llewelyn smiled.

"Just listen, lad; you will. You know, of course, that Welsh law divides a man's lands up amongst his sons. But how do you divide a kingdom, Llelo? It cannot be done. In the past, our law did but lead to needless bloodshed, set brother against brother. So it was with my own family; my father was slain by his brothers. And Gwynedd was torn asunder by their wars, bled white. I could not let that happen again. I had to keep my realm whole, could not let it be broken into fragments when I died. How else could we hope to stave off English attacks? We're at peace now with England, but it was a peace I won at sword-point, bought with blood. The moment we seem vulnerable, the English will seek to regain their conquests, and what could be more vulnerable than a land ravaged by civil war?"

Llelo reached over, picked up one of the arrow halves. "I think I see. You put Gwynedd first, did what you thought was best for Wales."

Llewelyn was delighted. "Just so, lad."

"But why did you choose Davydd? Why did you not want my papa to have Gwynedd? He was your firstborn. Why Davydd?"

That was the question Gruffydd had put to him, too. And he'd never been able to answer it to Gruffydd's satisfaction, never been able to make him understand. Would he have any better luck with the boy?

"A prince of Gwynedd must be practical, Llelo. He must be able to understand the limits of his power. No Welsh prince could ever hope to equal the might of the English Crown. To survive, to safeguard our sovereignty, we must come to terms with England. That is why every Welsh prince since my grandfather's time has sworn allegiance to the English king. But Gruffydd was never able to accept that. Over the years, his hatred of the English festered, until it was beyond healing. If ever he had my power, he'd start a war with England, a war he could not win. I do not blame him, Llelo; he cannot be other than as he is. But I could not let him destroy himself, and I could not let him destroy Gwynedd."

It was very quiet; Llewelyn knew that Ednyved, too, had been listening. Llelo had bowed his head, and Llewelyn could see only a crown of dark hair; it showed brown glints in the sun, but now looked as black as Llewelyn's own hair had once been. "Llelo?"

"Did you never try to make my papa understand? Mayhap if he knew why, if he did not think you loved Davydd more, then he'd . . . he'd be more content."

"Yes, lad," Llewelyn said. "I tried." Llelo asked no more questions, and after a moment, Llewelyn leaned over, quenched the candle flame.

"Llelo?" Ednyved spoke for the first time from the darkness. "I want to tell you something. Your lord grandfather spoke of a peace with England. What he did not tell you was that it was dictated on his terms. You see, lad, Llewelyn did what men thought impossible; he united the other Welsh Princes, got them to hold with him against England. Wales has never been stronger, more secure, and it is your grandfather's doing. He was too shrewd to lay claim to the title, knowing it would but stir up jealousies and rancors amongst the other Princes, but in truth, lad, Llewelyn is Prince of all Wales, Prince of all our people."

Llewelyn was taken aback. Ednyved was not a friend who flattered; his was an affection most often barbed by flippancy and sarcasm. "That is the sort of praise a man rarely gets to hear, Ednyved," he said wryly. "It is usually reserved for funeral orations!"

"Well, try not to let it go to your head, my lord. I just thought the lad ought to know."

No one spoke after that. Llelo snuggled deeper under the blankets. He was drowsy, not far from sleep. But his last conscious thought was one to give him great comfort. He need feel no shame for loving his grandfather. He was not disloyal. He knew now that his grandfather had never been his father's enemy.

LLELO awoke to darkness. The shutters were still drawn, and the hearth had gone out. The chamber was very cold; a thin crust of ice had formed over the water in the washing lavers. He knew instinctively that the abbey bells had not yet rung Prime. So why had he awakened? He yawned, then saw that his grandfather and Ednyved were stirring, too. Across the chamber, Llewelyn's attendants were rolling hastily from their blankets. Llewelyn sat up, and Llelo felt a throb of excitement when he saw the sword in his grandfather's hand. The intruder shrank back, gave a frightened bleat.

"I am Brother Marc! I intend no evil, God's truth!"

One of Llewelyn's squires had the wit to unlatch a shutter, revealing a glimpse of greying sky, revealing the white habit and black scapular of a Cistercian monk. Llewelyn's men lowered their swords in disgusted relief, muttering among themselves at the incredible innocence that had sent the monk bursting into a sleeping Prince's chamber, never thinking that his sudden, unsanctioned entry might well be taken for an assassination attempt.

"My lord, forgive me, but I did not know what else to do. I was on watch at the gatehouse when he sought entry, and he insisted he be taken to you at once. He says he has an urgent message from Lord Davydd and—"

"Christ Jesus, man, why do you tarry then? Bid him enter!" Flinging the blankets back, Llewelyn grabbed for his clothes. He was wide awake now, but baffled. Wales was not at war. The other Welsh Princes were his allies. Nor did he believe the English King was likely to violate the peace. A Marcher border lord? Again, not likely; they were like wolves, preyed upon the weak. But Davydd was never one to take alarm at trifles. So what . . . Jesú, Gruffydd! Had he risen up in rebellion again?

Llewelyn shot a troubled glance toward his grandson. And then an unshaven, begrimed man was kneeling before him, a man who'd obviously spent long, hard hours in the saddle, a man who could not meet his eyes.

"I bear grievous tidings, my lord. Your lady wife has been taken ill. Lord Davydd urges you to return to Aber with all haste."

Llewelyn had been buckling his scabbard; his hands froze on the belt. "Joanna?" There was shock in his voice, and disbelief, but no fear, not yet. "How ill? What ails her?"

"I know not the answer to that, my lord. But she burns with fever, and Lord Davydd said . . . he said you dare not delay."

The men dressed rapidly, wordlessly, casting sidelong glances at Llewelyn's graven profile. In his haste, Llelo pulled his shirt on backwards, nearly panicked when he could not find his boots, and then heard what he most dreaded, Ednyved's flat, dispassionate voice saying, "It might be best to leave the boy here with the monks."

"No! I want to come. I'll not slow you down, I swear!"

Ednyved looked into the boy's upturned face, and then over at Llewelyn. But Llewelyn's eyes were turned inward; he had no thoughts for Llelo, no thoughts for anyone but the woman lying ill at Aber. Ednyved hesitated, and then nodded.

The abbey at Llyn Eglwystl was more than fifty miles from Llewelyn's seacoast palace at Aber, but they covered the distance in less than two days, arriving at dusk on the second day. The men were chilled, soaked by hours of steady, winter rain, their horses lathered and mudsplattered, but none had protested Llewelyn's punishing pace. Llelo was in a daze, so exhausted that he'd not even noticed when Llewelyn lifted him onto his saddle; he'd settled back sleepily in his grandfather's arms, awakening only when rain dripped over the edge of his mantle hood, trickled onto his cheek. Now someone was reaching up for him, depositing him upon the ground. He staggered, and Llewelyn put a steadying hand on his arm, but the gesture was automatic; Llewelyn had already forgotten the boy, saw Davydd and only Davydd.

For two days Llewelyn had sought to convince himself that he feared for naught, that Joanna could not truly be in danger. But at sight of his son's ashen face, he heard himself say huskily, "She still lives?"

Davydd nodded, but then said, "Thank God you've come, Papa. We so feared you'd not be in time . . ."

"Why did you not summon me at once?"

"She would not let me, Papa. She swore it was but a chill, and indeed, at first it did seem so. When she worsened, it took us without warning."

Llewelyn had never been a man to shrink from hard truths; unless he knew the nature of his enemy, how could he know what strategy might stave off defeat? "Tell me," he said. "Tell me all."

"The chill was followed by fever, and despite all her doctors could do, it burns ever higher." Tears had filled Davydd's eyes, but he somehow managed to keep his voice steady. "She has pain in breathing, and a constant cough. The doctors have given her sage and vervain, wine with powdered anise and fennel, and Mama's confessor has not left the chapel all day, lighting candles to the Blessed Mary and to St Blaise. But Papa, I'll not lie to you. Nothing has helped, nothing. She grows weaker by the hour. The doctors . . . they hold out no hope."

"Devil take the doctors," Llewelyn said savagely. "Do you think I'll just stand by, let her die? She almost died before, giving birth to you. But I did not let it happen. I'm here for her now, and that will make the difference. I'll not lose her, Davydd. Whatever it takes to save her, I'll do. I'll find a way. I always do." He was turning away when Davydd caught his arm.

"Papa, wait. She . . . she's out of her head now with the fever. Papa, I doubt that she'll even know you."

Llewelyn stared at him, and then pulled his arm free.

His bedchamber had been draped with red, in vain hopes of banishing fever. Isabella, Davydd's young wife, burst into tears at sight of Llewelyn; so, too, did Nia, Joanna's maid. The doctors stood helplessly by; they looked exhausted, and not a little apprehensive. Llewelyn brushed them aside, leaned over the bed.

"Joanna? Breila, I'm here," he said, and then his breath caught in his throat as she turned toward the sound of his voice. Splotches of hot color burned high on her cheekbones, but her skin was bloodless, had taken on a frightening, waxlike pallor. Her eyes looked bruised, so deeply circled were they, sunken back in her head, glazed and unseeing, and even when he took her in his arms, held her close, he could find no flicker of recognition in their fevered depths.

LLELO awakened just before dawn. As early as it was, the great hall was already astir. Joanna had not been popular with her husband's people, but she was well-loved by those in her own household, and a pall had settled over the court. Even those who could not mourn Joanna, the unfaithful, foreign wife, even they grieved for the pain her death would give their Prince, and Llelo saw only somber, grim faces, saw people too preoccupied to pay heed to a bewildered eight-year-old.

Llewelyn had spent the night at Joanna's bedside, had at last fallen into a fitful sleep. When he awoke, it was with a start, with a sick surge of fear that subsided only a little as he glanced toward the bed, reassured himself that Joanna still lived. Her breathing was labored, rapid and shallow, but her sleep seemed easier, and he took heart from that. For much of the night, she'd tossed and turned, in her fever seeking to throw off the sheets, from time to time crying out his name, agitated, incoherent, imprisoned in a twilight world of delirium and shadows, just beyond his reach. But now she seemed calmer, and he leaned over, touched his lips to her forehead.

As he straightened up, he winced. His was no longer a young man's body, and his muscles were cramping badly, inflamed by the abuses of the past three days. He slumped back in the chair, for the first time noticed his grandson. The boy said nothing, shyly held out a clay goblet. Llewelyn took it, drank without tasting.

"Llelo, fetch me that casket on the window-seat." Llelo was in motion before he'd stopped speaking, and a moment later was watching, amazed, as Llewelyn dumped the contents onto the foot of the bed: a gleaming treasure-trove of gold and silver, garnets, amethysts, pendants and pins. "I once gave Joanna an amber pater noster. Help me find it, lad."

Llelo had the sharper eye, soon spied the yellow-gold prayer beads. "Here, Grandpapa! Why do you want it?"

"Men say that amber helps to ease fevers." Llewelyn leaned over, fastened the rosary around Joanna's wrist. Isabella had entered with a laver. Taking it from her, he sat on the bed, began to sponge cooling water onto Joanna's face and throat. When her lashes fluttered, he said soothingly, "I seek to lower your fever, breila." The words came readily, so often had he said them to her in the past twelve hours. But then the sponge slipped from his fingers, for her eyes had focused on him, no longer blind. "Joanna?"

"You came back . . . ." A joyful whisper, so faint that none but he heard. Only when he thrust the laver aside did the others realize she was lucid again.

"Hold me," she entreated, and he slid his arm around her shoulders, cradled her against his chest. "Llewelyn . . . I cannot remember. Was . . . was I shriven?"

"Indeed, love. Davydd did assure me of it, said your confessor administered the Sacraments whilst you were still in your senses." Brushing her hair back, he kissed her forehead, her eyelids, the corner of her mouth. "But it matters for naught now, breila, for you're going to recover. You need only—"

"My darling . . . my darling, not even you can . . . can deny death . . . ." The corner of her mouth twitched, tried to smile. "Davydd?" she whispered, and Llewelyn nodded, unable to speak.

"I'm here, Mama." Davydd came forward, into her line of vision.

"Right here." He saw her lips move, knew what she asked, slowly shook his head. "No, Mama. But Elen is on her way, should be here soon."

Joanna closed her eyes; tears squeezed through her lashes. So much she wanted to say, but she had not the strength. "Beloved . . . promise me . . ."

Llewelyn stiffened. She'd fought so hard to gain the crown for their son. Did she mean to bind him now with a deathbed vow? He waited, dreading what she would ask of him, to safeguard the succession for Davydd. Knowing there was but one certain way to do that—to cage Gruffydd again. And how could he do that to his son? How could he condemn him to a life shut away from the sun? But how could he deny Joanna? Could he let her go to her grave without that comfort?

"Llewelyn . . . pray for me," she gasped, and only then did he fully accept it, that she was indeed dying, was already lost to him, beyond earthly cares, worldly ambitions.

"I will, Joanna." He swallowed with difficulty, brought her hand up, pressing his lips against her palm. "You will have my every prayer."

"Bury me at . . . at Llanfaes . . ."

His head jerked up. He had an island manor at Llanfaes; it was there that Joanna had been confined after he had discovered her infidelity. "Why, Joanna? Why Llanfaes?"

Her mouth curved upward. "Because . . . I was so happy there. You came to me, forgave me . . ."

"Oh, Christ, Joanna . . ." His voice broke; he pulled her into an anguished embrace, held her close.

Llelo had been a petrified witness; at that, he began to sob. Isabella, too, was weeping. Davydd turned on his heel, bolted from the chamber. Ednyved took the boy by the arm. Gently but insistently, he ushered Llelo and Isabella into the antechamber. Then quietly he closed the door, left Llewelyn alone with his wife.

ELEN arrived at Aber in mid-afternoon, but by then Joanna was delirious again. She never regained consciousness, died in the early hours of dawn on Candlemas, February 2. At week's end, her body was ferried across the strait to the island of Môn, where she was buried, as she'd requested, in a seaside garden near Llewelyn's manor at Llanfaes.

It was a cold, blustery day, a day of wet winds and intermittent rains. Despite the raw, winter weather, there was a large turnout for the funeral of Llewelyn's lady; well-born Welsh lords stood shoulder to shoulder with Marcher barons as the Bishop of St Asaph performed the funeral Mass under a darkening sky. The Bishop had consecrated a burial ground within sight of the sea, and the people murmured among themselves, wondering why Llewelyn had chosen to bury Joanna here, rather than in the village church. They had their answer at the conclusion of the Mass, when Bishop Hugh announced that Prince Llewelyn had vowed to found a house of Franciscan friars at Llanfaes, to pray for the soul of the Lady Joanna.

None doubted the depths of Llewelyn's grieving; it was there for all the world to see in the haggard face, the hollowed dark eyes. But few had expected a gesture of such spectacular and dramatic dimensions. Llelo was standing close enough to hear his mother's indrawn breath. As inconspicuously as possible, he backed away, then circled around the mourners, at last reached his grandfather's side.

Llewelyn was standing with his son and daughter by Joanna's tomb. He'd put artisans to work day and night to complete it in time; the coffin lid bore his wife's effigy, was decorated with floriated crosses, foliage, a winged dragon. The coffin had been sprinkled with holy water; it was being splattered now with rain drops, with Elen's silent tears as she bent over, touched her lips to the cold, carven stone.

"My lord?" The Bishop of St Asaph waited at a respectful distance, knowing how difficult it always was for the living to bid farewell to their dead. "My lord Llewelyn, shall we return to Aber now?"

"Yes, go." Llewelyn did not move, though. "Take the others back, Davydd. You, too, lass," he said, when Elen would have objected. "I would have some last moments alone with her," he said softly, and his children no longer protested, left him there in the bleak, windswept garden.

The rain was coming down heavily by the time the mourners were ferried back to Aber. The great hall was soon filled to overflowing with cold and hungry guests. Davydd's wife had made herself ill with her weeping, had taken to bed, but both Davydd and Elen were still in the hall, accepting condolences with the brittle, prideful gallantry of noblesse oblige. Joanna's sister Nell had borne up with equal fortitude, but now her composure cracked and she covered her face with her hands, began to sob. Llelo was closest to her, but he did not know how to comfort, willingly relinquished the field to a French cousin of John the Scot. Simon de Montfort moved swiftly to Nell's side, gently led her toward the greater privacy of a window-seat, then hovered protectively nearby until Nell had regained composure.

Llelo retreated, but he could find no refuge, no way to outrun the memory of his grandfather, standing alone by a white stone coffin. Never before had Llelo experienced what it was like to identify with another's pain, and he did not know how to deal with the hurting, the shattering sense of helplessness. In his misery, he sought out his father.

Gruffydd had expected to rejoice on this day, for he'd hated Joanna with a passionate hatred that only death could satisfy. Now she was dead, but as he'd looked upon his father's stunned, silent grieving, he could feel no joy, only an unwilling sense of pity, pity his father did not deserve. He brooded now upon this, shamed by his weakness, by wayward emotions he did not understand, too troubled himself to see a small boy's distress.

As soon as the rain stopped, Llelo fled the great hall, fled the court. No one paid him any mind. Aber's full name was Aber Gwyngregyn— Mouth of the White Shell River—but the river was more in the nature of a stream. Following its meandering course, Llelo tracked it back to the cataract known as Rhaeadr Fawr—the Great Waterfall. It was more aptly named than the stream, a narrow spill of white water, surging more than a hundred feet over a sheer cliff. Llelo scrambled down the rocks until he stood at the base of the waterfall, close enough to feel the flying spray. Partway up the cliff, a crooked scrub tree struggled to survive, growing at an improbable angle out of the rock. Llelo amused himself by throwing stones at it, with occasional success. He was launching twig boats out into the foaming pool when the wind brought to him the sound of voices; instinctively, he dodged behind the rocks, a Welsh bowman awaiting the enemy's approach.

As they came into view, he flattened himself against the ground, the gameplaying forgotten. Senena and Owain came to a stop less than fifteen feet from his hiding place. He heard a splash, knew that Owain must have thrown a pebble into the pool.

"Thank you for coming with me, Owain. I could not endure that hall a moment longer, God's truth. If I'd heard one more fool babble on about Llewelyn's great gesture, I'd have thrown a screaming fit. To think of honoring that harlot with a Franciscan friary!" Senena's voice was trembling, so intense was her outrage. "Better he should have established a brothel in her memory!"

Owain laughed. Another rock thudded into the shallows, not too far from where Llelo crouched.

"I truly believe she was a witch, Owain. How else explain the way she ensorcelled Llewelyn, turned him against his own son?" Senena strode to the edge of the pool. "A pity," she said, "that it was not Llewelyn we buried today at Llanfaes."

"We'll have that pleasure, Mama, never fear. He's an old man, nigh on four and sixty. How much longer can he live?"

"I know. It is just that Gruffydd has waited so long . . ." Through a blur of tears, Llelo saw a flash of blue, his mother's mantle. He lay very still, scarcely breathing, until she moved away.

"Mama . . . do you ever wonder if Papa truly wants the crown?"

"What mean you by that, Owain? Of course he wants it!"

"Well . . ." The boy sounded hesitant, uncharacteristically uncertain. "When we talk about it, he does not seem as eager as he ought. Oh, he says he hates Llewelyn, says he'll never allow Gwynedd to pass to a weakling like Davydd. But . . . but sometimes, Mama, I wonder if his heart is truly in it."

Her son had inadvertently touched a very raw nerve, indeed, for Senena, too, sometimes found herself fearing that those years at Deganwy Castle had crippled her husband's spirit, had sapped his will to persevere, to fight for what was rightfully his.

"That is arrant nonsense, Owain! Never doubt this—that your father will one day rule in Llewelyn's stead."

"God grant it so," Owain said, with enough passion to placate Senena.

"He will, Owain. He will." She smiled at her son, linked her arm in his. "It is raining again; we'd best get back."

Their voices grew less distinct. After a time, Llelo heard only the sounds of the river and the rain. His face was wet, but he did not pull up his mantle hood, sat there huddled against the rock, his knees drawn up to his chest. He'd begun to tremble. The light was fading, night coming on.

2

Dolwyddelan, North Wales

April 1237

Gwladys de Mortimer reached her father's mountain castle of Dolwyddelan in mid-morning. She was accompanied by the armed escort that her rank and sex demanded; accompanied, too, by her small sons, Roger and Hugh, and—much to Elen's pleasure—Llelo.

Gwladys's children were now being fed in the great hall, while Llelo was hastening down the west slope toward the river, intent upon overtaking Llewelyn, who'd taken his dogs out for a run. From a window in Llewelyn's private chamber, Elen could track his progress; he vanished into a grove of trees, and she glanced back at Gwladys. "I'm right glad you've come. I shall have to return to Cheshire at week's end, and I'll feel better about leaving Papa now that you're here. Papa was not expecting you?"

"No. But he's been much on my mind these weeks past, and I've news, news that should cheer him." Gwladys moved to the window, too; it was unshuttered, offering a sweeping view of the valley, the serpentine course of the River Lledr. "Elen, tell me. How is Papa?"

"Heartsick," Elen said slowly, turning to face her sister. "His grieving is still raw, shows no signs of healing. He misses my mother so, and I've no comfort for him; no one has. I've been here a fortnight, but I've not had much time with him. He's ever been a man of remarkable energy, but never have I seen him push himself like this. He rises before dawn, labors till well after dark, seeks to fill every waking moment with activity. And if by chance he has no meeting scheduled with his council or his rhagnalls, he takes that new chestnut stallion of his out for long rides, does not come back till the horse is lathered, till he is utterly exhausted."

Gwladys sat down in the window-seat. "That sounds like a man trying to outrun his ghosts," she said, and Elen nodded bleakly.

"In truth. And I ache for him so, Gwladys. I doubt that he sleeps much; I know for certes that he is eating poorly. And sometimes at night in the great hall, a silence will fall, and there'll be on his face a look of such sadness . . ." Tears filled Elen's eyes; she blinked them back, mustered up a smile. "Well . . . what news have you for Papa?"

"I'm with child again."

Elen caught her breath; envy twisted like a blade, drew blood. "I am happy for you, Gwladys, truly I am."

Gwladys was quiet for some moments, dark eyes intent, reflective. "We used to be close, Elen. But not for years now—not since Joanna's infidelity." She saw the younger woman stiffen, said swiftly, "You need not fear; I shall speak no ill of your mother. In truth, I was fond of her once, thought of her as a friend. But I could not forgive her for causing Papa so much pain. Even after he forgave her, I never could." She rose, stepped toward her sister. "I should have, Elen. For Papa's sake, I should have made my peace with her. I see that now, too late. When I realized I was with child, I thought . . . well, I thought that if I have a girl, I could name her after Joanna. Do you think that would please Papa?"

"I think Papa would be very pleased." Elen turned back toward the window; talking about Joanna stirred up too many memories, too much pain. "There's Llelo," she said. "He's reached the river. How do you happen to have him with you, Gwladys?"

"I asked Gruffydd if he could visit with me for a while."

"You see it, too, then."

"See what?"

"His need."

Gwladys nodded. "Yes," she admitted. She leaned forward, pulled the shutters all the way back. In the distance Llelo vaulted over a log, as nimbly as a colt. "I think," she said, "that it will be good for Papa, too, having the lad here."

LLEWELYN had an old but erratic acquaintanceship with death. It had come into his life very early; he was still in his cradle when it claimed his father. But then it had shown an unexpected and inexplicable sense of mercy. The years passed and there were no further visitations. He lost friends in battle, but those he most loved were spared—until the summer of his twenty-ninth year. In the span of but three months, he lost his mother and Tangwystl, Tangwystl with her flame-bright hair and Gruffydd's green eyes, Tangwystl who'd given him love and four children. But after that summer of sorrow had come yet another mysterious reprieve. And as the years went by—so many years—it began to seem as if he'd been strangely blessed, able to walk in sunlight while other men trod in death's shadow.

It was not true, of course. Death offered no deliverance, only delay. For nine years now, it had hovered close at hand, demanding payment for debts long deferred. Rhys and Catrin, friends who'd shared all his yesterdays. Two of his daughters' husbands. The most steadfast of his English allies, Ranulf of Chester, uncle to John the Scot. Morgan, who'd been a father in all but blood. Adda, his brother. And then his son Tegwared.

Llewelyn knew he had been luckier than most men, for he'd sired eight children, buried but one—Tegwared. He'd been an amiable, cheerful youngster, quick to jest, easy to love, utterly unlike his brothers, lacking Davydd's ability, Gruffydd's passion. He'd grown into a placid, carefree young man, apparently content with the provisions Llewelyn made for him, and if he felt cheated that he was never in contention for a crown, if he had yearned to join in the lethal blood-rivalry between his half-brothers, none but he ever knew. But for Llewelyn there would always be an unease of mind, the awareness that he'd not been entirely fair to this third son of his, and two years after Tegwared's mortal illness, he still felt that of all death's claims, this had been the most merciless, and the most unjust.

An intimate enemy, death, capricious and cruel, ultimately invincible. But Llewelyn did not fear his own demise, and he truly thought he'd taken its measure, knew the worst it could do. And then death claimed his wife.

There was a Welsh proverb: for every wound, the ointment of time. To Llewelyn, it was an empty promise, a hollow mockery. Time would not heal. Till the day he died, he would grieve for Joanna. Now he sought only to learn to live without her. But so far it was a lesson that eluded him, for Joanna's was an unquiet grave. She came to him in the night, filled every room with her unseen presence, a tender, tempting ghost, beckoning him back to a past that was far more real to him than the joyless, dismal world he now inhabited. It had been more than two months, the longest he'd ever gone without a woman in his bed, but he felt no stirrings of desire. The woman he wanted was dead. It was April, and all about him were the miracles of new life. He looked upon this verdant, blossoming spring, a spring Joanna would never see, he looked upon a field of brilliant blue flowers—the bluebells Joanna had so loved—and at that moment he'd willingly have bartered all his tomorrows for but one yesterday.

His dogs had begun to bark, and his hand dropped to his sword hilt. But the barking had lost its challenging tone; the dogs had encountered a friend. Llewelyn waited, and within moments his young grandson burst into the clearing. "Grandpapa!" Llelo skidded to a halt, suddenly shy, and Llewelyn smiled.

"Come, give me a proper greeting," he said, and Llelo hurtled forward, into his arms. He swung the boy up into the air, pretended to stagger, slowly sinking to the ground under Llelo's weight. It was a game they'd occasionally played, but Llewelyn had not reckoned upon the enthusiastic participation of his alaunts. Both dogs joined eagerly in the fray, and Llewelyn was knocked flat, buried under one hundred sixty pounds of squirming, yelping alaunt, laughing for the first time in weeks.

"Wolf! You're squashing me!" Wriggling free, Llelo lay panting in the grass. "Aunt Gwladys brought me," he confided as soon as he'd gotten his breath back. "She says we can stay for at least a week, mayhap even till my birthday."

Llewelyn's mouth quirked. "I'm having a perilous day. First nearly smothered by these fool dogs, and now assailed by flaming hints."

Llelo grinned, unabashed. "You did say you had a bad memory for dates, Grandpapa."

"That I did," Llewelyn conceded. "Well, now that we happen to be talking of birthdays, I daresay you've a suggestion or two to offer."

"Just one. I would like you to take me hunting again," Llelo said promptly. But to his disappointment, Llewelyn shook his head.

"I'm sorry, lad. We'll have to wait; the season is past. But it'll be worth it, for the best time for hunting is during the summer, when the bucks are well grazed, fleshed out." Llewelyn smiled at the boy. "I remember instructing your father in hunting lore, too, more years ago than I care to count. The second season—for does—starts in November, lasts till . . . Candlemas."

The pause was so prolonged that Llelo looked up, saw that his grandfather's face had shadowed. He started to speak, then remembered. The Lady Joanna had died on Candlemas. He did not know how to comfort, at last said softly, "You must miss her a lot."

Llewelyn's eyes cleared, focused on the boy. "We'd have been wed thirty-one years next month. Nigh on half my life . . ."

"Grandpapa, do we keep on loving the dead?"

"Unfortunately, lad, we do." Llewelyn lay back in the grass, stared up at the sun; it soon blurred in a haze of brightness. He'd been troubled in recent days by sudden, severe headaches, could feel one coming on. "She was so much younger than I was, Llelo. I always expected to die first, never thought . . ." He stopped; a silence settled over the clearing.

Llelo wrapped his arms around his knees, coaxed one of the dogs within petting range, but he kept his eyes upon his grandfather's face, and he seemed to hear again his brother Owain's voice—How much longer can he live?

"Grandpapa, is sixty and four very old?"

Llewelyn turned his head; he looked amused. "Catch me on a bad day and I feel verily as old as Methuselah. But I'll share a secret with you, lad. No matter how gnarled the tree, ensconced within is the soul of a green sapling. The shell ages, Llelo, not the spirit."

"Then . . . then you're not going to die soon?"

There was fear in the boy's voice, and Llewelyn heard it. "No," he said, and he reached over, brushed grass from Llelo's hair. "Not soon. I promise."

Not long afterward, they rose, started back along the river bank. Llelo was—at Llewelyn's suggestion—gathering bluebells and woodsorrel for Elen and Gwladys. "What you said before, about sharing a secret. That was not a true secret, was a joke. But what if you had a real secret, Grandpapa? A . . . shameful secret? What if you knew that if you kept silent, bad things would happen? But if you spoke out, it might be worse. If you had such a secret, what would you do?"

"That is no easy question to answer. I suppose I'd weigh the evils, try to decide which would be the greater harm. Can you tell me more, Llelo?"

The boy looked up at him, then slowly shook his head. "No," he said, "no . . ."

Llewelyn knew better than to press. "As you will," he said, and they walked on. It had been a very wet March, a month of heavy rains, and the river surged against its banks, covered the mossy rocks that usually jutted above the water, stepping-stones that beckoned irresistibly to adventuresome youngsters. Llelo felt cheated; he'd often tested his nerve on those rocks, and he'd hoped to impress his grandfather with his daring. He bent down, searching for a large, flat pebble.

"Watch, Grandpapa," he said, and sent the stone skimming across the surface of the water. "Could you skip stones like that when you were my age?"

"I still can," Llewelyn said. "Find me a stone and I'll show you." Under his grandson's skeptical eye, he moved toward the bank. The sun was shimmering upon the water; the river had taken on a glittering, silvered sheen. It dazzled him, blinded him. The stone soared upward, much too high, splashed into the shallows, and Llelo gave a triumphant laugh.

"That was not even close! Grandpapa, you—Grandpapa?"

Llewelyn did not appear to hear. There was on his face a look Llelo would never forget, a look of utter astonishment. He stumbled, and then his left leg buckled and he made a wild grab for the nearest tree. But his body no longer took commands from his brain, and he fell backward into the damp spring grass.

"Grandpapa!" Llelo dropped to his knees beside his grandfather. "Grandpapa!" Llewelyn's face was flushed; his eyes were dazed, full of disbelief and fear. The corner of his mouth had begun to sag, and when he spoke, his voice was so blurred that he sounded drunk to Llelo. "Get help," he gasped, "hurry . . ."

Llelo snatched off his mantle, made a pillow for Llewelyn's head. "I will," he sobbed, "I will!" He gave one last terrified look over his shoulder, began to run.

ON a Saturday morning six days later, Gruffydd, his wife, and eldest son rode into the castle bailey, just as Davydd's wife, Isabella, emerged from the great hall. Isabella halted, irresolute, yearning to retreat. She'd been a child-bride, wed at ten, and even now, after almost seven years as Davydd's wife, she did not feel at home in Wales. Although her husband treated her well, his courtesy was impersonal, his kindness disinterested; theirs was a marriage lacking true intimacy, even in the marriage-bed. Isabella was grateful to Davydd, wanted to be a dutiful wife, a satisfactory bedmate, but she knew he did not love her. His mother, Joanna, she had loved, loved dearly. Llewelyn, she had come to respect. But Gruffydd—volatile, impassioned, unpredictable—Gruffydd, she feared. She glanced back toward the hall, but she'd waited too long; they were dismounting.

Gruffydd spared no time for social amenities. "What ails my father?"

he demanded. "Davydd's message said he'd been taken ill. Papa's never sick, never. What did—"

"A seizure," Isabella said faintly. "He suffered a brain seizure."

Gruffydd sucked in his breath. "Apoplexy?" He sounded stunned. "Christ Jesus!"

"Does he still live?" Senena's voice was so sharp that Isabella flinched; Senena, too, she feared.

"Oh, yes! He—" She had been about to assure them that Llewelyn was in no danger, but she checked herself, certain that was not what Senena—and possibly Gruffydd—wanted to hear. She stood alone, watching as Gruffydd hastened toward the castle keep, very thankful that she need not be a witness to the scene to come.

Llewelyn's bedchamber was still shuttered, lit only by cresset wall torches and a sputtering hearth fire. The bed hangings were closely drawn. Five people were seated at a table near the door: Davydd, Elen, Gwladys, Ednyved, and another man Gruffydd did not recognize. He never even noticed his younger son, slouched in the shadows of a window-seat. He strode into the room, stopped before Davydd.

"Your wife claims Papa had an apoplectic seizure. Is that true?"

Davydd's mouth thinned. "Think you that Isabella would lie about something like that? Yes, it is true."

"Why did you not tell me at once?"

"When I sent you that message, I did not yet know what ailed him."

"My lords, I must ask you to keep your voices down." The stranger rose, moved around the table toward Gruffydd. "Your lord father has at last fallen asleep, ought not to be disturbed."

"Who are you?"

The man smiled. "I am Einion ap Rhiwallon of Myddfai." The name was known throughout Wales; his was a family of doctors, celebrated for their healing arts. But Gruffydd did not react as expected.

"You're a doctor?" he said brusquely, and Einion's smile faded.

"My father was court physician to Prince Rhys Gryg," he said, somewhat stiffly. "I happened to be at Beddgelert Priory, and Lord Ednyved called me in to consult with Prince Llewelyn's physician, as I've had much experience in treating—"

Senena could wait no longer. "Do you expect Llewelyn to live?"

Einion's smile came back. "God willing, Madame, I do. Prince Llewelyn was fortunate, in that the seizure was a relatively mild one. He ought to make a good recovery."

Gruffydd drew back into the shadows, lest the others read his face. Why should he feel such relief? How could he still care?

Senena glared at the doctor. "Do not lie to us!"

"Madame, I assure you I am not lying!"

"A mild seizure! A good recovery! What sort of fools do you think we are? Apoplexy kills, it cripples, it affects a man's wits, his—"

"Not always, Madame, not in this case. It is true that Prince Llewelyn is showing some signs of palsy, some paralysis in his left arm and leg, but I feel that in time he will—"

"Paralysis—I knew it!"

Gruffydd was frowning. "Knew what, Senena?"

"Oh, think, Gruffydd, think! What happens if your father is disabled by this seizure, bedridden, unable to talk? Who do you think would then rule Gwynedd for him? Who would have control of the privy seal? They would!" She pointed at Davydd and Ednyved. "What is to keep Davydd from issuing orders in Llewelyn's name—orders for your arrest? Gruffydd, do you not see your danger?"

Gruffydd hadn't—until now. He swung about, stared at Davydd. How could he have been so blind?

Elen stopped striving for patience. "Davydd would never do that!"

"He'd do it," Gruffydd said grimly. "You think he has not been laying plans for Papa's death? He knows Papa's people would choose me if given half a chance, knows—"

Davydd shoved his chair back, rose to his feet. "I was a fool to send for you, a fool to think you'd want to know of Papa's illness. His suffering means nothing to you, nothing at all."

Gruffydd stepped toward him. "Damn you! I've had—"

"Grandpapa!" The cry was Llelo's; he alone had noticed the bed curtains being pulled back.

It was suddenly very still. Llewelyn's eyes moved slowly from face to face. "I think it best," he said, "that you keep this deathbed vigil elsewhere," and Senena's fear began to ease, for his voice had been low, but very distinct and very cold. So the doctor had not lied, after all. She'd nursed the sick often enough to recognize the distinctive aura of coming death, and she could not find it now in Llewelyn's face. How long, she marveled, was he to have the Devil's own luck? How long must they wait? But at least he'd not be Davydd's puppet. She sighed; thank Christ Almighty for that much!

The silence was a strained one; none of Llewelyn's children could meet his eyes. Elen was the first to recover; she moved swiftly across the chamber, bent over the bed. "Papa, we're so sorry! We never meant for you to hear that." She glanced back accusingly over her shoulder, said, "Do you want Gruffydd and Senena to leave?"

"Yes," Llewelyn said, but then he added, "I want you all to leave," and Elen straightened up in dismay.

"But Papa . . ." Her protest trailed off; Einion was already beside her.

"Madame," he said, politely but firmly, and she reluctantly let him escort her from the chamber. The others followed slowly.

No one spoke as they moved out onto the porch, crossed the narrow drawbridge that led to the stairs, descended into the bailey. But there Gwladys balked. She was turning to reenter the keep when Einion barred her way.

"I have to go back," she said. "I know how we must have sounded—like dogs squabbling over a choice bone."

"Worse—like birds of prey drawn by the stench of carrion," Elen interjected bitterly, and angry color rose in Senena's face.

Einion still blocked the stairs. "Madame, I understand. But now is not the time to talk to your lord father." He paused, speaking to them all. "I said I expected Prince Llewelyn to recover . . . and I do. But it will not be easy for him. You must try to understand how he feels—stunned, helpless, betrayed by his own body. He needs time to come to terms with it. What he does not need is another confrontation. My lord Davydd, I must speak bluntly. Your father was lucky—this time. But there is always the risk of a second seizure, and that one might well be fatal."

Elen paled. "What you are saying, then, is that Senena could have caused my father to have another seizure!"

"I did nothing wrong," Senena said heatedly. "I did but express fears for my husband's safety, well-founded fears! Do you think I can ever forget those years at Deganwy Castle?"

"Gruffydd forced my father to do that. Again and again he'd forgiven Gruffydd, even when Gruffydd took up arms against him." When Gruffydd would have interrupted, Elen turned to face him. "You know I speak the truth, Gruffydd. Papa loves you—even now—but you've given him naught but grief, you've—"

"He loves me?" Gruffydd echoed, incredulous. "Lest you forget, I spent six years in Deganwy's great keep at his command, my loving father, who would deprive me of my rightful inheritance, bestow it upon Davydd, the son of his Norman-French har—"

"Do not say it." Davydd's voice was even, dispassionate, a calm belied by the glittering hazel eyes. "My mother had nothing to do with your downfall. You brought it upon yourself. Papa found you unfit, to rule, and because he was not willing to sacrifice Gwynedd to spare your pride, you've done all you could to punish him, to make him suffer for your sins. But no more—not when it's now a matter of Papa's very life. I'll not let you put his recovery at risk." He paused. "Until he regains his strength, you are not to see him."

"You dare to tell me I cannot see my own father?" Gruffydd felt first shock, and then, murderous rage.

Davydd saw it, but had only a split-second in which to react. His first instinct was to order Gruffydd subdued. But the command died on his lips. The bailey was packed with people, exacting eyewitnesses who'd judge common sense as cowardice. He measured his brother with coldly appraising eyes; Gruffydd had the height and the reach, but he was quicker, younger, and as Gruffydd's hand dropped to his sword hilt, he, too, reached for his sword.

A woman screamed; people cried out, surged forward. But before Gruffydd's sword could clear its scabbard, a hand clamped down upon his wrist. Ednyved's voice was pitched low, but throbbed with fury no less intense than Gruffydd's.

"Enough," he snarled. "Davydd may not arrest you, but by Christ, I will! Do you think I'd let you do this to Llewelyn?"

Gruffydd jerked free. Ednyved raised his hand, and his household guards moved forward, waiting for orders. Davydd's sword was drawn, but lowered now; he, too, waited, warily. Owain was hovering a few feet away; he had his sword half-way up its scabbard, seemed at a loss as to what to do next. Gruffydd looked first at his brother, and then at his father's Seneschal.

Ednyved, too, was unusually tall; his eyes were on a level with Gruffydd's own; hard, unrelenting eyes. He was, Gruffydd well knew, not a man to bluff. "For once, Gruffydd, use your head. Do you truly want to see Deganwy again?"

"Gruffydd, he is right." Senena was beside him now, tugging at his arm. "Beloved, Davydd is not worth it. Please . . . let's go from here."

"Listen to her, Gruffydd," Gwladys implored. "Papa has a hunting lodge at Trefriw, just twelve miles from here. You and Senena can stay there whilst Papa regains his strength. As for this, it will be forgotten. Nothing happened. Davydd?" She turned challengingly toward her younger brother. "You would not want to trouble Papa for naught, would you?"

"No." Slowly, deliberately, Davydd sheathed his sword. "I agree with Gwladys, think it best you go to Trefriw. We'll send you word if Papa's condition worsens."

"I'll go and right gladly—but not to Trefriw. I'll withdraw to my own lands in Powys, and I will not be back." Gruffydd whirled, gestured to the closest of his men. "Fetch the horses."

Senena's relief was such that she closed her eyes for the briefest of moments, gave silent thanks to God and His angels, to the saint she'd adopted as her own. But she would not breathe easily until they were safely on the road south, and she glanced nervously toward her sons. "Owain, sheathe your sword. There is no time to saddle a mount for you, Llelo; you can ride behind your brother."

Owain did as she bade, but Llelo did not move. "No," he said, almost inaudibly. "No."

Senena turned. "What?"

Llelo hunched his shoulders, stared at the ground. "I'll not go. I'll not leave Grandpapa, not whilst he's so sick."

For Senena, it was almost a relief to have a tangible target for her rage. "You'll do as you're told!"

Llelo shook his head stubbornly, took a backward step, and then another. "I'll not leave Grandpapa," he repeated. "I cannot . . ."

Owain was regarding his brother with disgust, but no surprise. "Shall I fetch him for you, Mama?"

Senena, too, was staring at her youngest child. "You've always been willful, Llelo, and irresponsible. But I would not let myself believe Owain was right; I could not believe you were disloyal, too. And yet this is your answer to our Christmas Eve talk! You say you cannot leave your grandfather? Stay with him, then. But if you do this to your father, I will never forgive you—never!"

Llelo gasped, and the look on his face brought tears to Elen's eyes. But she did not dare intervene; she was the last woman in Christendom whom Senena would heed.

"Christ, woman, what are you saying?" Gruffydd was looking at Senena as if she'd lost her wits. "You know you do not mean that!" He did not wait for her reply, strode past her toward his son.

"I'll hear no more arguments from you, no more back talk. You'll come with us, come home where you belong. Do I make myself clear?"

Llelo swallowed. His eyes were brimming with tears, but again he shook his head. "I cannot," he whispered. "Please, Papa, I cannot . . ."

Gruffydd swore, reached for the boy, his fingers digging into Llelo's shoulder, jerking him forward, so roughly that Llelo stumbled. His face had lost all color; his eyes looked enormous, dark wells of such despair that Gruffydd's breath stopped. Slowly his fingers unclenched, his grip loosened. Until that moment, he'd not realized how much his son feared him.

Llelo's tears were falling free now. He brushed them away with the back of his hand, smeared his face with dirt. "Please, Papa . . . what if he dies? Please . . ."

Gruffydd said nothing; he stood there, looking down at the boy, and then caught the fragrance of perfume, felt a woman's hand touch his sleeve. "Let the lad stay, Gruffydd," Gwladys entreated, very softly. "I'll look after him. What harm can a few days do?"

Gruffydd's mouth twisted. "What harm, indeed? He's taken all else from me; why not my son, too?"

"Ah, Gruffydd . . ." Gwladys's hand tightened on his arm. "I'm not asking you for Papa's sake, but for Llelo's. If you must lay blame about, blame Senena, then, for sending Llelo to live at Papa's court. Blame Papa if you must. But not the boy, Gruffydd, not the boy."

Gruffydd stepped back, looked again at his son. "A fortnight," he said harshly. "But no longer. You understand, Llelo? No longer."

"I know not why it is so, my lord, but I've treated many apoplexy patients, and when the right side of the body is stricken, it is more likely that the powers of speech are also afflicted." The doctor waited, but Llewelyn gave no sign he'd heard. He hesitated, then said, "In truth, my lord, you were lucky."

That got a response; Llewelyn's eyes cut sharply toward him. "You find that a hard mouthful to swallow. But in time it'll go down easier. For you were indeed lucky, my lord. Apoplexy can maim, can leave men with their senses bereft, their tongues hobbled. But God has spared you that. Your wits are clear; so, too, is your speech. Your left arm and leg are benumbed, weak. But it may well be that in time you'll regain some use of them. I do believe that, my lord. You never lost consciousness; that is a good sign. And the muscles in your face were afflicted for but a few hours. That, too, bodes well for your recovery. But you must be patient, my lord. Above all, you must not lose heart."

Llewelyn did not reply, and after a few moments heard the doctor's retreating footsteps. But he was not yet alone; Ednyved still stood by the bed. "I know your thoughts," he said, not sounding like Ednyved at all; for once, there was no mockery in that quiet voice, no sarcasm.

"Do you?"

"Yes. You do not understand why the Lord God took Joanna from you, why He then did not take you. And as you lie there in that bed, you wish He had."

Llewelyn turned his head on the pillow, looked at the other man. "Could you blame me if that were so?"

"I, too, lost my wife within the past twelvemonth, but never did I love Gwenllian, not as you loved Joanna. Nor am I the one stricken with palsy. Blame you? No, Llewelyn, no. I can but tell you this. The ways of the Almighty are beyond our understanding. Why does He strike down the innocent with the guilty? Why does He claim a babe in its cradle? Why did He afflict my son with leprosy?" He leaned over the bed. "We need you still, Llewelyn. That is why the Lord stayed His hand. That is why you must not despair."

He stepped back. "Davydd, Elen, and Gwladys were sorely troubled by what happened this forenoon. They love you well, Llewelyn."

"I know," Llewelyn said, sounding so weary that Ednyved winced.

"Well, I shall leave you now, that you may rest." Adding reluctantly, "You must be told, though. Gruffydd has withdrawn into Powys." He received no answer, but then, he had not expected one.

LLEWELYN'S dream was disjointed, confused, but held such dark overtones of menace that he awoke with a gasp. The chamber was deep in shadows; he'd lost all sense of time, of place. But then he started to sit up, found himself wrenched back to the brutal reality of his plight, to the dead weight where his left leg should have been.

He raised himself up awkwardly on his elbow, threw off the coverlets. His body was still lean, showed the effects of a lifetime of hard activity, of riding, fighting. Across his ribcage, along his collar bone was the evidence of old wounds; the only serious sickness he'd ever known had been inflicted at sword-point. A third scar zigzagged down the upper thigh of his left leg. The leg was bent at the knee, angled away from his body, the muscles constricted, as if in spasm. He reached over, tracked the knotted path of the scar, felt nothing, as if he were touching foreign flesh, not his own. He'd begun to shiver; he pulled the blankets up, lay back against the pillow.

His left arm had drawn itself up to his chest. He stared at his hand, willed it to move, concentrated upon that to the exclusion of all else. His fingers twitched, slowly curved inward, formed a fist. He exhaled his breath, staring down at the hand, a stranger's hand. But no matter how he tried, he could not get his fist to unclench. At last he gripped those frozen fingers in his right hand, pried them apart; his eyes filled with tears.

A sudden creaking alerted him that he was no longer alone; the door had just opened. He wanted no witnesses, wanted no solace, no pity. "Get out," he said roughly. "Get out—now!"

No footsteps sounded; the door did not open again. All was still, the only sound that of his own uneven breathing. He grabbed for the bed hangings, jerked them back. In the center of the room a light flickered weakly, a horn lantern holding a single tallow candle. Above it he could just make out the chalk-white face of his grandson.

The boy had begun to back toward the door. "I'm sorry," he whispered, "I'm sorry," and Llewelyn struggled upright.

"Llelo . . . wait. Come back."

The lantern light swayed, seemed to float toward the bed. Llelo bent down, set it on the floor, almost as if he sensed that the man wanted no illumination, no close scrutiny.

"I brought you something, Grandpapa. I know your chaplain gave you a dispensation to eat meat whilst you're ailing. But when I was in the hall, I heard that you'd refused to eat the pasty the cooks made for you, even though it was stuffed with marrow and currants and dates . . ." There was wonder in Llelo's voice; he could not understand anyone spurning beef marrow, especially after so many weeks of meatless Lenten fare. "I thought you ought to eat, Grandpapa, so I went to the kitchen, and when the cooks were not looking, I smuggled this out." Lifting his mantle, he drew out a napkin, began to unwrap it. "See? I've got some ginger cake for you, two Lenten fritters, with apples and real sugar, and best of all, an angel's-bread wafer."

Llewelyn looked down at the crumbled cakes, felt his queasiness coming back. "Good lad. But that is too much for just one. Why not share it with me? You go ahead, and I'll save mine for later, when I get truly hungry."

"If you're sure . . ." Llelo whipped out his eating knife, conscientiously set about dividing his booty into equal halves. "I can get you more later," he offered, settling himself on the edge of the bed.

"No, thank you, lad." Llewelyn watched the boy eat. There was no need to talk. But a memory was slowly stirring. "Why are you still here, Llelo?" he asked suddenly. "Ednyved told me Gruffydd had gone. How is it you did not go with him?"

Llelo had stopped eating. He licked honey off his fingers, mumbled something about "staying behind."

"That I can see," Llewelyn said dryly, but his eyes were puzzled. "Gruffydd permitted you to stay?" As soon as he heard his own question, he realized the utter unlikelihood of that. "Llelo?"

The boy had averted his eyes. "I . . . I could not leave, Grandpapa. Not whilst you were so sick . . ."

"Jesú!" It was an involuntary exclamation, a belated and appalled understanding of the choice the boy had been forced to make, of yet another wound he'd unwittingly inflicted upon his son.

"Grandpapa?" Llelo was watching him with anxious eyes. "Grandpapa . . . do you not want me to stay?"

The sins of the fathers. Llewelyn reached out, took his grandson's small, sticky fingers in his own. "Yes, lad," he said. "I do want you to stay. More than I knew."

3

Llanfaes, North Wales

May 1237

GRUFFYDD reined in his horse at the edge of the wood, gazed out onto the beach. The narrow strait that separated the island of Môn from the mainland was swept by treacherous currents, the water surface churned by brisk winds. Llewelyn was sitting on the moss-covered spar of an old ship wreck, watching Llelo splash in the shallows. The boy gave a sudden shout, whirled and came running back to Llewelyn. The distance was too great for Gruffydd to see what he held; he thought it might be a crab. He watched as the man and boy bent their heads over Llelo's find; he could not remember his son ever running to him like that. They had yet to notice him; Llewelyn's dogs were upwind, ranging along the beach some yards away. Gruffydd's mouth tightened. You're getting careless, old man. You ought to have taken heed of me ere this. He urged his stallion forward, onto the sand.

They saw him now. Llelo took an involuntary step backward. The two weeks Gruffydd had grudgingly promised him had unaccountably lengthened into four and then six. Each morn he wondered if this would be the day his father would come for him, and as the weeks passed, a poisonous fear began to entwine itself around his reluctance to leave his grandfather, the fear that his mother had spoken no less than the truth, that she would never forgive him. "Papa . . . you've come to take me back?"

Gruffydd did not answer. He could not keep his eyes from his father, from the crutch Llewelyn had reached for as he rose to his feet. He thought he'd accepted the serious nature of Llewelyn's illness, but the sudden and irrefutable reality of that wooden crutch shocked him, shook him profoundly. He dismounted, handed the reins to Llelo. "Take my mount back into the woods, let him graze awhile."

Llelo reached for the reins, retreated with obvious reluctance, with many backward glances over his shoulder. The two men looked at each other; the silence spun out between them, a web made of memories.

"Are you in much pain, Papa?" This from Gruffydd, abruptly, awkwardly.

"No . . . not much." A faint smile touched Llewelyn's mouth. "Given that men call apoplexy the half-dead disease, I'd have to say that I took the honors in our exchange, was left with fewer battle scars than most."

"Is there nothing you'll not make light of—even that?" Gruffydd pointed an accusing finger toward that alien crutch. "You cannot make me believe this is easy for you!"

Llewelyn's eyes flicked from the crutch to his son's face. "I did not say it was easy, Gruffydd. I feel naked without a sword. A few minutes past, Llelo took hold of my left hand, but I'd not have known had I not seen him do it. I am weighed down by an anchor, one of my own flesh. I find myself hobbled, and—for the first time in my life—helpless. Is that what you'd have me say? Is that the truth you seek?"

Gruffydd blinked rapidly, spun around to look out over the strait. "No," he said, "no . . . " He strode to the water's edge before turning back to face his father. "Can your doctors do nothing?"

"I rather think they do too much," Llewelyn said dryly. "I've swallowed one noxious concoction after another, have had my flesh prodded and poked, have permitted them to bleed me and then wrap my leg in the skin of a newly killed fox. But when their potions and plasters failed, they wanted to apply a red-hot needle to my leg, to raise blisters that would drain off the bile—or so they hoped. They took it quite badly when I balked," Llewelyn said, the memory of his doctors' indignation evoking a grim smile.

"At that point," he said, "I decided to rely upon common sense. I've healed my share of lamed horses with flaxseed poultices and rest. But I've seen other men stricken with palsy, and unless they made use of their crippled limbs, the muscles would wither, become too feeble to support their weight. So as soon as I could, I sought to walk. Each day now I come down to the beach, and each day I find I can go a little farther."

That matter-of-fact statement was not an accurate accounting of the past six weeks, omitting as it did all mention of how very easily he tired, of the times he'd fallen, the times he'd despaired. But it was as much as he could share. "There has been some healing." He shifted his crutch. "God willing, there'll be more."

Gruffydd was still staring at the crutch. "I do want you to get well, Papa," he blurted out, then looked faintly surprised at his own words. "But I expect you do not believe that."

"Yes, I do, Gruffydd," Llewelyn said, wondering if he lied. He decided to gamble with the truth, added softly, "I very much want to believe you," and saw his son flinch. "You've come for the boy?"

Gruffydd shook his head. "No," he said, no longer meeting Llewelyn's eyes. "I've decided to let him stay awhile longer."

Llewelyn was taken aback. He knew the risk he took in admitting how fond he'd become of Gruffydd's son. But he felt he owed Gruffydd honesty for this unexpected generosity. "I cannot deny that I'm right pleased to hear that. May I ask why you changed your mind?"

"No," Gruffydd snapped, "you may not." His rudeness was defensive; he had no answer for Llewelyn. He could not admit, even to himself, that he would willingly share his son's love if that would ensure his father's recovery. Still less could he acknowledge his uneasiness about his wife's unrelenting attitude, her unreasonable hostility toward their child.

Gruffydd had been wed to Senena for nineteen years, had found contentment in marriage to his cautious, grey-eyed cousin. He knew that hers was the greater love, even sensed that hers was the quicker wit. He might well have resented her for that; instead, he'd come to rely upon her shrewd, unsentimental advice, upon her loyalty, loyalty that was impassioned, absolute. They rarely disagreed; it was all the more unsettling to him now that they should be so at odds over their own son. It baffled him that Senena could judge Llelo as if he were a man grown, making no allowances for his extreme youth, and he'd at last concluded that time apart might be best for both mother and son. But he felt disloyal to Senena even in harboring such thoughts, could not have spoken them aloud to anyone, least of all to Llewelyn. He turned away from his father's searching eyes, raised his voice. "Llelo! Come here!"

Llelo came on the run. "I tied your horse to a tree, Papa," he panted. "Do . . . do we go home today?"

"No, Llelo. I've decided to let you spend the summer at your grandfather's court."

"Truly?" There was so much joy on the boy's face that Gruffydd began to wonder if he'd not made a grievous mistake. "Thank you, Papa!" But then Llelo's smile wavered. "Why, Papa?" he said. "Does Mama not want me back?"

"Ah, no, lad!" Gruffydd knelt, put his hands on the boy's shoulders. "Never think that, Llelo. Your mother loves you," he said, "no less than I do." He saw his son's eyes widen, realized suddenly that he'd never said that to Llelo before, and then Llelo's arms were around his neck, clinging tightly. He held the boy close, gave Llewelyn a look that was at once challenging and oddly triumphant. *Just remember he is my son, not yours.* He did not say the words aloud, did not need to, for his was an easy face to read.

Llewelyn said nothing. The sight of his son and grandson together gave him no disquiet, only unexpected hope. He'd feared that Llelo's love would act as a knife, severing those last tattered shreds of the bond that linked him to his son. Now he dared to wonder whether the boy's love might instead act as a bridge between them.

There was shouting in the distance. As they glanced toward the sound, they saw that riders had ventured out onto the Lafan Sands, were signaling to the Llanfaes ferry. The boatmen were already rowing out, and Llewelyn, his son, and grandson started up the beach, for visitors to Llanfaes would be visitors for Llewelyn. Gruffydd could not help noticing how naturally his son slowed his pace to match Llewelyn's, and somewhat self-consciously, he, too, shortened his stride. The ferry had reached the Aber shore, was picking up several passengers. They had an impressive escort; fully a score of men were urging their mounts into the water. Slowly the ferry moved back toward the Llanfaes beach. Gruffydd could now make out the slender figure of a woman sitting in the bow. With recognition came a rush of resentment. He hated his father's marital ties to the English Crown, hated the bond Joanna had forged between Wales and its powerful, predatory neighbor to the east.

"It is the English King's sister," he said coldly. "A vain, flighty woman if ever there was one. But I daresay you'll make her welcome."

"Nell is Joanna's sister, too." Llewelyn's voice was no less cool. "I will indeed make her welcome."

Llelo looked from one man to the other in dismay, sensing the sudden tension, but unable to understand why it was so.

IT was a mild day; Welsh spring always came into flower first on Môn. Elen had removed her mantle and veil, and her long, dark hair was blowing about untidily. From time to time she'd brush it back impatiently, intent upon the task at hand. She was kneeling beside her mother's tomb. Putting her spade aside, she reached for the first plant, a blooming yellow primrose, removed the sacking from its roots and carefully lowered it into its waiting hole. The next plant was the vibrant gorse that was carpeting the island in gold. So absorbed was Elen in her work that she was oblivious of all else, unaware that she was no longer alone.

Nell was amused by Elen's wind-whipped hair, the grass stains on her skirt. She'd never known a beautiful woman as lacking in vanity as Elen. Nor did it surprise her to find Elen performing a chore she could more easily have entrusted to a servant. "I'm glad you chose the gorse," she said. "That was ever one of Joanna's favorite flowers."

"Nell!" Elen jumped to her feet, ran to embrace the younger woman. There were only eight years between them; in many ways, they were more like sisters than niece and aunt.

There was a wooden bench just a few feet from Joanna's tomb. Catching Nell's querying look, Elen said, "Davydd had it brought out, so Papa could rest when he visits Mama's grave. You've seen him already?"

"Yes, down on the beach. He told me where to find you." Nell unfastened her mantle, sat down on the bench. "When I first heard of Llewelyn's seizure, I feared the worst. But he seems much better, Elen, seems like to make a true recovery."

Elen nodded. "I'd say it was miraculous—if I did not know Papa so well. He's never been one to recognize defeat, and there's never been a foe he could not outfight . . . or outwait. Even when King John forced him to make that humiliating surrender at Aberconwy; within two years he'd won back all he'd been forced to yield to John."

Nell was neither defensive nor self-conscious when others spoke ill of her father, for she'd never known him; he'd died while she was still in her cradle. "I stopped at your manor in Delamere Forest on my way into Wales," she said, "and John gave me a letter for you."

Elen showed no great interest in her husband's letter. She'd joined Nell on the bench, now turned her face up like a flower, toward the sun. "I've been back in Cheshire but once since Papa's illness. I suppose John is growing restless for my return. Tell me, Nell. How long can you stay? You did not bring St Cecily with you, I trust?"

Cecily de Sanford had been Nell's governess, and later, one of her ladies in waiting. She was a deeply pious woman, a widow with an utterly unblemished past. But Elen detested her, for it was Cecily who had prevailed upon Nell to take a holy oath of chastity when Nell's husband died. To a grieving fifteen-year-old, so dramatic a gesture had proved irresistible, and Nell had been easily induced to follow Cecily's austere example. Both women had sworn their oaths before the Archbishop of Canterbury, put aside their silks for homespun, put upon their fingers the rings that proclaimed them brides of Christ. Cecily was well suited to a nun's life; she'd found great contentment in privation, self-denial, and celibacy.

Nell had not. She was a young woman who loved bright colors, sweetmeats, harp music, and laughter, a woman who liked the company of men, who'd come to yearn for the marriage and motherhood that her oath denied her. There'd been a time when she'd rush indignantly to Cecily's defense. Those days were past. Now she said only, "That is not kind, Elen," and then she grinned. "Do you know what Simon calls her? My very own dragon!"

Elen arched a brow. "Simon? Would that by any chance be Simon de Montfort, Earl of Leicester?"

"Who else?" Nell gave the other woman a sidelong glance. "What do you think of him, Elen?"

"Simon?" Elen smiled, shrugged. "Well . . . he is handsome enough, for certes. And he has a honeyed tongue, in truth. How else could he ever have coaxed John's uncle Ranulf into yielding up to him Ranulf's claim to the earldom of Leicester? Granted, Simon's claim was a just one. But how many men serve justice if it will take money from their own coffers? No, your Simon must have been remarkably persuasive!"

"He is, indeed," Nell agreed, and then, belatedly, "He is not 'my' Simon, though. But you've told me very little, Elen. He is John's cousin; surely you must know him better than that. What do you truly think?"

Elen reached down, picked a stray daisy. "I think," she said, after a very long pause, "that Simon de Montfort is a man of great ability— and even greater ambition."

She'd not meant that as a compliment, but she saw now that Nell had taken it as one. She was smiling, and as Elen looked at her, she felt a sudden protective pang. She started to speak, stopped. What was there to say? Nell knew the dangers, knew she could not allow herself to care for Simon de Montfort, to care for any man.

"Do you come from the court, Nell? How fares Henry?"

"Well enough. Although he still dotes shamelessly upon that child-bride of his." Nell made a comic grimace. "If she asked for the stars, I daresay he'd begin calculating how to harvest the heavens for her!"

Elen laughed. In the past year, Henry had finally wed, taking as his Queen the daughter of the Count of Provence. Eleanor was only fourteen, less than half Henry's age, but she was an undeniably pretty girl, high-spirited, well educated, and she'd utterly captivated Henry— if not Nell, who so far seemed immune to Eleanor's bright, brittle charm. By all accounts, Eleanor was indeed spoiled, but Elen suspected, too, that Nell felt some jealousy at seeing her place usurped by the young Queen, for Nell had long been treated as the first lady of her brother's court, the King's favorite sister.

"I think, Nell," she began, and then paused. "Did you hear—"

"Aunt Elen!" The voice was Llelo's, so shrill, so full of fear that Elen whitened.

"No, not Papa!" Coming to her feet so fast that she nearly tripped on her skirts, she started to run. She'd taken but a few strides before Llelo came into view. At sight of her, he slowed, caught at the garden wall for support.

"Grandpapa said to fetch you," he gasped. "A courier . . ." He could say no more, did not know how to deliver news so dire. "I outran him . . ." He pointed and Elen now saw the man hastening up the slope toward them. Her initial fear had begun to ebb, but it flared anew as the man came into recognition range—Fulke Fitz Alan, one of her husband's young squires.

"Fulke, why are you here? What is wrong?"

He had to struggle for breath. "You . . . you must come home, my lady. Our lord is taken ill . . ."

"Ill?" Elen's mouth went dry. Her husband was not a man to coddle himself; if he sent for her so urgently, he must be very ill, indeed. "Tell me," she said.

"It began with a chill, with pains in his head, his back. We did not worry, my lady, not at first. But he soon burned with fever. Then on the fourth day . . ." He looked her full in the face for the first time. "On the fourth day, he broke out in spots. All over his shoulders, then spreading down his chest, his arms, legs. The lesions were rose-colored, but they soon darkened, took on a mulberry coloration . . ."

"Dear God!" Elen was standing in the sun, but she'd begun to shiver. "Not spotted fever?"

He nodded mutely, and after that, there seemed nothing more to say, for the disease that they knew as spotted fever, that a later age would know as typhus, was one of the most mortal of all ailments.

LIKE all men of high birth and wealth, John the Scot was an avid hunter, and Darnhall was one of his favorite manors, for it was less than fifteen miles from Chester, yet deep within Delamere Forest. The River Weaver flowed peacefully past a mile to the east, and the green, shadowy woods that rose up around the manor offered refuge to roe deer, foxes, fallow deer, marten, red deer, rabbits. It was a tranquil setting, and Nell had enjoyed some pleasant days with John before departing for Chester and Wales. She returned now to find it a house of horrors.

John did not lack for doctors. There was Master Giles, who had attended the Earls of Chester since the days of John's uncle Ranulf. Walter de Pinchbeck, the Abbot of St Werburgh's abbey, had offered the services of Brother Eustace, who was skilled in the healing and apothecary arts. And when Elen returned to Darnhall, she brought with her Einion ap Rhiwallon. But Nell could not see that any of them had done much to ease John's suffering. They put her in mind of an old proverb, one that warned of too many cooks spoiling the broth, for they seemed to spend an inordinate amount of time arguing medical theories, disputing one another's treatment. And while they wrangled, John grew steadily weaker.

His fever had raged for a fortnight, resisting all efforts to lower it with sage, verbena, and sponge baths. He coughed continually, and his tongue was thickly encrusted, while a brownish slime formed on his teeth and gums faster than Elen could wipe it away. Watching as Elen and a servant gave John yet another sponge bath, Nell was shocked anew at sight of that wasted, emaciated body. John was only thirty-one, had always been a robust, stockily built man; Nell could not recognize that man in the one who submitted, apathetic, uncaring, to his wife's ministrations. To Nell, his body resembled nothing so much now as the hollowed woodwork of a lute, and she could only marvel that the disease could have made such lethal inroads in so short a time.

The doctors had bled him again that morning, murmuring uneasily among themselves at the dark color of his blood, but he seemed even weaker after their treatment. Nell suspected that they'd already abandoned hope. They continued to give him enemas, to brew herbal potions, whose ingredients they seemed loath to share, especially with one another, to study his urine and take his pulse. But each one had come privately to Elen, suggested she summon a priest.

Did Elen, too, realize her husband was dying? Nell did not know, for Elen shared none of her thoughts. She rarely left John's bedside, had slept so little in past days that Nell had begun to fear for her health, too. The sponge bath was done; kneeling by the bed, Elen began to apply a linseed poultice to the bedsores on John's thighs and buttocks. Nell had a sharp eye, yet try though she might, she could read nothing in Elen's face but exhaustion.

"Let me do that, Elen, whilst you get some rest."

Elen looked up; her mouth moved in a wan smile. "You need rest, too, Nell. I can never thank you enough for this, for all you've done . . ."

Nell flushed, for there'd been too many times when she'd found herself regretting her offer to accompany Elen, times when she'd wished herself a thousand miles away from this foul-smelling sickroom. "I would that I could do more," she said, in utter sincerity, and then, "Elen! Jesus God!"

There was no warning, just blood. It gushed suddenly from John's nose, soaking the sheets and pillows, spraying the bodice of Elen's gown as she sought frantically to staunch the bleeding with a towel; the towel, too, was soon splotched with red. Nell ran to the door, shouted for the doctors.

For a terrifying time, they feared John was dying, bleeding to death before their eyes. But at last that fearful rush of blood slowed, ebbed to a trickle. As the doctors applied fresh compresses, Elen sagged down on a coffer. For once she offered no argument when Nell insisted she change her bloodied clothes and then lie down; she nodded, moved numbly toward the door.

It was difficult to change the blood-stained linens with John in the bed, but Nell managed it with some help from a little kitchen maid. Nell was becoming increasingly grateful to Edith, for most of the servants were so terrified of catching the spotted fever that only the direst threats could get them into the sickroom at all. Nell had raged in vain, for their dread of the disease was greater than their fear of her. Nor were the servants alone in their alarm; Nell and Elen's ladies showed the same reluctance to cross that threshold. It was, Nell thought grimly, as if poor John had become a leper, and she decided that when she finally left Darnhall, she'd take Edith with her, give the girl a place in her own household.

"Do try to swallow, John," she coaxed, tilting a cup to his lips. He opened his eyes, but they were dulled, putting her in mind of quenched candles, lacking even a spark of light. The doctors had told her this eerie indifference was characteristic of his illness, but she found it strange, nonetheless, that he seemed not to care as he drifted closer and closer to death.

"Madame." One of the doctors was standing in the doorway. "Several lords have just ridden into the bailey. If you like, I'll sit with Lord John whilst you greet them."

Nell nodded, rose slowly to her feet. She'd never before been careless of appearance, but now she could not even bother to glance into a mirror. She untied her apron, relinquished her vigil to the doctor.

Although it was the last day of May, a fire burned in the great hall; it had rained steadily, relentlessly, for the past five days, and the men standing by the hearth were shrouded in dripping, hooded mantles. Nell felt no surprise to find no women among them; although both of John's sisters had been informed of his illness, neither had yet to arrive. Nor would they, Nell thought, with cynical certainty. John's sisters were no more willing than John's servants to brave the spectre of spotted fever.

One of the men had detached himself from the others, was moving swiftly toward her. There was something familiar about that tall, mantled figure, that quick, confident stride. Nell came to an abrupt halt. "Simon?" She rarely sounded so hesitant, but she was afraid to let herself hope. He jerked his hood back, and she looked up into intent grey eyes, eyes that showed sudden alarm as they took in her pallor, her startling dishevelment.

"I came as soon as I heard." He reached out, caught her hand in his. "Nell, you're not ill, too?"

She shook her head. "Oh, Simon . . . Simon, thank God you've come!"

JOHN's fever began to subside, but he showed no other signs of recovery. He was often delirious now, mumbling incoherently, plucking feebly at his coverlets, exhausting the last of his energy in agitated, sometimes violent, ravings. Elen moved a pallet into the bedchamber, slept there during those rare hours when she could be coaxed away from his bedside. "He needs me," she'd say whenever Nell or the doctors protested, and indeed, John did seem somewhat calmer when she sat by him, holding his hand.

Nell would always remember that first week in June as a waking nightmare. The rains had yet to abate, and the River Weaver was rising so rapidly that Simon set up a flood watch. In one of his brief lucid moments, John was shriven by his chaplain, and for a few hours afterward, he slept. But that night he was troubled again by fevered dreams, by sharp abdominal pains. The diarrhea soon became so acute that the doctors were not long in drawing the same bleak conclusion. For once in agreement about their diagnosis, they told Elen that her husband was in God's hands, beyond mortal help.

John was groaning, twisting from side to side. The sudden stench was overpowering; Nell had become accustomed to the fetid odors of the sickroom, but this was so foul, so noxious that she nearly gagged. She clapped her hand to her mouth, fought back her nausea as Elen called out for servants. They appeared within moments; Nell did not know what Simon had done, but the servants no longer balked at entering John's chamber, obeyed all commands with alacrity. Now they hastened toward the bed, quickly stripped off the soiled sheets, as Elen wiped her husband's wasted body with damp cloths, all the while murmuring wordless sounds of comfort, the way a mother might seek to calm a fearful child. Nell's eyes filled with tears; whirling, she bolted from the chamber.

Simon was coming from the stables as Nell emerged into the bailey. She heard him call her name, but she did not stop. Her steps quickened; by the time she reached the gatehouse, she was running.

She ran until she had no breath left, until she was surrounded by the utter silence of a woodland clearing. The sky was dark with rain clouds, and the oaks, hazels, and aspen trees were glistening, spangled with moisture. The grass was wet, but Nell was beyond caring about mud stains; she sank down beside a dripping oak. For a time, she sat very still, breathing in the scent of grass and honeysuckle. The silence had been illusory; she could hear now the soft trilling of linnet and lark, the harsh, clear cry of a mistle thrush.

"Nell?" Simon came through the trees, dropped down beside her in the grass.

"How did you find me?" she asked, and he smiled.

"You blazed quite a trail. You ought to ask those Welsh kinfolk of yours to teach you something of woodland lore." He was carrying a hempen sack, and as she watched, he pulled out napkins, thick chunks of cheese, and a loaf of manchet bread. "After you ran out, I stopped by the kitchen," he said, "grabbed whatever I could lay my hands upon. I've a flask of wine, too . . . here."

Nell took it gratefully, drank deeply. "My father died of the bloody flux, Simon. I always knew that, of course, but till now I never knew how he must have suffered. This afternoon I watched John's agony, and for the first time, I found myself thinking about my father—truly thinking about the man, about those last dreadful days and how it must have been for him . . ." She drank again. "I also found myself wishing John would die."

"Do not reproach yourself for that, Nell. For John, death will be a mercy, a blessed release." He reached over, handed her bread and cheese. "Eat," he said, "ere you fall sick, too."

"We ought to go back. I feel like a fool, running off like that . . ."

"You had cause. I've seen few women—or men—show the courage you've shown in these past days. In truth, Nell, I never suspected you'd make such an admirable nurse."

Nell smiled tiredly. "People are always surprised when I show I am competent or capable, not just—"

She stopped, and Simon finished for her. "—fair to look upon."

She blushed, then grinned. "As vain as it sounds, I was going to say that," she admitted. "But I'd be lying if I pretended I did not know I was pretty, and I've never seen the virtues in false modesty. I like the way I look. It is just that . . ." She hesitated. "I would never want people to think I'm like her, like my mother."

Nell's mother had been one of the great beauties of her age, a sensual sophisticate who'd left England when King John died, returning to her native Angoulême, where she'd wed her own daughter's betrothed. Nell had been just two when Isabelle departed; the only mothering she'd ever gotten had come from her older half-sister Joanna. For several months now, she and Simon had been conducting a cautious but intense flirtation; this was the first time she'd ever revealed anything so personal, giving him a sudden glimpse of the woman behind her flippant court mask. Twice she'd smothered a yawn, and he leaned over, put his arm around her shoulders. As she started to pull away in surprise, he said,

"When was the last time you slept? Lie back, Nell, and put your head on my shoulder."

"I ought not to . . ." Nell's dimple flashed. "But I will. I am bone-weary, in truth. A few moments, mayhap . . ." She snuggled back in his arms, and it was the true measure of her exhaustion that she felt no excitement at being so close to him, only a drowsy sense of security. Soon, she slept.

She awoke more than two hours later, and was both astonished and touched that Simon—so restless, so intense and energetic—should have found the patience to sit quietly, holding her while she slept. She was dangerously drawn to him, acutely aware of the strong sexual attraction that burned between them. But she'd not realized he could be tender, too.

They followed a woodland path back to Darnhall, their steps instinctively slowing as they neared the manor, not talking, reveling in the unexpected intimacy of silence. They were within sight of the manor gatehouse when thunder crashed over their heads and rain poured down in torrents. They ran for shelter, hand in hand; by the time they reached the great hall, they were both soaked to the skin. Laughing, they hurried toward the fire, leaving puddles in their wake.

"Simon, I'm half-drowned!" Nell jerked off her sopping wimple; even her long, blonde braids were drenched, dripping water onto the floor rushes. Still giggling, she glanced toward Simon. He'd already sobered, more sensitive than she to the atmosphere in the hall. Nell looked around her, saw only somber, disapproving faces, and sighed. Laughter was a sin of no small proportions in a house waiting for death.

Abbot Walter moved toward them. "My lord of Leicester, Madame. I regret I must be the one to tell you. Whilst you were gone, the Earl of Chester's earthly cares came to an end. He was taken to God nigh on an hour ago."

ELEN was sitting in John's favorite chair. She was so still she scarcely seemed to be breathing; her dark eyes were dilated, blind. She did not react to the opening door, to the sound of her name.

"Elen, I'm so sorry!" Nell knelt by Elen's chair, put her arm around the other woman's shoulders. "If only we'd been here," she said remorsefully, and Elen pulled away from her comforting embrace.

"I fell asleep," she said; her voice was toneless, flat, not like Elen's voice at all. "I did not mean to, but I was tired, so tired. And whilst I slept, he died."

"Ah, Elen, you cannot blame yourself for that. John would understand, truly he—"

"It is my fault," Elen said, still in that strangely muffled voice. "My fault."

"Elen, that is ridiculous! The Blessed Virgin herself could not have given John better care than you did. You've nothing to reproach yourself for, nothing!"

"You do not understand." Elen rose, moved toward the bed, where she stood staring down at her husband's body. "John had taken the cross, meant to depart this year for the Holy Land. I knew how dangerous such a pilgrimage would be; I knew how many died on such quests. And I could not help thinking that John might die, too. I let myself imagine how it would be if he did not come back, if I were widowed." Tears had begun to streak her face; she seemed not to notice. "I did not truly want his death, I swear I did not. I just wanted to be free. Was that so very terrible, Nell? That I wanted to be free?"

"No!" Nell's answer came unthinkingly, a cry from the heart. "No, of course it is not, Elen."

Elen had yet to take her eyes from her husband's face. "Then why," she whispered, "do I feel like this? Why do I feel as if his death is my doing?"

Nell was utterly at a loss. She turned, gave Simon a look of mute appeal, and he moved away from the door, joined Elen beside her husband's body.

"Do you think he was a good man?" he asked, and Elen nodded. "A good Christian?" She bit her lip, again nodded. Nell was beginning to look indignant; was this Simon's idea of comfort?

He reached out suddenly, grasped Elen's shoulders and turned her to face him. "Then why," he demanded, "do you think God would value his life so cheaply?"

"What?"

"Why should God punish you by taking John? That makes of him little more than a pawn, Elen. Does that not seem rather arrogant to you, that you should allot so much worth to your own soul and so little worth to his?"

"Simon!" Nell hissed. "How can you talk to Elen like this, now of all times!"

He ignored her, kept his eyes upon his cousin's widow. "John did not die because the Almighty wanted to punish you. He died because it was his time. That is the truth of it, Elen. To believe anything else is an insult to John, an insult to God."

"Simon, enough! How can you be so cruel?"

"No, Nell." Elen drew an unsteady breath. "It is all right," she said, "truly," and Nell saw that Simon's brutal common sense had somehow given Elen more comfort than her own sympathy.

Elen raised a hand to her face, seemed surprised when her fingers came away wet. "I shall try to remember your words," she said to Simon. "Now . . . now there is so much I must do. John must be buried at St Werburgh's; it was his wish. I must bathe him, must . . ." She faltered, and Nell said swiftly,

"I will take care of that for you, Elen. Simon and I will take care of everything, I promise. Come now . . . come with me. If you do not get some rest, you will not be well enough for the funeral."

She'd expected an argument, but Elen nodded. "Thank you," she said. "Thank you both for your kindness to my husband, to me." She moved back to the bed then, bent over and brushed her lips to John's forehead. Straightening up, she had to catch Simon's arm for support, and only then did they realize how close she was to physical collapse.

"John deserved a better death than this," she said softly. "And a better wife."

JOHN the Scot, seventh Earl of Chester, was buried on Monday, the 8th of June, before the High Altar in the Benedictine abbey of St Werburgh at Chester, the same church in which he and Elen had been wed more than fourteen years earlier.

Abbot Walter had turned over his private quarters to the Earl's widow. His great hall was crowded now with mourners. Servants passed back and forth among them, offering wine, ale, and cider, sweetmeats. The solemnity of the funeral Mass had slowly given way to the perverse cheer peculiar to wakes; people drank and ate with unseemly zest, shared news and gossip, speculated what would befall the earldom of Chester, for John's heirs were all female.

Nell would normally have enjoyed such a gathering, for she was the most sociable of beings, and she very much appreciated the attention a lovely woman could invariably command. But now her every thought was for Elen, Elen who moved amid the mourners like a wraith, so detached, so apparently aloof that she was giving rise to gossip, among those who did not know—as Nell did—just how frighteningly fragile Elen's composure was. As soon as she could, Nell drew Elen aside, led her toward the Abbot's private chamber at the south end of the hall.

"No arguments, not a word. As soon as I get your gown off, it's into that bed." Ignoring Elen's half-hearted protests, Nell soon had the other woman stripped to her chemise. Removing Elen's veil, she deftly uncoiled Elen's thick, black hair—a pity Elen's coloring was so unfashionable—and propelled Elen toward the bed.

"There, dearest, just lie back. You truly ought to rest awhile. I daresay you never suspected I could be so motherly!" Nell busied herself in fluffing the pillows, tucking the blankets in. "I think it is fortunate, indeed, Elen, that you are Prince Llewelyn's daughter."

Elen was not as surprised as she might have been; Nell's conversations were often enlivened by such seeming non sequiturs. "Why?"

"Because he'll look out for your interests, make sure your dower rights are protected. To tell you true, Elen, you'd best keep an eye on those sisters of John's. Their husbands cannot wait to get their shares; I actually heard them wagering upon how many manors John had held! I doubt that they'd be overly scrupulous of a widow's rights."

Nell could see no interest on Elen's face, and she said, more emphatically, "Elen, I know whereof I speak. My husband's family did their damnedest to deny me my share of William's estates." She frowned, and Elen was momentarily forgotten, for her resentment was a sharp blade, indeed, hurt to handle. She'd have been better off had Llewelyn been the one to speak up for her. A man like that would have been a shrewd bargainer; for certes, he'd not let Elen be cheated of her just due. Whereas Henry . . . She sighed. She did love her brother, truly she did. But why was he so weak-willed, so easily swayed by stronger men? He was the King, yet he'd let the Marshals rob her blind. Even now he did not curb the Marshals as he ought, allowed them to delay her dower payments, to offer feeble excuses for their disobedience. How lucky were those women who had men to stand up for them, men who were not afraid of giving offense, men with courage.

Vexed by Elen's indifference, Nell was mustering up new arguments, all her protective instincts now aroused, determined to save Elen from herself, when there was a knock on the door. She quickly reached up, drew the bed hangings, enclosing Elen in a cocoon of sarcenet silk. "You sleep; I'll get rid of whoever it is."

It was Simon. "One of John's cousins has just arrived, wants to pay his respects to Elen. I tried to discourage him, but he's remarkably persistent." He smiled apologetically, and Nell found herself suddenly paying more attention to the shape of his mouth than to what he was saying.

"Simon, I cannot let her see anyone now. Truly, I'd send the Pope himself away." John was related by blood or marriage to most of England's nobility; he was a first cousin of the Scots King, cousin to the Earls of Winchester, Arundel, and Lincoln, nephew to the Earl of Derby. But as she opened the door a little wider, Nell saw that the man standing at Simon's shoulder was not one of John's titled kinsmen. She knew Robert de Quincy on sight, but he was only a casual acquaintance, the younger brother of Roger de Quincy, Earl of Winchester.

As she started to close the door, he stepped forward. "I must see her, if only for a few moments."

Nell gave him a coolly reproving look, one mixed with curiosity, for in the past, his manners had always been impeccable. He was an attractive man, she conceded, not as tall as Simon, but with hair even blacker, and eyes of a truly startling blue. But he looked as if he'd not had much sleep, even less peace of mind. She'd not realized that he was so fond of John; their kinship was a distant one. "I am sorry, Sir Robert, but—"

To Nell's astonishment, he paid her no heed, pushed past her into the chamber. "Sir Robert, wait!" Simon was almost as fast as Robert de Quincy; he followed, started to put a restraining hand on the other man's arm. But at that moment, Elen jerked the bed hangings back.

"Rob?"

He froze where he was. For what seemed an endless moment, they looked at each other. And then, as if released from the same spell, they both moved. Elen swung her legs over the side of the bed, he started toward her, and they met in the middle of the chamber. As soon as his arms went around her, Elen began to weep.

"Rob, it was so awful. He suffered so . . ." She sobbed, and he drew her still closer, murmuring her name, kissing her hair, her temples, tasting her tears.

"I'm here, beloved, I'm here," he said, and Nell, an amazed witness, came abruptly back to reality. Jesú, the door! It had been wide open, giving all in the hall a front-row seat! She spun around, and then gave a sigh of sheer relief, blessing Simon for being so wondrously quick, for he'd whirled, slammed the door shut just in time, preventing those in the hall from seeing this lovers' embrace.

As Simon and Nell passed through the abbey gate out onto Northgate Street, Nell paused uncertainly. People were milling about in the street, dogs and children darting here and there, getting underfoot, reveling in the excitement. Although it was more than a fortnight until the city's annual fair, monks were already erecting stalls and booths in front of the abbey gateway. Some were there to trade their goods, others to witness secondhand the burial of a great lord. All stared openly at Simon and Nell, and it was this which made her hesitate, for she'd never been out amidst the common people without an escort, without the trappings and pageantry of rank. But Simon took her hand in his, and she soon decided she liked the novelty of it all, liked the bustle and color, even the admiring looks, for they were not entirely directed at her silk gown, at Simon's fine tunic and gilded scabbard.

We're a handsome couple, she thought, glancing sideways at Simon. It was usually easy to tell Welshmen from those of Norman-French descent, for the Welsh shaved their beards but retained their mustaches, while the Normans and Saxons were bearded. Simon was neither, was completely clean-shaven. Nell wondered whether this apparent disdain for fashion's dictates was an act of rebellion or one of vanity, and she tucked the thought away, to tease him with at a more appropriate time.

"You did not know about Elen and Robert de Quincy?"

Nell shook her head. "I knew her marriage was not a happy one. But no, I did not know that . . . that . . . ."

". . . she and de Quincy were lovers. That is what you are so loath to say, is it not?"

"Simon . . . try not to think too badly of Elen. I am not defending her sin, but . . . but she is so very Welsh, you see."

Simon gave her a look of faintly amused bafflement. "So? What are you saying? That the Welsh are truly as immoral as you English claim?"

"No, of course not. Adultery is no less a sin amongst the Welsh than amongst other peoples. But the Welsh treat their women differently. A Welshwoman has far greater freedoms than women of my England or your France. A Welshwoman cannot be forced to marry against her will; she has no less right than her husband to end an unhappy marriage; she cannot be beaten the way an erring English wife can. She can even divorce her husband if he brings his concubine into her home, Simon! Those are remarkable laws, you will admit, utterly unlike ours, unlike any in Christendom. And Elen grew up under them; she never learned proper obedience as an English girl would. So when she found herself trapped in a barren marriage, she felt free to . . . to look for happiness outside the marriage. Mind you, that is no excuse. But it does make her behavior more understandable, does it not?"

To Simon, it did not, but he did not want to hurt Nell by condemning her kinswoman, and so he shrugged, said lightly, "Had you been born a man, you'd have made a most persuasive lawyer." Adding, "But it would have been a God-awful waste."

Nell laughed. "In truth, I do not see what attraction de Quincy has for Elen. He is handsome enough, I suppose, but he always struck me as rather too easygoing, too carefree. Granted, I do not know him that well, but he seems to lack serious purpose, to lack ambition," she said, somewhat reluctantly, for she wanted to be fair to the man and she could think of few more damning accusations. "Though he is more than a match for Elen in recklessness! It is a miracle to rank with the loaves and fishes, that they did not betray themselves long ere this."

They were passing a street stall, and Simon stopped, fumbled for a few coins, and purchased two helpings of hot sausage. This, too, was a new experience for Nell, and she found herself envying Simon his wider horizons, the greater freedoms he enjoyed as a man. Reaching for her first taste of street sausage, she ate it with relish. Her innate honesty compelled her now to acknowledge that she was still much freer than most women her age, for she had no husband to answer to, to obey. But there was no longer joy in that freedom; she'd paid too high a price for it. Her gaze lingered on Simon's dark, laughing face, and in that moment she knew the full measure of all she'd lost, of what was forever denied her.

She looked hastily away, lest her heart show in her eyes. "I cannot imagine, Simon, that Elen would want to marry de Quincy . . . can you? After all, she is the King's niece, a Prince's daughter, now the widow of the richest Earl in the realm, and Rob de Quincy is but a knight. He's not a suitable match for her, could never— What? Why do you laugh?"

"I was amused," he admitted, "by the contrast. You look like a wayward angel, and then you open your mouth and you do sound practical enough to put a Cheapside fishmonger to shame!"

Nell bit her lip, sought to stifle her laughter. "You have queer notions as to what comprises a compliment, Simon de Montfort!"

"On the contrary," he said, "I just paid you the highest compliment a man can give a woman. I told you that you were beautiful . . . and clever. Do you not know, Nell, how rare a combination that is?"

She was used to bantering with men; her reputation as a flirt was deserved. But now she found herself suddenly tongue-tied, as flustered as if she were still a raw girl. She was accustomed to men looking at her with desire. But Simon was looking at her with approval, and that she found far more unsettling. "I want to thank you," she said hastily, "for what you did in the Abbot's chamber. It was kind of you, Simon; by your quick thinking, you saved Elen's good name. I know you did it for your cousin John, but Elen—"

"No," he said. "I did it for you, Nell. I did it because Elen is your kinswoman." He reached for her hand, brought it up to his mouth, pressed a kiss into her palm. He was not smiling. "Why do you think I came to Darnhall? Because Henry told me you were there, and I thought you might have need of me. There is nothing I would not do for you, Nell. Do you not know that?"

"Oh, Simon . . ." Nell's voice had dropped to a whisper. "Simon . . . whatever are we going to do?"

ON July 5, Elen had a Requiem Mass said for her husband on his month-mind. The next morning she made an early departure from Chester, rode west into Wales. In summer, travel was possible at a rapid pace, and she reached her father's manor at Aber two days later.

"Papa will be so pleased." Davydd came forward, helped her to dismount. "Why did you not tell us you were coming, though?"

"I was not sure you'd be here, Davydd. Were you not going to meet with the English King on Papa's behalf?"

"Our meeting was delayed." Although Davydd was not usually demonstrative, he embraced his sister. "Are you all right, Elen? You look tired," he said, and then realized how easily expectations could distort perceptions. In truth, she did not look tired at all, neither care-worn nor troubled. Those were the words that came to mind when one thought of a woman widowed but a month; they did not apply. For Elen looked radiant.

LLEWELYN watched as, one by one, the candles flared into life. He waited until the servant had withdrawn from the chamber, then beckoned to his daughter. "Come here, lass," he said. "Sit beside me on the settle."

She did, gave him a smile that caught at his heart, so loving was it, so like her mother's smile. "I was so glad, Papa," she said, "to find Llelo still with you."

"It means much to me," Llewelyn admitted, "having him here. But first, lass, I want to speak of you. I suspect, Elen, that the wolves will soon be gathering. John held land in ten shires, held two earldoms, a rich prize, indeed, to be up for the taking. I understand the husband of John's niece is laying claim to the earldom of Chester. It would not surprise me, though, if Henry is loath to let it go. For nigh on twenty years, Cheshire and Wales have been united, an alliance not in the interests of the English Crown. Whilst Ranulf and then John lived, there was little Henry could do. But now . . ." He was frowning, and Elen reached up, kissed him on the cheek.

"I am so sorry, Papa. I know how important that alliance was to you, to Wales."

It was indeed important; for Llewelyn, John's death had been cat-astrophic. He did not want to burden her, though, not so newly wid-owed, and he smiled at her, said, "Be that as it may, I do have good news for you. Henry has assured me there will be no difficulties about your dower rights."

"Thank you, Papa."

"Henry listens best to whoever reaches him last." Davydd spoke dryly from the shadows. "But Papa has been able to hold him to his word in the past, Elen, so I think your prospects look promising."

"Promising? Oh, yes, Davydd," she said, "yes."

Llewelyn was looking thoughtfully at his daughter. It was passing strange. He'd never thought she truly resembled Joanna; the resemblance had always been more pronounced in Davydd. But since her mother's death, she seemed more and more like Joanna. Of all his children, she'd been his secret favorite, so passionate, so stubborn, so vulnerable, the rebel to whom everything had always come so hard. "You have something to tell me, I think," he said.

"Yes," Elen said. "Yes, Papa, I have."

"You do not wear mourning."

She nodded. "Papa . . . I mean to wed again."

She heard Davydd draw a quick breath. Llewelyn's eyes narrowed. She'd seen that look before, had seen him change in the span of seconds from the fond, indulgent father to the Prince. "Go on," he said. "Is it anyone I know?"

She tried not to let his sarcasm sting, said as steadily as she could, "You've met him. Sir Robert de Quincy, brother to the Earl of Winchester."

"I can well understand why he'd want to wed you. He could not hope to do better. But you could, Elen. Surely you do know that?"

"I love him, Papa."

"Do you?" Llewelyn's voice was very cool. "Why? What sort of man is he, that he'd let you come alone to Aber? Is he so lacking in courage that he dare not face me? How can such a man be worthy of your love, Elen?"

"Rob is no coward!" Elen jumped to her feet, began to pace back and forth as she sought to get her rage under control. "He wanted to come with me, wanted us to see you together. I would not let him. I knew what would happen. You'd blame him, you'd not listen. I thought I had a better chance of making you understand."

She turned back to face him. "You know I did not want to marry John. Surely you remember, Papa, how I pleaded with you, how I wept? And so you told me I did not have to wed him, and then . . . then you explained how very important this marriage was for Wales, how important for you. I was fifteen, Papa, I yielded, did as you wanted. I married John."

Llewelyn was quiet, silenced by those echoes of bitterness. "You must know," he said at last, "that we never wanted to see you hurt. Your mother and I wanted you to be happy, Elen."

Elen's mouth softened. "I know, Papa, I do. I know, too, that I am disappointing you now. But try to understand. I have loved Rob for so long, for years. But as much as I loved him, I knew we could never have more than a few stolen moments. We could not run away together. I could not do that to John, could not hurt him like that, make him such a cruel laughingstock. I could not do that to you. I knew how much your alliance meant. And Mama . . . it would have raked up all the old gossip, the ugliness. Men would have said, 'Like mother, like daughter.' They would have remembered her mistake, judged her by my sin, judged her all over again. And Rob . . . you called him a coward, Papa, but that's not so. He would have run away with me anytime in the past four years; he would have ruined himself for me and never counted the cost. But I could not risk his life. John's honor was all to him, and he was Earl of Chester and Huntingdon, kin to the Scots King. Had I run away with his cousin, John would not have rested until he'd avenged himself upon Rob."

She knelt suddenly, took Llewelyn's hand between her own. "But now we can wed, Papa. We cannot hurt John or Mama now, and your alliance . . . it died with John." The hand she held lay still, unresponsive in hers; tears trembled on her lashes. But then he put his other hand upon hers, and she realized it was his left hand she held. "Oh, Papa . . ."

"Hush," he said, "hush," and he tilted her chin, looked for a long moment into her upturned face. "I'll not lie to you, Elen; I'll not pretend I do like it much. But you made one marriage to please me. It is only fair that you now make one to please yourself."

She'd not expected it to be so easy. She knew he loved her, but she knew, too, that he'd always put Wales first. "You've made me very happy," she said, and Llewelyn found for her a reasonably convincing smile.

"May your Rob de Quincy make you happy, too. Davydd, pour mead for us, and we'll drink to Elen's marriage, to Elen's homecoming." Llewelyn had always been adept at reading faces; for a prince, that was much more than a social skill. "What is amiss? Surely you intend to return to Wales whilst you mark your mourning time? Where else would you—"

"There will be no mourning time, Papa. Rob and I mean to wed as soon as the banns can be posted."

Both men were staring at her. Davydd spoke first. "If you mean that," he said incredulously, "then you are well and truly out of your mind!"

"Davydd, I have never meant anything more."

"You are no fool, Elen," Llewelyn snapped, "so stop talking like one. You may marry this man if you must, but not for a twelvemonth. To do otherwise would be to court disaster, to bring scandal down upon your name. A sudden marriage to a man of lesser rank would be taken as an admission of adultery. Not only would you besmirch your honor, you might well jeopardize your dower lands."

"Papa, I do not care about the lands!" She'd never dared say that before; they looked so startled that she gave a shaken laugh. "I know that sounds like heresy, but it is true, nonetheless. Rob's holdings are a mere pittance when compared to all John held, but he has manors of his own. We will not starve."

Davydd reached out, put his hand on her arm. "I believe you when you say the lands mean nothing to you. But are you equally indifferent to suspicions of murder?"

Elen's jaw dropped. "Murder? Davydd, that is ridiculous. No one could possibly believe that!"

Llewelyn was slowly shaking his head. "You are wrong, Elen. If you wed Robert de Quincy so soon after your husband's death, most people will conclude that he must have been your lover. A hasty second marriage plants ugly seeds. For too many, gossip is their meat and drink. And once men begin to see a death as convenient, there'll be those to see it, too, as contrived."

It was obvious to Llewelyn that his daughter was shaken. What an innocent she was. And de Quincy was just as blind. God help them both. For a moment he allowed himself to hope that he'd gotten through to her. But even as he watched, Elen's expression changed. He recognized the defiant jut of her chin, the sudden surge of color across her cheekbones. When she was a child, the easiest way to get her to do something she did not want to do was to dare her to do it. It seemed, he thought grimly, that she had not changed all that much.

"Those who know me would never believe that," she said tautly. "The others do not matter."

"I will not let you do this, Elen. I forbid it."

Elen stood very still. "I do not want to defy you, Papa. Nothing could lessen the love I have for you. I want your blessings for my marriage, but I do not need your permission. I am Welsh, am free to wed whom I choose. Our laws give me that right, Papa, you know they do."

Llewelyn started instinctively to rise, remembered just in time how cumbersome an act that now was. "Tell me this, Elen. You are willing to risk the loss of your dower lands, the loss of your honor. What if I cannot forgive you? Are you willing, too, to risk that?"

"Papa . . ." Elen's voice wavered. "Papa, please listen. Who can know how much time is allotted to us? You'd have me sacrifice a year with Rob when that could be the only year we'd have. That time is too precious, Papa. You of all men should understand that, with Mama but five months dead."

He was silent, and she saw him through a blur of tears. "I'll depart for Chester on the morrow. I shall bid you farewell ere I go, Papa." She waited, then turned, walked slowly toward the door.

Davydd crossed the chamber, poured mead for Llewelyn and for himself. Giving his father a brimming cup, he said, "Papa, how can you let her do this? How can you not stop her?"

"What would you have me do, Davydd? Put her under guard? Tie her to her bed?" Llewelyn looked down at the cup, then flung it from him, watched it shatter against the hearthstones. He at once regretted it; such ungoverned bursts of temper were not natural to him. "I am sorry, Davydd. My nerves are more on the raw these days than I like to admit."

"I was in the wrong, Papa, not you. For in truth, I do not know how to stop Elen, either." Davydd held out his own drink, and Llewelyn took it with a twisted smile.

"Go fetch her, Davydd. Bring her back."

After Davydd departed in search of his sister, Llewelyn leaned back upon the settle, took several swallows of mead. Although the chamber was empty, he did not feel alone. In this bedroom he and Joanna had consummated their marriage. Elen had been conceived in that bed, born in it, too. Joanna had died in it.

"What else could I do, Joanna?" he said. "How could I not forgive her?"

4

Odiham Castle, England

October 1237

IT was with a sense of foreboding that Mabel de Druual watched her lady read Simon de Montfort's letter. Color had risen in Nell's cheeks; her lips were softly parted. Since childhood, it had been so for her; her face was ever a mirror to her soul. Mabel had sometimes marveled at the irony of it, that King John's daughter should be so lacking in artifice, even caution. A widow who'd been with her since Nell's marriage to William Marshal, Mabel loved Nell for her candor, her impulsiveness, her high spirits. But it occurred to her now that those were the very qualities that were putting Nell so much at peril.

Nell looked up. "It is from the Earl of Leicester," she said, needlessly, for Mabel had recognized Simon's seal. "He has returned from York."

"That is twice this year that he has acted as the King's envoy, is it not? He must stand high, indeed, in the King's favor," Mabel said, because she knew how it pleased Nell to hear Simon praised.

"Yes," Nell agreed, "he does." She glanced down at the letter again, and her expression changed; her smile faded. "Simon has accepted my invitation to visit me here at Odiham," she said, and so grave was she that Mabel took heart. Mayhap it was not too late, she thought, and she knelt beside Nell's chair.

"Write at once to Lord Simon," she pleaded. "Tell him not to come."

Nell's brows drew together; when she started to speak, Mabel put up an imploring hand. "Please, my lady, just hear me out. You must know it is only my love for you that bids me be so bold. I fear for you, for I know how much you care for Lord Simon."

"Why do you say that, Mabel?"

"My lady, I have eyes to see. When you and he look upon each other, it is a wonder the air itself does not take fire. And now you would invite him here to your own manor. My lady, think what you do. Our flesh is weak; we are all daughters of Eve, sons of Adam, too susceptible to temptations, to Lucifer's whispers in the dark. If you have Lord Simon here, under your own roof, it is all too likely that ere the night is done, you'll have him in your bed, too."

Nell jumped to her feet, but she was not a hypocrite; her indignant protest died on her lips. Mabel rose, too. "I know the Church says that fornication is a mortal sin. But I truly think the Almighty looks upon it with a more tolerant eye than do His bishops, His priests, for could He damn so many for a sin so common? Adultery . . . that is a more grievous offense; few would argue that. But my lady, the sin you contemplate is one of the most serious of all. You have sworn a holy oath of chastity, knelt before the Archbishop of Canterbury and pledged yourself to Christ. How could you then give yourself to a mortal man? I fear there could be no forgiveness for a betrayal so great, Madame."

"You tell me nothing I do not already know, Mabel," Nell said, more sharply than she'd intended. How could she fault Mabel for caring?

"I am thinking not only of your soul, Madame. I am thinking, too, of your heart. The earldom of Leicester is not a lucrative one; Lord Simon is deeply in debt, is ever hard pressed for money. Twice now he has sought a wealthy wife, first the Countess of Boulogne and, last year, the Countess of Flanders."

"I know that, Mabel." Neither in Nell's voice nor in Mabel's was there condemnation or criticism. Marriages were very practical matters, based upon realistic considerations of politics and profit, not passion, and to both women, it was perfectly natural that Simon should seek to better his fortunes through wedlock. "What of it? What mean you to say?"

"What I am saying, my lady, is that the time will come when Lord

Simon must seek yet again to wed an heiress. What choice would he have, for how else could he hope to pay his debts, to fill his empty coffers? And could you ever endure that, Madame? Could you share him with another woman?" Mabel paused, but Nell bit her lip, said nothing.

"He may indeed love you well, Madame. In truth, I suspect he does. But there can be nothing between you but friendship. I beg you, do not risk so much for so little. Do not sacrifice your honor and chances of salvation for a sinful, stolen love."

Nell was still silent. She glanced again at Simon's letter, at the bold strokes of the writing, Simon's own hand, not that of a scribe. "You make it sound so simple, Mabel. But it is not." She looked up then, and Mabel saw tears in her eyes. "God help us both," she whispered, "for it is not."

SIMON arrived at Odiham at dusk on the third Friday in October. Supper was generally a casual, rather cursory meal, but for Simon Nell set a lavish table. Even the Friday fish menu had not daunted Nell's cooks; Simon and his men were served savory, highly spiced dishes of herring, lampreys, and oysters. Simon's squires were quite impressed by such rich fare, but they soon concluded that their lord was much more impressed by the Countess of Pembroke. The Lady Nell was clad in a gown of brocade silk, a vibrant ruby-red threaded through with strands of gold, and Simon had yet to take his eyes from her. His squires watched their lord, they watched the King's sister, and they were both awed and uneasy that Simon dared aim so high.

After the meal was done, there was dancing. Nell showed Simon about the hall; it encompassed most of the keep's second story, save for a small chamber to the north, which had been set aside for Simon's use. Nell was very proud of Odiham, and she told Simon that the castle had been built by her father, King John, "begun in 1207, the year of my brother Henry's birth."

"The year before I was born," Simon observed, and Nell suddenly realized that she'd not even known how old he was. It was a surprisingly unsettling thought, for it made her aware of how much there was that she did not know about Simon de Montfort.

"Your Lady Mabel has been eyeing me askance, but I've yet to see your dragon. Is Dame Cecily lurking about in the shadows? I cannot imagine her straying far from your side, not with a wolf prowling midst her flock."

"Is that how you see yourself, Simon?" Nell asked, and he grinned.

"No, but that is how your dragon does. Can you deny it?"

She shook her head. "Well, this is one lamb in no need of a shepherd. Dame Cecily is not at Odiham. I gave her leave to visit her son."

"I see," he said. Their eyes caught, held. "I daresay Dame Cecily was much beholden to you. I know I am," he murmured, and Nell's breath quickened.

The dancing was about to resume. Simon held out his hand, and Nell let him lead her out to join in the carol. When the dance ended, they shared a cup of hippocras, while Nell told him of Odiham's proudest hour, those fifteen days that the castle held out under a French siege in 1216. "They say the French were astounded when the garrison at last yielded and just thirteen men did march out to surrender."

Simon showed no surprise. "I've seen few castles better situated," he said. "King John had a good eye for defense. By placing the castle in a bend of the Whitewater, he made the river into a second moat."

"We do depend upon more than the river for our defenses. My lord father had trenches dug to the west, which could be flooded in times of danger, making the ground all but impassable," Nell said, and saw Simon's eyes kindle with a soldier's interest. She drank the last of the wine before saying, with studied nonchalance, "From the keep battlements, the canals are clearly visible."

She needed to say no more. Simon took the cue as if it had been rehearsed between them. "I should very much like to see these canals, for I've never encountered a defense of that sort. Could I persuade you to show me?" he asked, and Nell allowed herself to be persuaded. Mabel and Simon's squires sought to look noncommittal. No one ventured to comment upon the difficulties of inspecting a castle's defenses in the dark.

THE great keep of Odiham towered forty-five feet, afforded—by day—a spectacular view of the Hampshire countryside. A harvest moon lit the dark, a misty, mellow gold haloed by feathery, wispy clouds. The light from the heavens was so clear, so lucent that Nell found no need for her lantern. She set it down within the embrasure, began to point out landmarks to Simon: the slow-moving silver of the river, the castle moat, the marshes where John's defensive ditches lay, camouflaged by the night.

"To the northeast lies my deer park," she said proudly. "Henry gave me the castle and manor last year, but he only recently allowed me the park and hunting privileges. It offers good sport, Simon, as you may judge for yourself on the morrow. I've planned a hunt after dinner . . . if that meets with your approval."

"Everything you do meets with my approval," Simon said, to his own surprise, for he'd never been one to indulge in glib, shallow gallantries. What he'd just said to Nell was no less than the truth, although he did not know how to reassure her of that. They were, the both of them, treading an unmarked road, but wherever it led, it was too late to turn back.

The silence was making Nell uneasy; she could read too much into it. "I had a letter some days past from Elen de Quincy," she said. "She had good news for me. Her lord father has prevailed upon Henry, and an agreement has been reached as to her dower lands. Unlike mine, hers will be a fair settlement: manors in the shires of Bedford, Huntingdon, Middlesex, Rutland, and Essex."

"That marriage caused much talk, most of it ugly."

"I know," Nell admitted. "But I could find in Elen's letter no echoes of regret. She did a foolish thing, but also a brave one. It does take courage, Simon, to value love above honor."

"I should hope," he said, "that one could have love with honor."

Nell's smile flickered, sadly. "In an ideal world, so might it be." She leaned back against the parapet, let her eyes wander at will over Simon's face. How finely cut his mouth was, mayhap not quick to smile, but when he did . . . She sighed, said, "Elen had good news, too, about her father. Prince Llewelyn can now walk without the aid of a crutch. And he has picked up the threads of an old liaison, once again has a woman in his life. Elen spelled the woman's name as H-u-n-y-d-d, which should be said as Hiń-ith . . . I think. I confess, my tongue has ever tripped over Welsh!"

To Simon, it was only to be expected that Llewelyn should take a mistress; it had been more than nine months since his wife's death. But he knew women could be foolishly sentimental about such matters. "Does Elen resent this woman?" he asked, and Nell shook her head. Their hands rested together on the parapet wall, not quite touching.

"She says she did once—very much. This Hunydd was Llewelyn's concubine, you see, during those wretched months after Joanna's infidelity, when she was being held at Llanfaes. Elen detested Hunydd then, could not bear to see her in Joanna's place. But now she says she thanks God for her. She knows there is great danger in grieving too much."

"Did Llewelyn love your sister as much as that?" Simon asked, and then, "I expect he must have; how else could he have forgiven her?"

Nell longed to ask if he could have forgiven as Llewelyn did. But she did not, sensing that the answer would not have been to her liking. She said, instead, "Llewelyn loved Joanna well, and she him. I remember a visit to their court a few years past. One night the talk turned to remarriage. Few who lose a mate do not eventually wed again, and sometimes, with unseemly haste. Someone—Lord Ednyved's wife, I think—made mention of this to Joanna, mayhap in jest. But to Joanna, that was a joke bitter as gall. She always feared that Llewelyn would die ere she did, and she said, right sharply, that she'd take no husband after Llewelyn. It grew quiet, until Llewelyn dispelled the tension, made us all laugh. He said that he would want Joanna to wed again, would not begrudge her a second husband, no matter how young or handsome—provided that the man was utterly incapable in bed!"

Nell laughed; so did Simon. "My sister and Llewelyn were so lucky, Simon, so very lucky. They found together a rare love, a happiness few ever know. I . . . I would that I could have been so blessed."

"I never thought much about love," Simon said slowly. "I loved my mother, but she died ere I was thirteen. I can scarce remember my father. As for women, I suppose I've had my share. Some I fancied more than others. But I never met one to grieve over, I never thought to find one I'd need as I need bread to eat, air to breathe."

Nell's hand sought his on the parapet; his fingers closed tightly around her own. "And now, Simon?"

"Now I do want you, Nell, and only you."

"Simon . . ." Nell was not sure what she meant to say, never found out, for Simon was done with waiting. He took her in his arms. She raised her face to him, closing her eyes, and then felt his mouth on hers.

Nell had been wed against her will at the age of nine, given by her brother to a man much older than she. But William Marshal had been kind to her, and she'd learned to love him. When she was fourteen, they'd consummated their marriage, and he'd been kind then, too; her few memories of the marriage-bed were pleasant ones, memories of warmth and security and tenderness. Nothing in her past experience had prepared her for Simon.

He was kissing her mouth, her eyelids, her temples, removing her veil and wimple, kissing her throat, and Nell forgot her qualms, forgot her fears; she returned his kisses with abandon, with a passion to match his own. She loved this man. She loved him so much. How could she ever give him up?

Simon had not meant for their lovemaking to take fire so fast. But her response was so ardent, so eager that he found himself unable to hold back. Never had he been so aware of a woman's fragrance. It was subtle, elusive, clung to her hair, her skin; even the air seemed perfumed with a faint, flowery scent. She did not object as his caresses became bolder, more intimate, allowing him to pull the top of her bodice down, allowing him to fondle her breasts. Their kisses were hard, bruising, for there was in their desire a desperation, too, as if these fevered moments alone upon the castle battlements might be all they'd ever have.

When Simon suddenly released her, Nell was dazed, disoriented. She caught the wall for support. She felt drugged, focused with difficulty upon what he was saying. How strange his voice sounded, slurred and breathless. "No," he said, "not like this . . ." She leaned toward him, uncomprehending, and he grasped her shoulders. "For God's sake, Nell, stop. I am a man, not a saint. It will need but a few more moments for me to throw our mantles on the walkway, take you here and now, and I do not want it to be like that, not with you . . ."

Neither did Nell. There was nothing romantic in the image he'd just conjured up for her; the thought of such a hasty, frenzied coupling sounded sordid to her, shameful. She flushed, becoming aware of her dishevelment, and began to tug at the bodice of her gown. It frightened her now, the memory of that hot, heedless passion, and she confessed shakily, "I . . . I did not know . . ."

"It was not like that with your husband?" he said, and laughed when she mutely shook her head. "Where is your bedchamber, Nell?"

She hesitated. "Above the hall. Simon, I . . ."

He was not listening, had stooped to retrieve her discarded wimple and veil. "I'd be all thumbs; you'd best do this yourself. Nell, listen. We must go back to the hall. There'll be talk if we do not."

She nodded quickly. Yes, that was best. She needed time, time to think. She did love him . . . or did she? How often had she heard priests warn that lust could masquerade as love. And all knew that the Devil delighted in casting carnal snares for the unwary. She must be sure of her feelings, lest she barter salvation for a mere fever of the flesh.

"We'll return to the hall, and in time, we'll retire for the night—to our separate chambers. I will wait an hour, mayhap even two, till the castle sleeps. Then I'll come to you."

Nell did not speak, but she looked so uncertain that Simon smiled reassuringly. "It will be safe, Nell; you need not fret. None but my squires will know where I slept, and they'd never betray me." He leaned over, kissed her on the mouth, very gently this time. His eyes shone like silver in the moonlight, shone with elation and triumph and disarming tenderness. "How I love you," he said, and there was wonder in his voice.

Nell swallowed. "There . . . there is a second stairwell," she said softly. "In the northwest corner of the keep. It leads up to my chamber."

THE candle had been notched to show the passing hours, but no matter how often Simon glanced at it, he could not will the wax to melt. He paced to the window, then back again. When he reached for a wine cup, drained it in several swallows, his squires exchanged surprised and speculative looks, for Simon was a sparing drinker.

His squires were the sons of English noblemen, learning a knight's trade in Simon's service. Young men of seventeen and eighteen, they were as unlike in personality as they were in appearance, united only in their shared devotion to Simon. They'd been somewhat uneasy when they first joined his household, for Simon was known to have a notoriously quick temper. But they'd soon discovered that their qualms were for naught. It was true that Simon did not suffer fools gladly. That was not unusual in a man of rank and power. What was, though, was Simon's reluctance to direct his rages at the defenseless. And while he was a very exacting master, he was also scrupulously fair.

Baldwin and Adam were dazzled by Simon's lethal skill with a sword, awed by how easily he handled the most unruly horse. They admired his self-assurance, his boldness, came to treasure his rare compliments. And because they were at an age in which imitation was still the purest form of flattery, they took Simon as their example in all particulars. Simon was an avid reader, rarely traveled without a book in his saddle bags; Baldwin and Adam struggled, with indifferent success, to take this peculiar pastime of Simon's to heart. Because Simon never passed a beggar without giving a coin, his squires no longer mocked God's unfortunates. Like Simon, they professed to be scornful of the superstitions of ignorant men, and like Simon, they honored the Grey Friars above all other orders. Simon admired the friars for their austerity and piety, said they'd not been corrupted as the monks had, by rich living and worldly concerns; his young disciples said the same. They sought to mimic Simon's dry, sometimes caustic, wit, and they learned a difficult lesson in discretion, for Simon never boasted of his bedmates, had open contempt for men who did.

Even had they not known of Simon's distaste for such boasting, the squires would never have dared to jest about the Countess of Pembroke. They watched their lord stride back and forth, and they could only marvel at his rash courage, while fearing for his safety. The man who seduced a King's sister might well pay for his pleasure with his head; at the least, he could expect to forfeit the instrument of that pleasure. Even King Henry could not be indifferent to his sister's disgrace, would have to play a man's part should he learn of Simon's mad folly. The boys again exchanged anxious glances, and Baldwin surreptitiously crossed himself, for all knew the lady had pledged her honor to Christ. It would, he thought with a shiver, be almost like debauching a nun.

THE hall was dark; Simon could just make out the sleeping forms bedded down in the aisles. All was still. He encountered no one in the stairwell. He paused again before Nell's chamber, but could hear no sounds anywhere. The door swung open; Nell stood framed in soft firelight. She was still dressed in her gown of red silk, but her hair was unbound, tumbling about her shoulders. Simon had seen her hair uncovered by veil or wimple, but he'd never seen it like this, falling free down her back, and he wanted suddenly to feel its bright silkiness against his skin, to wrap it around his throat.

"Your hair looks verily like spun gold," he said, and then laughed. "I sound like every smitten lover since the world was green. Why must the language of love be so threadbare? There ought to be a way to tell you how I feel without evoking so many echoes, so many ghosts." He laughed again for the sheer joy of this moment, the joy of being here in this bedchamber with this woman. But when he reached for a strand of her hair, Nell pulled back, moved hastily to put space between them.

"I cannot do this, Simon," she said. "I cannot bed with you."

Color had risen in her face, but her voice was steady; she looked not so much remorseful as defiant. "I cannot bed with you," she repeated, and then waited, warily, for his anger.

It did not come. There were no explosions of outrage, no indignant recriminations, not even the reproaches she felt she deserved. Just utterly unnerving silence. His eyes seemed to have darkened, more slate now than silver. He made no move to approach her, but neither did he move toward the door. "What is wrong, Nell?" he said at last. "What do you fear?"

She'd braced herself for a dreadful scene, expecting him to rant, to call her all the ugly names men reserved for women who promised more than they could deliver. She realized now that she'd even wanted such a scene, wanted him to react with rage and injured pride. How much more dangerous was this quiet question of his.

"I know what some men say of me, Simon, that I am a wanton. It is true that I like to dance and flirt, that I wear silk, not homespun, and they dare to judge me for it. But they are wrong. I have held true to my oath. I have lain with no man since my husband's death."

"Do you really think you had to assure me of that? I know you, Nell, know full well that you've not violated your oath. Just as I know you were not playing a wanton's game with me, tonight on the battlements."

"I . . . I truly thought I could do it, Simon. I never meant to mislead you, I swear I did not. I'd not see you hurt for the world, for I do love you. No, Simon—do not! Please stay where you are. I do not think clearly when you are close to me," she said, managed a weak smile. "In truth, I do not think at all!" Although she trusted in his honor, she still thought it prudent to put some tangible barriers between them, and she slowly circled around the table.

"I do not know if I can make you understand, Simon. But as I sat here, waiting for you to come to me, I suddenly knew that I could not go through with it. As much as I want you, I cannot do this. Forgive me, Simon, but the sin is just too great. If I violate my oath, I am damned, am—"

"No," he said. "That need not be so, Nell. Do you think I would ever let you risk so much for me? I could not have you put your soul in peril; no earthly love is worth that. But there is another way. We can ask the Pope for a dispensation."

She stared at him, first in astonishment and then in anger. "That is not worthy of you, Simon," she said coldly. "The world is full of men who'll babble any nonsense that comes to mind, promise the sun and moon itself to coax silly women into bedding with them. But I expected better of you! Just how would you have me word this petition to the Pope? 'Will Your Holiness please deliver me from my oath so I might sleep with Simon de Montfort?' "

"Now you are the one to be talking nonsense," he said impatiently. "You must know that I seek more from you than a quick tumble in bed. I want to marry you, Nell."

"Marry?" she echoed faintly. She looked so stunned that he felt the first stirring of unease. He swiftly suppressed it, moved around the table and took her hands in his.

"Simon . . . Simon, it could never be."

"Yes," he said, "it could . . . and it will. Nell, listen to me. That day at Chester, you asked me what we could do . . . remember? In these past four months, I've thought of little else. We cannot bed together on the sly. But neither can I walk away from you. There is but one answer for us, Nell. We must seek a dispensation from the Pope, one that would free you from your vow, free us to wed."

"Marriage," Nell whispered, and for a brief moment she dared to dream it might be so, dared to envision herself as Simon's wife, able to bear his name, his children. But then her shoulders slumped. "That was cruel of you, Simon," she said dully, "cruel to give me such false hope. We could never wed. Even if the Pope could be persuaded to release me from my vow, that would mean only that I was free to wed again, not free to wed you."

Simon frowned. "Am I so unworthy a choice?"

"No, beloved, of course you are not. But I am the King's sister, and mine must be a marriage of state. Henry and his council would pick a husband for me, a husband of their choosing, not mine. Just as they did with my older sisters, so would they do with me. I would have to make a marriage for England's weal."

"I am Earl of Leicester and steward of England," Simon said stiffly. "My brother is Constable of France and Count of Montfort. My lady mother was a Montmorency. I need apologize to no man for my blood-lines, for my House is one of France's oldest and proudest."

"I know, beloved, I do," Nell said wretchedly. "But Simon, you are not a prince, and they would expect no less for me."

"They? Or you? I think I begin to see. It was not the vow at all. You do not think I am good enough for you."

"Ah, Simon, no . . ." Nell knew him too well now; she could see beyond his anger and pride, see how she'd hurt him. And she could not bear it. As he turned away from her, toward the door, she cried, "Do not go! I do love you, Simon, and I will marry you. Let Henry be damned, let them all be damned, I will marry you!"

Simon's hand froze on the door latch. He swung about, his eyes searching Nell's face. He found what he sought, and moved swiftly to her side. "Say it again," he said, and Nell smiled.

"I love you, Simon. I would be very proud to be your wife."

They looked at each other, and then Simon reached out, stroked her hair. When he touched her cheek, she closed her eyes, marveling that the same hand that so easily wielded a sword could be so very gentle, too. He slid his fingers under her chin, tilted her face up to his. The first kiss was soft, tender. The second one was not, for it took as little as that for the passion to flare between them again.

Simon wrapped her hair around his hand, burned kisses along her throat, and when he fumbled with the lacings of her gown, Nell's fingers were no less clumsy, no less impatient. The world beyond that bedroom door was forgotten; so, too, was the gold ring on Nell's left hand, the ring that symbolized her vow. It was as it had been on the battlements, but now they were all alone in a firelit chamber. Nothing was said; there was no longer a need for words between them. They helped each other undress, scattered their discarded clothes across the floor on their way to the bed. And then they were entwined together under Nell's linen sheets, and her last coherent thought was one so blasphemous she would later recall it with a shiver: that even if this was indeed a mortal sin, she could never repent of it.

The regrets were to be Simon's. After their lovemaking, he had rolled over, drawing Nell close and cradling her head in the crook of his shoulder. He could not convince himself that they had sinned; already, he thought of Nell as his wife. But still he knew they should have waited, for it was Nell who'd risked damnation.

He leaned over, kissed the pulse in her throat. She did not open her eyes, but the corner of her mouth curved, and he was swept by tenderness, a new and somewhat unsettling emotion for him. Nell was more than he'd ever dared to hope for, a woman beautiful and highborn and wealthy, a woman spirited and playful and passionate. But if she was indeed a remarkable gift from God, she was also a great responsibility. He was not easily frightened, but it frightened him now to think of Nell being hurt, and it frightened him to think of losing her. He let his fingers wander along the silken skin of her shoulder, stray into the tousled blonde hair. Was she having second thoughts? Could he blame her if so? He was only asking her to confront the Pope and defy the King, no more than that.

"Nell?" She made a wordless murmur, and he said, "What are you thinking of?"

"Our marriage." Nell propped herself up on her elbow. "We must not delude ourselves, Simon, must be prepared for much unpleasantness. Even after we have the dispensation in hand, there will still be those to disapprove, to charge we bought my freedom. And indeed, we will have to do just that; such a dispensation will be very costly."

Simon was cautious with money; he had to be, for he had so little of it. But now he found himself saying recklessly, "No price could be too high for you," and meaning every word of it.

"Money will be no problem," Nell said and smiled at him. "The lands Henry settled on me as my marriage portion give me two hundred pounds a year. My dower rights in William's Irish estates come to four hundred pounds a year, and I am entitled to another four hundred from my share of his English manors."

Simon was impressed, said so quite candidly, and Nell smiled again, with complacent pride. "So you see, my darling, I am indeed a marital prize. And that is why we shall have such a hard row to hoe. We must fight a war on two fronts, first with those who are appalled that I should have forsaken my vow, and then with those who are no less appalled that I should want to marry you. How jealous the other lords shall be, Simon! You are one of them, your estates are modest, and you're foreign-born, which seems to matter more and more these days. Those who fault Henry for showing too much favor to his Queen's foreign kindred will see our marriage in the same harsh light. There will be a loud and bitter outcry, none more so than from my brother Richard and my detestable in-laws. Richard will be sorely affronted that we would dare to wed without his approval . . . and with reason; he is Earl of Cornwall, after all, the second lord of the realm. And my brother-in-law, that wretch Gilbert Marshal, will do all he can to give us grief. So, too, will the rest of the Marshal clan. They know how shamefully they cheated me when William died. His estates are worth at least thirty-five hundred pounds a year, and my dower incomes fall far short of the one-third to which I am lawfully entitled. So they have uneasy consciences, and they will fear that you shall speak up for me, protect my rights as Henry failed to do."

"That you may rely upon, Nell," he said, and there was in his voice a grim resolve that did not bode well for the Marshals. Nell reached up, kissed him passionately on the mouth.

"Simon, tell me the truth. Do you truly believe we can prevail?"

"We will, Nell. We do belong together. But we'd best wed first and seek the dispensation after. It would be easier to thwart wedding plans than to untie a nuptial knot."

Nell at once saw the sense in that, and she nodded vigorously. "But there is one we must take into our confidence, Simon. Ere we wed, ere we petition the Pope for a dispensation, we must confide in my brother Henry."

"You would have us go to the King?" Simon sounded dubious. "Would he heed us, Nell?"

"Why should he not? He is right fond of you, and he loves me well. I cannot believe he would begrudge us happiness. But if we deceive him, he will not easily forgive us. I know my brother, Simon. He is not vengeful, but he can harbor a grudge. And where would we be without Henry's favor? Henry has never formally invested you with the earldom of Leicester. What if he declared your estates forfeit? And what of my dower lands? Are you willing to risk their loss?"

"No," he said, "of course I am not. We will need those incomes for our sons. You are right, Nell, we must have Henry as our ally. Who can afford to have the King as an enemy?"

" 'Our sons,' " Nell echoed. "Simon, how wonderful that does sound to me. And it must come to pass, it must!"

"It will," he promised. "It will, my heart." He began to kiss her, and she rolled over into his arms.

"Make love to me, Simon. But first tell me again that we will be wed." She put her hand on his chest, over his heart. "I could not bear it should I lose you now," she said, and he sought to reassure her with kisses and caresses, to reassure them both that their marriage would indeed come to pass.

HENRY Plantagenet was an attractive man of middle height, with his grandfather's reddish-gold hair, a neatly trimmed beard, and vivid blue eyes; his left eyelid drooped slightly, giving him an endearingly drowsy look. King John's eldest son, he had been crowned at the age of nine, in the midst of a bloody civil war. He was neither as clever nor as ruthless as his father, and he suffered in comparison with his younger brother Richard, who was shrewder, more practical, better able to deal with Henry's overbearing barons. Henry would have made a superior abbot for a wealthy Benedictine abbey, for he was urbane and pious and beneficent. But it was his misfortune to be a King whom few took seriously, and it was his greater misfortune that he knew it. In consequence, he was abnormally sensitive to slights, and although he was generous and kind-hearted by nature, he could also be capricious, petulant, his the perverse obstinacy of a weak man called upon to wield authority beyond his capabilities.

Henry loved pageantry and ceremony, and the Christmas season afforded him ample opportunity to indulge his passion for fêtes and revelry. On this chill night in mid-December, he was in good spirits, having at last selected his New Year's gifts for his young Queen: a heart-shaped silver brooch, a sapphire ring, and a reliquary containing a fragment of the True Cross. He was well pleased with his choices, already anticipating Eleanor's delight, and it was with pleasure that he watched now as Simon de Montfort and his sister Nell were escorted into the privacy of the Painted Chamber.

HENRY looked from Simon to Nell in disbelief. "Is this a jest?" he said, as if hoping it was, and Nell knelt by his chair in a flurry of silken skirts.

"Dearest, we are very much in earnest. Nothing has ever meant more to me, Henry. Simon and I love each other, and we wish to wed. We know that—"

"Are you mad? What of your vow?"

"We would not have Nell forsake her vow," Simon said hastily. "We intend to seek a dispensation from the Pope."

"What makes you think he would ever grant one?"

"I will make it worth his while," Simon said, saw Henry stiffen, and realized he had erred. He'd lived in England long enough to acquire some English prejudices; most Englishmen, no matter how devout, were convinced that the Pope saw England as a milch cow, one to be milked dry on behalf of the Roman Church, and few doubted that the papal court was a market place, where justice was dispensed to the highest bidder. But Henry had an impassioned reverence for the papacy, for he believed the Pope's support had helped to secure his throne for him during those first troubled years of his reign. He looked deeply offended now by Simon's cynicism, and said curtly,

"This is a pointless discussion. I see no reason why His Holiness would ever agree to set aside a vow of chastity. Such vows are not undertaken lightly, are not to be—"

"Henry, I was but fifteen! I did not know my own mind." Nell was becoming frightened, for she knew how stubborn Henry could be. "I know the Church teaches us that chastity is an exalted state, second only to virginity. But not all of us are destined for so holy a life. And marriage is an honorable state, too. What sacrilege could there be in a sacrament, Henry?"

It was a weak joke, failed to amuse her brother. Henry heard three Masses a day without fail, and he was genuinely shocked by his sister's irreverence, by her willingness to profane her oath. But she was looking at him so imploringly that he sought to soften his refusal somewhat. "Nell, I am sorry. But what you ask is impossible. Once you've had time to think, you'll recognize this request for what it is, a whim of the moment that could never be, that—"

"Henry, I love Simon! This is no whim, it is my very life!"

"I can make her happy, Henry, I swear it. And once we have the dispensation—"

"No!" There was anger in Henry's voice now, the anger of a man ensnared in a web not of his making. He did not want to hurt his sister. Nor did he want to hurt Simon. "You cannot marry my sister, Simon. Even if she were free to wed, that would change nothing. I could not give my consent to your marriage."

They looked so stunned that he winced. Why must they ask of him what he could not possibly give?

"I thought," Simon said, "that I was your friend."

"You are my friend. But that does not make you a fit husband for my sister!" Why was he having to do this, to elaborate upon the obvious? "My father and grandfather were Kings of England before me, Dukes of Normandy and Anjou. My grandmother was Eleanor, Duchess of Aquitaine. My sister Joan is Queen of Scotland. My other sister Isabella is Empress of the Holy Roman Empire. Need I truly say more, Simon? The very idea is absurd. In truth, you can be thankful for my friendship, thankful that I have not taken offense at your effrontery."

"I should be grateful that you think my love demeans your sister?"

"I did not say that, Simon! Or if I did, it was only because you forced me to it. I have never faulted you for your ambition. But this time you have over-reached yourself. And that is a warning you'd best take to heart. Have you no idea of the scandal this would cause in council? The King's sister and the Earl of Leicester? Christ on the cross!"

"I see," Simon said. "Then it is not Nell's oath and not my lineage. It is that you do not want to be discomfited before your barons. You'd truly sacrifice your sister's happiness for that? Because you lacked the . . . will to defend her?"

Henry flushed darkly. Like many timid men, he was morbidly quick to suspect slurs upon his courage, and Simon's pause had been a telling one. "This discussion is done," he snapped. "And so are your high-flying dreams of glory. You are not to see my sister again."

Nell had been listening, horror-struck. With that, she gave a choked cry. "Simon!"

He turned toward her, and she saw on his face her own despair and disbelief and a very dangerous rage. "I will have Nell as my wife," he said tautly, "with or without your approval."

Henry was accustomed to arguments and protest; even with the inherent powers of kingship at his command, he had never learned how to compel unquestioning obedience from other men. But such outright defiance left him speechless. He gasped, sputtered incredulously, and then shouted, "You marry Nell and you'll pass your wedding night in the Tower!"

Nell's fear suddenly gave way to fury. "If you imprison Simon, then you must imprison me, too!"

Henry had an inordinately strong sense of family; the thought of his sister in a prison cell was horrifying to him. "Jesú, Nell! Do you truly think so little of me, that you could believe me capable of that?"

For once, she was indifferent to his pain. She moved to Simon's side. "I think Simon is right," she said. "I think you do shrink from facing down your barons. It is easier for you if we do not wed, and you've ever been one for taking the easy way, Henry."

"You are fortunate, Nell, in that I do understand your anger, your disappointment. For I shall overlook your heedless words, shall do my best to put them from my memory. But you cannot marry this man, and I'll say no more on it. My patience is at an end."

Nell looked at her brother, seeing him suddenly with a stranger's eyes, seeing him with utterly unsparing clarity. She reached for Simon's hand, entwined his fingers in her own, for she knew now what she must do.

"No, Henry, you do not understand," she said, and was surprised that her voice could sound so calm, so cold. "You are right when you say there would be a great scandal if I wed Simon. But there will be an even greater scandal if I do not."

She felt Simon's hand tighten on hers; for a startled moment, his eyes sought hers, but he was quick to comprehend—and to approve.

Henry had yet to absorb the full impact of her words. "What do you— Nell, no!"

He sat down abruptly, the color draining from his face. But Nell felt no pity, no remorse. "Yes," she said, "I am with child."

It was a gamble of absolute desperation, a lie that risked all—perhaps even Simon's life—upon how well she knew her brother. "How could you?" Henry cried. "How could you shame yourself like that?"

"I love him," she said, as if that explained and excused all, and

Henry wondered suddenly if she could be bewitched, so unrepentant was she, so defiant.

"It must be true," he said, "what men say, that blood will tell. For God help you, you are indeed Eleanor of Aquitaine's granddaughter."

FROM the first Sunday in Advent until Epiphany no marriage Masses could be said. It was on the following day, January 7, that Simon and Nell were ushered into the Painted Chamber at Westminster Palace. There were no servants, no wedding guests, only the King of England to act as witness to their marriage. Henry had a private oratory in one corner of his bedchamber, and it was here that Simon and Nell knelt to be joined in wedlock by the chaplain of St Stephen's chapel.

When the Mass was said, the deed done, Simon poured wine for his King and for his bride. Drawing Nell aside, he gave her then his bride's gift, a ruby pendant set in heavy gold.

"Thank you, beloved!" Nell raised up, gave him a lingering kiss. "Mayhap Henry is right, mayhap I am shameless," she confided softly, "for I feel no more your wife now than I did that first night at Odiham. That was our true wedding night, Simon."

"You do not mind that our wedding was so hurried, so lacking in ceremony? I wanted more for you than this, Nell."

"I would willingly have wed you in a stable, Simon; do you not know that?"

"There was a time," he confessed, "when I thought we might be wed in a cell!" and they both laughed, the unsteady, exultant laughter of those who had wagered against all odds and somehow won.

"I will be such a good wife to you, Simon. I swear I will. But . . . but I doubt, beloved, that I can be a very dutiful one."

She looked so troubled that Simon burst out laughing. "I doubt it, too," he said. "I doubt it exceedingly."

"Simon, I will try, in truth I will. But I do not want to lead you astray with false promises, promises I cannot keep. I know my faults too well, you see. I am more willful than woman has right to be, and I am lavish with money, and I do not always think ere I speak; my tongue can be right sharp. We'll quarrel, Simon."

"Frequently," he agreed, and kissed her.

Across the chamber, Henry and his chaplain drank their wine in morose silence. The chaplain was wretchedly sure that he had sinned in performing this marriage, and he dreaded facing his superiors in the Church, having nothing to offer them but the feeble excuse that he had not dared to say nay to his King. He had shuddered when Simon placed a gold band upon Nell's finger, remembering another ring, one that pledged her to Our Lord Jesus Christ. No good could ever come of such a marriage; he did not doubt that Simon de Montfort and the Lady Nell would pay dearly for this day.

"My liege?" He cleared his throat awkwardly. "Will you be the one to inform my lord Archbishop of Canterbury?"

"No," Henry said hastily. "The Earl of Leicester shall have that signal honor." But he could take no comfort from that, for he knew the Archbishop would then demand to know how he could have permitted this marriage, how he could have allowed them to make of him a partner in their crime. He believed himself to be a good son of the Church, yet now he must risk the wrath of God, he must defend the indefensible.

And what of his council? His brother Richard? How outraged they would be, as much with him as with Simon and Nell. Henry hated confrontations; he knew there were men who thrived on discord and turmoil, but he was not one of them. Yet now, through no fault of his own, he found himself in the middle of a maelstrom. What, he wondered, was he to say? But what else could he have done? Let his sister shame them all by bearing a bastard child?

Simon and Nell were coming toward them, and Henry tried to find a passable smile. What was done was done, and this was Nell's wedding day. He would not spoil it for her.

"I drink to your happiness," he said, as heartily as he could, and held his wine cup aloft. The chaplain looked as if he'd been asked to quaff hemlock, but he gamely followed suit.

Henry kissed his sister on the cheek, but he could not help thinking that it was indecent for her to look so radiant, so joyous. Had she no conscience at all? His eyes shifted to his brother-in-law's face; a dark face, boldly featured, it was the eyes men first noticed, the eyes of a hawk, Henry thought, telling himself that Simon was his friend, that nothing had changed.

"When do you sail for France, Simon?"

They had decided that Simon should go to Rome, plead his case in person before the Pope. But Simon now said, "Not for some weeks yet. Nell and I talked it over, and we think it best if I wait until our marriage is revealed in council, until the dust settles." There was an involuntary, sardonic twist to his mouth at that last; he knew how Henry feared the uproar sure to follow, and as much as he wanted to be grateful for Henry's support, he could not deny that he felt, too, a certain contempt for the other man's timidity.

Henry was heartened by Simon's decision to remain; he could value in others qualities he knew he himself lacked, and he'd long admired

Simon's coolness under fire. "To my sister," he said, raising his wine cup again. "And to her husband. God keep you both in His favor." And he tried very hard to convince himself that he did indeed wish them well, that he had truly forgiven them for their betrayal, and that he bore them no grudge for all the trouble they were about to bring upon him.

5

Cricieth Castle, North Wales

July 1238

"IF you take much longer, Ednyved, moss will be forming on our chess pieces."

But Llewelyn's prompting was in vain; Ednyved refused to be rushed. "All things come to pass in God's time," he said sententiously, continuing his painstaking scrutiny of the chessboard, and Llewelyn glanced over at Hunydd.

"He always says that when he's losing," he said, and Hunydd smiled. He'd not noticed her doing it, but he saw that she'd brought a bowl of fruit to the table; her concern for his comfort was as constant as it was unobtrusive.

"Did you tell Lord Ednyved the news about Lady Joanna's sister?" she murmured, and Llewelyn returned her smile, his eyes lingering upon her face. She was Joanna's age, many years widowed, a serenely handsome woman who occasionally put him in mind of Tangwystl, Gruffydd's long-dead mother. He'd remained friends with Hunydd after their liaison was over; they were still friends, good friends who sometimes shared a bed. She had many qualities that Llewelyn admired; not the least of them was her utter lack of jealousy. She did not begrudge Joanna his heart, making mention of Joanna's name now without the slightest hesitation, neither self-conscious nor resentful, for she was too wise a woman to cast herself as Joanna's rival.

Ednyved reached for an apple. "What is the news about Nell?"

"I had a letter from Elen. She says that de Montfort was able to secure a dispensation from the Pope."

Ednyved's smile was sardonic. "I'd wager that cost him a right fair sum. But I suppose he feels it's money well spent, and I daresay most of it was Nell's!"

Llewelyn grinned. "I like Nell; I've always admired her pluck." He began to peel an orange. "Elen says de Montfort will not be hastening back to England, though. That marriage stirred up so much turmoil that Nell and de Montfort thought it best if he was away for a while, giving tempers time to cool. I understood poor Henry took so much abuse that he retreated to the Tower, refused to come out!" There was in Llewelyn's voice both detached amusement and faint sympathy, for while he had little respect for his royal brother-in-law, he did have a reluctant fondness for Henry; he'd often benefited from Henry's heartfelt affection for Joanna.

"According to Elen," he continued, "de Montfort has gone to aid his new brother-by-marriage, the Holy Roman Emperor, at the siege of Brescia. Marriage to Nell has suddenly given the man some truly illustrious kin, has it not? But he'll be back ere the first frost for certes; Elen says Nell is with child." Adding dryly, "To satisfy your unseemly curiosity, the babe is due in late November."

Ednyved made an elaborate show of counting upon his fingers. "Nigh on eleven months. I suspect that will disappoint a great many people!"

Llewelyn was no longer listening; he'd cocked his head, looking toward the window. It was unshuttered, and there came clearly to them now the shrieks of seagulls, squabbling over the garbage dumped behind the kitchen. There came also the sound of arrival; horsemen had just ridden into the castle bailey. "That will be Davydd and Isabella," he said. "They are due back today."

Ednyved knew that Davydd had been down in South Wales, meeting with the Princes of Deheubarth, Rhys Mechyll and Maelgwn Fychan. Rhys and Maelgwn were the sons of Llewelyn's former allies, and he thought, Llewelyn and I are outliving our friends as well as our enemies. But he was surprised by this mention of Isabella, for he knew no great passion burned between Davydd and his young English wife. "Did Davydd take his wife with him?"

"No, Isabella has been in South Wales for the past month, visiting her younger sisters. It was agreed upon that Davydd would escort her home once his council was done." Llewelyn glanced expectantly at the door, hearing eager footsteps on the outer stairs. But it was not Davydd and Isabella who burst into the chamber; it was Llelo and Gruffydd.

Llewelyn was delighted, but also surprised. He'd sent Gruffydd word of his arrival at Cricieth, asked to see his grandson, and he'd been hopeful that Gruffydd would agree, for Cricieth was just fifteen miles from Gruffydd's manor at Nefyn. He'd not expected, though, that Gruffydd would accompany the boy.

"We have good tidings, Grandpapa!" Llelo glanced back at his father. "Can I be the one to tell him, Papa?" and when Gruffydd nodded indulgently, he blurted out, "I have a baby brother!"

Gruffydd had told Llewelyn that Senena was not due till late August, but as Llewelyn's eyes sought his son's, Gruffydd grinned. "The babe was not willing to wait," he said. "Last Wednesday eve, just after Vespers, Senena was brought to bed of a fine, healthy son."

"That is welcome news, indeed." Llewelyn smiled upon them both, remembering just in time to query politely, "And Senena?"

"She is well, Papa." It had always irked Gruffydd that the brother he so detested should have borne the name of the most celebrated of Welsh saints, and he relished this opportunity to reclaim it for one of his own. "We named him Davydd." Adding quite needlessly, "After the saint, of course."

"He has reddish peach fuzz all over his head," Llelo volunteered, "and at first he was all puckered up, like a prune." His eyes had settled wistfully upon the orange in his grandfather's hand, for oranges had to be imported from Spain, were considered rare delicacies. Llewelyn proved himself to be adroit at mind-reading; he separated the fruit into halves, passed one to Llelo, who gave him a grateful grin. "The wet nurse suckles him every three hours, Grandpapa, so he gets four meals a day!"

Hunydd was pouring drinks for them all, mead for the men and watered-down wine for Llelo. She handed the first cup to Gruffydd, offering her good wishes, and he smiled. He approved heartily of this bedmate of his father's, although he probably would have approved of any woman who was not English and not Joanna.

As Gruffydd accepted Hunydd's congratulations, Llewelyn looked thoughtfully at his grandson. The Welsh practice of partible succession—dividing all equally among a man's sons—was in many ways a fairer system than the English one, which left all to the eldest son. But it was also a system to foster fratricide, for when a Welsh prince died, his sons inevitably fought each other for the succession, winner-take-all to the survivor; Llewelyn knew that his own uncommonly amicable relationship with his younger brother, Adda, had been possible only because of Adda's lamed right leg. Llewelyn had long believed that Wales was ill served by a practice that so turned brother against brother, that so often fomented civil war, and he'd dared to defy centuries of tradition, naming Davydd as his sole heir. He was heartened now by Llelo's delight in the birth of a baby brother; if change was to take root, what more fertile soil than childhood?

"It truly pleases you, Llelo, having a brother?" he asked, and Llelo edged closer.

"A baby brother," he corrected, and then confessed, "It was never much fun, being the youngest. But I can look out for Davydd, teach him things—how to make a whistle from a water reed, how to catch frogs, how to make a fire without flint. And I can tell him scary stories at night, the ones my sister used to tell me ere she got married." He grinned suddenly. "Then, too, now I will have someone to blame things on!"

Llewelyn laughed. "You sound as if you've given this much thought, lad."

Llelo nodded. "Being a good brother will be easy, Grandpapa. I need only remember what Owain did—and then do the exact opposite!" He was still smiling, but Llewelyn was not taken in; in this past year, he'd learned that Llelo often offered bald truths camouflaged as jests. He reached out, rumpled the boy's hair, and found himself thinking of an old Welsh proverb. Ni cherir yn llwyr oni ddelo'r wŷr. There will be no loving completely till the grandchild comes.

"I have another riddle for you, Grandpapa. Why do men make the oven in the town?" Llelo waited expectantly, and when Llewelyn shook his head, he said triumphantly, "Because they cannot make the town in the oven!"

Llewelyn was a good sport, groaned on cue, and then, as his eyes caught Gruffydd's, he laughed, remembering a time, so many years past, when Gruffydd, too, had a passion for childhood rhymes and nonsense riddles. Gruffydd grinned, and Llewelyn knew that he was thinking of those same memories. They laughed together, in a rare moment of ease, were still laughing when the door opened, and they saw Davydd and Isabella standing in the doorway.

Davydd's eyes cut from his father to Gruffydd, back to Llewelyn. He did not acknowledge his brother in any other way; they were long past the pretense of civility. "I wanted to let you know I was back, Papa," he said. "I have messages for you from both Rhys Mechyll and Maelgwn Fychan, have much to tell you."

Gruffydd set his cup down upon the table, so abruptly that mead sloshed onto the chessboard. He could see what was happening, could see how Davydd was taking upon himself more and more authority, acting in Llewelyn's stead more and more frequently. Soon he'd be Prince in all but name. "I brought news of my own," he said. "My wife has borne me yet another son. Do you not want to congratulate me, Davydd?"

Davydd's eyes filled with shadows. "Congratulations," he said, flinging the word down like a stone—or a gauntlet.

"Thank you. I do feel that I have indeed been blessed, for Senena has now given me a daughter and three healthy sons—whilst so many men have no sons at all."

Davydd stiffened, said nothing. But Isabella clasped her hand to her mouth, as if to stifle a cry; her eyes brimmed with tears. She spun around, and Davydd reached for her. She was too fast, though; his hand just brushed her sleeve.

"Isabella, wait!" Davydd started after her, stopped to look back at his brother. "You bastard," he said, and his voice was raw with rage, with such hatred that Gruffydd instinctively dropped his hand to his sword hilt. But Davydd had not waited; he plunged through the doorway, and they heard him call out his wife's name.

Gruffydd stared at that open door. He was a skilled archer; so why, then, did so many of his arrows misfire? He cared nothing for Isabella, had always found her to be timid and demure and cloyingly sweet. And she was English, Davydd's wife. But he would not have deliberately hurt her; he had only contempt for the man who would shoot a nesting duck, run down a newborn fawn. He turned reluctantly to face the others, defiant, daring them to object.

No one did. Nor did they meet his eyes. Ednyved's was not a face to give away secrets; impassive, he drank the last of his mead. Hunydd at once began to busy herself with the cups and flagons. But Llelo looked troubled, and Llewelyn suddenly looked very, very tired.

"I promised the boy he could stay," Gruffydd said, while staring into space above his father's head. "I'll send someone for him on the morrow."

"But Papa—Papa, you said you'd stay for dinner. Do you not remember?"

"Yes," Gruffydd said, "I remember," and the anger drained from his voice. He started to speak, then swung about, moved swiftly toward the door.

Llewelyn pushed his chair back, limped to the window. After a moment, Llelo followed, and Llewelyn reached out, put his right arm around the boy's shoulders. The window opened onto the bailey; beyond, he could see a sunlit shimmer, the silver-blue of the bay. Davydd had caught up with Isabella. They were standing together in the shadow of the great hall; it seemed to Llewelyn that she was weeping.

Llewelyn shifted his weight onto his good leg. His Church had been forced to find a way to reconcile the absolutism of the Sixth Commandment—Thou shalt not kill—with the realities of their world. And so the concept of a "Just War" had evolved. Rules were laid down, moral boundaries drawn. And all agreed that noncombatants were not to be harmed.

Women were to be spared, as were children, priests, diplomatic envoys, pilgrims. But Llewelyn knew better. In war, the innocent were usually the first to suffer.

As he and Llelo watched, Gruffydd rode through the castle gateway, without looking back. "I wanted Papa to stay," Llelo said softly. "I'd hoped . . ." His voice trailed off, and Llewelyn tightened his arm about the boy's shoulders.

"I know, lad," he said. "I know."

THE great castle of Kenilworth had been in the possession of the English Crown since the twelfth century. It was a formidable citadel, but it had never been one of Henry's favorite residences, and he'd temporarily turned it over to his sister. It was here that Nell had awaited Simon's return to England, and here that she now awaited the birth of their child.

It had been an unusually hot, dry summer, but a wet, chill autumn. A cold November rain slanted against the shuttered windows of Kenilworth's great hall. Richard Plantagenet, Earl of Cornwall, moved closer to the hearth. The other castle guests had also drawn their chairs nearer to the flames. Richard knew them all, although not well. Peter de Montfort was a Warwickshire knight, an intimate friend of Simon's, but no relation despite the fact they bore the same surname. The other men were all clerics, also friends of Simon's. Adam Marsh was a friar, rector of the Franciscan school at Oxford, a man with a notable reputation as a scholar, theologian, and mathematician. Walter de Cantilupe was the new Bishop of Worcester, and Robert Grosseteste the Bishop of Lincoln.

Richard was particularly impressed by the Bishop of Lincoln's presence, for the man was even more celebrated as a scholar than Adam Marsh. He was known to speak fluent Greek and Hebrew, he had been the first Chancellor of the University of Oxford, and he was admired as much for his piety and rectitude as for his intellectual accomplishments. Richard had heard that he was a friend to Simon, but he'd not realized how close the friendship was, close enough to bring the Bishop posthaste from Canterbury in a drenching rainstorm, a conclusive demonstration of loyalty for a man of Grosseteste's age and frail health.

"Have you known my brother-by-marriage very long, Your Grace?"

"We first became acquainted whilst I was still Archdeacon of Leicester, some six or seven years past, soon after Simon's arrival in England."

The Bishop's eyes shifted across the hall, followed Simon as he paced restlessly back and forth. There was such obvious affection in that glance that Richard found himself thinking Simon was lucky, indeed, to have so illustrious an ally as this honored and honorable Prince of the Church. For there were other clerics who still bitterly opposed Simon's marriage to Nell, clerics who had not been appeased by the papal dispensation.

Richard's eyes, too, now rested upon Simon. He acknowledged that Simon's relationship with the Bishop of Lincoln should not be suspect; a friendship of seven years was surely not open to charges of opportunism. But he instinctively searched for an element of calculation in all that Simon did, for he was still of two minds about his new brother-in-law, respecting Simon's abilities while remaining dubious about his motives. He had, however, made his peace with Simon, and whatever his private doubts, he'd not voice them aloud. The marriage was now a fact, and Richard no more quarreled with facts than he wasted time on idle regrets.

"How fares the King's Grace?" The query came from Peter de Montfort; he looked questioningly at Richard. "We here in Warwickshire were sorely distressed that the King might have come to harm in our very midst."

"Come to harm?" Simon echoed, having joined them just in time to catch the last of Peter's comment. "What harm?"

"The assassination attempt upon my brother the King this past September at Woodstock," Richard explained. "Nell did tell you?"

"Yes," Simon said, "she did." So had Henry, and at great length. He'd been very fortunate, for when the would-be assassin climbed into the window of Henry's bedchamber at his Woodstock manor, Henry was not there, having chosen to spend the night in his Queen's bed. One of the Queen's ladies had encountered the intruder; her screams had drawn others, and the man was quickly overpowered. But although Henry had escaped bodily harm, he'd been greatly shaken by the fortuitous nature of his deliverance, confiding to Simon that had he not fallen asleep, he'd have returned to his own bed.

Richard was telling them now of the fate of the assassin, ". . . taken to Coventry, where he was tied to horses and torn limb from limb. Henry chose not to witness it. Passing strange, for had it been me, I would have been there for certes."

Simon's eyes narrowed; the boasting rang false, for Richard's reputation was for aloof competence, not derring-do or lordly swagger. It seemed that Richard and Henry were not as unlike as he'd first thought; they shared the same fondness for high-flown language, for suspect bravado. But no, that might well be too harsh a judgment. He did not want to be unfair to his wife's brothers. He could not deny, though, that they puzzled him. There were but fifteen months between them, fifteen months that had cost Richard a crown. Did Richard ever resent Henry for that? Simon wondered. He did not doubt there was a genuine bond between the brothers, but neither did he doubt, too, that Richard believed himself capable of being a far better King than Henry could ever be.

As he looked at the other man, Simon suddenly found himself remembering a bleak February morning, the day he'd gone to ask Richard's pardon for his clandestine marriage to Richard's sister. It had not been easy for him. Even knowing as he did how crucial Richard's support was, he might not have been able to do it had it not been for the Bishop of Lincoln. Simon respected Robert Grosseteste as he did no other man in Christendom; when Grosseteste urged him to make peace with Richard, he listened to the Bishop's advice, and then reluctantly acted upon it. Richard was known to have an extremely healthy regard for material gain. So when Simon sought a truce, he did not come empty-handed. It had taken some finely bred stallions and silver plate, had taken some equally well-crafted words of apology and assurance, but Simon had inveigled Richard's grudging consent. It had to be done; Simon knew that. But it was not a memory he cared to dwell upon.

Simon's eyes strayed again toward the door. When he looked back, he discovered that they were all watching him. "Why is it taking so long?" he said, and Richard smiled indulgently.

"Let me give you some advice, Simon. I've gone through three such birth vigils, so I know of what I speak. You must be patient, and hope for the best, all a man can do at these times."

"Nonetheless," Simon said. "I think I'll seek Elen out again."

"If you keep running back and forth in the rain, you'll catch your death of cold," Richard predicted, "whilst getting nothing from Elen. Women like to make much mystery of the birthing process; they give away no female secrets. In truth, Simon, you need not fret so. Nell may look as fragile as gossamer, but as her brother, I can assure you she is actually as tough as hemp! She—" He stopped, for Simon was no longer listening; he'd already turned away.

Nell had chosen the main room of the castle keep for her lying-in chamber, so each time Simon went to check upon her progress, he had to cross the bailey. The rain was falling heavily, and he was shivering by the time he reached the forebuilding. He rapidly mounted the stairs to the second story. It held a small chapel, but he did not pause there, moved toward the door of Nell's chamber. He had to knock several times before it opened, just a crack. Mabel peered out, eyeing him warily. It seemed to Simon that it took an inordinately long time before Elen joined him in the chapel.

"I'm beginning to think," he said, "that I'd find it easier to gain entry into a convent of Benedictine nuns."

Elen laughed. "You make them nervous, Simon. Whilst I do understand your concern, there is nothing yet to tell you."

"But it's been nigh on eleven hours!"

"The babe will come in its own good time, Simon. All is progressing as it ought, truly. And it should not be long now. Nell's water has broken," she said, having earlier explained the significance of that to Simon. "You'd best go back to the hall. I shall send for you as soon as the babe is born, I swear it."

"I would rather wait here, in the chapel," he said, and Elen gave him a sympathetic smile, vanished back into his wife's chamber. He stood there for a time, and then crossed to the altar, where he knelt and prayed for God's forgiveness if he had indeed sinned by marrying Nell, prayed that if punishment was due, it should fall upon him and not upon Nell, not upon their innocent child.

AS the pain subsided, Nell looked over at Elen, and the other woman reached for a soft cloth, began to blot away the sweat streaking Nell's face. "Simon is in the chapel," she said. "I think he is having a harder time than you are, Nell!"

"Indeed, Madame," Mabel chimed in. "Each time he knocks on the door, I fear he will come bursting right in!"

Between pains, Nell had been sipping wine laced with feverfew. She took a swallow, tried to smile.

"My father actually did that," Elen said. "My mother had been in labor with my brother Davydd for fully a day and night, and she'd begun to lose strength, to lose heart. When one of Mama's ladies told Papa that she'd begun to bleed, he forced his way into the chamber, stayed with her till Davydd was safely born."

Mabel and the midwife looked so appalled that Elen laughed. Nell managed another smile, this one more convincing; that story was folklore in her family. "Only Llewelyn would have dared," she whispered. "Or Simon—" She gasped, and the women hovered helplessly around her, waiting for the pain to pass.

"Soon, Madame," the midwife soothed. "Soon now. Here, take this." She thrust a small, silvery rock into Nell's hands. "Eaglestone has wondrous powers, my lady. Hold it tight when the pains come."

In the corner was a shaft, leading down to the cellar well. Mabel crossed to it, helped a young maid servant to operate the pulley, to draw up another bucket of well water. Elen stayed by Nell's side, offering what small comfort she could, words of encouragement and affection.

The midwife poured thyme oil onto her hands, knelt before the birthing stool, and raised Nell's skirt.

"It is coming, Madame! I can just see the crown of its head," she exclaimed, and made haste to pull off Nell's soiled and bloodied chemise. Nell was groaning, writhing upon the stool; the eaglestone had fallen into the floor rushes. The contractions were constant now, and the midwife put her hands on Nell's thighs, spread them farther apart.

"No, lass, no," she warned. "You must not bear down, now, lest you tear yourself. Do not fight the pain, my lady. Let the babe do the work now . . ."

She kept up these continuous murmurings, seeking to lull Nell with the rhythm of her words, knowing the sound was as important as the sense. Nell groaned again, and the midwife gave a triumphant cry, for the baby's head was emerging. She swiftly leaned over, made sure that the navel cord was not caught around the infant's neck, and Nell had the first glimpse of her child, saw a small, wet head, surprisingly dark.

"It's Simon," she gasped, and then her body contorted again, and the child's shoulders were free. The midwife held out her hands, caught it deftly as it began to cry.

"You are right, Madame," she said, and turning the child over, she cupped the small genitals for them all to see. "It is indeed a son!"

Nell held out her arms, and the midwife laid the baby on Nell's stomach. His cries had increased in strength and volume, but as he nestled against his mother's warm flesh, he began to quiet. Nell stroked his drenched, black hair, ran her hand along his back, reassured herself that his tiny fingers and toes were all intact, that her son was perfect in all particulars. The other women watched, sharing in the wonder. But this idyllic spell was soon broken; there was a sudden, insistent pounding on the door.

"What does that man have, second-sight?" Elen marveled, and crossing the chamber, she slid back the door latch.

"I thought I heard a babe cry. Did I?" Simon demanded, and when she nodded, he could wait no longer. Shoving the door open, he shouldered Elen aside, strode into the room.

The midwife gave a horrified shriek, sought with her own ample girth to block his view of Nell. "No, my lord, you cannot come in yet! You must withdraw; this is no sight for male eyes!"

"That is ridiculous," Simon snapped. "I was there for the planting, so why should I not be there for the harvesting?" Thrusting her out of the way, he came to an abrupt halt at sight of his wife and child. "Is it a boy or girl? Is it whole, healthy?" he asked anxiously, glancing back toward the women.

Elen was laughing too much to talk, and the midwife and Mabel were still too flustered to respond. It was left to Nell to reassure him, which she did with a weary but elated smile. "I have given you a son," she said, "a beautiful little son . . ."

Simon quickly covered the space that separated them, knelt by the birthing stool. "A son," he said softly, staring in awe at the cord that still bound the baby to his wife; when he touched it, he could actually feel the blood pulsing through it.

"He looks as if he was dipped in wet flour, Nell. What is this white, sticky stuff?"

Nell did not know; she'd never witnessed a birth before. She glanced up at the midwife, and the older woman swallowed her resentment as best she could. "You need not worry, my lady. Babies are ofttimes born covered with this substance. I expect it must protect them in the womb."

She'd given Nell a cup of salted water to drink; Nell took a swallow and grimaced. "Why must I—" She broke off in dismay. Her mouth twisted, and then, to Simon's horror, blood gushed between her thighs.

"Nell! Christ, do something for her!"

But to his surprise, the women did not seem perturbed by this sudden flow of blood. Elen reached for string and scissors, saying calmly, "It is only the afterbirth coming. Simon, do step aside. I think one reason you men are barred from the birthing chamber is just to keep you from getting underfoot!" As she neatly tied and cut the cord, the midwife placed her hand on Nell's abdomen, began to tug gently on the cord.

"It is coming," she said, and Simon leaned forward to see, for he'd heard many stories about the mystical, magical properties of the afterbirth; it was widely believed that it could even attract demons. It was something of a disappointment, though; he thought the afterbirth resembled nothing so much as a chunk of raw liver.

While Elen and Mabel sponged the blood and mucus from Nell's thighs, the midwife carried the baby to the table, where the maid servant had prepared a basin of warm water. Simon followed, watched his son have his first bath, so obviously fascinated that the midwife began to thaw somewhat. Laying the infant on a soft towel, she gently rubbed his skin with salt, while he proved again that his lungs were in superb operating order. When she dipped her finger in honey, Simon caught her hand.

"May I do that?" he asked, and she surrendered unconditionally. Under her guidance, he carefully inserted his finger in his son's mouth, brushed those tiny gums and palate with honey. The baby seemed surprised at first, but soon began to suck upon his finger, and Simon burst out laughing.

The midwife laughed, too. "Whilst I swaddle the babe, my lord, will you carry your lady to the bed? And do not let her sleep for a while; that can be dangerous."

Propped up by pillows, with her husband beside her and her son in her arms, Nell experienced a sudden sense of unease, for how could she ever know a moment of greater happiness? "I am not yet twenty-three years old," she said, "and the rest of my life is bound to be a letdown, Simon, for nothing could possibly surpass this day for me." And then she laughed. "Just a twelvemonth past, I had no Simons at all, and now by the grace of God Almighty, I do have two!"

They had agreed upon the names for their child: Joanna for a daughter, Simon for a son. But now Simon shook his head. "No," he said, "not Simon. I think we should name him after the man who made this day possible for us. When I look at you, Nell, at our son, I can fully realize for the first time, I think, just how much I do owe him. I want to name our son Henry, after your brother."

Nell nodded. "You are right. We do owe Henry a great deal, beloved."

Simon leaned over, kissed her gently. "Look," he said, and Nell smiled, for the baby had grasped Simon's finger, was clinging tightly. But then she saw the tears in her husband's eyes.

"You are a constant surprise to me, Simon," she said slowly. "In truth, I did not think it would mean so much to you."

Simon glanced up at her, then down again at his son. "In truth," he confessed, "neither did I."

THE Welsh Princes had come to the Cistercian abbey of Ystrad Fflur in response to Llewelyn's summons. There in the Chapter House of the monastery, they gathered to pledge oaths of fealty to Llewelyn's son Davydd.

It should have been an occasion of great satisfaction to Llewelyn. It was not. He'd wanted more for Davydd, much more. It had been his intent to have the Welsh lords swear homage to Davydd. But the English had reacted with alarm, had forbidden Davydd to accept oaths of homage.

Llewelyn had once committed a tactical error of monumental proportions; he had overestimated his own power and underestimated that of the English Crown. It was a mistake that had almost cost him his life and the sovereignty of Gwynedd. He had been spared by the grace of God and a ruthless King's love for his daughter, for Joanna had interceded with her father and John had listened. That memory was twenty-seven years past, but Llewelyn had not forgotten; nor had he made that mistake again.

He was troubled now not so much by the need to back down, to defer to the English Crown, as by the implications for Davydd. The other Welsh Princes had done homage to him in the past. That the English were applying two different standards—according him concessions they were not willing to concede to Davydd—did not bode well for Davydd's future. Once he was dead and Davydd was in power, the English Crown would begin whittling away again at Gwynedd, seeking to reclaim all he'd won, to overthrow a lifetime's work. What sort of a legacy was he leaving his son?

The Abbot had brought in heavy, oaken, high-backed chairs for Davydd and Llewelyn; they sat side by side as the Princes of Deheubarth and Powys and the lords of Llewelyn's Gwynedd came forward, knelt and swore formal oaths of fealty to Llewelyn's heir.

Gruffydd stood apart, watching as Ednyved and his sons pledged fealty to Davydd. His bitterness was twofold, that it was Davydd who was being acknowledged as the next Prince of Gwynedd, and that Llewelyn should have yielded to English pressure yet again. This was an old and festering grievance, for he would never understand how a man of his father's proven courage could allow the English Crown to meddle in Welsh affairs. He had hated John, was scornful of Henry, would have defied them both had the power only been his.

"Gruffydd?" Senena had come quietly through the crowd, slid her hand into his. "Remember, beloved," she said softly. "It is just empty words, no more than that."

For a moment, his eyes held hers. "It is a holy oath," he said, "sworn before God."

Senena's hand tightened. "An oath sworn under duress, Gruffydd. The Church does not hold a man to such an oath, beloved. Nor will the Almighty."

He said nothing, but he knew she was right, knew what he must do. Near the dais, he saw his sons, Owain and Llelo. As unlike as they were, they shared now a remarkably similar expression, one of anxious unease. He smiled reassuringly at them, and then heard his name echoing across the chamber. He drew several steadying breaths, walked slowly toward the dais.

As he knelt before Davydd, his brother silently handed him a sword. It was specially crafted for such swearing ceremonies, with a hollowed hilt that contained the most sacred of relics, a tooth of St Davydd and a scrap of cloth from the mantle of the Blessed Mother Mary. Gruffydd's fingers closed gingerly around the hilt, never quite making contact. He knew how Davydd must be relishing this moment, but the younger man's face was utterly inscrutable. He had always envied Davydd that uncanny self-control, for he knew his every emotion blazed forth upon his own face for all the world to see.

The silence was becoming awkward. Never had Gruffydd been so preternaturally sensitive to his surroundings. No detail of the scene escaped him; he noticed how the floor tiles were patterned with pallid sunlight, how his father had leaned forward in his chair, even how mud was caking Davydd's boots.

"Well?" Davydd said at last. "Are you going to swear?"

And with that, Gruffydd's tension was gone. He felt strangely calm, almost peaceful. "No," he said, "I am not." Rising without haste, he very deliberately dropped the sword at Davydd's feet. "I will not swear fealty to you. Not now. Not ever."

It was a moment of appalling familiarity to Llewelyn, as if time had somehow come full circle. Ten years ago an embittered quarrel with Gruffydd had flared into a harrowing test of will. Gruffydd had refused to recognize Davydd as the heir, had promised civil war, and he had responded as the Prince of Gwynedd, had ordered his eldest son's confinement at Deganwy Castle. It had been the most difficult act of his life, and as he looked now upon his defiant, dangerous firstborn, he knew suddenly that he could not summon up the strength to do it again.

"That is your choice," Davydd said, quite coolly, and Llewelyn realized that Davydd was not at all surprised. He had expected Gruffydd to balk, for he'd always understood Gruffydd better than Gruffydd understood him. "But every choice carries with it consequences. After defying our lord father and his council, you cannot expect to be entrusted with so much of Lower Powys. You may retain the lordship of Llŷn. But you have just forfeited the commotes of Arwystli, Ceri, Cyfeiliog, Mawddwy, Mochnant, and Caereinion."

"I've forfeited nothing! It is my father who still wields the power in Gwynedd, not you!" Gruffydd took a step toward the dais, but toward Llewelyn, not Davydd. "Tell him, Papa. Remind him who is the Prince of Gwynedd!"

Llewelyn's throat closed up. He swallowed, said as evenly as he could, "Davydd speaks for me in this." Knowing he could say nothing else, but knowing, too, that he'd be haunted till the end of his days by the memory of his son's stricken face.

DAVYDD was sitting in the window-seat of the abbey parlor, drinking directly from a flagon of highly spiced red wine. It stung his eyes, burned his throat. He glanced up as the door opened, then held out the flagon to Ednyved. "I could not find any wine cups."

Ednyved came forward, reached for the flagon. "You handled that well," he said, and Davydd's mouth twisted.

"Liar," he said amiably. "Since when do you approve of half-measures? You know as well as I what I ought to have done. I ought to have given the order then and there for his arrest." He reclaimed the flagon, drank deeply. "But I just could not do that to Papa."

Ednyved sat down beside him in the window-seat. "Pass the flagon," he said, and they drank in silence.

When Llewelyn entered the parlor, Davydd rose to his feet. "I had no choice, Papa. I could not allow Gruffydd to defy me. If I had, I'd have forfeited the respect of every man in the chamber."

"I know, Davydd." Llewelyn lowered himself onto the closest bench. "These four years that he's been free, I tried to mend the breach between us," he said wearily. "I sought to convince him that I still loved him. And I succeeded too well. I saw that on his face this afternoon, saw that he'd persuaded himself I might relent. Instead . . . instead I betrayed him yet again."

"You did not betray him, Papa."

"He thinks I did. And he'll not forgive me. Not this time."

Davydd put his hand on his father's shoulder. He would never know what meagre comfort he might have offered, for just then the door opened. Llelo was panting, as if he'd been running; he looked flushed and disheveled. "I can stay but a moment, Grandpapa. My father is leaving the abbey and . . . and I must go with him."

"Yes," Llewelyn said. "I know, lad."

Llelo moved closer. "I do not think he will let me visit you again."

"No, Llelo, I do not expect he will."

Llelo was near enough now for Llewelyn to see his tears. "In less than four years," he said, "I shall be fourteen. I'll have the legal right then to make my own decisions, to see you as often as I want."

Llewelyn nodded wordlessly. But four years seemed an eternity to a ten-year-old boy just at the beginning of his life and a sixty-five-year-old man coming to the end of his. Llelo flew forward into his grandfather's arms, and for a long moment Llewelyn held him close. "Grandpapa, if you come to Cricieth," he pleaded, "I can still see you. It is not far from Nefyn; I can slip away for a few hours, and none need know."

He'd feared that Llewelyn might seek to dissuade him, to make an adult's arguments about obedience and patience. But Llewelyn did not. "Till Cricieth, lad," he said huskily, and gave Llelo one final farewell hug.

Llelo blinked back the last of his tears; as young as he was, he was already learning that tears were an indulgence he could ill afford. At the door he paused, dark eyes seeking Llewelyn's face. "I do not understand," he said, "why it must be like this."

6

London, England

August 1239

SIMON looped his wife's hair around his hand, slowly pulled it taut, until she laughed and rolled back into his arms. "Each time," he said, "you always cry out my name, and you always sound surprised."

"Do I?" Nell thought it a pity that none but she would ever know Simon's smile could be so tender. "That proves I do not yet take you for granted," she said. "But I daresay you've scandalized the entire household, seducing your wife in the middle of the day!"

"Was that a seduction? I rather thought it a reconciliation."

Nell grimaced. "A deft thrust, my lord, right to the heart. I am sorry we quarreled, Simon; I always am. You must admit, though, that I did warn you. I cautioned you on our wedding day that I did not think I could be a dutiful wife."

"Yes, you did," he agreed, "but not until after we'd already said our vows," and Nell hit him with a pillow. He grabbed for her, and she squealed, but then they heard a discreet cough; Simon pulled the bed hangings back, saw his squire standing in the doorway.

Adam coughed again; it never failed to amaze him that his serious-minded, prideful lord was the same man who indulged in pillow fights and tickling matches in the privacy of the marriage bed. Allowing himself one circumspect glimpse of Nell's white shoulders and flaxen hair, he said politely, "Dame Mabel asked me to remind you, my lord, that the Queen's churching is set for mid-afternoon, lest you be late."

While Simon was scrupulously punctual, Nell was invariably tardy, and Simon's squires often wagered as to whose habit would prevail. Now as Simon rose from the bed, signaling for his clothes, Nell settled back comfortably against the pillow, and Adam grinned, thinking his money was as good as won.

"Eleanor will have a magnificent churching," she said, somewhat wistfully. "Henry will spare no expense now that she's finally given him a son." Sitting up, she shook her hair back. "I've never fully understood the churching ceremony, Simon. The priests say that until it is done, a woman is impure, that she cannot touch holy water or make bread or serve food. But why should childbirth make a woman unclean?"

Simon paused in the act of reaching for his shirt, momentarily diverted, for he was fascinated by theology. "I do not know," he admitted. "I shall ask Bishop Robert when next we meet. Now bestir yourself, Nell. Your study of Scriptures can wait; your brother the King cannot."

Henry had leased the Bishop of Winchester's bankside manor house to Simon and Nell, and it was but a short journey upriver to Westminster Palace. Simon hastened his wife along the King's wharf, across the New Palace yard, not slowing stride until they entered the great hall, saw that the procession to the abbey had yet to begin. Only then did Simon relax, pausing to speak to Richard Renger, London's Mayor, for he was no less intrigued by political craft than he was by canon law. The Mayor greeted him warmly; when Simon's interest was sparked, so, too, was his charm. Nell continued on toward the dais, where she curtsied to her brother's teenage Queen.

Eleanor was dressed in regal splendor; Nell's eyes moved hungrily over the iridescent cloth-of-gold gown, the plush velvet mantle, the necklet of emeralds and rubies. There was no ease, no affection between the two young women; each one envied the other's hold upon Henry's heart. They made stilted but courteous conversation, drawing upon their only common interest: motherhood. Eleanor spoke lovingly of her newly born son, Edward, and Nell no less proudly of her Harry, now entering his ninth robust month. A dark imp, she said fondly, who was already trying to stand erect. Eleanor smiled politely, thinking that for certes her little Ned would be no less forward than Nell's wonder-child. She brightened at sight of Simon approaching, for she was like Nell in one other way, she preferred the company of men to that of women.

She extended her hand for Simon's kiss, while feeling a twinge of conscience. She genuinely liked Simon, who was handsome and spoke the French of the Île-de-France, not the bastardized Norman-French of Henry's court, and she hoped she had not gotten him into Henry's bad graces. Favoring Simon with a dazzling smile, she began to complain of Henry's tardiness.

"That man will be late for his own wake," she sighed, and pouted prettily. "Simon, will you not go to his chamber, hasten him along? He listens to you."

"Make yourself easy, Madame," Simon said, and both women watched as he began to thread his way through the crowded hall, Nell with possessive pride and Eleanor with a satisfied smile.

"I think I managed that quite well," she said. "Henry is rather vexed with Simon, and now they'll have a chance to talk in private, to make peace ere the churching begins."

"Why should Henry be vexed with Simon? You must be mistaken, Madame, for Simon has never stood higher in Henry's favor."

"Then why did Henry fly into such a rage when I made mention of the debt Simon owes my uncle?"

Nell was frowning. "What debt?"

Eleanor shrugged. "All I know is that Simon somehow owes my uncle Thomas a large sum of money, and he bade me ask Henry to seek payment from Simon. Which I did, and Henry became remarkably wroth."

Nell was remembering. "You must be referring to the debt Simon owed his cousin Ranulf. He was the late Earl of Chester, John the Scot's uncle," she added, for even after three years in England, Eleanor had yet to untangle the bloodlines of the English aristocracy. "Upon Ranulf's death, the debt passed to the Count of Brittany, and then to your uncle, the Count of Flanders. It was two hundred pounds at the outset, but with interest accrued, it is now more than two thousand marks. So much," she said resentfully "for the Church's stricture that Christians must never engage in usury! But why should Henry be angry over an old debt? That makes no sense."

"That is why I wanted Simon and Henry to talk together, to—" Eleanor stopped in dismay, and Nell turned, saw her brother entering the hall.

Henry came to an abrupt halt at sight of his brother-in-law. "You are not welcome here," he said, "not at my court and for certes not at my Queen's churching."

Simon's smile faded. "My liege?" he said, sounding so astonished, so innocent that Henry's rage—too long untended, smoldering in the dark—flared up like parched kindling, flaming out of control.

"This is a holy ceremony," he snapped. "Only those who know God's grace deserve to take part in it."

Simon felt no anger yet, only disbelief. "How have I offended you?"

"You know full well how you have offended me! You do owe my wife's uncle two thousand marks, and yet you refuse to pay, you—"

"That is not so," Simon cut in sharply. "That matter is pending before the papal curia, and I will abide by whatever decision they render."

"I am sure His Holiness the Pope will be relieved to hear that! But how do you expect to make payment? I gave you the earldom of Leicester, and yet your debts continue to mount, to—"

"And we both know why. King John took the earldom from my father in 1207; it was not returned to me until 1231." Simon had not heard Nell's approach, suddenly felt her hand upon his arm. But he could not stop himself; his grievance was too raw. "And in those twenty-four years, the lands were mortgaged, the revenues wasted, the forests cut down. Yes, you gave me back our earldom, well nigh ruined!"

Henry flushed. "Ah, no, you're not going to blame me for your debts! If you did not keep such a princely household, if you curbed your wife's lavish spending as you ought, your coffers would not be empty, and you could pay your debts as a man of honor should!"

Nell gasped; her extravagances were of minor moment when compared to those of Henry's Queen. "If I find no fault with my wife's spending, why should you?" Simon said coldly, and she gave him a grateful look, before turning indignantly upon her brother.

"It is your fault that Simon and I are so hard pressed," she cried. "You are the King, my eldest brother, and yet you allowed the Marshals to cheat me of my dower rights. You still allow them to delay payments, to offer excuses instead of money. And then . . . when Simon and I were wed, you denied me my marriage portion!"

"You did not deserve it! That marriage was a mockery, a sinful—"

"My liege!" Simon's voice was shaking with fury, for to challenge their marriage now was to cast a shadow upon their son's legitimacy. "Need I remind you that the Pope did grant us a dispensation?"

"Only because you lied to him! You bribed his counselors, got them to give him false facts, else he never would have consented, and you know that! You lied to His Holiness, just as surely as you lied to me!" Henry swung about, faced his sister. "I would never have agreed to your marriage had you not deceived me, had you not sworn you carried this man's child!"

There was a sudden and utter silence, remarkable in a hall that size. For a moment frozen in time, Henry looked no less horrified than Nell and Simon. He seemed to hear his own words, echoing over and over in the eerie stillness. His sister was staring at him, but he could not meet her eyes. "Get out." He swallowed, said more loudly, "I want you both gone from my sight, from my court." He looked at Simon as he spoke; it was easier that way. "Get out!"

Simon reached for Nell's hand. She was trembling, but she matched her step to his. Holding hands, they walked slowly toward the door, as if oblivious of the whispers, the stares, the scandal.

❧

SIMON poured red wine into a cup, passed it to Nell. "Drink," he said, and she obediently took a swallow, then set the cup down.

"How can I ever return to court?" she whispered. "How could he do it, Simon? How could he shame me like that?"

He gave her one brief, burning glance. "Hold me," she entreated, and he took her in his arms, but for a few moments only, no more than that. He could not be still, paced the chamber as if it were a cage, and as she watched, she discovered that his pain was harder to bear than her own.

"My lord . . ." Adam stood in the doorway, and Simon whirled, for he'd given orders that none were to enter the solar. "Do not be angry, my lord," the boy pleaded. "I had to seek you out, for the city sheriffs have come. They await you in the great hall."

Simon knew both of the sheriffs, John de Coudres and John de Wylehale. They looked surprisingly ill at ease, for he knew them to be men not easily discomfited. But before he could speak, John de Coudres said hastily, "You should know, my lord, that we are here at the King's will, not our own."

Nell was standing beside Simon. She regarded the sheriffs with composure, with polite curiosity, but her fingers were digging into Simon's arm. "And what," he asked, "is the King's will?"

De Coudres glanced at his companion, back at Simon. "I might as well say it straight out. You cannot stay here any longer, my lord. This is the King's house, and he has ordered us to turn you out."

"My God . . ." Nell had never felt faint in her life, but she did now, was suddenly dizzy and light-headed. She caught the back of a chair, leaned on it till her breathing slowed. The King could do that, could take from them all that was theirs. The King had the power. But where was her brother? How had she lost Henry?

Simon had turned away, moved to the window. After some moments, Nell followed. "Beloved, listen to me," she said softly. "We must return to court. We must see Henry, must seek to put this right." He looked at her, saying nothing. His eyes glinted, took the shadows but none of the light. She knew what he was feeling; without words, she knew. "Please," she said.

ELEANOR had been anticipating the churching for weeks. But the ceremony was utterly overshadowed by Henry's shocking public quarrel with his sister and her husband. Instead of being the center of attention, Eleanor found herself all but ignored. Upon their return from the abbey, she fled to her own chamber, where she threw herself down upon the bed, heedless of her new finery, and burst into tears. Henry retreated to his private apartment, the sunlit green room known as the Painted Chamber, and all others dispersed to discuss the astonishing scene so many had witnessed in Westminster's great hall.

AS Simon and Nell approached the entrance of the Painted Chamber, an embarrassed usher stepped forward to bar the way. "I am sorry, my lord of Leicester," he said. "The King's Grace has given orders that you are not to be admitted to his presence."

"I see." Never had Simon felt such rage; never had he felt so frighteningly impotent. All knew Fortune was a fickle bitch, but had any man ever lost her favor so fast?

Nell was gazing coolly at the usher. "Did my brother the King issue any order barring me?" And when he shook his head, she said, "You may announce me, then." Her eyes cut quickly to Simon, eyes full of entreaty. "Will you wait for me?" she asked, and he nodded, for he knew what was at stake, too much for false pride.

The Painted Chamber, the lesser hall, and St Stephen's Chapel intersected to form a spacious courtyard. Beyond, the ground stretched down to the river wall. People were wandering about in the late afternoon sun; as he walked down a graveled pathway, Simon could feel their eyes following him. None were neutral about Simon. Men either liked him very much or not at all, and more than a few were taking satisfaction in his sudden fall. But even those who sympathized did not dare to express it in so public a setting. He was left alone in the garden, gazing up at the oriel windows of the Painted Chamber, windows defaced by incongruous iron bars, installed in all of Henry's manors after the assassination attempt at Woodstock.

"Simon!" He turned, saw Elen and Robert de Quincy hastening toward him.

When they reached him, there was a moment of awkward silence, for they'd been in the hall. "Nell is with Henry," he said. Color rose in his face, but he forced himself to add, "He would not see me. And . . . he turned us out of Winchester House."

"Jesus wept!" Elen shook her head in disbelief. "I do understand none of this," she confessed. "Simon, I thought you and Henry were on the best of terms."

"So," Simon said grimly, "did I," and another silence fell. It was Rob who saw Nell first. She paused in the doorway, then started toward them. Simon knew her as no one else did, could read failure in the prideful tilt of her chin, the rigid set of her shoulders. He was close enough now to see the tears glistening on her lashes; they seemed to cling by sheer force of will.

"He would not listen. As soon as he saw me, he began to shout and rant like . . . like a madman. He insisted there was nothing more to be said, and when I tried to plead with him, he became even more agitated, ordered me from the chamber." There was a faint tremor to her voice. "Take me away from here, Simon," she said, and he nodded, his hand closing tightly on hers.

"I will," he said, but his assurance sounded hollow, even to him, for where was he to take her?

As the same thought occurred to Elen, she opened her mouth, but Rob was even quicker. "Elen and I have leased a riverside manor," he said, "not far from Castle Baynard. Come back with us, Simon."

Simon gave the other man a look of surprised reappraisal, and then he smiled. "Thank you, Rob. I feel fortunate, indeed, to have such a kinsman."

With a fine disregard for propriety, Elen wrapped her arms around her husband's neck, gave him an impassioned kiss. "I shall make a Welshman out of you yet, Robyn," she laughed. "For my people know that kinship counts for all."

Nell was staring up at the Painted Chamber's bleak, barred windows, and there was on her face both bewilderment and despair. "I always thought," she said, "that Henry believed that, too."

NONE of them had much appetite; a supper of stewed apples and eels had gone virtually untouched. The de Quincy manor was not far from the church of St Martin le Grand, and sitting in a solar window-seat, Nell could hear its bells tolling curfew. Eight o'clock; the city gates would be shutting. But people would not be making ready for bed yet, not until the last of the light faded. Only then would they venture indoors, ignite oil lamps. The taverns and ale-houses would close, and the city Watch would take to the empty streets. The routine of London life would not vary. Tonight would be as it had been on any of a thousand summer nights. As if nothing had changed, Nell thought, as if the world had not gone mad.

Elen refilled their wine cups. "What shall you do, Simon?" she asked, and he gave a weary shrug.

"On the morrow we shall fetch our son from Kenilworth. Then we shall withdraw to one of my manors in Leicestershire, or mayhap to Odiham Castle." But Simon knew even as he spoke that he was deluding Elen, deluding himself. What did it matter that those manors were his, that Odiham was Nell's? The humiliation at Winchester House could be repeated at any time; all of his lands could be forfeited if that were the King's pleasure. And who knew what would please this King?

Nell suddenly tensed. "A barge has just tied up at your dock, Rob," she said. "Now what?"

"Given how the day has so far been going," Simon said, "that is probably one of the city sheriffs with an order for my arrest."

His attempt at gallows humor did not amuse his wife in the least. "Do not say that," she cried, "not even in jest!" and he made amends with a rather strained smile. But then, at the sight of the man being ushered into the solar, Nell sprang to her feet, ran to embrace her brother.

"Oh, Richard, thank God!" For an irrational moment, she found herself fearing that Henry's inexplicable lunacy was somehow contagious, that it might even have infected Richard, too, and her relief was considerable when he hugged her back.

"I had a devil of a time tracking you down," he complained. "But I want no servants on hand, not for what I have to tell you."

Nell clutched his arm. "What is it? What else could possibly happen?"

Richard waited till the servant withdrew, then glanced over at his niece. "What is it you Welsh say, Elen? 'Troubles may ofttimes be so dire that they cannot get better. But they are never so dire that they still cannot get worse.' That says it all quite well. You see, Simon, Henry ordered the sheriffs to place you under arrest, to take you to the Tower this very night."

Simon sucked in his breath. Nell made a smothered sound, whirled toward him, arms outstretched, almost as if she would protect him with her own body. "No! Henry cannot do that, he cannot! Name of God, Richard, help us!"

Richard was faintly disconcerted, for he'd meant only to dramatize his own part in Simon's deliverance, not to terrify his sister, and he made haste to say, "I will, Nell. Indeed, I already have."

"In truth?" she said dubiously, and he nodded.

"Luckily for you, Simon, I was present when Henry gave that command. For once a cooler head prevailed—mine. I was able to persuade him to rescind the order."

It was very quiet then. Simon reached for his wine cup, took a deep swallow, then another. "Thank you, Richard," he said flatly. "I am grateful that you did speak out on my behalf. I would, though, that you'd found a way to tell us without giving Nell such a needless fright."

Richard frowned. "You do exaggerate, for certes," he said, beginning to bridle, and Elen decided she'd best take the helm, for the conversation was fast veering into rough water.

"No, Richard, Simon did not exaggerate; you gave us all a scare. Uncle, when you do have good news and bad news to deliver, it is usually more merciful to deliver the good news first," she said and smiled. "But Simon . . . if a man is drowning and another man throws him a lifeline, ought the drowning man to quibble over the color of the rope?"

The combination of evenhandedness and calculated candor worked, as Elen had known it would; there were times when a woman might say with impunity what a man could not. She turned her head, winked at Rob, as Nell said tautly, "Richard, will you not tell us what happened?"

He did, painting for them an unnerving portrait of a very distraught man, a King on the far reaches of self-control. "And so," he concluded, "it did take the veritable patience of Job, but when I left him, Henry had grudgingly agreed that Simon had done nothing to warrant a stay in the Tower."

Simon had begun to pace. "I find it hard to believe he could be so false. Since our marriage, he has treated me as a friend, a brother. At Candlemas, he formally invested me with the earldom of Leicester. He stood godfather to my son, and just six weeks past, I stood godfather to his son. Yet all the while, he was dissembling, biding his time!"

Richard gave a derisive laugh. "No wonder you're in such trouble with Henry if you understand him as little as that. Do you truly believe that outburst today was calculated? Henry does not plan ahead from one day to the next!"

They were all staring at him. "Jesú, it is so plain; am I the only one to see it? What happens if a wound fails to heal as it ought? Proud flesh forms, it begins to fester. And even a light touch can break it open, freeing all that poison and pus. Poor little Eleanor did that today, quite unwittingly, found a very raw wound, indeed."

"But . . . but why?"

"You should know that, Nell, better than anyone. You played Henry for a fool, did you not?"

"No!"

"Henry thinks you did. He told me about that resourceful lie of yours, Nell," Richard said, and was both surprised and amused when his sister blushed. "He pointed out—accurately—that he could have acted quite differently, that scandals have been muffled behind convent walls, buried in dungeons. But he cared for your happiness. And because he did, he brought upon himself trouble and grief in no small measure . . . only then to discover that you'd deceived him, made a mockery of his trust."

"Richard, it was not like that! Yes, I lied, but not out of malice, out of desperation. I loved Simon, could not bear to lose him. If you take me to Henry, I could talk to him, try to make him understand—"

Richard was shaking his head. "It is too late, Nell. You did Henry a wrong, but today he did you a far greater one, and he knows it. You cannot believe he ever meant to blurt out the truth like that . . . before half the court? He is sick with shame at what he's done, and he cannot own up to it. That is not Henry's way, not any king's way. All he can do is to take refuge in rage. Why else would he have ordered you to the Tower, Simon? He is trying very hard to convince himself that he is blameless, that you brought all of this upon yourself."

Simon studied his brother-in-law, impressed in spite of himself. "And so where does that leave me?"

"In peril," Richard said bluntly. "You have your share of enemies, Simon, men who begrudged you the King's sister. Even as we speak, one of them could be with Henry now, all too eager to salt Henry's wound anew, to goad him into punishing you as he so wants to believe you deserve. I was there to dissuade him today; tomorrow you might not be so fortunate." He paused. "I've sent a man to the docks, told him to engage passage for you on the first ship sailing for France."

Simon glanced at Nell, saw her face mirror his own shock. "You truly think my danger is as great as that?"

"Yes," Richard said, "I do. I would not see you made the scapegoat for Henry's shame. Nor would I see Henry do that which he'd regret for the rest of his life. As long as you are in England, within reach of Henry's rage, you are not safe—and neither is Henry."

"Simon!" Nell closed the space between them, flung herself into Simon's arms, and as he watched, Richard's eyes—as blue as Henry's but more analytical, less innocent—lost some of their detached distance.

"You'd best withdraw at once to Odiham, Nell," he said quietly. "Give Henry time to heal."

"Odiham?" she echoed, incredulous. "Do you truly believe I would re-main in England whilst my husband is forced into exile? I go with Simon."

Simon forgot the others, saw only Nell. He touched her face with his fingers, his eyes searching hers. "Are you sure, Nell? Truly sure?"

"How can you even ask that, Simon? You are mine no less than I am yours. Whatever happens, I will not be parted from you."

She turned then, toward Richard. "But we cannot sail so soon, not tonight, not until we have our son."

"Nell, Simon would be in the Tower now had I not been there when Henry gave the order. You have no time to spare, no margin for error. As for the child, I have a suggestion. Why not send him to my wife, have him join my household at Berkhamsted—"

"No!" Simon and Nell spoke at once, sounding so distraught that Elen's eyes began to burn with tears. But if she could never have what

Nell did, a child born of her body, born of love, she could ease Nell's fears for that child.

"Nell, listen. On the morrow Rob and I will go Kenilworth, will take your son back to London. You may entrust Harry to us; we will—" The rest of her promise was lost. Nell embraced her, clung to Elen for a revealingly long moment; only then did Elen discover how Nell was trembling. "Simon," she said, "my lord father will make you welcome in Wales."

Simon had long since revised his earlier unfavorable opinion of Elen; her adultery seemed of little consequence when measured against her absolute, unswerving loyalty to Nell. "That is a generous offer, Elen, and no less than I'd expect from you. But if I agreed, I'd be paying you back in false coin. I cannot put another man at risk, would not have Henry turn his wrath upon Llewelyn."

Just a few short months ago, Simon's elder brother Amaury had paid a visit to the English court, had been fêted by Henry, and left much impressed by Simon's soaring fortunes. The thought of returning as a fugitive, his splendid future in ruins, lacerated Simon's pride as surely as any knife blade could. But what choice had he? "I will take Nell to France," he said. "To my brother's castle at Montfort l'Amaury."

RICHARD had found only two ships ready to sail at such short notice, a sturdy cogge and a lighter, faster esneque. The cogge was the larger of the two, but this particular ship must have been built during the reign of Nell's father or possibly even her grandfather, for it could offer no better shelter from the weather than a faded and frayed canvas tent. Simon chose the esneque; however cramped its rear-castle chamber, it would at least provide Nell with some small degree of protection and privacy.

Darkness had descended upon the city. Now and then a flickering light floated by, as they passed another boat. An occasional riverside house gave off a dim glow. But ahead the Southwark bank seemed ablaze. Simon's mouth tightened; he watched until Winchester House had receded into the distance. It was with a sense of utter unreality that he realized it was less than ten hours since he and Nell had been making love in the Bishop's bed.

Nell was standing alone near the bow. He crossed to her, wrapped his mantle around her shoulders. "The ship's master tells me it may take a few days to navigate the river, but he says that if the winds are with us, we should make it from Dover to Wissant in nine or ten hours."

"Where is Montfort l'Amaury?" It was too dark to see her face and he could read little in her voice.

"It is about thirty miles south of Paris. I always meant to take you there, Nell. But not like this."

"I know," she said. "I know . . ."

An immense, imposing wall suddenly seemed to loom ahead, and Simon slid his hand along Nell's arm. "We are about to shoot the bridge. Mayhap you ought to go aft, wait with Mabel in the rear-castle," he suggested, for the bridge acted almost as a dam and the current surged through its arches with awesome force; a year never passed without some unlucky Londoners drowning as their boats splintered against the massive piers. "Nell," he said, "it can be right dangerous."

"I'd be more frightened if I was unable to see what was happening," she said, and he put his arm around her, drew her close. Nell tried not to look at the rushing water, stared instead up at the ship's towering mast, at the drawbridge opening above their heads. The ship gave a sickening lurch, the arch enveloping them on both sides. Nell felt as if they were in a dark, wet tunnel, and she shuddered, clung to Simon. And then they were through, the bridge was behind them, ahead only open water. Nell put a hand up to her face. "We're drenched in spray," she said, and then, almost inaudibly, "I hate boats, hate the sea. When I was a little girl, I'd dream sometimes of drowning . . ."

"Nell . . . Nell, I am so sorry—" he began, and she reached up, put her fingers to his lips.

"No, Simon. You've nothing to be sorry for, nothing!"

Lights lit the dark to their left. They turned, stared up at the steep outer walls, the whitewashed, moonlit silhouette of the Tower keep. Richard believed that time was their ally. Henry would have such a queasy conscience, he insisted, that eventually he would have to make amends, and he would do it the only way he could, by pretending nothing had ever happened, by welcoming Nell and Simon back at his court as if their estrangement and exile had never been. That was a frail reed to cling to, yet it was all Nell had. But now, as she watched the Tower slowly slide past, she thought, What if Richard is wrong? What if Henry never relents? What would become of us, then? What future would our Harry have?

"Simon . . ." She swallowed with difficulty. "Simon, might all this be retribution? Mayhap our marriage was indeed a sin, mayhap we did grievously offend the Lord when we wed . . ."

"I find it very hard to see Henry as the instrument of the Almighty," he said, with such bitterness that Nell shivered. Even if Henry does relent, she thought, nothing will ever be the same again. Simon will never be able to forgive Henry for this, never. And sheltered by the darkness, with only Simon to see, she at last allowed herself to weep.

7

Nefyn, North Wales

March 1240

GRUFFYDD leaned over the cradle, gazed down at his infant son. Rhodri was a remarkably placid baby; amidst all the tumult in the hall, he slept as soundly as an overfed cat. So easily contented was he that Gruffydd occasionally worried lest he lack for attention. Davydd's birth—coming so many years after Llelo's—had been a source of incredulous joy, a rare blessing. In contrast, Rhodri seemed almost like an afterthought, the fourth son . . . the forgotten son.

Gruffydd touched his finger to the baby's cheek, then turned toward a sudden squeal of laughter. Davydd and Llelo were squatting by the hearth, where Llelo had cleared a space amidst the floor rushes. He was skillfully whipping a top, and as it spun, Davydd laughed again. Gruffydd smiled. Davydd's hair was the burnished shade of October bracken, his eyes the color of rock moss, full of light and devilry. He kept the household in turmoil with his pranks and persistence and curiosity, but few begrudged him his moments of mischief; the boy's charm was all the more potent for being so artless, so innocent.

The heads of the two boys were almost touching, bright against dark, a sight to give Gruffydd pleasure. But as he watched, the game came to an abrupt end. Owain strode toward the hearth, swung Davydd up into the air. As Davydd shrieked with laughter, Llelo's face shadowed. He let the top spin out, rose slowly to his feet. Too often Gruffydd had seen the jealousy flare up like this; even their love for Davydd was tainted by the rancor of their rivalry. He would have had it otherwise, but did not know how to mend the rift. For what could he say to them? He, too, loved his brother not.

Owain had put Davydd back upon his feet, ignoring the child's protests. "Papa," he said, and Gruffydd turned, watched the men being ushered into the hall. He recognized them both—Hywel ab Ednyved, the newly consecrated Bishop of St Asaph, and his brother Goronwy— and his suspicions ignited. Ednyved had nine sons, several of whom were Gruffydd's long-time companions. But he'd never counted Hywel or Goronwy among his friends. So why, then, had they ventured into his lands? He was not at war with his father—not a declared war. In the months after their confrontation at Ystrad Fflur, he had sought in vain to stir up the embers of rebellion. Men who might willingly fight Davydd on his behalf were not so willing to defy Llewelyn Fawr. Gruffydd had raged at his comrades for their cowardice, but for all his taunts about aging lions, he'd accepted defeat too readily for Senena and Owain; it was their unspoken fear that Gruffydd was no more eager to war upon his father than were his allies.

To Gruffydd, courtesy was a needless indulgence when dealing with the enemy. "Why are you here?"

"We have come at Prince Llewelyn's behest. It is his heartfelt wish that you accompany us back to Aberconwy Abbey." The Bishop paused. "You and the lad," he said.

Gruffydd felt a sudden surge of anger. Why would his father not let him be? And when would he ever learn to harden his heart against these overtures? He sought to gain time with the first query to come to mind. "Why is my father at the abbey?" No sooner were the words out of his mouth than he regretted them, for the question was too obviously transparent, too obviously a delaying device. His father had always favored the White Monks, often accepted their hospitality; why should he not be at the abbey? But the answer he got was totally unexpected, shocking him profoundly.

"Prince Llewelyn does dwell there now. A fortnight ago he did take holy vows."

Gruffydd's jaw dropped. It was true his father had always been devout. It was no less true that his concerns had always been more secular than spiritual in nature. He was no man to relinquish power. Gruffydd felt certain of that, so certain that he dared to call a Bishop of his Church a liar. "Why should I believe you?"

Goronwy began to bristle. "If my brother's word is not good enough—"

Hywel put a restraining hand on the other man's arm. "I spoke true. There comes a time when even the most worldly of men must put aside earthly pleasures, think only upon God. Your lord father understands that, has—"

"He is ill?" Gruffydd demanded roughly, and the Bishop nodded.

There was a sudden silence, broken at last by Owain. "He'll need more than a monk's cowl to get through Heaven's gate," he jeered. "Mayhap he truly is ill. Mayhap not. This could well be a ruse, Papa, a cowardly trick to lure you back to his court, into his power."

"That is not so," Llelo said hotly. "Grandpapa has been ailing for months—" Too late did he realize his mistake, realize he'd just betrayed himself. But much to his relief, neither his mother nor Owain seemed to have understood the significance of his words. He expelled his breath, then braced himself to look at his father. When he did, he saw that his father had known of his clandestine afternoons at Cricieth, had known and said nothing. Guilt rose in Llelo's throat like bile. He could not even promise Papa he'd never go again to Cricieth, for it would be a lie. But . . . but would Grandpapa ever come back to Cricieth now? Mayhap he'd stay at the abbey with the monks, and if so, when would they see each other again?

Senena glanced impatiently at her husband; how could he be so slow to see the truth? "What you are saying is that Llewelyn is dying, are you not?"

The Bishop resented her bluntness, would have preferred to break the news more gently, for the boy's sake. "Yes," he said reluctantly. "He is dying."

"Dying?" Gruffydd sounded so stunned that Senena felt both pity and irritation; did he think the old man was immortal? She would have gone to him, but Gruffydd had begun to pace. He moved to the hearth, did not turn back to face them as he said, "He had another seizure?"

"No." The Bishop looked toward Llelo, then said slowly, "In recent months Llewelyn has begun to suffer from pains in his chest. At first they would subside if he rested awhile. But as Lent drew nigh, they became more frequent, more severe. The last attack was a bad one; he was in pain for several hours. He is better now, but he knows not for long. A man with heart-pain counts his days, does well to take each moment as it comes."

He waited, but Gruffydd was silent. "My lord? Will you go to him?"

"No." Gruffydd had yet to move from the hearth. "No."

Hywel was not surprised. "As you will."

But Goronwy could not dissemble so well. "Are you sure that is a decision you can live with?" he said scornfully, and Gruffydd spun around.

"You have your answer! What more do you want from me?"

Hywel caught his brother's eye, shook his head. "What of the lad?" he asked. "Have we your permission to take Llelo back with us?"

Llelo had yet to move, to speak. At mention of his name, he raised his head. Senena was startled by his sudden pallor; he'd lost color so quickly that he looked ill. She stepped toward him, then saw the tears glimmering behind his lashes, tears for Llewelyn. "No," she said curtly, "indeed you do not, my lord Bishop. Llelo is not going to Aberconwy."

"Yes, Mama, I am."

Senena stared at her son. "I am thinking of your safety, Llelo. When a man lies near death, his influence wanes very quickly. It is Davydd whose commands do matter now. Harm might well befall you if—"

"Would you truly care?"

Senena gasped, and Llelo swung about, toward his father. "Papa," he said, "tell her I can go."

The boy was taut; to Gruffydd, he seemed very like a wild colt, ready to bolt at the slightest movement. But he was not pleading, and his eyes never wavered from Gruffydd's face. Gruffydd nodded. "Yes," he said, "go ahead, lad."

"Gruffydd . . ." Senena bit her lip, bit back her protest. Gruffydd was already turning away.

THE wind was blowing in from the west, a wet, sea-borne wind that held no hint of coming spring. Gruffydd had left his mantle in the hall and he stood shivering in the bailey, staring up at the darkening sky, a sky adrift in smoke-color clouds. They hung low over the horizon, blotted out the last traces of day. There'd be a storm soon, he thought, and it would be a bad one.

"Papa." Llelo was standing several feet away; how had he not heard the boy approach? "Papa," Llelo said again. "Come with me . . . please."

Gruffydd discovered his throat was suddenly tight; the words had to be forced out. "I cannot, Llelo." His voice sounded strange to him, too, thick and scratchy. "I cannot . . ."

LLEWELYN's lashes flickered. A woman was bending over him; a long, black braid swung loose, lightly brushed his cheek. "Joanna?" he murmured, and his daughter flinched.

"No, Papa,'" she said, as steadily as she could. "It's Elen."

He opened his eyes. "So it is," he said, sounding drowsily amused. "I was dreaming of your mother, lass," he explained, as if he'd read her mind, her fear that his wits had begun to wander. "It seemed so real," he added, "and, I regret to say, not at all the sort of dream I ought to be having, not after taking holy vows."

Elen found herself smiling through tears. "You always could make me laugh, Papa." As much as she'd mourned her mother, she knew her grieving would be even greater for Llewelyn. Even now, forced to face the mortal nature of his illness, she could not truly imagine a world in which he no longer walked or laughed, and as she clasped her father's hand in hers, she felt not like a woman grown, a woman with a husband and life of her own, but rather like a child lost in the dark.

Gwladys stepped from the shadows surrounding the bed. "Papa, do you think you could drink some of this?"

The wine was bitter, so strongly flavored was it with marigold and rosemary and lemon juice, other herbs he could not identify. Llewelyn drank these potions without complaint, more to please his daughters than his doctors, and now he forced himself to take several deep swallows before Gwladys reclaimed the cup. "Jesú, what a waste of good wine," he muttered, heard a low laugh, and felt no surprise when his son moved into his line of vision. Davydd rarely left his bedside; sometimes he even kept vigil at night.

"Do not fret, Papa," he said. "I've some mead in my chambers, and I promise to smuggle it past your doctors."

Gwladys glared at him, for she'd yet to give up hope. Davydd knew better. Llewelyn was smiling, but they all could read the question in his eyes, and none wanted to answer him. Elen finally said, with forced cheer, "Marared and Angharad arrived whilst you slept, Papa."

That meant all of his children would be at his deathbed, save only Gwenllian, who was in Ireland . . . and Gruffydd, who could not forgive. Llewelyn lay back against the pillow, closed his eyes. "I never truly expected him to come," he said wearily. "But I'd foolishly let myself hope that he might send the lad . . ."

LLEWELYN awoke with a gasp. He lay still for a time, listening to his own labored breathing. More and more his lungs were putting him in mind of a broken bellows, for he never seemed to get enough air. He wondered almost impersonally how long they could operate at such a crippled capacity. He wondered, too, how long his spirit would be tethered like this.

A log still burned in the hearth, and as his eyes adjusted to the flickering firelight, he saw a shadow move. "I'm awake," he said, glad of the company, and then, when he realized who was keeping vigil, his smile flashed, sudden, radiant. "I'd almost given up on you, lad," he confessed, and Llelo moved forward, sat beside him on the bed.

"My mother tried to stop me," he said, "but Papa . . . he understood."

"Gruffydd did not come with you . . . did he?"

"I think he was afraid to come, Grandpapa, afraid he could not forgive you."

Llewelyn's mouth twisted down. "Or afraid he could."

Llelo looked startled, then thoughtful, and Llewelyn reached out, rumpled the boy's hair. "What do you hold there, behind your back?" he asked, and Llelo moved closer, showed him a small clay vial.

"Whilst the monks were at supper, I went into the church, filled this with holy water. I thought, Grandpapa, that we could rub it on your chest. It might make you better." His words were coming faster now, rumbling out in a breathless, urgent rush, as if to forestall Llewelyn's refusal. "Why not, Grandpapa? What can you lose?"

Llewelyn was quiet for some moments. "Of all the books of the Scriptures, I've always found the most comfort in Ecclesiastes. It tells us that time and chance happen to all men, that—"

"I know what it says, that everything has its season, its time—even death. Is that what you'd have me believe, Grandpapa, that it is your time?"

"Yes." Llewelyn shoved a pillow behind his shoulders. The pain was back—by now an old and familiar foe—spreading down his arm, up to his neck. But he did not want the boy to know. He found a smile, said, "It has been more than three years, after all. Joanna grows impatient—and I've never been one to keep a lady waiting."

Llelo's head jerked up. "How can you do that? How can you jest about dying?"

He sounded angry. Llewelyn looked at him, at last said quietly, "What other way is there?"

Without warning, Llelo's eyes filled with tears. He sought without success to blink them back, then felt his grandfather's hand on his.

"Try not to grieve too much, lad. I've not been cheated; I've had a long life, with more than my share of joys. I sired sons and daughters. No man had better friends. I found two women to love, and a fair number to bed with. And I die knowing that Wales is in good hands . . ."

Llelo frowned. "Davydd?" he mumbled, and his grandfather nodded.

"Yes, Davydd . . . and you, Llelo."

He heard the boy's intake of breath. "Me?"

"Davydd has no son. God may yet bless him with one. But if not, he'll need an heir. And in all of Christendom, he could do no better than you, Llelo."

As young as he was, Llelo had learned some hard lessons in self-control. But he'd never felt the need for defenses with his grandfather, and Llewelyn could see the boy's confusion, could see the conflict of pride and excitement and guilt.

Llewelyn shifted his position; the pain was starting to ease somewhat. He was very tired, and not at all sure that he should have shared his dream with the boy. But then Llelo said, "Do you truly have so much faith in me?" and there was wonderment in his voice.

Llewelyn swallowed with difficulty. He nodded, then leaned forward and gathered his grandson into his arms. Llelo clung tightly; he made no sound, but Llewelyn could feel him trembling. "I'd be lying if I said I had no regrets, Llelo. But I was not lying when I told you that I believe it is my time." After a long silence, he said, very softly, "I should have liked, though, to have seen the man you will become."

LLEWELYN had hoped to see one last Easter; he missed it by but four days. He died at twilight on the eleventh of April, as the abbey bells were summoning the monks to Vespers. He was laid to rest before the High Altar in the abbey he'd loved, and men came in great numbers to mourn.

As she emerged from the church, Elen saw her brother and the Lord Ednyved standing apart from the other mourners. They shared a like expression, one so grim that she quickened her step.

"There is trouble," she said. "Tell me."

"You might as well know; all will soon enough." Ednyved sounded very tired; to Elen, he seemed to have aged shockingly in the days since her father's death. "We just learned that Owain led a raid upon our granges at Dolbadarn and Nant Gwynant. They burned the barns, ran off the cattle, and killed more than a dozen men."

"They could not even wait until my father was decently buried!" There was so much bitterness in Davydd's voice that Elen winced. She knew how deeply he'd loved their father, and it seemed monstrously unfair to her that he should be denied even a single day to mourn.

They'd been joined now by Ednyved's sons, Bishop Hywel and Goronwy. The former sighed, said sadly, "So it is to be war," and none disputed him. He remembered, then, the boy. "What of Llelo?" He had pledged the honor of his Church for Llelo's safety, but he did not remind Davydd of that now, saw no need. Nor did Davydd disappoint him.

"Send the lad home, Hywel," he said, turned and walked away. The others knew enough not to follow.

Elen roused herself with an effort. "Llelo is still in the church. I'll fetch him," she said, thinking that Llelo, too, would have little time to mourn.

The church was quiet; the scent of incense still lingered. Elen encountered neither monks nor mourners as she moved into the nave. Her father's tomb was encircled by flaring, white Syze candles. It had been constructed during Llewelyn's lifetime, was as impressive a sepulchre as Elen had ever seen. She looked at the arms emblazoned upon the side of the tomb, and Llewelyn's lions blurred in a haze of hot tears.

Llelo had turned at the sound of her footsteps. "It is a fine tomb, one befitting a great Prince." He reached out, gently stroked one of the enameled red lions. "Not that Grandpapa needs a monument of marble," he said huskily. "Men will remember him."

"Yes," Elen said, "they will." She moved closer, dreading what had to be done. "Darling, you can no longer stay at the abbey. Your brother Owain has attacked two of my father's—two of Davydd's granges. Your father will want you back at Nefyn. Davydd will provide an escort, and I'm sure Bishop Hywel will accompany you if—".

"No," he said, "that will not be necessary," and what Elen found saddest of all was that he did not seem surprised.

Llelo had yet to move. He was reluctant to leave Llewelyn's tomb, knelt and whispered one final prayer for his grandfather's soul. Rising, he said, very low and very fast, "Aunt Elen, shall we still be friends?"

"Yes," she said, "oh, yes, love!" She knew he'd placed his crucifix in Llewelyn's coffin, and she fumbled with the clasp of hers. "Here," she said, "I want you to have this, Llelo."

Llelo took the proffered cross, carefully tucked it away inside his tunic. "Llelo is a boy's name. I'm twelve now, old enough to be called by my given name—Llewelyn."

Elen's throat closed up. She nodded mutely, then held out her hand. He took it, and they walked in silence from the church.

8

Abbey of St Mary and St John the Evangelist, Reading, England

April 1240

Henry shifted in his seat. There were few if any men whom he trusted more than these two, his Chancellor, John Mansel, and his brother Richard. He knew their advice was sound, would have to be followed. But he could not stifle his pangs of conscience, wondered why he was so often faced with such unpalatable choices.

"I know, I know," he said impatiently. "Davydd is vulnerable right now, and we'd be mad not to take advantage of his plight, not to extract all the concessions we can. But I take no pleasure in it. He is Joanna's son, our kinsman, Richard. I'd much rather offer him our aid in putting down Gruffydd's rebellion."

Richard and John Mansel exchanged weary glances; Henry's sentimentality was often a severe trial to them both. "We are in agreement, then?" Richard persisted, and Henry gave a grudging nod.

"Yes, yes. But no more of this now." He had begun to smile, and Richard, turning, saw why, saw Eleanor approaching with Edward, Henry's ten-month-old son.

Richard had a well-loved son of his own, a frail five-year-old named after Henry, cherished all the more for being the only one of Richard's four children to survive infancy. But he felt Henry's devotion was excessive, and he watched disapprovingly as Henry dandled little Edward upon his knee, utterly indifferent to his royal dignity.

John Mansel rolled his eyes, knowing there was little chance now of keeping Henry's mind upon affairs of state. The sound of Eleanor's giggling set his teeth on edge, for he thought her a frivolous, vain young woman, a bad influence upon Henry. Richard found it easier than the priest to understand the appeal of a pretty, vivacious seventeen-year-old, but his own wife was just three months dead. He'd once contemplated divorcing her, fearing she could not give him an heir, but he'd been sincerely attached to her, mourned her still, and the sight of Henry's domestic bliss rubbed raw against his nerves, stirring feelings of resentment no less intense for being illogical, and he followed Mansel as the Chancellor moved away from the dais.

"Has Henry given you the news yet?" he murmured. "Eleanor is with child again, and already Henry is laying out plans for new nurseries at his favorite manors. He has even given orders to prepare a luxurious lying-in chamber for her, although the babe is not due till after Michaelmas!"

"Yes, he told me," the priest said glumly. He was pleased, of course, that Eleanor had satisfactorily performed her primary duty as a Queen, bearing a healthy male heir, for Henry was so uxorious a husband that Mansel feared he would not have parted with her even had she proved barren. Fortunately, that fear had been laid to rest. Mansel welcomed this second pregnancy. While Edward seemed to be a sturdy, robust child, death came so often for the young that it was well to have sons to spare. But he also knew that Eleanor's pregnancy would distract Henry even more than usual.

Richard was still pondering the problem posed by Wales. "As soon as they got word of Llewelyn's death, the Marshals crossed into Ceredigion. They'd not have dared whilst Llewelyn still lived—to give the old lion his due. But their timing suits us well, puts all the more pressure upon Davydd. I do not see how he can—'' He stopped, gave the priest a curious look. "What is it?"

Mansel was staring across the hall. "Jesus wept," he muttered. "When did he return to England?"

Richard peered about, but the abbey hall was crowded and he was very near-sighted, one of the reasons why he had so little enthusiasm for battlefield heroics. "Who?" he demanded, and Mansel gestured.

"Simon de Montfort," he said, sounding far from pleased.

Richard caught his breath. "Devil take him, whatever is he thinking of?"

Simon was striding toward the dais, a path opening before him as if by magic; a man in the King's disfavor was shunned like a leper. Richard glanced back at Henry, then hurried to intercept his brother-in-law.

"What are you doing here? I told you Henry would need time—"

"It has been eight months, time enough, I should think."

"But I've had no chance to prepare Henry for your return! Christ, Simon, why must you be so reckless?"

Men had often accused him of that failing, although Simon could never understand why; by his lights, he was just doing what had to be done. But he did not resent Richard's aggrieved, peevish tone, for he knew Richard's concern was genuine. "I've never held patience to be a virtue," he said, and then the corner of his mouth curved. "Mayhap because I have so little of it," he admitted, and Richard swore under his breath. He had little patience himself with men who made jests in the face of disaster.

"In that, you and Nell are remarkably well matched. At least you had the common sense to keep her away. Go on, then, seek Henry out. I wash my hands of it," he warned, but as Simon moved away, he made haste to follow.

Henry was tickling Edward, while the child wriggled and squirmed happily. He was slow to become aware of the silence, was not alerted until Eleanor squeezed his arm. At sight of Simon, blood rushed to his face; his mouth puckered strangely. He looked so stricken that Simon almost felt a flicker of pity—almost. "My liege," he said, began to kneel. But the sound of his voice shattered Henry's trance.

"Simon! No, do not kneel. Come up here, onto the dais. How it gladdens me to see you," he exclaimed, and then, to Simon's astonishment, he found himself embraced by his King. His recoil was instinctive, but if Henry noticed, he gave no sign. "We've missed you at court . . . have we not, Eleanor? But where is Nell? Is she not with you?"

Simon shook his head. He was not easily flustered, but he was utterly discountenanced now by the warmth of Henry's welcome. He'd come prepared to accord Henry the respect and honor due his rank. But he did not know how to deal with this, did not know how to fake friendship. While he did not begrudge Henry a King's homage, he could not share Henry's pretense, could not blot out memory of the past eight months. He thought of Nell, of the nights she'd wept in his arms, grieving for their son, for the shame Henry had brought upon them. He thought of his brother Amaury, of his humiliation in having to ask Amaury for shelter. And he felt anger begin to stir, that Henry would deny them both their dignity like this, force upon him this charade, this hollow mockery of a reconciliation.

He had yet to speak, did not know what to say. But before his silence became awkward, Eleanor raised up, kissed him on the cheek. "We have indeed missed you, Simon," she said gaily, while her green eyes pleaded for his cooperation, his complicity, and the moment thus passed when Simon could have objected, could have salvaged his pride.

Richard had mounted the dais, too. He was somewhat chagrined that Simon had not needed his help after all, but he felt honor-bound, nonetheless, to do his part. Simon looked strangely grim for a man just restored to the royal favor, and Eleanor's merriment had a brittle, edgy sound to it. But Henry's smile was dazzling; he was beaming fondly at Simon, as if genuinely joyful at his return. In time he would almost convince himself of that. Role-playing was Henry's reality. Richard knew it, wondered if Simon did.

THAT spring had been a dry, mild one, and as Richard de Clare, Earl of Gloucester, left London and rode west, he found the roads crowded with fellow travelers: merchants, itinerant peddlers, pilgrims, an occasional fast-riding courier. When he stopped for lodging in Oxford, he was pleased to discover that Elen de Quincy had also sought shelter with the Franciscans, and when he learned that she, too, was heading for the river port of Gloucester, he suggested that they travel together. Elen agreed readily, grateful both for the company and the added protection, and they passed the remainder of their journey quite pleasantly, troubled neither by outlaws nor by the notoriously erratic May weather.

Richard de Clare glanced often at Elen as they rode. He knew, of course, of the faint scent of scandal that clung to her. She was the King's niece. But she was also half-Welsh, and when she'd made the shockingly unsuitable marriage to Robert de Quincy, there were many who explained it in terms of her tainted blood. Richard knew she was no longer young, for she had confessed quite nonchalantly that she was in her thirty-third year. Nor did she measure up to their society's concept of beauty. Her hair was midnight-black instead of flaxen, her eyes were dark, and her skin seemed sun-warmed all year round; by English standards, she was an undeniable exotic. Yet for all that, Richard thought her quite the most fascinating woman he'd ever seen, her appeal all the more alluring for its unsanctioned, sinful nature. But it had not occurred to him to make improper advances; he was just eighteen and too well-bred to envision so highborn a lady as a bedmate. Moreover, Elen was known to be blazingly outspoken, and he shrank from putting her Welsh temper to the test.

Elen had gone straight from her father's funeral to one of her dower manors in Essex, and so was not that conversant with current London gossip. Richard happily brought her up to date, informed her that the Earl of Warenne was ill unto death, that her uncle Richard, Earl of Cornwall, would soon be ready to depart upon his long-planned pilgrimage to the Holy Land, that four Norwich Jews accused of circumcising a Christian boy had been torn asunder by wild horses.

"They say most of Norwich was there to watch." Richard was surprised when Elen grimaced; he'd not have thought her to be the squeamish sort. "It is well that women have softer hearts than men," he said, quite earnestly, "but pity ought not to be wasted on Jews, Lady Elen. They deserved to die."

"Did they?"

He swung about in the saddle to stare at her. "How can you doubt it? Jews are the Devil's disciples, the enemies of the True Faith. Think upon the evil that they do. They steal the Eucharist, stab it till it bleeds. They lure Christian children away and then sacrifice them in vile rites. They poison wells, Lady Elen! Surely you know all this?"

"I know men say it is so." Elen slowed her mare. "I know, too, that Englishmen claim the Welsh are a godless, barbaric people, who couple like beasts in the field and know nothing of honor. Some of them even fancy we have tails, Richard."

He flushed deeply, and she relented; he was, after all, very young. He did not understand, but that did not surprise her. She knew none who did.

They rode in silence for a time, Richard wondering how he had offended, and Elen thinking of the four Jews who'd died at Norwich. Had they truly circumcised the boy? And even if so, did it warrant such a ghastly death?

She was troubled from time to time by such questions, questions with no answers, questions no Christian should even pose. John the Scot had called her perverse; so did Rob, although he said it with pride. Neither man had understood how lonely it could be. Once she'd realized how deviant, how irregular her thoughts were, she rarely shared them with others. Even with Rob, whom she loved, there was much she left unspoken.

Her wayward sympathy for the Jews was but part of a disquieting pattern; somehow she seemed ever out of step with her fellows. Holy Church taught that women must be subservient unto their husbands; English law guaranteed it. But such unquestioning obedience did not come easily to a daughter of Llewelyn Fawr; she'd always been one to balk at fences. Welsh women had rights of their own; Welsh law held that a woman was "to go the way that she willeth, freely." Why were the ways of her people wrong? Could it not be the English who were in error? Or even the Church?

At times it seemed to her that she was at war with her world. She was convinced that Welsh law was more just than Church law, too, in the treatment of bastard children, for she did not believe it was Christian to deny any child his birthright. Nor did she believe that women were by their very nature more susceptible to the Devil's wiles. She did not understand why her Church so scorned man's carnal needs, why St Jerome had admonished a grieving widow to mourn the loss of her virginity more than the loss of her husband, or why St Augustine had contended that, even in marriage, sexual intercourse could not be wholly free from sin. She did not—could not—believe that a baby who died unbaptized would be forever denied entry into Paradise. She could accept the existence of demons, but not dragons. She doubted that the wounds of a murdered man truly bled in the presence of his murderer. She felt certain that vervain would ill protect a man in battle, that rosemary was of little use in warding off lightning bolts. And she did not in her heart believe that the Jews were the veritable Antichrists.

Now she looked over at Richard, at last said, "Rumors are the easiest of all crops to tend, Richard. You need only sow a few seeds about and in no time at all, you'll reap a harvest of hatred. Have you never noticed that when men are goaded into attacking a Jewry, they are invariably led by those who owe debts to Jewish money-lenders?"

"Who can blame them," Richard protested, "when the Jews charge such outrageous interest rates?"

Elen frowned. This was a familiar argument. She'd even heard it from Simon de Montfort; when she'd asked him why he'd expelled the Jews from Leicester, he'd replied that he'd acted to keep Christians from falling into the hands of Jewish money-lenders. No one, not even Simon, seemed to see what was, to Elen, the obvious connection between those high interest rates and the precarious position of the Jews, aliens and outcasts dangerously dependent upon the dubious good will of their Christian neighbors.

"I never knew you felt so kindly toward the Jews," Richard said suddenly. Before she could respond, he added, "But I'll not speak of this to others. And . . . and I think it best if you do not, either, Lady Elen. People would not understand."

"No," Elen conceded. "I do not suppose they would, Richard." She laughed then, but without amusement. She was enough of a misfit as it was. Even before she'd defied convention by wedding Rob, the English had looked at her askance. In her own way, she was no less an object of suspicion than were the Jews.

Richard was fumbling for a safer topic of conversation. "Why did your husband not accompany you to Gloucester?" He hesitated, then ventured a maladroit gallantry. "Were you my wife, I'd never let you wander about unescorted."

Elen ducked her head so he'd not see her smile. "Rob was not free to come with me. An Essex neighbor of ours was found dead a fortnight ago, and Rob and several other knights were requested to hold an inquest, to try to determine the cause of death. But I could not wait; I knew Davydd would be meeting with Henry on the fifteenth . . . today."

"Well, we ought to reach Gloucester by the morrow," Richard said, and Elen nodded. She was not sorry she'd be a day late; she'd not truly wanted to watch as her brother was compelled to do homage to the English Crown.

IT was midday when Elen and Richard de Clare rode through St Mary's gate into the precincts of the Benedictine abbey of St Peter at Gloucester. Richard was impatient to reach the guest hall, but Elen halted her mare before the Abbot's house, for she'd caught sight of a familiar face. "You go on, Richard," she said, "and take my servants with you. I see a friend."

She did think of Ednyved ap Cynwrig as just that. He'd been more than her father's Seneschal, he'd been Llewelyn's lifelong companion, had always been on hand whenever any of her family had need of him. She was glad to find him here at Gloucester, glad he was standing by Davydd in her brother's time of trial, and she slid from her mare, moved swiftly toward him.

"Well, now," he said, "if you're not a sight to gladden these aging eyes. Llewelyn and I never could figure out how he'd managed to sire such handsome children."

Elen's smile was sad. "Papa casts a long shadow," she said softly, and he nodded.

"Most of all for Davydd. I miss Llewelyn, lass, miss him like I'd miss an arm. But Davydd . . . he has to measure up to Llewelyn now, and that is a lot to ask of any man."

"Tell me about the peace, Ednyved. Were Henry's terms harsh ones?"

"He did not ask us to harvest the moon or cull the stars from the sky," Ednyved said grimly, "but he stopped just short of it. Davydd had to agree to submit any Marcher claims to arbitration; that could call much of Llewelyn's conquests into question. And no Welsh lord may do homage to Davydd, only to Henry. Llewelyn was the uncrowned Prince of all Wales, but the English seek to make of Davydd a mere vassal of the Crown. They did not even accord him a title, Elen, referred to him in the treaty documents as Davydd, son of Llewelyn, former Prince of North Wales."

Elen had no divided loyalties. She might love an Englishman, live in England, but she was utterly and passionately Welsh. "Damn them!" she spat. "They are like vultures, the lot of them, always hovering about, preying upon Welsh weakness. Well, let them rejoice; it will not be for long. I know Davydd better than they do. Whatever he's had to yield today, he'll retake on the morrow."

"You need not argue that with me, Elen. I agree with you. Davydd shall prove to be an unpleasant surprise to the English—if he's given the chance."

Elen stared at him. "What are you saying? That you truly think Gruffydd might prevail? Never!"

"I would I could be as sure of that, lass," he said, sounding so bleak, so somber that Elen felt a sudden chill of fear.

"Davydd has to win," she said. "God pity Wales if he does not . . ."

AFTER learning from Ednyved that Davydd was at Gloucester Castle, Elen wasted no time in seeking her brother out. Crossing the moat into the castle bailey, she came upon a scene of utter chaos. Henry was constructing new quarters for his Queen, and carpenters and masons were rushing about, clambering up onto shaky scaffolding, dropping tools, exchanging curses and sarcasm. It was not unheard of for Henry to supervise his building projects, but now he was nowhere in sight. Elen was glad, for he was the last person she wanted to see at the moment. She guided her mare toward a horse block, and the nearest man hurried over to help her dismount.

She thanked him, then asked, "Where will I find Prince Davydd?" making defiant use of her brother's title.

"I do not know." The man didn't recognize her, but he added

"Madame" for safety's sake; her gown and mantle were of high-quality wool. He pointed. "Mayhap the Earl of Leicester might know."

"Simon!" Elen was delighted. "I got your letter, so I knew you were returning to claim your son, and wait until you see how much he's grown! But I would not have expected to find you at Gloucester. Have you and Henry been reconciled, then?"

Simon was no less pleased to see her. He smiled, kissed her cheek. "Well, I am here with Henry, am I not?"

Elen gave him a searching look. "So is Davydd," she said, "but not by choice."

Simon laughed; her candor was comforting after the hyprocrisy of Henry's court. "He acted as if nothing had ever happened, Elen. He even said he'd missed me!"

He sounded bemused, but bitter, too. Elen understood exactly how he felt. "Why did you not bring Nell?"

"I thought it best to face Henry myself. His quarrel was never with Nell." Simon paused; his smile flashed again. "She is with child; did she write to you?"

Elen nodded. "I am glad for you, Simon, glad for you both. Nell also wrote that you've taken the cross, mean to go on pilgrimage to the Holy Land."

"Yes," he said. "I came back for my son, for we were not willing to entrust him to others on so long and perilous a journey. But whilst I am here, I hope to sell some of my lands to raise funds for my pilgrimage. I do not intend to tarry longer than need be in England, though. I plan to sail with Harry within a fortnight's time."

"What of Nell? Now that you are welcome again at Henry's court, will you send Nell back to England whilst you go on crusade?"

"You ought to know Nell better than that, Elen. She intends to go with me, at least as far as Italy; there she'll await the birth of our child. If not for that, I daresay she'd have insisted upon accompanying me to the very gates of Jerusalem." Simon's smile was wry. "I have to confess, though," he said, "that I did not try to dissuade her as much as I ought. I rather like having her with me."

Elen laughed at his understated admission; coming from Simon, she thought, that was like the most impassioned of declarations. "Nell's grandmother, Queen Eleanor of Aquitaine, went on crusade, so why not Nell? She must— Davydd!"

Simon watched as Elen and her brother embraced. Davydd was a stranger to him; they'd met only twice. But he was Nell's kinsman, Elen's brother, and Simon felt some sympathy for his plight. Had he known Davydd better, he might have thought to caution him about Henry, to warn him that despite Henry's generous nature and kind heart, any man who trusted him was one of God's great fools. Simon suspected, though, that such a warning would have been wasted. Davydd did not strike him as the trusting sort.

DAVYDD and Elen had sought privacy by the River Severn. Some yards away, their horses grazed. Behind them rose the walls of the castle bailey; ahead lay one of the wooden bridges that spanned the Severn. Davydd picked up a handful of pebbles, let them drop one by one into the muddy water. Elen waited, with uncommon patience, for him to speak.

"Did Ednyved tell you what they demanded of me?"

"Yes," she said, and he dropped another pebble into the river, watched the ripples widen.

"The English tried for years to get Papa to arbitrate Marcher claims, tried and failed. What they could not get from him, they got from me, Elen, within one month of Papa's death."

"What choice did you have? You cannot fight Henry and Gruffydd both. Not even Papa could do that." Elen moved toward him. "Davydd, look at me. Ednyved told me that the Marshals have captured Cardigan Castle, that Ralph de Mortimer is laying claim to Maelienydd. You had to end the war, had to come to terms with the English. And you know that, else you'd not be here today in Gloucester. So why are you blaming yourself like this? The English took advantage of your need and extorted some promises from you. What of it? Our people have a saying, Davydd, one you know well—rare is the promise that is kept."

Davydd looked at her for a long moment. "As ever, you go right to the heart of things, Elen. I had to yield to Henry; I could not fight two wars at once. I know that. But knowing makes it no easier."

Elen caught his arm. "Forget Henry!" she said fiercely. "It is Gruffydd who matters now. Davydd, you have to defeat him. Not just for your own sake, for Gwynedd, for Wales. He is not fit to rule, would bring us all to ruin if ever he had the power."

"Not all of the Welsh would agree with you, Elen."

"For the love of God, Davydd! You can ill afford hurt pride. Yes, some of the Welsh would prefer Gruffydd if given the choice. People fear change; they cling mindlessly to the old ways, to what they know. When Papa broke with tradition, named you as his sole heir, it frightened them. Let them be frightened, the sheep! You do not need them, Davydd. You will prevail without them."

For the first time since his arrival at Gloucester, Davydd smiled. "Your faith is heartening, Elen. And not ill founded." From the corner of his eye, he caught a flash of bright blue, turned to watch as a kingfisher streaked by, all but skimming the surface of the river.

"What will you do, Davydd?"

"I mean to win this war." Adding dryly, "I cannot well afford not to win, can I?"

9

Cricieth, North Wales

September 1240

THEY had followed the coast road since dawn, but the sun was high overhead by the time they caught their first glimpse of Cricieth Castle. Like all Welsh castles, it sprang up without warning, was suddenly there before them, an awesome, grey stone silhouette rising against the vivid September sky. It seemed haloed by clouds, so high was its hill, and afforded sweeping views of the Llŷn Peninsula, the distant heights of the Eryri mountain range, the brilliant, blue waters of the bay. But the beauty before him was wasted upon Owain, for he saw only the banner that flew from the castle's Great Tower—the quartered lions of Davydd ap Llewelyn.

He nudged his horse closer to his father's mount. "I still do not understand, Papa, why you have agreed to meet with Davydd."

"How often do I have to tell you?" Gruffydd said impatiently. "I did agree because the Bishop of Bangor asked it of me."

To Owain, that was a highly unsatisfactory answer. And what, he wondered, if the Bishop asked you to ride off a cliff, Papa? But so disrespectful a question could never be voiced. It was not fear that silenced him; Owain feared only leprosy and demons. Yet if he did not fear his father, he did love him, and that love effectively hobbled his tongue.

The Bishop of Bangor had overheard their exchange, urged his mount up alongside them. "Holy Church has pledged both your safety and that of Lord Davydd. So what, then, can you lose by this meeting?"

Owain's mouth twisted. The Bishop did but belabor the obvious; of course their safety was assured. But he was wrong to think there was nothing to lose. What if Davydd offered his father half of Gwynedd?

What then? For as much as Owain wanted to believe his father would scorn the offer, he shrank from seeing Gruffydd put to such a tempting test.

Despite himself, Gruffydd felt a sudden unease as he passed through the castle gateway; Cricieth was a place of unpleasant memories for him. It was here, on an August afternoon twelve years past, that he had goaded his father into riding an unbroken stallion. Llewelyn had been thrown, but suffered no serious hurt, and Gruffydd had felt a shamed sense of relief. But afterward, the hatred that had long burned between his brother and him had at last flared into violence, into a sudden brawl. He was then thirty-two to Davydd's nineteen; the victory had been his. At sight now of Davydd, awaiting them by the stairs of the Great Tower, Gruffydd drew a sharp breath, swore silently that this victory, too, would be his.

Owain demanded to be present at the meeting, as if daring Davydd to object. But Davydd merely shrugged, then led the way up into the Great Tower. The Bishop, Gruffydd, and Owain followed.

The trestle table was laden with food: cheese toasted on thin slices of bread, cold Michaelmas goose, sweet wafers. But no servants were in evidence. "I thought we'd speak more freely amongst ourselves," Davydd said. Moving to the sideboard, he began to pour mead into waiting cups, as the men settled themselves around the table. Owain alone showed interest in the food. Reaching for a caus pobi, he bit deeply into the melted cheese, washed it down with a large swallow of mead.

"You set a good table, Uncle," he drawled. "I suppose you learned such niceties from your kin at the English court." His rudeness was calculated; it had occurred to him that if he could provoke Davydd into a rage, he might bring this council to an abortive end. But his sarcasm was ignored; neither Gruffydd nor the other men so much as gave him a glance.

"Well?" Gruffydd leaned back in his chair, watching Davydd as he drank. "What have you to say to me?"

"He wants to buy peace, Papa; what else?" Owain interjected, and this time his father silenced him with an abrupt gesture.

"Your son is right," Davydd said, and Gruffydd stiffened. "What are you offering?"

"If we come to terms, I will allow you to retain the lordship of Llŷn, and I will restore to you two of the commotes you forfeited at Ystrad Fflur: Arwystli and Ceri. In time, I might be willing to restore the other four commotes, too."

"Might you be willing, indeed!" Although Gruffydd's outrage was real enough, it was threaded through with relief, too. He still believed his cause was just, his war was winnable. But what if Davydd's had been a genuine offer to share power, to share Gwynedd? Better that he never know. "You want my answer? Rot in Hell," he said, started to push away from the table.

The Bishop caught his arm. "You are too hasty, my lord. When you seek to strike a bargain, do you make your best offer first?" Adding in an undertone, "Trust me, Gruffydd. We're not done here yet."

"He gives you good advice, Gruffydd," Davydd said, but he was looking at the Bishop, not his brother. "I find it interesting," he said, "that you do champion Gruffydd's rights. It was my understanding that the Church refuses to recognize sons born out of wedlock."

"Welsh law holds otherwise," the Bishop snapped, not comfortable with the unexpected turn the conversation had taken. He had his reasons for backing Gruffydd. Wales was unique among Christian nations, in that under its laws, the Church was subordinate to the State. To the Bishop, that was heresy, and he hoped that Gruffydd would be more malleable than Davydd in this regard, less likely to challenge Church doctrine. Gruffydd might hate the English with a demented passion, but at least he'd always shown himself to be a good son of the Church, and the Bishop thought he'd be receptive to the right approach, the right adviser. He'd known Gruffydd long enough to determine that the Welshman was as straightforward as he seemed. But subtlety was not likely to be lacking in the grandson of King John, and there were few qualities that the Bishop mistrusted more.

"I find it curious that I should be upholding the position of the Church," Davydd murmured, "whilst you, my lord Bishop, do argue for the old laws of Wales," and his smile was sardonic enough to bring a flush to the Bishop's face.

"We digress, my lord," he said coldly. "What ought to concern us is the good of Gwynedd. For nigh on six months now, this war has been waged between you and the Lord Gruffydd. Neither of you has been able to gain an advantage, but the country has been bled white, and every day good men die so that one of you might be Prince. What purpose does it serve to continue this strife?"

"There is truth to what you say," Davydd conceded. "But you do not fully understand our problem." He looked, then, at Gruffydd. "If I were to offer you half of Gwynedd, would that end your rebellion?"

Taken aback, Gruffydd gained time by reaching for his wine cup, swallowing a generous measure of mead. "No," he said at last. "I fight not just for myself, but for Gwynedd. You could not be trusted to defend our land against the English. You've already proven it by that accursed deal you struck with them at Gloucester, that craven agreement to arbitrate Marcher claims."

Davydd showed neither surprise nor resentment. Instead, he nodded. "I expected no less. Whatever our other differences, Gruffydd, I've never doubted your sincerity." And then he startled Gruffydd by smiling, a strange smile, for to Gruffydd, it seemed to be mocking them both, and yet somehow sad, too. He was puzzling over it as Davydd turned back toward the Bishop.

"Do you see the problem now? Gruffydd is convinced that I am not a worthy Prince for Gwynedd. Unfortunately, I feel no less strongly that he is utterly unfit to rule, that he would be a disaster for Gwynedd, for Wales, for us all. That does not give us much room for compromise, does it?"

"Compromise be damned!" Owain emphasized his opinion with a sweeping gesture, too sweeping; his arm struck his empty wine cup, sent a platter of wafers crashing to the floor. "Damnation," he muttered, sounding faintly embarrassed. "How did I do that?"

Gruffydd felt embarrassment, too, on his son's behalf, but also annoyance. Owain had a notoriously poor head for wine. To Gruffydd, that was no excuse, though; Owain should have known better than to gulp mead like water, today of all times. "Here," he said brusquely, shoving a platter toward his discomfited son. "Eat something."

Owain obediently picked up a caus pobi, only to drop it hastily. "I . . . I'd best not," he said. "I feel queasy of a sudden, and light-headed, too . . ."

Gruffydd swore under his breath. But his son's pallor was quite pronounced now, and he'd begun to sweat. "Lie down for a while," Gruffydd said, jerking his head toward Davydd's canopied bed, and then glared at Davydd, daring him to jeer at Owain's folly.

If Davydd was amused by Owain's gaucherie, it did not show on his face. The Bishop was less tactful, though, could not repress a grimace of disgust. Owain rose unsteadily, yawned, and shambled toward the bed.

The Bishop decided it was time he took the helm. "It grieves me that brothers could be so filled with hate, that you should so disregard the example of Our Lord Jesus Christ. You both share the blood of Llewelyn Fawr; I think it time you remembered that. If you cannot come to terms, the Church might have to compel a settlement."

Gruffydd set his cup down with a thud. "I think not! I'll not be coerced into acting against my conscience, not even for the Church." His defiance might have had more impact, however, had it not been punctuated by a loud snore from his son.

Davydd rose, moved to pour himself another drink. "I think you'd best consult with the English King ere you issue any ultimatums, my lord Bishop. I rather doubt that Henry shares your desire for peace.

This war betwixt Gruffydd and myself serves none better than the English, and well they know it."

The Bishop was becoming more and more convinced that his instincts had been right, that Davydd ap Llewelyn would bear close scrutiny, indeed. He changed his tack, no longer spoke of his Church's power, spoke, instead, of its compassion. They must forswear the example of Cain and Abel, he argued earnestly, must put aside their grievances and work together for the good of Gwynedd, for their Welsh brothers and sisters in Christ.

Gruffydd was hard put to hide his impatience. While he'd always shown the Bishop every respect, it was the priest he honored, not the man. He knew the Bishop had his own axe to grind, even if he was not yet sure what the Bishop hoped to gain. For now, he was willing to accept support where he could find it, but he thought that having to listen to an interminable sermon upon brotherhood was a high price, indeed, to pay for that support.

Only one of the windows was unshuttered; the chamber seemed very stuffy to Gruffydd. As the Bishop droned on, he actually found himself dozing off. He hastily gulped the last of his mead, but it did not seem to help. He'd begun to sweat, tasted salt on his upper lip. How hot it had become! Mayhap he ought to open another window. But when he rose to his feet, he discovered, to his astonishment, that his legs would not support him. He sank back weakly in his chair, and the Bishop gave him a look of sudden concern.

"Gruffydd, are you ill?"

"I . . . I am not sure. I feel strange, in truth . . ." It took an effort to form the words, to get them out without slurring. The Bishop was leaning across the table, asking if he wanted to lie down. He did, craved nothing so much as to sink into a deep, deep sleep. He sought desperately to clear his head of cobwebs, to get his thoughts back into coherent order, but it was hard, so hard. The Bishop was looking alarmed. Davydd, too, was watching him. He was standing near a wall sconce; his eyes caught the light, seemed to take on golden glints. Cat eyes, intent, unblinking. King John's eyes.

Gruffydd's gasp was audible to both men. He swung around, stared at the bed. His eyes darted to his empty wine cup, back up to Davydd's impassive face. "Christ, you poisoned us!"

The Bishop recoiled. "Mother of God," he whispered, staring in horror at his own wine cup.

"No," Davydd said, "not poison." His denial did not even register with Gruffydd. Lurching to his feet, he fumbled for his sword. He managed to get it free of his scabbard, but almost lost his balance, reeling back against the table. The trestle boards separated, overturning the table; the Bishop scrambled clear just in time. Davydd had not moved. He stood watching as Gruffydd staggered toward him, two steps, three. But then Gruffydd's knees were buckling. The sword slipped from his numbed fingers, clattered to the floor. Gruffydd's last awareness was of falling, of plummeting down into the dark.

Davydd crossed the chamber, picked up the sword. He knelt then, by Gruffydd's body, unsheathed his dagger. The Bishop still stood as if frozen, made mute by shock. Davydd straightened up, moved swiftly to the window, and beckoned. Within moments, one of his men had answered his summons. He did not even glance at the body on the floor, listened intently to Davydd's low-voiced commands. The Bishop could catch an occasional word ". . . out-numbered . . . tell them . . . their lord's life does depend upon their cooperation . . ." And the Bishop realized that Davydd was giving orders to seize Gruffydd's men, awaiting him in the great hall.

As the man withdrew, Davydd strode toward the bed. Owain still snored, did not stir as Davydd bent over him, claimed his sword and dagger, found a hidden knife in his boot. Even now, the Bishop could not help noticing how economical Davydd's every movement was, how deliberate, not a wasted motion. He edged his way around the wreckage of the table, moved slowly toward Gruffydd's body.

"Jesú, you . . . you killed them!" he said incredulously.

"No," Davydd said. "I gave them an uncommonly potent sleeping draught, well laced with henbane, but not enough to kill. They're likely to feel utterly wretched when they awaken, but they'll live." He crossed to the window again, jerked the shutter back. Whatever he saw seemed to give him satisfaction. He said, almost inaudibly, "It is done, then."

The Bishop knelt by Gruffydd, with some difficulty managed to turn him over onto his back. Gruffydd's breathing was heavy, stentorian, but the Bishop's searching fingers found a steady pulse, and he sighed with relief. He was still struggling with disbelief, for it was inconceivable to him that anyone would dare to defy the Church. "Have you gone mad? Do you not realize what you've done? Jesus God, you swore a holy oath that you'd not harm him!"

Davydd turned from the window. "I lied," he said.

The Bishop's jaw dropped. Gruffydd was forgotten. What was at stake now was far more important than the fate of one man, it was the very authority of the Church. "You'll be damned for this, damned for all eternity! That I swear, by all I hold sacred in this life. I shall see to it, shall excommunicate you myself!"

Davydd nodded slowly. "Do what you must, my lord Bishop," he said. "Just as I must."

ALTHOUGH she had been the lady of the manor for almost six months, Isabella still did not feel completely comfortable dwelling in Llewelyn's shadow. That was particularly true here at Dolwyddelan, which had been Llewelyn's favorite residence. Even now, she found herself half-expecting him to enter, demand to know what she and Davydd were doing in his private chamber.

In fact, the room still looked much as it had when Llewelyn and Joanna had lived in it, for Isabella had made but one change, replacing Joanna's old settle with one of finely carved oak. Davydd was slouched upon it now, idly strumming a small harp. He played well, as he did most things, but Isabella doubted that his mind was upon his music. He had the remote, inward look that was all too familiar to her, that so effectively shielded his thoughts, shut her out.

Isabella had a cushion cover spread across her lap; ostensibly, she was occupied in embroidering an elaborate floral design. But her needle remained poised over the linen. She was actually engaged in watching her husband, casting him covert, troubled glances whenever she thought he wasn't looking.

After a time, he caught her at it. Their eyes locked. "You might as well say it, Isabella," he said, and she flushed, bent hastily over her sewing.

"I'm sure you—you had good reasons for what you did, Davydd. But . . ." She bit her lip, let her words trail off.

Davydd finished the thought for her. "But it was less than honor-able," he said softly.

Isabella looked up quickly, but she could not tell if he was mocking her or not. She lowered her gaze to her embroidery, began to stitch. Needlework was one of her proudest accomplishments. Yet now she wielded her needle so awkwardly that soon she drew blood. Davydd had resumed playing, a lively, buoyant little melody that seemed an ironic selection under the circumstances. A tear suddenly splashed upon Isabella's wrist. She and Davydd had been wed for ten years. She thought herself to be far more fortunate than most wives, for Davydd never maltreated her. He begrudged her nothing. They rarely quarreled. But they were strangers to each other. She knew no more of the secrets of his heart than he did of hers.

She was relieved when the Lord Ednyved was announced a few moments later. "I'll leave you alone to talk," she said, once greetings had been exchanged. Mayhap Davydd could unburden himself to Ednyved, his father's friend, as he could not to her. Did he even feel such a need? She did not know.

As soon as the two men were alone, Ednyved's smile faded. "I think," he said tersely, "that you'd best find yourself another Seneschal."

Davydd had been about to rise. He sat back on the settle, his eyes searching the older man's face. "I see," he said. "So you, too, want to talk of honor."

"No, not honor—honesty! If you could not trust me enough to confide in me, how can I continue to serve you?"

"I would trust you with my very life," Davydd said, so simply that some of Ednyved's anger began to ebb.

"Then why did you not tell me what you meant to do?"

"Because I knew what my action would cost me. No man defies the Church with impunity. Had you been involved, the curse of excommunication would have fallen upon you, too."

Ednyved expelled his breath. Mollified, he stepped forward, straddled a chair. "If we are going to work together, lad, you'll have to curb these motherly instincts of yours," he said, and Davydd laughed.

"Need I explain myself, Ednyved?" he asked, felt an intense surge of relief when Ednyved shook his head. "If you do understand, you may be the only man in Christendom who does. Tell me, do you remember that Saracen saying you brought back from the Holy Land, something about tigers?"

Ednyved looked bemused, but nodded. "Not Saracen, though; men said it was a folk wisdom from Cathay: He who rides a tiger dares not dismount. Is that the one you had in mind?"

"The very one," Davydd said. There was something about the tilt of his head, the sudden, self-mocking grin that took Ednyved by surprise. For a fleeting moment, he so resembled his father that Ednyved's eyes filled with tears. He blinked them away, but made no attempt to hide them. He felt no shame; Llewelyn was worth grieving for.

Davydd was watching him. "You are thinking of my father," he said, and he leaned forward, put his hand on Ednyved's arm. "I cannot fail him, Ednyved. No matter what it costs, I must keep faith with him . . . I must!"

Ednyved had never heard him sound so impassioned; emotion was an indulgence Davydd rarely allowed himself. "You do know," he asked, "that it is not over?"

"Christ, yes." Davydd rose, moved restlessly toward the hearth. "There will be those to make of Gruffydd a martyr, to—" He stopped, frowning, then crossed quickly to the window.

Below, the bailey was in turmoil. Men were crowding about, dogs barking. Several of Davydd's teulu, his household guard, had surrounded an intruder, who was struggling to break free. Davydd shoved the shutter aside. "Let him go," he said sharply. He did not wait to be sure his command would be obeyed, took that for granted. Turning back to Ednyved, he said, "It is Llelo."

They could now hear footsteps thudding on the outer stairs. A moment later, Llelo burst into the chamber. He was muddied and disheveled, so out of breath that he had to lean against the door. "Is it true?" he demanded. "Did you take my father prisoner?"

"Yes."

Llelo moved forward into the room. "You swore a holy oath to his safety, swore upon the surety of your soul! How could you break such an oath? Do you truly think he would approve of such a betrayal?"

There was no need for Davydd to ask who *he* was. "I do not know, Llelo," he admitted. "I can only hope he would have understood."

Llelo's eyes narrowed. "Well, I do not understand," he said bitterly. "I will never understand—or forgive!"

Ednyved got stiffly to his feet. "Davydd knew he would be excommunicated, Llelo. But he was willing to risk eternal damnation to put an end to this dangerous war."

Llelo looked at him, then away. "My name is Llewelyn, not Llelo." His eyes flicked back to his uncle's face. "I want to see my father," he said. "So does my lady mother."

Davydd's gaze did not waver. "No, lad, I cannot allow that. Not yet."

Llelo's breath quickened. "You lured my father and brother into a trap. What of me? Do you mean to imprison me, too?"

Davydd shook his head. "No. You are free to go."

Llelo was at a loss, even let-down. He'd been expecting hostility, not honesty, found it disconcerting and somewhat bewildering to have Davydd treat him not as an enemy, but as an adult. Defiant, confused, desperately unhappy, he began to back toward the door, keeping his eyes upon Davydd all the while. "You've not won," he said, horrified to find his voice was no longer under his control. "You'll be sorry for this, I swear it!"

Not surprisingly, Llelo slammed the door behind him. The two men looked at each other in silence. Ednyved finally moved to the table. Picking up a wine flagon, he said, "In just a year and a half, Llelo will be fourteen. When Llewelyn was fourteen, he celebrated his new-found manhood by beginning a civil war. You do know that you are taking a risk with that lad?"

"Yes, I know. But some risks are worth the taking."

Ednyved paused in the act of pouring wine. Until that moment, he'd not known that Davydd, too, looked upon Llelo as a potential heir.

"Have you never thought of divorcing your wife?" he asked, quietly enough not to offer offense. "Another woman might be able to give you a son."

Davydd shrugged. "Another man might be able to give Isabella a son."

Ednyved's brows rose. Even though all knew of women whose first marriages were barren, second marriages blessed with babes, conventional wisdom still faulted the wife, not the husband, for failure to produce an heir. "Why are you so sure that the problem lies with you and not Isabella?"

Davydd took one of the wine cups. "I lay with my first woman when I was nigh on sixteen. In less than two months, I will be thirty-two. And in all those years, Ednyved, no woman of mine has ever gotten with child. When we breed horses, if a stallion fails to get his mares in foal, we find another stallion. But when a marriage is barren, we find another wife."

Another silence fell. Ednyved's eyes had softened. Reaching over, he clinked his wine cup against Davydd's in a rueful, mock salute. "You do not ever believe in taking the easy way, do you, lad?"

Davydd gave him a taut smile. "You've noticed that, have you?" He drank deeply, staring into his cup as if it held answers, not wine. "It was not enough to cage Gruffydd. As long as he lives, he will be a threat, a rallying point for rebels and malcontents. I should put him to death, Ednyved. I know that. And yet knowing is somehow not enough. For Christ help me, but I cannot do it."

10

Shrewsbury, England

August 1241

By the time they rode through the gatehouse and into the abbey precincts, Senena was taut with apprehension. For so many months she had labored ceaselessly with but one objective in mind—to gain her husband's freedom—and now that it seemed within reach, she was suddenly terrified that something might go wrong at the last moment, that the English King might refuse her plea.

Ralph and Gwladys de Mortimer were waiting for her by the entrance to the guest house, but Senena was too preoccupied for courtesy. She ignored Gwladys, and as Ralph came forward to help her dismount, she said abruptly, "Has the English King arrived yet?"

"No, he is not expected till noon. But Walter Clifford, Roger de Montalt, and the Princes of Powys are within, waiting for you."

Senena beckoned to the nearest of her servants. "See to the unpacking." But before she could enter the hall, Llelo slid from his saddle, ran toward her.

"May I come with you, Mama?"

"No," she said, turning away.

Senena's youngest brother, Einion, winced, for Llelo was thirteen, old enough, in Einion's opinion, to be permitted some small part in his father's rescue. But Einion was only twenty himself, and had too cheerful, too placid a nature to relish crossing wills with his sharp-tongued elder sister. He gave his nephew an apologetic pat upon his shoulder, followed Senena and Ralph de Mortimer into the hall.

Einion was not the only one to sympathize with Llelo. Gwladys was finding it harder and harder to overlook Senena's indifference to her second son. She had never been shy to speak her mind, but she was too well-mannered to make a public scene. Recriminations could wait; Llelo's need could not.

Llelo had watched until his mother entered the hall, then turned back to check upon his little brothers. Both children had long since fallen asleep, did not stir even as servants lifted them from the horse litter. It puzzled Llelo that his mother should have wanted them here for her meeting with the English King, but he was too grateful to question the whys and wherefores of his deliverance, so great had been his fear that he'd be left behind in Llŷn.

Gwladys had come to stand beside him. "Whilst Ralph meets with your lady mother, shall we take a walk into the town?" she suggested, and was rewarded with a radiant smile. Their ride through Shrewsbury had been too rapid for Llelo to see very much, and he was eager to explore the town at closer range. He'd had no experience with towns; there were none in North Wales.

Llelo was fascinated by the bridge that spanned the River Severn, a massive structure of red grit stone, complete with heavy drawbridge and portcullis; most Welsh rivers had to be forded. "The English must be very rich," he marveled, as they turned into the street Gwladys called Sub Wila.

Everywhere Llelo looked, he saw sights to astonish. The streets were very narrow, shadowed by the over-hanging stories of timber-framed houses, and they were packed with people, more people than he'd ever seen in all his life. Gwladys told him that Shrewsbury held nigh on two thousand inhabitants, a figure that seemed impossibly vast to Llelo. When his aunt laughed and said London had a population more than ten times the size of Shrewsbury, Llelo could only shake his head in disbelief.

If London was truly so immense, he did not care to see it. As little as he liked to admit it, he was not comfortable amidst so many people. They crowded about him, jabbing him with their elbows, smelling of sweat and sour ale, assailing his ears with their loud, incomprehensible babble. It disconcerted him to discover that the citizens of Shrewsbury spoke a tongue entirely alien to him, for he'd studied Norman-French for fully five years.

"Many speak French, too," Gwladys explained. "For certes, the provosts and merchants do. But English has remained the language of the common people. Passing strange; it ought to have died out by now. It is nigh on two hundred years, after all, since William the Bastard defeated the Saxon thanes. French is undoubtedly a far more cultured tongue, but it is useful, too, to know some English, for the peasants cling to it so. My husband speaks it; so do most of the Marcher lords. None of their kings have, of course, but Henry plans to have his son tutored in English. He . . ."

Llelo was no longer listening. The crowds were parting, men squeezing up against the stalls that lined both sides of the street. When Llelo saw why they were retreating, he, too, shrank back. Two black-garbed figures had come into view, shaking latten clappers to warn of their approach; never had Llelo heard a sound so doleful.

Gwladys made the sign of the cross. "Lepers," she said and shuddered. "Poor souls. At least they fare better in Shrewsbury than in many places. They have a lazar house beyond the abbey grounds, and King John granted them a portion of all flour sold in St Alkmund's market."

"Poor souls," Llelo echoed softly, thankful that their cowled hoods shadowed their faces, hid their ravaged flesh.

Gwladys was fumbling in a small leather pouch that swung from her belt. Withdrawing a few coins, she walked toward the two lepers. Llelo felt a surge of pride as his aunt calmly wished them Good Morrow, dropped the coins into their alms cup.

Unfortunately, she then found herself besieged by beggars. She scattered a handful of pennies into their outstretched palms, then moved on. Her servants kept the beggars at a respectful distance, but they continued to trail after her, pleading their poverty in loud, importunate voices. Llelo was shocked at their numbers, for beggars were rare in

Wales, where every man's hearth was open to those passing by and the kinship of the clan was a sacred trust.

To Llelo, the most unnerving aspect of Shrewsbury was its noise. Church bells pealed out the hour, summoning Christ's faithful to High Mass, tolling mournful "passing bells" for dying parishioners. Men wandered the streets shouting "Hot meat pies" and "Good ale," seeking to entice customers into cook-shops and ale-houses. Itinerant peddlers hawked their goods, offering nails, ribbons, potions to restore health, to bestir lust. People gathered in front of the cramped, unshuttered shops, arguing prices at the tops of their voices. Heavy carts creaked down the street, their lumbering progress signaled by loudly cracking whips. Dogs darted underfoot, and pigs rooted about in the debris dumped in the center gutter. Apprentices, pilgrims, cripples dragging about on crutches and wooden legs, would-be thieves, Shropshire villagers come to watch the King's procession to the castle, people come to trade at St Alkmund's weekly market, an occasional Black Friar—it was all rather intimidating to a youngster country born and bred.

Gwladys seemed to sense Llelo's unease, for she began to talk, telling him that his grandfather had captured Shrewsbury in 1215, that the red and gold lions of Gwynedd had flown from the battlements of Shrewsbury's royal castle. "He rode right up this very lane—known to some as Gomsall Street, to others as Haystrete. The provosts were awaiting him at the stone cross, offered to surrender if he'd warrant the townspeople's safety, which he did, Llelo." She caught herself, too late, smiled ruefully. "I did forget again—Llewelyn."

Llelo shrugged, unoffended by her lapse. At least she tried, which was more than the rest of his family did. The knowledge that Shrewsbury had been conquered by his grandfather was a sudden source of comfort, and he looked about with renewed confidence. To his left lay an open stretch of ground, a dark, foul-smelling pond. A crowd had gathered at the water's edge, and Llelo gasped at what he saw now—a man trussed up with rope, bound to a wooden plank, about to be lowered into the pond.

"Jesú! Aunt Gwladys, look! They mean to drown that man!"

Gwladys merely laughed. "No, just a good dousing. When a brewer is caught watering down his ale, or a baker weighing his loaves too lightly, the culprit is dragged to the ducking pond for a quick, albeit wet, chastisement."

Now that he knew the man was in no danger, Llelo watched with considerable interest as he was pulled, sputtering and choking, from the murky pond. A sudden stench warned that they were nearing the Shambles, the butchers' row, but as they passed a narrow alley, Llelo's attention was caught by a woman lounging in an open doorway. What first drew his eye was her spill of wind-blown, bright hair; only young girls went bare-headed in public, yet this woman wore neither veil nor wimple. Nor had Llelo ever seen hair the color of hers, a harsh, metallic gold, a shade never intended by nature. She was drinking from a wine-skin, beckoned to a discomfited passer-by, and made a lewd gesture when the man continued on his way.

Llelo's eyes widened. He forgot his manners, stared openly, never having seen a harlot before. He kept craning his neck, glancing over his shoulder, so intent upon keeping the whore in view that he walked right into a pig, almost fell over the animal's back. Gwladys laughed, and he flushed, then grinned self-consciously, wondering if she'd noticed the whore, too.

"And that is known as Grope Lane," Gwladys said dryly, "for obvious reasons. There are other streets that have bawdy houses, too, but Grope Lane has more than its share."

Llelo knew, of course, that there were Welsh whores, too, "women of the bush and brake." But he'd not known that there were houses for whores, that English harlots lived together just as nuns did. The comparison was so unexpected, so ludicrous, that his embarrassment yielded to amusement, and he began to laugh.

Gwladys stopped a peddler, bought Llelo an apple. "You missed your aunt Elen by one day, I fear. She and Rob de Quincy came to Shrewsbury to talk to my husband; Elen hoped to persuade him not to take part in the coming campaign, not to pledge his support to Gruffydd. But she had no more success with Ralph than she had with King Henry. When she could not sway Ralph, she and Rob departed for the White Ladies Priory, to the north of here, where they will wait for word on the war's outcome."

Llelo was keenly disappointed, for he'd not seen Elen since his grandfather's funeral. He hastily looked away, but not in time; Gwladys saw.

"She did not know Senena was bringing you, Llewelyn, else she'd have waited. Elen is right fond of you."

He very much wanted to believe that, but he was learning to live with doubts. He said nothing, ate the last of the apple, and threw the core to the scavenging pig. They turned into the Shambles, walked for a time in silence.

"There." Gwladys pointed. "That is the cross where the provosts waited for your grandfather, where we will await Henry's arrival. The provosts and the town's common council are already gathering."

Llelo barely glanced their way. His enthusiasm for Shrewsbury and its marvels was fast waning. So swiftly had his mood soured that he felt only guilt; how could he take such pleasure in trifles when so much was at stake? "Nothing is more important than freeing my father from Cricieth Castle—nothing!"

Gwladys nodded, waited, and at last he said, very low, "But . . . but was there not another way to do it? My grandfather fought all his life to keep the English out of Wales. And now an English army is about to invade Gwynedd—at my mother's invitation."

Gwladys did not know what to tell him. Her father would have been appalled by what Senena meant to do. She was not even sure that Gruffydd would approve. And she knew why the Marcher lords were allying themselves with Senena. Roger de Montalt, Walter Clifford, her own husband—they all stood to gain by Davydd's defeat. A weakened, divided Gwynedd was what the other Welsh Princes sought, too. They had not shared the dream of Llewelyn Fawr, his belief that for Wales to retain its independence, it must be united. The Princes had long chafed at Gwynedd's dominance, hoped now to restore the balance of power among the Welsh principalities.

"I'll not lie to you, lad," she said slowly. "Yes, your mother is taking a great risk. But to whom could she go if not to the English King? And in truth, I find it hard to fault her for it, for I, too, want Gruffydd freed."

Llelo nodded. He understood quite clearly that this might be his father's only chance for freedom. But he could not stifle an uneasy suspicion that Gruffydd's good and Gwynedd's good might not be one and the same. "It is just that I know what Grandpapa would have said, that we are inviting a wolf in to protect our herd from foxes."

Gwladys did not dispute him. "Desperate needs require desperate remedies," she said and sighed. "And loyalties . . . what a tangled coil they make. I am a Welshwoman wed to a Norman-French lord, have borne him five children. Am I Llewelyn Fawr's daughter—or Ralph de Mortimer's wife? Sister to Gruffydd—or to Davydd? I would to God I knew . . ."

There was a sudden stir in the crowd gathered about the cross. One of the provosts, recognizing Ralph de Mortimer's lady, sauntered over to explain the raised voices, the rumblings of discontent. "Some of them claim they heard a trumpet fanfare, whilst others insist they are but deluding themselves. Tempers are growing short; it has been a long wait, under a hot sun. That loud-mouthed blacksmith wants someone to climb the cross, keep watch for the King, but he can find no one nimble enough—or sober enough—to attempt it."

"I will," Llelo said promptly, and the provost grinned.

"Good lad," he said, and before Gwladys could object, Llelo was being ushered toward the cross, where he was at once surrounded by approving Englishmen. He could not understand their speech, but their smiles needed no translation. Within moments, he was boosted onto the blacksmith's shoulders, scrambled up onto the cross.

The sun was shining directly into his eyes, and Llelo clung with one hand, raised the other to shield the glare. The houses blocked most of his view of Shrewsbury's streets, but he could see beyond to the river, see the long, serpentine line that wound its way up the Abbey Foregate. Chain-mail armor was not meant for long rides, and the chivalric code had been amended accordingly, adding the caveat that it was not honorable to attack a knight unless he was fully armed, thus freeing men of the need to spend stifling hours in the saddle. But Henry had wanted his entry into Shrewsbury to be a memorable one, and his knights were clad in sun-blinding mail, brilliantly colored surcoats. Heralded by high-flying, bright silk banners, by trumpets and pipes, the English army stretched as far as Llelo's eye could see. It took his breath, raised a sweat that had nothing to do with the heat of the summer sun.

He abandoned his perch so hastily that he almost fell, would have if not for the blacksmith's quick reflexes. Sliding to the ground, he said, "They come," and when the provost translated from French to English, the spectators raised a cheer.

Whatever argument there might be about Henry's abilities, all conceded that he was in appearance an ideal king. He wore a rich red gown, a jewel-encrusted hat, seemed impervious to heat and dust. Elegant and urbane, he showed no impatience with their slow progress through the crowded streets. Henry thrived upon pageantry and panoply, enjoyed the ceremonial aspects of kingship far more than he did the actual exercise of power.

As Henry approached the cross, he saw the provosts, ready to welcome him into Shrewsbury. But then he abruptly drew rein. "Lady de Mortimer," he said, and the people looked at Gwladys with sudden interest, that she should be signaled out for the King's notice.

"Your Grace, may I present my nephew, Llewelyn ap Gruffydd?"

Prompted by Gwladys, Llelo came forward, knelt in the dusty street. "Ah, the Lady Senena's son," Henry said and smiled. Llelo could find nothing to say. He stared mutely at the English King, unable to think, to see anything but that endless column snaking its way across the Shropshire countryside: knights, men-at-arms, supply carts, siege weapons. My God, Mama, he thought. My God, what have you done?

HENRY was particular about his accommodations, and those at the castle were not to his liking. He chose, instead, to stay at the Benedictine abbey of St Peter and St Paul, in the Abbot's private domicile. His household had to be lodged, too, and the abbey was soon filled to capacity. So, too, were the castles and inns, as Shrewsbury sought to absorb the King's army.

Henry met several times in the days that followed with Senena, the Marcher lords, and the Princes of Powys and Deheubarth. But Senena refused to satisfy Llelo's curiosity. Once it was settled, she said, she would explain everything to him, and Llelo had to be content with that grudging promise.

He saw no reason, though, why he should not seek to ferret out facts for himself, and he soon discovered that his youth and nationality offered unsurpassed opportunities for spying. He could mingle with Henry's lords, eavesdropping with impunity, for on the rare occasions when he was challenged, he need only look blank, mumble in Welsh, and he was once more invisible.

He was frustrated, though, by what he heard, for the English lords showed little interest in discussing the captive Welsh Prince or his hostile half-brother. Instead, they passed the hot August days gossiping about Simon de Montfort and the Lady Eleanor of Brittany, cousin to the King.

Llelo knew Simon de Montfort had gone on crusade to the Holy Land. Now he learned that a great honor had been conferred upon him there. He had so distinguished himself that the barons, knights, and citizens of the kingdom of Jerusalem had petitioned the Holy Roman Emperor to have Simon act as Governor of their realm. Llelo's memories of the Lady Nell had become rather blurred and misty with time, but he still remembered her low laugh, the way she'd turn all heads upon entering a room, and he felt mildly pleased that her husband had won such acclaim.

The news about the Lady Eleanor was altogether different, spoke not of earthly honors, but of man's mortality, for she had recently died at Bristol Castle, where she'd been confined for decades. Llelo did not understand why a highborn woman, first cousin to the King, should have been a captive, and he'd gone to Gwladys for enlightenment. From her, he learned that the Lady Eleanor and her brother, Arthur, had been John's only rivals for the English Crown. When they'd fallen into John's hands, Arthur had vanished into one of John's castles, never to be seen again, and Eleanor had been sent to England. For thirty-nine years, she had been kept in comfortable confinement, at various royal castles, first by John and then by Henry, until finally freed by death. Llelo was horrified by her sad story, for he could not help envisioning the same fate for his father.

As he wandered about the abbey grounds, alert for any mention of Gruffydd, Llelo learned that Henry's lords did not hold their King in high esteem. They thought him erratic of purpose, too easily swayed, too indulgent a husband. Llelo soon determined that Henry's foreign Queen had found little favor with his subjects, that they blamed her, however unfairly, for many of Henry's shortcomings. Generosity was expected of every great lord, but Henry's English barons faulted him for that very virtue, resented how lavishly he'd bestowed largesse upon Eleanor's kindred. He'd managed to have one of her uncles chosen as Archbishop of Canterbury, had conferred the earldom of Richmond upon another uncle. As there were six more uncles to be provided for, it was questionable which would be exhausted first, the patience of Henry's barons or the royal treasury.

But there was no talk of the forthcoming war. The English treated the Welsh campaign with insulting indifference. They acted as if Davydd's defeat were a foregone conclusion, as if Henry had only to cross into Wales to bring Davydd to heel. And Llelo made a disconcerting discovery, that he did not want to see a Welsh Prince humbled before an English King—even Davydd, his uncle, his enemy.

At supper in the Abbot's hall on the third night after Henry's arrival, the King announced that he had reached an accord with the Lady Senena, and amidst laughter and cheering, men raised their wine cups high, drank to Gruffydd's freedom, to Davydd's defeat.

Llelo had hoped his mother would now honor her promise, but no sooner was supper over than she disappeared into her chamber with her brother and Ralph de Mortimer. Llelo restlessly roamed the monastery grounds, seeking to keep boredom at bay. He paid a visit to the stables, then wandered down to the abbey water mill, but the monks were gone, the sluice gate in place. He ended up in the gardens by the abbey pool, lying on his stomach by the water's edge, listening to the twilight sounds of summer: frogs, crickets, the sharp chack of jackdaw, the cooing of woodpigeons. An occasional splash made him wish he had a fishing pole, but the monks would hardly be happy were he to poach their carp. After a time, he fell asleep in the grass.

He was awakened by voices close at hand. He started to sit up, recognized one of the voices just in time. Cautiously he wriggled toward a blackthorn hedge, found a viewing hole amidst the spiny branches. They were standing in a circle of moonlight: the English King; his Chancellor, John Mansel; Queen Eleanor's unpopular uncle, the new Earl of Richmond; a fourth man Llelo could not identify.

From their conversation, it appeared the stranger had just arrived at the abbey. Henry called him Richard, called him brother, and that caused Llelo some confusion, for he knew the King's brother Richard was in the Holy Land, like Simon de Montfort. As they talked, however, the boy was able to sort it out, to realize that this man was Richard Fitz

Roy, one of King John's numerous illegitimate sons. Richard Fitz Roy had occasionally been to the Welsh court, for he'd been close to the Lady Joanna, his sister. Llelo remembered now that he held a barony in Kent; King John had always done well by his bastards. But it appeared to be another futile eavesdropping endeavor, for Henry and Richard Fitz Roy were not discussing the campaign, were talking, instead, of their brother-by-marriage, Simon de Montfort.

Henry was telling Richard that Simon would not be accepting the governorship of Jerusalem, would be returning to England, at which point John Mansel muttered, "More's the pity."

The other men laughed, but Henry said mildly, "You must admit, John, that it was an uncommon honor they paid Simon. For certes, he does make an impression upon men, is not one to pass unnoticed."

"He sees to that," Mansel said caustically. "There is no one who values Simon's abilities more than Simon."

"Well, he has reason for pride," Henry said, and Llelo, listening, thought he'd never heard a man defended with so little conviction. It grew quiet then. Llelo scratched himself trying to peer through the blackthorn tangle, at last risked a quick glance around the hedge. John Mansel and the Earl of Richmond had withdrawn; Henry and Richard were standing several feet away.

"Well?" Richard asked. "Did you agree to aid Senena?"

"Yes," Henry said. "She is a remarkable woman, that one."

"She is a bitch," Richard said flatly. "She gave our Joanna naught but grief; I've not forgotten. So . . . tell me. What did she promise? Or more to the point, what did you promise?"

Henry chuckled. "She is to pay me six hundred marks. I have promised to free Gruffydd and their son Owain. She agrees that England shall determine what share, if any, Gruffydd should have received of his father's inheritance. She agrees, on Gruffydd's behalf, to pay the Crown three hundred marks a year if he is restored to his half of Gwynedd. And as her pledges, she offers no less than three Marcher lords and five Welsh Princes."

"She could offer the Lord Christ Himself as a pledge and I'd still not believe her. I know Gruffydd, know how he hates the English. Senena could swear in her own blood and it would avail her naught, Henry. You cannot believe he'll hold to this agreement once he is free?"

"Senena realized I would have my suspicions. She sought to allay them by agreeing to yield up her younger sons as hostages."

Richard drew an audible breath. "She actually agreed to that? You astonish me, in truth. It is not that many years, after all, since those Welsh hostages were hanged at Nottingham."

"A deed ill done," Henry said indignantly, "and one that shamed our father, both as King and as Christian. But are you suggesting I would ever do the same? I would never harm a child, never!"

"Of course you would not. I know that, Henry, for I know you well. But Senena does not. How could she be sure?"

Henry's anger faded as quickly as it had flared. "I suppose," he said, "that it is a measure, then, of her desperation, that she did agree. Gruffydd is lucky, indeed, to have so devoted a wife."

"Henry . . . ere we go in, there is something I would say to you. I understand why you have agreed to intervene on Gruffydd's behalf. Once Davydd had Gruffydd securely caged, he balked at honoring the arbitration agreement. Morever, this is a rare chance to regain all we lost to Llewelyn Fawr. A great man, few would deny it. Fortunately for England he was also mortal; a far easier task it is to confront the lion-whelp than the lion. But I do have qualms about this deal you have struck with Senena. I may sound an utter innocent for saying so, but I cannot help remembering that Davydd is Joanna's son."

Henry smiled. "There is no shame, Richard, in that. Indeed, I value you all the more for such feelings. You may rest assured that I share your sentiments. Davydd needs to be taught a sharp lesson. But I would not see our sister's son brought to ruin if it could be avoided, and I think it can."

They were moving away, their voices growing fainter. Still, Llelo did not move. He'd dropped down upon the ground, lay for a time with his face pressed into the grass. As the men withdrew, a starling whistled shrilly; its mate answered. Soon the garden air was alive again with the sounds of the night. Llelo was deaf to it all, seemed to hear only the wild, erratic beating of his own heart.

The stables, laundry, brew-house, bake-house, and kitchen were ranged together just to the north of the abbey pool and gardens. When Llelo rose, he moved instinctively in that direction. The few people he encountered never even glanced his way; he found it very easy to sneak into the huge, stone chamber where the abbey cooking was done. It was deserted; the monks had long since retired, for they would rise for Matins at 2:00 A.M. Llelo tripped over a large mortar and pestle, bumped bruisingly into an enormous empty cauldron. He froze in fear, but none heard the noise. Finding a hemp sack upon the chopping block, he began methodically to fill it with food: large cheeses, apples and pears, even a jar of plum jelly. He then moved on to the abbey bake-house, where he took loaf after loaf of freshly baked bread, manchet for Henry and his lords, maslin for the monks. In a last gesture of sudden defiance, he appropriated an entire plateful of angel's-bread, wafers baked expressly for the English King.

Until now, he'd acted without conscious deliberation, as if watching from a distance as his other self stuffed the sack with pilfered food. But as he gazed across the garth, saw the lights burning in the abbey guest house, his shield cracked, and he began to tremble. He knew, as did all the Welsh, of the hangings at Nottingham Castle. Twenty-eight hostages had died that day, dangling from a makeshift gallows in the middle bailey, died at King John's command. Only Llewelyn's sixteen-year-old son had been spared, only Gruffydd.

Llelo knew, too, of the other hanging. Another Welsh hostage, the seven-year-old son of Prince Maelgwn ap Rhys. He'd died that same August, before Shrewsbury's stone cross, died because the English King had willed it so.

The guest house was filled to capacity, and men were milling about in the great hall, upon the stairs. But none paid heed to youngsters; Llelo passed unnoticed up to the chamber alloted to his mother. The door to her room was still shut, a murmur of voices coming from within. He wasted precious moments staring at that closed door, then moved into the chamber he and his brothers shared with Einion. Neither Einion nor the children's nurses were within; the room was dark, quiet. Llelo knelt in the moonlight by Davydd's pallet, looked down at the sleeping child.

"Llelo?" Davydd yawned, gave his brother a sleepy smile. "You woke me up," he said, but without reproach. His eyes alighted upon the sack. "What is that? Are you going away?"

Llelo nodded, and Davydd yawned again. "Where? Can I go, too?"

For a mad moment, Llelo actually considered it. But Davydd was only three and Rhodri not yet two. His throat too tight for speech, he shook his head. As young as he was, Davydd was remarkably strong-willed, given to tantrums when his wishes were thwarted. Now, however, he was too sleepy to protest. "When will you be back? Tomorrow?"

Llelo did not answer. Fumbling with Elen's crucifix, he jerked it from his neck, pulled it over his brother's head. "I'm sorry," he whispered, "so sorry . . ."

"Why?" But Davydd was admiring his new possession, not really listening. Llelo reached into the sack, drew out two sugared wafers.

"Here," he said huskily. "Keep these for when you awake; one is for Rhodri." He dared not remain longer. At the door, he looked back, in time to see Davydd secrete a wafer under his pillow, begin to munch contentedly upon the other one.

The abbey gatehouse was closed, but Llelo had noticed a small postern gate in the east wall. Only after he unbarred the door, slipped through into the dark did he give in to his fear, begin to run. He lost all sense of direction or time, ran until he had no more breath, until the abbey was no longer in view and the only light came from stars, until he was alone in the silent, shadowed woods.

11

Gwern Eigron, North Wales

August 1241

Fᴏᴍ Shrewsbury, Henry and his Welsh allies rode north. After passing six days at Chester, the English army moved into Wales. No Welsh prince could hope to match the might of the English Crown. They depended, instead, upon the awesome wildness of their homeland, turning their mountains into fortresses, deep woods into barricades, rivers into moats. Davydd prepared to do battle as his people had always done. He razed Deganwy Castle to keep it from falling into enemy hands, made ready to withdraw into the impenetrable fastness of Eryri.

But in his time of need, he found himself forsaken not only by his Welsh allies, but by God. For the past four months, Wales had suffered under a severe drought. Crops shriveled in the fields; rivers that once surged were now sluggish under a relentless sun. Lakes grew muddy; fish floated belly-up in the shallows. Day followed day, and the sky remained bleached of color, barren of clouds. The great marsh of Rhuddlan was no longer the vast, tidal wetlands that had always proved such an obstacle to invasion. The English army crossed the quagmire with such astonishing ease that Davydd was caught by surprise, his retreat blocked by the fast-moving Welshmen of Gruffydd Maelor. Cut off from the sheltering heights of Eryri, abandoned by his Welsh allies and many of his own people, outnumbered and alone, facing a foe who had even the weather on his side, Davydd yielded to the inevitable, sent Henry word that he would come to the latter's encampment at Gwern Eigron, there surrender to the English King.

ᴛʜᴜʀsᴅᴀʏ, August 29, dawned hot and very humid; the air was utterly still, the sky such a metallic blue-white that it hurt to look up at it. They moved slowly east along the coastal road, turned south at the mouth of the River Clwyd. If Davydd even glanced toward the English banner that flew over Rhuddlan Castle, none of his men saw it. Within two miles, they reached the junction of the River Elwy. Ahead lay the English camp, where Henry awaited them.

Ednyved raised his arm, blotted sweat with his sleeve. From the corner of his eye, he could see his son Goronwy. His other son, Hywel, rode almost at his stirrup. No Christian was to befriend or break bread with an excommunicate, yet Hywel, Bishop of St Asaph, had not wavered in his loyalty to Davydd, and for that, Ednyved was very proud of his son. As their eyes met, they exchanged grim nods, each man dreading what was to come. For Ednyved, there was an eerie sense of familiarity about this day, so similar did it seem to another riverside surrender, another Welsh Prince, another English King. He spurred his stallion forward, caught up with Davydd.

"I have something to say to you," he said, and guided his mount away from the path, into a shadowy grove of alder trees. Davydd followed, drew rein, and waited.

"It was in August, too, when your father had to yield to John at Aberconwy," Ednyved said abruptly. "As hot as Hades it was, as hot as today. Thirty years ago, but still like yesterday to me, so well do I remember. John had agreed to spare Llewelyn's life. That much he would do for his daughter, but no more. He made Llewelyn's surrender as public as possible, as humbling, as painful as he could. And his terms were harder to swallow than wormwood and gall. He claimed twenty thousand cattle in tribute, demanded thirty hostages and damned near half of Gwynedd. That had to be one of the worst moments of Llewelyn's life. But he survived it, Davydd, he learned from it, and within two years, he'd won back all he'd been forced to yield."

Davydd's face was expressionless. "I know that," he said. "What point do you seek to make?"

Ednyved frowned, slowly shook his head. "No point, lad." There was nothing more he could say. Davydd had his father's courage. He had Llewelyn's dream, his vision, possibly even his ability. But Llewelyn had one great advantage over Davydd. He'd known how to forgive himself.

Henry's camp by the River Elwy was crowded with both Welsh and English. It was an additional bitterness for Davydd that so many of his own countrymen had fought against him. Almost at once he saw the Princes of Powys, Gruffydd ap Gwenwynwyn and Gruffydd Maelor. They had done as much as any man there to bring him to this moment, and the irony was that they had been his father's enemies, not his. Gruffydd ap Gwenwynwyn had grown up in English exile, forced to flee when his father lost Lower Powys to Llewelyn a quarter century past. And Gruffydd Maelor had nursed a grudge against Llewelyn ever since one of his brothers had murdered the other. Llewelyn had promptly punished the fratricide, and Gruffydd Maelor had neither forgotten nor forgiven the Prince of Gwynedd's intervention into the affairs of Upper Powys. But neither Prince had dared to challenge Llewelyn. They sought, instead, to gain from the son what they could never have gotten from the sire. And they had, Davydd thought. They had.

But if the Princes of Powys were enemies he'd inherited, ahead were those he'd earned, clustered around the King of England's oaken chair. Senena's two brothers, Einion and Gruffydd ap Caradog. The Bishop of Bangor. Senena. Her brothers were openly gloating; the Bishop, too, was showing a most unchristian satisfaction. But there was no overt triumph upon Senena's face, only hate. It was a potent force, Senena's hatred; Davydd could almost feel it, no less scorching than the sun, no less implacable.

Surrounded by such intense, virulent hostility, Henry seemed almost benign by contrast. He was grave, as befitting so solemn an occasion, but his eyes were shining. It wasn't often that one of his political ploys met with such unqualified success.

Dismounting, Davydd handed the reins to one of his men. He kept his eyes upon his uncle, ignored the others as best he could. Unsheathing his sword, he handed it to Henry, then knelt, saying in a low voice, "I submit myself to the King's will."

Henry accepted the sword, passed it to John Mansel. His happiness had honed his powers of observation. He saw the flicker of Davydd's eyelids, the sweat beading his temples, the secret signs that belied his nephew's outward calm, and he felt a nostalgic tenderness for his dead sister, a surge of pity for her son. Rising, he said, "I think we will be more comfortable in my tent."

That was a mercy Davydd had not expected; he'd braced himself for the worst, for the most public of humiliations. He rose, followed Henry into the tent; so did Ednyved and John Mansel. But when Senena, the Bishop, and the Princes of Powys would have entered, too, Henry held up his hand. "I regret there is room only for the four of us." An English king suffered few hardships, even while campaigning; Henry's tent was spacious enough to accommodate a bed, table, coffers, and fully a score of witnesses. Before the tent flap dropped, Davydd had a quick glimpse of outraged faces. But for all that he had spoken pleasantly, Henry had given a command, and they had no choice but to obey it.

The coolness within the tent was a welcome relief. Henry gestured and they seated themselves at a trestle table of polished oak. John Mansel began to fill their cups. When Davydd tasted his, he discovered that Henry had even thought to provide mead, a drink unfashionable in England but still popular among the Welsh. Henry was watching him, a faint smile playing about his mouth; he looked so expectant that Davydd said, "Thank you." That was the best he could do, but it seemed to satisfy Henry.

"I saw no reason," he said, "to turn your surrender into a spectacle. Now . . . shall we speak freely? You are in no position to balk at any of my demands, Davydd. You do understand that?"

He waited, got an all but imperceptible nod of the head in reluctant response. "Very well, then. Let me tell you what I want from you. You must surrender Mold Castle to Roger de Montalt. Lower Powys is to be returned to Gruffydd ap Gwenwynwyn. The cantref of Meirionydd is to go to the sons of Maredudd ap Cynan. For the Crown, I am claiming the commote of Tegeingl . . . and Buellt Castle." He paused, anticipating objections, for Buellt Castle was Isabella's marriage portion. He did not feel comfortable about penalizing Isabella, but Buellt was one of the most strategic castles in South Wales, too strategic to leave in the hands of a Welsh Prince. He was rather relieved, therefore, when Davydd said nothing.

"Nor is that all, Davydd. You must also assume the costs of my campaign. And lastly, you must surrender to me the castle and manor of Ellesmere in Shropshire."

"Ellesmere was my mother's marriage portion," Davydd said, and Henry no longer met his eyes. John Mansel made haste to interrupt, for he had long ago learned how unpredictable Henry could be. If given time to reflect, he might well decide that since he would not have taken from Joanna whilst she lived, he could not in conscience do so now.

"You must also yield up ten or more highborn hostages, my lord," he said, and Davydd's hazel eyes focused upon him with an unblinking, almost feline intensity. But at that, Henry leaned forward.

"You need not fear for them, Davydd," he said, quite earnestly. "They shall be well treated; you do have my word on that."

A silence fell. To Mansel, Henry's assurances were absurd, for it was the threat that made the taking of hostages so effective a stratagem. But he knew better than to remonstrate with Henry. Henry never forgot who was King, never forgave a slight to his royal dignity. The man who wanted to manipulate Henry had to do so by indirection, had to plant his seeds and then wait patiently for them to take root, for Henry to conclude those first green shoots were the fruit of his own imagination.

Davydd's head was throbbing. There was an air of amiable unreality to this entire conversation that Henry should be savaging Gwynedd with a smile. He did not know the rules to this game. Should he be grateful that Henry meant to shackle him by the wrists and not the neck? "What of Gruffydd?" he said. "What happens to him?"

"He must be turned over to the English Crown. So must Owain, and the other men you are keeping at Cricieth Castle."

Davydd had not realized he was holding his breath. "And then?"

A parchment scroll lay on the table. Henry reached for it, slid it over to Davydd. Ednyved moved closer so he could read, too. It was written, of course, in Latin, and the Welsh names had been hopelessly mutilated in the translation process; at the bottom of the page were attached the seals of Gruffydd, Senena, and the English King. Davydd scanned it rapidly. "Agreement made at Shrewsbury, on the Monday before the Assumption . . . whereby the said Senana undertakes on behalf of Gruffino, her husband . . . that the King may deliver the said Gruffino and Oweyn, his son, from prison . . . that the King shall cause him to have justice, according to Welsh law . . . Senana shall give to the King Dauid and Rather, her sons, as hostages . . ." Davydd looked up at that. "Why not Llelo?"

"It was intended that he, too, should be a hostage. But the lad disappeared from Shrewsbury, and Senena had no luck in finding him."

Davydd slid the charter roll back across the table. "So Gruffydd is to have his freedom," he said, "and half of Gwynedd, too." And try as he might, he could not keep the bitterness from his voice.

"Well," Henry said, "that is Senena's understanding."

Davydd and Ednyved exchanged glances. "And your understanding, Uncle?"

"Such a decision cannot be made in haste. I shall need time to ponder all the implications, the consequences, ere I can make up my mind. And whilst we deliberate, we think it best that Gruffydd remain in confinement. I have made arrangements, therefore, for Sir John Lexington to escort Gruffydd and Owain to London, to the Tower."

If Henry had expected Davydd's reaction to be one of relief or reprieve, he was disappointed. The younger man set his wine cup down. He had, Henry decided, an unnervingly direct gaze, one that seemed to see too much. "So Gruffydd and I both lose," he said, quite tonelessly.

GRUFFYDD ap Llewelyn was forty-five years old, and had passed eleven of those years as a prisoner. His most comfortable confinement had been his six years in the great keep of Deganwy Castle, for he'd been permitted the company of his wife and children, all the material solace his wealth could provide. He'd been treated most harshly by the English King. In contrast to John, Davydd at least allowed him certain basic amenities—baths, clean clothing, mead, even a chess set and dice. But for Gruffydd, such favors were trifles, mere flickers of light amidst the all-enveloping dark. Cricieth was the worst ordeal of all.

During his imprisonment in England, he'd had hatred to sustain him—and hope. The young always have hope. He'd never utterly despaired, never given up his belief that one day he'd be free. Now . . . now he stared out at the distant silhouettes of Eryri, and knew these were the sights he'd see till the day he died, for Davydd would never let him go. And he hated Davydd no less for his forbearance than for his treachery, hated Davydd for denying him the mercy of death.

So the days had passed for him, one into the other, yesterdays indistinguishable from tomorrows. The months changed, the seasons changed; nothing else did. And then, on a morning in early September, they were awakened before dawn, ordered to dress, and within the hour, they were riding toward a horizon aglow with light, riding into the most vivid, vibrant sunrise Gruffydd had ever seen.

He could only conclude that they were being transferred to another of Davydd's castles, although he did not understand why Davydd would take such a needless risk, for his brother was no fool—had he only realized that eleven months ago, he might not have walked so trustingly into Davydd's trap. As they moved inland, he prayed, as never before, that Senena had been foresighted enough to keep Cricieth under surveillance. But the sun rose over the mountains, they moved through narrow ravines ideal for ambush, emerged unscathed. By the time they reached the valley of the River Lledr, Gruffydd no longer deluded himself, knew that no rescue would be forthcoming. It was up to him.

Unfortunately, their guards were seasoned soldiers, cat-quick and as wary as wolves. By day's end, they'd given neither Gruffydd nor Owain opportunity for escape. They took no chances, from time to time would check their prisoners' bonds, and they kept Gruffydd and Owain's horses on tight leads. While they stopped fairly frequently to rest in the heat of midday, they untied their prisoners' wrists only to allow them to urinate, and then kept watch in a circle, swords drawn—although they'd not crowded in quite so closely after Owain had urinated upon the nearest pair of feet. But even so deliberate a provocation had failed to crack their icy composure. The men remained tight-lipped, aloof, unfriendly—and ever watchful.

Gruffydd had thought at first that Dolbadarn or Dolwyddelan would be their new prison. But when they moved into the wide, wooded valley of the River Conwy, he realized that he was to be caged again at Deganwy, Deganwy, which held for him so many ghosts, so many phantom griefs. Davydd had a hunting lodge at Trefriw, but they pressed on, bedded down for the night by the bank of the river. Gruffydd had lain awake for hours, gazing up at a sky aglimmer with pinpoint lights, with as many stars as he had regrets. The deepest regret of all lay asleep beside him, mouth ajar, fair skin mottled by so much sudden exposure to the sun. Gruffydd shifted on his blanket, at once attracting the eyes of those guards keeping a sleepless vigil. Turning awkwardly on his side, for he was bound hand and foot, he gazed for a long time at his sleeping son. Owain would never have come to Cricieth if not for him, would not have forfeited eleven months of his life had he not been so blind, so willfully, unforgivably blind. How could he have so misread his brother?

Before dawn, they were on the road again, reached the Cistercian abbey of Aberconwy by mid-morning. Ahead lay the great rock of Deganwy. But the castle Gruffydd so hated was in ruins. Blackened and scorched timber palisades lay smoldering in the sun; the wooden buildings within the bailey had been burned to the ground. Gulls wheeled overhead, occasionally shrieking, but no other sound intruded upon the eerie, death-like silence that overhung Deganwy. Gruffydd had rarely seen a sight so desolate, or so baffling. Who had destroyed it? And why?

Owain sought for a time to elicit answers from their taciturn guards, in vain. They moved on, once more heading into the sun. By late afternoon, they were within sight of the walls of Rhuddlan Castle. Rhuddlan had a checkered past. There had been a castle at the mouth of the River Clwyd for nigh on two hundred years; it was Welsh or English according to the vicissitudes of war. Owain's sight was keenest; he saw it first. "Jesú," he gasped. "Papa, look!" And Gruffydd gazed upward, saw the banner flying from the castle battlements—three golden lions on a blood-red background—the royal arms of England.

The castle bailey was filled with men, but not the men Gruffydd expected to see. The red and white livery of the King was everywhere present. Yet amidst the bearded English faces were mustached Welsh ones, too. No sooner had they ridden through the gatehouse than the Welsh surged forward; within moments, the riders were engulfed. A babble of voices rose up around Gruffydd, an incongruous mesh of three tongues, English, Welsh, and French. Men were shouting his name, making of it an exultant battle cry. He looked about in bewilderment, then saw a familiar figure shoving his way toward them: his young brother-by-marriage. Einion was only of average height, seemed to be struggling against a rising tide, but he finally thrust through the crowd, grabbed at Gruffydd's boot.

His mouth was moving, but Gruffydd could not catch his words. "What are you doing here, Einion? What has happened?"

"You are free! Senena . . . she struck a deal with the English King. You are both free, Gruffydd!"

Owain heard enough to let out a jubilant yell. Gruffydd stared down at his brother-in-law. "Free?" he echoed. He sounded stunned. "At what price?"

Einion hesitated, then said, "No higher than need be." Relieved when Gruffydd's guards cut their conversation off, he followed them into the hall. Let Senena be the one to tell him. Not me, he thought, no, by God, not me!

The great hall was no less crowded than the castle bailey. Gruffydd's guards formed a phalanx, bulled their way toward the dais. Gruffydd caught a glimpse of bright gold hair, recognized the English King. He was heartened at sight of the Princes of Powys, standing behind Henry upon the dais; he was not so friendless as he'd first thought. And then he saw his wife. Even as a young girl, Senena had never been a beauty. But there was such joy upon her face that she held the eye of every man in the hall. She was the acknowledged heroine of the hour, and when she started down the dais steps toward her husband, a path at once opened for her.

While she'd proven herself to be a passionate bedmate, she'd never been demonstrative in public. But now she threw her arms around Gruffydd's neck, and when he lowered his head, she kissed him full on the mouth. She embraced Owain next, and then kissed Gruffydd again. "You are safe, beloved," she murmured. "Safe at last . . ." Her laughter was a soaring sound of triumph. "And we have won, Gruffydd, we have won!"

But belief did not come easily to Gruffydd. "Is it true, Senena? You made a deal with the English King?"

"Yes," she said, "I did. I would have bargained with the Devil himself if that was what it took to free you."

Gruffydd looked into those luminous grey eyes, at that red mouth, no longer laughing. "The Devil demands souls," he said tautly. "What does Henry want?"

She would have to tell him, of course. But not now, not here. "That can wait, beloved. First we must cut these bonds." She saw the protest forming on his lips—he was nothing if not single-minded—and added hastily, "Davydd is here."

Gruffydd's eyes narrowed, swept by her, raking the hall. She knew by his indrawn breath when he'd located his brother, and she gave his arm a supportive squeeze. "In time, love," she said, "all in good time," and then she turned back toward the English King.

Senena had no more regard for the English than did Gruffydd, but she believed in honoring her debts, and the smile she now gave Henry was unforced, genuinely grateful. "May I borrow your dagger, my liege? Let Gruffydd be freed by your knife—and my hand."

She stretched out her arm, palm up, but Henry did not unsheathe the dagger. "I regret, Madame," he said, "that it will not be possible to free your husband—not just yet."

He'd spoken so quietly that many in the hall had not heard his words. But they had only to look at Senena's face to know that something was terribly wrong. She was suddenly ashen. "What are you saying? You promised me that Gruffydd would be freed. You gave me your sworn word!"

Henry had the grace to look embarrassed. "I am not saying he will not be freed, Lady Senena, only that his release must be delayed. You did agree, after all, that we were to determine his legal rights under Welsh law. Well, that will take time. But until I can reach a decision, I will personally see to it that your husband and son lack for no comfort, that they—"

The rest of his sentence was lost. As Gruffydd's supporters realized that they had been duped, they began to voice their shock, loudly and indignantly. Of all the Welshmen in the hall, Gruffydd alone was not surprised. "Where?" he demanded, his voice cutting sharply across the rising murmurs of protest. "Where do you mean to hold me?"

There was so much raw emotion in that question that Henry winced. "London," he mumbled, temporizing in vain, for there was not a man there who did not know what he truly meant—the Tower.

"No!" The scream was Senena's and it acted as a catalyst, unleashed pandemonium in the hall. The echoes of her scream were still reverberating as Gruffydd lunged at the nearest of his guards, made a desperate grab for the man's dagger. But they'd been anticipating just such a move, and he was swiftly subdued. Owain, too, was struggling now, but to no avail. Some of Henry's men had unobtrusively augmented Davydd's force, and they made haste to defuse a dangerous situation, began to drag their prisoners toward the door behind the dais.

The Welsh were in an uproar. Both Princes of Powys were remonstrating angrily with Henry. Others were taking out their frustration and fury upon the closest targets, and English-Welsh quarrels were breaking out across the hall. Several men had hands on sword hilts, but the Welsh were hopelessly outnumbered. It was that sense of their own helplessness that gave such an edge to their rage. A few tried halfheartedly to intervene upon Gruffydd's behalf, were shoved back by his guards.

Gruffydd had cut his hand upon the guard's dagger, and the sight of his blood had so demoralized Senena that she'd stood frozen, watching in horrified disbelief. But then the guards reached the door, thrust their prisoners through, and again she cried out, darted forward to follow. One of the men pushed her aside. She staggered backward, fell to her knees, to the utter outrage of those close enough to see. Henry leaped to his feet, hastened down the steps of the dais.

"How dare you?" he raged. "I'll not have any man maltreat a lady in my presence, not ever!" But when he sought to help Senena up, she gave him a look of such hatred that he recoiled. Stepping back, he said curtly, "She has my permission to accompany her husband. Is that understood?"

Senena's mouth contorted. Getting slowly to her feet, she looked at Henry, then spat upon the floor. Only then did she turn, follow after her husband and son.

Amidst all the turmoil, the two men standing against the far wall seemed somehow out of place, for they alone had remained calm, detached eye-witnesses to disaster. After a time, they attracted the attention of Gruffydd Maelor, Prince of Upper Powys. He pushed his way toward them, his eyes flicking accusingly from Davydd to Ednyved, back to Davydd again.

"So you won, after all," he said bitterly.

Davydd looked at him, saying nothing; he'd never realized that silence could be such an effective weapon. But when Davydd did speak, it was with such blistering contempt that the Prince of Powys could never forget it, nor ever forgive. ·

"I've won, you say? When the English can now use Gruffydd as a sword at my throat, a threat to extort whatever they damned well please? They know I dare not balk at their demands, for they need only release Gruffydd to start another bloody civil war, to tear Wales asunder again. There was but one winner here at Rhuddlan, the King of England, and if you cannot see that, you deserve what is like to befall you. Unfortunately, your people do not, although they will be the ones to suffer for your stupidity. Till the day he died, my father fought to hold the English at bay. And he did, he kept them from overrunning Gwynedd and yes, your Powys, too, as they had Deheubarth. If not for him, much of Powys would be an English shire by now. Yet his dream did survive him by just sixteen scant months. His life's work is in ruins about us, and I must bear my share of the blame for that. But if I have reason to rue this day, so do you, Gruffydd Maelor. You are going to learn a very hard lesson about English power and Welsh consequences."

12

White Ladies Priory
Shropshire, England

September 1241

THE guest house of the Augustinian nunnery lay to the north of the priory church. Elen's maid was standing in the sun before their chamber; she smiled at sight of her lady, and they entered together. Aveline was making idle conversation about the delightfully warm September weather, but almost at once Elen signaled for silence. Surprised, Aveline complied, a little hurt until she saw Elen's husband asleep on the bed.

Rob had removed only his shoes and sword. He looked utterly at peace, and in repose, very youthful for a man in his mid-forties. Aveline smiled, thinking that if he were her man, it would have been fun to fluff his pillow, to tiptoe about the chamber whilst he slept. Elen, too, was smiling down at Rob, but with none of Aveline's maternal solicitude. She was dressed in the Welsh style, wore a veil but no wimple. Reaching up, she unpinned the veil, let it flutter to the floor. "Help me," she whispered, beginning to unbraid her hair.

Although she obeyed without question, Aveline was shocked; lovemaking in the middle of the day seemed somehow sinful to her. Almost as if reading her thoughts, Elen laughed, gestured for Aveline to unlace her gown. These past six months had been a revelation to the younger woman. Marriage was an immutable fact of life, every woman's fate, but until joining Elen's household, Aveline had not known that a marriage could be like Elen's, that a wife need not be beaten, that a man and woman could take genuine joy in each other.

Elen dropped her dress into the floor rushes, slid into bed. When Aveline started to draw the bed hangings, she shook her head. "It will be too hot," she said softly, and Aveline blushed, moved rapidly toward the door.

Rob had yet to stir, but as Elen moved closer, breathing into his ear, molding her body to his, he sighed, buried his face against her breasts. "Rosamund," he mumbled, and Elen nipped his ear lobe between sharp, white teeth. He laughed, rolled over on top of her. But almost at once, he jerked back, nearly falling off the bed, so abrupt was his recoil.

"Jesú, Elen, for a moment I did forget! Are you all right, love?"

"Aside from being squashed as flat as a water reed? I—Rob, I was but teasing! You must not treat me as if I am a frail flower, else I'll start to take shameless advantage of my condition. Unless, of course, you would like to wait upon me hand and foot for the next six months?"

He grinned, lay down beside her. "The next time I get the urge to pamper you, I'll fight it," he promised, and Elen rolled over into his arms, gave him a lingering kiss that was no less of a promise.

"I know you've been impatient to get back to Essex, Rob, but it meant much to me, spending these weeks here. White Ladies holds special memories for me."

"You were here as a little lass, were you not?"

She nodded. "During a troubled time in my parents' marriage. John had just hanged the Welsh hostages, and my mother was seeking to come to terms with it. I was but five, yet my memories are still as sharply edged as your best sword. I remember my mother's despair, my homesickness, remember the day my father came for us. Their marriage could have broken apart on those rocks, but they somehow managed to salvage it. They reconciled in this very chamber, probably in this very bed!" She grinned, slipped her hand into Rob's shirt. "In later years, my mother always spoke of White Ladies with fondness, and when her eyes would meet Papa's, they'd share a very private moment. I thought if I were to come back, that I'd feel close to them both, that it would be almost like telling them . . ."

Rob reached over, laid his hand upon her abdomen. "Your belly feels as flat as your aforesaid water reed. Elen, you are sure . . . ?"

She understood his doubt; her smile was tender. "My flux first came at twelve, Rob, and in the years since, I've been as reliable as the lunar tides. Not once have I ever missed a flux, and now I've missed three. And then there is my morning queasiness. Not to mention the wonderful way my bosom has been swelling of late. I never did think I'd gotten my fair share, but better late than never!" She laughed, then slid her chemise down her shoulder, slowly baring one breast. "Lastly, see how the circle round the nipple has darkened?"

"No," he said, "I think I need a closer look," and Elen's chemise soon joined her gown in the floor rushes. Rob sat up to free himself of his tunic. Elen then took his hand, placed it again on her belly. He leaned over, kissed the soft skin below her navel. "Is it too early," he asked, "to talk of names?"

"Would we be tempting fate?" She shook her head, so vehemently that cascading black hair swirled upon the pillow. "No. It would be an act of faith, love. As soon as I began to suspect, I began, too, to think of names. If it is a boy, I want to call him Robert," she said, saw by his smile how much she had pleased him.

"And if it is a girl?" he prompted. "Joanna, I expect."

To his surprise, she shook her head. "After I awake each morn, Robyn, there is a moment when memory comes flooding back, when I think to myself: It is no dream; I truly am with child. And the wonder does strike me anew, as if for the first time. Who could blame me for doubting? As John's wife, I was barren for nigh on fifteen years. And it has been four years since we wed. I'd long ago given up all hope. That I should conceive at last, in my thirty-fourth year . . . it seems nothing less than miraculous to me, beloved. What can it mean but that the Almighty has forgiven our adultery? I think, therefore, that if I have a daughter, we ought to name her Anne, after the mother of Our Lady."

"Anne or Robyn it shall be then," Rob agreed. "And for the next one . . ."

But to Elen, that *was* tempting fate. She hastily put her fingers to his mouth. "One babe at a time," she murmured, and kissed him.

They'd gotten rid of his shirt, were fumbling with the cords fastening his braies to his chausses when they heard the door open. Rob swore, raised up to jerk the bed hangings into place. At sight of his squire, he scowled. "For your sake, Gervaise, you'd best be here to warn me the priory is afire."

Gervaise shifted his feet. Rob was such an easy master to serve, so rarely riled that his household had little practice in dealing with his tempers. "I am indeed sorry, my lord, but I thought you should know that there is a youth out in the garth, demanding to see you at once. An impudent rascal he is, and I'd have sent him on his way with a few bruises to nurse had he not claimed to be your lady's nephew. I do not believe him, in truth; as bedraggled and filthy as he is, he looks more like beggar than prince. Still, I thought it best to—"

"Llelo?" Elen's head poked through the bed hangings. Unable to reach her gown, she snatched up the chemise, instead, and a moment later tumbled out of bed. Brushing past Gervaise, she ran out into the garth, Rob following much more slowly. The men reached the door just in time to see Elen embrace a very scruffy-looking youngster, utterly heedless of her astonished, scandalized audience.

Equally unfazed, Rob leaned back against the door and grinned at his squire. "I think, Gervaise," he said, "that we can safely assume the lad spoke true."

"I once owned a mastiff who could bolt down a shank of beef at each meal and still look for more. I must say, though, Llelo, that he could not hold a candle to you!" No sooner were the words out of his mouth than Rob regretted them, for he did not know Llelo well enough to risk teasing him. For certes, the lad's father had never been noted for his sense of humor! But Llelo glanced over his shoulder, gave him a quick grin between bites.

"Pay him no heed, Llelo. You can eat a whole cow if you've a mind to!" Elen had deferred to propriety to the extent of putting on her shoes and gown, but she had not bothered to braid her hair, and as she leaned over to ladle more venison frumenty onto Llelo's trencher, she looked far more like a young hoyden than the lady of the manor, so disheveled and yet so desirable that Rob found himself sorely lamenting Llelo's sense of timing.

This was Llelo's second meal in as many hours. He'd eaten a full plate of roast beef, an entire loaf of bread, and a fat carp from the priory fish-pond. After a desperately needed hot bath, he was now devoting all his attention to a generous helping of venison stew. Vowing she meant to burn his clothes, Elen had given him one of Rob's tunics to wear; it was too big, of course, but did not dwarf him as much as she'd expected.

To Elen's surprise, Llelo was now taller than she, endearingly awkward, as if he'd not yet grown into this new body of his; the long legs he'd entangled under his chair were as cumbersome as any colt's, but his shoulders had begun to broaden, and when she sought to wipe dirt from his upper lip, she discovered that the smudge was the first faint shadow of a mustache.

Not having seen Llelo in the seventeen months since her father's funeral, Elen had missed the day-by-day changes, and she felt cheated somehow. Do not grow up so very fast, lad, she wanted to say. She did not, of course; instead, she watched Llelo gulp down a goblet of strong cider. In just seven short months, he would be fourteen. Too young, she thought, too young to take on the burdens of manhood, and she hoped suddenly that the child she carried within her would be a girl.

Llelo put down an apple-filled wafer, half-eaten. "I cannot eat as much as I thought I could. You knew, then, that I was missing?"

"Of course we did. Your mother had men out scouring the entire countryside for you, lad." And it seemed inutterably sad to Elen that the boy should look so obviously surprised.

"That did not occur to me," he admitted. "But I did fear the King's men might be in pursuit, that they might even send lymer hounds after me. So I waded in Meole Brook to throw them off the scent, and at first, I traveled only at night, stayed hidden during the day."

"Hidden, indeed! It was as if you'd vanished into blue smoke. Where have you been all these weeks, Llelo? How did you fend for yourself? What did you eat?"

"Whatever I could find," he said, and grimaced. "After my food ran out, I foraged where I could. I found blackberries and elderberries in the woods. I caught a few fish and frogs. One time I came upon an orchard, though the apples were so green I got a right sharp belly ache! I roasted chestnuts, once even snared a rabbit, and whenever I could find them, I plundered English gardens. Of course I had to watch out for dogs, and—"

"But how?" Ellen was astonished by the matter-of-fact tone of his voice. "How could you make fires? Or catch fish? Or hunt? How could you manage without proper weapons?"

Llelo looked quizzically amused. "I had my knife," he pointed out patiently. "What more did I need? I made fish hooks from thorns, and fishing lines from vines; what could be easier? A rabbit snare is simple to make; you need only watch for tracks, then set the loop along the trail. As for making a fire without flint, I've known how to do that since I was eight years old. You find a hard stone like agate or quartz, hit your knife against it till you strike sparks. With shredded birchbark for tinder, it flames up right quick. Were you never taught such tricks, Aunt Elen?" he asked, in some surprise, and she slowly shook her head.

"The different worlds in which men and women live," she marveled. "But I suspect it could not have been as simple as you make it sound, lad. And I should like to know where you've been all this time. White Ladies is no more than twenty-five miles from Shrewsbury, if even that. It should not have taken you a full month to get here."

"I got lost," Llelo confessed. "Aunt Gwladys said it was to the north, so I headed north. But she was wrong, Aunt Elen. White Ladies is east of Shrewsbury, not north! I'm just lucky I did not end up in Scotland."

Elen laughed, then reached across the table, took his hand. "Tell me," she said, "the good and the bad. Were you never scared, Llelo?"

Llelo hesitated only briefly. "All the time," he said softly. "I was scared that the King's men might find me. I was scared that I'd not find you, that I'd not get to White Ladies in time, that you'd be gone and I'd have nowhere else to go." He slumped back in his chair, the role-playing forgotten, no longer the hero of his own adventure saga, just a thirteen-year-old boy out of his depth.

"Being hungry was not so bad," he said. "I got used to it. The worst was the loneliness. Once I was well away from Shrewsbury, I thought

I could risk asking people how to get to the priory. But I could find no one who understood French."

It had been fun to swagger a bit, to gild his exploits with what he fancied to be adult bravado. But it could not compare to the utter relief of speaking the truth. "Do you know what my greatest problem was, Aunt Elen? Lack of water, for the drought has dried up so many of the brooks and ponds. Sometimes I even had to put pebbles in my mouth. And one day I could not find any streams, any ponds at all. Finally I came upon a hamlet, just a few houses and a church. I waited till dark, but the village dogs were loose, and I could not risk approaching their wells. At last I went into the church."

He looked down into his goblet, back up at Elen. "I suppose it was a sin to steal from gardens, but I thought God would understand. I am not sure, though, that he would understand what I did in the church, Aunt Elen. I drank from the font, drank holy water."

Elen fought back a smile. "Darling, if that is the only sin you ever have to answer for, you'll never even see Purgatory, will go straight to Paradise!"

"There is more," he said. "You see, after I drank the holy water, suddenly it began to rain—for the first time in months! I knew God was telling me something, but what? I stayed in the church, waiting for the rain to stop and then I fell asleep. When I awoke, it was morning and the priest was standing over me."

Llelo smiled suddenly. "That was not the best way to begin my day! He was very wroth at first, too. I think he suspected I was a runaway serf," he said reluctantly, frowning in recollection of such an insult. But once I spoke French to him, he realized that I was no peasant, that I must be of good birth. Unfortunately, he knew no more than a few words of French. Is there anyone in this blessed country who does speak that language?"

They laughed, and Llelo ate the rest of the wafer before resuming. "The priest fed me, gave me a bed in return for doing chores. I passed a few days with him, days I could ill afford to spare. Then on Sunday, he said Mass for the villagers, and I realized how foolish I'd been. But I'd never thought to try Latin. I could scarcely wait for Mass to be done. Only . . . only he did not truly speak Latin, did but chant from memory." Echoes of remembered disappointment crept into the boy's voice, and bafflement, too, for the only priests Llelo had known were cultivated chaplains of the Welsh court, princes of the Church like Bishop Hywel.

"He did understand, though, that Dominae Albae meant White Ladies, and it finally dawned upon him that I sought the priory. It was only then that I learned White Ladies lay to the east of Shrewsbury, that I'd long since passed it by. The priest gave me a sack of apples and some bread, drew a map for me on the sack, and I set off again. It took me another six or seven sunsets—I lost count—and I had no adventures worth recounting, but I got here." He looked from Elen to Rob, back to Elen again, and said, with quiet yet intense satisfaction, "I got here."

Elen had so often wished that Llelo could have been her son and not Gruffydd's, but never more so than now. "I am so proud of you, lad."

"Aunt Elen, there is something I must ask you, and I must have the truth. I heard the English King swear that he'd never harm a child. Are my little brothers safe with him? Did he speak true?"

"Yes," she said, "I do believe he spoke true."

There had been no hesitation before she spoke, and Llelo took heart from that; Elen was one of the very few people whom he did not believe would lie to him. "I pray God you are right," he said. "I'd have taken them with me if only I could, hope they'll understand that one day. My mother will not understand, though . . . not ever. She'll never forgive me for running away, for putting her plans in jeopardy." He caught the look, quick as it was, that flashed between Elen and Rob, and stiffened, throwing his head up as a colt would, scenting danger. "What is it? What has happened?"

Elen looked very troubled, but she did not mince words. "I'm afraid your mother's plans did go awry, Llelo, but through no fault of yours. A fortnight ago Davydd was forced to surrender to the English, to turn Gruffydd and Owain over to Henry. But Henry then broke faith with the Welsh. Instead of freeing Gruffydd, he sent Gruffydd into England, to the Tower of London."

"Jesú . . ." It was little more than a whisper; Llelo's teeth had bitten into his lower lip. For a long moment, he stared at Elen, then pushed away from the table, so violently that his chair tipped over, clattered to the floor. Elen rose to her feet, too, but then she hesitated. Llelo had turned away from them both. He was standing by the window, shoulders hunched forward, head down, and Elen found herself at a loss, unable to decide which was greater, his need for comfort or his need for privacy.

"Llelo?" He did not respond, and as the minutes trickled away, it seemed to Elen that the last of his childhood was ebbing away, too. And as she watched him, she remembered a conversation she'd long since forgotten, remembered his plaintive request on the day of her father's funeral, that he be called by his given name, his grandfather's name.

"Llewelyn?" she said huskily, and he turned to face her.

He had lost color, and his lashes were wet and tangled, but his eyes were dry. "Will you take me to my father?" he said.

❧

EVEN after more than a fortnight, Senena was not yet accustomed to the splendor of her husband's prison. Until recently the great chamber and hall in the White Tower had been the King's residence. But with the completion of the magnificent, octagonal Blundeville Tower, Henry had no need for the keep's great chamber. Moreover, he did feel some genuine conscience pangs for having so betrayed a lady. In consequence, Gruffydd and Owain found themselves in a very gilded cage, indeed.

Following a guard up the stairwell in the northeast turret of the White Tower, Senena paused in the doorway. The top story of the keep contained an enormous hall, now blocked off, an elegantly austere chapel, and Henry's great chamber, a spacious, well-lit room with soaring ceilings and numerous windows, encircled overhead by the most impressive mural gallery Senena had ever seen. The chamber afforded not only luxury, but privacy, too, partitioned off by a large, oaken screen.

Emerging from behind the screen, Owain was hastening toward her, a jaunty smile of welcome upon his face. "I was beginning to fear you were not coming, Mama!"

"How is your father, Owain?"

His smile faded. "The same," he said, saw her lashes sweep down. "Ah, Mama . . . Mama, do not do this to yourself. You are not to blame for what happened."

She neither agreed nor argued. As close as they were, he could see how hollowed were her eyes, webbed by worry lines, bloodshot from lack of sleep. "Mama, listen to me. I'll not deny that when I first realized I was to go to the Tower, I was chilled to the very marrow of my bones. But look about us. Who could find fault with such a prison? Life is far better here than at Cricieth, that I can say for certes."

As he spoke, he was drawing her toward the nearest window. "Henry is a more generous gaoler than Davydd, God rot him. Time does not hang so heavily on my hands here. Davydd did allow us books, but I've never been much of a reader, and neither is Papa. Now we can play at tables, or dicing, or draughts. We've a servant to tend to our needs, even our own cook. Best of all, we can have visitors, can write and receive letters. We can learn what is happening beyond these walls, after nigh on a year of silence, of never knowing."

He gestured toward the window. "At Cricieth, we had nothing to do, nothing to watch but sea gulls. But Henry's palace is right across the bailey, so there is constant activity, tradesmen and servants and soldiers milling about. I do not feel so cut off here, feel like I'm still part of the world. Above all, I feel safer here. Henry needs us alive. Davydd needed us dead. I never could understand why he did not have us put to death, and I'd much rather trust to Henry's self-interest than to Davydd's forbearance."

At that, she nodded. "Not a day passed that I did not fear for your lives," she confessed. "Not an hour . . ."

"You must see then that you've nothing to reproach yourself for. It is better here in all ways, Mama. Henry's guards speak no Welsh, so Papa and I have far more privacy, need not watch every word. And our English guards are friendly, treat us like lords. Davydd's men acted as if we were lepers, but I sometimes dice with our guards now, and they tell me all the court gossip, will share a flagon if I offer it." He could see her disapproval that he should socialize with his inferiors, with his enemies, and he lowered his voice even though no one was within earshot. "The day could well come when a friendly guard might be a godsend, Mama."

"You are right," she conceded. "By all means, cultivate these men if you can." Reaching for a small leather pouch that swung from her belt, she held it out toward him. "Ere I forget, here is the money you asked for. To pay some of those dicing debts, I daresay?"

Owain grinned, but did not answer. He carefully tucked the pouch inside his tunic, for he meant to put it to much better use than gambling. One of the guards had boasted that he knew a young whore with hair the color of silver-gilt, and he'd promised to bring her up into the keep if Owain made it worth his while. "The guards say I can have a pet if I've a mind to, Mama. Do you know what I'd like? One of those trained monkeys. I understand you can ofttimes find them offered for sale at the Smithfield Horse Fair, or down by the wharves, where foreign ships come in."

"I'll find you a monkey, Owain, never fear. Now . . ." Senena drew a steadying breath. "Let us go in to your father."

The partitioned-off portion of the great chamber was still spacious enough to contain two large, canopied beds, a table and chairs. Gruffydd was sprawled in a window-seat, staring out into the Tower bailey. He looked up as his wife and son entered, but did not speak.

"Good morrow, beloved." Senena leaned over, kissed the corner of his mouth. He did not respond, but neither did he pull away, as he'd done in the past, and she took what meagre encouragement she could from that. As she sat down beside him, though, she could not keep from casting a wistful glance toward Gruffydd's bed, could not help wondering if he'd ever take her behind those canopied curtains, if he'd ever forgive her.

"I have news," she said, forcing a smile. "I need no longer stay at that noisome Southwark inn, have leased a house in Aldgate, not far from here."

"We are glad, Mama." Owain returned her smile, but Gruffydd said nothing. He was fiddling with a wooden ball and cup, a child's toy, flipping the ball into the air and catching it in the cup. Senena yearned to reach out, to stroke his cheek, his hair, noticing suddenly how many silvered hairs were scattered now amidst the red.

"Yesterday," she said, "I paid a visit to Davydd and Rhodri. They are well, Gruffydd, and . . . and they seem quite content."

His hand jerked and the ball bounced into the floor rushes. Senena reached over; her fingers just brushed his sleeve. "Gruffydd, listen to me. They are safe, I swear it. And they need not live at the King's court, need not follow Henry on his journeys around the realm. He has agreed to keep them at Westminster, so I may see them often."

"How very magnanimous of him," he said, so bitingly that color flooded her face. "So we have no cause for concern, then. Henry shall take our sons to his heart. They are safe, you say, they are well, they are even content. I wonder, though, how content Llelo is. I suppose you could ask, Senena—that is, if you knew where to find him!"

"You are not being fair! Do you not think I care about Llelo's whereabouts? I've had men searching all of Shropshire for the past month. What more would you have me do?"

He gave her such a burning look that her breath lodged in her throat, and Owain made haste to intervene. Even knowing as he did that their guards could not eavesdrop, he was embarrassed, nonetheless, by their raised voices; quarrels sounded the same in any language. And as uncomfortable as he felt, being trapped like this between them, he found most of his sympathy flowing toward his mother.

"I think Mama was right in what she did. Our lives were in peril; the lads' lives are not. There are worse fates, Papa, than to be a hostage of the English Crown, and I think you are over—"

"What do you know about it?" Gruffydd flung the wooden cup from him with such force that it splintered against the far wall. Rising to his feet, he swung about to confront his son. "You were not at Nottingham Castle the day John hanged the Welsh hostages. You were not trussed up like a pig for butchering, you did not lie for hours on a dirt-strewn floor, listening as your friends were taken out to die, expecting at any moment your own summons to the gallows. You did not hear their pleading, or see their bodies, swaying back and forth, see their black, swollen faces . . ."

Gruffydd's mouth twisted; he swallowed, spat into the floor rushes, said, "There were children amongst them, boys of nine or ten. So do not tell me that it is safe to be a hostage of the English King, do not tell me that youth is a shield and none would harm a child. I know better. I was there!"

Senena, too, was on her feet now. "Henry is not John! Why can you not see that? Henry is not capable of his father's cruelties, would never murder a child!"

"You sound so sure of that, Senena. But then, you were sure, too, that Henry would honor his bargain with you, that he'd set me free!"

Senena turned away, leaned for some moments against the door leading into the chapel. Neither Gruffydd nor Owain spoke. It was only then that they heard the footsteps approaching the partition.

It was the most amiable of their guards, the freckled youth who claimed to know a whore with silver-gilt hair, and evidenced in both his blood and name the mingling of two cultures, two heritages, the ancient Saxon of Edwin, the proud Norman-French of de Crecy.

"You have visitors," he said. "Sir Robert de Quincy and his wife, the Lady Elen."

Gruffydd was taken aback; Elen had long ago pledged her loyalties to Davydd. But Senena reacted at once, with utter outrage.

"No, by God! There may be much I have to endure, but I'll not let that bitch come to gloat. Send her away."

"No," Gruffydd snapped. "I will see them." And when his wife would have protested, he silenced her with an impatient, "Use your head, woman. If Elen is here, it can only mean she has word for me, and it might well be of Llelo."

Senena opened her mouth, shut it again. "You are right," she said, sounding somewhat abashed. "I never even thought of that . . ."

As the guard motioned them to come forward, another of the guards · stepped in front of Llelo, holding out his hand. The boy looked at him blankly. Only when the man gestured, did he understand, slowly unsheathe his knife and hand it over. He gave Elen a crooked smile, then began to walk toward the partition. His feet were making an inordinate amount of noise, scuffling through the rushes, and he was suddenly very thirsty. His throat seemed to have closed up, so tight had the muscles become; he had not even enough saliva to spit.

He halted in the screen doorway, not knowing what to expect. He heard his mother cry out his name, but his eyes were already riveted upon his father. He'd never seen Gruffydd with a beard before; he was both astonished and disconcerted that it should be so streaked with grey. For one dismaying moment, he felt as if he were staring at a stranger. And then Gruffydd smiled. .

"Thank God," he said simply. That was all, was more than enough. Llelo forgot his fears, his qualms, even his guilt, moved forward into his father's arms. But when he stepped back, there was a sudden awkwardness. He looked at his mother, not knowing what to say. She, too, seemed at a loss, seemed no less uncertain than he.

"Come here," she said at last. But the embrace was forced, unfamiliar, gave neither of them the comfort they sought. Senena's fingers brushed Llelo's cheek, smoothed his untidy, dark hair, while her other hand tightened on his shoulder. "Do you know what a scare you gave us, Llelo? I think you have some explaining to do!"

Llelo tensed anew, but his father was shaking his head. "No, Senena," he said, "he does not." His eyes cut from his son to the woman now standing in the doorway. "Is it safe for him to be here?"

Elen nodded. "You need not fear; he has a safe-conduct. Rob and I are leaving now, Llewelyn, will await you in the bailey."

"That will not be necessary." Senena's was a poisoned politeness, for she was seething with rage, with aggrieved and baffled resentment that her runaway son should have turned to Elen, to Elen of all women. "My son belongs with me, will be returning to my house in Aldgate."

Elen's eyes narrowed. "That," she said, "will depend entirely upon the lad!"

Llelo flushed, stared down at the floor, and Gruffydd made haste to say, "Thank you, Elen, for taking care of my son." Putting his arm, then, around Llelo's shoulders, he said, "Come with me, lad," and Llelo followed him gratefully into the chapel.

There Llelo came to an abrupt halt, dazzled by what he saw. The King's chapel of St John the Evangelist was splendid beyond all expectations, a superb crafting of man's skill and God's spirit. Henry had recently ordered it white-washed, and the stone walls glowed with ivory light. It was the windows that caught Llelo's gaze, however, for three of them were set with costly stained glass, brilliantly shaded depictions of the Virgin and Child, the Holy Trinity, and St John the Evangelist. Crimson and emerald and purple—the panes shimmered and sparkled, until even the shadows held flickers of lavender and rose-tinted sunlight.

Against the west wall was Henry's private pew. Gruffydd pushed the gate aside, sat down deliberately upon Henry's plush velvet cushions, gesturing for Llelo to join him. "Tell me the truth," he said. "You ran away from Shrewsbury because you learned you were to be offered up as a hostage, did you not?"

Llelo nodded, and Gruffydd grinned. "Good lad! Now tell me the rest," he said, and Llelo did. He was accurate, but not entirely honest. The account he'd offered Elen was far closer to the truth than the version he now spun out for his father, sketched in fact but colored by imagination. What Gruffydd got was a tale of high adventure, one utterly lacking in dark shadings, and when it was done, Gruffydd said again, "Good lad," in tones of pride and approval.

"Papa . . . what happens now?"

"I would that I knew." The boy looked so troubled, though, that

Gruffydd roused himself. "As much as it galls me to be a prisoner of the English, the truth is, lad, that I am probably better off here than at Cricieth. Davydd would never have set me free. Henry would free me tomorrow if he thought it served his interests to do so. In that sense, my prospects are not as bleak. And then, too, there are other ways out of prison. Not even Merlin could have managed an escape from Cricieth, so tightly was that bottle corked. But here . . ." He laughed scornfully. "As lax as Henry's guards are, I could be gone fully a day ere I'd even be missed!"

"Aunt Elen told me that a Bishop once escaped from the Tower, from your very chamber, by sliding down a rope, as slick as you please." Llelo hesitated, then said reluctantly, "What do you want me to do, Papa? Would you have me go home with Mama?"

"Yes," Gruffydd said, pretended not to see the boy flinch. "Your rightful place is, of course, with your mother. But I would not have you remain in England any longer than need be, will not truly breathe easy till you are back in Wales. Gwladys and de Mortimer are in London, plan to return to the Marches within the next fortnight or so, and when they go, you are to go with them."

Llelo's relief was soaring. Although he would have preferred living with Elen, he was quite content to stay with Gwladys, would have turned to her for help had her husband not been one of Senena's pledges. "I'd as soon live in a lazar-house as in London," he confessed, and Gruffydd gave him a grimly amused smile.

"You did not let me finish, lad. I do not mean for you to stay with Gwladys. Send word to Senena's brothers, and they will come for you, take you back into Gwynedd. My war is not done, will not be as long as I draw breath. But since I cannot fight it, it is up to my friends—and up to you, Llelo."

"You want me to war upon Davydd?"

Gruffydd misread the boy's dismay, said swiftly, reassuringly, "You will not be alone, lad. Senena's brothers will be there to counsel you; Einion in particular is well worthy of your trust. So, too, is Gruffydd Maelor of Powys. But it is you whom men will rally to, lad. The men who would fight for me will fight now for my son—for you."

Llelo got to his feet, moved into the brightest patch of sunlight. According to Elen, Henry was already building a new stone castle at Disserth. How many more English castles would be rising up from Welsh soil? How many crops did Henry mean to harvest from those bitter seeds sown at Gwern Eigron? And it was Davydd who stood alone against him, Davydd who was Gwynedd's only bulwark against further English conquest. Yet now, with the dike so dangerously weakened, leaking like a sieve, Papa would act, not to shore it up, but to tear it down, to let the flood waters engulf them all!

Gruffydd had risen, too, disturbed by his son's silence. "Well? I need you, Llewelyn, need you to play a man's part, to do what I cannot. You'll not let me down?"

Never before had he called Llelo by his given name. The boy turned slowly to face him. "No, Papa," he said, "I will not let you down, will do whatever you ask of me."

He looked so somber, though, that Gruffydd felt a conscience pang, could only hope he was not burdening the lad too unfairly, too soon. But there was no help for it.

"Your mother meant well, but she was wrong to offer our sons as hostages, and she was wrong to put her trust in Henry. Take this lesson to heart, lad, and never forget it, never—that the world's greatest fool is a Welshman who trusts an English King."

IN October, Henry summoned Davydd to London, where he did homage to the English King, ratified the Treaty of Gwern Eigron, and was forced to yield all rights to Deganwy Castle to the English Crown.

The sun was low in the sky, sinking toward the west, as Davydd emerged from Henry's palace into the inner bailey of the Tower of London. He stood motionless upon the steps of the great hall, seemingly blind to the chaos swirling about him. Tradesmen come to sell their goods mingled with servants from the royal brewery and bake-house and dovecote, grooms from the stables exchanged banter with men herding doomed pigs toward the kitchen stock-pen, while soldiers and small boys gathered to watch a drover struggling to free his mud-mired cart, and the ever-present stray dogs prowled about, hopeful for hand-outs. Davydd was oblivious to it all, did not move even as their horses were brought up; he'd made use of the land-gate, for like most Welsh-men, he had little regard for river travel. Still, he stood there, staring unseeingly at his own restive stallion, as his men shifted uneasily, began to murmur among themselves.

Ednyved had followed Davydd down the steps. He'd rarely felt so tired or so dispirited or so heavy with years, yet he stood by patiently, willing to give the younger man the time he needed. But then he saw the boy.

It was not by chance; Llelo had been waiting for more than two hours for his uncle to emerge from the King's private chambers. He'd had more than two hours, though, in which to rehearse what he would say. He'd had more than a year, the thirteen months since he'd confronted Davydd at Dolwyddelan Castle.

Ednyved frowned, reached and touched Davydd's arm in warning. "Llelo is below, watching for you."

Davydd seemed to sigh, then shrugged. "So be it," he said wearily, moved down the steps toward his nephew.

The words were already forming on Llelo's tongue, blistering, accusatory, what he felt he should have said at Dolwyddelan and hadn't, words scathing enough to banish all doubts, all qualms. He never said them, forgot them all as he looked into Davydd's face.

"What is wrong?" He swallowed, aware only of fear. "What has the King demanded of you?"

"That if I die without heirs of my body, Gwynedd passes to the English Crown." Davydd sought, and failed, to keep his voice even. "Do you not want to ask if I agreed?"

Llelo jerked his head toward the Tower keep that rose up behind them. "What choice did you have?"

That was a generosity Davydd had not expected, not from a thirteen-year-old boy, not from Gruffydd's son. He repaid it the only way he could, with unsparing honesty. "My father would never have agreed."

"Yes," Llelo said, "he would. He'd have given them their accursed oath, and once he was back in Wales, he'd have disavowed it."

Davydd said nothing, turning aside and swinging up into the saddle. But then he reined in his stallion. His slanting hazel eyes—the most haunted, disquieting eyes Llelo had ever seen—came to rest upon the boy's face, and then he raised his hand in a silent salute.

Llelo stood watching as Davydd and Ednyved rode slowly through the inner gateway, not moving until he heard his name, a whip-lash sound that spun him around in instinctive alarm.

Senena was standing by the stairs of the keep forebuilding. "Stay right there," she warned, and he knotted his hands into fists, tasted the salt of sweat upon his tongue as he waited for her to reach him.

"I cannot believe what I just saw." Senena's voice was breathless, full of shock. "I came out of the keep, and what did I find? My son—passing the time of day with Davydd ap Llewelyn!"

"No, Mama, you do not understand. Something dreadful has happened. Henry has forced Davydd to agree that if he dies without heirs, Gwynedd will pass to the English Crown!"

"God in Heaven! You dare to tell me that you feel sorry for that hell-spawn, for the man who betrayed your own father?"

"But . . . but Mama, do you not see? It is not Davydd, it is Gwynedd!"

"Oh, indeed, I see. I see that you're not to be trusted out of my

sight! It was not enough that you ran away, put your father's release at
risk, made a fool of me before half of Wales, and gave us all a nasty
scare. No, you then had to go to Davydd's sister for help. It is a bloody
wonder you did not go to Davydd! And the worst of it is that I cannot
even say I'd have been surprised if you had, for I cannot remember a
time—not even once—when you have not given us grief, when you
have not been a disappointment to us."

Llelo was too stunned to protest, to offer any defense at all. He
took a backward step, then whirled and fled across the bailey, and
Senena's rage drained away, leaving her sick and shaken. She'd said
more than she ought, and would have called her words back if only she
could. Llelo had not gone far. He had stopped by the east curtain wall,
was standing in the shadow of the stables, and something about his
stance put her in mind of Gruffydd. So alone did he seem, so forlorn,
that she was suddenly remorseful. It had never been easy for her to
admit errors, to offer apologies. After a time, though, she squared her
shoulders and crossed the bailey, sought out her son.

"Llelo," she said. But when he turned, she saw that she'd waited
too long; his hurt had congealed into ice.

"I was not a disappointment to Llewelyn Fawr," he said defiantly.

13

Brindisi, Apulia
Kingdom of Sicily

February 1242

Nell awoke at dawn. From her bedchamber
window, she watched as the last of the night shadows faded and the
day was born. Along the horizon, the sky glowed with golden light,
and the sea was slowly lightening, shading from a fathomless ink-blue
to a luminous silver. As the sun rose above the town, it slanted off the
flat, white roofs, cast the shadows of palm and oleander upon the powdery sands, and Nell thought she could have been looking out upon a
Saracen city, so alien and colorful and exotic did the scene below her
seem.

Church bells had begun to peal, summoning Christ's faithful to worship; it was Candlemas, feast day of the Purification of the Virgin Mary, one of the most holy days in the Church calendar. Nell listened to the bells chime, and suddenly tears filled her eyes. She had never been one to cry easily or often, but in the past six weeks she'd found herself constantly on the verge of tears, for it was just six weeks ago that she'd learned of the death of her sister Isabella.

The sea was now a vivid, translucent turquoise; a ship had entered the outer harbor, flaunting a sail as red as the sunrise. "Simon," she whispered, "oh, Simon, why have you not come back . . . ?"

NELL caused a stir in the town by choosing to hear High Mass not in the Cathedral but in the ancient church of San Giovanni al Sepolcro. Throughout the service, heads kept turning in her direction, eyes seeking a glimpse of the Norman-French lady of the castle, wife to a Christian crusader, sister by marriage to their own lord, Frederick II, Holy Roman Emperor, King of Sicily. Even after a year and a half in their midst, Nell found herself the center of attention whenever she ventured forth from the castle, for she scorned the custom of Frederick's realm, did not go veiled in public.

Brindisi was an embarkation port for the Holy Land, and scarcely a week went by that a ship did not drop anchor in the harbor, bringing Christian knights back from crusade. Nell welcomed them all, entertained them lavishly at her brother-in-law's castle. Life was lonely in Brindisi, and she enjoyed the company; moreover, one of these returning pilgrims might have news of Simon, occasionally even a letter. But in the past few months, the flood had ebbed, slowed to a trickle. Nell's castle was empty of guests, and she felt free, therefore, to take advantage of this mild, sunlit day, to choose the beach over the somber silence of the great hall.

It was unthinkable that a woman of Nell's rank should ride out without an impressive escort, even for a pleasure jaunt, and they made a large, rather unwieldy party as they rode north along the coast. There were Nell, and her two small sons, Harry and Bran. There was Mabel, her long-time maid and confidante. There was Dame Kathrein, who'd joined Nell's household after the December death of her lady, Nell's sister Isabella. There were Rhonwen, Harry's young Welsh governess, and Philomena, who was wet-nurse to sixteen-month-old Bran. Then there were six knights of Nell's household, who'd accompanied their lady more for status than safety; even in those lawless times, few men would have been so foolhardy as to molest the sister-in-law of so formidable a lord as Frederick. Lastly, there were two grooms and several castle dogs and even a few village children, trailing at a cautious but curious distance.

Kathrein was not surprised that Nell should have chosen to dine outdoors; in an age in which lords moved frequently from one manor to another, it was quite common to eat meals by the roadside. What did surprise her, though, was that Nell had thought to include her young sons. It was Kathrein's experience that ladies of noble rank were not attentive mothers; nor were they expected to be. Yet here was Nell, the King's sister, Countess of Leicester and Pembroke, kneeling in the sand by the water's edge, helping three-year-old Harry to build a soaring castle of sand and shells. Kathrein could only marvel.

"Here, lad," Rhonwen said, handing Bran half a peeled orange. "Try not to drop it into the sand." She watched the little boy totter toward his mother, then lay back comfortably on the blanket. "How warm it is. A fair land, this Apulia, but so flat! I miss the mountains of Eryri."

Mabel did not answer; she did not approve of Rhonwen, thought her to be lazy and cheeky and altogether too Welsh. Kathrein said, "There are mountains to the north," but merely out of politeness; she was still watching Nell play with her children. "I'd not have expected a lady so highborn to be such a doting mother," she confessed, and Rhonwen shrugged.

"I'd never given it much thought. Mayhap it is because she misses Lord Simon." The day was unseasonably balmy, even for Apulia, and Nell and Rhonwen had removed their veils and wimples. Several shepherds were now coming up the road, driving some malnourished goats. They were young and darkly handsome, and Rhonwen could not resist giving them a sidelong smile, hoping to shock Mabel. But they did not even notice; their eyes were riveted upon Nell's flaxen-silk hair. Rhonwen gave a sigh of mock regret; blondes were even rarer here in Apulia than in her Wales. She helped herself to the rest of the orange, then glanced over at Kathrein. "Were you with your lady very long?"

"Six years. I was London born and bred, but I came out with Lady Isabella at the time of her marriage to the Emperor."

Rhonwen leaned forward. "Are the tales told of him true? Does he really keep a harem of Saracen harlots?"

"Indeed he does, and cares not a whit who knows it! Whilst my poor lady, may God assoil her, was kept sequestered, verily like a nun. The day after the wedding, he sent all her English maids away, save only Dame Margaret, her old nurse, and me, and then he handed her over to his Saracen eunuchs, who watched her like hungry hawks!"

This was gossip, not revelation; the Emperor's scandalous private life was an open secret throughout his domains. Rhonwen's eyes flicked toward Mabel. "My French . . . it is not always so good," she said innocently. "Tell me, what is this . . . eunuch?"

Mabel's mouth tightened noticeably, but Kathrein grinned, entered willingly into the spirit of the game. "A eunuch is a poor wretch who still suffers from the most common of male itches, but who has lost the wherewithal to scratch it," she said, and both women laughed. Mabel said nothing, turning to make sure the knights were out of earshot.

Rhonwen had reached under her skirt, was stripping off her stockings. She wriggled her feet luxuriously in the sun-warmed sand, then offered the rest of the orange to Mabel, a peace offering the older woman coldly spurned. Rhonwen shrugged again, popped an orange slice into her mouth. "Tell me of your lady. Was she young, fair to look upon like our Lady Nell?"

Kathrein's smile faded. "Very fair, and too young to die. She was twenty-seven, just a twelvemonth older than Lady Nell."

"It was God's will," Mabel said sadly. "Scriptures say, 'In sorrow shalt thou bring forth children.' "

"Sorrow she had, in plenitude." The sand had muffled the sound of Nell's footsteps. She stood for a moment looking down at them, then sat on the blanket. "Enough sorrow for a lifetime," she said bitterly, "even such a pitifully brief lifetime as hers. God's will—or Frederick's?"

Isabella was Frederick's third wife to die young, the second to die in childbirth, and his enemies were already putting about malicious rumors of poison. The three women stared at Nell in shocked silence, but only Rhonwen dared to ask. "Do you think, Madame, that Frederick killed your sister?"

"If you are asking whether I think he murdered her, of course not. But yes, he did kill her. His jealousy killed her, Rhonwen. What sort of life did he give her? Henry might as well have wed her to the Caliph of Baghdad, for he'd have kept her no less cloistered. Four children in six years, cut off from all she knew and loved, her family, her friends, banned from his court, never seen in public, always under the eyes of his God-cursed eunuchs, his spies. My brother Richard spent four months with Frederick at Terni on his way home from the Holy Land, and he was allowed to see Isabella but once in those four months—her own brother!"

There was anger in Nell's voice, but there was pain, too, and the other women hastily sought to offer comfort, each in her own way. Mabel pointed out that woman's lot is rarely an easy one, while Kathrein felt constrained by fairness to say that Frederick had provided Isabella with great luxury. Rhonwen sat up, gave Nell a probing look. "I would die if I were caged up like that; my very soul would shrivel. I suspect,

Madame, that so would yours. But mayhap your lady sister had not our need for freedom. She had a crown, after all, was surrounded by splendor. It may be that was enough for her."

But Nell's imagination, while undeniably vivid, was flawed in that she measured all griefs, all needs, by her own. "How could it be?" she demanded, so passionately that none dared dispute her. "You think a crown is a magic talisman, that it warrants happiness? I daresay Isabella could have told you otherwise! So could my sister Joan, for she found precious little contentment as Queen of Scotland. On her last visit, just ere she was stricken with that fatal fever, she begged Henry to let her stay in England. Of course he could not allow it, would have sent her back to Scotland had she not sickened, died . . ."

Her voice trailed off. She turned, stared out to sea, toward the sun-bright silhouette of Sant' Andreas Island. "First Joanna, then Joan, and now Isabella. In just four years, I've lost all my sisters . . ."

That was not true; she had four half-sisters, born of her mother's second marriage to Hugh de Lusignan. But none of the women were so foolish as to remind her of that now. Mabel reached over, touched Nell's arm. "At least the Lady Joanna's life was a happy one."

"But of course it was! After all, she did marry a Welshman," Rhonwen interrupted, to Mabel's annoyance and Nell's amusement. "And all know Welshmen make the best husbands and lovers." Adding impishly, "Although I've been told that Frenchmen do right well, too!"

"Yes," Nell said, "they do, indeed." But her smile was fleeting. They knew why, understood her fears. Her brother Richard had returned from the Holy Land months ago; so had her cousin, the Earl of Salisbury. Why had Simon not returned, too?

"I am sure your lord is safe and well, Madame," Kathrein said, as reassuringly as she could. "You must not despair, must not torment yourself for naught."

Nell picked up a handful of sand and sifted it through her fingers, let the wind blow it away. "For naught, Kathrein? My husband's brother, Amaury, died on crusade; many men did. I have not heard from Simon for two months. For all I know, he may be dead, too."

Mabel and Kathrein were silent, too honest to deny that Death's favorite hunting ground was the blood-soaked soil where Christ once walked. Rhonwen, however, heeded voices more mystical, more intuitive. "You love him, Madame," she said. "You know his heart, the secrets of his soul. As his joy is yours, so, too, is his pain. If he were dead, you would know it. You'd not need to be told; you would feel it."

Nell's mouth curved in a shadowy smile. "Ah, Rhonwen, belief comes easily to you, for your people are poets. But the Plantagenets spring from less visionary stock. And yet . . . and yet I do think that if Simon were dead, I would know. Somehow I would sense it. How could I not?"

She reached then for the basket, withdrew a wine flagon. "Rhonwen, will you fetch Philomena and the boys? And Kathrein, you tell the men it is time to eat."

Rhonwen rose languidly, brushing sand from her skirt. But she'd taken only a few steps before she stopped. "Look, Madame, someone is coming."

Mabel shaded her eyes, but could see only a blur of sun-bleached sand. Hopelessly myopic herself, she much resented Rhonwen's claims to vision an eagle might envy. "What do you see, Rhonwen?" she asked maliciously. "More Sicilian shepherds?"

"A knight is coming up the road. My guess, Madame, is that he seeks you, bears a message of some urgency."

"How could you possibly know all that?" Mabel snapped. "Your Welsh second-sight, I daresay?"

Rhonwen smiled, quite unfazed. "He is too well mounted for a local villager, so he must come from the castle. And I can tell he is a knight from the way the sun strikes his hauberk; can you not see that, too, Mabel?"

Nell had risen reluctantly to her feet. "You'd best help me with my veil and wimple, then, Kathrein. He does come on fast; I wonder what—" She stopped so abruptly that she drew all eyes. The flagon slipped from her fingers, spilled onto the sand. "My God . . ." And then she picked up her skirts, began to run.

"Madame!" Her knights had been dicing on a level stretch of sand. The game forgotten, they scrambled to their feet in alarm, hastening after Nell. But she ignored their shouts. Her hair had come loose about her shoulders, and she splashed heedlessly into tidal pools, soaking her skirts to the knees, never taking her eyes from the man on the white stallion. He reined in before her, sending up a spray of sand, and then reached down, in one smooth motion lifting her off her feet, up into his arms, much to Rhonwen's delight.

"Well done!" she cried. "Did you see that, Mabel? He rides like a Welshman, in truth, like one born to the saddle—" At a sudden tug of her skirt, she looked down, into Harry's bewildered blue eyes.

"Mama is kissing that man," he said, and Rhonwen laughed.

"That she is, Harry, that she most certainly is!" She laughed again, then gave the little boy a hug. "Come, lad, let's go meet your father."

Harry took her hand, clung tightly. His mother had often talked to him of his father's exploits, his battlefield bravery, and he'd been yearning for Simon's return. But now that Simon was actually here, a dark, gaunt stranger in a travel-stained surcoat, surrounded by laughing, jostling knights, his arm possessively around Nell's waist, Harry felt suddenly shy, uncertain, no longer sure he wanted this man to come back, this man he did not remember.

"Harry!" Simon smiled at his son, but to his disappointment, the child shrank back. Nell looked no less distressed. It was Rhonwen, however, who was the first to comprehend.

"You're so tall, my lord," she murmured. "I think it scares him." Seeing that his son was indeed staring up at him as if his head were scraping the clouds, Simon reached down, swung the boy up into his arms. Harry was startled, for a moment seemed about to resist. But he was a good-natured child, and his protest died on his lips as he realized that he was now taller than his mother, her maids, most of the knights.

Philomena had just joined them, holding Bran by the hand. Simon set Harry back upon the sand, knelt by his second son. "Well, now," he said, "so you are Simon."

The child scowled. "No," he insisted, "no, I am Bran!"

Simon turned quizzically toward his wife, and Nell stepped forward, put her hand on his arm, as if needing physical reassurance of his return. "Did you not get that letter then? We christened him Simon, as you know. But so dark he was that Rhonwen began to call him Bran, saying his hair was black as a crow's wing, and it seemed to stick. You do not mind, Simon? It does spare us the confusion of having two Simons under one roof, love!"

Simon looked down at his small son, who stared right back. Bran did not have Harry's bright blue eyes; his were grey, darker than Simon's, almost black, narrowed now in sudden suspicion. Simon grinned, said, "Bran you are then," and when, after a moment, the little boy grinned back, Simon felt—however absurdly—that he had passed some sort of test.

Nell's household knights were crowding around, eager to welcome Simon home. Nell was content to cling to his arm, to caress his face with her eyes. He looked thin to her, and very tired, in need of a shave. She did not at first pay heed to what he was saying; she did not care when his ship had dropped anchor in the harbor, cared only that he had come back to her.

"Are you hungry, Simon? We have a basket full of food, a cured ham the local people call prosciutto, fruit, Gallipoli wine, and—"

Simon was shaking his head. "We have to return to the castle, Nell. I sailed with the Duke of Burgundy, and he awaits us back in the great hall."

Nell felt a sharp stab of disappointment; she wanted nothing so much now as to be alone with her husband. But so highborn a guest could not be neglected. She was making a mental list of all that must be done for his comfort when Simon said, "We will be returning to Burgundy with him, and he does not want to tarry in Brindisi. I told him we could be ready to depart in two days' time; I assume that will present no problems?"

There was a collective catch of breath from the women; to move a household the size of theirs was a massive undertaking, only somewhat less complicated than the transport of troops to the Holy Land. Nell's maids now eyed her apprehensively, but she managed to choke back her indignant protest. "Ere we return to the castle, Simon, I would have a word with you in private."

They walked hand in hand to the ocean's edge. "I've never seen any waters as blue, as clear as these southern seas," Simon said. "I wondered at times if my memory was playing me false, but your eyes truly are as blue as Il Mare Adriatico. I brought you back a sapphire-star necklet; your eyes will put it to shame."

Even while courting, he had not been lavish with compliments; she'd learned to treasure them all the more for their infrequency. Yet now his words barely registered with her, so intent was she upon what she must ask of him.

"Simon . . . these past fifteen months have been the most lonely, the most wretched time of my life. I cannot bear to be parted from you. Promise me, beloved, promise me you'll not leave me again."

His hands tightened on her shoulders. "Nell, I cannot. Even ere I sailed from Acre, rumors had reached us of the coming war between England and France. Henry is my King, my liege lord. When he calls upon me for help, would you have me refuse him?"

Nell had not truly expected any other answer, but it hurt, nonetheless. She made an enormous effort, mustered up a plaintive smile. "Must you always be so unsparingly honest? Just once, could you not comfort me with a lie?"

"Men who say possession slakes passion do not know whereof they speak. I missed you, Nell; to be honest, far more than I expected. Never doubt that you hold my heart," he said softly, and then his mouth quirked. "Or any other body parts that you care to claim!"

Nell's laughter was rueful. "Oh, Simon, how ever are we to wait until tonight?"

A loose strand of hair had blown across her face, veiling her in a sudden mist of sun-burnished gold. He entwined the bright threads around his fingers, slowly brushed them back from her cheek; her skin felt hot to his touch, and very smooth. "We'll not wait," he murmured, saw her lips part in a dazzling smile.

"But what of the Duke of Burgundy?"

"Hugh is young. Once he sees you, he'll understand," Simon said, and Nell laughed again. He slid his fingers under her chin, along her throat, and she sighed, leaned against his encircling arm.

"Let's go back," she said huskily. "Now . . ." But then he felt her body stiffen, saw those blue eyes wide in dismay. "Jesú, I did forget! Simon, we cannot make love this day; it is forbidden by the Church."

Simon was no less dismayed. But according to the teachings of their Church, a menstruating woman was unclean, and no man could lay with his wife at the time of her purgation; if he did, he must then fast forty days in penance. "How many days must we wait?"

"Days? Oh, no, love, I do not have my flux. But it is Sunday, and even worse, it is Candlemas!"

Simon was silent for a moment, considering. Under Church doctrine, a man could not have carnal knowledge of his wife on any holy day, on Fridays, Sundays, or Wednesdays, during Advent or Lent or on Rogation Days. But Simon suspected that this particular Church stricture was flouted more than any other. It was, he thought, for certes the most difficult discipline the Church did demand of her sons and daughters.

"Simon?" There was such longing in the look Nell now gave him that he made up his mind. It had been so long, so many nights when he'd lain awake, stifling, hot nights in which memory perfumed the air with Nell's favorite fragrance and Brindisi had seemed a world away.

He reached out, drew her back into his arms. "I think," he said, quite seriously, "that God will understand, too."

14

Pons, English Gascony
Duchy of Aquitaine

June 1242

HENRY's war was not popular with his English barons. They balked at financing yet another attempt to regain the lost Angevin empire. Most saw no justification for breaking the truce with France, and they were to a man highly suspicious of the motives of

Henry's chief allies, his mother, Isabelle, and her husband, Hugh de Lusignan, Count of La Marche; Hugh and Isabelle had a deplorable history of betrayals and double-dealing, had too often sought to play Henry off against Louis, the young French King. But Henry overrode all objections. After extorting money from the Jews and draining the Irish Exchequer, he sailed on May 9 from Portsmouth, taking with him his pregnant Queen, his brother Richard, six Earls, three hundred knights, and thirty casks of silver pennies.

SIMON and Nell had been forced to detour far to the south, for all Poitou north of the River Charente was now in the hands of the French King. It was not until early June, therefore, that they reached Pons.

As they rode into the castle bailey, they were effusively welcomed by its seigneur, Reginald de Pons, one of Henry's inconstant Poitevin allies. The next face they saw, though, was one dear to them both.

Rob de Quincy did not even wait for greetings to be exchanged. "A girl," he exclaimed, "born on Shrove Tuesday!" Accepting their congratulations, he prepared to talk at length of his baby daughter. "I think she'll have Elen's brown eyes, though Elen says it is too early to tell—"

Simon made haste to interrupt. "We are indeed happy for you, Rob. Tell me, what news of the French? The last I heard, they were laying siege to Frontenay Castle."

"It fell six days ago. Even worse, Hugh de Lusignan's cousin Geoffrey has yielded Vouvant Castle to Louis without a struggle."

Simon shook his head in disgust. "Now why," he said, "does that not surprise me? I know local legend claims the de Lusignans trace their descent from the fairy Queen Melusine, but I'd wager you could find Judas somewhere in their family tree, too."

That brought laughter, directly behind them. Turning, they saw William Longsword, Earl of Salisbury, striding toward them. Will was Nell's first cousin, for his father had been an illegitimate half-brother to King John. He had become quite friendly with Simon during their months in the Holy Land, and Simon was very pleased to see him here, for he was beginning to suspect that they were in need of all the seasoned soldiers they could find.

Will was grinning widely. "Loath as ever to speak your mind, eh, Simon? If nothing else, this should be a right lively campaign!"

"Do not go far, Will; I want to talk to you about the campaign. But now my wife and I must seek out the King . . . and her lady mother." Simon glanced at Nell as he spoke, read such reluctance in her face that he at once made an excuse to take her aside.

"Nell? What is amiss?"

Nell bit her lip. "You'll think me foolish, Simon, but I find myself uneasy at the thought of facing her. I've not seen her for twenty-four years. What do I say to her?"

"She is the one who should feel discomfort, not you, Nell, for it was she who made the choice to leave her children, to return to Angoulême."

"She is a stranger to me, Simon, and—and I do not think I shall like her. The stories I hear—her tempers, her arrogance, her treachery. And yet she was not like this whilst she was wed to my father. What changed her so? I know she found it hard to be merely a Countess when for sixteen years she had been a Queen. And then, too, she and Hugh have so many children; mayhap it is concern for their prospects that has made her so grasping . . ."

Simon was touched by the echoes of bewilderment in his wife's voice; at that moment she looked very young to him, and open to hurt. "Who can say what causes a spirit to sour? But I think we need look no further than her marriage bed. During all the years of her marriage to John, she never meddled in English politics, never interfered in the governance of the realm. Yet no sooner did she wed de Lusignan than she began to intrigue, to lure Henry into foolhardy schemes against the French, to aid and abet de Lusignan in all his knavery. So it would seem that there is truth in the adage 'Qui cum canibus concumbunt cum pulicibus surgent.' "

Nell looked blank, for her education had not been as extensive as his, and he smiled at her. " 'He who lies with dogs will rise with fleas.' " Adding under his breath, "I do hope to God that will not hold true for Henry, too."

Now it was Nell's turn to offer assurance; she knew how pessimistic he was about this campaign. She squeezed his hand, then lifted her chin. "Come," she said. "Let us find my mother."

THERE had been a period in Nell's life when she'd become intensely curious about the mother who'd left her so long ago, and she'd pressed all who'd known Isabelle to plumb their memories on her behalf. To Joanna, Isabelle had been "the loveliest sight that ever filled my eyes." Henry had spoken wistfully of a woman "fair as any angel, who always smelled of roses." But it had been Llewelyn's response that had lodged in Nell's memory. "Isabelle," he had laughed, "did always put me in mind of a very sleek and very contented, cream-fed cat."

Within ten minutes of meeting her mother, Nell found herself silently saluting Llewelyn's insight. Isabelle did indeed seem like a cat. But John's pampered and cosseted pet was now a high-strung, wary creature, inscrutable, elegant, haughty, claws never fully sheathed. Although in her mid-fifties, Isabelle was still a handsome woman. Her veil and wimple were softly draped, disguising the inexorable inroads that aging had made upon a once-breathtaking beauty of face and figure. The body was still slim, testified to the iron discipline of a woman who'd learned to measure every mouthful, and the face was artfully made up. But there was no contentment in the sapphire-star eyes, no peace, and that, far more than the passing years, had been Isabelle d'Angoulême's most implacable enemy.

"I've been looking forward to your arrival," Isabelle said to Simon, revealing a still seductive smile. "I've heard some intriguing tales of your exploits in the Holy Land. Although I suspect you stir up turmoil wheresoever you go!" The blue eyes flicked back to her daughter. "I've been eager, of course, to meet you, too, Nell. I've been told that, of all John's children, you are the one most like me."

"I have your coloring," Nell said politely.

Isabelle's laughter was faintly sardonic. "Yes . . . that, too," she murmured. "Well, I suppose you must be curious about your half-brothers. I'll present them to you at dinner, now will just point them out to you. There is Hugh, my firstborn; he did turn twenty-one but a few weeks ago. And that is Guy, over by the hearth. I do not see Geoffrey at the moment, but he looks like his brothers, tall, fair-haired. Whatever else my enemies say of me, I do have very handsome children!"

Even as she spoke, a strikingly lovely young girl was approaching them; she so resembled Nell that Simon knew at once she must be another of Isabelle's brood. "You are just in time, dearest. May I present my daughter Isabella?"

Nell's social graces now stood her in good stead, allowed her to acknowledge the introduction with aplomb, to show none of her inner agitation. It was not that uncommon for Norman-French lords to bestow the same Christian name upon legitimate and illegitimate offspring, as King John had done with Richard Plantagenet and Richard Fitz-Roy. But this was not such a case. Nell looked at the girl, at the wide-set blue eyes, the skin like rose petals, the somewhat sulky red mouth, and she could think only of the dead sister who'd been cheated of so much— even her own name. How had Isabella felt when she'd learned of her mother's choice? Had it seemed like a repudiation to her? It did to Nell.

"What are your plans for the campaign, Nell? Shall you return with me to Angoulême, there await the outcome of the war?"

"Thank you, no," Nell said hastily. "Simon thinks it would be safer for me to accompany Henry's Queen to Bordeaux." Isabella had drawn Simon aside, was flirting with him so blatantly that Nell's temper flared.

Simon seemed more ironically amused than bedazzled, but Nell felt a jealous pang, nonetheless. Her mother was watching her watch Simon and Isabella; annoyed that Isabelle had noticed her distraction, Nell forced a tight smile. "My sons are in Bordeaux already, awaiting my arrival. I have two boys, named after Henry and Simon."

"And a third one on the way, no?"

Nell was taken aback. "I was so sure I did not show yet!"

"Dearest, if there is any subject with which I am all too familiar, it is childbirth! In addition to the four here at Pons, I have five more back in Angoulême, the youngest just eight."

Nell did some swift calculations, concluded that her mother had continued to give birth until well into her forties, and she wondered suddenly if some of Isabelle's discontent might not be attributable to all those pregnancies, year after year, unwieldy, uncomfortable, and life-threatening.

There was a sudden stir in the hall; Henry was entering with Eleanor, then in her seventh month of pregnancy. Henry was beaming, but Eleanor looked rather tired and tense to Nell; as loyal as she was to Henry, she could not have welcomed this war, for her elder sister, Marguerite, was wed to the French King. In the confusion, Nell drew back. She was as uneasy about this meeting with her brother as she had been about her reunion with Isabelle, for she and Henry had last seen each other three years ago, on that dreadful August day at Westminster Palace. Henry gravitated at once into Isabelle's orbit, and Nell found herself wincing on his behalf, so naked was his need.

It was some moments before Henry noticed Nell. They stared at each other across the most perilous of terrains, a pitfall made of memories. Nell took the first step; it was easier than she'd expected.

"My liege." But when she would have curtsied, Henry held up his hand.

"Nay," he said, "greet me not as your King, but rather as the brother who loves you well," and she came toward him, into his outstretched arms.

Once they were together in a sunlit window-seat, however, their silence was heavy with all that lay unspoken between them. "Ought we not to talk about it, Henry?" Nell asked at last.

But Henry's way was denial, not confrontation. "I missed you, Nell. My court was a sadder place for your going. I want you and Simon to come back to England; I want you to come home."

"Of course we will come home, Henry." Nell smiled at her brother, but she felt no relief, only a sorrowful sense of loss. When a shadow fell across them, she knew even before she looked up that it would be Simon's.

"Your mother asked me to fetch you, Henry." Simon's smile was wry. "And when she asks, men tend to obey."

Henry laughed. "That they do!" He was already on his feet. Across the hall, Isabelle beckoned with a smile.

Simon watched in bemusement. He'd not deny the woman spun a subtle web, but this was the third time that Henry had blundered into it. "How old was he when she left England, Nell?"

"Ten," Nell said softly. "He was ten . . ."

THE River Charente shimmered in sunlight; deep and fast flowing, it was the only barrier between the French and English armies. Henry had fortified the crossing at Tonnay, but to Simon's frustration, he had done nothing to secure the bridge at Taillebourg, a few miles north of Saintes, where the English were encamped.

They were discussing Henry's failing now as they rode north along the river bank, Simon and Will of Salisbury and Rob de Quincy and the knights of Simon's household. Two of the latter, Baldwin and Adam, were in particularly high spirits; Simon's former squires, they had been knighted by Simon less than a fortnight ago, and the euphoria had yet to fade. And Simon's new squires, Miles and Luke, eager youths of fifteen, were delighted to be included in this adult scouting expedition. But the men did not share their excitement. Grimly, wrathfully, they were reviewing the events of the past six weeks, tracing the trail of errors that had so far marred their King's campaign.

"What I cannot understand," Will complained, "is why Henry did allow the French to seize the offensive. We landed at Royan on May thirteenth; it is now the twenty-first of July, and what have we accomplished?"

"Nothing," Simon said flatly, "nothing whatsoever. The Gascons have failed to capture La Rochelle. The Count of Toulouse has yet to join our ranks. And most unforgivably of all, Henry has made no attempt to take Taillebourg."

"Has he not been negotiating with the Lord of Taillebourg?" Adam ventured. "Baldwin and I heard that Geoffrey de Rancogne had given the King reason to think he'd refuse the French entry into Taillebourg."

"And that," Simon said bitterly, "is the greatest lunacy of all. Rancogne does despise Hugh de Lusignan, so much so that he even swore an oath that he'd not shave or cut his hair till he'd revenged himself upon Hugh. Do you truly think such a man will join forces with Henry and Hugh? He is playing Henry for a fool, whilst giving the French time to reach Taillebourg. But do you think I could get Henry to see that?"

"You did try, Simon." Rob considered himself to be too old, at forty-five, to be squandering a summer in this meaningless fashion; he cared only that he should return safely to his wife and daughter. But he knew that Simon could not be so stoical, for war was what Simon knew best, and this badly botched campaign had outraged his sensibilities, affronted his soldier's pride.

"For naught, Rob." Simon gestured toward his right, toward the river. "Had we crossed at Tonnay, we could have taken Taillebourg with ease. At the very least, we ought to have burnt the bridge. But no, Henry would wait at Saintes, and now if our scouts have told us true, it may well be too late."

"My lord father once told me that King John was the unluckiest of battle commanders," Will remarked, signaling to his squire to pass him a wineskin. "But Henry, God bless him, is surely the most inept."

None could dispute him. They rode in silence for a time. Although they were not wearing the heavy, cumbersome helms that had begun to replace the old conical helmet with nose-guard and the brimmed kettle hat, they'd thought it prudent to put on their chain-mail armor, and their surcoats only partially shielded their hauberks from the sun's glare. The day grew hotter, the road dustier, their tempers more strained.

"Simon!" Peter de Montfort had ridden ahead. He was now heading back in their direction, coming at a hard gallop. "The French," he gasped. "That whoreson Rancogne has opened the town gates to the French army. The fleur-de-lys is flying from the castle keep. Taillebourg is theirs—and so is the bridge!"

LIKE a small city sprung up overnight, the tents of the French army spread out along the north bank of the Charente, as far as the eye could see. Henry abruptly drew rein, staring across at the enemy encampment. He looked stunned, as if doubting the evidence of his own senses. "We . . . we just have to hold them here," he said, gesturing vaguely in the direction of the narrow stone bridge.

Will stared at him in disbelief, then glanced about in search of Henry's brother. Unlike Henry, who was subject to occasional fits of martial fervor, Richard had never shown much zest for battle, and Will could not quite understand why, for Richard was no coward. But although Richard might never distinguish himself as a battle commander, at least, Will thought, the man does know how to count!

His confidence was not misplaced. Richard needed but one glance to see that the English were dangerously outnumbered. "Mayhap we ought to consider retreating," he began cautiously, for he knew better than any man there how important it was to let Henry save face.

But no de Lusignan had ever been acclaimed for tact. Hugh had been gazing gloomily across at the French army, thinking of all he'd done to give offense to the French King, provocations that were suddenly taking on new and alarming proportions. "Hold them here?" he echoed incredulously. "How? Do you English expect God to favor you with a miracle or two? I suppose He could always smite Louis with a thunderbolt, but—"

"Do not blaspheme," Henry said coldly, for nothing roused his ire quicker than ridicule. "Need I remind you that 'we English' would not be here at all if not for you? Had you not balked at paying homage to Louis's brother, had you not besought my help, swore you'd provide the men if I provided the money—"

To Henry's astonishment, and the indignation of every Englishman within earshot, Hugh de Lusignan snapped, "Indeed I did not!"

"Dare you deny it?" The lie was so brazen that Henry was at a loss. "What of your letters, your pleas—"

"If you're laying blame about, much of it must go to your mother. Isabelle wanted this war fully as much as I did, even more. It was to please her—"

The rest of Hugh's denial was lost; all heads were turning toward the south, all eyes focusing upon Simon de Montfort. Simon reined in before Henry. "I rode upstream a few miles, and it was just as I suspected. The French are building a second bridge, and it's nigh on done. They are about ready to cross, my liege, and when they do, they'll cut off our line of retreat, cut us off from Saintes."

Henry whitened. "What do you suggest, Simon?"

"Your safety must be our first concern. If we fight this day, I do not see how we can keep you from falling into the hands of the French. Let me go to the French King, try to get us a truce."

"You'd do that for me?" Henry asked, and Simon nodded.

Richard guided his mount forward. "Simon is right. We must somehow gain time enough for you to retreat. But you are French-born, Simon, and there may be those who feel you're fighting on the wrong side. Better that I be the one to go. When I was in the Holy Land, I was able to secure the release of a number of French crusaders, and that might well stand me in good stead."

Henry glanced from Simon to his brother. "You are both brave men," he said quietly. "I am indeed well served."

Carrying only a pilgrim's staff, Richard crossed the stone bridge, walked alone into the French encampment. No sooner had he gone than Henry began to fret, to regret allowing him to take such a risk. His regrets were multiplying by the moment. Nothing was happening as it ought. Louis would not harm Richard. Henry told himself that repeatedly, told himself that Louis was an honorable man. He knew that to be true. So why, then, was he making war upon Louis? Trapped there on the banks of the Charente, having to trust to an enemy's honor, Henry found that was a question he could no longer answer.

SIMON reached for a pen, only to have the quill point split. He tossed it aside impatiently, accepting another from his squire.

> Done at the priory of St Eutrope at Saintes, on this the 22nd'day of July, feast day of St Mary Magdalene.

To my dear wife, greetings.
Henry was almost captured yesterday at Taillebourg, but God was with us and Richard was able to gain a brief truce from the French King, making it possible for us to retreat to Saintes. I do not know what will happen next. I think Henry is beginning to realize the folly of having heeded so faithless a man as de Lusignan, but he is stubborn and proud, never more so than when he is in the wrong. And yes, I know that those failings are mine, too! I will write again when I can. God keep you well.

He signed with a flourish, handed the parchment to Miles. "Use my signet to seal it. Tell the courier he is to deliver it to the Countess of Leicester, at the Dominican friary in Bordeaux. Then he is to—"

Simon paused, frowning. The shouting drew louder, and he followed Miles to the window. Black-robed Cluniac monks had halted on the cloister paths, looking puzzled, as knights began to spill out of the guest hall, struggling with hauberks, shouting for their squires, for their horses. Simon jerked the shutter back, saw the Earl of Salisbury running across the grassy inner garth. "Will! What has happened?"

"That lunatic de Lusignan!" Will slowed but did not stop. "He has attacked a foraging party sent out by the French. The Count of Boulogne came to their aid, and a battle is now taking place even as we speak, in the vineyards north of the town!"

PILGRIMS on their way to the holy shrine of St James at Compostella were accustomed to seek lodgings in Saintes, and a small band of these penitents had been unfortunate enough to blunder onto the battle. They scattered in panic, but in fleeing the fighting, three of them just missed being trampled by the knights of Simon's household. The men were skilled riders, though, and managed to turn their horses aside in time, cursing, kicking up clouds of thick red dust. The pilgrims—two women and a youth no more than thirteen—huddled together in terror, too shaken to run.

Simon had swerved off the narrow road. He was astride his favorite war-horse, a high-strung, blooded roan stallion, and it took him some moments to get the destrier back under control. The women were sobbing, pleading for mercy, and he said hastily, "You've no cause for fear." And then he smiled, for he did not want his young squires to accompany him into battle. Although squires were by tradition banned from the actual fighting, their presence upon the field would still put them in some peril. Simon had always found his squires to be a distraction at best, a danger at worst; on more than a few occasions he'd found himself at risk, seeking to make sure of their safety—and Miles and Luke were younger, more untried than most.

He beckoned to them now. "These women are in need of our protection. I want you to escort them back to the town, let no harm befall them."

Both boys looked keenly disappointed; this would have been their first battle. But they knew better than to object, dismounted, and stood watching glumly as the men disappeared around a bend in the road.

Coming onto the fighting, Simon swore in dismay, for all was chaos. Under a blinding noonday sun, men were grappling with one another, stumbling and sliding down the rock-strewn slopes, crying out to St Denis or St George, crashing through the barrier hedges of thorn and bramble, into the fields of ripening grape vines. To Simon, it looked more like a brawl than a battle, a wild mêlée lacking any order or discipline. And as more and more soldiers hastened upon the scene, unable to tell which side was theirs, the confusion spread; men began to die by mistake.

Glimpsing the banner of the Count of Artois, Simon gestured to his men. "There, toward the fleur-de-lys!" He had only ridden a few yards, however, before he veered off, for he'd caught sight of a man much in need of assistance. If given a choice, knights scorned foot soldiers as unworthy opponents, preferred to cross swords with other knights. But the lure of ransom made lords and well-armed knights tempting targets. This particular knight was braced against a large tree, seeking to hold off three circling assailants, lashing out so wildly that it took only a moment for Simon to comprehend the true nature of his plight. Every knight's dread—the man's helm had been knocked awry, his eye-sights wrenched askew, effectively blinding him.

Simon spurred his horse forward, leveling his lance. He was upon them before they realized their danger. As the first man whirled, the lance caught him in the throat. Simon swung his stallion around, but a man afoot was no match for a mounted knight; the other two attackers were already in flight.

The knight had taken advantage of the respite to yank off his helm. His eyes flicked from the dying man at his feet to the fork-tailed lion emblazoned across Simon's shield. "My lord of Leicester, I am in your debt."

Simon dipped the lance in acknowledgment, then let it clatter to the ground; it would be useless in close-quarters fighting. Passing his left arm through the loops of his shield, he drew his sword, for a knight was bearing down upon him from the right. The man's helm hid his face, and he had neither shield nor surcoat, making it impossible for Simon to know whether he fought for England or France. He had no choice, though, moved to meet the charge. But at the last moment, the knight sheered aside, pointed at Simon's arms, and raised his hand in a jaunty gesture of apology.

Simon gave his stallion its head, galloped toward the thick of the fighting. Just ahead of him, he saw Adam unhorse a knight, and felt a throb of pride. Not far away, Will was exchanging blows with two French men-at-arms; he was more than holding his own, though, so Simon didn't stop. An arrow pierced an English soldier in the eye; he screamed, toppled backward, right into the path of Simon's stallion. The horse gathered itself, cleared the body in one smooth leap, and Simon gave it an approving pat. He'd sighted the enemy, a man whose white surcoat flaunted the blood-red cross of the Knights Templar, the "soldiers of Christ," the most militant of all the orders of knighthood.

Simon shouted, and his stallion lengthened stride. The Templar was turning to meet him; they came together with a jarring clash of swords. A second time they circled. The Templar's sword bounced off Simon's shield; Simon's counter-thrust sliced through the other man's reins. The third rush was more deliberate, for by now each had taken the other's measure, knew he was well matched. As the Templar swung, Simon twisted sideways in the saddle. Again they circled. But this time Simon's roan stallion swerved into the other horse, teeth bared, raking a bloody ridge along its neck. The second stallion screamed in rage, reared up wildly, and Simon's sword slammed into the Templar's chest. The chain-mail deflected the blade, but the force of the blow rocked the man backward. Caught off balance, he had no chance of saving himself, hit the ground hard.

Simon reined in his stallion, but his foe lay stunned, helpless. Simon grinned, then patted the roan again. Were they not so hard-pressed, he'd have claimed the man as a prisoner. Not only was he forfeiting a ransom, but a good destrier, too. A pity. He gave the Templar one last regretful look, then sent the stallion charging into a phalanx of cross-bowmen. Prudent men all, they scattered.

The roan had overshot its mark, splashed into a chain of the shallow fish stews that the luckless vineyard owner had dug for drainage. Simon slackened the reins, allowed the destrier to drink from one of the ponds. He was very thirsty himself, but while his helm was liberally punctured with air holes, it made no provisions for drinking. Or for wiping sweat away. He could feel it trickling down his forehead, stinging his eyes; grimacing, he tasted salt on his tongue. His pulse was still racing. But he knew how vulnerable an armor-clad knight was to the heat of the sun, and he forced himself to take deep, deliberate breaths, to give his stallion—and himself—this brief pause. Where was Henry? This was not a battle they could hope to win. Much too many French.

The stallion snorted; its head came up sharply, scenting the air. Cursing himself for his lack of care, Simon turned in the saddle, already knowing what he'd see. The three men were rapidly closing in. The soldier on the left looked to be the weak link in the chain, and Simon aimed the stallion toward him. The man gave ground; Simon would have broken through had the middle man not thrust his halberd toward the destrier's face. Screaming defiance, the stallion reared up. Simon suddenly realized their intent, threw his weight forward to bring the roan down, but not in time. The first man darted under the flailing hooves, drove his sword into the animal's unprotected belly. The horse screamed again, lurched to its knees, and Simon flung himself out of the saddle.

He hit the ground rolling, a trick taught him in his youth by his brother Amaury, one that served him well now, carrying him out of sword-range, giving him the precious seconds he needed to regain his feet.

They advanced warily. Simon kept his eyes on the man with the halberd; he was the most dangerous, his weapon having the longest reach. "You cannot take all of us," he said in a thick Flemish accent. "You're a lord, can afford to buy your freedom. Use your head, yield whilst you can."

"No." There were no trees at hand. The best Simon could do was to try to keep the pond at his back. A risky gambit, for if they ended up in the water, the weight of his armor would drag him down. He watched them come on, without haste; they knew what they were about, mercenaries, most likely. This was a fight to be won fast, or not at all. He waited, letting them get closer, within striking distance, closer still. He feinted suddenly toward the halberdsman, then whirled upon the man moving in on his right. His sword—three feet long, honed sharp enough to split a thread in midair—came down upon bone, with all the force of Simon's body behind the blow. There was a shriek; the man reeled backward, his hand severed at the wrist.

Simon spun around, his sword dripping blood. But the halberdsman was shaking his head; he'd begun to back away. The injured man clutched his stump, rocked back and forth, staring dumbly at his mangled hand. It had fallen into the mud; the fingers still twitched. He seemed in shock, as if not yet comprehending what had befallen him. The third man looked no less horror-struck.

"Fulke! Christ! You bastard, you maimed my brother!" he screamed, and lunged at Simon. It was a wild blow, ill aimed, yet as luck would have it, it connected. The sword slashed at Simon's upper arm, and the point caught upon several of the metal links of his hauberk. As the blade twisted, the rings gave way; pain seared up Simon's arm.

The man called Fulke had dropped to his knees, retching. The halberdsman was gone, in search of easier prey. Simon circled slowly around the last of his assailants. "I'll kill you if I must." He was panting, could feel blood trickling down his arm. "Take your brother and go."

In answer, the man swung again. Simon easily parried the blow. But as he stepped back, he stumbled on the wet grass. The other man flung himself forward, and they both crashed heavily to the ground. For several frenzied moments, they thrashed about by the pond's edge, neither able to gain an advantage. But then Simon managed to roll over on top, and the added weight of his hauberk and helm enabled him to pin the man long enough to unsheathe his dagger. The man gave a frantic heave, carrying them both into the shallows, and Simon thrust the knife up under his ribs. He gasped, his body jerked, and Simon broke free. The water was fast turning red. He gasped again, began to choke. Simon grasped his belt, dragged him back onto the grass. A bubble of blood had formed in the corner of his mouth. As his eyes clouded over, Simon made the sign of the cross, then rose slowly to his feet.

The man he'd maimed continued to moan, oblivious of all but his own pain. Simon ignored him, crossed to where his dying stallion lay. He knelt, rested his hand on the horse's head. The destrier's eyes rolled; its legs kicked weakly, and it made a valiant, futile effort to regain its feet. "Easy," Simon said, "easy, Smoke." His throat tightened; he stroked the muddied forelock, and after a moment or so, he brought up his dagger, drew it swiftly across the animal's throat.

A knight afoot was not likely to survive for long. He'd have to find a loose horse, and fast. He turned back toward the battlefield, stopped abruptly at the sight of the men. They stopped no less suddenly, taking in the graphic scene before them: the two men sprawled in the grass, the dead horse, the blood still wet on Simon's sword. "Do not mind us," the first one said. "We're but passing by!" Giving Simon a very wide berth, they headed for the body of his horse, where they crouched, sought to pry the ivory cantle from the saddle.

Simon watched them wearily, too tired to object. Sheathing his dagger, he started to walk. He'd not gone far, though, before he saw a knight riding toward him. The chivalric code held that it was dishonorable for a knight to ride down a fellow knight, but Simon had no expectations that his attacker would dismount for a fair fight. He stood where he was, and waited, feeling an enormous reluctance to hamstring a horse, yet knowing he was likely to have no choice. The knight was almost upon him before he recognized the six gold lions embossed upon his shield.

Will reined in beside him, his eyes taking in Simon's crimson-stained surcoat. "I trust most of that blood is not yours?" When Simon shook his head, he said, "Christ Jesus, Simon, this is no battle, is more like a God-cursed circus! Half of our men seem to be blundering into each other instead of the French. As for the looting, I swear I saw bodies stripped clean ere they hit the ground. And this you'll not believe, but I even saw a couple of whoresons rutting with a peasant wench, though how they found a woman amidst this madness . . ."

"An unlucky pilgrim. But you're right, Will; this is madness. Where is Henry? We must get him away from here whilst—" Simon stopped, for Will had begun to laugh.

"I'll wager my cousin the King has long since fled the field. His men would see to that!"

Simon frowned. "What are you saying, Will? Are you calling Henry a coward?"

Will was no longer laughing, for there was no more serious charge than to impugn a man's courage. "No," he said. "No, I am not. I had forgotten; you've never fought with Henry ere today, have you? Henry . . . how can I say this? You know how he is, Simon, how easily he gets flustered. Well, on the battlefield, he seems to lose his head altogether. If you'd ever seen him, flailing about with his sword, for all the world like a windmill gone berserk . . ." Will laughed again, ruefully this time. "The Lord God in His wisdom made Henry a King, but He for certes made him no soldier!"

Simon could not help grinning at the image Will had just conjured up. "That is all the more reason, then, to see to his safety," he pointed out, and Will nodded.

"Do not go wandering away," he said. "I'll be back." And he was as good as his word, returned shortly thereafter leading a blood-streaked bay.

Simon and Will could catch no glimpse of the royal arms of England. But they did see a banner flying the silver-crowned lion of Richard of Cornwall, and beneath it they found not only Richard, but John Mansel. Mansel had just murmured a prayer over a dying soldier, all the while clutching a morning-star mace, the favorite weapon of warrior-priests seeking to evade the Church's stricture against "smiting with the edge of the sword." Under his kettle hat, his face was grey with fatigue, but the blood splattering his surcoat was not his own. He told them that Henry was on his way back to Saintes with a bodyguard of one hundred twenty sergeants, and he did not quarrel with Simon's terse verdict, that the battle was lost. The French battle cry of "Montjoye!" now echoed from all quarters of the field.

"If we begin a withdrawal back toward the town, can you hold them here?" he asked, and Simon nodded.

"For a time, yes. Just try not to let the men panic."

It was Mansel's turn to nod. He had odd, amber-colored eyes, heavy-lidded, sharp with suspicion, but as they came to rest now upon Simon, they showed a fleeting, grudging respect. "I hear you fought well this day."

Simon gestured toward the blood-caked spikes of Mansel's mace. "So did you."

Despite Simon and Will's best efforts, the retreat soon turned into a rout. In their haste to reach safety at Saintes, the outnumbered English broke ranks and ran, although others did rally to Simon and Will, and some of the bitterest fighting took place within sight of the city's stone walls. A few of the French became so caught up in the passion of the chase that they foolishly pursued the English into the city itself, only then to find themselves trapped in the town. The French army withdrew in triumph to their encampment across the river, and an eerie silence settled upon the vineyards of Saintes, where so many men had fought and died such a few short hours before.

ONCE they'd pulled his hauberk over Simon's head, his squires saw that the sword's blade had slashed cleanly through his leather gambeson, too. The wound was not deep, but it had laid the skin open from shoulder to elbow, and there had been a fair amount of bleeding. Simon's shirt was so stiff with dried blood that the boys were reluctant to peel it back from the wound, and Simon ended up having to jerk it off himself.

Wincing as if the pain were their own, they made haste to obey when he bade them fetch verjuice, pour it over the injury. Blood was oozing out again, and they would have torn a perfectly good pillow cover into bandages had Simon not tossed them his bloodied shirt, suggested they make do with that. Now that he was stripped to the waist, they could see the ugly bruises spreading across his ribs, discoloring rapidly, and they began to argue as to which salve could best ease their lord's discomfort. Simon slumped back in his chair, closed his eyes. After a time, a wine cup was pressed into his hand; he glanced up, saw Peter de Montfort smiling down at him.

"Men are talking of your exploits, Simon. You gained glory for yourself this day."

"But alas, not so much as a farthing of ransom money," Simon said dryly. Seeing Baldwin standing in the open doorway, as if hesitant to enter, Simon beckoned to him. "You acquitted yourself well, Baldwin. All in all, we did our best. Though I lost Smoke . . ." He sighed, only belatedly became aware of the younger man's silence. In the five years they'd been in his service, Baldwin and Adam had become inseparable companions, so constantly together that those in Simon's household had jokingly begun to call them Sun and Shadow. And now Baldwin stood alone in the doorway, tears welling in his eyes.

Simon pushed his chair back. "Adam? He is dead?"

Baldwin blinked. "I do not know, my lord. I . . . I saw him fall . . ."

The squires froze, not daring to move. Peter made a sorrowful sign of the cross. All watched Simon. He had begun to pace. "Christ wills it," he said, very low. But his rage was growing, a hot, heedless rage born of grief, blind to consequence. "Had he died in the Holy Land, it would have been for the glory of God Eternal. But to die in a wretched village vineyard, and for what? For a King's folly, a rebel baron's greed! Where is the justice in that?"

"Simon!" The hurrying footsteps, the raised voice were Rob's. "You'd best come to the King's chamber. Simon, the man intends to hold Saintes against the French!"

Simon's eyes were very dark, utterly opaque. "Has he gone mad?"

"I can only tell you what he says, that he'll not retreat—"

Simon was no longer listening. Grabbing a tunic, he started for the door, as Miles cried out a plaintive protest. "My lord, wait! We've not yet bandaged your wound!"

But his plea was cut off by the slamming door. Rob turned toward Peter, who said bleakly, "Simon just learned that Adam is dead."

Rob swore. "Christ keep us all, for I've just made a grievous mistake."

HENRY's anger was threaded through with unease. His decision to defend Saintes had been an impulsive one, the response of raw pride. The reaction of his barons was so adverse, though, so resistant that he'd begun to have second thoughts. To a man—his cousin Will, his brother Richard, the Earls of Winchester and Norfolk, the young Earl of Gloucester, Hugh de Lusignan, even John Mansel—they insisted that the town was indefensible, so vehemently that Henry found himself wondering if they might be right. But he'd staked out a position for himself, did not know how to retreat with grace.

"The lot of you suddenly sound as timid as nuns," he said testily. "I'm not asking you to defend a rabbit hutch, but a town I've spent six weeks fortifying. The city walls are made of sturdy ashlar stone, not Ruayn cheese!"

Hugh de Lusignan gave a loud snort. The day's defeat had brought home to him just how vulnerable he was to the wrath of the French King. Henry could sail blithely back to England, but he'd have to come to terms with Louis, and he knew how harsh, how humiliating those terms would be. He was not feeling charitable, saw no reason to indulge his stepson's posturing now that Henry had proved such a worthless ally, and he said scornfully,

"We'd be better off with the Ruayn cheese; at least that would fill our bellies. Just how do you expect to feed our army? Mean you to go from door to door, plundering every larder? Even then, we'd run out of food long ere Louis ran out of soldiers. Christ, within a fortnight we'd count ourselves lucky to be eating rats!"

With the sole exception of the indignant Henry, the men agreed with Hugh, though it galled them to admit it. Even had Hugh not been so arrogant, they would have disliked him, but he made it easy for them. Will spoke for all when he drawled, "Speaking of rats, mayhap you can tell me if it is true, my lord, what men say, that rats are ever the first to abandon a sinking ship?"

Hugh leaped to his feet. "Say what you mean, Salisbury!"

Will's smile was cold. "I thought I did."

"Enough!" Henry glared at them both, but neither man seemed daunted by his displeasure. They continued to eye each other with undisguised rancor.

The Earl of Norfolk shifted impatiently in his seat. He'd distinguished himself on the battlefield that day, was now bruised and sore and short-tempered in consequence. Glancing toward Richard, he said, "You talk to him, my lord, make him see the folly of this."

Richard looked troubled, started to speak. But Henry forestalled him. "The decision is not my brother's to make, my lord Norfolk. It is mine."

The ensuing silence was an uncomfortable one for Henry. However much he sought to feign indifference, he could not be impervious to their disapproval. Their criticism rankled, and their doubts were contagious. He moved toward the table, gestured for Mansel to pour from the flagon. His was the right of command. So why must he have to argue for the obedience that was his due? But what if he was wrong, if Saintes could not be held?

When the door opened suddenly, Henry felt a flicker of relief at sight of Simon. He'd put it to Simon, let Simon persuade him—reluctantly—that they should retreat. None could fault him for paying heed to Simon's advice, for even Mansel admitted that Simon was a brilliant battle commander. He smiled at his brother-in-law, said, "It is my belief that we ought to make our stand here, at Saintes. But I value your opinion, Simon. Tell us what you think."

"Why not show you?" Simon said, so curtly that Henry's smile faded. There was a chessboard on the table. Simon strode toward it, picked up one of the ivory chess pieces. "We have here the King of England," he said, and Will sat up straight in his chair, for Simon had selected the pawn. Henry noticed that, too, and color began to rise in his face. Simon reached next for the wine flagon. Flipping up the lid, he poured red wine onto the hearth. By now the silence was absolute, all eyes riveted upon him. "The city of Saintes." He dropped the pawn into the flagon. "The English King has taken up position. The French King then acts—thusly." He slammed the lid shut, with a resounding clang. "Behold," he said, "the battle of Saintes."

Henry was as darkly flushed as the wine dripping down the hearth stones. "How dare you speak to me like that! I find this little game of yours highly insulting. Disagree with me if you will, but by God, you'll show me the respect due me, as your King!"

"Even the Almighty has been known to anoint a fool. The French were once cursed with a King so foolish he was known as Charles the Simple. He finally had to be confined for his own good." Simon heard Henry gasp, but he continued on, relentlessly. "Your chambers at Windsor Castle have barred windows to ward off assassins, but I expect they could be put to other use if need be."

Henry found it almost impossible to believe that anyone would dare to speak so contemptuously to him. "I . . . I never heard such wild talk! Are you threatening me?"

"You did ask for my opinion," Simon said harshly. "Now you have it." He felt no remorse, but his anger had peaked, leaving him suddenly drained, sapped of all emotion, his an exhaustion both of body and soul. He was turning away when Henry grabbed his arm.

"Damn you, de Montfort, get back here! You'll go nowhere till I give you leave!"

Simon swung around, wrenching free of Henry's hold. But Henry had already recoiled; he was staring down at his hand. Will had risen in alarm. He, too, now saw the darkening splotch along the sleeve of Simon's tunic.

Henry's eyes at last shifted from his bloodied palm, up to Simon's face. "Men died for you this day," Simon said, and when Henry did not speak, he turned, walked from the chamber.

No one else moved. After an interminable time, Henry crossed to the table, moving like a man in a daze. There he splashed wine onto a napkin, scrubbed until his hand was clean.

"Get out," he said. "All of you, get out!"

One by one, they did.

THE man in the bed was young; limp, fair curls and a smattering of freckles made him look even younger, gave an added poignancy to his plight. Drenched in sweat, his lips bitten raw, he was mumbling incoherently, drifting in a fevered darkness, in that dangerous twilight between sleep and death. "Is that Adam?" Rob asked softly, and Simon nodded.

Rob had heard that the French King had sought a brief truce so both sides could recover their dead and wounded. "What are his chances, Simon?"

"The doctor says that he is in God's hands." Simon's eyes were deeply circled, shadowed with weariness, bereft of hope. "His arm was so badly mangled it could not be saved. We had to get him drunk, hold him down whilst the doctor cut it off at the elbow . . ."

Rob grimaced, waved away a squire's offer of ale. "Simon . . . Henry has just given the command to withdraw from Saintes, to fall back upon Pons."

Simon had been about to bite into a slice of honeyed bread. He paused, then set the bread down untasted. Glancing again at the delirious man in the bed, he beckoned to the doctor. "When the French take the town, tell them that the Earl of Leicester will stand good for this man's ransom."

The doctor nodded, started to ask if Simon would also assume the costs of burial, but thought better of it. Simon moved to the window. It was just past sunrise, and the grass still glistened with night dew. The sky was a softly shaded blue, fleeced with wisps of cotton-white clouds.

Rob had joined them; they stood for several moments breathing in the familiar scents of a summer dawn. "At least he did change his mind, Simon. At least he did listen."

Simon's mouth twisted. He said nothing. Church bells were sounding; Morrow Mass was about to begin.

AT Pons, Hugh de Lusignan slipped away; two days later, he and Isabelle humbly submitted to the French King. So did most of Henry's Poitevin allies.

Henry moved on to Barbezieux, where a French crusader ransomed by Richard in the Holy Land sent a warning that the French meant to surround the city, to take Henry captive. The English hastily retreated toward Blaye, in such disorder that the road south was strewn with broken carts, lamed horses, even the wounded. From Blaye, Henry fled to Bordeaux, where his Queen had just given birth to a daughter. There he holed up, saved only by the vagaries of fate; the pursuing French army was stricken with the bloody flux, forced to withdraw to the healthier lands of the North.

A sweltering, humid August passed into a dry, sun-scorched September. Henry's disgruntled lords lost all patience with their King. Roger de Quincy, Earl of Winchester, was the first to go, soon followed by his brother, Rob, and the Earl of Hereford. Henry quarreled bitterly with his brother. He had given Richard the county of Gascony as reward for his service at Taillebourg Bridge; now he revoked the grant, and the Earls of Norfolk and Gloucester departed from Bordeaux in disgust, sailed for England. The English forces dwindled daily, while the French sang mocking ballads of Henry's Poitou campaign:

> "They did not stop to spin a tale,
> The English with their barley ale,
> But all of France did dance and dine,
> For barley ale is not worth wine!"

It was early afternoon when Simon and Nell rode into the outer garth of the Benedictine abbey of Sainte-Croix. Simon was helping Nell to dismount in front of the Abbot's lodging when they heard Simon's name called.

Will was hastening toward them. "You are just in time to bid me farewell. Henry wants me to lead an expedition to Périgord." He saw the query in Simon's eyes, and shrugged. "Aye, I agreed. Why not? The pleasures of Bordeaux are beginning to pall!"

"And Henry's fortunes are at ebb tide," Simon suggested, and Will gave a sheepish grin.

"If you make me sound noble, Simon, I'll never forgive you." He kissed Nell's hand with an exaggerated flourish, gave Simon a jolting slap on the shoulder, then turned back. "Henry had another quarrel with Richard this forenoon; we could hear the shouting clear out to the cloisters. You can tell me if it is none of my concern, Cousin Nell, but gossip has it that the Queen was responsible for Henry's change of heart. Is there truth to that?"

Nell nodded. "For once the gossips do speak true. Eleanor did not want to see Gascony go to Richard, felt it should be part of her son's patrimony."

"And who is to hold off the French till the lad is of an age to fight for it? Sometimes I think these southern climes do addle men's brains! Just keep your guard up, Simon, my lad. Cousin Henry is like to be in a foul temper, and you'd make a tempting scapegoat, indeed!"

With a wave and a loud laugh, Will was off. They watched him go, and then Simon said, "Henry sent for me, not you, Nell. There is no need for you to accompany me."

"No?" Nell linked her arm in his. "Had we lived as Christians in ancient Rome, do you think I'd have let you face the lions alone?"

"If my memory serves," Simon said, "the lions always won." But he was secretly glad to have Nell with him. Never had he and Henry been more in need of a mediator than in these strained weeks since Saintes.

Henry looked haggard, his eyes red-rimmed, his mouth pursed. "Richard is returning to England," he said, "leaving me to fight this war alone. What of you, Simon? Are you going to abandon me, too?"

Nell's hand was resting on Simon's arm; she could feel the muscles tense, contract under her fingers. But when Simon spoke, his voice was even. "No," he said. "You are my King. I will stay as long as you have need of me."

Henry expelled an audible breath. "Thank you," he said simply.

Across the room Eleanor and John Mansel watched in disapproving silence. "Henry is too good." Eleanor kept her voice low, but it throbbed with indignation. "How can he forgive Simon after the disgraceful way he behaved at Saintes?"

Mansel, who'd so often deplored Eleanor's influence over Henry, now found himself welcoming it, for a loved Queen could prove a formidable ally, indeed. "Do not fret, Madame," he said, and smiled thinly. "Henry may have forgiven, but you can be sure he has not forgotten."

BELLS were chiming, summoning the friars to Matins. That meant it was well past midnight. Nell sighed, and beside her, Simon stirred.

"Nell? Is it the babe?"

"He's restive tonight." She reached for his hand, placed it on her abdomen. "See for yourself."

Simon propped himself up on his elbow, fascinated by the rippling movement of her skin. "You think you've another lad tucked away in there?"

She smiled. "Did I not tell you about Rhonwen's test? She pricked my finger over a cup of spring water, and when the drop of blood sank, she said that was proof I carried a son. I think she may well be right. This one kicks like a mule, just like Harry and Bran."

Simon gave her his pillow, propped it behind her back. She made herself as comfortable as her pregnancy would permit; she hated feeling so ungainly, so bloated, and she sighed again. Simon reached for her hand, pressed a kiss into her palm.

"I can blame my sleeplessness on our little lad. But what of you, Simon? What keeps you awake at such hours? Beloved, I know you are troubled. Do not shut me out. Share your thoughts with me."

"I cannot," he said softly. "Henry is your brother."

Nell's hand closed over his. "Yes," she said, "Henry is of my blood. But we are of one flesh, you and I, joined in the holy sight of God. Tell me, my heart. Tell me."

Simon turned toward her, moving into a bright splash of moonlight. Although he was not yet thirty-four, he had a streak of silver just above his left temple; Nell liked to tease him about it, claiming he put her in mind of a raven daubed with whitewash. But now the sight touched a protective chord. She realized it was foolish; if any man was well able to look to his own interests, it was surely Simon. And yet it was her secret that sometimes her redoubtable husband seemed very vulnerable to her.

Simon's continuing silence came not from reluctance; he'd been deciding how best to answer her, to make her understand. "I know," he said slowly, "that Christ said we should forgive our enemies not seven times, yet seventy times seven. But it has never been easy for me to forgive a wrong done me or mine. I hardened my heart against Henry, could not forget how he shamed us, forced us into exile. That failing is mine; I freely admit it. Bishop Robert has often cautioned me that a haughty spirit goeth before a fall."

While Nell could find Simon's inflexibility truly infuriating at times, she could never bear to hear him criticized, even if he was the critic. "Yes," she said, "you are a prideful man. But you have reason, my love, more reason than most."

Simon shook his head. "This is different, Nell. What I've seen during these past months . . ." He frowned, searching for the right words. "After that day at Westminster Palace, I could no longer think of Henry as my friend. Yet he was still my King, my liege lord. Allegiance does not depend upon affection. But a King ought to be accountable, too; he has responsibilities as well as rights. And this summer has shown me that I have pledged my honor and loyalty to a man not worthy to rule."

HENRY remained in Bordeaux through the autumn and winter. When his supplies ran out, he had no choice but to rely upon credit, and both Simon and Will incurred heavy debts on their sovereign's behalf. In April 1243 a truce was finally concluded, permitting the French to keep all they'd conquered, and obligating Henry to pay a thousand pounds a year in tribute to his brother-in-law, the French King. Still, he lingered on in Gascony, not departing for England until the following September. Just before he sailed, he outraged the English with a flamboyant gesture of forgiveness, granting the castle of Saintes to his faithless mother and his de Lusignan half-brothers. He landed at Portsmouth on October 9, a staggering 350,000 marks in debt, and demanded a victory procession into London. His English subjects were not amused.

15

Tower of London

February 1244

Senena's arrival in the Great Chamber interrupted Owain's dice game with Edwin de Crecy. She was flushed with the cold, snow melting on her lashes and cheeks, looking for the moment more like an exuberant, lithesome girl than a tense, too-thin woman in her forties, and the young guard was not surprised when Gruffydd took her in his arms, gave her an uncommonly passionate welcome. As they headed toward Gruffydd's curtained bed, Edwin got to his feet. It amused him that Owain always wanted to leave the chamber when his parents were making love; what more privacy could a couple need than linen bed hangings? But he liked Owain enough to humor his quirks. "Lead the way, lad," he said airily, and Owain acknowledged his indulgence with a self-conscious smile.

Behind the bed hangings, Gruffydd and Senena sat very still, listening as the footsteps receded behind the screen. Although they did not need to fear eavesdropping, for Edwin spoke no Welsh, they both felt more secure with him gone, what with so much at stake. "Well? Did you bring it, Senena?"

Reaching into the bodice of her gown, she withdrew a small leather pouch. "Henbane, darnel, black poppy, and dried briony root."

Gruffydd reached for the powder. "You did not go yourself to the leech?"

"No, of course not. I sent the most trusted of our men; I sent Alun."

Fingering the pouch, Gruffydd began to laugh. "I daresay this is the same sleeping draught that whoreson Davydd used at Cricieth. What a rare jest, that it should be his scheme that sets me free!"

It had been so long since Senena had heard him laugh like that. She slid her hand into his. "I bring you naught but good news this day. Alun has found our man—one of the King's servants. He has agreed to unbar a door into the great hall." She saw him frown, and her grip tightened. "It should be safe enough, love; Henry is not in residence, remember? You and Owain need only enter the hall, then make your way into the Blundeville Tower. There is a small postern gate just before you reach the Tower stairwell, Henry's private entrance. It will take you out onto the dock, take you to freedom. I'll have a boatman at the dock, ready to row you across to Southwark, where I shall be waiting. By the time we lose the night, we'll be miles from here, well on our way into Wales."

"Mayhap . . ." Gruffydd sounded dubious. "I would that there was another way. I can put no faith in an Englishman, Senena. I'd not have trusted Our Lord Christ Himself had He been born English. I still think my idea is safer."

"Beloved, we've gone down this road before. Yes, the Tower grounds cover twelve acres, more than enough to shelter two men in search of a hiding place. But Gruffydd, then you'd have to wait till dawn, till the Tower gates were unlocked. Enough tradesmen and servants and soldiers go in and out; you might well be able to mingle with them, mayhap hide in a cart. But my darling, what if you were missed? As soon as your guards discovered that you'd escaped, they'd seal off the Tower, let no man leave the grounds. We cannot take that risk. This way, you'll be gone long ere the sun comes up."

"Only if this man does not betray us. Why should he not just keep the money?"

"There is no greater lure than greed, Gruffydd. He is to get half now, the rest afterward."

That did reassure Gruffydd somewhat. But he'd have gone ahead with their plan in any event. "So be it, then. Make ready to go two days hence."

Senena felt a sudden prickling, excitement indistinguishable from apprehension. "So soon?"

"It has been two and a half years, Senena. Yesterday could not be too soon," he said, and grinned at her, the carefree, devil-be-damned grin of his lost youth, a smile to banish qualms, to break hearts.

"Monday, then," she agreed breathlessly. "I have one more gift for you, my love." And raising her skirt, she showed him the narrow dagger strapped to her thigh.

Gruffydd's eyes seemed as luminous to her as any cat's, a pale, glittering green. He bent over, kissed the soft skin just above the sheath.

SENENA's sleeping draught was as potent as the men could have hoped. Gruffydd and his son looked at each other over Edwin's prone figure, exchanged triumphant grins. Edwin was snoring, did not stir as Gruffydd unbuckled his scabbard. It was a sweet relief, indeed, to feel the familiar weight of a sword at his hip again. "I'll get him into the bed," he said softly. "You fetch the bindings."

"Use this, Papa." Owain was holding out a green tunic. "I never did like that color," he said cheerfully, and Gruffydd used Senena's dagger to cut ties, soon had Edwin securely bound and gagged.

Dropping to his knees, Owain pulled their makeshift rope from under the bed; over the past week, they'd torn all their sheets into strips, painstakingly knotted the pieces together. Gruffydd was pulling down the wall tapestry, and Owain jerked the linen cloth from the table, began to rip it in half. "I'm glad we needed our bed covers for appearance's sake," he said, "else we'd have been sleeping stark-naked!"

Gruffydd laughed. "Life in the King's gilded cage has made you soft, lad. Take care, lest you end up like an Englishman, unable to sleep without a mattress of down and a pillow!"

Owain laughed good-naturedly, although he did wonder if there was truth to his father's jest, for he felt an embarrassing reluctance to leave his pet monkey. He gave the little creature a hazelnut before tossing Gruffydd the braided tablecloth. He had noticed that his father had not found it easy to move Edwin. Too proud to ask for help, he'd been red-faced and panting by the time he'd dragged the guard across the chamber, heaved him up onto the bed. And Owain found himself wondering if his father, too, had not grown soft in captivity, a blade dulled by disuse. As big-boned as he was tall, he carried the added weight better than most, but even on so large a frame, the excesses eventually showed, the thickening middle, the jowled chin—symptoms of boredom, rich food, and the torpor of long confinement. Gruffydd had always assumed heroic stature in Owain's eyes, but there was no denying that he was past his prime, a man just a few weeks shy of his forty-eighth birthday, an age that seemed vast, indeed, from the vantage point of Owain's twenty-five years.

Feeling his son's gaze, Gruffydd looked up, smiled, and Owain flushed. "Fetch that water bucket, lad. These knots will hold better once they're wet."

Owain was quick to comply, and within a few moments, they collected their mantles, moved into the chilled shadows of St John's Chapel.

Gruffydd crossed to the altar, knelt, and murmured a brief prayer. Rising, he said, "I was asking St Davydd to bless our efforts with success. And I know he listened. It's past midnight, which means that this is March first, his name-day."

Owain had forgotten; much cheered, he said, "That is indeed a good omen. Papa . . . Papa, let me be the first one down the rope."

"Do not get motherly on me, lad!" Gruffydd laughed, poked Owain playfully on the arm. With freedom now so close, he felt as if he could get drunk on expectations alone. Scrambling up into the window, he unlatched it, signaled for Owain to tie their rope to one of the heavy, stone columns.

The night air was bitter cold; he felt as if he were inhaling ice. He'd passed all his life upon the alpine heights of Eryri, but as he looked down at the snow-blanketed ground so far below him, he experienced a dismaying jolt of dizziness. He closed his eyes for a moment, then smiled at his son. "Once it's your turn, do not tarry, lad, for it's cold as a witch's teat!" And he swung his legs over the ledge, pushed out into space.

While planning all aspects of their escape, he'd not given much thought to the climb itself, had seen it merely as the means to an end, to freedom. That had been a mistake. Within moments, his arms felt as if they were being wrenched out of their sockets, and every muscle was in rebellion against this unaccustomed abuse. His body had always done what he demanded of it. It had never occurred to him that a time might come when it could fail him, when will alone would not be enough. He fought back this surge of panic, sought to get air into his laboring lungs. He'd make it. Slow and easy. He'd make it.

Already badly winded, he had to rest, and he found a foothold, turning his body sideways as he sought to ease the ache in his arms. The wind caught his mantle, tore him loose from his perch, slamming him into the wall. As he'd balanced himself on the window ledge, he could clearly hear the roaring of Henry's lions, caged down by the wharf. Now he heard nothing but the blood thudding in his own ears, his gasping, broken breathing. He could see Owain's face above him, bleached by the moonlight, and he managed a twisted smile of assurance, made ready to shift his handholds.

When it happened, it was without warning. The ripping noise the rope made as it gave way was muffled by the wind. There was a sudden slackness, and then Gruffydd was falling, plunging backward into blackness. There was a moment or two of awareness, but mercifully no more than that. The last sound he heard was a man's scream, but he never knew if the scream came from him or from Owain.

❧

SENENA had kept a futile, increasingly frantic vigil all night. By the time the horizon had begun to pale, she was shaking with the cold, and with fear. With the coming of light, her boatman had rowed back to Southwark, and he and the other men were watching Senena now, none daring to suggest they return to Aldgate. It was a blustery, overcast day, and the wind gusting off the river knifed through the thin wool of their mantles, sent their hats spiraling up into an ominously grey sky. Shivering, half-frozen, they could only blow upon their chapped hands, stamp their feet, seek to soothe their equally miserable mounts—and wait.

Alun at last braced himself to approach their mistress. "Madame, let us take you home."

"No." Senena was staring across the river. She had yet to take her eyes from the massive stone silhouette of the Tower. "No, you are to take me there."

"Madame, you cannot. The risk is too great. Something must have gone wrong, and if you appear at the Tower so early in the morn, you'll but turn suspicion upon yourself."

"Now," she said.

It was an unpleasant crossing; by the time they'd reached the north bank, they were drenched in icy spray. The water-gate gave them entrance into the outer bailey, and they had to wade through knee-deep snow to reach the gateway into the inner palace ward. The entrance into the White Tower lay to the south, through a stone forebuilding. They had just turned the corner as Edwin de Crecy emerged from the forebuilding stairway. His pallor was evident even at a distance, tinged with the sickly greenish hue of one awakened too abruptly from a drugged stupor. His eyes were swollen and bloodshot; they narrowed now at sight of Senena.

Alun tensed, for the man's hostility was confirmation of all his fears. Senena gave a soft cry; it sounded strangely like a whimper. But as Alun turned, he saw that she was not looking at Edwin de Crecy. She was staring beyond him, staring toward her right. "Madame?" Alun murmured, and then, "Christ!" for he, too, had seen it, now—the trampled snow, the pool of dark, ice-encrusted blood.

SPRING had come late to the River Lledr valley, but on this sunlit Saturday in early May, the wooded hills surrounding Dolwyddelan Castle were aglow with the brightest of nature's colors. Hawthorns were in snowy bloom, and buttercups and rockroses and bluebells were scattered about in dazzling profusion. The river bank was hedged in purple, row upon row of plum-tinted comfreys. Sycamores seemed garlanded, as if for

May Day, in trailing streamers of yellow-gold. Like feathers of orange and blue, butterflies floated upon the morning breeze. One, fanning wings of speckled pearl, even brushed Davydd's cheek. He laughed, lingered a moment longer upon the stairs, his eyes drawn irresistibly to the cloud-sheathed peak of Moel Siabod.

"My lord?" The man hastening across the bailey was one of his grooms. "You may well think me mad, but I know how much stock your lady sets by little 'uns . . ."

That was true enough; Isabella was absurdly fond of animals, to the point where she even refused to take part in hunts. "What have you found this time, Padrig, another baby rabbit?"

Padrig grinned. "Nay, something much more outlandish!" And opening his hands, he showed Davydd his prize, a ball of brightly burnished fur that now revealed itself to be a newly born fox kit. "It's not as if the pelt would be worth anything," he said, as if to excuse his soft-heartedness.

"People find it odd that my wife makes pets of cats. Know you what they'll say about a fox?" But Davydd was already reaching for the tiny cub.

He found Isabella alone in their bedchamber, demanded she close her eyes, and then deposited the kit into her outstretched hands. "Davydd, how sweet!" The fox nipped at her fingers, but she just laughed. She had a gentle, calming way with animals, could establish a remarkable rapport with any creature if given a chance, and Davydd did not doubt that the fox would soon fall under her spell. "It's not weaned," she said. "Cricket is still nursing her last litter; do you think I could get her to accept it?"

"You got her to raise that kitten. So why not a fox foundling?" Davydd knew the fox's future was not promising; if it wasn't killed by one of the castle dogs, it would eventually start raiding the henroost. But he said nothing, not willing to spoil his wife's pleasure in her new pet. She'd not believe him, anyway; reality always seemed to take Isabella by surprise.

Ednyved was expected at any time, and the table was laden with freshly baked wafers, fragrant fruit tarts. Davydd helped himself to one, leaned over to study the map covering one end of the table. Isabella stopped stroking the fox cub, watched her husband, instead. "Davydd, how long ere you go to war?"

"I expect we'll be in the field within a fortnight." He looked up. "Does it bother you, Isabella, that I shall be making war upon the English?"

"No," she said slowly. It was not that she did not want him to fight the English. She did not want him to fight anyone. But that was not a confession she could ever make. War was an inevitable aspect of life; she might as well rail at the coming of winter. Men fought, and women waited. "I know naught of politics, Davydd," she said. "If you say this war must be, I accept that. It is not for a wife to meddle in those matters best left to men."

Davydd laughed. "I was just remembering," he said, "the flaming fights my parents had about 'those matters best left to men.' I've known few women who were not eager to 'meddle.' My mother, for one. My sister Elen, for another. Senena—for certes! My sister Gwladys. Nell de Montfort. Even Henry's Queen. I suspect that a truly docile woman would be as hard to find as Diogenes's honest man!"

Isabella knew he was teasing her, but she felt a faint unease, nevertheless, for she could not keep from wondering if he'd have preferred a woman less dutiful, more spirited. Almost as if he'd read her mind, he crossed the chamber, drew her into his arms, kissed away her qualms. She wrapped her arms around his neck, thinking that it was a dreadful thing to find pleasure in a man's death, for certes a sin. But she could not help it. Davydd was happier this spring than he'd been in the four years since his father's death, and she rejoiced in it . . . even if it meant that she valued Davydd's happiness higher than Gruffydd's life.

Ednyved was to have arrived at noon, but he was now past seventy, afflicted with the "joint evil," and it was well into the afternoon before he and his son Goronwy reached Dolwyddelan. They brought Davydd welcome news. Bitter over his expulsion from Kidwelly Castle, Prince Maredudd ap Rhys Gryg of Deheubarth was now willing to throw his lot in with Davydd.

"That means," Davydd said, "that Gruffydd ap Gwenwynwyn and Gruffydd Maelor will stand alone. Even their kinfolk are with us. I had a message two days past from Gruffydd Maelor's younger brother, Madog Fychan. When we take the field against the English, he'll be there."

"The Welsh are slow to learn, our country's curse." Ednyved propped a cushion behind his aching back. "But even the greatest fools are coming to understand that we hang together or one by one. They've seen what the English Crown has done in these three years past, the castles erected, the forests cleared, the roots put down in Welsh soil. I've spent my entire life striving to keep them out of Gwynedd, as did your father, Davydd, but the fight never ends . . ."

Davydd signaled for a servant to give Ednyved a revitalizing drink of mead. "I think the tide turned for us when Henry appointed those justices to hear Marcher and Welsh pleas. Jesú, it was so brazen! Offering the royal courts as an alternative to the courts of the Welsh Princes, the Marcher lords—Henry might as well have signed a confession of conquest."

Goronwy tossed a tidbit to one of Davydd's dogs. "Have you had any word, Davydd, about Senena? We know how enraged Henry was. Did he punish Senena for her part in that botched escape attempt?"

"I daresay he found much to say to the Constable of the Tower, those hapless guards. But Henry has never been one to turn his wrath upon a woman. Senena was not held accountable."

"Is she still in London?"

Davydd shrugged. "As far as I know; her sons are there. Not surprisingly, she took Gruffydd's death very hard. I was told she fainted at sight of his body."

"Little wonder. When a man falls from a height like that . . ." Goronwy had heard some grisly stories about Gruffydd's death, and he would have liked to ask Davydd if it was true that Gruffydd had been nearly decapitated in the fall. But Isabella was sitting within earshot, and he knew that was not a topic Davydd would wish to discuss in front of his sensitive wife. Curbing his curiosity, he said, instead, "What of Owain?"

"He did feel the brunt of Henry's anger, is being held in close confinement."

Ednyved had been watching Davydd. Leaning forward, he said, "The Abbot of Aberconwy means to petition the King to have Gruffydd's body interred next to Llewelyn's, in the abbey church. Henry has so far refused, but he might relent once his anger cools. What of you, Davydd? Would you object?"

Davydd set his wine cup down. Isabella, too, was waiting for his answer. "No," he said, "I would not object. Gruffydd should be buried in Welsh soil."

There was a moment's silence. To Davydd's relief, he saw that they understood, neither read too little nor too much into his answer. Reaching for the map, he used his dagger to pinpoint his target. "I think we should move first against Henry's new castle at Disserth."

"We ought to make a few raids into Powys, too," Goronwy suggested. "Let Gruffydd ap Gwenwynwyn learn what it'll cost him to be an ally of the English King." Crossing to the window, he opened the shutter, curious as to the sudden clamor. "Damn me if it's not Llelo!" Turning toward Davydd, he said, "Did you not hear me, Davydd? Does that not surprise you any?"

Davydd shook his head. "I've been expecting him."

Ednyved smiled at that, but Goronwy looked skeptical. "Davydd, the lad's been in rebellion against you for the past two years! Granted, he's not done much damage, but he did closely ally himself with Ralph de Mortimer, Senena's brothers, the Bishop of Bangor, men who love you not. Every discontented knave along the Marches found his way to

Llelo's manor at Maesmynan, almost as if it were a court in exile. And yet you say you expected him to come to you?"

"Yes," Davydd said, "I did. In your own words, his rebellion did little damage. Why not? Because his heart was never in it."

"My lord!" The guard was one of Davydd's household teulu; he looked no less startled than Goronwy. "Your nephew, Llewelyn ap Gruffydd, has just ridden in, and alone, by God! Will you see him, and if so, shall we disarm him first?"

"Yes to your first question, no to your second." Davydd got to his feet. Ednyved rose, too, limped to his side.

"No son of Gruffydd's would ever lack for courage," he said. "But Senena will never forgive him for this."

"No," Davydd agreed, "probably not. But I expect he knows that."

Llewelyn's appearance was a surprise to them both. The unhappy, gangling boy Davydd had last seen in the Tower bailey was a tall, wary youth well on the way to manhood. But to Ednyved, it was as if time's boundaries had blurred, giving him a brief, precious glimpse of a beloved ghost lost in memory these fifty years past. "My God, lad," he said, "if you're not the very image of Llewelyn at sixteen!"

Llewelyn gave him one swift, guarded glance, and the illusion faded. The coloring was there, and the stance, the body language. But the boy was more tightly coiled than the man had ever been, far more defensive, and—as young as he was—more deeply scarred. Ednyved smiled sadly, suddenly feeling very old and very tired. Deferring to Davydd, he stepped back, sank down in the window-seat.

Llewelyn slowly unsheathed his sword, just as slowly walked forward. Silently he held out the sword, knelt before his uncle. "I would make my peace with you. Punish me as you will."

He made it sound more like a challenge than a submission, but Davydd understood the raw pride of sixteen. He reached for the sword, then reversed it, handed it back to the boy.

Llewelyn rose, looking not so much relieved as suspicious. "You pardon me? Just like that? Why?"

"Why did you rebel against me?"

Llewelyn frowned, said nothing.

"Because your father asked it of you. Am I right?"

"Yes." A grudging answer, but honest.

"And why do you want to make peace with me?"

This time there was no hesitation. "Because," Llewelyn said, "England is the enemy," and the faintest of smiles touched his uncle's mouth.

"Do I still need to explain why I pardoned you?"

Llewelyn shook his head. But it had been too easy, and it was with a trace of defiance that he said, "I admit I was in the wrong. Say of me what you will. But I'll let no man speak ill of my lord father, not now, not ever!"

"Fair enough," Davydd said quietly, and Llewelyn was at last able to draw an unconstricted breath. Ednyved was looking at him with heartening good will, and he could now offer a smile of his own.

"Tell the lad what you've done, Davydd. Show him the Pope's letter."

"The Pope?" Llewelyn sounded so bewildered that the men laughed. Isabella rose, brought Davydd an ivory casket. Davydd easily found the letter he sought, but he was not sure if Llewelyn's Latin was adequate for the task, and rather than embarrass the boy, he said,

"It is simple, in truth. We need allies, and who better than the Pope? When I was fourteen, my father was able to secure papal recognition of my claims to the principality of Gwynedd. I reminded His Holiness of that, arguing that I had in effect been made a ward of the Church, and offering to hold Gwynedd as the Pope's vassal."

Davydd had said his plan was simple, but Llewelyn was dazzled by its daring. "And the Pope has agreed to this?"

"Well, he did accept the five hundred marks I tendered as my first payment." Davydd no longer feigned nonchalance, acknowledged the extent of his triumph with a sudden grin. "When King John turned England over to the Church, he reaped some remarkable benefits, for the Pope at once forbade the French to invade England. It is too much to hope that Innocent might lay such a stricture upon Henry. But in the Pope's letter, he did say, Llelo, that he was planning to appoint the Abbots of Aberconwy and Cymmer as inquisitors, to have them investigate my claims against Henry. And that is a beginning."

There was no warmth in the look Llewelyn now gave Davydd, but there was no small measure of respect. "No one calls me Llelo anymore," he said, without belligerence. Davydd nodded agreeably, and when Llewelyn asked, passed him the Pope's letter. Llewelyn read rapidly; he was fluent in French, Welsh, and Latin, had begun to learn English. The letter confirmed all that Davydd had said, opened up resplendent vistas for Wales, offered hope. And although he knew that his father would not have understood, could not have forgiven, for the first time since Gruffydd's death Llewelyn felt at peace.

16

Deganwy Castle
North Wales

September 1245

For a time it had seemed as if Davydd's bold gamble would succeed. The Pope appointed the Abbots of Aberconwy and Cymmer to investigate Davydd's grievance against the English King, and Henry was summoned to defend himself in the Welsh village of Caerwys. Outraged, Henry sent his agents to Rome. Embroiled in a bitter feud with Frederick, the Holy Roman Emperor, the Pope was now seeking to have Frederick formally deposed, and he welcomed the news that the English clergy would vote his way at the upcoming Council of Lyons. He then reassessed Davydd's claim, and withdrew the papal protection from the Welsh Prince.

It was on a cool afternoon in late September that Simon returned to the King's encampment on the banks of the River Conwy. England and Wales had been at war for more than a year, but Henry had not bestirred himself until August; a month ago, he had led an army into Gwynedd, where he set about rebuilding at Deganwy the castle razed by Davydd four years earlier. As Simon dismounted in the bailey, he saw that some progress had been made; the great hall had been roofed. But the castle still had a raw, unfinished appearance, looked to be what it was, an alien outpost in an enemy land.

Dispatching his squires to unsaddle their horses, Simon mounted the steps into the great hall. His friends were seated at a wooden trestle table—Will, Peter de Montfort, and Humphrey de Bohun, son and heir of the Earl of Hereford. Stopping a servant, Simon ordered wine, then crossed the hall.

Will was the first to see him. "No! You truly were crazed enough to come back?"

"I gave Henry my word that I would," Simon said, and sat down. "What has happened whilst I was gone?"

They all grimaced. Will was, of course, the one to give voice to their discontent. "Just the usual pleasures of a Welsh campaign. We're running out of provisions again. It's gotten so bad that a soldier with a farthing loaf can sell it for fivepence. So we get to dine on stale bread and hard cheese. And we get to fight off Welsh attacks at any hour of the day . . . or night, since the Welsh know nothing of the rules of warfare, make raids when all men of common sense are abed. Then we get to chase them into the woods, where they can ambush us. What do the Welsh call this accursed land of theirs—Cymru? Had they only asked me, I'd have suggested Purgatory."

"Welsh wars are always ugly," Humphrey de Bohun said trenchantly, "if only because there's so little profit in them. But this one is bloodier than most. We hanged some Welsh hostages and now they take no prisoners. Just as Will said, our supplies are nigh on gone, and our men's spirits are scraping the bottom of the barrel, too. Most would head for home tomorrow if they had a say in it. As for me, I'm beginning to envy Rob de Quincy his back ailment!"

They all laughed at that, all but Simon. Few believed Rob's excuse for not joining the campaign; his injury was too convenient to be credible. But few begrudged his reprieve, or blamed him for being loath to fight his wife's brother, for Rob was generally well liked, not being ambitious enough to make lasting enemies. Simon was very protective of his friends, however, and he said, somewhat defensively, "Rob had good reason for wanting to stay close to home. His wife's birthing was a hard one; he almost lost her."

This was news to them all, and a matter of mild concern to Will, for Elen was his cousin. "I knew she was with child again, but not that her time was nigh. Was she able to give Rob a lad this time?"

Simon shook his head regretfully. "Another lass."

There was a moment of sympathetic silence, broken by Humphrey. "Well, Rob's a younger son, with no title to pass on. Mayhap a son is not so needful for him."

It was an ill-chosen remark, for Will had never been formally invested with the earldom of Salisbury, and the legal tangles surrounding his title were such that it was at least likely that his son would never inherit it. He scowled, not so much at Humphrey as at the lunatic complexities of the law, and Peter de Montfort, ever the peacemaker, said swiftly, "What of your lady, Simon? When is her babe due?"

"November, around Martinmas."

Will grinned; it never took much to restore his good humor. "Another lad, I'll wager. Are you going to name him after me?"

Simon's mouth twitched. "I might name a hunting dog after you, Will, but for certes not an innocent babe. Nell and I have decided upon Joanna for a lass, and Amaury for a lad, after my brother." He looked about in vain for a wine-bearing servant. "That means," he concluded, only half in jest, "that we have just six weeks to win this war. I got back from Rome in time for Harry's birth, I delayed sailing for Acre until Nell was brought to bed of our son Bran, and Guy, of course, was born whilst we were at Bordeaux. I promised Nell I'd be there for this one, too."

"I'll tell Henry of your need," Will said dryly. "But who'll tell Davydd?"

Davydd and Humphrey de Bohun were brothers by marriage—his wife was Isabella's younger sister—but at mention of the Welsh Prince's name, he looked as if he'd tasted something sour, for the de Bohuns were Marcher lords, their fortunes rooted deep in the disputed soil of Wales. "Did you know," he said indignantly, "that the whoreson is daring to call himself Prince of Wales?"

Simon merely shrugged. "If ambition be a sin, we can all expect to burn. Davydd may call himself the King of Jerusalem for all I care. My concern is to make the best of this botched campaign, to gain what concessions we can, and to get back to Kenilworth by Martinmas."

"Best of luck to you, lad. I've long since reached the sorry conclusion that wars with the Welsh are unwinnable."

"Not so, Will." Simon leaned forward, no longer indifferent. "The Welsh could be defeated by the right man, the right strategy. But an English king bent on conquest would have to be willing to spend vast sums of money, to spill a veritable ocean of blood. First he ought to put a total embargo on those goods the Welsh get from England, blockade the Welsh coast. Then he should strike at Wales in a triple thrust, from our bases at Chester, Montgomery, and Carmarthen, a three-pronged attack from the east, south, and west. And as he advances toward the heart of Gwynedd, he must build castles to hold what he's won. At the same time, he ought to take advantage of the great weakness of the Welsh—their quarrelsome, jealous nature—and stir up dissension amidst the other Welsh princes. Lastly, he should fight the Welsh on their own terms, make lightning raids and retreats, use lightly armed troops just as they do. I'd also train our men in the use of the Welsh longbow; it can fire half a dozen arrows in the time it takes one crossbowman to take aim."

Simon paused for breath, pleased by how attentive his audience had become; even Will looked impressed. Having just coolly laid out a plan for the annihilation of Wales, he now confessed, "But to be honest, I hope it never comes to that, for I would rather befriend the Welsh than destroy them."

Humphrey gasped, his outrage at such heresy so obvious that Simon laughed. "I know," he conceded. "I might feel differently had I lands in Wales; I admit as much. But the fact is that neither Nell nor I have holdings in the Marches, just a manor or two in Worcestershire, and so I can afford to be objective. I have no grievances with the Welsh. I admire their grit, their pluck, their mad gallantry. Nor can I fault them for wanting to curb Henry's influence in Wales. I would that there was a way to curb his influence in England!"

Will burst out laughing, but Humphrey and Peter were not amused. Peter winced visibly. "Jesú, Simon! If anything ought to be curbed, it is that reckless tongue of yours."

Simon shrugged again. "A man should be able to speak his mind with his friends, Peter."

Will gave a hoot. "Then you must count all the souls in Christendom as your friends, Simon, for you speak freely to every man, be he carpenter or cardinal . . . or king."

Simon was unrepentant. "I'm not good at dissembling," he said, in so sweeping an understatement that Will laughed again. The servant had finally arrived with wine. Simon's throat was parched, for he'd been in the saddle for most of the day, and he took a deep swallow, gagged, and spat the wine into the floor rushes. "What was that swill?" he gasped.

Will laughed till he choked. "Henry's butler swears it is white wine, but we suspect it could be anything from verjuice to goat's piss. A land of milk and honey, this Wales!"

"Well, I'd best find Henry, let him know I'm here—" Simon paused, frowning, for he had acute hearing. "Someone is shouting," he said, just as two men burst into the hall. Simon knew them both, John de Grey, Constable of Deganwy, and Sir Alan Buscell, one of the knights in Richard of Cornwall's household. He and Will were the men of highest rank in the hall and the newcomers headed their way.

"One of our Irish supply ships . . ." Buscell was badly winded, almost incoherent, and so it was de Grey who gave them the unhappy news.

"That fool pilot," he panted. "He ran the ship aground as he tried to enter the estuary—on the Welsh side of the river!"

Simon and Will exchanged grim looks. "We'd best make haste, Simon. The Welsh will swarm over that ship like bees out of a hive, pluck it cleaner than a Michaelmas goose!"

Will often mixed metaphors, although rarely with such abandon, but Simon had no time now to savor his friend's eccentricities of speech. "Tell the King and Earl Richard," he instructed de Grey, then glanced back at Will. "I have not even unpacked yet," he said wearily.

❧

HASTENING down to the estuary, Simon and Will saw that de Grey and Buscell had not exaggerated the ship's plight. The Welsh had been keeping Deganwy under constant surveillance, and they were not slow to take advantage of this gift from the sea. They were further favored by the timing of the accident, for it was low tide, thus enabling them to approach the ship from the landward side. Some had already succeeded in boarding the crippled vessel, were scuffling with the ship's crew. The English had begun launching small boats out into the estuary. Simon and Will joined the rush, scrambled into a rapidly filling flatboat. Soon more than three hundred men were crammed into all available boats, a motley mix of Norman-French knights, Gascon crossbowmen, Welsh mercenaries, English foot-soldiers, a rescue force that far outnumbered the Welsh attackers.

The Welsh at once broke off their assault, were in flight by the time the first boats reached the shore. Several boats headed toward the disabled ship, the others for the beach. But as men splashed into the shallows, they reeled backward under a hail of arrows. A lethal weapon, the longbow; it now confirmed all of Simon's suspicions as to its superiority over the English crossbow. Faster than the eye could follow, arrows fanned the air, found targets of flesh and bone; men screamed, began to die.

Yet the aerial onslaught was a holding action, no more than that. The Welsh bowmen knew they could slow down but not stop the enemy advance, and they soon abandoned the attack, retreated toward the surrounding woods. After some confusion, the English survivors set out in wrathful pursuit.

Ahead lay the Cistercian abbey of Aberconwy, and some of the fleeing Welsh disappeared into the monastery grounds, but most vanished into the woods. Following at as fast a pace as the weight of their armor would allow, the English soon found themselves alone in an unfamiliar forest, dark and silent.

It was the silence that was so disquieting to Simon, for he knew that it was deceptive, that all around them were wary, watching eyes. The autumn trees of oak and birch, the thickets of aspen and hedges of hawthorn provided an impenetrable shield for the denizens of these deeply shadowed, dangerous woods: stoats, weasels, foxes, deer, rabbits brought over by the Normans for their sport, deadly and unpredictable wild boar, wolves that no longer roamed English hills—and waiting Welsh bowmen?

Their great helms might deflect a lance, but they limited vision, too. Simon was acutely aware that he could be leading his men into a lethal trap. He estimated that they'd covered about two leagues in this mad plunge of theirs, which put them two leagues too far into the enemy's terrain. Raising his hands, he signaled for a halt. The quiet was absolute, eerie; even the woodpigeons were stilled.

"I've learned to trust my sixth sense," he said softly to Will, "and it is telling me that we're doing just what the Welsh want us to do. I think we'd best get back to the ship."

Will needed no convincing. "Right gladly. A soothsayer once promised me that I'd die in the Holy Land, and I'm damned if I'm willing to settle for Wales."

Their men were no more eager than Will to chase after ghosts, and welcomed Simon's command with obvious relief. They had less than an hour till sunset, and they retraced their steps with nervous haste, casting back over their shoulders the uneasy glances of hunters who might now be the hunted. The ground was scattered with acorns, broken branches, dried leaves; the forest seemed to echo with the sounds of their retreat, floating on the wind toward unfriendly ears. So intent were they upon possible pursuit or ambush that they did not at once smell the smoke, catch sight of the black clouds that spiraled up through the trees ahead.

It was Simon's squire Miles, with the sharp eyes of youth, who was the first to notice the smudged sky. "My lord, fire!"

The men came to an abrupt halt. There was a moment of hushed silence, and then a confused babble of voices. But for Simon, there was no need to speculate. As he gazed up at the billowing smoke, he knew. "Christ Jesus, those fools have set fire to the abbey!"

Long before they were in sight of the abbey walls, Simon's fears had been borne out. Most of the English soldiers had not been as diligent in their pursuit as Simon and Will, and once the Welsh faded away into the woods, they had fallen back upon the abbey. It had begun with a few men breaking into the buttery in search of wine, had rapidly gotten out of hand. After plundering the abbey casks of wine and ale, the soldiers had stripped bare all the shelves of the bake-house, created havoc in the kitchens. Inevitably, some of them began to want more than bread or ale.

A soldier's life was not an easy one, but many thought it gave them a license to loot. And few had any great liking for monks; the Cistercians in particular were viewed with suspicion, for they were known to co-operate closely with the Welsh Princes. Men began to mutter about gold, to swap stories of abbots who lived like fine lords. Soon they were ransacking the Abbot's house, the guest hall, the monks' dorters, wherever they thought they might find coins, silver plate, jeweled rings. The monks had so far offered no resistance, but then a few soldiers drunker or bolder than their fellows forced the church doors, sought to steal from God. An outraged monk tried to stop them; his body was later found crumpled in the shadow of the marble tomb of Llewelyn Fawr. No one seemed to know who set the first fire. But by the time Simon and Will came upon the scene, most of the abbey buildings were in flames, and the garth was filled with smoke, with gleeful looters no longer caring about the worth of what they stole, grabbing at anything that could be carried away.

Simon was appalled. He plunged into their midst, shouting for them to stop, but few paid him any heed. Will, too, attempted to reassert discipline, rather half-heartedly, for he knew that, once begun, looting was almost impossible to check. Like plague, it infected at random, few were immune, and men could only wait for it to run its course. But Simon was not willing to wait, not when he saw soldiers carrying off church candlesticks and chalices, even the sacred silver pyx that held the Host. He grabbed for this last man, and the pyx went spinning through the air, bounced along the ground like a pig's-bladder football. Before Simon could retrieve it, though, another looter snatched it up, darted away.

In the doorway of the church, one of the monks was struggling with a soldier, clinging desperately to an ivory reliquary. "No," he panted, "you'll not have it," refusing to relinquish his hold even as the other man beat him about the head and shoulders. Simon reached them just as the English soldier lost all patience, fumbled for his dagger. Before he could unsheathe it, Simon grasped his arm, spun him around and sent him sprawling. He rose spitting oaths, but at sight of Simon's drawn sword, he decided that Simon was a more formidable foe than the aged monk and retreated, cursing them both.

The monk did not thank Simon. Clutching the reliquary to his chest, he said defiantly, "This casket contains our greatest treasures, a lock of St Davydd's hair and straw from the Christ Child's manger. You'll have to kill me to take it."

While Simon would have dearly loved to possess such sacred objects, he could imagine few sacrileges so great as the theft of holy relics. "Take the reliquary back into the church," he said. "Hide it well."

The monk was badly bruised; the white of his tunic was almost as dark as his scapular, so smudged and soiled was it with smoke and cinders. One eye was blackened, swollen shut, but the other blazed with feverish fury. Looking past Simon to a soldier brandishing one of the abbey's cherished chalices, he cried, "God smite you English for this! May He curse you one and all, shrivel your crops in the field, dry up your wells, strike down your firstborn sons just as He destroyed the sons of Egypt! May He—"

Simon crossed himself, backed away. He was too stubborn to concede defeat, though. Long after another man would have given up, he still sought to turn the tide, swearing and shouting at soldiers too drunk to listen, even striking about him with the flat of his sword. What at last brought him to his senses was not Will's plea to "let it lie," but the sudden heat upon his face.

"The wind has shifted, Will!" He gestured toward the burning bakehouse, at the sparks and cinders swirling up into the darkening sky. "Unless we have men sober enough to fight the fire, it'll spread to the church. We've got to get back to the camp."

When they reached the river, they saw that the Irish supply ship was now safely in English hands. But the beach was littered with bodies. Simon recognized the coat of arms on a surcoat stiff with blood. Turning the man over, he removed the helm, stared down into the face of Alan Buscell. Even after twenty years of war, he still found himself shocked by the random suddenness of death, found himself remembering the knight who a few short hours before had run into the hall to warn them of the Welsh attack. Reaching out, he closed the dead man's eyes, then gestured for his men to enter the nearest boat.

Dusk was fast falling. As their boat pulled away from the shore, Simon gazed back over his shoulder at the surging, wind-blown flames. He did not doubt that Henry would heed his appeal, dispatch men to save the church. But why did Henry need to be asked? The fire must be visible from the castle. Why did Henry never take action on his own? Why did he not act as a King ought?

They had almost reached the east bank when the screaming began. Suddenly the beach was full of fleeing men, shouting and shoving as they sprinted for the boats. But most were too drunk to run far, were reluctant, too, to discard their plunder, and they were soon overtaken by the Welsh riders who now galloped out onto the sands. What followed was a slaughter.

Some of the quicker, more sober soldiers had managed to launch boats, but they were not yet out of arrow range. They were endangered, as well, by their own comrades, for the estuary was full of drowning men, men who clutched at oars, sought to clamber into boats already riding low in the water. As one swamped boat tipped over, hurling all its occupants into the river, Simon exclaimed,

"We've got to go back for them!" When Will protested, voicing the opinion of them all that the whoresons deserved to drown, Simon gestured toward one of the floundering men. "That is Humphrey de Bohun," he said, and ordered his reluctant oarsmen to row toward the sinking flatboat.

Humphrey had kept enough wit to abandon his great helm, but he was still weighed down by thirty pounds of chain-mail, and he clung desperately to the side of the boat, measuring his life in minutes until he heard Simon's shout. He managed to tread water just long enough to grasp an outstretched oar, was hauled, gasping and choking, into their boat. They plucked a few fortunate others from the river, too, before their own craft began to lurch dangerously. Abandoning the others to their fate, they rowed rapidly for the far shore.

The cries of dying men followed them, carried clearly across the water. Back on the beach, the Welsh were triumphant. Some were helping the monks to fight the fire, while others were surveying the ship. Watching from a safe distance, Simon found himself admiring the military precision of the Welsh assault; he knew it was no easy task to muster a counter-attack with such speed. Granted, the Welsh had a powerful motivation—outrage—for Aberconwy Abbey was their Canterbury. But their rapid response spoke also of a shrewd grasp of martial tactics, and Simon was soldier enough to recognize it, and to salute it.

Will was equally impressed. "That was a rally worthy of Llewelyn Fawr."

Humphrey had been slumped in the bottom of the boat, having vomited up a remarkable amount of river water. He roused himself at that, mumbled, "His grandson."

That information meant more to Simon than to the other men, for Elen was his window to the Welsh world, and he'd often heard her speak fondly of her young nephew. "Llewelyn ap Gruffydd? Are you sure, Humphrey?"

"That's his household guard, his teulu." Humphrey sat up, pointed. "There . . . that youth on the sorrel stallion. Now there's one Welshman worth taking; he'd fetch a prince's ransom."

Almost as if he knew they were speaking of him, Llewelyn reined in his stallion at the water's edge, looked across the river toward them. He turned then, gestured to a nearby bowman. They watched as the archer fit an arrow into the linen string, bent back the elm bow, but without alarm, sure they were beyond range. A moment later an arrow thudded into the stern of their boat. Behind them, the sun sank into the sea, and darkness descended upon the vale of Conwy.

FROM Deganwy's battlements, Henry had an unobstructed view of the river estuary—and the abbey. In the soft light of dawn, the devastation was even more dreadful than Henry had anticipated. Some of the buildings still smoldered and the church was smoke-blackened; down on the beach, he could see bodies, stiffened in the ungainly sprawl of death. He had never seen a sight so sad. He leaned over the parapet, not moving until Simon joined him on the walkway. They stood in silence for a time, gazing across at the abbey ruins. The sun was rising over the mountains; a sea-salted breeze stirred up foaming breakers out in the harbor. It should have been a beautiful day.

"Simon . . . do you think that God was punishing us?"

"Yes," Simon said, but then could not keep from adding, "With some diabolically inspired help from the Welsh."

Henry's head swiveled around; after a moment, he gave a wan smile. "It is a terrible sin to burn a church," he said mournfully, "to burn God's House . . ."

There was sudden activity across the river. Now that the tide was going out, the Welsh were making another attempt to seize the ship. From their triumphant shouts, they had just discovered what Simon and Henry already knew, that the ship was deserted. The besieged crew had waited till high tide, then sneaked down into the waiting boats and paddled to safety under cover of darkness. But they'd had to leave the cargo behind, and Henry and Simon could only watch helplessly as the Welsh laid claim to the corn and flour and bacon meant for Deganwy's larders, Henry's soldiers.

"What a botch," Henry said, almost inaudibly. "What a bloody botch . . ."

"More than you know, Cousin." They turned at the sound of Will's voice, watched as he hastened up the walkway toward them. "I just talked to that whoreson of a captain," he said, before letting loose with a particularly profane oath, one that earned him a frown from Henry. Will didn't even notice. "There was more than food on that ship," he said, making an obscene gesture in the general direction of the beach. "There were sixty casks of good wine, and those God-cursed Welsh got all but one!"

THE rains came in October, and the English encampment soon began to resemble a quagmire. Men huddled miserably in their tents, having neither warm winter clothing for their backs nor full rations for their bellies. Cold, homesick, and hungry, Henry's army was denied even restful nights, for the Welsh were still determined to thwart the construction of Deganwy Castle, and they soon learned that their raids were most demoralizing when made in those unsettling early hours before dawn. No soldier with any sense ever looked forward to service in Wales, a land without towns or villages, a poor place to plunder, to find women, but an easy place to die. Yet rarely had a campaign been so wretched as this one, and as the days grew shorter, as snow began to appear on the heights of Eryri, scarcely a soul in Henry's encampment—save Henry himself—believed that this was a war he could win.

Although it was only noon, the clouds were so thick and the rain so unrelenting that it seemed more like dusk. Even a blazing fire in the center hearth could not keep the chill from the hall, nor could it dispel the gloom. For more than an hour, Henry had listened as his barons voiced their complaints about the Welsh war. He was reminded that all they'd gained was a partially constructed castle, that their foraging parties were ambushed every time they ventured from camp, that their larders were as barren as their expectations of victory. They pointed out that his scheme to divide the Welsh by making use of Gruffydd's son Owain had so far come to naught; he had released Owain from the Tower, granted him a house in Cheshire, but few rallied to his cause. They argued that they were not equipped for a winter campaign, and they pressed Henry from all sides, demanding that he lead them home.

Henry was not surprised by this lack of support. More and more, he was convinced that there were none he could rely upon, none he could truly trust. None who understood why he was so reluctant to retreat. None who understood his hunger for a victory, his need to blot out the shaming memories of his last military campaign, that costly, inglorious war with France.

He had moved closer to the hearth, although this was a chill of the spirit as much as of the body. Now he turned back, let his eyes move slowly from man to man, but not finding what he sought. Theirs was a common discontent; he saw it mirrored in the faces of his brother Richard, his cousin Will, the Earl of Winchester, even Marcher lords like the Earl of Gloucester and Humphrey de Bohun. As ever, he thought, I stand alone.

It was Richard's resentment that bothered Henry the most. He could acknowledge that Richard had some cause for disgruntlement; Alan Buscell was the third of his household knights to die in Wales. But from the first, Richard had shown little enthusiasm for this campaign, had voiced his opposition so freely that rumors had begun to circulate, rumors that had Richard siding with his nephew Davydd rather than his brother the King. Henry knew better than that. The irony of such rumors was that he was probably more sympathetic to Davydd's plight than Richard, for family ties had always meant more to him, and as angry as he was with his nephew's intransigence, as determined to punish the Welsh, he had never sought Davydd's utter destruction.

But as Henry looked at his silent brother, he felt an unease that went beyond Richard's objections to this war, for he knew that there lay between them the shadow of Gascony, Gascony that he had promised to Richard, only to renege at Eleanor's urgings. Upon their return from France, Richard had married Sanchia, Eleanor's younger sister, and he and his new wife were often at Henry's court. On the surface, their quarrel seemed to have been forgotten, peace restored . . . or so

Henry had tried to believe. Yet he could never quite stifle a secret fear—that of all he'd lost in France, his greatest loss was not to be measured in terms of money spent or lands forfeited, but in the distance he now saw reflected in his brother's eyes.

A sudden gust of rain-drenched wind turned all heads toward the opening door. Henry's sense of foreboding only intensified at sight of his brother-in-law. Logically, he ought to be able to count upon Simon's support, for how many men had been so favored by their King? But as he made ready to ask Simon for his opinion, he was already bracing himself for bad news, for betrayal. "My lords think we ought to abandon the campaign, withdraw into England. What say you, Simon? Are you in agreement with them?"

"Of course I am," Simon said, sounding faintly surprised that the question should even be raised, for he could envision no greater lunacy than attempting to fight a winter campaign in Wales.

His tone was not lost upon Henry. As if he thought that men of common sense could not differ on this. As if his way was the only way. As if he did not owe his King better than this.

"I am astonished by your ingratitude, Simon, yea, and grievously disappointed. When I think of all I have conferred upon you . . . I gave you an earldom, even gave you my sister. Last year I granted you custody of Kenilworth Castle, one of the most formidable fortresses in the realm, and agreed to give Nell a marriage portion of five hundred marks a year. Just a year ago I gave you the lucrative wardship of Sir Gilbert de Hunfrunville's son, even though my brother, too, wanted it, and I excused Nell from paying one hundred pounds she owed a Jewish money-lender. How can you then turn on me like this?"

If he'd hoped that this tallying up of the benefits he'd bestowed upon Simon would stir in Simon a sense of shame, he had miscalculated. Simon had listened, first in astonishment, and then in anger. An accusation of ingratitude was perilously akin to one of disloyalty. The charge stung all the more because in the past year Simon had violated his conscience in Henry's behalf. When the English clergy had refused Henry's demands for additional moneys, Simon had reluctantly agreed to act as one of Henry's spokesmen, a role that had brought him into conflict with the Bishop of Lincoln, the friend whose opinion Simon valued above all others.

"Turn on you?" he echoed coldly. "I came to Wales to fight for you, did I not? What more do you want from me?"

"I want your respect!"

To those watching, it was difficult to decide who looked more startled, Simon or Henry. Henry clasped his hand to his mouth, a gesture as involuntary as the words themselves had been. His discomposure was painful to look upon, and yet disarming, too. Simon felt his anger ebbing away, and he did not make the obvious cruel retort, that respect could not be commanded, must be earned. But his silence was eloquent in itself, and no less wounding to Henry.

No one spoke; no one knew what to say. Henry swung about, able to escape their eyes but knowing he could never outrun the memory of this moment, that every man here would remember it, he most of all. He summoned up the shreds of his dignity, said bitterly, "So be it, then. I cannot fight this war alone. We shall withdraw from Deganwy by week's end."

ON the 28th of October, the English army retreated, leaving behind a garrison to hold Deganwy Castle. They then laid waste to the Welsh countryside in hopes of creating famine, and ravaged the neighboring English shire of Cheshire as well, so that the Welsh could find no succor there for the hunger that would soon stalk their land. Henry imposed a strict embargo on corn, salt, iron, steel, and cloth, and vowed that the war was not done.

From Chester, Henry and Richard returned to London. Will and Humphrey de Bohun rode toward their respective estates in the West Country. Peter de Montfort headed for his manor in Warwickshire. And Simon raced for Kenilworth Castle, arriving in time for the birth of his fourth son.

In Wales, they suffered, and they waited for the spring, when the English army would return.

17

Maesmynan, North Wales

January 1246

LLEWELYN was too tense to sit for long. He kept wandering to the shuttered window, back to the hearth, over to the trestle table, set for two. Reaching out, he realigned the trenchers, adjusted the spoons and knives. Napkins! Rummaging about in a coffer, he finally unearthed two linen squares. Righting an hourglass, he watched time trickle away, one grain after another. Where was she? Had she changed her mind?

The knock was so light, so tentative, that he could have imagined it. In two strides, he was at the door. She was enveloped in a long, dark mantle, a fragile wraith camouflaged in shadow. She smiled at sight of him, but seemed hesitant to cross the threshold. Llewelyn took her hand, drew her into his bedchamber, into the light.

"I alerted my servants. You had no trouble gaining admittance, Melangell?"

He so liked the sound of her name that he said it again. She shook her head, let him take her mantle. Her gown, a plain homespun, had been newly dyed forest-green, embroidered around the neckline. Llewelyn, who'd never paid any mind to women's clothes, now found himself unexpectedly touched by the sight of that decorative stitching. He could imagine her huddled by the fire in her father's cottage, laboriously seeking to adorn her gown—to catch his eye. The first time he had seen her, she'd been kneeling by the river bank, barefoot, hair in curly disarray, singing softly to herself, as if she took joy in scrubbing a shirt. That was the girl he'd hoped to find tonight, a laughing river nymph, not this solemn stranger, hair demurely braided, eyes downcast. Never had they been so shy with each other. But never had they been alone in a firelit chamber, just a few steps away from a bed.

"I have something for you, Melangell."

The locket was delicately crafted, engraved with a slanting *M*, exquisite enough to dispel Melangell's unease. With a cry of wonder, she began to trace the *M* with her fingertips, in the way that Llewelyn had seen the blind explore the unknown. "Never have I seen anything so fine. These markings . . . they have meaning?"

He nodded, and then, inspired, he led her toward the table. Picking up a sheet of parchment, he scrawled a large letter *M*. "*M*—for Melangell." As she watched, enthralled, he filled in the rest of her name. She had never seen it spelled out before, and she sought to trace the parchment as she had the locket, recoiling in dismay when her fingers smeared the ink. Llewelyn hastily recopied her name, then added his own beside it, like parallel branches on the same tree. Beneath he inked in the date of his birth—April 1228—and when he explained the meaning of these new scribblings, she laughed aloud.

"But that is my birthday, too! I was born in April just as you were, in 1230, at the time of the great scandal, when your lord grandfather's wife was caught with her English lover."

The parchment was forgotten. They smiled at each other, marveling at this most amazing of coincidences, that they should share the same birth-month.

Llewelyn reached out; his fingers followed the curve of her cheek. "How fair you are to look upon . . ."

He could feel heat rise in her face. "No," she said regretfully, "I am not. When the bards sing of great beauties, such women always have hair like flax, lips like cherries, and skin like snow."

"Then the bards are blind," he said, "for you are beautiful." He hesitated, compelled to honesty, yet fearing its consequences. "I would not lie to you, Melangell. You hold my heart. But I cannot wed you."

She had long-lashed brown eyes, eyes that widened now in astonishment that he should even mention such an impossibility. "I know that, my love. You are a Prince and I am a tanner's daughter. I am not worthy—" She got no further; Llewelyn kissed her.

In the past, their kisses had been stolen, furtive; this was a kiss of possession. She did not protest when he began to loosen her primly coiled braids, shook her head playfully, and gave him back his river hoyden. "You said your father will be in Bangor until Thursday? I shall go to him upon his return, shall promise him that I will take care of you, that you'll want for nothing. And if . . . when we have children, I shall be proud to recognize them as mine. On that, he will have my sworn word, Melangell."

Melangell felt a sweet, sweeping relief, for as much as she'd needed such a guarantee, she'd been loath to broach the subject herself. Now her future—and more important, that of their children—was assured. "Is it true," she asked, suddenly shy again, "that the English do not provide for children born out of wedlock? I've heard it said, but can scarce give it credence, so cruel it seems . . ."

"It is true, nonetheless. Even if the father acknowledges a child as his, the child has no legal rights of inheritance under English law. It is a hard land, hardest of all upon bastards and the women who bear them."

"Bastard" was a word that had no sting in Wales. Any children born to Melangell and Llewelyn would be no less his heirs than those subsequently born in wedlock, in the marriage of state she knew he must one day make. She slid her arms up his back, feeling an enormous sense of pity for those English girls who must live in a society that made them either wives or whores. "I am so lucky, Llewelyn, lucky to be Welsh, lucky to have been on the river bank that day you passed by . . ."

Llewelyn's elaborate dinner plans came to naught; neither could eat a bite. But he poured wine with a lavish hand. Melangell drank gratefully. It was highly spiced and potent; one cupful and she felt warmed, mellowed. She'd never been on a feather mattress before; she clung to it as if it were a thick, fleecy cloud likely to float out from under her.

Llewelyn was not having much success with the lacings of her gown. His fingers were too eager, so clumsy that she could not help giggling. When he sought to remove her chemise, though, she put her hand on his chest.

"Llewelyn, wait. I must tell you . . ."

She was suddenly flushed. Llewelyn propped himself up on his elbow, looked intently into her face. "This is your first time?"

She nodded. "And you?" she whispered.

"No." He leaned over, kissed the curve of her mouth. "Ere I came to terms with my uncle Davydd, I ofttimes stayed with my aunt Gwladys on her Shropshire manors. Every now and then, I would accompany her husband's squires to Shrewsbury on errands, and whilst there, we'd go to the bawdy houses in Grope Lane." He kissed her again. A familiar fragrance clung to her hair, her skin, sweet-smelling basil and rosemary, spices of the kitchen, the only perfume she could afford. "I love you, Melangell," he said, and her eyes filled with tears.

Her skin was a warm, dusky color, and her hands were work-roughened, her nails of necessity clipped to the quick, for vanity rarely found a dwelling place in a tanner's cottage. She was right; she was no knight's ideal of ethereal blonde beauty. But when she pulled her chemise over her head, the body she revealed to Llewelyn was, to him, perfection. He touched a scrape on her knee, then bent over, put his mouth to the full, smooth breasts, and she wound her arms tightly around his neck as they sank down into the softness, into her cloud.

For Llewelyn, what followed was a revelation. His few hurried, awkward couplings with the whores of Shrewsbury had given him both satisfaction and shame. In the practiced embraces of bought women bored with a boy's greenness, women who kept their eyes open as the candle burned down toward his allotted time, his body's needs would soon blot out all else, even the scratchy straw mattress, the smell of sweat, the grunting from nearby cubicles. All too soon, there would be relief, of the sort gained by shooting an arrow skyward, and then he would lie quivering, much like that spent bow, aware again of the itch of flea bites, the stench from chamberpot and sour ale, the woman's indifference. At seventeen, sex was not yet a pleasure, was rather a burning, urgent hunger that was neither convenient nor dignified, but impossible to deny.

Now he shared a bed with a girl his own age, a girl with trusting eyes, a soft, clean body, and he discovered that her youth and innocence and adoration were far greater aphrodisiacs than mead or oysters or pomegranates. He wanted to be gentle, wanted to please Melangell. But his need was too intense, the fire too hot. He gave himself up to it gladly, came back to reality with reluctance, dazed and euphoric and drenched in sweat. It was then that he saw the tears glistening on her lashes, felt the warm stickiness of her blood on his thigh.

He was at once horrified, contrite. "Melangell, I am sorry, I swear I am. I never meant to hurt you . . ."

"It . . . it is supposed to hurt, I think." There were echoes of tears in her voice, but she managed a wan smile. When he put his arms around her, she found in physical intimacy the pleasure that had eluded her in the sexual act itself. He was very tender, murmuring endearments and reassurances, and she decided pain was a small price to pay for this quiet contentment. She was innocent but not ignorant, knew that the hurting would lessen now that he'd pierced her maidenhead. She knew, too, that many women took great joy in laying with a man. While she could not yet comprehend how that could be, she remembered vividly how Llewelyn had shuddered and groaned, and she felt a pride she'd never experienced before, that she'd been able to give him such pleasure.

When he wanted wine, she insisted upon fetching it for him; she meant to take care of him now that he was her man. He seemed to share her sentiments, for as soon as she got back into bed, he said, "Melangell, what can I do for your family? If I offered your father five milk cows, would he accept?"

"Oh, yes!" Her father was a proud man, but these were lean times, and she had four younger sisters.

Llewelyn was pleased, although not surprised. This was the hardest winter he could recall. "I suppose it was to be expected that the English King would ravage Gwynedd ere he led his army back across the border. But I will never understand, Melangell, how he could then have laid waste to Cheshire, too. It served his purposes, increased our suffering, but the people of Cheshire are English, his own subjects. Did he care naught for them?"

That was not a question Melangell could answer; she knew nothing of politics, nothing of kings, and until now, nothing of war. But that would have to change. In the spring, the English army would return, and Llewelyn would be amongst the first to answer Prince Davydd's summons. She looked at her lover, and for a moment of heart-stopping horror, she could actually see him lying dead on a blood-soaked battle-field. "Llewelyn, tell me the truth. Do you think Prince Davydd can win this war?"

Llewelyn was torn between an instinctive desire to protect her and the need to speak his mind freely and frankly to one he could truly trust. "Yes," he said, because he had to believe that. Then he added, "But I am not sure that my uncle Davydd does. As ever, he keeps his own counsel, yet it is so obvious that he is sorely troubled, Melangell. He looks drawn and haggard, looks like a man who has forgotten what it is like to get a good night's sleep. He picks at his food as if suspecting poison, and he hoards his words like the most mean-spirited of misers. In truth, I do not know why King Henry should cast so long a shadow; men say he is a pitiful soldier. But Davydd is no coward, and yet I see fear in his face."

Davydd's fear meant nothing to Melangell, but Llewelyn's distress meant everything. Yet she had no comfort to offer, for his was a world beyond her ken. She experienced a moment of panic; how could she hope to hold him? And then she leaned over, kissed him on the mouth, a kiss that had nothing in it of passion, but a great deal of tenderness and some measure of despair. He returned the kiss, with the passion she lacked, and as his desire flared again, she felt dismay—so soon— and yet pride, too, that it took as little as that, just one kiss. This time it did not hurt as much, and afterward, she soon fell asleep, cradled and safe in Llewelyn's arms.

He lay awake beside her, stroking her hair, marveling how perfectly her small body fit into his. She stirred as his hand slid down her back, gave a sleepy sigh. He was not so love-blinded that he could not see how mismatched they were. She'd said she was no worthy wife for him; in the eyes of others, she was no worthy mistress, either. Llewelyn, grandson of Llewelyn Fawr, knew well the value his people placed upon blood. His father had been born out of wedlock, but to the daughter of the Lord of Rhos. His mother would never accept Melangell. Nor would the rest of his kin, not his uncles Davydd or Einion, nor his brothers, his aunts, his clan.

But he had not seen his mother for more than four years. He and Davydd were allies, not friends, with Gruffydd's ghost forever between them. He had alienated Einion by making peace with Davydd. Owain was in Cheshire exile, his younger brothers in London. Until the war with England was done, his aunts might as well have been in Cathay. He had none to hold him accountable, none to protest the tanner's daughter he'd taken to his bed. His was the independence of solitude, of indifference. It seemed strange indeed to him that never had he felt so alone as he did now, with Melangell's warm body nestled beside him. Drawing her closer still, he murmured, "I do love you," and drifted into sleep.

His dreams, peaceful at first, soon grew fragmented, foreboding. He awoke with a start to find Melangell already sitting up, clutching the sheets to her chin. He could hear the pounding now, interspersed with plaintive cries of "Llewelyn! Llewelyn, wake up!"

When he would have risen from the bed, though, Melangell grabbed his arm. Theirs might be an honorable liaison, but she was not yet ready to have others find her naked in his bed.

By now Llewelyn had recognized the importuning voice. "You need not fret, beloved. It is only my cousin." He swung his legs over the side of the bed, but then paused, seeing she was still in need of reassurance. "My father and Davydd had a half-brother, Tegwared, who died ten years ago. That is his son and namesake at the door."

The hearth log had burned down so low that the air was icy. Snatching up his bedrobe, he crossed the chamber, slid the bolt back. Tegwared must have been leaning against the door, for he all but tumbled into the room. It was just the sort of slapdash entrance Llewelyn would have expected him to make; he was fond of his young kinsman, but never had he known a soul so clumsy, so hapless. Now, as he introduced Melangell and Tegwared, he shot his cousin a wordless warning, for although Tegwared had no malice, he had no guile either, and Llewelyn did not want to take any risks with his unbridled tongue.

Much to Llewelyn's surprise, Tegwared never even glanced toward the girl in the bed. He sank down upon the nearest coffer, struggling for breath. "Lord Ednyved . . . he bade me fetch you straightaway to Aber. Jesú, Llewelyn, something dreadful has happened!"

"What? Tell me!"

"It is our uncle Davydd. He has been taken ill." Tegwared's shoulders slumped; the face he turned up to Llewelyn's was freckled and dirt-smeared and frightened. "Llewelyn, it is serious. You know how Aunt Isabella is; she'd flood Aber with her tears for a kitten's cries or a torn gown. But Lord Ednyved could face down the Four Horsemen of the Apocalypse without qualms, and yet when he told me to get to you, he said . . . he said not to spare my horse."

ISABELLA had been sobbing steadily since Llewelyn's arrival; he marveled that she still had tears to shed. Ednyved had not moved for hours, sat staring into the hearth as if it held the answers the doctors had yet to give them. Llewelyn rose restlessly, crossed to a window-seat. So did Tegwared, who'd become as adhesive as his own shadow. "Llewelyn," he whispered, "what if he dies?"

That was a fear to be ignored at all costs; recognition might give it reality. Llewelyn said sharply, "Do not talk nonsense!"

Ednyved's son Goronwy brought his father a cup of mead. He drank, as he did all else, with deliberation. When he spoke, it took them all by surprise, as if silence had become natural, safer. "You never suspected he was ailing?"

Only belatedly did Isabella realize that she was the one being addressed, the one who must answer. Ednyved's tone was flat, reflected only exhaustion. But she flinched away from the words, as if from weapons. "I knew he was troubled," she sobbed. "He's been sleeping so poorly, and losing weight. But he had no appetite. I thought it was this accursed war . . ."

Whatever else she meant to say was lost, so bitterly was she crying. She was clad in a scarlet gown, an incongruous shade for the sickroom, and looked to Llewelyn like a brightly colored butterfly, innocent and ineffectual. He pitied her grieving, yet found himself yearning for his mother's taut, gritty competence, yearning for someone to take charge. What would befall them if Davydd did die? He'd sometimes indulged in daydreams of power, envisioning himself as Gwynedd's Prince, hearing again his grandfather's dying declaration of faith. But such fantasies were safely set in a distant future. Davydd was only thirty-seven; he'd never given serious thought to his uncle's mortality. Now, watching Davydd's weeping wife, watching Edynved age before his eyes, watching that closed bedchamber door, he could think of nothing else.

Ednyved had summoned Einion ap Rhiwallon, one of the famed physicians of Myddfai, an unwelcome ghost from Llewelyn's past, stirring up too many memories of his grandfather's seizure. When he finally emerged, his face was utterly blank, a mask of such resolute stoicism that Llewelyn's hand closed roughly, involuntarily, upon Tegwared's arm. Isabella got to her feet, but did not speak. It was left to Ednyved to say in a dulled, tired voice, "Well?"

Einion's eyes did not linger on Ednyved's face, focused instead on the far wall. "Prince Davydd's court physician has been treating him for what he believes to be a disorder of the liver. After closely examining the Prince, and testing his urine, I find myself in agreement with his doctor."

"A liver disorder." Isabella echoed the doctor's words with no emotion, like one parroting a foreign tongue. "What can you do to ease his pain, to make him well?"

"His doctor has been giving him potions of dandelion root. I would continue that treatment. Even though January is not an auspicious month for blood-letting, I would still recommend it. And there are herbs we can try: vervain, centaury, chickweed, poultices of burdock."

Those were herbs familiar to Isabella, too familiar, the ingredients of recipes for headache, coughing fits. She wanted more than home remedies for Davydd, wanted exotic, alien cures, wanted the medicine of magic. She drew several ragged, shallow breaths before repeating, "And that will make him well?"

Einion at last forced his eyes to her face. "Madame . . . one's health depends upon the proper equilibrium of the four humors, those of blood, phlegm, white bile, and black bile. Should that balance be disturbed, men sicken. Some of the most grievous ailments result from a surfeit of hot, black bile. We call them melancholic ulcers, cancers—"

He saw the blood drain from Isabella's face, saw her lashes flutter, and darted forward as she swayed. Goronwy was even closer, and no less quick-witted; he caught her just in time, steered her toward the settle while shouting for her ladies.

Ednyved had yet to move. He watched for several silent moments as Einion ministered to Isabella, then turned abruptly, limped from the chamber. When Einion straightened up, he found Llewelyn standing but a few feet away.

"What can we do for my uncle?" he asked softly, and the doctor seemed to sigh.

"You can pray for him, lad," he said. "You can pray for him."

DAVYDD's dreams had become so troubled that his doctors had begun to give him peony seeds in hot wine. He'd been skeptical, but had just passed one of the few restful nights he'd known in weeks. He did not remember the particulars of his dream upon awakening, only the precious sense of peace. He lay still for a time, eyes closed, for he could hear people moving about the chamber. As February ebbed away in a relentless deluge of icy winter rain, he was finding it harder and harder to rally his dwindling strength, to make the effort that the presence of others required.

Like flotsam cast up on the receding shores of memory, a sudden image came to him, vividly, as he lay there. Behind his closed eyelids, a woman's face was taking form, floating above the bed, haloed by candlelight. He remembered now. In his dream, he had been ill, burning with fever, and then his mother was there, summoned by his need, keeping vigil through the night, keeping time and death itself at bay.

The irony of such a dream was not lost upon him, but neither was its poignancy. He bit his lip, unsure whether he meant to stifle laughter or curses, and then opened his eyes as he heard a woman's step approaching the bed.

He was braced for the sight of his wife, whose need for comfort was beyond him, a burden he could no longer bear. He was wretchedly aware that Isabella and he were both victims of his mortal illness. But the woman now bending over the bed was no stricken blonde Madonna; she had level, clear brown eyes, dark braids swinging free—the one person in Christendom he'd most wanted to see ere he died—his sister Elen.

He caught his breath in disbelief. "Are you truly here? How can it be?"

She sat on the bed, with her habitual disdain for sickroom protocol, took his hand. "What, and did you think the small matter of a war would keep me away? For shame, Davydd, you ought to know me better than that! Rob accompanied me to the border, where Ednyved had an escort waiting. So simple it was, I wonder we did not think of it sooner. I would have brought my girls, too, had I but—" She stopped, for his hand had tightened upon hers.

"You are talking too much," he said, and saw her eyes fill with tears.

"I know," she said, and leaned over, kissed him on the forehead.

For some moments, neither spoke. Elen's tears had broken free, were trickling down her cheeks. She made no move to wipe them away, her grieving so matter-of-fact, so natural, that she relieved him of the need to respond to it, no more than he had to respond to the rain he now heard slanting against the roof.

"You were here last night," he said suddenly. And when she nodded, he smiled. "I sensed your presence. Only . . . only I thought it was Mama . . ."

Elen's throat closed up, cutting off all speech. She gained time by turning toward the bedside table, pouring for him a cup of mead. It was as strong as men could make it, for he refused to take sleeping draughts during the day, and the mead was his only defense against the pain. She took a deep swallow herself before leaning over, helping him to drink.

"Mama died in February, too," he murmured, and then his despair broke through. "Christ Jesus, Elen, why? If I had but a little more time . . . What is going to happen to Wales?" His mouth twisted. "Almost, I could believe that God must be English!"

She was shocked neither by his bitterness nor his blasphemy; she, too, had cried unto the heavens, had railed against Fate, even God, upon learning that he was dying. But she summoned up a smile. "You need not fear for Wales, Davydd. You have stalwart allies in Papa's greatest friend and his grandson. Who could you better entrust Gwynedd to than Ednyved and Llewelyn?"

A man enfeebled by the burden of seventy-three winters. A green lad of seventeen. But Davydd choked back the words, for Elen would give him hope, not a gift to be scorned. If it was pretense, it was noble pretense. "Yes," he agreed, very low. "Between them, they'll serve Wales well."

WHEN Llewelyn had come to terms with Davydd, he unwittingly opened the door to his brother's cage. Henry and his council decided that Owain might be more useful as a rival Prince than as a prisoner, and he had been released in July 1244. He had proven to be an unsuccessful lure, for the Welsh stayed loyal to Davydd. But Henry had not revoked his freedom; he had been dwelling for months now at Henry's manor of Shotwick in Cheshire. It was there that he got word of Davydd's death. Within the hour, he was riding west into Wales.

The messenger, sent by an old ally of Gruffydd's, told him that Davydd had died at Aber that Sunday past, that he was to be buried at the abbey of Aberconwy. The messenger had confided that Davydd had taken holy vows upon his deathbed, just as his father had done. Owain had laughed when told that, sure it would avail Davydd naught. No more than it had availed Llewelyn Fawr, burning in Hell these six years past, or so he most fervently hoped.

Owain blamed Davydd for all the griefs that had befallen his family, and he rejoiced in Davydd's death. But above all, he rejoiced in his return to Wales. After so long and bitter an exile, he was going home, home to claim a crown.

He reached Aberconwy Abbey at dusk on Thursday. The monks recognized him on sight, even after an absence of five years. From childhood, he had been called Owain Goch—Owain the Red—and not even a winter twilight could dim the fiery luster of his hair. When the hospitaller murmured a deferential saint's day greeting, he almost laughed aloud, for he had forgotten the date. The first of March. St Davydd's Day. Two years since his father's death. It suddenly seemed very symbolic to him that he should arrive at the abbey on this, of all days, seemed the most promising of portents. I could not avenge you, Papa, he thought, but I can rule Wales for you, and by God, I will. He turned toward the hospitaller. "Where," he demanded, "is the Lord Ednyved?"

The nave of the abbey was lit with flickering funeral candles; beyond, all was blackness. Ednyved was standing on the steps of the High Altar, close enough to reach out, touch the cold marble tomb of Llewelyn Fawr. He watched impassively as Owain strode toward him, looking so ravaged by time and too many sorrows that Owain almost did not recognize him.

"You do not seem surprised to see me," he said, and the older man shrugged.

"I am not. I was expecting you."

"Were you, indeed?" Owain took a step toward the High Altar. "I am here," he said, "to claim what is mine, the crown that Davydd, damn his soul, stole from my father."

"Liar!" Elen stepped from the shadows. Starkly clad in mourning black, her eyes circled by darkness, aglitter with anguished rage, she made a dramatic, compelling figure, one to give Owain pause, for no son of Senena would ever dismiss women as the weaker, softer sex. Had he sensed her presence, he would have chosen his words with greater care, for he did not begrudge her the right to grieve for her brother. He decided that the etiquette of bereavement demanded he accord her the last word, and turned, instead, back to Ednyved, saying defiantly:

"Are you challenging my right to the throne of Gwynedd?"

"I am." Like Elen's, this voice, too, came from the shadows behind him. Owain spun around, watched warily as this new threat moved into the light. It took him a moment or so before he realized he was facing his brother.

"Well, well." He shook his head, smiling sourly. "I almost did not recognize you, Llelo. You've grown some, in truth, have even begun to shave, I see."

"I recognized you straightaway, Owain. You've not changed . . . not at all."

There was an echo of mockery underlying the innocence of the words, a coolly ironic tinge to the tone, neither of which gibed with Owain's memories of an annoying, irksome little brother. He gave Llewelyn a second, appraising look. It was a distinctly unpleasant shock to find their eyes were level; Owain had always been rather proud of his uncommon height.

Ednyved had been watching the two of them watch each other. "Today I buried my Prince, a man I loved. I have no patience for game-playing. Let us settle this—now. None would deny the validity of your claim, Owain." Before Owain's triumphant grin could blossom further, he added, "But your claim is no better than Llewelyn's."

"Llewe—" Owain's eyes flicked toward his grandfather's tomb. "You mean . . . Llelo?" His laughter was loud, but not as hearty as he'd hoped. "That is absurd! He's but a raw boy!"

Llewelyn could have pointed out that in less than two months, he would be eighteen. He could have argued that he'd enjoyed Davydd's trust, that he was Davydd's rightful heir. He said, "As ever, you are slow to grasp the obvious, Owain. We cannot fight the English and fight each other, too. We bear for each other as much brotherly love as Cain bore Abel. But Henry is the enemy. If you cannot see that, you are indeed a fool."

Ednyved saw the expression on Owain's face change, first incredulous and then outraged, and he said swiftly, "If you force our people to choose between you and Llewelyn, you'll sorely regret it. Some might well choose you. But most will choose your brother. Whilst you lived on the King's bounty at Shotwick, Llewelyn was fighting to expel the English intruders. As young as he is, he has gained a name for himself. Men know he had Davydd's support, and they know he has mine. Should it come to war between you, he will prevail. But the Wales he'd win would be a prize not worth having, bloodied and impoverished, easy prey for the English King."

He moved down the steps of the High Altar. "Llewelyn loves Gwynedd enough to share it. What of you, Owain? Do you?"

"Yes, damn you, yes!" Owain's cry was spontaneous, heartfelt; Ednyved's taunt about his Shotwick manor had drawn blood. He could feel other eyes upon him; the shadows were astir with witnesses, Ednyved's sons, the Abbot of Aberconwy, influential men all, willing him to agree, to accept his accursed little brother as an ally, an equal. He yearned to scorn Ednyved's warning; he could not. There was too much truth in what the old man said.

"So be it," he said bitterly. "First we must fight the English. Then . . . then we shall see." Turning on his heel, he stalked up the aisle, vanishing into the darkness of the nave.

One by one, the others departed, too, leaving at last only Ednyved, Llewelyn, and Elen standing in silence before the twin tombs of their dead. Reaching over, Elen squeezed Llewelyn's arm. "Henry is going to get a right sharp surprise," she said. "As for Owain, I do hope Henry gave him title to that Shotwick manor; he'll be needing it again by and by."

Somehow she always knew just what to say, what he most needed to hear. Llewelyn wished he knew how to comfort her in kind. "I think my greatest fear has been of letting Grandpapa down. Now . . . now I pray to God that I do not."

"I am so glad you made peace with Davydd, lad. I think it eased his mind a little, knowing you shared his dreams for Wales, knowing those dreams need not die with him . . ." Elen's voice wavered. She dared not talk further of her brother. She would mourn him later when she was alone, would mourn him all her life.

"I know Davydd asked you both to look after Isabella," she said huskily. "He asked the same of me. I think she might want to return to England. After the funeral, she made mention of Godstow, a Benedictine nunnery near Oxford. She's still so distraught that I doubt if she knows her own mind yet. Without Davydd, she's like a lamb without a shepherd—" She broke off, no longer trusting herself. Turning as abruptly as Owain had done, she, too, retreated into the shadows.

Llewelyn hesitated, casting a sorrowful look back at Davydd's tomb.

Slowly he made the sign of the cross, as much a gesture of respect as of piety, a final farewell, and then followed Elen's receding footsteps up the nave.

Ednyved walked stiffly down the remaining steps, paused before the other tomb. Slowly, very slowly, he knelt as if to pray, instead rested his cheek against the gilded, enameled lions of Llewelyn Fawr.

"They love each other not, those grandsons of yours. But I got them to see what was at stake. Llelo did not take much persuasion, a good lad . . . Owain, he needed more convincing. I yoked them into a harness sure to pinch, Llewelyn, but I gained time for us . . ."

He raised his head, heard only the rasping sound of his own breathing. "My last service for Wales," he whispered, "my last service for you. This is one task I cannot see through to the end." Above his head, the candles blurred, shivered and shimmered in a halo of tears. "I know what lies ahead, but I am ailing, and so very tired. It will have to be up to the lad, Llewelyn. God help us, all up to him . . ."

18

Woodstock, England

April 1247

Llewelyn's unhappiest birthday had been his twelfth, coming as it had so soon after his grandfather's death. But his nineteenth birthday was no less dismal, for he marked it on the road to Woodstock, where he and Owain were to make a total and humiliating surrender to the English King.

The war's outcome was inevitable. Disheartened by Davydd's untimely death, weakened by famine, abandoned by their countrymen, the Welsh of Gwynedd had little chance of thwarting the English Crown; the surprise was that Llewelyn and Owain had been able to hold out for fourteen months. The knowledge that they had put up a valiant defense gave Owain a small measure of solace. Llewelyn was denied even that meagre comfort. He had failed his grandfather. In his moment of truth, he had been found wanting. And it consoled him not at all that his failure was also Owain's; Owain, he could forgive.

His despair was all the greater for being a burden he must bear alone. After Davydd's death, he had reconciled with his uncle Einion, yet neither Einion nor Tegwared rode by his side as he approached Henry's Oxfordshire manor. He had wanted no witnesses to what was to come. He missed them, though, as he splashed into the shallows of the River Glyme, for fears echoed too loudly in solitude. Above all, he missed Ednyved's ice-blooded sangfroid, his shrewd counsel. But Ednyved's blunt tongue was stilled. He had died in the heat of high summer, on St Margaret's Eve, as lightning split the sky asunder and hailstones shredded the leaves from trees, sent birds plummeting to the ground and men hastening for rosary beads, a gale of such savagery that people knew it must be an omen of ill fortune, a harbinger of doom. And as he rode through the Woodstock gateway, it seemed to Llewelyn that Gwynedd's fortunes had plummeted no less fatally than those storm-slaughtered birds.

At first sight, the royal manor of Woodstock resembled a town, for around Henry's lodgings were clustered a kitchen, buttery, larder, almonry, stables, a smithy, other buildings Llewelyn could not identify. They were as rich as Croesus, the English kings; what Welsh prince could hope to equal such vast revenues? Llewelyn felt a sudden chill. Nudging his mount closer to Owain's, he murmured, "Shall we lay a wager upon where we'll be come Ascension Day? Back in Gwynedd— or at the Tower?"

There was no malice in his jest; he'd always been one for whistling past graveyards. But Owain gave him a baleful stare, for he, too, put little credence in the English King's safe-conduct. "I doubt you'll find it so amusing once you're mewed up in an English castle keep!"

Had it been anyone else, Llewelyn might have apologized; Owain was hardly the ideal audience for jokes about the Tower. But with Owain, the most he could manage was strained civility, and that was more than Owain even attempted. "Do you know what I most admire about you, Owain? Your unfailing good humor," he said flippantly, thus earning himself another irate glare.

The bailey was overflowing with curious spectators, and Llewelyn remembered having read that Romans had turned out in large numbers to watch as the Christians sought to convert the lions. In the next moment, though, all else was forgotten. "Jesú, Owain! It's Mama!"

Senena was waiting by the stairs of the hall porch, flanked by two young boys. With a shock, Llewelyn realized that these strangers were his brothers. Owain was already dismounting, embracing first his mother and then the boys. It was not so easy for Llewelyn. Owain had maintained contact with Davydd and Rhodri during his confinement at the Tower; Llewelyn had not seen the boys since the autumn of 1241. Rhodri hung back, still in his brother's shadow. Davydd showed no such shyness. He was a handsome youngster with bright chestnut hair and Gruffyd's eyes; they were as green as a Welsh mountain cat's, and as remote, too opaque, too wary for the eyes of an eight-year-old. The eyes of a hostage.

The change in Senena was no less unnerving; Llewelyn was stunned to see how much she'd aged. Wimples had never been a Welsh fashion, and the brown braids that hung down from her veil were threaded through with grey. Her face was free of cosmetics, a mirror to the bleakest, more barren of terrains, the rock-strewn, arid wasteland of widowhood. The grey eyes were dry, tearless, as frozen as the mouth denied the leavening of laughter. Not even now could she summon up a smile; that was a forgotten skill, withered with disuse.

"You need feel no shame," she said in a low, fierce voice. "You did your best against a far stronger foe." For the most fleeting of moments, those grey-ice eyes cut toward Llewelyn's face, her first acknowledgment of her second son's presence. "You did not shame yourselves," she repeated tautly. "You did not shame your father."

Owain caught her elbow, drew her aside. "Christ Jesus, Mama, why did you bring the lads?"

For once, Llewelyn found himself in full accord with his brother; why make the boys unwilling witnesses to a Welsh defeat? "Could you not have spared them this, Mama?" he asked, and saw that he'd been wrong; she could still smile—a twisted grimace of mirthless mockery.

"Do you think it was my doing? Nay, they were summoned at the royal command. Henry," she said, drawling out the King's Christian name with a truly terrible contempt, "thought it would be a kindness, a magnanimous gesture from the victor to the vanquished."

Llewelyn could more easily comprehend an enemy's vengeful rancor than such misguided benevolence. "Can you keep the lads here, Mama?" he asked quietly, and when she nodded, he turned, and without waiting for Owain, mounted the stairs into the hall.

Llewelyn paused in the doorway. There was an unnatural stillness about the scene before him, an unsettling air of unreality. He welcomed it, though, for how else could he endure what was to come? Mere playacting, he thought. Henry the complacent conqueror, regally clad in red velvet. He and Owain the penitent Welsh Princes. Rehearsed speeches, words that floated on the air like feathers, with no more weight or substance. And then he saw Elen.

She was standing near the dais, her dark, prideful gaze shining like

a beacon across the crowded hall, a gaze that held such utter and unqualified love that his throat tightened. He would have sworn he'd
wanted no witnesses. But Elen had known him better than he knew
himself, had known he would need her here, Elen who shared his
grandfather's dream, who did not blame him for having betrayed it.
Their eyes held, and it was to Elen that he looked rather than to Henry
as he moved toward the dais, knelt before the English King.

THE great hall was festively adorned with spring blossoms and brightly
woven wall hangings, lit by fully a score of flaming torches. Llewelyn
was awed by the luxury of Woodstock; many of the chambers were
wainscoted in fine oak, and all of the windows were set with expensive
glazed glass panes. The sight of such splendor only intensified his despair. How could he hope to compete with Henry when Henry had so
much wealth, so much power? How in Christ's mercy had his grandfather managed to outfight or outwit two English Kings?

And yet it had not lasted. A lifetime's work now lay in ruins. All
his grandfather had won for Wales had been lost this afternoon. He and
Owain had been forced to yield the four cantrefs of the Perfeddwlad to
the English Crown, all of Gwynedd east of River Conwy. They'd had
to agree to provide Henry with one thousand foot-soldiers and twenty-
four knights should the King call upon them for military aid. Never had
Gwynedd been so tightly yoked to the English Crown.

Across the hall, he could see Owain, in earnest conversation with
their mother; he knew without being told that to join them would be
an intrusion. Neither Davydd nor Rhodri was in sight. Nor was Elen.
Llewelyn's sense of isolation had rarely been so overwhelming. Not that
he was being ignored. From the moment he'd entered the hall, he'd
found himself the focal point of all eyes. The stares were uncomfortably
obvious, obtrusive, the sort of stare men turned upon lepers and lamed
beggars. As if, Llewelyn concluded bitterly, being Welsh was a defor-
mity, too. He had rarely been so ill at ease, but pride held him in the hall,
just as pride kept him away from Senena and Owain.

Henry's laughter floated across the hall, exultant, joyful laughter
that salted Llewelyn's wounds anew. Henry was lavishing a conspicuous
amount of attention upon several young men and a girl in her mid-
teens, all of them flaxen-haired, uncommonly fair to look upon. Many
of Henry's courtiers were casting these new favorites disgruntled glances,
but Llewelyn was too distracted to fathom English undercurrents or
eddies. He wanted only for this wretched night to end.

He didn't hear the woman's approach. It was her perfume he noticed first, an intriguingly exotic fragrance, subtle yet haunting. He turned,

wondering how he might obtain some of this elusive, elegant scent for Melangell, and found himself gazing into beguiling blue eyes.

"Do you remember me?" she asked. Her tone was friendly, even faintly flirtatious, and he readily returned her smile.

"Is a man likely to forget the King's sister, the Countess of Leicester? Although I suspect that you would be remembered, Madame, were you but a crofter's daughter."

Nell laughed. "Llewelyn passed on more than those dark eyes, I see. He could be very gallant when he chose, to Joanna's dismay, for the women bedazzled by that honeyed tongue were legion."

Llewelyn laughed, too, for the first time since his arrival at Woodstock. He wanted Nell to stay, for not only was she fair, she was his grandfather's sister by marriage, and he hastily sought a topic of conversation. "Those people clustered about the King, the ones he has been favoring all evening, who are they?"

Nell's smile faded. "Guy, William, Aymer, and Alice de Lusignan— Henry's half-brothers and sister." She saw Llewelyn's brow quirk at "*Henry's* half-brothers," and although he did not say anything, a slight flush rose in her cheeks. "They have come to live at Henry's court, now that their father is joining the French King's crusade." She hesitated almost imperceptibly before saying, "Their mother—and mine—died last year. I expect you heard?"

Isabelle had died that past June at Fontevrault Abbey, after having been accused of attempting to poison the French King. Whether there was truth to the accusation, Nell did not know, did not want to know. The only certainty was that the accusation had frightened Isabelle enough to send her fleeing to Fontevrault. Nell's mouth tightened, and she looked challengingly now at Llewelyn, waiting tensely for his response.

He had, in fact, heard of Isabelle's disgrace; so great was the scandal that it had penetrated even into the fastness of Eryri. His face remained impassive, though, and Nell relaxed, favored him with another smile.

"I sought you out at my husband's behest. He withdrew to our own chambers some time ago, having no taste for court fêtes. He would very much like to meet you, though. Might I lure you away?" She saw him wavering, for he was admittedly curious about the Earl of Leicester, and clinched his acceptance by adding, "Elen is there."

HENRY had founded the borough of New Woodstock half a mile north of his manor, so that his courtiers might have adequate lodgings. But Simon and Nell were enjoying, with his blessings, the use of Everswell, a nearby manor built by Henry's grandfather for his beloved courtesan, Rosamond Clifford. As he gazed about at the bubbling springs, the starlit gardens, Llewelyn decided that Simon must stand high, indeed, in Henry's favor.

Simon's chamber was filled with friends, almost as if he were holding court himself. Of the other people present, Llewelyn was most impressed with Robert Grosseteste, the aged Bishop of Lincoln, for that venerable churchman's fame had spread as far as Wales, and with a tall, wind-burned man who looked as if he'd be more at home in tavern brawls than at the royal palace. When Simon began to introduce him, Will interrupted with a grin. "We've met before . . . at Aberconwy Abbey, where our paths crossed, if not our swords. Your battle tactics were first-rate, lad. I'd have told you that then, but the timing did not seem quite right!"

Even an hour ago, Llewelyn would have insisted that he could never find humor in the sacking of his grandfather's burial place. But an hour ago, he had not yet encountered Will. His mouth twitched, he laughed in spite of himself, and thus entered into an unspoken truce with two of his English enemies.

Simon and Will wanted to dissect the campaign in great detail, and Llewelyn was more than willing to join in, having recognized the kinship that soldiers the world over share. Once they'd refought the battle to their mutual satisfaction, they permitted the women to redirect the conversation, and the talk then ranged farther afield, to the earthquake that had rocked London two months past, to the arrival at the English court of Henry's de Lusignan kindred, and to the Pope's offer to Henry's brother Richard of the kingdom of Sicily.

Since the Pope's avowed enemy, the Emperor Frederick, was firmly in control of Sicily with no intention of abdicating, the Pope's offer was one that only Henry had taken seriously. Richard had responded with none of Henry's enthusiasm, remarking caustically that the Pope might as well offer him the moon.

Amidst the ensuing laughter, Llewelyn marveled that Henry's judgment could be so flawed. Would he truly have Richard entangle himself in a war he could not win, all for the glimmer of false gold? Nor was that Henry's only blunder. Llewelyn had not been long in concluding that Henry's blatant preference for his de Lusignan siblings was stirring up resentment. It was not surprising; the court was a natural breeding ground for envy. Henry should have anticipated a backlash. That he hadn't was significant to Llewelyn, offered him his first flicker of hope since his arrival at Woodstock.

All the talk was now of the French King's upcoming pilgrimage to the Holy Land, for crusading fever was running high. Virtually every man present was vowing to go; even Nell announced that she, too, would take the cross, accompany Simon to Palestine. Llewelyn listened, somewhat bemused. As much as he regretted the fall of Jerusalem to the Saracens, he could not share their enthusiasm for crusading; his enemies were in London, not Cairo or Damascus.

"Of course you Welsh need not roam so far afield to find infidels," Simon observed, reading his mind with such unerring accuracy that Llewelyn caught his breath. But then he saw that Simon's eyes were silvered with laughter, and he grinned. It came as something of a shock to realize that he was actually enjoying himself.

During a lull in the conversation, he drew Elen aside to ask her about Godstow Abbey. "It is close to Oxford, is it not? I ought to call upon Davydd's widow, Isabella, for courtesy's sake—Elen? What is amiss?"

"Ah, love, I thought you knew. Isabella is dead. I was told it was a wasting fever, but I think she lost heart. Poor lass, she—" Elen paused, turning like everyone else, toward the door.

Simon was no less startled than were his friends by the King's sudden and unheralded appearance in his chambers, but he rose at once, moved to make Henry welcome. Henry acknowledged the courtesy somewhat distractedly, and as soon as greetings were exchanged, he blurted out, "Simon, is it true what I've just heard? That you mean to take the cross?"

"Indeed, I do. I expect—"

"But you cannot! You must not go to the Holy Land, not whilst I have need of you. I want you to accept the governorship of Gascony."

Simon frowned. "Henry, I am sorry, in truth I am. You are my King. But I serve God, too, and Jerusalem must be restored to Christian control."

Nell had moved to Simon's side, but their guests discreetly withdrew to the far end of the chamber in order to give Simon and his King some privacy. Llewelyn was glad to retreat. It seemed strange to him that Henry should have come himself rather than summoning Simon to his presence, almost as if Henry were the supplicant and Simon the sovereign, and when Elen joined him, he said as much to her, secure in the knowledge that no one but she spoke Welsh.

"Exactly," she agreed softly. "The wrong man wears the crown, and God pity them, they both know it."

"And yet all seems amicable between them. Henry let Simon lodge here at Everswell, and they treat each other with perfect courtesy . . ."

"Indeed. But that courtesy is like the ice that glazes over a winter pond. It obscures what is truly happening beneath the surface, and a man ventures out upon it at his own risk."

Llewelyn gave her a searching, sideways glance. "You are fond of Simon."

"Yes . . . but not at first, though. I'd never met anyone as free of doubts as Simon; he raised all my hackles!"

"A man free of doubts sounds truly blessed to me," Llewelyn said, so wistfully that she laughed.

"No, love, not so. Too much certainty is more often a curse than a blessing. A man blind to shading, oblivious to subtlety is a man who cannot compromise, a battle commander likely to take too many risks, a crusader for Christ who looks upon the Jew, the heretic, and the infidel as the enemies of God, a seeker after perfection in a world of mere mortals."

"Those are traits that most men would hold forth as virtues," Llewelyn pointed out playfully, and she nodded.

"I know, lad," she said wryly. "Well do I know."

"Tell me of Gascony. It is a province in Aquitaine, the last of the English possessions upon the Continent, no? Do you think Simon will agree to forsake his crusade, to rule Gascony for the King?"

"Yes . . . eventually."

"And will the King then be grateful to Simon?"

Elen was silent, watching Simon and Henry. "No," she said at last. "No, I think not."

19

Westminster, England

January 1251

EPIPHANY was by tradition a day of great festivity at the English court. But this year's celebration seemed sadly lacking in splendor to Eleanor. So hard-pressed was Henry for money that he'd even refrained from giving the members of his household their customary gifts of Christmas clothing, a humiliating economy for so luxury-loving a King. To Eleanor, who was no less extravagant than her spendthrift husband, his new-found frugality was particularly galling during the holiday season.

"Henry has so generous a nature; I know it vexes him to deny us the comforts we deserve. But his priorities are skewed. He still manages to find great sums of money for the rebuilding of Westminster Abbey. It is a good thing to honor the Almighty, of course, but the abbey had a perfectly adequate church, Sanchia. There was truly no need for Henry to assume such an awesome undertaking. His masons have been laboring for nigh on six years already!"

Her sister shrugged. "Did you not tell me just last week that Henry had coerced a rich Jew of York into giving him fourteen thousand marks, money he then turned over to you?"

"Well, yes, but . . ." Eleanor had begun to bridle. With an effort, she curbed her annoyance. Was Sanchia being malicious? Or merely indifferent? After a moment, she sighed. Richard had been bedazzled by Sanchia's beauty, but once they were wed, her allure had faded. How else explain Sanchia's moodiness, her peevish tongue? For certes, her sister had not found with Henry's brother the contentment she had found with Henry.

At least Sanchia had now been able to give Richard a son. When her first child died, her grieving had been painful to Eleanor, for that was a sorrow embedded in her own heart. Earlier that evening, their nurses had ushered her children into the hall to bid her good night: Edward, her favorite, a handsome, swaggering lad already in his twelfth year; ten-year-old Margaret, who was to wed the young Scots King ere the year was out; Beatrice, a fair, giddy child of eight; Edmund, her baby, not yet six. But two pitiful little shadows had trailed them into the hall, Richard and John, the sons born after Edmund, the sons who had not survived.

The brightness in the hall dimmed. "The loss of a child is mayhap the most common of griefs," she said softly, "and yet it is the wound hardest to heal . . ."

"What I do not understand," Sanchia confessed, "is why some women are spared such grief. I've lost one, you've lost two, Richard's first wife lost three of her four. But Henry's sister is blessed with babe after healthy babe. How many has Nell borne de Montfort now, six? Seven?"

"Six, I think." Eleanor paused, counting on her fingers. "Harry and Bran and Guy and Amaury, that's four. Then she had a fifth son, Richard, two springs ago, after she'd accompanied Simon to Gascony. And her lass, Joanna, was born last June. I have to agree, Sanchia; she's luckier than she deserves. But her children are a likable lot, nonetheless. The older boys have been my Edward's companions since their cradle days, and— Speaking of babes, I almost forgot to tell you! Henry's niece, Elen de Quincy, has been brought to bed of her third, another lass, sad to say."

"Elen? Ah, yes, the Welshwoman," Sanchia said, with another shrug, one of dismissal. "Henry beckons to us from the dais. I marvel he noticed us, so taken up is he with those de Lusignan kinsmen of his. Do you never tire of their constant presence? Were I you, I'd fear lest I'd find one secreted under Henry's bed!"

Although she needn't fear eavesdroppers, for Sanchia's arrow had been launched in langue d'oc, the language of their native Provence, Eleanor was irked, nonetheless, by her sister's sarcasm. "Henry loves his family well," she said coldly. "Can you fault him for that?"

"They are not worthy of Henry's favor, Eleanor. None at the court can comprehend why Henry dotes upon them so, for no one else can abide their arrogance and avarice and haughty ways, not even Richard or Nell. Yet Henry has done naught but lavish honors upon them. It was disgraceful enough when he wed Alice to the Earl of Surrey's heir and gave William the earldom of Pembroke. But to force the monks of Winchester to elect Aymer as their Bishop—that is an outrage, Sister! Aymer is twenty-three years of age, a boastful, unlettered rakehell, ignorant of the Scriptures, of—"

"Enough! Think you that I do not know how unfit Aymer is to wear a bishop's mitre? These de Lusignans have naught to recommend them but handsome faces and Henry's blood. They stir up dissension at the court, make enemies with awesome ease, and they give nary a thought to Henry's welfare. I cannot begin to count the times they have brought shame upon him. Just a fortnight ago, Guy de Lusignan returned from the Holy Land, and on his way to London, he passed the night at Faversham Abbey, where the Abbot was kind enough to lend him horses for his journey—horses that Guy never returned! But what matters my opinion as long as they hold Henry's heart? I understand it no better than you do, Sanchia. Mayhap they stir up memories of Henry's mother . . . I just do not know! I do know, though, that I will not grieve my husband by seeking to separate him from his kinsmen. Nor will I allow anyone to speak ill of him in my presence."

Sanchia did not reply, and Eleanor relented, satisfied that she had made her point. "I know my enemies accuse me of influencing Henry unduly. To hear them talk, John Mansel and I are the puppeteers and Henry our hapless puppet. Well, that is arrant nonsense. Naturally I seek to counsel Henry, but he is very much his own man, and those who think—" She swallowed the rest of her complaint, for they had reached the dais, and she found a sweet smile for Henry, a spurious one for his brothers, Aymer and William de Lusignan. She did not have long to endure their company, however, for within moments Richard was moving toward them.

"I've just been told," he said, "that Simon de Montfort is on his way into the hall."

Henry swung around. "That cannot be! Simon is in Gascony!"

Richard shook his head. "My servant says he was riding a well-lathered horse, accompanied by only three men," he said, and Henry frowned uneasily.

People were already turning, staring. Simon did not even pause to acknowledge the surprised greetings of friends. He strode toward the King, leaving a trail of whispers in his wake. As he knelt before the dais, Henry felt a prickle of resentment that Simon should dare to come before him like this, unshaven, boots muddied, mantle dark with dust. Although bloodshot, glazed with fatigue, Simon's grey eyes were smoky, burning with such intensity that Henry's protest froze on his lips.

"Your Grace," Simon said, "I bring you grievous news. Gascony is at war."

THEY had withdrawn from the great hall in urgent haste, seeking the privacy of Henry's Painted Chamber. There they listened in shocked silence as Simon told them that Gascony was aflame with rebellion, a revolt led by Henry's own kinsman, Gaston de Béarn, in alliance with the lords of Fronsac and Albret and Bordeaux's powerful del Soler family.

Henry's dismay found expression in angry reproach. "Jesú, Simon, how could you fail me like this? Your task was to bring the rebels to terms, to quell—"

Simon's exhaustion overrode deference. "By God, your memory is pitifully short! I did just that upon my arrival in Gascony. I negotiated truces with France and Navarre, I besieged and captured the rebel castles of Fronsac and Gramont, and then I sent Gaston de Béarn to you for justice. A rebel, a traitor to his liege lord, a brigand who'd preyed upon his own vassals, shamed women and plundered towns without pity, a man who bloody well deserved to hang. But you saw fit to pardon him, to restore him to power, to send him back to Gascony, did you not? The self-same Gaston de Béarn who is once more in rebellion against the Crown!"

Henry flushed darkly. "Gaston is my wife's first cousin, and he swore upon his honor that he would keep faith with me!"

"And you believed him? A man more false than the serpent, more treacherous than Judas? Henry, how could you be so trusting? Gaston de Béarn is my kinsman, too, for he wed the daughter of my brother's widow. But had he been my very brother, I'd not have winked at his crimes. I'd have hanged him higher than Haman, and had you done that, this rebellion would never have happened."

"Whether I erred or not in pardoning Gaston, it is done and beyond recall. Mayhap had you not treated the Gascon lords so harshly, they'd not have been so quick to join forces with Gaston. As it happened, Gaston sent his chaplain to court barely a fortnight ago, with a saddlebag full of complaints against your rule. Gaston claims that you have been arbitrary and unjust, that you have imprisoned lords without trial, seized their castles, and destroyed their vineyards. What say you to these charges, Simon? Do you deny them?"

Simon had been listening in astonishment. "That I have been unjust, indeed I do deny—upon the surety of my soul! But for certes I do not deny that I imprisoned the lords of Gramont and Soule, or that I seized their strongholds. How else would you have me deal with rebels? These men call themselves lords, but in truth they are no better than brigands. You want to know if I have succeeded in restoring order to Gascony? Ask, then, the common people, ask the pilgrims and townsfolk and merchants who can now travel the roads without fear of ambush, who can sell their goods for fair prices, who need no longer hide their women when their lord rides into town—ask them if I have been unjust!"

The discussion was not going as Henry wished; somehow arguments with Simon never did. "That may well be," he said cautiously, "but surely you cannot expect me to dismiss the testimony of viscounts and barons. The word of a lord must count for more than the word of a carpenter or a blacksmith, Simon."

"If memory serves, Our Lord Christ was a carpenter," Simon could not resist gibing. He immediately regretted it, for Henry's face splotched with angry color, and he said swiftly, "Wait, my lord. I ask that you hear me out. Of course I am not saying that all men have equal rights. I believe no less than you do in a nobility born of blood. But privilege carries with it obligations. A lord has a responsibility to those of lesser rank. He must not abuse his power, he must not persecute the weak, and he must safeguard his people as best he can. In return for their loyalty and obedience, a lord pledges his protection to his subjects. It is a debt of honor," Simon concluded passionately, for what he had just articulated was his concept of kingship. He waited now for Henry to agree with him, to avow his own adherence to these same principles of power, waited in vain.

Henry was frowning. Once, years ago, Henry had summoned a Jewish rabbi to his court, demanded of the man why so few Jews came to the conversion houses he had set up throughout the country. Henry had wanted to know why the Jews were so loath to convert to the True Faith, why they shunned salvation, and he had listened intently, if uncomprehendingly, as the rabbi spoke of Yahweh, the God of Israel. Neither Simon nor Henry had been able to understand why people should cling so obstinately to a false faith, but it seemed to Simon now that the look upon Henry's face was the same as upon the day he'd confronted the aged rabbi, his the baffled expression of one encountering an alien philosophy, a creed both mysterious and menacing.

"I am King by God's Will," Henry said slowly, "not by the approval of my subjects. My covenant is therefore with the Almighty, not with my people. But I do, of course, desire for my subjects the King's Peace. If these barons are as lawless as you say, mayhap they deserve the punishment you have meted out to them. Yet not all of the complaints come from the highborn. What of the del Soler family?"

Simon was silent, grimly weighing the implications of Henry's words. He was uncommonly well-read for a man of his rank, knew that even King John of ill fame, Henry's notorious father, had possessed a sense of noblesse oblige. A king who did not was a king unfettered by duty, counseled only by his own conscience. For all Henry's piety and good will, was his conscience enough to sustain the burden of government? Simon thought not.

Only when Henry repeated his question did Simon rouse himself, say impatiently, "My liege, you know the offenses of the del Solers fully as well as I. When an election eve mêlée broke out in Bordeaux between the city's two rival factions, the del Solers and the Colom family, I hastened to the scene, ordered the fighting to cease. The Coloms heeded my command, but the del Solers did not, had to be subdued by force. I thought you were in agreement with me, for when Gaillard del Soler fled to England, you ordered him to be remanded into my custody and imprisoned."

"Not precisely," Henry snapped. "We determined that Gaillard del Soler and his confederates should be tried before a Gascon court. But you did not bother with such legalities; you simply cast the man into prison!"

"What if I did? Christ Jesus, Henry, I was fighting a war—your war!"

Henry could not deny the truth in that. Simon had moved to his side, and Henry took a backward step. He was five feet, nine inches tall, and usually quite comfortable with his height, but not now, not next to Simon, the last man in Christendom he wanted to look up to. "I am not defending the del Solers, Simon," he said, in a more conciliatory tone. "I seek only to find out all the facts. From what I've heard, that rioting in Bordeaux was bloody, indeed; I know some of your own household knights died in the fray. But the del Solers claim that you did favor the Coloms from the very first. Is that true?"

Simon nodded. "Yes, I did. Shall I tell you why? Because the Coloms are wine merchants, dependent upon trade with England. They have a vested interest, therefore, in maintaining close ties with the Crown. Whereas the del Solers are no longer engaged in trade, and they have allied themselves with the local lords, with outlaw barons like Raimond, Viscount of Fronsac. Can you find fault with my reasoning?" he demanded, and when Henry reluctantly shook his head, he followed Henry to the hearth.

"I did not seek the office of Seneschal. This was a burden you thrust upon me, Henry. I had taken the cross, was about to depart for the Holy Land when you entreated me to delay my pilgrimage, to go, instead, to Gascony and govern it for you. It was agreed that I should serve a seven-year term, with absolute authority to act on your behalf. You violated that agreement when you pardoned Gaston de Béarn, and now you show yourself willing to listen to my enemies, to give credence to traitors and rebels."

Simon drew a sharp breath, reluctant to reveal how deeply affronted he was by Henry's accusations; he had far too much pride to admit he felt betrayed by his King's lack of trust. "Shall I resign my command? I will relinquish it this very night if that be your wish, and resume my crusader's vow, asking only that you reimburse me for the heavy expenses I have incurred in your service. If, however, you wish me to continue as Seneschal, I will do so, but only if I have your full support. The choice, my liege, is yours."

Henry hated nothing so much as being backed into a corner. He glanced unhappily at Eleanor and Richard, silent witnesses to his clash of wills with Simon, but neither showed any inclination to intercede. His hesitation was only momentary, though; despite his dissatisfaction with Simon's performance, he knew of no one who could do better. Moreover, to accept Simon's resignation would be to admit that his appointment had been a mistake, just as his brother Richard had once argued.

"I want you to continue as Seneschal," he said. "It was no easy task I set before you; I know that. You have my every confidence, and to prove it, I shall grant you an additional three thousand marks to quell the rebellion."

That was not the answer Simon had wanted. "So be it, then," he agreed, sounding so weary that Henry finally noticed just how utterly exhausted he looked.

"Good Lord, Simon, did you sleep at all on your way from Dover? You truly should get some rest. But first, stay and sup with us. We're having a special mummery, a pageant about St George slaying the dragon."

Simon mustered up a smile. "Thank you, but no. Right now I seek only a bath and then a bed, for I depart at dawn for Kenilworth, where I hope to raise additional moneys by selling some of my forests. And then, of course, I want to visit His Grace, the Bishop of Lincoln; Nell and I entrusted our two eldest sons into the Bishop's keeping, so that they might be properly educated." As he spoke, Simon moved toward Eleanor, kissed her hand, and Henry's ring. He was at the door before Henry cried out.

"Simon, wait! I have grievous news for you. We have learned that my cousin, the Earl of Salisbury, is dead."

"Will?" Simon swallowed, then leaned back against the door. His eyes remained dry, but the pupils had dilated so suddenly that the irises seemed utterly black, bereft of all color, all light. Henry had rarely seen him so shaken, and he was at once contrite.

"I ought not to have blurted it out like that, but I'd forgotten you were such friends. He died well, Simon, died a hero's death. We can all be proud, can glory in his martyrdom."

Simon nodded mutely. Making the sign of the cross, he turned, swiftly departed the chamber.

Henry was not at all satisfied with the outcome, yet he did not know exactly what he'd wanted from Simon, and that uncertainty only intensified his frustration. "It is troubling enough," he complained, "that Simon can see only blacks and whites. But he also demands that all men be as color-blind as he is!"

"You know I bear no love for Simon de Montfort," Eleanor said, after a long pause. "But I do think he is right in this, Henry. Rebels must be punished, and retribution must be swift. Whatever his other faults, Simon does understand that."

This was not the first time that Henry had found himself at odds with his wife. It never failed to surprise him that so feminine, so delicate a woman could be so resolute, so remorseless. He could not help envying her absolute certainty, her sure sense of right, and he worried sometimes lest she think him unmanly, for he knew she made a more implacable foe than he. She'd insisted he was too lenient with the Welsh, she shared none of his concerns about converting the Jews, would have gladly expelled them all from their realm, and he knew she cared no more than Simon that rebels were denied due process of law. In truth, Henry was not all that disturbed himself by the illegality of it, would not have objected had he not been forced to deal with the aggrieved complaints of those who felt wronged by Simon's summary justice.

Turning away from Eleanor, Henry looked challengingly at his brother. "Am I to assume from your silence that you, too, disapprove?"

"In fact, I agree," Richard said coolly. "Now that you've committed yourself to Simon, you have to support him. You owe the man that much. That does not mean, however, that I've changed my mind. I told you more than two years ago that de Montfort was the wrong man for the task at hand. He is more than capable of conquering a province, utterly incapable of pacifying it afterward. Whilst Simon excels at breaching walls, your Seneschal should be able to mend fences, too. But you paid me no heed, you would have yourself a soldier. Well, that is what you got, one of the most celebrated soldiers in Christendom. I daresay he'll quell this latest rebellion soon enough; I've heard it said that the Gascons 'fear the Earl of Leicester more than lightning.' It is what you wanted, Henry, is it not? So do not complain to me because your soldier does not act like a statesman."

"And I suppose you would have been the ideal choice? The truth is, Richard, that you've never forgiven me for revoking that grant, for giving Gascony to my son instead of to you!"

Richard rose, stalked to the door. "Take heart, Henry. If all else fails, you can always go to Gascony yourself. I'm sure the rebels would surrender at once, for who would dare to defy the victor of Saintes?"

Henry flinched, but Richard didn't see; he'd already slammed the door. Eleanor came hastily to her husband's side. "Pay Richard no mind, beloved. Gascony is part of our Edward's inheritance. It belongs by right to him, not to Richard."

"I know," Henry said morosely. "But he is my brother, and it grieves me that we should be at odds over this. Damn him! Damn him and Simon both!"

He had slumped down in the closest chair, straightened up hopefully as the door flew open. But it was not a repentant Richard, it was his son. Henry's spirits soared at sight of the boy. He adored all his children, but Edward held a special place in his heart, Edward, his firstborn, Edward who gave every promise of one day being as tall, as fair, and as fearless as his famous grand-uncle, Richard Lionheart.

"I heard that Uncle Simon was here! Is it true, Papa? Has he come back from Gascony?"

Henry stiffened. Striving for nonchalance, he said, "Yes, lad, he is back. You just missed him, in fact."

"Mayhap I can still catch him then," Edward exclaimed, and whirled, bolting from the chamber as precipitately as he'd entered.

"Ah, Henry . . ." Eleanor reached out, sought without success to knead some of the tension from his neck and shoulders. "You must not let it hurt you, beloved. Edward is just at that age when lads are easily bedazzled by swordplay, by battlefield heroics, and Simon is . . ."

She did not complete the sentence. She did not have to; Henry finished it for her. " '. . . the greatest soldier in Christendom,' " he quoted bitterly.

✦

FROM the south solar window of the Bishop of Lincoln's palace, Simon gazed down upon Danesgate. Sleet had been falling since mid-morning, and two carts had just collided on the steep, icy hill, spilling wine kegs and crated chickens and sacks of flour into the street. A crowd soon gathered, drawn by the creative profanity of the drivers. But Simon was oblivious to the chaotic scene below him. He was seeing the sun shimmer upon the muddy waters of the Nile, above an empty, copper-colored sky.

"Mansourah," he murmured, turning away from the window. "That was the name of the village. The French King's hot-headed brother led the raid. Will warned him that they were badly outnumbered, but he paid no heed. Then when the Saracens attacked, he tried to flee, only to drown in the Nile. Not Will, though. He held his ground, refused to yield, saying he'd die ere he surrendered to infidels. So impressed were the Saracens with his courage that the Sultan of Babylon saw that he had an honorable burial."

Taking a seat across from the Bishop, he said softly, "I am proud to have called him friend. Few men are given such a glorious ascent into Paradise. But I shall miss him, more than I can say . . ."

"And you wish with all your heart that you had been there to fight beside him," the Bishop said, eliciting from Simon a startled smile.

"Have you turned soothsayer now? How well you know me. Not that I yearn for martyrdom! But at least Will died in the service of the Almighty; his death had meaning. I had three near-misses with death myself in the past twelvemonth," he admitted, somewhat to the Bishop's surprise, for he rarely shared secrets of risk. "All men die, of course, and no Christian should fear death. But should my wife be made a widow, my children made fatherless, what comfort would they have, knowing I died for a fickle King's favor?"

"But did the King not promise to support your efforts against the rebels?"

Simon gave a mirthless laugh. "Do you remember the legend of the birds of paradise? Surpassingly beautiful and dazzling to watch on the wing, but they could never land, for they lacked feet. Well, Henry's promises soar upward, too, in flights of golden rhetoric, but they never make it back to earth. Today he pledges me his eternal gratitude. To-morrow he may well lend an ear to Gaston de Béarn again." Simon had reached for a wine cup, but now he set it down with a thud. "Gaston has no more loyalty than Lucifer, is hand-in-glove with the Kings of Navarre and Castile. His sworn word is spit on the wind. So how, then, can Henry give credence to anything he says? It is almost as if Henry wanted to believe ill of me!"

"Mayhap he does, Simon. Although in fairness to Henry, I have to say that other voices besides Gaston de Béarn's have been raised against you."

Simon was stunned. "I never thought I should have to defend myself to you, my lord."

"Nor do you." The older man leaned across the table, laid his hand upon Simon's arm. "I do not fault you for treating brigands as they deserve. These Gascon lords hate you because you sought to uphold the King's rights and to defend Christ's poor. I do regret, though, that you have been so inflexible, so loath to listen—"

"When? What have you heard?"

"The King's Seneschal always came to the town of Saut to take the townsmen's oaths of fealty, a privilege they held very dear. But you insisted that they come to you at Saint-Sever, and when they refused, you—"

"Had I gone to Saut for the oath-taking, the other towns would have demanded the same privilege. It just was not practical, made no sense. I all but slept in the saddle as it was!"

The Bishop nodded. "I do not doubt that you were hard-pressed for time. But sometimes, my son, there are other considerations than practicality. You are the best horseman I've ever seen, for you know how to guide your mount with the slightest pressure of your knees, whilst keeping a light hand on the reins. If you could but learn to use the same sure touch with men, Simon, you'd find them less likely to balk."

Simon was quiet for a time. The Bishop's criticism was not as easily dismissed as Henry's, for if Henry's judgment was dross, Bishop Robert's was unalloyed gold. Moreover, he was deeply touched by the Bishop's fond use of "my son." "As ever, you counsel wisely," he said at last. "My temper does catch fire too fast, and I too often let my stubbornness lead me astray. I have tried to learn patience, but my resolve takes me only so far. In truth, my lord, I do not think I can change my nature."

The Bishop's smile was still compelling, belying the burdens of ill health and age. "No," he conceded, "probably not. Try to remember, though, that neither can Henry. Now . . . no more lectures. You have a Christian's conscience and a knight's honor; betwixt them, they shall see you through to a safe harbor. Let us talk, instead, of more cheerful matters, of your sons. They are fine lads, Simon, mayhap not the scholars I would wish; Latin in particular seems to elude them. But they have good hearts and more than their share of pluck. At times they can be too boisterous for an old man's liking, but we expect blooded stock to have spirit. I think you will be well pleased with their progress."

Harry and Bran looked uncommonly neat and well-scrubbed to

Simon. Harry was twelve now, and Bran ten, and Simon was amazed at how fast they'd grown in the six months since he'd seen them last. They'd seemed somewhat subdued as they entered, as if expecting to be called to account for found-out sins, but at sight of their father, they abandoned all decorum, flung themselves upon him with joyful shrieks. "Papa! You're back! For how long? Is Mama with you? When can—"

"Enough!" Simon laughed. "I cannot answer if you assail me both at once. Your mother is back in Bordeaux with your little brothers and sister, but I brought you her latest letter and some surprise packages. I expect to be at Kenilworth for just a month or so, however long it takes me to raise funds. Whilst I'd not want to interrupt your studies, I would like you to spend some time at Kenilworth with me. Now . . . other questions?"

The boys exchanged glances, elected Harry as spokesman. "Papa . . . when you go back to Gascony, can we go with you?"

Simon slowly shook his head. They knew better than to beg, but they looked so disappointed that Simon actually found himself wavering for a moment. "You know that is not possible, lads. I see no reason, however, why you cannot take a brief respite from your lessons, pass a fortnight in London with your cousin Edward. That is, if Bishop Robert agrees?" he added, and the Bishop gave an amused nod, marveling anew that Simon, of all men, should be such an indulgent father.

Simon's sons politely expressed their thanks, but it was obvious they considered London a poor substitute for Gascony. It was Bran whose discipline broke first. "Why must you go back to Gascony, Papa? Why can you not come home to stay?"

"Because I gave the King my word, Bran."

Bran bit his lip. "I know you say a man must keep his word, Papa. But the King does not always keep his word! So why, then, must you still serve him?"

Simon was taken aback, gave a rueful laugh. "Amidst your study of Latin and arithmetic and geography, have you taken up law, too?" But that was an evasion, and he owed the boy better than that. Reaching out, he drew Bran to him. "I serve Henry because he is the King." Bran said nothing; it was clear, though, that he found it an unsatisfactory answer. Simon looked over at the Bishop and shrugged. He was not yet ready to admit, even to himself, how unsatisfactory an answer it was to him, too.

THE sky was beginning to lighten in the east; the last stars were fading from sight. April had been a month of sudden, chilling rains, slowing down Simon's assault upon Castillon Castle, but it was May now and the siege was drawing to an end. Peter de Montfort had no doubts of that, for Simon had told him this would be the day that the castle fell, and Peter had learned to trust Simon's military judgment. Castillon had dominated the River Dordogne since the ninth century, but it was not so formidable a stronghold as Fronsac and Gramont, castles said to be impregnable, castles captured by Simon. Peter felt certain that the rebel Viscount, Pierre de Castillon, would be a prisoner or a corpse before this day was done.

Now, however, his immediate concern was for Simon. Mining was the slowest means of taking a castle, but the most effective, and once they had broken through Castillon's outer defenses, Simon put his men to work with picks and shovels. Day by day, the tunnel snaked forward, while Simon kept the defenders distracted with a relentless barrage from mangonel and trebuchet. At last the mine was ready, having been cautiously and laboriously dug across the inner bailey, up under the southwest corner of the castle keep. Rising by cover of night, Simon's men had stuffed the tunnel with brushwood, with the bodies of newly killed pigs, and they were about to set the fatal fire. Fueled by the lard, the flames would swiftly engulf the timbers used to shore up the tunnel roof, and when the tunnel collapsed, so, too, would the section of the keep above it.

Peter did not expect the mine to fail. But he was disturbed that Simon had insisted upon going down into the mine himself while the fire was set, for he thought that was a needless risk. Peter hated mines, could not endure such close confinement, and he was well aware of their dangers; it was not uncommon for them to collapse upon their builders, and the image of a flame-filled mine seemed to him verily a description of Hell.

The entrance to the mine was concealed by a wooden structure called a cat. Much to Peter's relief, he finally heard running footsteps, and men began to scramble up to safety. Simon's face was smudged with smoke and soot, but he was grinning. He coughed, laughed, and coughed again. "We've a right beautiful bonfire going, Peter. I'll wager those sluggards will still be abed when the keep comes crashing down around them!"

Simon had been up for most of the night, making ready for the final assault. He took time now to eat a hasty breakfast of bread and cheese, washed down with a spiced red wine, all the while giving last-minute instructions to his captains. "When Castillon falls," he predicted, "so, too, will the rebellion. They'll all come on the run, seeking terms."

"They already offered terms," Peter reminded him, and Simon grinned again.

"Yes," he said, "but now the terms will be mine," and he signaled for the bombardment to begin. The mangonels heaved boulders into the inner bailey, and the trebuchets hurled the dreaded Greek fire, which not even water could extinguish. The castle came rapidly to life; men appeared, yawning and cursing, upon the roof battlements, at the narrow arrow slits.

Simon had been both besieged and besieger, and he knew how unpleasant conditions must be for those mewed up within the keep, denied light or fresh air, unable to escape the pungent stink of the latrines, having to ration every swallow of water, to count every mouthful of food. "I think we've been able to locate the underground spring that feeds their well," he said. "If the mine does not work, we can salt the spring. That should bring a surrender in short order!"

But there was no need for contingency planning. The underground fire soon set the timbered roof ablaze, and when the tunnel caved in, the corner foundation of the keep cracked, split open in a shower of rock and mortar and ash. A few died in the collapsed rubble, more died trying to keep Simon's men from gaining entry at these gaping holes in the wall. But the defenders were outnumbered, and the momentum was with the attackers. Simon's men soon had control of the lower floor. Fighting his way up the stairwell, Simon discovered that the Viscount had barricaded himself in his private chamber, and Simon's demand for surrender was met with a volley of verbal abuse.

William Pigorel, Simon's Gascon lieutenant, joined Simon in the stairwell, suggested that he remind the Viscount that the rules of warfare permitted the hanging of an enemy garrison if they held out after all hope was gone.

Simon shook his head. "From what I know of Pierre de Castillon, he'd not turn a hair if we hanged his entire family from the battlements, as long as his own skin was safe. No, I've a better idea. Send some men up on the roof. Let's see what happens if we stuff burning brands down the louvres."

They soon heard a commotion from within the chamber, as the trapped men sought frantically to put out the fires, and while they were thus occupied it was simple enough for a stout soldier with an axe to split the door asunder. Simon was among the first into the chamber.

"De Castillon!" he challenged, and the Viscount moved to meet him. But no sooner had they crossed swords than Simon knew he was facing an inferior opponent, one who was, moreover, on the verge of panic. He easily parried the other man's thrust, with enough force to stagger them both. Recovering first, Simon lunged, and his sword neatly sliced through the overhead bed hangings. De Castillon reeled backward, suddenly enveloped in billowing folds of Tripoli silk. He bumped blindly into the bed, sprawled into the rushes, much to the amusement of Simon's soldiers, and by the time he managed to free himself from the shrouds of bedding, Simon was standing over him, sword poised above his windpipe.

"You may yield," Simon said calmly, "or you may die," and de Castillon gasped, "I yield," his sword clattering to the floor.

Afterward, there was much to be done. Simon's men had to make sure that the tunnel fire was extinguished. There were prisoners to be counted, and ransoms to be calculated, wounded men to be tended, and messengers to be dispatched, bearing word of Castillon's fall. Much to Pierre de Castillon's annoyance, he found himself shunted aside, utterly ignored, as if he were a person of no importance. He fumed in silence for a while, then demanded that he be taken to Simon, and he was so insistent that his guards finally grew tired of listening to his complaints, escorted him up the stairs into his own bedchamber.

His resentment flared even higher to find that Simon had appropriated his private quarters. Nor did his temper improve any when Simon disregarded his presence, continuing to dictate letters and give orders.

"Put the wounded in the hall until the smoke clears from the downstairs chamber. The cellar is still intact? Good, we'll use it for a dungeon. You'd best set men to digging grave pits, Peter, and—" Simon paused, looking up as the Viscount wrenched free of his guards, pushed toward him.

"My lord of Leicester, how much longer do you mean to keep me waiting? Your manners, sir, are insufferable. I demand to know what ransom you seek."

Simon's eyes narrowed upon the other man's flushed, sweaty face. "That, my lord de Castillon, will depend upon your allies of the moment. In the meantime, you may make yourself comfortable with the rest of your men—in the cellar."

Castillon's mouth dropped open. "You cannot be serious! You'd imprison me with the common soldiers? I am a lord, am entitled to be treated with the respect due my rank!"

Simon merely looked at him. "Men of honor I treat honorably," he said tersely. As his delighted soldiers shoved the sputtering Viscount toward the door, one of his squires knelt by his chair.

"My lord Simon, may I bandage your hand now?" the youth entreated, and Simon leaned back in his chair, glancing toward de Castillon with a sardonic smile.

"Indeed, Philip. God forbid that I should bleed all over my lord de Castillon's bedchamber." He nodded, and his men dragged their outraged prisoner into the stairwell. Suddenly realizing that he could not remember when he'd last slept, Simon made a gesture of dismissal. "I'd

best get some rest whilst I can. Peter, you are in command. Be merciful,
though, and do not awaken me unless we come under attack. No, lads,
do not bother," waving his squires away when they would have helped
him undress. "Just remember to clean the blood from my sword . . ."
That was his last coherent thought; flinging himself down upon the bed,
he fell asleep almost at once.

It seemed only moments later that someone was shaking his shoulder, but as he sat up, Simon saw that shadows had spilled from the
corners; daylight was done. Peter was bending over the bed. Although
Simon could not make out his face, his voice sounded strained. "Simon,
wake up. Your lady has sent her sergeant . . ."

Simon went cold, for Nell would not dispatch Andrew de la Brach
on a routine errand. "Those whoresons have not dared to besiege the
castle at Bordeaux?"

There was a flare of light as someone struck a flint, and Simon's eyes
flickered to Andrew's face. He was a taciturn man in his mid-fifties, utterly loyal, utterly imperturbable. Now he looked even grimmer than usual.

Kneeling in the darkness by the bed, he said, "My lord, it is not
your lady. It is your daughter, your babe, Joanna. She has been taken
right bad, and Lady Nell . . . she begs you to come with all haste."

IT was dawn by the time Simon came within sight of the city walls of
Bordeaux, but the sky remained shrouded in thick, grey clouds. As early
as it was, the city was already stirring, and as Simon rode through the
Medoque Gate onto Rue Sainte-Catherine, people stopped and stared,
for even the smallest child recognized the King's Seneschal on sight.
The looks directed at Simon were both admiring and resentful, in equal
measure, for the town was divided between those who saw Simon as
a saviour and those who saw him as Satan. Peter was acutely aware of
the stares; Simon was not. He could think of nothing but his ailing child,
could hear nothing but Andrew's ominous words, "taken right bad . . .
all haste." And yet he could not believe that his daughter might be
dying. His son Amaury had once fallen ill with the tertian fever, but
he'd recovered, even after the doctors had despaired. So, too, would
Joanna.

The castle known as Ombrière occupied the east bank of the River
Garonne, site of a stronghold since the days of the Roman Empire. The
ancient rectangular keep called the Arbalesteyre dated from the eleventh
century, had little of the comfort and none of the luxury to which Nell
was accustomed. But Ombrière was safe, and that was what mattered
to Simon. As he rode through the gatehouse, a cry went up and people

hastened out into the bailey. Simon saw none of them; his eyes had fastened upon the man standing by the entrance to the keep.

Geraud de Malemort was the Archbishop of Bordeaux, and it should have seemed natural that he'd be here in Nell's time of need, ready to offer solace, the comfort of their Church. But Simon knew better, for he knew Geraud de Malemort. The Archbishop was a politician, not a priest, little given to succoring the sick, and he was no friend to Simon.

He came forward, halted by Simon's stallion. "The ways of the Almighty," he said, "passeth the understanding of man," and it was in the unsympathetic eyes of an enemy that Simon learned of his daughter's death.

OMBRIÈRE's chapel was ablaze with torches and candles, at Nell's insistence, for Joanna had been afraid of the dark. Simon had lost all track of time, did not know how long he had been kneeling by his daughter's coffin. For once, prayer had failed him. Rising stiffly to his feet, he confessed, "No matter how often I tell myself, 'Thy Will be done,' I cannot stifle a voice that cries, 'Why?' "

Nell was standing on the other side of the coffin, gazing down at their child. "She could be asleep," she whispered, and then looked up at Simon. "The Archbishop of Bordeaux told me that too much grieving was an affront to the Almighty, for it showed that I lacked faith, that I doubted Joanna had been taken to the bosom of Our Lord Christ. I told him, in turn, that he was one of God's great fools."

Simon joined her beside the coffin, saying grimly, "Good lass."

Nell reached down, smoothed her daughter's blanket. "It was not our first quarrel. Were he not a Prince of the Church, I'd have had him ejected from the castle. You see, when Joanna . . . when Joanna was stricken, I sent for the doctors of Saint Jacques Hospital, but they could do nothing for her. I remembered that when Guy had been afflicted with the same cough, we'd boiled water, made a tent of blankets and let him breathe in the hot vapors. We tried that, too, with Joanna, but she steadily worsened. I'd heard that there was a Jew in the town, a man skilled in the healing arts, so I . . . I sent for him, which did outrage the Archbishop mightily."

Seeing that she had shocked her husband, too, Nell said defensively, "I know the Church forbids Christians to seek out Jews for healing, but in truth, I did not care! I would even have turned to an infidel Saracen doctor, had I thought he could save Joanna. But she died . . . died ere we could find him."

Her hand had clenched upon the edge of the coffin, whitened to the bone, and Simon quickly covered it with his own. "I ought to have been there for her, for you."

"For your sake, I am glad you were not. It was dreadful, Simon. She . . . she suffered so. I thought sure each coughing spasm would be her last. She could not breathe, kept crying, 'Mama, Mama . . .' " Nell had begun to tremble, but she had no more tears to shed. "I could do nothing for her. She was my child and I could do nothing for her . . ."

Simon pulled her into his arms, into a despairing embrace so tight that she gave an involuntary gasp. The chapel door was pushed ajar; they were being watched by their sons Guy and Amaury. Amaury, who was just five, whimpered, and Guy put his arm around his brother's shoulders. But neither boy dared to venture into the chapel, for they had never seen their father weep before.

20

Bordeaux, Gascony

April 1252

NELL was dictating a letter to her scribe when Simon returned to Ombrière. She had not seen her husband for a fortnight, as he'd been refortifying the castle at Cuzbac, and the letter was forgotten. It was not until several hours later that Simon happened to notice it lying upon the table in their bedchamber. "What is this, Nell?"

"I was writing to Bishop Robert. Shall I delay dispatching it until you have had a chance to add your own greetings?" she suggested, and Simon nodded.

"I do not want to repeat our news. What have you told him so far?"

"About the latest troubles with Henry. I told him that when we returned to England at Christmas, you offered again to resign your command, asking only that Henry reimburse you for your expenses, but Henry refused to pay, in clear violation of your agreement!" Three months later, echoes of indignation still colored Nell's voice. "I told Bishop Robert that even Henry's Queen was disquieted by his duplicity.

And then I explained how, whilst we were still at York, Henry received more complaints from those Gascon renegades, and he decided to send Henry de Wingham and Rocelin de Fos to Gascony. How very like Henry that, after you succeeded in quelling the rebellion for him, he should then reward you by appointing a commission of inquiry into your conduct!" Nell drew a calming breath; it didn't help. "Lastly, I told Bishop Robert that Henry's commissioners concluded that you had indeed treated some of the Gascon lords harshly, but no more than they deserved, and I expressed the hope that Henry would now cease his witless meddling."

"That hope," Simon said caustically, "is a broken straw. Any man who long serves Henry comes to understand exactly how Sisyphus must have felt." Anticipating her query, he added, "Sisyphus was a King of Corinth who displeased a pagan god of the Greeks. According to the legend, he was condemned to pass all eternity laboring to roll a huge boulder up a steep hill, only to have it roll down again as soon as he'd reached the summit."

"A man may be God's anointed and yet an idiot, too; my brother is living proof of that. But let's speak no more of Henry, beloved. Come, sit beside me on the settle, for I have news for you, news that not even Henry's foolishness can tarnish." Taking Simon's hand, she said, "I am with child again."

Nell was right; her news drove all thoughts of Henry from Simon's head. "This is the seventh time you've told me that, and each time it is like the first. We have in truth been blessed, Nell. When is the babe due?"

"October. Now . . . lie back, Simon, and rest, whilst I tell you all the London gossip, culled from Elen's latest letter." He did as she bade, pillowing his head in her lap, and she told him that Richard had received a pair of water buffalo for his menagerie, much to Henry's envy, for such creatures had never before been seen in England, that their de Lusignan half-brother William had poached deer from the Bishop of Ely's private park, and then forced his way into the Bishop's Hatfield manor, where he and his men plundered the Bishop's wine cellar, and that a two-year-old child in a Kent village had shown powers to heal the sick. Simon listened in silence, only the flicker of his lashes assuring her he did not sleep. His eyes snapped open, however, when she murmured, "And then, of course, there is the scandal about Henry's Queen, now that her love affair with Llewelyn of Wales has become common knowledge."

"What?" Simon relaxed again, lay back in her lap. "You caught me out," he confessed. "I was not listening. But I was thinking of you . . . and this babe. Do you remember, Nell, what I vowed on our wedding night? That I would keep you close, that I would keep you content, and that

I would keep you safe. Well, seven children in fourteen years is proof that I've kept you very close, indeed, and I think I've managed to content you—most of the time. But there has been precious little peace in our marriage. Too often you've found yourself torn between husband and brother, too often found yourself my hostage to Henry's enmity, and neither of us expected that on the day we exchanged vows. In truth, Nell . . . no regrets?"

A flippancy was already forming on Nell's tongue, but it was so unlike Simon to ask such a question, even in jest, that she heard herself saying, instead, "No, Simon. No regrets at all."

He reached for her hand, held it against his cheek. They'd had more than their share of quarrels in recent months, reflecting the strain of Simon's increasingly precarious position, and this moment of quiet and utter intimacy was both a healing and an affirmation. They remained together on the settle, not moving even as the chamber began to fill with shadows. And then the message came from the King.

Simon was forewarned by the very first words, for Henry had dispensed with the stock phrases of friendship, the conventional courtesies. The letter was addressed not to "The King's faithful and well-beloved brother-in-law," but simply to "The Earl of Leicester." Moving toward the last burning candle, Simon began to read. Watching from the settle, Nell saw the blood drain from his face. "Simon? Jesú, you look— What is wrong?"

"Henry has summoned me back to England. I am to appear before his royal court, to defend myself against the charges made by the Gascon lords."

"Mother of God . . ." To Nell, there was an appalling familiarity about this moment. It was as if she were reliving that ghastly August day twelve years ago, when Henry had suddenly turned upon Simon, shamed them both before his court, and banished Simon from England. "Simon . . . Simon, what shall you do?"

Simon swung around. "What do you think I'll do? I shall return to England, confront those who've slandered me. If they have accusations to make, then by God, let them make them to my face!"

UPON their arrival in London, Simon and Nell were heartened by how rapidly their friends rallied to their support. The Bishop of Durham offered them the use of his riverside manor, and when their barge headed downriver toward the Tower, where Henry was currently in residence, they were accompanied by Walter de Cantilupe, Bishop of Worcester, Peter de Montfort, and Rob and Elen de Quincy. Elen was surprised by how often people along the bankside, recognizing Simon's Silver Lion, raised a cheer. Nell, needing the distraction, was more than willing to enlighten her.

"Several years ago," she explained, "Henry enraged the citizens by granting a fair to the abbey of Westminster and then ordering the townsmen to close all city shops whilst the fair was in progress. Their discontent festered and two springs ago became outright defiance. Luckily, Simon was then in London, and he and Richard interceded with Henry on the city's behalf. Londoners do not forget a wrong done them. Nor do they forget their friends."

Elen followed Nell's gaze, toward the stern of the barge where Simon was listening to the Bishop of Worcester. Lowering her voice, she touched Nell's bejeweled fingers with her own. "Nell . . . how are you and Simon bearing up? Is there naught I can do?"

"You're here; that counts for much." Nell's eyes were still probing her husband's face. "Simon is lucky," she said softly, "for he has his anger to sustain him. My anger burns brightly by day, but night quenches its flames, and my fears . . . they are legion, Elen. I fear for my children's future. I fear that Simon will not be able to hold his temper in check. I fear the King's disfavor. And I fear that the day might well come when I will learn to hate my own brother."

Henry refused Simon's request for a private audience, and when Simon and Nell were ushered into the Blundeville Tower, they found Henry's chamber packed with hostile eye-witnesses. Henry was seated in a heavy oaken chair, fashioned like a throne, and beside him stood Geraud de Malemort, the Archbishop of Bordeaux, and the Viscounts of Fronsac and Castillon.

Simon strode forward, knelt before the King. "These men have spoken against me, and they have lied, my liege. I demand the right to defend myself against their slander. I demand the right to be heard."

"You shall be heard, my lord of Leicester," Henry said coldly. "The trial begins at Ascensiontide, the ninth of May, in the refectory of the abbey at Westminster."

Simon looked at Henry, then at the Gascon lords, and his temper flamed, even as Nell's hand tightened upon his arm. "How is it that you are so eager to give credence to traitors? You know I have served you faithfully; no man dares say otherwise. So why, then, does my word count for less with you?"

Henry's head came up. "If your innocence is so evident, my lord, why fear an inquiry? Indeed, your fame should shine all the brighter for it."

And after that, there was nothing more to say.

❧

"MY liege, my lords, I am Gaillard del Soler, son of the one-time Seneschal and Mayor of Bordeaux, Rostand del Soler, may God assoil him. I am here not to speak in my own behalf, but of the wrongs done my father. He was forcibly seized by the Earl of Leicester's men, cast into prison despite his age and ill health, and held there until his death. My father did not deserve such a fate, for he was a good Christian, a loyal subject, a man respected by all. It is too late for him, but you can do justice to his memory. You can censure the man who treated him so harshly and unfairly, and I earnestly entreat you to judge the Earl of Leicester as he deserves."

"Thank you, Messaire del Soler." Henry shifted in his seat, looked challengingly at Simon. "My lord of Leicester, do you wish to respond to these accusations?"

"Yes, Your Grace, I do." Simon rose, moved toward the dais. "To hear Messaire del Soler tell it, I seized his father at random, on a mere whim. A most affecting tale, but he has omitted a few significant facts. Rostand del Soler was taken as a hostage in consequence of the bloody rioting that broke out in Bordeaux in June of 1249. Men died in that rioting, including the city's Mayor and three of my own household knights, because the del Solers refused my order to disperse. But far from being treated harshly, Rostand del Soler was lodged in the royal castles of Ombrière and Roquer, where he was permitted servants to tend to all his needs. Does Messaire del Soler dare to deny that? Need I summon witnesses to confirm this?"

Gaillard del Soler gave Simon a look of naked hatred. "My father died at Roquer Castle! Dare you deny that?"

"No. Rostand del Soler did indeed die in my custody. Shall I tell the court why? When your father fell ill, he asked me if you could take his place. I was agreeable to this." Simon paused; he had an instinctive sense of timing. "But you were not willing," he said, "were you?" And when Gaillard del Soler did not answer, Simon glanced back at Henry. "I think," he said, "that I have responded to the accusations."

"I am Raimond de Fronsac, here under safe-conduct of the English King. I do have numerous grievances against the Earl of Leicester, as do my neighbors, the Viscounts of Gramont and Soule. He seized my castle of Fronsac, holds it to this day. He laid siege to Raimond Brun's castle at Gramont, then cast the Viscount into prison without benefit of trial. He also imprisoned the Viscount of Soule, and last summer he did capture the Viscount of Castillon's stronghold, whilst detaining the Viscount for ransom, and the castle still remains in his hands. He destroyed our vineyards, our main source of income. He paid no heed to our complaints, treated us as if we were peasants, men of low birth. And all of this I am willing to swear upon the most sacred of holy relics."

"I am Sir Peter de Montfort of Beaudesert in Warwickshire, liegeman to the Earl of Warwick. It was my privilege to serve in Gascony for the past three years with my lord of Leicester. I am a witness, therefore, to those events described by the Viscount of Fronsac. Earl Simon did indeed seize the Viscount's castle; the man was in rebellion at the time! The Viscount of Soule was imprisoned after he refused to appear before the Seneschal's court. The Viscount of Castillon was no less of a rebel, no less of a traitor. These men claim their income is derived from their vineyards, but that is a lie. They are, in truth, brigands, who prey upon passers-by and pilgrims."

There was an angry murmur from the Gascons, but Peter ignored them. "The Viscount of Fronsac is a brigand," he repeated, "and his past is a bloody one. He ravaged the region of Labour, sacked the town of Blaye, gave shelter to Gaillard del Soler and his brother Pierre, who were then fugitives from royal justice, having fled Bordeaux after the rioting."

"Fugitives from Leicester's justice!" Gaillard del Soler interrupted hotly, and Peter snapped,

"The Earl of Leicester was the King's Seneschal, his regent in Gascony, appointed to act in the King's stead. What he did, he did in the King's name, on the King's behalf."

"Then why," Pierre de Castillon jeered, "was he summoned to defend himself before the King's court?"

Peter turned, looked directly at the King. "Why, indeed?"

"I am Pierre de Lignan, Abbot of the Benedictine Abbey of Sainte-Croix in Bordeaux. I would tell you this, my lord King. The Earl of Leicester has caused needless suffering in my city. He unfairly favored the Coloms over the del Solers, raising serious doubts about his neutrality. After he demanded hostages from the del Solers, he destroyed Rostand del Soler's house, in violation of city statutes, and when challenged, he disregarded our complaints, saying that the King had instructed him to put down a rebellion and by God, that was what he meant to do. I ask you, do not send him back to Gascony."

"YOUR Grace, I am Amanieu Colom, Mayor of Bordeaux. I have been listening with a troubled heart these weeks past, as the Earl of Leicester has been defamed by men unworthy to stand in his shadow. The testimony of the del Solers is tainted, my lords. There has long been bad blood betwixt our families, and they resent my lord of Leicester for not giving them a free hand in the city. They do not speak for Bordeaux. I have here a letter from the commune. May I read a portion aloud? 'The Earl of Leicester has governed with patient strenuousness, with prudent circumspection, with just moderation, with persevering clemency, assisting loyal subjects and punishing rebels, without danger to any or profuse expenditures.' That, my lords, is the verdict of the Bordelais.''

"SINCE my lord Gaston, Viscount of Béarn, could not be present before the court, I am authorized to speak for him. The Earl of Leicester has treated the Viscount of Béarn with unrelenting hostility, and it is our belief that this hostility is of a personal nature. The County of Bigorre is claimed by Gaston's wife, Mathe, and by Esquivat de Chabanais, who happens to be de Montfort's kinsman. We suspect, therefore, that—''

"That is a damnable lie!" Simon was on his feet. "When the Countess of Bigorre died last year, she bequeathed her lands to her grandson, Esquivat. Whilst I agreed with her choice, that did not affect my dealings with Gaston.''

The Archbishop of Bordeaux smiled, not pleasantly. "Naturally you would say that, my lord.''

"When men want to throw hounds off a scent, they drag a herring across the trail. That, my lord Archbishop, is precisely what you seek to do here today. By impugning my motives, you hope to distract the court, to turn attention away from the man who ought to be on trial, Gaston de Béarn. The man who plundered the town of Dax. The man who shamelessly intrigued with the King of Navarre. The man who disavowed allegiance to England, to the King who then pardoned him!''

Henry jerked upright in his chair. "I had my reasons for pardoning him!''

Simon moved forward. "Tell us then, my liege. Tell us what they were. I daresay every man here waits with bated breath for your revelation.''

"I am not answerable to you, de Montfort! I am not answerable to any man!''

In the silence that followed, Henry sensed that he had somehow erred, somehow played into Simon's hands. His barons were exchanging glances; their disapproval was a palpable thing, a sudden presence in the court. Simon said, "As you say, my liege,'' returned to his seat.

"MY name is Bertrand Lambert, my lords. I am a citizen of Bordeaux, where I have an apothecary shop, close by the Hospital Saint-Jean. I am here to speak on behalf of the Earl of Leicester. Ere he came to Gascony, the land was in turmoil. Men were loath to travel the King's roads, for the lords of Fronsac and Gramont set up barriers, charged unlawful tolls. They gave shelter to outlaws and felons, and turned them loose upon the countryside to rape and pillage. They refused to pay merchants fair prices for their goods. They put men in fear for their lives, for their women. And then the Earl of Leicester came, and it all changed. My lords, think you that the Gascon people care that the Viscount of Gramont was cast into prison without a trial? We cheered when my lord of Leicester ordered these brigands hanged. Would that one dangled from every tree in Gascony!"

"WE, the deputies of Bayonne, do humbly urge Your Grace not to send the Earl back to Gascony. We do not grieve for the rebel lords he imprisoned; they well deserved it. But the Earl confuses dissent with disloyalty, ignores legitimate complaints, and treats our land like a conquered province. Our citizens long for peace, and the Earl by his very presence stirs up controversy, even amongst men of good will. His task is done, Your Grace. We beseech you to heed our pleas, to banish the Earl from Gascony."

"MY lord of Leicester, do you wish to address the court?"

"I do, Your Grace. Gascony has long been a thorn in the English Crown. Its lords are known to be the most faithless in Christendom, men who barter their honor like whores. Three Seneschals in succession had failed to restore order to the duchy. At the King's urgings, I undertook to crush the rebellion. I have listened as men complained that I was too harsh, too unyielding, and indeed, I make no apology for it. I know no other way to fight a war. Granted, I was not always scrupulous about observing legal formalities. But as I see it, men who defy the law do put themselves beyond the law. If I have given citizens reason to doubt my good intentions, I do regret it. Ask me not to shed tears, though, for rebel lords like the Viscount of Gramont, or those who allied themselves with him, like the del Solers. They well deserved any grief they got, and if there was justice, Gaston de Béarn would be rotting now in Hell."

For a moment, Simon's eyes swept the chamber, coming at last to Henry's face. "I sought to serve my King, to protect the powerless, and I am willing to submit myself to the judgment of my peers, to the judgment of the Almighty. I do not doubt that I shall be fully vindicated, indeed am ready to try my innocence upon the field, in trial by combat, if my accusers be willing." He paused. "I see they are not. Well, then, let my actions speak for themselves. I acted in good faith, and no man can do more than that."

"MY lord of Cornwall, you have something to say?"

"Yes, my liege, I do." Richard rose to his feet. "For five weeks now, we have been listening to testimony, weighing evidence. I think it is time we reached a decision. I know I have heard enough. What say you, my lords?"

Henry was caught off balance, none too happy at having the initiative taken away from him like this. But his lords were already murmuring their assent, looking to Richard.

"It is my opinion," Richard said slowly, "that the Earl of Leicester deserves no censure. I think he has proved beyond question that he was but following the King's ŏrders."

Henry sucked in his breath. That Richard could so betray him like this! Did the loss of Gascony mean so much to him, that he'd side with de Montfort against his own brother, against his King?

The Bishop of Worcester swiftly followed Richard's example, proclaiming Simon's innocence in ringing tones. That was no more than Henry would have expected, for he knew the Bishop was an intimate of Simon's. He seethed, but felt no surprise when the Earl of Hereford now declared for Simon; Hereford's eldest son was Humphrey de Bohun, another of Simon's friends. But the Earl of Gloucester was getting to his feet, and Henry's confidence began to return, for he knew Gloucester had no liking for Simon. He was stunned, therefore, when Gloucester said,

"My liege, I can find no fault in the Earl of Leicester's conduct. As I see it, you sent the Earl to Gascony to quell a rebellion, and he did just that."

Henry often had dreams of betrayal. Now he found himself unable to awaken from one, as his barons and Bishops continued to speak out in Simon's favor. Roger de Quincy, Earl of Winchester. Roger Bigod, Earl of Norfolk. Walter Kirkham, Bishop of Durham. Men he'd trusted. But his wife's uncle, Peter de Savoy, Earl of Richmond, had yet to be heard. Peter was known to be an eloquent orator, and Henry clung to the last tendrils of hope as he rose; mayhap Peter could still sway them, make them see Simon as he truly was, stripped of his aura of invincibility and righteousness.

"My lords, I am not surprised we are in full agreement, for the facts permit no other conclusion. I can but echo the findings of Your Grace's own commission of inquiry, the one you chose to disregard, that the Earl of Leicester did treat certain lords quite severely, but no more than they deserved."

After that, Henry ceased to listen. Never had he felt so alone. A deliberate affront, he had no doubt of that. His lords were making use of de Montfort to diminish the powers of the Crown. Well, they'd not get away with it. He could still override them all, impose his own will upon them, as his father would have done. He raised his hand for silence. But as he gazed out upon a sea of expectant faces, his resolve wavered. "I have heard your judgment . . . ," he began, and then his courage failed him. He simply could not summon up the fortitude to defy them all, de Montfort, his own council, the Church, his barons. "It would appear," he faltered, "that the Earl of Leicester has proven his innocence to the satisfaction of this court," and as he slumped back in his seat, he knew that he'd carry to his grave the bitter memory of Simon's triumphant smile.

SIMON and Nell had celebrated into the early hours of the morning, and as they entered the abbey refectory the next day they looked tired, but content. Henry did not appear to have gotten much sleep, either. His blue eyes were puffy, and a tiny muscle was twitching in his cheek, an infallible sign of stress.

"My lord King." Simon approached the dais. "Whilst I am, of course, gratified by the judgment of your court, I think it might be best if I now renounced my command. I am willing to resign this day, provided that I am indemnified for the heavy expenses I incurred in the governance of Gascony. If, however, you wish that I continue as Seneschal, I am willing to serve out the three remaining years of my term."

"Are you willing, indeed? Most magnanimous, my lord Earl. As it happens, however, I choose to reject both of your offers. I have no intention of paying your debts. Nor do I wish you to return to Gascony."

The last of Henry's speech was almost drowned out in the sudden uproar that swept the court. Men were all talking at once, in rising tones of astonishment and indignation, and Henry had to struggle to make himself heard.

"Silence, whilst your King speaks! Last night I did give much thought to the problem posed by Gascony, and I have reached a decision. It has long been my intent to give that realm to my firstborn son, Edward. In less than a fortnight, Edward shall be thirteen. On that day, I mean to invest him with the duchy. Furthermore, a truce is to be declared, from now until Candlemas, at which time I hope to go myself to that troubled land. The Earl of Leicester is not to resume his former authority; I shall send a bailiff to take control of the government. I hereby order the Earl of Leicester to release those Gascon lords he is holding as hostages. He is also to surrender the castles of Fronsac, Castillon, and Sault de Navailles, and as I have issued an order for the release of the Viscount of Gramont, that lord's castle is to be turned over to Pierre de Bordeaux forthwith. Then—"

"Pierre de Bordeaux is Gramont's cousin!" Simon's disbelief exploded into outrage. "You're telling me I must allow those castles to become outlaw strongholds again? For what purpose, then, did I spend four wretched years in Gascony? For what purpose did I endure this trial at Westminster? To have you annul the court's verdict at your whim?"

On a nearby table lay the court exhibits, the documents and sworn affidavits that had been presented in the course of the trial. Reaching for a charter bearing the King's seal, Simon thrust it toward Henry. "This is the covenant we made four years ago. It clearly states that I am to be given full authority to govern Gascony, and that you are to assume responsibility for my expenses. I demand, my liege, that you keep faith with me, with this charter. You owe me, and well you know it, for I have impoverished my earldom for the sake of your honor. You gave me your sworn word! Are you now saying that the King of England's word is worthless?"

Henry grabbed the parchment, crumpled it in his fist, and flung it to the floor at Simon's feet. "I'll not keep these promises! I'll not keep any promises to a traitor!"

The court erupted in pandemonium. In two strides, Simon was up on the dais, and Henry jumped to his feet in alarm. "That is an accursed lie," Simon said, slurring the words in his rush to get them said. "If you were not shielded behind the dignity of the Crown, this would have been an evil hour for you! Had any other man dared to call me traitor, he'd have paid for that insult with his life."

"You dare—" Henry looked around wildly for the captain of his guards. "I want this man taken to the Tower, want him—"

"No, Henry, you do not!" Few had seen Richard move with such speed; in the blink of an eye, he was on the dais, too, between the two men. "For the love of Christ, brother, think what you do!" Lowering his voice, he ignored Henry's attempt to shake off his restraining hand. "Look around you, Henry. Do you think these men are going to allow you to arrest de Montfort? Yesterday he was exonerated in this very court, by your own council, by the most powerful lords of your realm, by the prelates of the Roman Catholic Church. And yet today you call him a traitor, proclaim your promises have no value, and want to have him imprisoned! What do you seek to do, provoke a rebellion here and now? Do you not know what can befall a king abandoned by his own lords?"

Other voices were being raised now. The Bishop of Worcester and Peter de Savoy had begun to echo Richard's arguments, and John Mansel, appearing as if from nowhere, hissed urgently, "Sire, you cannot do this!"

Henry pulled free from Richard's grasp. His eyes darted from face to face, seeking support, finding only hostility. "Get away from me, all of you!" he cried. "You are luckier than you deserve, de Montfort. Never have I regretted any deed so much as I regret that I ever permitted you to make England your home, to possess lands and honors here."

"At last," Simon said, "you do speak the truth. I've long known that you wished me ill. I suspect that the whole purpose of this trial was to enable you to declare me a traitor, thus allowing you to bestow my estates upon your de Lusignan half-brothers!"

Henry gasped, for he had indeed considered the possibility of confiscating Simon's lands. But he had discussed it only with Eleanor and Richard, and so negative had their responses been that he'd never gone beyond wistful conjecture. Now he whirled, gave Richard a look of enraged reproach, and Simon said scornfully, "No one needed to tell me. I know you."

Henry had not inherited the notorious Plantagenet temper, the savage fury that spawned a legend, that these Angevin Kings did claim descent from the Devil. Henry's rages were less spectacular, less irrational, more ineffectual. Now, however, he felt such hatred that he feared he might choke on it. "Go to Gascony, then!" he shouted. "If you crave war so much, seek it out! Go and be damned!"

"I will indeed go to Gascony, and I shall not return until—ungrateful though you are—I have subdued your enemies, flung them at your feet!" With that, Simon turned his back upon his King, stalked from the chamber.

Nell followed in haste, caught up with him some moments later, alone in the Chapter House. Another of Henry's projects, it was nearly completed, and ablaze with summer sunlight, for Henry's stained-glass panes had yet to be installed in the soaring windows. Simon was standing by the lectern, and when she reached him, she found that he was still trembling with rage.

"Simon, do not do this," she pleaded. "Do not let him goad you into going back."

"What would you have me do, Nell, just walk away? What of the debts I owe? You well know what it cost me to garrison those castles, to hire men-at-arms. Would you have me beggar myself on Henry's account?" Adding ominously, "And I do have some scores to settle in Gascony."

Nell knew it was futile to argue further, but she would have persisted, nonetheless. Just then, however, their son Harry appeared in the doorway.

"Papa . . ." He came forward hesitantly, keeping his eyes imploringly on Simon. "Papa, take me. Take me with you when you go back to Gascony."

Simon looked at the boy, and then nodded. "All right," he said, and Harry let out a jubilant yell, which echoed eerily in the vast, empty chamber.

Nell bit back a cry of her own, one of protest. In just five months, Harry would be fourteen; it was time he began his schooling as a squire. Nor could he have a better teacher than his father. But it would be hard to let him go. It would be hard to let them both go, for she and Simon had decided that if he returned to Gascony, she would wait out her pregnancy at Sutton, her manor in Kent. Now, faced with the prospect of losing both her husband and son, thinking of the lonely nights she faced, thinking of the uncertainty, the fears for Simon's safety, she could not blink back the tears, hot, angry tears that streaked her face and startled her husband and son, for she was not a woman who easily wept.

Simon's "Nell?" and Harry's "Mama?" echoing in her ears, she shook her head impatiently, backed away from them. "Damn Henry!" she cried. "Damn him to everlasting Hell!"

HARRY was delighted when Simon summoned him to La Réole. Harry had fretted all summer long, watching his father's war from the safety of Bordeaux. But La Réole's castle had been repeatedly besieged by the rebels, and Harry was hopeful that it might come under attack again. Since his arrival, he'd passed many happy hours prowling the battlements of the round towers, peering down at the River Garonne and envisioning himself the hero of an enemy assault. But on this rainy afternoon in early September, the weather confined him to the keep, and once his chores were done, he wandered about restlessly, until he found Peter de Montfort in his father's bedchamber.

Harry could not remember a time when Peter had not been a part of his father's life, for their friendship stretched back more than twenty years, to the time of Simon's arrival in England, a young knight of twenty-two, ambitious and impoverished. Harry liked Peter well enough, but he'd wondered sometimes why his father should have befriended a man who seemed to be his utter opposite in all particulars: cautious, self-contained, easily overlooked. Or so Harry had thought—until that May morning in the refectory at Westminster, when Peter dared defy the King. After that, Harry had decided there must be truth to the old adage, the one about still waters running deep.

"We heard many stories in Bordeaux of Papa's campaign, but you were there, Uncle Peter. Tell me what it was like. Tell me about the ambush gone wrong and the siege of Montauban."

Peter was sharpening his sword on a whet-stone, slowly and deliberately, as he did all things. "Fetch me that rag, lad. Well . . . the ambush. Now, that was a day. Your father had set a trap for the Gascon rebels, but they got wind of it, and attacked the men lying in ambush. Several of Simon's men were captured, including Baldwin de Grey, the knight in command. I'm sure you know him; he's been long in Simon's service. One of the men managed to escape, reached Simon with word of the ambush. Simon was less than two miles away, and he at once set out in pursuit. We were hard put to keep pace with him, in truth! He struck the Gascon rebels like a lightning bolt, lad, scattering them in all directions, and slashing the ropes of his captured men, he set them free."

Peter glanced up, smiled into the boy's star-filled eyes. "It was a sight to see, Harry. But then the Gascons rallied, and cut Simon off from the rest of his men. They'd recognized him, you see, knew that his capture or death would win their war, and Simon found himself overwhelmed by numbers. He kept them at bay for a time, but then they killed his stallion. He was in grave danger, lad. But Baldwin and the men he'd freed flung themselves into the fray, held the Gascons off until Simon could mount another horse."

"And then?"

"Why, Simon won the battle, of course," Peter said. "A bloody battle it was, too, lasting half a day, but the victory was ours, and amongst the prisoners taken, one was a del Soler."

"What of Montauban? Is it true that Papa was nearly captured?"

"Indeed. Montauban is a formidable castle, but when we reached it, we discovered that it was poorly garrisoned, its larders nearly empty. The rebels, learning of Simon's presence, laid siege to the castle, and it did look grim for a time. We had to yield some of the prisoners we'd taken earlier, much to Simon's dismay. But the devotion of his soldiers saved him, saved us all. Men are right willing to fight for Simon, lad, will follow him even unto the far reaches of the netherworld, and they—"

"Good God, Peter, what sort of nonsense are you filling the lad's head with?"

"Uncle Peter was telling me about your triumph at Montauban, Papa, about—"

"Triumph? We did escape with our skins, by the grace of the Almighty. Heaven spare me too many more triumphs like that," Simon said dryly, but when Peter laughed, not taken in by Simon's protestations, Simon laughed, too.

"The rain has let up, Harry. Come out to the bailey, and I'll give you another lesson in swordplay," Simon suggested, and laughed again, for Harry had jumped to his feet so eagerly that he almost fell over Peter's whet-stone. But as they emerged from the stairwell, the King's messengers were being escorted up into the keep.

Simon knew the first one, Rocelin de Fos, Master of the Templars. The other man identified himself as Nicholas de Meuilles. They both showed the edginess of men bearing unwelcome news, but Simon expected nothing else from Henry, and he was not surprised to be told that Henry was insisting he honor the truce with the Gascon rebels. He heard them out, then shook his head.

"Quite impossible. Were the Gascons honoring the truce when they besieged me at Montauban? I just succeeded in raising the enemy siege here at La Réole, and the rebels are still in the field. Not even Henry can expect me to lay down my arms in the midst of a war."

The men exchanged troubled glances. "The King thought you might say that, my lord. He therefore instructed us, should you refuse, to inform you that you are relieved of your command."

Harry gave a stifled cry, jammed his knuckles against his mouth. Simon's men gathered around him, closing ranks against the enemy. Simon alone seemed unperturbed. "Under the terms of our agreement," he said coolly, "the King does not have the authority to dismiss me. I'd never have accepted this command if I had to serve at the King's pleasure."

Nicholas de Meuilles sighed, reached into his tunic and drew out a parchment scroll. "You say he cannot dismiss you, my lord, but he says he can, and he has. Here, see for yourself. These are letters patent, bearing the King's own seal."

Simon reached for the scroll, scanned it rapidly. "This changes nothing. The King cannot dismiss me, and I do not choose to resign." Crossing to the hearth, he thrust the letter into the flames, then turned back to face the astounded messengers. "Tell the King," he said, "that if he wants my resignation, he'd best make it worth my while."

MUCH to Harry's excitement, Simon agreed to take the boy along when he laid siege to Guilhem Seguin's castle at Rions. Their assault only confirmed Harry's conviction that war was great fun, for the Gascons had put up feeble resistance, and Simon was soon master of Seguin's stronghold.

When the messenger galloped into Simon's encampment, Harry followed him into the castle keep, for his mother's time was nigh, and any day now they might get word from England. He found Simon by the hearth, an open letter in his hand, and his step quickened.

"Papa? Is the letter from Mama? Has the babe been born?"

"No, lad, the letter is from your uncle Richard. He writes to tell me that when parliament assembled, the King sought in vain to rouse the lords against me. Richard reports that Henry now realizes he has no choice but to buy back my command. He offers seven thousand marks, and agrees to pay the debts I incurred in his service."

Seven thousand marks sounded like a lot of money to Harry. "Will you accept, Papa?"

"Yes," Simon said. "Right gladly."

He did not look glad to Harry, though. "Papa, what will you do then?"

"We shall withdraw into France, you and I. And once your mother has the babe, she and your brothers will join us there."

Harry had never lived in France; England was the only home he'd ever known. "Papa . . . will we be going back to England?"

"No, Harry," Simon said. "We will not be going back."

21

Paris, France

October 1253

"Simon, think what you do! Do you not realize what a great honor has been bestowed upon you? Accept the French offer, be their Seneschal. It would mean that, until the French King's return from crusade, you'd be the virtual Regent of France!"

"I know that, Nell." Simon's patience was fraying fast. "But I cannot accept. I've pledged my allegiance to the English King. How, then, could I serve the King of France? It would not be honorable."

Nell slammed her hairbrush down upon the table. "This is strange talk, indeed, from a man who swore he'd never again set foot in England!"

"That was said in anger. Like it or not, Nell, our future lies in England, lies with our lands."

"I am not saying we should abandon our estates. You know me better than that! But I do not understand why the Earl of Leicester cannot also be Seneschal of France. I do not understand why you must sacrifice so much for your pride, why—"

"Enough! It was my decision to make, not yours, and it is done. Now let that be an end to it!"

"I know I cannot expect to change your mind, for your stubbornness would put a mule to shame. But at the very least, you can hear me out!"

"When do I not hear you out? If there's a way to silence you, short of stuffing a gag in your mouth, I've yet to discover it. But this argument is senseless, for you ought to welcome my decision. Henry is your brother, not mine!"

"Damn you, my loyalties are yours and yours alone!"

Simon's anger vanished, as if by alchemist's magic. "That is the most hostile declaration of love I've ever gotten," he said, with a grin, and as he studied his indignant wife, honey-colored hair cascading about her shoulders, blue eyes aglitter, cheeks flushed, he was suddenly conscious of how desirable she looked. His eyes followed the rapid rise and fall of her breasts, moved up to her face, and saw that she was well aware of the erotic turn his thoughts had taken.

"No," she warned, "not this time. This is one quarrel that's not going to end in bed!"

"Were you not so fair," he pointed out, "I'd not be so easily distracted. A pity you were not plain as a hedge-sparrow, for I daresay we'd then have far more satisfying fights!"

The deliberate lunacy of that logic almost earned him a smile— almost. Although Nell was amused, she was not yet mollified. When she started to say so, Simon silenced her with a lingering kiss, one that did not end until she'd entwined her arms around his neck. But as he drew her toward him, she suddenly pushed against his chest, shoving him backward onto the bed. Yet even off-balance, his were the reflexes of a soldier, and as he fell, he grabbed her wrist, pulling her down on top of him.

"Simon!" Nell scowled at her husband. "Jesú, you're as quick as a fox," she complained, "and just as sly." But she made no attempt to free herself, and the corners of her mouth were curving upward.

Simon kissed that suggestion of a smile, slid his leg between her thighs. "It appears, Madame, that you're my prisoner. Shall we discuss terms?"

Nell ran her fingers caressingly along his throat, then pricked his skin with her nails. "No surrender, my lord. I might, however, consider a brief respite, rather like a Christmas truce, with the understanding that hostilities shall resume after—"

"Lord Simon, an urgent— A thousand pardons!" Footsteps echoed a hasty retreat, a door slammed.

Simon reluctantly swung his legs over the side of the bed. "I dare not bid a servant to enter," he said, "for you look far too wanton to be a wife."

Nell assumed an even more provocative pose, while favoring him with a mockingly seductive smile. "Fortunately for you," she said, "I am both a wanton and a wife," and Simon laughed, moved toward the door.

Nell took advantage of his brief absence to strip off her gown, chemise, and stockings, and when Simon returned, he found her waiting in their bed, reclining in an artful tangle of sheets and silken blonde hair. But the effort was wasted; he did not even notice. "Of all the men to be sending me urgent messages," he said, "for certes Henry ought to be the last one in Christendom!"

Nell was not as surprised. "Henry," she said caustically, "has ever had a rotten sense of timing. No, Simon, do not read it . . . not yet. Whatever he has to say, it will but sour your mood. Put it aside till later."

Simon could not deny the common sense of that, but still he hesitated. "I hear," he said, "that since his arrival in Gascony, Henry has been sore beset on all sides, has had naught but troubles."

"As well he should! Unchristian it may be, but I can find no pity for his misfortunes; he has earned each and every one. When that wretch Gaston de Béarn rebelled again and allied himself with the King of Castile, it did seem like divine retribution to me! Now do let that letter be, Simon. Henry can wait. I cannot." She pressed her point home with some strategic slippage of the covers and succeeded in luring Simon back to bed.

But curiosity could exert a potent pull of its own, and when Nell noticed that Simon had brought the letter with him, she gave up the struggle. "You might as well open it. I absolutely refuse to have you making love to me and thinking of Henry!"

"I daresay you'd hold my attention," Simon said, managing to be both wry and gallant, but he was already breaking Henry's seal. Nell watched his face change as he read, astonishment and satisfaction and amusement and suspicion blurring, one into the other. Looking up, he said, "It is a plea for help. Henry wants me to come to his camp at Bénauges, to aid him in his war against Gaston de Béarn."

"Simon, be serious! What does Henry truly want?"

"Nell, I am not jesting. Listen for yourself: 'We command and request you to come to Gascony and discuss matters with us; if you think that it befits neither our honor nor yours to remain with us, you can withdraw when you please, without incurring our indignation.' Need I read further?"

"God and all His angels! May I see?"

Simon passed her the letter. "I will never understand the workings of Henry's brain. Were our positions reversed, I'd have willingly endured the rack ere I asked him for help!"

"Henry is either an idiot or an utter innocent. I can never make up my mind which—" Nell stopped abruptly, staring at her husband. "Mother of Christ . . . you're going to agree! You're going to come to his rescue!"

It was one of the few times that Nell had seen Simon look self-conscious. "His need must be grave, indeed, for him to ask me for help, Nell. But you may be sure that we'll not lose by this. My services will not come cheaply."

"That is well and good," Nell conceded, "but . . ." She frowned, not knowing how to articulate her unease, her instinctive sense that it would be better for Simon to distance himself from her brother the King. "Do you not see?" she cried. "Henry does not deserve your help!"

"I'd not dispute that, Nell. But I do not do it for Henry. I do it for myself, because it is what I ought to do."

Nell started to speak, stopped, and looked for a long moment into his eyes. Then she sighed, entwined her fingers in his. "Whatever am I going to do with you, Simon?"

He pressed a kiss into the palm of her hand, another into the hollow of her throat. "I have a suggestion or two," he murmured, and Nell forgot she was playing a wanton, began to giggle like a little girl. "You are wicked, my lord," she chided softly, and ducked modestly beneath the sheets. Simon followed, and when they surfaced for air, amusement had given way to urgency. Throwing off the covers, they rolled over into the center of the bed, where she assisted him in removing his clothing, tearing his tunic in her haste, a rip he would later delight in teasing her about. Henry's letter was crushed beneath their naked bodies, at last fluttered to the floor, where it lay forgotten amidst the rushes of basil and mint, not to be retrieved till the morning.

∞

UPON getting word of the Bishop of Lincoln's illness, Nell hastily took ship at Boulogne. But she was not in time. Bishop Robert died at Buckden Palace on the 9th of October.

THE de Quincy manor of Stevington was only a day's ride from Buckden, and there, at least, Nell's arrival could not have been better timed, for she found Elen abed and in need of comfort, having almost miscarried on St Edward's Eve.

Elen's chamber was bright with sun, and Nell resisted, with difficulty, the urge to slam the shutters upon the light and air so fatal to a sickroom. But if ever Elen's eccentricities should be indulged, now was the time, for Nell thought it unlikely that Elen would be able to carry this baby to full term.

That fear was Elen's, too. "This is the second time I've bled, Nell. All my pregnancies have been difficult, but in less than a fortnight, I'll be forty-six. If I lose this babe . . ."

"Of course you'll not lose this babe! I've known women who birthed healthy babies until they were nigh on fifty. My own mother was older than you when her last was born. I want you to promise me you'll not fret. That will do neither you nor this little lad any good," Nell said, patting Elen's abdomen and eliciting from Elen the flicker of a smile.

"I am glad you are here, Nell. It is good of Simon to spare you . . ."

"I'll stay as long as you have need of me, dearest. I ought to warn you, though, that my Bran will have your household in constant turmoil!" Elen's smile was sleepy, and Nell leaned over, kissed the older woman on the forehead. "Rest now, you and the little one . . ."

Descending the stairs into the hall, Nell took up pen and parchment, began a letter to Simon, explaining that she and their son would be delaying their return to France. She wondered if he'd gotten her other letter, the one informing him of Bishop Robert's death. She hoped not, hoped he had a day or two yet ere he must grieve. Bishop Robert had been seventy-eight, in ailing health, and died in God's Grace, but Simon had loved him well. She reached again for the quill. She'd tell Simon about the bells that the Bishop of London claimed to have heard on his way to Bishop Robert's deathbed, bells chiming in a deep wood miles from any church. Mayhap Simon could take comfort in that.

"Mama!" Bran was gasping for breath, reeled to a stop before her chair. "Riders are approaching, and they're Welsh, Mama, I could tell by their mustaches! Do you think it could be a raid?"

"Of course, darling. What could be more likely than that the Welsh would choose, after six years of peace, to ride hundreds of miles into

England and attack the Bedfordshire manor of their own kinswoman?"

Bran grinned, unfazed by her sarcasm. "I did not really think so," he admitted, "but I could always hope . . ."

Nell reached out, rumpled his hair. To her amusement, he quickly smoothed it back into place; at thirteen, he was suddenly showing an interest in his appearance. Moving to the window, she discovered that for once Bran had not allowed his imagination to embellish his accuracy; the riders entering the bailey were indeed Welsh. After a moment, she smiled, then glanced back over her shoulder at her son. "You'd best mind your manners, lad. We are about to entertain a Prince."

"ELEN shall be so joyful when she awakens, finds you here."

Llewelyn smiled. "We have a saying amongst my people: Eilfam modryb dda; a good aunt is a second mother. Elen is very dear to me. Since my aunt Gwladys died, she is all the family I have. Save Davydd and Rhodri, of course."

Despite Nell's reputation for compulsive candor, she was not utterly without tact, and she made no mention now of Senena, Llewelyn's very-much-alive mother, reputed to be residing in Owain's half of Gwynedd. Instead, she looked across the hall, toward Llewelyn's young brother. Davydd was restlessly swinging a shutter back and forth, but he came readily when she beckoned.

"Davydd, mayhap you'd like to go out to the garden, join my son and the Lady Elen's daughters. Hawise and Joanna are just babes, but Anne and my Bran are near your age, and—"

"Madame, I doubt that I'd have much in common with children." Davydd's voice throbbed with such convincing indignation that it was a moment before Nell caught the gleam of laughter in his eyes.

"Alas, I have mortally offended you," she murmured, with such mock remorse that Davydd conceded her the game.

"I would forgive so beautiful a lady right gladly," he declared, mixing callow gallantry with a genuinely engaging grin, reminding Nell anew what a mercurial age fifteen was, so precariously balanced between child and man.

Davydd glanced at his brother. "When we passed through the village, I happened to notice a girl drawing water from a well. I think I ought to go back and offer her my help."

"The soul of chivalry," Llewelyn drawled, waving him on. Davydd's grin widened; he was gone in a flash.

"He's a handsome lad, your brother. But I'd wager he's a handful, too. How long has he been back in Wales?"

"Five years. Your brother the King freed Rhodri and Davydd the year after Woodstock. And in truth, he is a hellion. But so was I when I was young."

"And now you're all of what . . . a staid twenty-four? An aged twenty-five?"

A sudden shriek floated in from the gardens, sending them both rushing to the window. Llewelyn smiled at sight of Elen's daughters. Aged three, eight, and eleven, they so resembled their mother that it was as if he'd been given a magical glimpse of a young Elen he'd never known, at varying stages of her childhood. The girls were gazing up at a huge apple tree; only belatedly did Llewelyn notice the boy swinging from branch to branch, a good twenty feet above the ground.

"Bran! Get down ere you break your fool neck!"

Tree-climbing did not seem so great a sin to Llewelyn; he could not help laughing. "Speaking of hellions . . ."

"One I could withstand, but five?" Nell's smile was rueful, and yet perversely proud, too. "Harry, my firstborn, is not as willful as Bran, but he's just as reckless. And Guy, God love him, not a day passes that Guy does not get into trouble of some sort. Whilst my last two changelings . . ." Nell stopped, then laughed. "But I doubt that you're waiting with bated breath for me to chronicle the woes of motherhood!"

"My lady, you could read from your steward's account book and still hold my interest. Now . . . I believe congratulations are due you, for I seem to remember Elen mentioning that last year you gave birth to a daughter."

Nell nodded. "A beautiful lass she is, too, if I say it who should not. Simon wanted to name her Eleanor after me, but I favored Isabella, after my sister. So we did compromise—upon Eleanor."

"A variation, I believe, of Helen, no? Did you know that's Elen in Welsh?"

Nell nodded again. "That is what we call her—Ellen. I never could brook Eleanor and we cannot have two Nells."

"And your lord husband? He is not with you, then?"

"No. Simon is in Gascony . . ." Nell paused mischievously, before adding, ". . . fighting beside my brother the King."

She got the response she wanted; Llewelyn's jaw dropped. "I see that surprises you. I cannot imagine why, for my husband has a very forgiving nature."

Llewelyn's mouth twitched. "A saint, in truth," he agreed, no less blandly. "Not being a saint myself, I can only guess at this, but I'd wager there must be enormous satisfaction in being begged for help by a man who so wronged you."

For a moment, he thought she might take offense, but then she grinned. "Well, there is that, too," she admitted. "But all jesting aside, when Henry asked my husband for help, Simon willingly gave it, and how many men would have done so in Simon's place?" They'd resumed their seats, and Nell reached over, touched his hand. "So far the talk has been all of my family. What of yours? Do you have any children of your own yet? No? A wife, then? Why ever not? I daresay Wales is full of girls dazzled by those dark eyes of yours, but you truly ought to have a wife. I think— What? Why do you laugh?"

"Because," Llewelyn confessed, "I cannot decide whether you are flirting with me or mothering me!"

Nell was taken aback; then she, too, began to laugh. "Both, I suspect! I suppose I could have a son nearly your age, for I shall be thirty-eight in December," she said, hers the confident candor of a woman still sure of her allure. "And I've ever been a flirt, that I cannot deny."

"And your husband, he's not jealous?"

"Regretfully not. Which vexed me when first we wed, I admit. Not that I was ever so foolish as to try to provoke his jealousy, but I did feel slighted, nonetheless. Until I realized why. For a woman, there can be no greater sin than infidelity. To Simon, the very suspicion would be an insult, as if he believed me capable of such dishonor. And whilst such faith might not be as much fun as an impassioned fit of jealousy, it is a far greater compliment, do you not think?"

Llewelyn nodded. "What I think," he said, "is that Simon de Montfort is a most fortunate man."

"So I keep telling him! But no . . . I am the lucky one, Llewelyn, for I have been blessed with two good marriages, albeit as unlike as chalk and cheese. With William, it was a . . . a refuge, like being nestled before the hearth on a winter's eve. I was very young when he died, and mayhap that kind of contentment might have palled in time, but I cherish my memories of William. Now marriage to Simon . . . well, that has been an altogether different experience, that has been bonfires and lightning bolts and shooting stars, and whatever you do, never repeat that to another soul!"

It had been a while since Llewelyn had laughed so much. For too long, his relationships with women had begun and ended in bed; he'd forgotten that conversation could hold pleasures of its own. "So, then, you'd choose tumult over tranquillity, passion over peace?"

"Poetically put, but yes, of course! Who would not?" Nell leaned across the table, propped up on her elbows, her face cupped in her hands, a pose of calculated charm. But it was with genuine curiosity, not coquetry, that she said, "And what of you? I am not talking of bedmates now; what man does not have his share of those? But has there never been a woman who mattered to you? A woman to haunt your memory?"

Llewelyn set his wine cup down. "Yes . . . there was one. But we were very young, and what drew us together did not prove strong enough to keep us together. Mayhap if we'd had a child . . ." He shrugged, then raised his eyes to Nell's. "You did take a great risk, Lady Nell, in marrying for love, a foolhardy risk . . ."

"Yes . . . I suppose I did." And then she flashed a vivid, impish smile. "But what is a thing worth, Llewelyn, if it comes with no risk?"

"HOW long must you stay abed?"

Elen grimaced. "Lord pity me, the midwife says at least a week! So your company is indeed a godsend, Llewelyn. Sit beside me on the bed so we may talk. I'm surprised that Davydd agreed to accompany you; I very much doubt that Senena ever spoke kindly of me!"

"I daresay you're right, but whatever Davydd's opinion of you, Aunt Elen, he's not shared it with me. I would that he did, would that I knew what goes on in his head. He's quick to laugh, quick to jest, but not to confide. We've never once talked about his years as a hostage. If he nurtures a grudge, blames our mother for making that Devil's deal with Henry, none but Davydd knows it. He divides his time betwixt my lands and Owain's, comes and goes as he pleases, the way a cat does—always on his own terms."

Elen smiled. "A cat . . . I like that. It fits Davydd well—independent and beguiling and inscrutable. Your grandfather played a game like that as a lad, matching people and animals, and I often play it with my lasses. Now Henry would be . . . what? A peacock, resplendently feathered, yet unable to fly very far. And his Eleanor, a swan—beautiful, but bad-tempered, and oh, so vain. Owain? There you have me, lad. Your brother has ever been an enigma to me. I'd have wagered a king's ransom that he'd war on you after Woodstock, so sure was I that he'd seek to claim your share of Gwynedd."

"So was I," Llewelyn admitted. "Remember, though, that he was content to dwell all those months in Cheshire, not returning to Wales until your brother died. You ask what beast Owain might have been? What of a cob? A hardy breed, with strength and endurance, but happiest in harness, not one for forging ahead on its own."

Elen laughed, but Llewelyn was in earnest. "I've come to believe that, if left to his own devices, Owain is content to amble along at a sluggish pace. But that may well change, for I fear he has found a rider to apply the spurs—our mother."

Elen's smile faded. "Tell me."

"When Davydd turned fourteen last year, he reminded us—prompted by my mother, I daresay—that under Welsh law, he was entitled to a share in the governance of Gwynedd. Owain agreed to cede to him the commote of Cymydmaen on the Llŷn peninsula. But he is no longer content with that. He now argues that he deserves no less than a full third of Gwynedd. And Owain has agreed to this madness. Mayhap he truly believes it is just, most likely he seeks merely to spite me, but whatever his reasons, he is adding fuel to a fire that might well engulf us all."

"For you cannot agree."

"How could I? Wales has never been so weak, so vulnerable to English conquest. If we were to split Gwynedd into three separate, petty principalities, Christ Jesus, but we might as well cede Wales to the Crown here and now!" Llewelyn drew a sharp breath. "But Davydd is too young to understand that. I love my brother, do not want to see him estranged from me. Yet I very much fear it may come to that. If only— Aunt Elen? What is it?"

Elen had gone grey; sweat suddenly stood out on her forehead, her upper lip. "Fetch Nell," she gasped, and doubled over, her body contorting. "Hurry . . ."

BRAN wandered over to the stairs, gazing up at Elen's bedchamber door. It seemed to him that his mother and the midwife had been closeted with Elen for an eternity. How utterly, eerily quiet it was! He glanced uneasily at Elen's husband, slumped in a chair by the hearth. How could the man just sit there? Bran was not sure what Rob ought to do, but he felt certain his father would have taken action of some sort.

Hawise and Joanna were in bed, but on the settle Anne sat very still, hands clasped in her lap, head bowed so that Bran saw only a spill of dark hair, as shining-black as his own. He wished she would go upstairs like her sisters; pity was not an emotion he knew well, and he averted his gaze, not knowing what to say to her. Moving back to the table, he occupied himself in scraping his thumbnail through the wax splattered around a brass candelabra. When Davydd joined him, they passed some moments in silence, eyeing each other warily.

Bran made the first overture. "If you are the Lady Elen's nephew and I am her cousin, does that mean we are kin, too?"

That had never occurred to Davydd. If he was Bran's cousin, did that make him a kinsman, too, of the English King? "I suppose it does," he conceded grudgingly. "But of course you do not have Welsh blood."

Bran raised his chin. "Who'd want it?"

But they'd forgotten Llewelyn was within earshot. "You are just jesting, of course, for neither of you could be so ill-bred as to be squabbling at a time like this," he said, with enough ice in his voice to send shivers up two youthful spines. They were mumbling hasty assent as the bedchamber door opened.

Rob sprang to his feet. "Nell . . ."

Nell came slowly down the stairs, holding onto the railing as if she needed the support, and even before she stepped into the light, they knew. "Rob, I am so sorry. But we could not stop the bleeding. She lost the babe . . ."

Rob flinched and his eyes closed; after a moment tears began to squeeze through his lashes. Nell, fighting back tears of her own, put her arms around him, but he pulled away, moved toward the stairs.

No one spoke until the midwife emerged onto the landing; at that, Anne began to sob. Nell drew the child to her, held her as she wept. When Anne would have started for the stairs, though, Nell shook her head.

"No, darling, not yet. She . . . she is very distraught, Anne, needs to be alone now with your father."

Bran was hovering helplessly at his mother's elbow, standing so close he was almost treading upon the hem of Nell's gown, standing close enough to hear her whisper. It sounded to him as if she said, "It is a dreadful thing to lose a child," but he wondered why she called Anne by her sister's name, why she called her "Joanna."

NELL's dream was muddled, lacking coherence, but disturbing enough, nonetheless, that awakening was a relief. The chamber was dark, dawn still hours away. She started to sit up, remembering just in time where she was. As Stevington had only one bedchamber and a small loft for the children, the women were sleeping in Elen's chamber while the men bedded down in the hall. Nell's eyes were adjusting to the shadows, and she could distinguish now the sleeping forms of their ladies, stretched out on pallets by the bed. Elen was having a restless night, too; Nell could feel the bed shifting under her weight.

"Elen?" she said softly. "Elen, I'm awake. Would it help to talk?" There was no response. Elen had flung the covers off, although the room was chilled. Leaning over, Nell drew the blankets up over Elen's bared shoulder.

"Merciful God!" She gasped, staring down at the other woman in horror, for her fingers still throbbed with heat. Elen's skin was searing to the touch.

A DOCTOR was urgently summoned from nearby Bedford, and he did his best, but Elen's fever did not abate. As the infection spread, she grew progressively weaker, drifting in and out of delirium, responding neither to herbal potions nor sponge baths. Nell had often suspected that Elen was the core, the very marrow of the de Quincy family, and now Rob was like a ship without a rudder. He spent every waking hour at his wife's bedside, and the burdens of Elen's illness fell not upon him, but upon Nell. It was she who kept the household functioning, who gave instructions to the stricken servants, who nursed Elen and comforted her terrified children. And it was Nell who finally sent for the village priest.

He was very young, this his first parish, and exceedingly sorry to have been summoned, for the dying woman was not just the lady of the manor, she was the niece of the King. What if she did not regain her wits? She could not be shriven if she could not confess her sins, answer the Seven Interrogatories. But if she did not receive Extreme Unction, she would be damned. If he so failed the King's kinswoman, what would be his fate, his punishment?

All day his little church had been pealing passing-bells, alerting his parishioners to pray for the soul of a sister Christian in her hour of need. But at dusk, Elen stirred, and to his heartfelt relief, her dark, feverlit eyes held a spark of recognition.

"Rob . . ."

"Here, love." Shouldering the priest aside, Rob bent over the bed. When Elen reached out to him, her fingers twitched, but then fell limply back upon the blanket, and she looked at her hand in bewilderment, as if puzzling why it no longer obeyed her brain.

"Bells . . . I dreamed of bells," she whispered; why was it such an effort to talk? "But I still hear them. Rob . . . ?" Her husband's eyes were red-rimmed and swollen; he covered her hand with his own, squeezing so tightly that she gasped. The candles seemed inordinately bright, blurring and wavering, casting foreshortened shadows. Elen looked past Rob, her gaze wandering the room, moving from Nell to Llewelyn and then back to the priest.

"Sir Robert . . ." The priest cleared his throat, began again, saying with as much authority as he could muster, "You must withdraw now, leave me alone with your lady so she may make her peace with Almighty God and Christ the Redeemer." Setting down the pyx that held the Host, he fumbled for his vial of holy water, sprinkled it upon the bed, and launched into the formula he knew by heart. "Thou shalt sprinkle me with hyssop, O Lord, and I shall be cleansed. Thou shalt—"

"No!" Elen was shaking her head, turning it weakly from side to side. "I cannot be dying, not now, not yet . . ."

How often had he heard that. To Christians, death offered deliverance; why did they cling so to life's sorrows and woes? "It is God's Will, my lady."

"No!" Elen tried to sit up, sank back against the pillows. "I have a three-year-old daughter. She'd . . . she'd not even remember me! How could that be God's Will?"

He had no answer for her. He shook his head mutely, watched helplessly as Rob knelt by the bed, gathering Elen into his arms. In the silence that followed, they could hear Rob's voice, murmuring broken words and endearments. As desperately as he wanted to see Elen safely shriven, the priest could not bring himself to intrude upon a moment of such despair.

"Madame . . ." He turned at the sound, saw that the children's nurse had slipped into the room, was conferring quietly with Nell. Catching a few words, he guessed the rest, and gave an involuntary cry of protest.

"No! God must come first!"

But Nell ignored his outburst, brushing past him and approaching the bed. "Elen . . . dearest, do you want to see your daughters now?" When Elen nodded, she leaned over and, with a corner of the sheet, gently blotted the tears from Elen's face.

THE young priest fidgeted, pacing a path to the hearth and back. He could feel Llewelyn's dark, brooding gaze upon him all the while and that only intensified his unease, for in his heart he was convinced the Welsh were pagans, false Christians. Elen's daughters had been up with her for at least an hour, mayhap the last hour of her life. When at last he heard Nell's footsteps on the stairs, he hastened forward, only to come to an abrupt halt at sight of her, for her face was blanched of all color, a mask of such desolation that he impulsively put out a supportive hand, remembering just in time that she was the King's sister.

"Madame, you must fetch the children. There is no time—"

"Are you mad? Think you that I would deny Elen this meagre comfort?"

"Madame, Lady Elen is dying! All that matters is her immortal soul. She's been out of her head with fever for days, but she is lucid now, and that time is too precious to waste like this. She must make her confession ere the fever returns, for she cannot be shriven if she is not in her senses."

Nell stared at him, and he wondered if she, too, might be feverish, for hectic patches of color suddenly stood out across her cheekbones. "She will be shriven," she said huskily. "You will see to that."

"My lady, you do not understand—"

"No," she said, "you are the one who does not understand." Reaching out, she caught his arm. He had never seen a hand so elegant, fingers long and tapering, nails perfectly manicured, a hand that had never known hard manual labor. He stared at it in fascination, accustomed to the broken nails and swollen knuckles of the village women, thinking that Nell's hands were verily as white and smooth as the marble statue of the Blessed Lady he'd once seen in a Canterbury church. But those delicate, bejeweled fingers had a surprisingly strong grip, and as he looked up, he found himself frozen by what he saw in her eyes.

"Elen shall have this time with her daughters," she said. "Then you shall hear her confession, see that she is shriven, and if she cannot make the proper responses, you will make them for her. You will give her the holy viaticum, and you will do all you can to ease her last hours. Above all, you will never even hint to Rob or her children that you have any doubts whatsoever as to the validity of these Sacraments."

The priest was appalled. "But . . . but Madame, you are asking me to—"

"I am asking nothing. I am telling you that should you fail Elen in this, you will find that the Almighty's mercy is far greater than mine."

The priest swallowed. All knew the stories told of King John, that he was of the Devil's brood, that the Plantagenet seed first took root in the womb of a witch, the demon Countess of Black Fulk of Anjou. He looked now at the woman before him, King John's daughter, and even as he nodded, he thought, All true, Christ keep me safe, the tales be true!

BRAN awakened shivering, for the hall fire had long since gone out. Reaching for his clothes, he dressed hurriedly under the blankets, for he lacked a chamber pot and would have to go outdoors to relieve himself. But as he got to his feet, he noticed his mother, seated alone at the trestle table. Snatching up a man's mantle from a nearby sleeper, he crossed the hall. Nell was leaning forward, her head buried in her arms, and he thought she slept. But as he draped the mantle about her shoulders, she raised her head. "Bran? Is it dawn yet?"

He nodded. Her gown was badly wrinkled, stained with sweat and water splotches. Even her hair had lost its lustre; spilling from an untidy chignon, it framed her face in stray wisps and tangled tendrils, lacking color or sheen in the harsh morning light. The mother Bran knew best was a glamorous, worldly creature, high-tempered and high-spirited, by turns sarcastic and merry, but always elegant, always unpredictable, utterly unlike the drab, ordinary mothers of his less-fortunate friends.

This haggard, disheveled woman seemed a stranger. But if her sudden vulnerability unnerved him, it also fired his protective instincts, and when she rose, he trailed her across the hall.

Llewelyn was stretched out upon the settle. Nell leaned over, shook his shoulder. "Llewelyn, it is dawn." He opened his eyes, and she saw that he had not slept, either. He was sitting up as the bedchamber door opened.

The young priest came wearily down the stairs. "It is over," he said, making the sign of the cross. He had dozed during the night in a chair by Elen's bed, so great was his relief that he had been able, after all, to administer the Last Rites, thus offending neither the Almighty nor the Countess of Leicester. But his position had been a cramped one, and his muscles were constricted and sore. As he sank down on a bench, his gaze fell upon the platter of food, flaky pasties filled with cheese and beef marrow, stone-cold, flecked with congealed grease, but still rich fare to an impoverished priest, and irresistible to a man who'd not eaten since noon the day before. Tucking a napkin into his cassock collar, he helped himself to a pasty, and then another.

"She was at peace, at the end, all her thoughts given over to God," he volunteered, the falsehood not weighing heavily upon his conscience, for it was what he was expected to say, what the bereaved wanted to hear. "My lady . . . mayhap you might mention to your royal brother that I was the priest who ministered to his niece? It would be such an honor, that my name might be known to the King . . ." Nell's response was not encouraging; she merely looked at him. Deciding it would not be seemly to push further, he sighed, swallowed the last mouthful of pasty, and gestured politely toward Llewelyn. "My lord, if you could pass me that flagon of ale . . . ?"

Llewelyn reached for the flagon. It was full and the ale sloshed over the rim as he lifted it. His fingers clenched around the handle, and then the flagon was slamming into the wall with such force that men scattered in all directions, seeking to evade the flying shards. The priest scrambled to his feet in alarm, but Llewelyn never even glanced his way. He was gripping the edge of the table, staring at the platter heaped with pasties. With a wild sweep of his arm, he sent it spinning to the floor, and then brought his fist down upon the table, again and again, not stopping until the trestle boards buckled.

His breath was coming fast and uneven; he could hear it now, echoing in his ears. He could even hear his heart beating, no less rapidly, for so still was it of a sudden in the hall. He looked up, saw the silent men, the fearful priest, the watching women. No one spoke, but the manor dogs crept from hiding, began to feast warily upon the pasties strewn among the floor rushes. Davydd pushed his way toward Llewelyn. His eyes were wide, filled with wonder. As he passed the priest, he murmured, "Did no one tell you? My brother cannot abide ale," and a few men laughed nervously.

Nell jerked the napkin from the priest's neck, stepped toward Llewelyn, and it was only then that he became aware of the blood trickling down his wrist. He stood without moving as she bandaged his hand, then turned, walked toward the ash-filled hearth. Nell watched him go; no one else dared to follow.

As men began to clear away the wreckage, Nell laid claim to a soldier's flask, tilted it up and drank deeply of the pungent, spiced wine, then startled the priest by passing the flask to him. He accepted gratefully, but it took several swallows to nerve him to approach Nell again.

"I am sorry, my lady," he blurted out, "sorry I was not of more comfort, sorry I must now trouble you further. But the little lasses, they must be told. I daresay they're awake by now, for this din was for certes enough to raise the dead—" He bit his lip; a lamentable choice of words! "My lady, Sir Robert is sore crazed with grief; never have I seen a man so stricken, in truth. I doubt that he can . . ." His words trailed away. For an awful moment, he feared that Nell might expect him to be the one to tell Elen's daughters. But then Nell got slowly to her feet.

Unlike the open, wooden stairway that led to Elen's bedchamber, this was a narrow, spiral staircase, giving access to the roof, the battlements, and the small loft squeezed under the eaves. Gazing upward, Nell could not detect a glimmer of light, nor a whisper of sound. She lifted her skirts, put her foot on the first step, but could go no farther. Clutching the rope railing, she faltered, then sank down upon the stairs.

At approaching footsteps, she looked up reluctantly. But it was Llewelyn, not the priest, and when he held out his hand, she readily took it, let him help her to her feet.

They stood quietly in the shadows of the stairwell. From the sound of her breathing, he suspected that she wept. He put his arm around her shoulders and she leaned against his chest. After a time, she said softly, "There can be burdens too onerous, too painful to be borne. Whenever I feel that I cannot . . . cope, I try to think what Simon would do. I know he'd find the strength to do what he must, and knowing that, I can somehow find the strength, too. Until now . . ."

Since his frenzied outburst, his futile, rending denial, Llewelyn had felt nothing, only exhaustion, numbness. Now a surprising emotion flickered faintly—envy for Simon de Montfort, for how many men were ever loved so passionately? But then there came to him his last memory of Rob, his desperate deathbed vigil. Rob had been well loved, too. Yet what man in his right senses would envy Rob now? Llewelyn drew a constricted breath. God pity Rob, God pity all who gave their hearts with such reckless abandon. "Nell . . . do you want me to go up with you?"

"No. No, it is best that a woman be the one to tell them." Nell stood for a moment longer in his embrace, and then, lifting her skirts again, she started up the stairs.

22

Beddgelert Priory North Wales

June 1255

T HEY'D been roused from sleep, and they stumbled, yawning, into Llewelyn's bedchamber, blinking at the sudden flaring of torch-light. Llewelyn stood motionless in the shadows, listening in silence as his scout told them what he already knew—that his brothers, Owain and Davydd, were leading an invading army into his lands.

He watched them intently, saw their faces change, their sleepiness vanish. Only his cousin Tegwared seemed truly startled; Tegwared inhaled optimism as naturally as he did air. Gruffydd and Goronwy ab Ednyved had followed in their father's footsteps, wielding their swords in the service of Gwynedd's Prince. Like Ednyved, they were shrewd, cynical, and utterly unsentimental, not to be surprised by a brother's betrayal. His uncle Einion showed no surprise, either, only dismay. Llewelyn understood, and felt honor-bound to offer a reprieve.

"This is no quarrel of yours, Uncle, not when you'd find kinsmen on both sides of the battlefield."

"Ah, but that is the Welsh way, lad." That was too true for humor, though; only Einion smiled. He was greatly tempted to take advantage of Llewelyn's generosity. It would be no pleasant task, explaining to Senena that he'd backed the wrong son. Moreover, he sympathized with Davydd's claim, for in his heart he believed that Gwynedd ought to be divided equally amongst all of Gruffydd's sons, as the ancient

Welsh laws decreed. But his affections ran contrary to common sense, and he heard himself saying, "It is an easier choice than you think, Llewelyn. I have never liked Owain."

This time Llewelyn did smile. "Neither have I," he said, no more than that, but Einion needed no more. He returned his nephew's smile and for the moment, at least, his sister, Senena, was forgotten.

Llewelyn moved into the light. "Mayhap it was inevitable that Owain and I would have a day of reckoning. Now that it has come so be it. But I want our men to understand this, that Davydd is not to be harmed."

Tegwared and Einion nodded approvingly, but Llewelyn caught the skeptical look that passed between Ednyved's sons, and he could not keep a defensive note from creeping into his voice. "As young as Davydd is, he does not fully comprehend the consequences of what he's done."

Goronwy carefully avoided his brother's eye. He'd have wagered that Davydd was no innocent; even as a lad, he had been one for poking sticks into hornets' nests. But he knew better than to argue. Instead, he said, "What mean you to do, Llewelyn?"

Llewelyn crossed to the table. The map was crudely drawn, but that didn't matter. He'd had twenty-seven years to learn the lay of his land, knew the depths of every river, the twistings of every mountain trail.

"They circled around Cricieth Castle, are now heading north. To get from Eiffionydd into Arfon, they'll use the Bwlch Mawr Pass." He gestured toward the map, then said grimly, "And there they will find us waiting for them."

IT was not lack of sleep that had soured Davydd's enthusiasm. He was still young enough to savor novelty, and camping out under the stars seemed part of the adventure. Nor was he fazed by the weather. It was surprisingly hot and humid for June, and rain had been falling intermittently since dawn, but rain was so common an occurrence in Wales that Davydd never gave it a thought. It was his quarrel with his brother that rankled.

Davydd had tried to be tactful, but Owain had flared up almost at once, pointing out scathingly that, as he was thirty-six whilst Davydd still lacked a fortnight till his seventeenth birthday, his battlefield experience was considerably greater than his brother's. Davydd could not dispute that, but it did occur to him that Owain had fought two wars, one against their uncle Davydd and one against the English King, and he'd lost them both.

Davydd still felt that their campaign was being conducted in a haphazard, needlessly risky manner, lacking clear objectives. So far they'd plundered Llewelyn's lands in Eiffionydd, to no great effect, and this morning they'd pillaged the abbey grange at Cwm, for Owain believed the Aberconwy monks to be too favorably inclined toward Llewelyn. But Davydd wondered what they'd accomplished, aside from scattering a flock of panicked sheep.

Pitched battles were rare in Wales, where warfare most commonly consisted of hit-and-run raids. It might well be that Llewelyn would yield before their show of force and offer terms; Davydd fervently hoped so. But he thought it was at least as likely that Llewelyn would choose to confront them. They had the greater numbers, but he would be able to choose the time and the terrain, and Davydd felt they should be taking more precautions, posting additional guards at night, sending out scouts to range farther afield. Suggestions that had seemed eminently sensible to him, but to Owain presumptuous enough to spark their most serious altercation, one that still smoldered after several hours of morose silence.

Rain had begun to fall again; the peaks of Bwlch Mawr and Mynydd Craig Goch were shrouded in grey mist. Owain could hear his men beginning to grumble; they'd soon have to call a halt. Glancing over his shoulder, he sighed. Davydd's face was too expressive for his own good. So the lad was still brooding. He eased his stallion, waited for Davydd to catch up. "We'd best give some thought as to how we'll be dividing Gwynedd. I'll have all of Môn and Llŷn and Arfon, but the rest is up for the taking. Just remember, ere you put in your bid, that we must make some provisions for Rhodri, too."

"Do you mean to leave nothing to Llewelyn, then?"

Owain smiled. "I'd leave him enough ground to be buried in, I suppose."

Davydd swung about in the saddle. For certes, Owain was jesting . . . or was he? "I do not want Llewelyn killed!"

Owain forgot at times just how young the boy was. "I do not seek Llelo's death. But I know what can happen on a battlefield. This is no game, Davydd." Drawing rein, he reached over, put his hand on his brother's arm. "I thought you wanted this, lad. I thought you wanted what is rightfully yours."

"I do! But . . . but I would that there was another way."

"There is not," Owain said, then raised his hand for silence, frowning. By now Davydd heard it, too. Heads were turning, men straining to see. One of their scouts was galloping toward them, gesturing wildly.

"There's an army at the head of the pass, my lord," he gasped. "Your brother's army, waiting to do battle!"

There was a moment of stunned silence, and then all within earshot began talking at once. Owain's captains were shouting questions, but his response was drowned out by a sudden clap of thunder. Davydd's mount shied as thunder sounded again, directly overhead this time, and he had to waste precious minutes calming the animal before he was able to push through to his brother's side.

"Owain, you've got to send a man out with a flag of truce, offer to talk!"

Owain looked at him as if he'd lost his senses. "Talk? I'll let my sword do my talking for me!"

"Owain, we've got to gain time! Our men are not ready to fight. They need to get their blood stirred up first, you know they do. Send word to Llewelyn that you want to negotiate, to—"

"And have Llelo think I fear him? I'd be damned first!"

"Owain, wait—" Davydd was never to know, though, if he might have prevailed, for Llewelyn had no intention of giving them the time they so needed. Even as they argued, his army was advancing. Owain swung his mount about, began to shout commands. Davydd found himself alone, forgotten.

Not knowing what else to do, he sought to follow his brother. But it was his stallion's first battle, too. Already unnerved by the storm, the horse panicked at sight of the running, yelling men. It swerved suddenly, then bucked, and Davydd, taken by surprise, went flying over its head.

His first reaction was utter disbelief; he could not even remember the last time he'd been thrown from a horse. He shouted, but the stallion was already in full flight from the battlefield. Becoming aware of his danger, Davydd scrambled to his feet, unsheathing his sword.

He was shocked by what he saw. He had been prepared for a battle to be violent and bloody, but not so chaotic. Gazing about him at this seething mass of men, he wondered despairingly how he could even tell who was the enemy. Only lords wore heraldic devices; so who fought for Owain and who for Llewelyn?

He moved forward, caught up in the current. The rain was coming down heavily now, and the ground was growing slippery; men were losing their footing, stumbling in the muddy marsh grass. From the corner of his eye, Davydd saw a man fall. Before he could regain his feet, another soldier was astride him, wielding an axe. Davydd yelled and the man whirled to meet this new threat. As his would-be victim rolled out of range, he swung at Davydd; the blade sliced through the air only inches from Davydd's helmet. He was raising the axe again when Davydd's sword thrust through his leather gambeson, up under his ribs.

Davydd was no stranger to death; he'd seen executions, and once, a man murdered in a London street brawl. But those deaths lacked the awful intimacy, the immediacy of the battlefield. Splattered by the blood of the man he'd just stabbed, Davydd had to fight back a sudden queasiness. But at the same time, he felt a surge of pride. He'd matched his wits and his training and his courage against another man, and he'd won.

"My lord!" The soldier he'd saved was beside him now, grinning his gratitude. Only then did Davydd recognize him as one of their sentries, but that was something he meant to keep to himself. If the sentry survived the battle, he'd tell and retell the tale of his rescue. It never occurred to Davydd that he himself might not survive.

The ground squished under his feet, for they were well away from the road by now. Davydd knew there were extensive marshes between Mynydd Cenin and Bwlch Mawr. There were patches of quicksand, too, but he tried not to think of that. Sheets of silver rain were obscuring visibility; he could only speculate as to the whereabouts—or the well-being—of Owain and Llewelyn. Lightning seared the sky to the west, and he ran his hand uneasily along the metal links of his hauberk. As if he did not have enough worries at the moment!

A soldier was bearing down upon him, sword already well-bloodied. Davydd parried the man's thrust, numbing his arm from wrist to elbow. The soldier staggered, regained his balance and lunged again. Again Davydd deflected the blow. He had always begrudged those tedious hours of tiltyard practice. Now he had only a moment to thank God for them, and then the man was once more pressing the attack.

They circled cautiously. When Davydd swung, his sword encountered only air, for the other man was as quick as a ferret. They were so intent upon the stalk that they didn't realize the ground was becoming soft, not until the soldier took a backward step and found himself sinking up to his knees. He spat out a startled oath, and when he looked at Davydd, for the first time there was fear on his face.

Davydd was no longer a threat, though; he, too, was mired in the thick, viscous mud. He experienced a flash of instinctive panic, but froze until it passed, until he could slowly start to work his way back to firm ground. By the time he had extricated himself, he was panting, relieved out of all proportion to the danger posed by the quavering, sodden sands.

The soldier had also kept his head, and together they struggled back onto solid footing. For a moment or two they eyed each other warily, but they'd both lost the stomach for further killing. The soldier, moreover, was now looking beyond Davydd's height and man's build, seeing the boy.

"Get away whilst you still can, lad," he said. "There is no madness like dying for a cause already lost."

"Lost?" Davydd frowned, and the soldier gestured impatiently.

"Look around you. Owain ap Gruffydd's men are on the run. Looting of bodies has begun, the surest sign yet that it's done, and no surprise, for my lord Llewelyn is twice the soldier Owain could ever hope to be." With that, he turned away, seeking to gain what he, too, could from the dead.

Davydd pulled off his helmet, ran his hand through his sweat-soaked hair. The sky was clearing; the storm had passed them by. So, it seemed, had the battle. His brother's army—what was left of it—was in flight, some wading across the shallows of the River Desoch, some scattering toward the wooded slopes of Bwlch Mawr, others bogged down in the rain-drenched marshlands, easy prey for Llewelyn's pursuing soldiers. Davydd found himself alone on a muddy field with the dead, the dying, and the looters. No one paid him any mind, and he did not know what to do next. At last he decided to head west, for there was a monastery a few miles away at Clynnog. Once there, he could then try to reach his own lands down in Llŷn. After that? He had no idea.

As it threaded its serpentine way through the marshes, the river gained in silt what it lacked in depth, and its color was an unappealing yellow-brown. But Davydd was too thirsty to care. Kneeling, he cupped the brackish water in his hands, drank greedily.

"Cadell, that's him!"

"You're daft, man! He's a lord, would be mounted."

"I'm telling you, it's him. I've seen him often enough to know!"

Davydd did not like the sound of that. He jumped to his feet and spun around. Two men were approaching him, one from each side. He took an instinctive step backward, and nearly slid down the embankment into the river.

"Careful, lad!" One of the men was reaching out, as if to offer a hand, but retreated when Davydd raised his sword. "We mean you no harm, God's truth! Our lord has promised a gold ring to the man who sees to your safety."

"Llewelyn did that?" Davydd was startled enough to let down his guard. Both men nodded vigorously, and he felt a sudden pang of remorse, remembering Owain's callous joking about graves. They saw his hesitation and the younger one held out his hand. It was a gesture as disarming as it was courageous, and Davydd impulsively lowered his sword, then offered it, hilt first.

They accepted it gravely, and for a moment all three of them took pleasure in the solemn formality of surrender, evoking as it did echoes of those tales told around campfires and winter hearths, tales of chivalry rooted in the Welsh legends of Arthur and his knights of the Table

Round. Then the older soldier let out a gleeful whoop, clapped his companion on the back. "You stay here, Cadell, whilst I fetch our lord!"

He was off like a shot. Cadell looked suddenly uncertain. Glancing shyly at Davydd, he asked, "Have I your word, my lord, that you'll not try to flee?" Much relieved when Davydd nodded, he unfastened a flask from his belt, passed it politely to Davydd.

Sitting down on the river bank, they shared the flask, and Davydd found himself quaffing the warm ale as if it were vintage wine. Cadell was very young himself, and somewhat awed, for he'd never expected to be in such intimacy with one of his Princes. "This was my first battle," he confessed, "and I cannot say I fancied it much. It was not at all as I thought it would be."

Davydd reclaimed the flask. "The first time I lay with a whore," he said, "that was a letdown, too. I wondered afterward why men craved women's flesh more than meat or mead. But it did not take long to develop a taste for it. Mayhap it is the same with battles."

Cadell laughed. "War and women . . . they both do heat the blood for certes. But between the bed and the battlefield, it's not much of a choice. I know a lass called Enid who can light a bonfire just by . . ."

Davydd smiled, but he was no longer listening. He was thinking of the coming confrontation with his brother. Llewelyn was the very last man in Christendom whom he wanted to face right now. With that realization, he began to think of ways to avoid it, shooting Cadell a sideways, appraising look. No longer two against one. Moreover, his identity was in itself an invincible shield; Cadell would never dare to draw a sword upon his lord's brother. He rose, stretched as casually as he could, and then reached over, snatched up his sword.

Cadell at once tensed. "What is it? Where do you go?"

"I just remembered a pressing need to be elsewhere. Convey my regrets to Llewelyn."

But what Davydd had not anticipated was Cadell's outrage. Jumping up, he cried, "You gave me your sworn word!"

Davydd shrugged, then leveled the sword. "That is far enough," he warned. Cadell paid him no heed, continued to advance, and Davydd discovered that he could not thrust his blade into the other youth's belly. With an oath, he flung the sword aside, and swung at Cadell. The blow never connected; Cadell was quicker than he looked, and as he ducked, Davydd's fist just brushed his chin. They traded punches, then grappled until Cadell slipped in the wet grass, dragging Davydd down with him.

They rolled about, pummeling each other. Davydd's was the greater weight and he was eventually able to pin Cadell down. "Will you yield?" he panted, but Cadell stubbornly shook his head.

"You gave me your word," he repeated, as if nothing else mattered, and Davydd swore again. Neither he nor Cadell had realized they'd gathered an audience, not until Davydd turned his head, caught a glimpse of muddied boots. He struggled to sit up, his heart thudding wildly, for he already knew what he would see. The stallion was a smoke-grey, well lathered, its mane smeared with blood, Llewelyn's favorite destrier. Davydd's breath froze in the seconds before he forced himself to meet his brother's eyes. Llewelyn's face was shadowed by his helmet; he sat motionless on the grey stallion, staring down at Davydd, saying nothing, until the silence itself became more intolerable to Davydd than any reproaches Llewelyn could make.

He got slowly to his feet, began to walk toward Llewelyn. He made no attempt, though, to wipe the mud from his face, hoping it might camouflage some of the hot color burning his cheeks and throat. "I've always heard tales," he said, "about men emerging from battle covered with glory. But I cannot remember anyone ever mentioning mud!"

He'd long ago learned that humor was a most effective defense, particularly with Llewelyn; amusement, no less than charity, covered a multitude of sins. But now he searched his brother's face in vain, could find not the least glimmer of a smile, and as they looked at each other, Davydd began to realize that he had at last committed an offense which could not be laughed away.

THE rain had not dissipated the heat, and Llewelyn's tent was stifling. When Davydd rose, the guards tensed, watching him intently as he crossed to a coffer. Picking up a flask, he retraced his steps, thrust it at his brother. "Drink," he said. "If ever we had an excuse to get drunk, it's now."

Owain accepted the flask with the indifference that had characterized his every act since the moment of his capture. Still utterly stunned by the magnitude of his defeat, he seemed in a state of shock, and the grey eyes that now focused upon Davydd were dulled by disbelief. "I will never understand," he said, "how God could so favor Llelo."

Davydd bit back the tart reply that God usually favored the better battle commander. "It could be worse," he pointed out. "You could have been horribly maimed, skewered through like a stuck pig and left for dead with your guts spilling out into the mud. There are worse things to lose than a battle, Owain—like your head, or Jesú forfend, your privy member!" His mock shudder was not entirely feigned. He grinned, then said, more seriously, "At least you are alive, Owain."

Owain gave him a sourly patronizing smile. "For the moment," he said, investing his words with such ominous portent that Davydd lost patience.

"For the love of Christ, Owain! You cannot truly believe Llewelyn would have you put to death?"

At that moment, the tent flap was pulled aside and Llewelyn entered, followed by Goronwy ab Ednyved. At sight of his brother, Davydd cried, "Tell him, Llewelyn. Tell him his life is in no danger!"

Llewelyn's eyes cut toward Owain. "I am not Cain," he said tersely. Davydd was about to utter a triumphant "I told you so" when Llewelyn added, "You'd best make yourself ready, Owain. Your guards are waiting to escort you to Dolbadarn Castle."

Owain rose to his feet. "Post your guards," he said. "It will avail you naught, for your prison will not hold me for long."

Llewelyn merely shrugged, and Davydd glanced uneasily from one to the other. The enmity between his brothers had always been a secret source of amusement to him, and it had fed his sense of superiority that Llewelyn should nurture childhood grudges, that Owain should obstinately cling to the use of "Llelo" as if a boy's name somehow diminished his brother's manhood. Davydd had long ago learned how to turn their rivalry to his own advantage, had become adroit at playing them off against each other to his benefit. But his fondness for them both was genuine, and only now was he realizing how greatly he'd underestimated the depths of their rancor.

"How long do you mean to keep Owain at Dolbadarn?" he demanded, had his answer in Llewelyn's silence. "My God, Llewelyn, you cannot—"

"Davydd!" Owain grabbed his arm, swung him around. "Do not beg for me," he said fiercely, "not now, not ever!"

"But it is my fault!"

"No." Owain's grip loosened; he shifted his hands to Davydd's shoulders. "No, lad," he repeated, "it is not. I knew the stakes even if you did not."

Davydd did not know what to say, and watched mutely as Owain followed his guards from the tent. Llewelyn ignored his departure, keeping his eyes upon his younger brother. Davydd reached for Owain's forgotten flask, drank until he'd gotten his bravado back.

"What now? What happens to me? Am I to be imprisoned, too?" "Yes."

Davydd dropped the flask. "For how long?"

"That depends upon you, Davydd. I'll release you as soon as I can be sure you comprehend the consequences of treason."

Davydd flushed. "It is not treason to claim what is rightfully mine!"

"It is," Llewelyn said, "when you lose."

He gestured and the guards moved forward. Davydd did not balk, but as they led him from the tent, he shouted defiantly, "I'll never say I'm sorry, never! My only regret is that we lost!"

Llewelyn said nothing. For a time, neither did Goronwy. Bending down, he retrieved the flask, handed it without comment to Llewelyn. "You ought not to have promised him his freedom," he said at last. "Better to have kept him in suspense."

"I know," Llewelyn admitted. "But I had to give him that reassurance, Goronwy. You see," he said softly, "beneath all that bluster, he was afraid."

ALTHOUGH Anian, the Abbot of the Cistercian abbey of Aberconwy, was both friend and ally to Llewelyn, he was not pleased to be told that Llewelyn had just ridden into the abbey garth. The abbey had benefited in no small measure from the favor of its greatest patron, Llewelyn Fawr. It was he who had generously absolved the White Monks of the need to entertain the princes of Gwynedd or their households. As no prince traveled without a large retinue, this was no insignificant saving to the abbey larders. But it was a privilege rarely invoked, for abbots were not political innocents—if they were, they weren't abbots—and there was nothing politic in refusing hospitality to one's liege lord. Anian could only hope that Llewelyn's entourage would not be too numerous, or too hungry.

He forgot all about the abbey larders, though, at sight of the woman. He was too pragmatic to deny entry to his Prince's concubine, but he was enough of a moralist to want to, and he could not help giving Llewelyn a look of wordless reproach. When he did, Llewelyn burst out laughing.

"I know how heartsick you'll be," he bantered, "but we cannot accept your hospitality. We're on our way down the Conwy valley to Trefriw, where I have a hunting lodge."

Anian laughed, too, from sheer relief. "How then may we serve you, my lord?"

Llewelyn's smile faded. "I've come to visit my grandfather's tomb."

"YOUR lord father is buried here, too, is he not?"

Llewelyn nodded. "The English King finally gave his consent and he lies now where he belongs, with his kinsmen."

Eurwen arched a brow. "I do hope he does not lie too close to your uncle Davydd," she murmured slyly, "else they'd get precious little Eternal Peace."

Llewelyn grinned, slid his arm around her waist as they entered the abbey. The women in his life were usually slim and dark, sweet-tempered bedmates who evoked unconscious echoes of the gentle Melangell. Eurwen was an anomaly, therefore, as she was cheerful and cheeky, uncommonly tall for a woman, with a vigorous brisk stride, a buxom hour-glass figure, and masses of thick, tawny hair which more than did justice to her name, for "Eurwen" was derived from the Welsh word for "gold." Llewelyn was fonder of her than he had yet to admit, and he was suddenly glad that she was here with him, sharing the culmination of his victory in the mountain pass at Bwlch Mawr.

Eurwen seemed to sense his mood, for she came to a sudden halt, then said with unwonted seriousness, "I think your grandfather would be very proud of you this day."

Llewelyn nodded. "Yes," he agreed softly, "I think he would."

The abbey was not utterly dark, for the Cistercians believed stained-glass windows to be sinfully ornate. But coming in from sun-dazzling daylight, Llewelyn and Eurwen were momentarily blinded. They did not see the woman standing in the shadows of the choir, and they both jumped when she suddenly spoke.

"I knew you'd come here sooner or later," she said.

As she stepped forward, Eurwen understood why they'd not noticed her, for she wore, like a cloak of invisibility, the stark black of mourning. She wondered who this aging widow was, that she dared to speak to Llewelyn with such familiarity, and then the woman said, "Get rid of your harlot. We need to talk."

Eurwen gave a gasp of pure outrage, started indignantly down the nave. But Llewelyn put a restraining hand on her arm. "Your grievance is with me, Mother," he said coldly, "not with Eurwen. Do not take out your anger on her."

Eurwen's eyes widened. She glanced quickly at Llewelyn, then at Senena. "I'll await you in the cloisters, my lord." He nodded and she moved reluctantly up the aisle, casting numerous glances back over her shoulder.

"I demand that you free your brothers. I want you to give the order for their release now, this very day."

"I will release Davydd right gladly—once he's shown he can be trusted. I cannot free Owain, and you well know it, Mother."

Senena's hand closed upon his arm. "What if I can persuade Owain to agree to your terms?"

"Even if—allowing for miracles—you did get him to agree, he'd never hold to it. Once free, he'd devote every waking hour to vengeance, and that, too, you know."

Llewelyn looked for a long moment into his mother's face. "Wales is not yet whole," he said. "All of Gwynedd east of the Conwy still lies in English control. I mean to remedy that, to regain what was stolen from us at Woodstock. But I cannot fight the English and Owain, too, not if I can help it—and I can."

But the passion in that answer was lost upon Senena; she heard only the refusal. "Damn you, Owain is your brother! Are you telling me you'd have him pass the rest of his days shut away from the sun?"

Llewelyn moved away, crossed to his grandfather's massive tomb. He stared down at the enameled lions, the emblem he'd taken as his own. "If the battle had gone to Owain and I was the one being held at Dolbadarn, would you now be pleading with Owain on my behalf? I doubt it."

Senena followed him, again caught his arm. "What do you want from me? Do you want me to beg? Forget Owain, then; do not do it for him. Do it for me, because I am your mother and I ask it of you."

She felt the sudden tautness in his arm, felt a quiver of tension contracting the muscles, and thought she'd won. But then he raised his eyes to hers.

"No," he said, and Senena stepped backward, struck him across the face. He was much taller than she and could easily have avoided the blow, merely by jerking his head away. But he did not, and somehow that seemed to Senena the ultimate rejection.

Tears of rage and disappointment filled Senena's eyes, but she willed them not to fall. Even in the subdued church lighting, she could see that Llewelyn had lost color; the imprint of her slap showed on his cheek like a brand. He made no attempt to stop her, though, as she turned to go. She took a few steps, swung back to face him.

"You are going to pay a great price," she said, "for Llewelyn Fawr's dream."

Discretion had taken Eurwen as far as the door, but curiosity had then diverted her toward the shelter of a large, stone pillar. Now she hastily crossed herself, for Senena's last words sounded to her almost like a curse. She shrank back behind the pillar as Senena passed, not venturing out until the older woman had left the church.

Llewelyn was still standing by his grandfather's tomb. He did not move, not even when she said his name. "I could not help overhearing," she confessed. "Do you want to talk about it, love?" But she felt no surprise at all when he shook his head.

23

Isleworth, England

September 1256

FROM his father, Hugh de Lusignan had inherited the county of La Marche, and from his mother, the rich lands of Angoulême. He alone of his brothers was not despised by the English people, for he alone had made no claims upon Henry in the name of kinship. Henry was not as fond of Hugh as he was of William, Aymer, Geoffrey, and Guy, for their relationship was not one of need. But he was determined, nonetheless, to make Hugh's first visit to England a memorable one, never thinking that to indulge in lavish spectacles might not be wise in a year of poor crops, rain-rotted harvests.

SEVEN miles west of London lay Richard's favorite residence, his riverside manor at Isleworth. After a bountiful noontime dinner meant to lull Hugh into an agreeable frame of mind, Richard was taking pride in showing his guests the luxuriant gardens and elaborately constructed fish ponds.

The ground was muddy, for it had been raining almost daily since mid-August. Richard's wife, Sanchia, lagged behind, complaining of the soggy footing, and Nell felt constrained by courtesy to keep pace with her. She was grateful when Simon lingered, too, for Sanchia was not a companion of her choosing.

Richard and Hugh had continued on, and now their voices drifted back upon the humid September air, quarrelsome echoes that brought a frown to Sanchia's face. "Jesú," she muttered, "if they are not arguing again about that poor child killed by the Jews!"

"What child?"

Nell jumped, for she'd not heard her son's approach. "Where did you come from, lad? I thought you were watching your brothers in the tiltyard."

Amaury was not yet eleven, but he was already displaying a single-mindedness many an adult might envy. Refusing to be distracted, he repeated with polite persistence, "What child, Mama?"

Nell hesitated. She did not believe in sheltering her children, gave honest answers to even the most awkward questions. But she did not look forward to offering an explanation under Sanchia's hostile eye; in defending the Jews, she found herself torn between her sense of fairness and her faith.

"It happened in Lincoln," she said slowly. "A Christian child's body was discovered in a cistern close by a Jew's house. The Jew was arrested and confessed that he and other Jews had abducted the child, then crucified him in a vile ritual meant to mock Our Lord Jesus. He implicated a hundred others, and Henry ordered them taken to London for trial, where all but three were found guilty. Eighteen were put to death last Christmas, but twenty-one were freed this past May, at your uncle Richard's behest."

Amaury was not shocked by the crime itself, for he had often heard people gossiping of ritual killings done by Jews. Although such murders were always set in conveniently distant parts of the country, Amaury did not doubt them, for his chaplain had taught him that the Jews were in league with the Devil. But he was very shocked that his own uncle should have condoned such evil, and he gasped, "Why, Mama? Why?"

"Because Richard believed them to be innocent, lad."

"But . . . but they were Jews!"

Nell sighed. "I cannot pretend that I understand a people who willfully reject Our Saviour. It may be that the Lord God put them in our midst as a test of our own faith. But we must not assume a man is guilty merely because he is a Jew, Amaury. In this sad case, there were doubts about their guilt and so—"

"Nonsense," Sanchia interrupted. "One of the Jews confessed, did he not?"

"Under torture." But Simon had no interest in arguing with Sanchia, for he'd long ago dismissed her as vain and frivolous. It was his son's view that mattered. "Can you tell me, Amaury, who is the greatest sinner—a Jew, an infidel Saracen, or a heretic?"

That was a question Amaury could answer with ease; so well versed was he in his catechism that his parents were considering for him a career in the Church. "The heretic, of course, Papa, for he knew Christ and then denied Him."

Simon nodded. "Just so. But even the heretic has legal rights. As does the Jew. It is true that the Lincoln Jews were found guilty. But doubts remained, for what a man says on the rack is not reliable, lad. Not all believed the verdict was just. Brother Adam Marsh did not, and convinced me that justice had not been done. He felt compelled to speak out on the Jews' behalf, as did his brother friars, even though they incurred much abuse for it. And so it has been for your uncle. He would have gained from their deaths, for last year the King was so hard-pressed for money that he sold all the English Jews to Richard. Had they been hanged, Richard would then have inherited all their estates. Instead, he secured their release, and Londoners will not soon forgive him for it. That was an act of courage, Amaury."

"That was an act of lunacy," Sanchia snapped. "Till the end of his days, men will look at him askance, and all for what? If Henry would only have heeded Eleanor, expelled the Jews from the kingdom as he ought, none of this would—"

She stopped in mid-complaint, for Richard and Hugh de Lusignan were coming back. Richard looked so disgruntled that it was obvious he'd been defending himself to Hugh with little success. Nell saw all their carefully laid plans going up in smoke, and she hastily suggested they move on to the tiltyard.

There Nell and Simon's sons, Harry and Bran, had been taking turns at the quintain with their cousins, Edward and Hal, Richard's eldest son, while Guy de Montfort and Gilbert de Clare, the Earl of Gloucester's son, watched enviously. Now that they had a more distinguished audience than two eager thirteen-year-olds, the youths launched into mock warfare. In the first run, Bran unhorsed Hal, much to Simon and Nell's delight, for Bran was but sixteen to Hal's twenty-one. In the next run, all were surprised when Harry's lance hit Edward's shield with enough force to send Edward sprawling into the sawdust.

"So much for Henry's bragging." Hugh laughed. "To hear him talk, that lad of his was born to the saddle, and handles a sword with the skill of Charlemagne."

"Henry was not exaggerating Edward's prowess," Richard said, rather coolly. "Edward is a fine swordsman, and he won high honors at his first tournament in June. You're not seeing him at his best. He quarreled bitterly with Henry yesterday and I expect it is still much on his mind."

"You mean Henry actually took the lad to task for some misdeed? I thought he'd see that as sacrilege!" Hugh laughed again. "In truth, I've never seen such a doting father. It is understandable with Edward, for he's a likely lad. But Henry coddles all his brood, even that little lass of his, and her deaf as a post and mute as a swan! Yet he shows nary a qualm about keeping her at court."

He shook his head in bemusement, oblivious to the frozen silence. As lord of La Marche and Angoulême, he'd never needed to develop a sensitivity to atmosphere.

Nell bit her lip, reminding herself that they wanted this man's good will. "I would advise you not to speak ill of Katherine in Henry's hearing," she said flatly. "He cherishes her no less for being a deaf-mute, mayhap more. He once overheard one of his chaplains bewailing her birth, saying it was not fair that God should punish the King and Queen with a dumb child. Never have I seen Henry so wroth. He cursed the priest roundly, said God had given them Katherine not as punishment, but because she would need more love than other children."

Hugh was in his mid-thirties, the eldest of Isabelle's de Lusignan offspring, and the handsomest; he had his mother's sapphire eyes, hair like sun-silvered flax, and now his smile was dazzling. "Henry is moonstruck, in truth. I suppose if he had an idiot child, he'd find cause for pride in that, too!"

Nell's head swung toward her husband. With the utter certainty born of eighteen years of wedlock, she knew precisely what Simon was about to say—that Hugh might well be right, for Henry did seem to take pride in his idiot half-brothers. She could already hear the sardonic inflection, the scorn Simon could wield like a whip. She caught her breath, and then discovered that mental telepathy worked both ways. As her eyes met Simon's, she saw his mouth twist down. "I think Edward is in need of cheering," he said, in a voice husky with rage, and turning abruptly, he strode away.

Edward was wiping mud from his face, ignoring Harry's gleeful gibes. Theirs was a rivalry that stretched as far back as the cradle, a bond of more than blood. Edward was not a gracious loser; he'd had too little practice. But he was not too proud to learn from his mistakes, and despite his evident chagrin, he listened intently as Simon pointed out where he'd gone wrong.

At seventeen, Edward was already taller than Henry, taller than most men. He'd inherited from his father a drooping left eyelid and, as a child, Henry's fair coloring. But his hair had begun to darken as he approached manhood, and in temperament, he could not be more unlike his insecure, erratic father.

As they watched him conferring with Simon, the same thought was in all their minds. It was Hugh who put it into words, saying dryly, "That boy might well make me believe in changelings. Whatever did he do to incur Henry's disfavor—rape a nun?"

Sanchia thought that a jest in very poor taste, and she, too, turned away, upon the pretense of watching Bran cross lances with Harry. Richard and Nell did not have that option. They exchanged glances, concluded the time was now.

"Edward has been running wild for some months," Richard said reluctantly, for he was fond of Edward, did not relish laying bare his weaknesses before Hugh de Lusignan. But there was no help for it; Edward was becoming part of the problem.

"At first it was more mischief than malice. Edward and the youths in his household would race through village streets at midnight, sending panicked sleepers flying to their windows. Or they'd take a man's wagon, later leave it in a cemetery. But their behavior soon grew more unruly, more offensive. They began to molest women, to harass monks, to stop travelers on the road and seize their horses and goods. Earlier this summer, Edward came to my castle at Wallingford, in the Thames valley. As it happened, I was absent, and he and his companions then invaded the nearby priory, where they despoiled the buttery and wine cellar, beating those monks who dared to object. I urged Henry to chastise him, but Henry insisted it was merely youthful high spirits."

"There was some truth in that," Nell conceded. "I daresay my own sons have sins on their souls that I'd rather not know about. But what Edward did upon his return from Wales last month can in no way be dismissed as mere high spirits. He became irked with a man he encountered on the road; mayhap the man did not readily yield the right of way. But whatever the man may have done, he did not deserve the punishment inflicted upon him. Edward ordered his servants to seize the poor wretch, and at his insistence, they cut off an ear, gouged out an eye."

Hugh had listened impassively. "The man was lowborn, was he not?" And when Richard nodded, he shrugged. "Well, then," he said, letting the sentence trail off significantly.

"That made it all the more outrageous, that the man was so defenseless," Nell said sharply, and Hugh grinned, winked at Richard.

"I'd wager," he said, "that I'm now about to get a sermon on the ethics of power, as decreed by Simon de Montfort."

Richard saw the pupils of Nell's eyes contract, and he reached for her arm. But she shook off his hand. "My husband does indeed believe that power is entrusted to man by the Almighty, and the protection of Christ's poor is an inherent obligation of that power. But I am quite capable of speaking for myself. You may fail to see it, but the implications of Edward's behavior bode ill for him, for Henry, and for England. The common people have begun to fear what sort of king he shall be. They wonder if he would abide by his coronation oath, which promises peace and justice to all Christians, even the lowly born. They suspect he would not honor the Runnymede Charter, that he would rule by whim, not law. And they blame Henry for yet another failing."

Richard gave his sister an approving look, pleased that she had not allowed her anger to divert her from the purpose at hand. "Nell is right," he said. "Edward has given men another stone to fling at Henry's door. They quote from Scriptures, that a man who spareth his rod loveth not his son. And they say it is no surprise that Henry should be found wanting as a father, just as he has been found wanting as a king."

Hugh prided himself upon the fact that little surprised him. But this did; he'd not expected such unsparing candor. "I see," he said. "So we're telling the truth. Very well, that's a game I can play, too. Either we assume the Lord is not always infallible, after all, or Brother Henry is a private celestial joke. But what of it? What do Henry's shortcomings have to do with me?"

"Not Henry's shortcomings, his troubles. I doubt that you realize just how precarious his position has become. Ever since he came of age, Henry has been at odds with his barons, but never like this. First his duplicity over the Castilian invasion, then the Sicilian madness. As a result, he has utterly lost the trust of his lords, and trust—"

"I know about the 'Sicilian madness,' as who in Christendom does not? Ever since the Emperor Frederick's death, his empire has been unraveling faster than the eye can follow. I understand the Pope tried repeatedly to coax you into accepting the crown of Sicily, an offer you declined, quite sensibly, since Frederick's bastard son, Manfred, is firmly in possession of Naples. But when the Pope then made the same offer to Henry on behalf of his younger son, Edmund, Brother Henry snapped at the bait like a starving trout. He would," Hugh said and laughed derisively before adding, "I do not give a farthing for Sicily. I would like to know, though, if the rumors be true about the rest of Frederick's domains. Is it true that you are seeking the German crown for yourself? 'King of the Romans,' a fine, high-sounding title! What of it, Richard? I've laid a wager with Aymer that you are, indeed, angling for a kingship. Is my money safe, my wager won?"

Richard could not hide his displeasure. "You ought to know better than to pay heed to common gossip," he said stiffly. "I would that I could share your indifference about Sicily. But Henry has entangled himself so deeply in the Pope's web that I see no means of escape. He has pledged to send an army to Sicily, and if that were not enough, to pay all the papal expenses of the war against Manfred, 135,000 marks, more than twice the annual revenues of England!"

"It would take a veritable miracle for Henry to raise that kind of money," Nell said. "But if he does not, the Pope will excommunicate him and lay all England under Interdict!"

Hugh laughed again. "Henry must be a source of constant and abiding comfort to his enemies! So much for his Sicilian folly. What was this talk about Castile?"

Nell shook her head. "It was not Henry's finest hour. He was in Gascony at the time, after he'd been forced to ask Simon's help in putting down Gaston de Béarn's rebellion. Richard and Eleanor had remained in England, acting as regents in his absence, and he sent them an urgent request for money, claiming that Gaston de Béarn's ally, the King of Castile, was about to invade Gascony. But it was not true; although no one in England knew it yet, Henry had dispatched John Mansel to Castile with a peace offer. Unfortunately for Henry's scheme, whilst parliament was debating his demand, Simon happened to arrive unexpectedly in England. He was astonished by this talk of invasion, and explained that negotiations were in progress for Edward's marriage to the King of Castile's sister. Simon was right, of course; the marriage took place ere the year was out. But Henry's barons never forgave him for so blatant a lie. Now he could swear upon the Holy Cross itself, and I doubt they'd believe him."

"You are sure Henry is King John's flesh and blood? How any son of John's could be so inept at intrigue . . ." Hugh shrugged. "I daresay we could stay here till Vespers, swapping droll stories of Henry's blunders. But I suspect you had more in mind when you lured me down from London. Just what is it that you want from me?"

Richard could not help bridling. "I assure you we were not making sport of Henry's weaknesses. We were seeking to convince you that he has ventured out beyond his depth, that he right desperately needs someone to throw him a lifeline. We hoped it might be you."

Nell found no encouragement in Hugh's skeptical smile, but she was determined to try. "Henry is more vulnerable than he realizes, Hugh. Things cannot continue as they are now. Unless Henry agrees to make reforms, they are going to be forced upon him. But he still has time to mend his ways, and he could help himself immeasurably by reining in his de Lusignan half-brothers, your brothers."

Richard was nodding grim agreement. "You must understand, Hugh, just how hated they are. To be honest, even had they been saints, they'd have stirred up jealousy, so lavish has Henry been with his gifts, wardships, benefices. But believe me when I say they have acted more like men possessed than saints. Not even a bishopric has sobered Aymer. So bitterly has he quarreled with his monks at Winchester that he went so far as to lock them in the abbey church, kept them confined without food for a full three days! Christ Jesus, how can you laugh? You find that fitting behavior for a Prince of the Church?"

Nell was equally outraged. "I wonder," she said, "if you will find this story amusing, too. When one of Henry's cooks somehow offended your brother Geoffrey, he had the man seized, taken to Guildford, where he entertained himself by hanging the man by his heels, then having every hair plucked from his head. The man died, Hugh, and Geoffrey dismissed the killing with jests about bad cooking!"

Hugh was no longer laughing. "I assume complaints were made to Henry?"

"Yes," Nell admitted. "Henry's master of cooks came to him, as did the poor soul's family. Henry . . . he refused to take any action."

"Then what, pray, do you expect me to do?"

"Henry is unwilling—or unable—to curb their excesses," Richard said slowly. "You're their elder brother; they might listen to you. If they care naught for Henry's welfare, they must care for their own. If they continue to act in so lawless and unchristian a manner, they might well find themselves answering to men far less indulgent than Henry."

"They've feathered a right soft nest for themselves," Nell interjected bitterly. "I doubt that they'd want to lose it. If you tell them that, Hugh—"

"No," he said, "I think not. They are Henry's problem, not mine, and I'd as soon keep it that way. Better they should be in England, bleeding Henry white, than back in Poitou, bleeding me white!"

Nell stood watching as Hugh headed toward the manor, with Richard trailing him like a laggard shadow, shackled by the bonds of hospitality. Not so Nell. She turned, wandered down the slope toward the river. Rows of ash trees lined the bank, deep-green foliage feathered with clusters of amber, the seeds of autumn. Occasionally she trod a leaf underfoot. The sky seemed boundless, putting her in mind of a seascape, one that lacked even a single sail. She could see not a wisp of clouds, but it was a September blue, too bright and metallic for summer indolence.

She'd never given much thought to the seasons. She'd always taken her world just as it was, a world vibrant and vital and earthy and at times implacable, shy of nuance, alien to subtleties. But now she found herself caught up in an inexplicable surge of sadness, a nostalgic longing that seemed somehow rooted in her sudden awareness of the ebbing summer.

"Nell?"

"Simon?" She spun around. "Hold me," she said, surprising herself as much as Simon. She saw a dark brow arch upward, but he put his arms around her, drew her under the wavering shadows of a nearby ash.

"At the time, I thought it best not to linger," he said. "I did not trust myself, in truth. Was I wrong, Nell? Ought I to have stayed?"

"No, Simon. We did but waste our time, waste our breath." She said no more, and he asked no questions; he'd known their appeal would fail. Nell slid her hands up his back; she could feel the tautness of muscle, the body less supple than in his youth, but no less lean, the flesh still firm. A body she knew better than her own. She still found it hard to sleep in a bed alone, needing to be able to reach out to him, to hear his breathing in the dark.

"Did de Lusignan's refusal distress you so much, then?" he asked softly, bending his head so that he could touch his lips to the downcast curve of her mouth.

"No, it's not that. This will sound foolish, but of a sudden I felt so very sad, as if I'd suffered a loss." In the distance, Nell could hear voices, loud and youthful, boisterous; their sons were approaching. She released Simon's arm and stepped back, no longer the lover, once more the practical helpmate, the political partner.

"I did learn something whilst we talked, Simon, and it is not good. I think the rumors are true. I think Richard does mean to gain for himself the German crown."

"I'd feared it was so," he confessed. "I've no reason to wish Richard ill, but for England's sake, I hope he fails. Without him, Henry will be a ship without a rudder."

"You see a storm gathering," she said, and he nodded.

"Yes," he said. "I can tell you that for a certainty, Nell. I can tell you, too, where it will break first—over Wales."

RHODRI ap Gruffydd arrived at Cricieth Castle on a drear, blustery afternoon in mid-October. The sea churning the shore was a dull, leaden grey, and the rain was constant. Rhodri was not surprised to get a sullen, ungracious welcome from his brother; on such a dismal day, not even a saint could have mustered much cheer.

Davydd showed no interest in Rhodri's gossip, and he brusquely refused his brother's offer to play chess or tables. After a few sarcastic rebuffs, Rhodri lapsed into a faintly offended silence. He thought he deserved better; he'd ridden through a rainstorm for Davydd, after all. But he had to admit that Davydd was generally good company. Captivity had not repressed his flippant, irreverent humor, and even within the confines of Cricieth Castle, he somehow found material for ribald, comical anecdotes and practical jokes. Rhodri wondered how he could be so blithe, so cocksure after more than fifteen months at Cricieth. But then, Davydd had always been an enigma to him. He loved Davydd, envied him, by turns resented and admired him. Yet he'd never understood him.

It was not even the natural rivalry of brothers so close in age, for he could not remember a time when Davydd had not utterly overshadowed him. He'd heard that Davydd had distinguished himself in the fighting at Bwlch Mawr, would have expected no less. Davydd never lacked for courage, had always raced recklessly ahead while he hung back. He could not change his nature, could not help being cautious, deliberate, introspective, not traits to be scorned by any means, but traits that seemed dull, bland—even to him—when compared with Davydd's hell-for-leather dazzle.

Was that why Davydd had garnered all the love, all the approval? Rhodri had no memory of his father, but he had few illusions about the other members of his family. His mother had never paid him much mind, and for his brothers, it was always Davydd who mattered, Davydd who came first. When, three years after the Treaty of Woodstock, the English King had demanded that Owain and Llewelyn again yield up a brother as hostage, Rhodri knew they'd never even considered surrendering Davydd. He, Rhodri, was the last-born, the after-thought, the expendable one. And so he had returned to England, passed four more years at Henry's court, comfortable years, not unpleasant ones. But always the question remained, a query to come to him in the early hours of dawn, in moments of solitude. Why was it always Davydd? Why Davydd and never him?

As he stretched his muddied boots toward the hearth, Rhodri's eye was drawn to an object half-hidden in the floor rushes. Leaning down, he fished out a woman's garter. "Yours?" he said, and Davydd grinned.

"The lass who does my laundry. We were wondering where she left it." Reaching for the garter, he deftly tucked it away under his pillow.

"I think you could find a woman in a Benedictine monastery," Rhodri said, and Davydd grinned again.

"From what I've heard about some of the monasteries, that would be no great trick!" Davydd's spirits were beginning to rise; he could never be depressed for long. Sprawling upon the bed, he said, "Have you seen Owain?"

Rhodri nodded. "I was at Dolbadarn a fortnight ago. He's doing as well as could be expected." The words sounded stilted, even to him; he saw Davydd's eyes flick toward him, then away. "Davydd . . . how long do you intend to stay here?"

"That is a question you ought to be asking of Llewelyn, not me."

"You hold the key to that door, and you well know it. Llewelyn would have released you months ago if you'd only curb your temper and your tongue. He does care for you, Davydd."

Davydd glanced up, and Rhodri marveled that his eyes could seem so luminous one moment, so frigid the next. "I suppose he does," he said. "But he put Gwynedd first, Rhodri. Owain put me first."

"What are you seeking to prove, Davydd? How does it help Owain to have you caged, too? I never knew you had such a craving for martyrdom!"

Davydd scowled, but his mouth was twitching, and in a moment, he was laughing. "I know how you like to lecture me, but I suspect there's more to this than you're telling. What do you know that I do not?"

Rhodri's smile was sheepish. "You always did read me too well. You're right, I have found out something. Llewelyn is coming to see you again. I thought that if you had advance warning, you'd have time to think, to realize what is at stake. For God's sake, Davydd, tell him what he wants to hear and he'll set you free. It is as simple as that!"

Davydd leaned back against the headboard, then slowly shook his head. "You are wrong, Rhodri," he said. "Nothing is as simple as that."

LLEWELYN dismissed servants and guards before turning toward his brother. Davydd was leaning against the table, his pose a little too calculated, his nonchalance not quite convincing. Llewelyn shut the door. "We need to talk, Davydd."

Davydd's shoulders shifted, a half-shrug. "It's fortunate, then," he said, "that you happened to find me in."

Llewelyn parried the thrust with ironic agreement. "Very fortunate." He moved into the room, not halting until Davydd was but an arm's length away. "What do you know of the Lord Edward's dealings in Wales?"

That was not the opening Davydd had anticipated. "The English King's son? That's a right odd question; Cricieth is no hermit's cell, after all. Edward has held the crown lands in Wales for nigh on two years now, and I could almost believe he was secretly in your pay, so faithfully has he been sowing seeds of rebellion."

That mordant appraisal drew from Llewelyn an involuntary smile. "Your arrow just hit the target dead-center," he said approvingly. "Edward has indeed played into my hands at every turn—appointing corrupt or inept officials, entrusting so much authority to Geoffrey Langley, a man foolish enough to think he could treat Welsh freemen like English serfs."

Despite his determination to remain aloof, Davydd felt his interest catching fire; something was in the wind. "I always thought Langley would eventually make one mistake too many. Has he?"

"He seeks to introduce English law into the Perfeddwlad. He would scorn the ancient laws of Wales, would govern our cantrefs as if they were part of Cheshire. He would make our people aliens in their own land, and they'll have none of it. There were some who hoped Edward would see his folly, but this August he paid his first visit into Wales, and nothing changed. Now . . . it will. The men of the Perfeddwlad have come to me, have asked my help in ridding them of these English intruders. I told them I would."

Davydd's eyes had begun to shine. "So it is to be war," he said, and Llewelyn nodded.

"I expect to be ready to cross the River Conwy by All Saints' Day. I'd like to have you at my side when I do, Davydd."

"And what do I have to do first?" Davydd demanded. "Grovel? Beg forgiveness? Swear a blood-oath of loyalty?"

"No."

"No? Just like that?" Davydd's unease flared into an emotion he was more comfortable with—anger. "Why?"

That was a reaction Llewelyn had expected, though; he was still young enough himself to remember that at eighteen, pride could burn higher than any fever. He waited, saying nothing, and Davydd finally blurted out, "So I am to be released, restored to favor. What else?"

"Is that not enough?" Llewelyn asked dryly, already knowing the answer he'd get.

Davydd raised his chin. "No," he said, greatly daring, and then his brother's smile told him that he had in truth risked nothing at all.

"The lordship of half of Llŷn, and the cantref of Dyffryn Clwyd."

Davydd sucked in his breath. "Christ, Llewelyn, if you'd only offered that a year ago . . ." He turned away, almost at once swung back to face Llewelyn. "I will be accountable to you, of course. But what of the revenues? They'll be mine?"

Llewelyn nodded. "You'll earn them," he said. "Lest you forget, Dyffryn Clwyd is still infested with the English. We'll have to evict them ere you take possession, lad."

Davydd grinned. "That," he said, "will be half the fun!" But even as he spoke, a shadow crossed his face. "What of Owain?"

"I cannot trust him, Davydd," Llewelyn said quietly. "You know I cannot."

"Can you trust me?"

"I suppose I'm about to find out, am I not?"

Something flickered in Davydd's eyes, too quick to catch. "You're taking a great risk," he said. "You do know that?"

"Yes," Llewelyn said, "I know. But a beautiful woman once told me that there's nothing worth having without risk, and who am I to dispute a lady?"

"I never thought women were ones for risk-taking."

"This one is—Nell de Montfort," Llewelyn said, and smiled at the boy's surprise.

"I met her at Stevington. She is the King's sister, no?"

"Yes, she is that. But first and foremost, she sees herself as Simon de Montfort's wife."

It was not working; banter could not dispel ghosts, could not exorcise Owain's presence, and they both knew it. Davydd's eyes narrowed, caught the light like a cat's. "And how do you see yourself, Llewelyn?" he said, with sudden bitterness. "As the Saviour of Wales?"

Llewelyn's gaze did not waver. "I think I'd prefer Holy Redeemer," he murmured. "It has more of a ring to it, would probably look better on charters."

A heartbeat's pause, and then they both were laughing. Llewelyn opened the door and, still laughing, they left the chamber, emerged into the mild October sunlight, within sight and sound of the sea.

FROM the pen of a thirteenth-century Welsh monk, in *The Chronicle of the Princes:*

Edward, son of King Henry, came to survey his castles and his lands in Gwynedd. And then the magnates of Wales, despoiled of their liberty and reduced to bondage, came to Llewelyn ap Gruffydd and mournfully made known to him that they preferred to be slain in battle for their liberty than to suffer themselves to be trampled in bondage by men alien to them. And Llewelyn was moved by their tears. And at their instigation and by their counsel, he made for Perfeddwlad and gained possession of it all within the week.

24

Westminster, England

April 1258

NATURE was occasionally bountiful, but never kind, and for two years now, the people of England and Wales had been suffering cruelly from its vagaries. Severe winters followed by late, cold springs had played havoc with the harvests, and famine soon stalked the unhappy land. When Richard, now King of the Romans, dispatched from Germany fifty ships heavily laden with grain to ease his countrymen's misery, Henry provoked a torrent of outrage by seizing the ships and offering the cargos for sale at inflated prices; so infuriated were the Londoners that Henry was forced to back down. It was in this climate of ill will and mutual mistrust that the Hoketide parliament was scheduled to meet, to consider Henry's urgent need for money and the no-less-urgent problem posed by the insurrection in Wales, where Llewelyn ap Gruffydd now reigned supreme.

EDWARD paused in the doorway of the great hall, looked back at his parents. He understood their somber demeanor, for the anniversary was approaching of their daughter Katherine's death, and they were discussing with Henry's chaplain their plans to mark Katherine's year-mind. Edward knew they still grieved for the little girl, grieved, too, for the son they'd lost that same year, a sickly infant who passed, too quickly, from cradle to coffin. But Edward was not yet nineteen, too little schooled in grief himself to comprehend the sorrow of a parent for a dead child; it seemed to him that they ought to have come to terms with their loss by now, and he watched them with the inarticulate, impatient sympathy of the very young.

"Edwardo?" Eleanora was looking at him with concern, and he found a smile for her. He'd not yet bedded her, for she was just thirteen, but she was sweet-tempered, easy to please, so obviously adoring that he was confident she'd prove herself a most satisfactory wife, and he'd done what he could to ease her homesickness for Castile. Taking her hand, he led her out into the April dusk.

"They've aged so in the past year," he said.

She knew whom he meant. "How old are they?"

"I'm not sure about my lady mother; she never would tell! She's still of child-bearing age, though, and my father . . . he'll be fifty-one come October."

"But that is very old, Edwardo," she pointed out, so earnestly that he had to smile.

"I know, lass, but it is more than age. It has not been a good year for them, or for England . . ."

She nodded. "The King was distraught by his failure in Wales—" She caught herself, but not in time. Wales was a sensitive subject, for it had been Edward's failure, too. That past August he and Henry had led an army into Gwynedd, but their campaign had ended in disaster. They'd gotten no farther than Deganwy Castle, had been forced to retreat in less than a month, leaving Llewelyn ap Gruffydd in uncontested control of Edward's Welsh lands. "I am sorry," she began shyly, but Edward shrugged, leaned down to kiss her cheek.

"You are leaving?"

"I'm supping tonight with Hal and the de Montforts." He beckoned to the captain of his guards, hovering within earshot, then raised Eleanora's hand to his lips in a more formal farewell. He noticed neither the disappointment in her eyes nor that she stood there for some moments, watching him cross the New Palace yard.

"No, Giles, not to the stables, to the wharf. We need my barge, no horses this night; we're for Southwark."

The other man paused in the act of signaling to the waiting guards, looked at Edward in surprise. "Southwark? I thought, my lord, that you said you were meeting your cousins?"

Edward grinned. "I am—at the Half-Moon."

The captain grinned, too, for the Half-Moon was one of the better known of the bankside brothels. "This is one night," he said, "when those men not on duty will be right envious of those who are!"

EDWARD could have predicted what he would find at the Half-Moon, for he knew his cousins well. There was no sign of Hal, who was late again. Bran was in the midst of a noisy, high-stakes dice game, while Harry had managed, as always, to snare the prettiest whore in the house, a surprisingly fresh-faced lass who'd yet to lose her country-girl bloom, and whose hair was not only the shade of newly churned butter, but even looked reasonably clean. Seated on Harry's lap, she was occupying most of his attention, and he did not notice Edward's approach, not until Edward leaned over, claimed his tankard of ale.

Unfazed by the theft, Harry looked up, gave his cousin a wide, welcoming grin. He was slightly drunk, but his good humor was not dependent upon ale; he had none of his father's intensity or fervor, none of his brother Bran's perverse unpredictability. Harry was by far the best-liked of the de Montfort sons, for he had a happy-go-lucky disposition, a cheerful outlook, and a generosity of spirit that enabled him to defer to Edward's compulsive need to command. Because he was also willing to accept any dare, willing to follow Edward into the seediest bankside tavern, to defy the City Watch and take part in midnight horse races, heedless of risk, he had long been Edward's favorite companion, and their friendship had not yet suffered from the increasing animosity of their fathers.

With Bran, it was not so simple; he and Edward had a much more erratic relationship. There was affection on both sides, and a mutual, grudging admiration, but their rivalry was constant, for tension was inevitable with both youths so unwilling to relinquish the reins. Bran acknowledged Edward's entrance now with a casual wave, but did not come over; he would not leave the game as long as he was winning.

Edward took a seat opposite Harry, signaling to one of the girls for more ale. Brothels were not allowed to serve food or drink, but Edward's ale was delivered with dispatch; he and his de Montfort cousins were known here, and treated with an uneasy mixture of awe and apprehension.

Within the quarter hour, Hal hastened in, flushed and out of breath. He had arrived only that morning from his father's manors in the West Country. With Richard in Germany, much of the responsibility for maintaining his vast English estates had fallen upon Hal, and he at once launched into a humorous account of his troubles with guileful bailiffs and unruly tenants. He showed no resentment, though, when Edward interrupted. Although he was twenty-two, he seemed much younger—given to sudden enthusiasms, readily influenced, Edward's eager echo.

"We've more important matters to discuss, Hal. Harry, get rid of the wench."

"Go to the Devil," Harry said amiably, slipping his hand into the girl's bodice. But when Edward persisted, he gave an exaggerated sigh. "What is your name, sweetheart?" When she murmured "Maud," all three of them looked at her with new interest, for harlots invariably chose for themselves fanciful names like Clarice and Petronilla. Maud was real, spoke of an innocence but recently lost. Harry pressed a coin into her palm, coaxed a promise to wait, and as she slid off his knee, he shot Edward a look of warning. "You'll have much to answer for, Ned, if I lose that one!"

"She'll keep," Edward said. It was probably true; he could not deny that Harry had a way with women, even with whores, who were usually as sentimental as horse-traders. "Hal needs to know what has been happening whilst he's been gone."

"That's easy," Harry said. "Parliament met, Uncle Henry sought money to pay off the Pope, the lords balked, and all Hell broke loose."

Edward ignored Harry, kept his eyes upon Hal. "Right from the opening session, there was trouble. John Fitz Geoffrey leveled charges against our de Lusignan uncle Aymer, claiming that Aymer's servants attacked his manor at Shere, killing one of his men. He demanded justice of my father the King, and when my father was loath to bring charges against Aymer, most of the barons took Fitz Geoffrey's side. But it was our Welsh woes that stirred up the most commotion."

"Is it true what I heard in the West Country, that Llewelyn ap Gruffydd has made a pact with the lords of Scotland?"

Edward nodded grimly; his memories of their abortive summer campaign still rankled. "Llewelyn is drunk on delusions, which the Welsh fancy even more than mead. There are rumors that he now dares to call himself Prince of Wales."

"What you call delusions, Ned, Llewelyn doubtless calls victories." None had heard Bran's approach, not until his voice cut through the smoky air above their heads. "He did drive Gruffydd ap Gwenwynwyn out of Powys, did overrun the Perfeddwlad, and did send your army reeling back across the border . . . did he not?"

This was the sort of razor-edged banter in which they all engaged, but Bran's mockery had a sharper bite than usual, cut a little too close to the bone; he, too, had been drinking. Edward regarded him with unfriendly eyes, then turned back to Hal.

"William de Lusignan was sorely affronted by Llewelyn's triumphs, and—"

"Of course," Hal interrupted, nodding knowingly. "He has the most to lose, after all, what with his wife being heiress to the Pembroke estates in South Wales." He had an unfortunate penchant for belaboring the obvious; all knew William de Lusignan was Earl of Pembroke by right of his wife—that being the most controversial of the lucrative marriages Harry had made on behalf of his de Lusignan kindred, and Hal earned himself an impatient look from Edward.

But the name of William de Lusignan had acted upon the de Montforts as a goad. Harry no longer slouched bonelessly in his seat, and Bran made a sweeping gesture, came close to knocking the candle from the table into Hal's lap.

"That whoreson de Lusignan claimed that the other lords lacked the will to fight the Welsh," he said tautly. "He accused my father and the Earl of Gloucester of having a secret understanding with Llewelyn, and then . . . then he even dared to call my father a traitor!"

Hal whistled through his teeth; he could not imagine any man having the courage to challenge his uncle Simon like that, not to his face. "He said that and still lives?" he asked, amazed, and Harry nodded.

"Regretfully, yes. Papa would have killed him then and there had the King not thrust himself between them!"

"What I'd not have given to see that!" Hal's eyes sparkled. Harry and Bran did not share his amusement; they passed some moments indignantly denouncing William de Lusignan. Hal was tempted to tease, to remind them that William de Lusignan was their uncle, too, but decided against it; Simon's sons were unlikely to find any humor in that particular blood-bond.

The young harlot was back, whispering something in Harry's ear that brought him swiftly to his feet. "It's now or never," he said dramatically, and swaying slightly, headed for the stairs, his arm around the girl's waist. A moment later, Bran rose, too, and as Edward and Hal followed his gaze, they saw why. Hal pointed. "That lad, there, is that not your brother Guy?"

Bran grinned. "Harry and I thought it was time he ploughed his first furrow. He is fifteen, after all. But I think he's had his fill of ale. If he gets too greensick, this visit may not only put him off ale, it could put him off whores, too!"

They joined in his laughter, watched as he made his way across the crowded common chamber toward Guy. And then Edward leaned across the table. "I've more to tell you, but I had to wait till we were alone. There is a meeting being held this very night, one that bodes ill for my father. I do not know all their names yet, but our uncle Simon and the Earls of Gloucester and Norfolk are the leaders."

Hal was impressed. "How did you find out about this meeting, Ned?"

Edward shrugged. "How do you think? I have eyes and ears where I need them; money loosens most tongues. I do not know what their intent is, but I like it not. They are men whose voices would be heeded, and they have long been disgruntled with my father's government."

"Ned . . . do not take this amiss, but we all know there is a need for reforms of some sort. Even you have said as much. So why oppose them now, why not—"

"Why not? Would you let these men dictate terms to my father, to the King? A king is responsible for his subjects, not to them. It is true that a king ought to be ruled by the laws he makes, but no man can force him to obey the law. A king's transgressions must be left to the judgment of God. For certes, he is not accountable to self-seeking knaves like Gloucester!"

"But what of Uncle Simon? Do you not believe he is sincere?"

Edward hesitated; his feelings for Simon were clouded with ambiguities and ambivalence. "Yes," he said, "I do believe Simon is sincere. And that, Hal, might well make him the most dangerous of the lot." But he saw that his cousin did not comprehend. Reaching across the table, he caught Hal's hand. "Swear to me," he said. "Swear that whatever happens, you'll stand by me."

"Jesú, Ned, of course I will!"

"No," Edward said, with such intensity that Hal's smile faded. "Not like that. Swear to me not as your kinsman, but as your King-to-be."

His fingers were digging into Hal's wrist; they were perilously close to the candle flame. Hal felt a thrill of edgy excitement, a sense that they were on the verge of momentous happenings. He nodded, said with self-conscious gravity, "I do so swear." Neither youth noticed that they were being watched. Across the chamber, Bran drank and bantered with his companions, but kept his eyes upon his cousins all the while.

IT was Simon's turn to take the oath. He came forward, picked up the crucifix, and for a moment his eyes flicked from face to face—solemn, shadowed by torch-light. Richard de Clare, Earl of Gloucester, no friend of his. Roger Bigod, Earl of Norfolk, England's Marshal. His younger brother, Hugh. Their brother-in-law, John Fitz Geoffrey, so recently wronged by the de Lusignans. Peter of Savoy, Earl of Richmond, for they'd found a surprising ally in the Queen's uncle. And, as always, Peter de Montfort. Simon closed his fingers around the crucifix, held it up to the light.

"I do swear," he said, "as you have done, to help one another and those belonging to us, against all people, doing right and taking nothing that we cannot take without doing wrong, saving faith to our lord the King of England and to the Crown."

ON the last day of April, they came in full armor to Westminster. Although they put aside their swords before entering Henry's presence, he was so alarmed that he blurted out, "What is this? Am I your prisoner?" The Earl of Norfolk hastened to assure him that was not so, but then set forth their demands, that Henry and his heir, the Lord Edward, swear upon the Holy Gospels that they would accept the counsel and advice of "twenty-four good men of England." Not for the first time, Henry shrank from confrontation, reluctantly swore that he would accept their reforms—much to Edward's dismay—and it was agreed that parliament would reconvene on June 11 in the Dominican friary at Oxford.

BOTH sides came armed to Oxford, under the pretext of preparing for war with Wales. More than a hundred barons gathered for the opening session of parliament, more than twice the usual number. After selecting the committee of twenty-four, twelve chosen by the barons and twelve by the King, they began to air their grievances. Henry was accused of violating the Runnymede Charter, of not keeping his promises, of favoring aliens over his own subjects, of allowing corrupt sheriffs to sell justice and plunder their shires, of refusing to consult with his lords, even of forbidding Chancery to issue any writ that was adverse to his half-brothers' interests. Sicily. The de Lusignans. The complaints were vociferous, irate, and—to Henry—brazenly presumptuous.

But Henry could do naught but listen, and inwardly seethe, as his barons appointed Hugh Bigod as Justiciar, as they declared that henceforth parliaments would meet three times a year, as they declared that sheriffs were to be chosen by the local gentry of each shire and serve for only one year. It was, for Henry, a profoundly humiliating experience.

It was no less of an ordeal for his de Lusignan half-brothers. William de Lusignan, in particular, was in a continual state of embittered, impotent fury, and as he dismounted in the friary garth, it took only a glimpse of the one white-robed monk amidst the black-clad Dominicans to put him into a murderous rage.

"There's that Welsh bastard now," he said, loudly enough to turn heads. The Abbot of Aberconwy turned, too, but Anian then offered the ultimate insult, letting his eyes pass over William with utter indifference as he paced sedately toward the Chapter House. William swore again, far more profanely this time. Of all that he'd so far endured in these ten days at Oxford, it was the truce with Llewelyn ap Gruffydd that he found most intolerable.

"You tell me, Geoffrey, that those misbegotten whoresons were not in league with Llewelyn from the beginning! That puking priest's safe-conduct was dated June second, nine full days ere parliament began, and who just happened to escort him to Oxford? Leicester's lap-dog—Peter de Montfort!"

Geoffrey shrugged. Unlike William, he had no lands in Wales, and in consequence, he did not share William's obsession with Llewelyn ap Gruffydd's ambitions. "A murrain on Wales, on all the Welsh," he said impatiently. "What of our interests in England? What ails Henry? Why did he ever agree to this accursed parliament? When I confronted him, he claimed there was no other way to get the money he needs. He rambled on about the Pope's threat to excommunicate him, insisted he had to accept these reforms to get any aid from his barons. Why does he not just demand that they obey him? Sometimes I wonder how the man walks erect, lacking all backbone as he does!"

"Henry has a backbone. It just happens to be made of wax." William's riposte drew a chuckle from his brother, but he was frowning, for he'd just noticed the man approaching.

John de Warenne, Earl of Surrey, was both their cousin and their brother-in-law, for eleven years ago he'd wed their sister Alice, and the relationship had survived her death. Ordinarily, the sight of de Warenne would have been a welcome one, for he was one of the few allies they had at court. While Edward and Hal had been taking their side at Oxford, their motives were political, not personal. But de Warenne was a friend, and they needed just one look at his face to know the news he brought was bad.

"You'd best get to the Chapter House," he said, "and right quick! They have sprung upon us an act of resumption, which would compel all those of foreign birth to relinquish any castles and manors given to them by the King!"

William paled, for an act of resumption would take from him not only Hertford Castle, but the royal demesne manors of Essendon, Bayford, and Bampton. With Geoffrey hard on his heels, he started for the Chapter House at a dead run.

There they found the chamber in turmoil. Men were yelling, swearing. Their brothers Aymer and Guy were offering dismayed, blustering defiance. So was Edward, who saw this action as an intolerable constraint upon the powers of kingship. No one thought to appeal to Henry; he sat, forgotten, as the debate raged on about him.

William strode to the center of the room, by sheer perseverance managed to shout down the others. "Is it true that you would deny to men of alien birth the right to hold English castles?" He got a resounding roar of assent; fully a dozen voices cried out it was so. He whirled then toward the man he most blamed for their plight, pointing an accusing finger at Simon de Montfort.

"What of Leicester? He's no more English than I am, yet he holds the most formidable castles in all of England! Suppose you explain, my lord, why this act does not apply to you. Tell us how you can justify keeping Kenilworth and Odiham!"

Simon rose without haste. "I have sworn an oath," he said, "to uphold the Provisions we have agreed upon here at Oxford. I will, therefore, yield Odiham and Kenilworth to the King. I would—" He got no further; the chamber erupted into cheers and laughter, for all—Simon's enemies as well as his friends—took malicious pleasure in the de Lusignans' discomfiture.

William de Lusignan was, for the first time in his life, literally speechless. It was Aymer who came to his assistance, saying scathingly, "My lord of Leicester may, indeed, surrender his castles. For all I care, he may even take a holy oath of poverty, beg his bread by the roadside! But do not expect us to follow in his footsteps. Our manors and lands were given to us by our brother the King, and he and he alone has the right to ask for their return."

Henry looked acutely unhappy; his answer was almost inaudible to many in the chamber. "I have agreed to be guided by the advice of my lord barons," he mumbled, refusing to meet the eyes of either his outraged brothers or his incredulous son. He'd tried to explain his predicament to them. Did they not realize that he faced excommunication if he failed to pay the Pope? Could they not—just this once—put themselves in his place? How sick he was of conflict, bone-weary of this constant wrangling, this endless strife. But that was not something he could ever confess, for he knew they'd never understand—Edward least of all.

The Earl of Gloucester, no less furious now than the de Lusignans, was glaring first at Aymer, then at William, as if unsure which one more deserved his loathing. "I daresay you never expected a day of reckoning. But it is here and it is now. Fifteen of the King's castles are in the hands of foreigners, and we say—enough!"

William had recovered his aplomb. "Say what you will, but we'll never agree to relinquish our castles, our lands—never! And that, my lord, I do swear to you on the very wounds of Christ!"

Men muttered angrily, but the de Lusignans held firm, and Simon at last lost all patience. "The choice is yours, my lords," he interrupted. "Either your castles or your heads."

And that brought silence to the chamber, for none who heard Simon could doubt he meant exactly what he said.

EDWARD was tense, defensive. "I suppose," he said, "that you think ill of me now, that I've earned your scorn for refusing to abide by the Provisions."

To his surprise, and somewhat to his relief, Simon shook his head. "No," he said, "a man should not offer his word lightly. If you have doubts, better you resolve them first, for an oath, once given, is inviolate."

Edward's eyes flickered. "Are you so sure, Uncle, that I'll come around to your way of thinking?"

"Yes," Simon said, and softened the arrogance of that answer with a smile. And then he was on his feet, turning toward the door, for he'd heard the sound of boots on the stairs, coming too fast for a commonplace errand.

Harry burst into the room, out of breath, but flushed with excitement. "Papa . . . they've fled! The de Lusignans and de Warenne, they're gone!"

WOLVESEY Castle, official residence of the Bishops of Winchester, had withstood a savage assault in the twelfth century, but the luxury-loving Aymer had preferred a palace to a fortress, and when the barons followed the fugitive de Lusignans to Winchester, Aymer and his brothers discovered that they had neither the supplies nor the will to endure a prolonged siege. To resist would be to give the barons what they most wanted, an excuse to reduce the castle to rubble, to treat its defenders as rebels. Their sense of self-preservation prevailed over pride, and Aymer reluctantly gave the order to surrender.

They met in the great hall, and when Aymer, acting as spokesman for his brothers, announced that they had reconsidered, would now be willing to honor the Oxford Provisions, he garnered only a burst of derisive laughter.

That was most magnanimous, the Earl of Norfolk allowed, but too late. They'd had their chance at Oxford. Now . . . now they were no longer welcome in England, were to be banished from Henry's domains, never to return.

Henry's brothers were stunned, but when they appealed to Henry, they had their answer in his averted eyes, in his wretched, shamed silence.

THE weather continued its perverse disregard for seasons, and famine and plague hovered dangerously close at hand. July saw the departure of the de Lusignans for France, after a disastrous farewell banquet at Aymer's Winchester manor. A number of the highborn guests were afterward stricken, and several died, including the Abbot of Westminster and the Earl of Gloucester's brother. Gloucester himself fell ill, and for a time there were fears for his survival. Inevitably, suspicions of poison followed. Although proof was lacking, most men were only too willing to believe the worst of the de Lusignans. Their banishment was welcomed with widespread and heartfelt joy. Henry alone mourned.

The day had begun with a hint of hazy sun, and Henry had morosely agreed to John Mansel's suggestion. Mayhap Mansel was right; mayhap a leisurely excursion on the Thames would raise his spirits. But no sooner were they heading downriver than the wind began to rise. The sky darkened so suddenly it was as if night had fallen. As a youngster, Henry had once been trapped out in a thunderstorm of awesome violence; it had so scarred his memory that, even now, a sky streaking with lightning would evoke uneasy echoes of that child's fear. He ordered his boatmen to make for shore, but the tide was against them, and by the time they tied up at the Bishop of Durham's dock, Henry was soaked to the skin and shivering uncontrollably.

The Bishop came out to welcome his unexpected guest, and after one look at Henry's pallor, made haste to escort him into the hall, shouting for servants to light a fire for the King's Grace. Henry followed gratefully, only to come to an abrupt halt in the doorway. In his anxiety to escape the storm, he'd completely forgotten that Simon de Montfort always stayed at Durham House while in London.

Simon had been sharing a flagon of wine with the Franciscan Adam

Marsh and the Bishop of Worcester. Simon's affinity for clerics had long been a source of embittered wonderment to Henry; it invariably put him in mind of the old adage, the one about the Devil quoting Scriptures. With the possible exception of Peter de Montfort, Marsh and Worcester were the men who stood closest to Simon, companions, confidants. Henry hated them for that. They greeted him with concern, and he hated them for that, too.

Simon was holding out a wine cup. When Henry didn't move, he said, "Take it, my liege, and make yourself easy, for the storm is passing."

Henry yearned to knock the cup from Simon's hand. "I am indeed fearful of lightning, I'll not deny it. But far more than any storm, I do fear your ambitions, de Montfort!"

He heard an intake of breath, Adam Marsh's involuntary, shaken protest. But he could read nothing in Simon's face. Simon turned, set the cup down upon the table. "Your greatest failing, my liege," he said curtly, "is that you've never learned to tell your friends from your enemies."

"Do you dare to call yourself my friend?" Henry demanded, incredulous, and Simon slowly shook his head.

"No," he said. "But I need not be your enemy."

"You are my enemy—admit it! You've done all you could to poison men's minds against me, against my brothers. You harried them mercilessly, and even after you brought about their utter ruin, that was not enough for you. No, you had to send your son after them, had to—"

"My son?" Simon was frowning. "What in God's Name are you talking about?"

"As if you did not know! Your Harry followed my brothers to Boulogne, so stirred up the people against them that they had to take refuge in a local priory, to appeal to the French King for aid!"

"Harry did that?" Simon's astonishment was so obviously unfeigned that Henry decided that, in this at least, he may have wronged Simon. But then Simon laughed, and Henry choked anew on his hatred.

"I know what you seek—to make of me a crippled King. I know all about your plotting. I know that you tried to get the London aldermen to take an oath to your precious Oxford Provisions, and when they balked, you and Norfolk summoned the citizens to the Guildhall, where you got them so wrought up that they acclaimed the Provisions as if they were Holy Writ." Simon's continuing popularity with Londoners both baffled and infuriated Henry, and it was with real venom that he added, "Go ahead, pander to the rabble if you have so little pride! It will avail you naught!"

"Simon." Adam Marsh's voice was deceptively calm; his eyes gave away his anxiety. But for once Simon seemed to have his temper in check. He glanced at his friend, then back at his King.

"I took an oath to keep faith with the Provisions. Need I remind you that you, too, swore such an oath?"

"No," Henry snapped. "I remember."

"For all our sakes," Simon said softly, bleakly, "I hope you do."

25

Paris, France

June 1259

Neither the English nor the French yearned for a lasting peace, but their sovereigns did, Henry because he had more than enough enemies at home and Louis because he believed that Christian kings were natural allies. Although it took Henry and his brother-in-law, the French King, fully five years, it was at last agreed that Henry would renounce his claims to Normandy, Anjou, Touraine, Maine, and Poitou, and, as Duke of Aquitaine, do homage to Louis for Gascony, all that remained of the once-vast Angevin empire. Louis, in turn, promised to pay Henry the sum necessary to maintain five hundred knights for a two-year period, the knights to be employed only in the service of God, the Church—or the welfare of England.

The impending peace was not popular with the English, even less so with the French, but it was not public disapproval that threatened to sabotage the treaty—it was the will of one woman. Henry's sons, Edward and Edmund, were required, too, to renounce their claims to the lost Angevin domains, and so were King John's other surviving children, Richard, King of the Romans, and Nell, Countess of Leicester. Much to Henry's chagrin, Nell balked, refusing to make any renunciation until Henry paid her the considerable sums due her as widow of the Earl of Pembroke. Despite the unrelenting pressure brought to bear upon her, Nell remained adamant—no renunciation without repayment—and if her resolve caused any embarrassment for Simon, who'd been one of the chief English negotiators, none but he knew it. Henry fumed in vain, Simon supported his wife, and Louis seemed likely to need every particle of the patience for which he was so celebrated.

FROM the dais, the French Queen had an unobstructed view of the entire hall, and she had no difficulty in locating Simon and Nell de Montfort. They were, as always, encircled by friends and admirers, although this evening they were sharing center stage with their nephew, the Lord Edward. Marguerite lowered her voice, glancing toward her husband. "Well? Had you any luck this afternoon? Were you able to make Nell see reason?"

Louis shook his head. "Those who dismiss women as the weaker sex," he said mildly, "have never met the Countess of Leicester."

Marguerite frowned. "Has she no thought for her brother? She is making poor Henry look a right proper fool. I even heard people jesting about it this forenoon, saying that if Henry lacks the wherewithal to be a man, his sister for certes does not!"

"I would that she'd not chosen to hold the treaty hostage, and cannot sanction her methods. But in truth, my dear, her grievances against Henry do have some merit. She was but fifteen when she was widowed, and it was Henry who negotiated on her behalf with her husband's brother. Their Runnymede Charter provides that an English widow is entitled to fully one-third of her late husband's lands. But Henry accepted six hundred marks a year for Nell, when by rights she ought to have gotten two thousand. He then permitted the Marshals to delay payments, to fall far into arrears. And once the Pembroke earldom passed to his de Lusignan half-brother, he even took it upon himself to waive some payments altogether. No, for all the affection I bear Henry, I must confess that some of his actions passeth all understanding."

"I'll grant you that Henry has been remiss. Even so, where does Nell get the gall to defy two Kings and the Church? Do not ever tell my sister this, for Eleanor would never forgive me. But at times I find myself admiring Nell's sheer pluck!"

Louis smiled. "Yes," he said, "I like her, too."

"Not too much, I trust," Marguerite murmured archly, for Nell was, even at forty-three, still a very handsome woman. "Since we are making confessions, I might as well admit that I enjoy Simon's company, too. To hear Henry talk, the man is verily the Prince of Darkness, but in truth, I—" She paused, alerted by her husband's frown. "Louis?"

"The Earl of Gloucester just entered the hall," he said, and she gave a comprehending nod.

"You fear trouble with Edward? Why are they so at odds?"

"Conflicting claims to Bristol Castle, I believe. Moreover, they like each other not. But Simon, too, bears Gloucester a grudge."

Louis signaled for wine, waited until his cup-bearer withdrew from earshot. "Gloucester and Simon were allies by expediency, not choice, and they were not long in falling out. I've been told they quarreled bitterly during the February parliament over their Oxford Provisions. Gloucester wanted the reforms to apply only to the King, whilst Simon insisted that they should apply as well to the barons themselves. Gloucester is a great landholder, and he was not eager to have the reforms extended to his own tenants. It probably could have been settled amicably, but Simon lost his temper, as usual, and he and Gloucester had a blazing row. The Earls of Norfolk and Hereford prevailed upon Gloucester to make peace with Simon. But it was a false peace, in truth, and in this past month they've spent as much time wrangling with each other as they have negotiating the treaty."

Marguerite found the prospect of a public quarrel exciting, but for decorum's sake, she sought to sound disapproving as she said, "Do you truly think they'd argue here and now, before all the court?"

Even as she spoke, voices were rising, heads turning. "Yes, my dear," Louis said dryly, "I do," and came hastily to his feet. Marguerite rose, too, eager to see. "How ill-bred the English are," she marveled, remembering, too late, that Simon was French.

Simon was regarding the Earl of Gloucester with undisguised contempt. "You are mistaken, my lord," he said, managing to imply that Gloucester's "mistake" could only be the result of moral obtuseness or evil intent. "The Oxford Provisions are neither extreme nor radical. We seek only to counsel the King, to restore harmony to the realm, and to see that no man be denied justice. Any problems that have since arisen may be traced to the unwillingness of some to put aside their self-seeking and think of the common good."

"Self-seeking?" Gloucester sputtered. "By God, you've a droll wit, de Montfort! That you, of all men, would dare to accuse another of self-seeking! What of the treaty?" Swinging about, he pointed an accusing finger at Nell. "For months we have labored to reach an accommodation with the French, only to have this woman—your woman—set our efforts at naught! Were she my wife, you may be sure she'd do as she was bidden, and right quickly. But you, my lord of Leicester? Not only do you indulge her willfulness, you argue in her behalf! Which means either that you cannot control your own wife, or that she acts in this as your puppet, and neither explanation does you credit! If she does not—"

"My lord." Simon's voice was suddenly soft, and those who knew him best tensed. "Think carefully ere you complete that sentence. Do you mean to threaten my wife? Because if you do, my lord of Gloucester, I trust you are willing to accept the consequences."

Gloucester hesitated; although he was not intimidated, Simon's reputation did warrant a certain degree of caution. "Of course I am not threatening the Countess of Leicester," he said impatiently. "I was but—"

"—being offensive," Edward interrupted, more than willing to put his oar into these turbulent waters. "I think you owe His Grace of Leicester an apology. You do, for certes, owe one to my aunt!"

"What I owe you," Gloucester began heatedly, but at that moment, Louis reached them.

"My lords," he said, "this is not seemly." And it took no more than that, for Louis had long ago mastered that art which still eluded Henry, the ability to command respect, both as a man and monarch. Moreover, Gloucester and Simon now became aware of their amused audience, for the French court was highly entertained by this diverting display of English bad manners. Summoning up what grace they could, both offered apologies to Louis. Neither one apologized to the other, but Louis was too much of a realist to expect that. Instead, he engaged Gloucester in conversation, deftly piloting him away from Simon and Edward.

Simon said nothing; he was too angry, did not yet trust himself to speak. Edward claimed the nearest man's wine cup, drank deeply. It was left to Bran to articulate their shared outrage. "That man," he said bitterly, "has a poisoned tongue. It would give me great pleasure to cut it out by the roots."

"You always were a greedy sort, Bran." Harry was fumbling for a coin. Flipping it up into the air, he said, "Call it." The jest was a grim one, but it worked; some of the tension was dispersed by laughter.

"Simon?" Nell was so flushed that Simon took her arm, drew her aside. "Simon," she said softly, "I am so sorry. The last thing I wanted was to give your enemies a weapon to use against you."

He shrugged. "Whilst I was in the Holy Land, I learned a Saracen proverb: The dogs bark, but the caravan passes on. That may be infidel wisdom, but it is wisdom all the same."

"Yes, but . . ." She bit her lip, and Edward, close enough to overhear this brief exchange, stepped toward her. He was very fond of Nell, for unlike his father, he did not blame her for her loyalty to Simon. Since both Church law and common law bound a woman to obey her husband, Edward did not see how Nell could do otherwise than support Simon, and whilst he would not have tolerated Nell's volatile spirits in his own Spanish bride, he found it easy enough to indulge a favorite aunt. But he could not resist teasing, even as he put an affectionate hand on Nell's arm.

"Does this mean, Aunt Nell," he murmured, "that you no longer care about your dower payments, that you'll make the renunciation?"

"No!" The answer was so unpremeditated, so lightning-fast that both Simon and Edward laughed.

Looking about for a secluded corner, Simon's eyes lit upon a heavy, carved screen. "Come with me," he said, and steered Nell toward the privacy of that oaken partition. "Now . . . tell me. Do you not believe your grievance against Henry is a just one?"

"You know it is, Simon! Henry has cheated me not only of my dower, but of my share of our mother's inheritance. To please her, he agreed to relinquish any claims to her lands in Angoulême, which was his right—but then he dared to renounce my claims, too! And what of the vast sums he's borrowed from us over the years, money never repaid, and—" She stopped, for Simon had put his finger to her lips. After a moment, she managed a smile. "The answer to your question," she said, "is yes."

He nodded. "Then what more need be said? We both know Henry's sworn oath is worthless. A Christian would keep a vow made upon the True Cross; even a Jew would hold to an oath sworn upon his own holy book. Henry would be false in either faith, and I'd sooner grapple with an eel than try to keep him to his word. But this treaty is a forked stick, enabling us to pin him to the ground. In truth, Nell, we'd be fools not to make use of it."

"I know. But Simon, I do not want to see you hurt on my behalf!"

"Would you have me fear Gloucester? That stoutheart might have been sired by a weather vane, so faithfully does he follow the prevailing winds!" Simon reached out, put his hands on Nell's shoulders. "Believe me, Nell, when I say I am not loath to uphold your rights. Whatever you can gain for our children gladdens me. Moreover, I do owe you this. For all of our marriage, you have stood by me, and that loyalty cost you a brother's love, a King's favor. So it gives me pleasure, my heart, to do this now for you."

"Ah, Simon . . ." His endearments were rare, all the more cherished in consequence. "There are times," she said, "when I could right cheerfully push you down a flight of stairs. But there are other times, like now . . ."

He grinned. "Hold that thought," he said, "until tonight," and taking her hand, he led her back into the hall.

They were joined at once by Edward and their sons, which did not pass unnoticed. Marguerite frowned, touched her husband's arm. "It seems to me," she said, "that Edward is too much in Simon's company these days. Henry would not approve."

"No, he would not. It is not surprising, though, that Edward and Simon should seek each other out. Simon could have no more valuable ally than the King's son. And Edward, for all his youth, has a fine grasp of military tactics. Divide and conquer, no? If he could somehow win Simon away from the other disaffected barons, he'd be doing Henry a great service."

"Do you think Edward might succeed?"

"Should God so will it. But I think it unlikely, my dear. In all the years that I've known Simon de Montfort, only two men were able to influence his thinking, the sainted Bishop of Lincoln and the Franciscan Adam Marsh, and both are dead."

"Well, then, is there any chance that Simon might sway Edward? He is only twenty, after all."

"My first inclination would be to say no; we both know how headstrong Edward is, and how willful. But Simon ought never to be misprized, not a man who could win himself an earldom with his tongue! Nor has he changed much over the years; he still burns with all the zeal and ardent conviction of his youth. It is a contagious infection, Simon's passion, and a dangerous one, for he can imbue the most ordinary task with all the color and allure of a holy quest. As to whether Edward will be immune, only time can tell."

"I pray to God he is," Marguerite said, "lest he break Henry's heart."

Louis nodded somberly. "Whatever happens," he said, "I very much fear that naught but strife and discord lie ahead for the English."

Even after twenty-five years of marriage, Marguerite could find herself surprised by her husband's lack of rancor. "Given the bad blood between our two countries, most French kings would welcome English dissension. Is there no man, Louis, whom you count your enemy?"

He considered the question gravely, as if it had been seriously posed; humor was no less a foreign tongue to him than English. "The Jew, the heretic, the infidel, all who deny the Lord Christ," he said, "they are my enemies."

"But not the King of England."

"No, not Henry." And then he smiled. "And not Simon de Montfort, either."

AT the insistence of the French King, fifteen thousand of the marks to be paid to Henry were set aside, to be held while Nell's claims were submitted to arbitration. Nell then agreed to make the necessary renunciation, and the treaty was finally ratified in Paris on December 4, in the presence of both monarchs.

THE Oxford Provisions stipulated that there were to be three parliaments a year, and in late January 1260, Simon and Nell sailed from Normandy. But Simon's haste was for naught. The Candlemas parliament could not meet, for Henry was still in France. There were urgent matters to discuss—Llewelyn of Wales was besieging Edward's castle at Buellt, and there were reforms still to be implemented—but nothing could be done in the King's absence. As long as Henry remained in France, he effectively paralyzed the opposition.

"I would be heard," Simon said, striding toward the center of the chamber. "I have listened as you berated the King, accused him of bad faith, and bewailed our plight. But we are not as powerless as some of you seem to think. There is an obvious solution, so simple I marvel that none of you have thought of it. We no longer wait for the King; we hold the parliament now."

There was a shocked silence; more than one lord looked at Simon as if he'd suddenly lost his senses. Hugh Bigod, the Justiciar, was shaking his head in disblief. "You cannot be serious!"

"Indeed, I am. What could be more logical? Are we to permit the King to cripple all our reforms merely by fleeing to the French court? If so, my lords, the Oxford Provisions will be meaningless, will—"

"But to summon parliament in the King's absence?" Bigod was not the only one to seem stunned; even some of Simon's supporters looked uneasy. "My lord of Leicester, think what you are suggesting. The King would no longer be the ship's captain, would be no more than a figurehead, carved upon the ship's prow!"

"Nonsense," Simon said impatiently. "To put it in your terms, we are only asking for a say in plotting the ship's course. If we have no right to meet except at the King's pleasure, we are utterly at his mercy. Is that what you want, my lords?"

Glancing about the chamber, Simon saw that the younger lords were beginning to nod agreement. The Earl of Surrey had made a complete turnabout since the expulsion of his de Lusignan brothers-in-law, was now one of Simon's more fervent disciples, and he and the young Earl of Derby were caught up in the sudden excitement, echoing Simon's arguments to their neighbors. But Simon knew they were too youthful, too callow, to influence the others. "What say you, my lord Bishop?" he asked.

Walter de Cantilupe, Bishop of Worcester, was a friend, but a man of such integrity that his opinion would not be suspect. Getting slowly to his feet, he said, "My lord of Leicester is proposing a radical reform, one not to be undertaken lightly. And yet . . . and yet, how else can we redeem the Provisions?"

Looking about him, Hugh Bigod saw, to his dismay, that Simon might well prevail. Most of the men present lacked Simon's imagination, his audacity, but they did share his frustration, and as Simon now explained it, his proposal began to seem more and more reasonable. Men repeated the Bishop's query: what else, indeed, could they do?

"I do not know what alchemy you work here," Bigod said softly to Simon. "But I'll not let you infect us with your madness." Raising his voice, he said, "The Lord Edward sent me word that he would be attending this session. He ought to be here within the hour. Which of you wants to tell the King's son that you mean to hold parliament in his lord father's absence, against his lord father's express wishes?"

Edward's fiery temper was already becoming a byword, and Bigod saw disquiet flicker from face to face. As he'd hoped, Simon's spell began to waver before the reality of Edward's outrage, and Bigod turned triumphantly to face Simon, sure that he'd won—until he saw Simon's smile.

"I think you will be most interested in what the Lord Edward has to say," Simon said, raising his hand for silence. "You see, he and I are in agreement. He, too, thinks that parliament ought to meet."

THOROUGHLY alarmed by the reports coming across the Channel, Henry took the French King's advice and hastily returned to England. Accompanied by armed mercenaries, he arrived in London on Friday, April 23.

William Fitz Richard, the city's Mayor, and both city sheriffs were summoned to the Bishop of London's manor, where they were confronted by a very angry, very distraught King, who ordered them to bar the city gates to the Earl of Leicester and the Lord Edward, his son and heir.

Henry's brother was a silent, disapproving witness to this harangue. Richard was accustomed to Henry's histrionics, but even he had been shocked by this latest tangent of his brother's, and as soon as they were alone, he said incredulously, "Henry, you cannot mean this! How could you possibly believe that Edward has been plotting to depose you?"

"You think I want to believe that? Blood of Christ, Richard, we're talking of Edward, my flesh-and-blood, my firstborn! But what else can I think? Has he not allied himself with that treacherous, swaggering hellspawn? He does de Montfort's bidding, Richard—my own son! He backed de Montfort's treason, agreed to have parliament meet in my absence, and when de Montfort and his lackeys dared to dismiss my wife's uncle, Peter of Savoy, from the royal council—my own council— Edward even agreed to that, too! He is evil, Richard, evil, and damned to everlasting Hell for his double-dealing, that I swear to you upon the very bones of St Edmund!"

"Who?" Richard said coldly, "Edward or de Montfort?" and Henry gave him a startled, reproachful look.

"De Montfort, of course. Jesú, Richard, what ails you?"

"Henry, do you ever listen to yourself—truly listen? The man is infuriating, arrogant, and Lucifer-proud, but the Antichrist he is not, Brother. And in all honesty, you've done your share to poison that well, too."

"That's a damnable lie! I've been more than fair to that whoreson."

"By selecting Gloucester as one of the men to arbitrate Nell's dower claims? I'd say you have a right quaint concept of fairness." Richard shook his head wearily. "So far you've called de Montfort a whoreson, a traitor, a liar, a hellspawn. Have you forgotten that he is also our sister's husband?"

"And have you forgotten that he brought hired mercenaries with him from France? Or that he holds Kenilworth and Odiham, two of the most formidable castles in England—castles he swore to surrender to the Crown! The man is a menace, Richard, a danger to us all; how can you not see that?"

"He did yield the castles," Richard pointed out. "The barons then returned them to his custody." But his heart was not in his defense; he was furious with Simon, too. "Henry, this serves for naught; we can argue about de Montfort from now till Judgment Day. But what of Edward? How can you doubt his loyalty? Do you not realize how much Gloucester hates him? Since Gloucester's return to England, he and Edward have quarreled each time they've met, twice almost coming to blows! Whatever he has told you is suspect, Henry, is—"

"There was a time when you were right fond of Gloucester!"

"Do you truly think I need you to remind me that the man is my stepson? Yes, I was once wed to his mother, and yes, I was fond of him. He was a likable lad—then. But now I'd sooner trust a Gascon, and I'd believe a converted Jew ere I would Gloucester. Lest you forget, he was one of the lords responsible for the Oxford Provisions. Yet this is the man who now seeks to curry favor with you, the man who would poison your mind against your own son!"

"Edward's actions speak for themselves," Henry muttered, and turned away to pour himself wine.

Richard followed, unrelenting. "Tell me again," he demanded. "Tell me you mean to hold to this madness, refusing to see your son."

Henry spun around. "Do you not think I want to see the lad? But I dare not, Richard, I dare not. For if I were to see him, I could not keep from embracing him, from forgiving him any sin, even treason . . ."

There were tears in Henry's eyes, and Richard's irritation ebbed away. It was fifteen months since he had returned from Germany, and while he did not repent of his decision to stand by Henry in his time of need, his resentment had begun to fester, for Henry had taken his homecoming for granted. But he had not consolidated his hold on Germany; the King of Castile was a rival claimant for the German crown; and the Pope was no longer offering his unqualified support. Richard thought it the ultimate irony that, in seeking to secure Henry's throne, he might well have sacrificed his own. Looking at his brother now, though, he felt a sharp throb of pity.

"I'm going to Edward," he said. "If he can satisfactorily explain his behavior—and I'd wager the surety of my soul that he can—I am then bringing him back here, so he may make his peace with you. Do you agree?"

Henry swallowed. "Yes," he whispered. "Please . . ."

"HOW could he believe that of me?" Edward sounded stunned. "That I meant to depose him and rule in his stead—Christ, that is madness!"

"Kings are prone to madness of that sort," Richard said grimly. "But in his heart, lad, he knows you'd not betray him, wants only to be reassured of that."

"This is that whoreson Gloucester's doing!"

Richard nodded. "Gloucester baited this hook with care, and Henry could no more resist it than he could fly, for the mere mention of Simon's name can throw him into a frenzy. In truth, lad, where Simon is concerned, he is like one possessed, so consumed with suspicion that it has clouded his wits, allowing him to think the unthinkable."

"No matter how much he hates Simon, how could he ever suspect me? What I've done, I've done for him!"

Edward had begun to pace. "My uncle Simon would never plot to depose the King; in that, my father wrongs him. But he is besotted with those damnable Provisions, so much so that I think he's gotten them confused with the Commandments. When he began to feud with that Judas, Gloucester, I sought to turn their discord to our advantage. And I did, Uncle! Simon trusts me now, confides in me. He— Why do you look at me like that? Do you not believe me?"

"Yes, lad, I believe you. I do not doubt that was your intent. But you are no longer traveling that road, Edward, have been led astray, into—"

"What are you saying, Uncle? That I've become Simon's puppet? Think you that I am so weak-willed, so simple?"

"No, Edward, merely young. You are not the first one to misjudge de Montfort's ability to bedazzle. I've watched him for nigh on thirty years, and even I do not fully understand how he so easily inflames the imagination. But again and again I've seen him—"

"With all due respect, Uncle, that is nonsense!"

"Is it? Tell me this, then. Why did you support Simon's demand to hold parliament in your father's absence?"

"Because," Edward said angrily, "Papa had miscalculated, and badly. I do not understand how he can be so short-sighted. Better to deny a right altogether than to grant it and then seek to disavow it. By agreeing to hold regular parliaments, and then reneging, Papa did needlessly stir up rancor and resentment. It is dangerous to make men feel cheated; that is not the way to handle them. Give them nothing and they have nothing, then, to lose. Rather, give them a little, lest they ask for a lot, just enough to content them, not enough to whet their appetites for more. Jesú, Uncle, it is so simple! Why can my father not see that?"

"So you were seeking only to repair the damage done by Henry's foolishness? Fair enough. But answer for me one question. How did holding that parliament serve your interests as the next King of England? What happens once you're on the throne and your lords want to follow Simon's example?"

"You said one question, Uncle, not two." But Edward's sarcasm was defensive, and color was rising in his face. "The answer is easy. Once I am King, I would forbid it, of course. Men will not defy me as they do my father."

"But did you not just argue—very convincingly—that it was a great mistake for a king to confer a privilege and then revoke it? Simon's parliament would set a dangerous precedent, one to haunt future kings, to haunt you, Edward. He took from you a measure of your authority, even made of you an accomplice in his usurpation. And yet you'd have me believe that you'd not been infected by Simon's zeal, that you were totally immune to his blandishments!"

Edward turned away without answering, and Richard relaxed in his seat, content to wait until Edward's pride would permit him to ask how he could make peace with his father. He was well pleased with what he had accomplished, for Henry's breach with his heir had to be healed at all costs, and if in the process, he'd just sown some lasting seeds of enmity between Edward and Simon de Montfort, so be it.

"YOU are not being fair!" Edward's indignation was colored with genuine surprise, for his past experience had led him to expect people to accept any excuse he deigned to offer, even to make the excuses for him. "I thought you would understand," he said, and Simon shook his head.

"No," he said, "I do not. In these past months, we've spent count-less hours discussing the Provisions. You agreed wholeheartedly that they must be upheld, that there was an urgent need for reform. Yet after just one meeting with your father, you are now willing to disavow all our efforts?"

Edward's mouth tightened. "I love my father too much to cause him further grief," he said, and Simon reached out, grasped his wrist.

"If you truly love your father, lad, do not abandon him to evil counsel, to men like John Mansel and Gloucester. Use your influence, Edward, lead him back to the right path. Set him an example, show him that a king must keep his oath, that he must think of the common good, for even the least of his brethren are deserving of justice. If the Lord God pays heed even to the fall of a sparrow, can the King do less? These are lessons he must learn, Edward, lessons you alone can teach him."

As flattering as Simon's appeal was, the message itself was alien to Edward. As far as he could determine, Simon's politics seemed to be a peculiar form of Christian chivalry, in which the ideals of knighthood were sanctified by faith, and he'd quickly concluded that Simon had paid too much heed to the visionary Bishop of Lincoln, for such an uncompromising code of ethics belonged in Camelot, not England in God's year 1260. It was never Simon's political theories that Edward had found so seductive; it was the blazing sun of his enthusiasm, the ca-maraderie of a shared quest with the greatest soldier of their age. But that singular sense of comradeship was no more; that, his uncle Richard had destroyed, utterly and for all time, leaving behind a residue of bitterness, self-reproach, and resentment.

He jerked free of Simon's hold. "I am beginning to think that your enemies do well to suspect your motives. What would you have me do, fight my own father?"

Simon stepped back. "I would have you honor your word. Is that too much to ask of you? Of a sudden, I think it is."

Edward flushed. "It is not for you to criticize me, my lord Earl. A man may be judged only by his peers, his equals. I am a King's son, and therefore I am answerable only to my father, the King of England, and my uncle, the King of the Romans. Not to you!"

Simon was now flushed, too. "Yes," he said scathingly, "you are indeed Henry's son!"

"I am also the grandson of King John, a man who did not forget his enemies. You'd best bear that in mind!" Edward's anger had blinded him to all but Simon. Turning, he brushed past Nell as if she were not there, stalked from the chamber.

There was an involuntary cry of "Ned!" from Harry, and then the slamming of the door. Simon had moved to the hearth. Nell followed, put her hand on his arm. He shrugged it off, but she forbore to take offense, for she knew the depths of his disappointment. "You tried," she said. "What more could you do?"

"He never believed in the Provisions, Nell. If he had, he could not have renounced them with such ease. Lies, all lies! He cares naught for the Provisions, naught for our common enterprise. So he does not forget his enemies? Well, neither do I!"

Simon swung about, reaching for his mantle, and Nell cried, "Where do you go at such an hour?"

"Wherever my horse takes me," he said brusquely. "I need the air, need time for my anger to cool. Do not wait up."

She did not like the idea of his riding abroad, alone, at night, but she knew it would be futile to protest. "Just do not jump any fences," she shouted after him. "Last time you almost broke your neck!"

An unhappy silence settled over the chamber, for Harry and Bran were no less troubled than Nell by this sudden rupture with Edward. But Guy appeared unfazed. "I am Edward and answerable only to God," he said mockingly, "for I am surely a sovereign's son!" He was a clever mimic, but a cruel one, too, for Edward did have a slight lisp. Bran's mouth twitched, Nell frowned, and Harry snarled:

"Curb your tongue, you impudent whelp!"

Guy had inherited his full share of Simon's volcanic temper, and at seventeen, he was still exploring the outer boundaries of manhood. "I take no orders from you, Harry!"

Nell was not pleased, but she did not interfere. She and Simon believed their sons should settle their own disputes, and intervened only when blood seemed likely to flow.

It was Bran who acted as peacemaker, in his own inimitable way. "I've got ten marks, Mama, that says the cub knocks Harry on his arse."

Harry snorted. "If you've got ten marks," he gibed, "it means you filched my purse again!"

"I most certainly did not," Bran said. "If I was going to steal from anyone, it would be from Amaury!" As Amaury was the one miser in a family of incorrigible spendthrifts, that got a laugh. But then Bran's grin faded. "Why be so quick to defend Ned, Harry? How can you justify what he's done?"

"I do not! But I find it easier than Papa to understand. We would be loyal to Papa unto death. So how, then, can we fault Ned for being loyal to his father?"

Nell saw that he'd scored some points with Bran, who looked suddenly thoughtful, but not with Guy, who said, "Yes, but Papa is in the right and Uncle Henry in the wrong!" And that no de Montfort would dispute.

Harry and Bran drifted over to the hearth, where they began a low-voiced discussion of Edward's defection, laying plans to bring him back into the fold. Guy watched, looking both left out and sullen, and Nell gave him a curious glance. "You do not like Ned, do you?" she asked, and saw his eyes—grey like Simon's—become suddenly wary.

"No," he said, no more than that, and Nell decided not to press further. Returning to her seat, she picked up her account book. But she found it difficult to keep her mind upon household expenses, for her ears still rang with Edward's angry warning, that he did not forget his enemies. Was that how he truly saw Simon now—as an enemy?

"Mama."

Glancing up, she smiled. Her three elder sons so resembled Simon that she often found herself indulging them more than she ought, caught by a sudden grin, a familiar gesture, by tantalizing glimpses of a ghost, the young Frenchman who'd so long ago won her heart. Her youngest son, eleven-year-old Richard, also bore Simon's stamp, while her girls, Ellen and the daughter buried in Bordeaux, had inherited her coloring. But Amaury was the anomaly. With his sturdy frame, his curly chestnut hair, he bore so little resemblance to his dark, long-legged, boisterous brothers that Guy occasionally called him a changeling. Amaury responded to such taunts with serene indifference, thus confirming to Simon and Nell that they'd been right to choose for him a career in the Church.

The Archbishop of Rouen had offered Amaury a prebend, and the boy was to sail for Rouen that summer, where he would be installed in his new benefice, continuing his studies under the Archbishop's benevolent eye. Nell was delighted that they had secured so prestigious a post for Amaury, but she would miss him, too, more than she could admit, for their society expected sons to be sent away from home at early ages, expected mothers to acquiesce in long separations.

Amaury looked troubled; he, too, had been a witness to his father's confrontation with his cousin Edward. Nell gestured for him to sit upon her foot stool, waited with unwonted patience for him to confide his concerns. He fidgeted, then blurted out, "The King hates Papa!"

"Yes," Nell said slowly. "I fear he does."

"He does not mean to honor his word, does he, Mama? He is not going to abide by the Provisions."

"I would hope he does, but his attempt to thwart parliament does not bode well for the future, lad."

"Mama . . . will there be war?"

"Jesú, no!" Nell stared at her son. "Whatever Henry has done, he is still the King, and your father has sworn an oath of fealty to him. Think you that Simon could forget that?"

"But Papa has sworn to defend the Provisions, too, Mama. What if he has to choose?"

"God willing, it will never come to that, Amaury," Nell said, firmly enough to forestall further questions. Amaury looked relieved, soon wandered over to engage Guy in a game of tables. But as Nell stared down unseeingly at her account book, the seed planted by her son took root, for with a fourteen-year-old's forthrightness, Amaury had been the first one who dared to put Simon's dilemma into words. What if he had to choose? Despite her assurances to her son, it was not a question Nell could answer. She doubted that Simon could have answered it, either.

HAVING reconciled with his son, Henry then sought to bring Simon to trial, charging him with perjury and lèse-majesté. But his council balked, and the French King was dismayed by Henry's bad faith, dispatching the Archbishop of Rouen to England to speak in Simon's defense. Henry was forced to back down.

He then took a page from his father's book of tricks. Just as King John had persuaded Pope Innocent III to annul the Runnymede Charter, Henry now appealed to Pope Alexander IV, and in June 1261, he triumphantly made public the papal bull invalidating the Oxford Provisions.

But he had misjudged the mood of his countrymen. His barons were outraged; even the Earl of Gloucester rallied to the opposition. Simon, Gloucester, and the Bishop of Worcester went so far as to summon three knights from each shire to St Albans, a truly revolutionary step, for this was the first time that men other than lords were to be given a voice in the affairs of state. Edward cleverly countered their move by having Henry hastily summon the knights to meet with him on the same September day at Windsor, and the confused knights chose the safer course, stayed home. Both sides began to recruit foreign mercenaries; conflict seemed inevitable.

And then the Earl of Gloucester once again switched sides, came to a private understanding with Henry. The barons were so shaken by his defection that Simon's "common enterprise" began to fall apart. Appalled, Simon cursed his irresolute allies in vain. Declaring that he'd never known a people as faithless as the English, he withdrew to France in a fury, vowing to go on crusade.

In Simon's absence, the barons agreed to submit their dispute with Henry to the judgment of his brother Richard, and in May of 1262, Richard found in Henry's favor. In July, Henry followed Simon to France, where he sought to have Simon arraigned before the French King. Again, his attempt failed.

As 1262 came to a close, it seemed that Henry had won. The barons were in disarray, Simon in voluntary exile, the Oxford Provisions declared null and void. But Simon refused to repudiate the Provisions, and such was the shadow he cast that until he did, Henry's victory was in doubt. The country was uneasy. In November, there were ugly anti-Semitic riots in London, for as always in times of stress, the unfortunate Jews served as scapegoats. Along the Welsh Marches, strife flared up again. Charging the English with violations of the truce, Llewelyn laid siege to Edward's castles of Deganwy and Disserth. And all men turned their eyes toward France, wondering how long it would be before Simon de Montfort returned to England.

26

Dolbadarn, North Wales

April 1263

"I TELL you, Owain, England totters on the very brink of civil war!" Davydd gave an excited laugh. "Edward and the young de Montforts spent last year in France, fighting in tournaments and ale-houses. Henry was at the French court, doing what he could to give grief to de Montfort, whilst his brother Richard was chasing a phantom crown the length and breadth of Germany. But they are all back in England now—even that de Lusignan half-brother of Henry's."

Owain yawned. "Aymer?"

Davydd frowned. "William—the Earl of Pembroke," he said with strained patience. "Do you not remember, Owain? Aymer died in Rome. So . . . the stage is set. But the principal actors are still biding their time, for the play cannot begin without de Montfort. All of Christendom now looks to France, waiting for de Montfort to make up his mind—as if there is any doubt what he'll do! Henry has alienated most of the young lords, Gloucester and de Warenne and even his own nephew, the Lord Hal, and they've been entreating de Montfort to lead them, to—"

"I thought Gloucester backed the King," Owain said, and Davydd slammed his mead cup down upon the table.

"Jesus wept, where are your wits? Gloucester died last summer!

It is his son I speak of, Gilbert de Clare. Do you not read my letters?"

Owain flushed. "For certes I do. But English affairs now hold little interest for me, Davydd. What is the point, after all? Whether Gloucester allies himself with the King or de Montfort, it is all the same to me. Whatever these English lords do, the morrow will find me still here at Dolbadarn, will it not?"

Davydd winced. He did not begrudge Owain his anger, but there was more self-pity than bitterness in Owain's lament. In recent months, Davydd had noted a marked deterioration in his brother's spirits. Senena's December death had struck Owain a telling blow. He alone of Senena's sons truly mourned her passing, and his grieving had yet to show signs of healing, for his yesterdays were all he had.

The silence was so prolonged that Owain at last became aware of it. "So tell me, lad," he said, too heartily. "How is that red-haired lass of yours? What is her name—Meryl?"

"Meriel. But that was over months ago. My current lady's name is Eleri." Davydd rose, crossed to his brother. "When I was speaking of the English King's woes, I was not just making idle conversation. The English turmoil matters, matters more than you know. Will you hear me out?"

When Owain nodded, Davydd gestured toward the closest bench. "Sit then, whilst I refresh your memory. When Gloucester died last year, his son hastened to Boulogne, where he sought to persuade Henry to give him seisin of the de Clare estates. Henry balked. Legally, he was within his rights; Gilbert was just nineteen then, two years shy of his majority. But politically, his refusal was madness, yet another of Henry's self-inflicted wounds. Let me tell you about the young Earl. Men call him 'Red Gilbert,' for like you, he has fiery hair . . . and like you, a fiery temper. Henry made an enemy in Boulogne, and needlessly. Moreover, he succeeded in estranging Richard's firstborn, for Hal counts Gilbert as a friend."

"So Gloucester is nursing a grudge? What of it?" But Owain's indifference was feigned; he was listening in earnest now.

"Three days ago, Edward crossed into North Wales, bringing supplies to his garrisons at Deganwy and Disserth. It will avail him naught, of course, for both castles will fall to Llewelyn sooner or later. You'll not like hearing this, Owain, but I daresay our brother has given Edward some sleepless nights of late. You see, he now poses a threat twice-over to England. No Welsh prince ever wielded the power he does, not even our grandfather. Moreover, he and Simon de Montfort are much too friendly for the English Crown's comfort. Once de Montfort returns from France, he'll seek Llewelyn out, and that is an unholy alliance in truth, one to put the fear of God into any English king, much less a timid soul like Henry!"

"Do you truly think I want to hear you laud Llelo's prowess on the battlefield?"

"But if he were not so formidable a foe, Owain, Edward and Henry would not be in such desperate need of Welsh allies." Davydd's smile was sudden, sardonic. "Our grandfather profited right handsomely from the last English civil war. I expect to profit no less from this one."

Owain's eyes widened. "What mean you to do, lad?"

Davydd's smile lost its edge. "I mean," he said, "to set you free."

THERE were just thirteen months between Gilbert de Clare and his younger brother, Thomas, and they could have been taken for twins, for they had inherited the same stocky build, the same flaming red hair, and an apparent infinity of freckles. But Thomas lacked Gilbert's irascibility, his prickly pride, and Edward found him to be a more amiable companion than the young Earl of Gloucester. Thomas was intelligent, Oxford-educated, but he had a full measure of common sense, too. Above all, he was a good sport, and while he'd voiced some qualms about this midnight meeting of Edward's, he was now riding at Edward's stirrup.

"Do you trust him?" he asked, casting an uneasy glance over his shoulder, for the Welsh woods were utterly black. They seemed to have entered a long, leafy tunnel, bereft of even the faintest glimmer of starlight, but alive with unseen eyes.

Edward grinned. "Trust a Welshman, Tom? Are you daft?"

"Then what are we doing out in the middle of the forest, in the middle of the night?"

"Because he could not come to me. Would you have him ride into Deganwy, brazen as you please? With Llewelyn's men keeping vigil day and night?"

Thomas said nothing. Edward had logic on his side, but Thomas had an uncomfortable suspicion that Edward relished the intrigue, even the risk.

Their Welsh guide now reined in his mount. "We are here," he announced, although to Thomas this glen looked like every other woodland clearing they'd passed through since leaving Deganwy. Edward signaled for his men to wait, and he and Thomas dismounted.

Thomas immediately tripped over a hidden root, nearly falling flat, to his chagrin and Edward's amusement. "I can just see us," he grumbled, "waiting out here till dawn, whilst this phantom ally of yours is comfortably abed back at Aber. This is just the sort of perverse jest to appeal to a Welshman!"

The laughter startled them both. They spun around, hands groping for sword hilts, as Davydd, still laughing, stepped from the shadows.

"If I'd meant to lure you out here under false pretenses," he said, "it would not be for a jest, but for an ambush."

Edward was annoyed; the initiative seemed suddenly to lie with Davydd. "Tom, meet Davydd ap Gruffydd, brother of the Prince of Gwynedd."

"I do believe Llewelyn calls himself Prince of Wales these days," Davydd said dryly, and Edward shrugged.

"He can call himself Prince of Palestine. But that is not a title recognized by the English Crown."

Now it was Davydd's turn to shrug. "Your recognition might matter in London, but west of the River Dee, it is Llewelyn's writ that holds sway. And you, my English lord, well know it. Why else would you have agreed to meet me tonight? Because you had an urge to take a midnight ride by moonlight?"

Thomas began to bristle, for he'd taken an immediate dislike to this arrogant Welsh rebel; even if Davydd's treachery was to their benefit, he could not respect a man who so blithely betrayed his own brother. But Edward gave a loud, ringing laugh.

"I was told you had a tongue sharp as a Fleming's blade. By God, now I believe it!"

"And I was told you're one for getting right to the heart of a matter. Shall we talk of my brother's intended alliance with Simon de Montfort—and what you're willing to do to thwart it?"

Edward had now taken the measure of his adversary, had begun to enjoy himself. "If you ally yourself with me, I'll make it worth your while; we both know that. What I do not yet know is why you are willing to forsake your brother, to take up with his sworn enemies."

"The answer to that is simple," Davydd said. "I want my brother Owain freed from Dolbadarn Castle."

Thomas abruptly revised his unfavorable estimation of Davydd, finding it truly admirable that Davydd should favor a brother powerless and forgotten over one who wore a crown. But Edward was regarding Davydd with a skeptical smile.

"I see," he said. "So it's to be a holy crusade to rescue Owain ap Gruffydd from his unjust confinement. Fair enough; every war needs its reason, and that will do as well as any, might even rally the Welsh to your side. But I am no unlettered Welsh herdsman, so spare me any heartrending tales of Brother Owain's suffering. Men do not fight wars for love. They fight for vengeance or for power. Which spurs you on?"

Davydd's face was utterly in shadow, but his voice was full of mockery. "God forbid that I should offend the King's son, but why should I care whether you believe me or not?"

"Should I assume, then, that you seek nothing else for yourself?

Your only demand is your brother's freedom?" Edward murmured, no less mocking.

There was a silence, and then Davydd laughed. "I'm no unlettered Welsh herdsman, either, my lord. What do I want from you? As much as I can get, of course. In my place, would you ask for less?"

"No," Edward admitted. "I'd ask for the moon. But I think we can come to terms. We'd find it acceptable for you and Owain to rule in Llewelyn's stead. And what of Llewelyn? He's kept you on a tight rein these six years past. Do you want him dead?"

"How you English fancy the blood-feuds of the Welsh! You are never happier than when we are fighting one another, are you? But I'm afraid I must disappoint you. I would see Llewelyn lose his crown, not his head. I cannot, of course, answer for Owain."

Edward nodded. "That sounds straightforward enough. Which at once arouses all my suspicions!"

Davydd grinned. "I see," he said, "that we do understand each other right well!"

MOST men coordinated their labor with the sun; they rose at dawn, worked during the hours of daylight, and with the coming of darkness, they slept. But Llewelyn followed his own inner clock, devoting most of his waking hours to the governance of Gwynedd. It was not at all unusual for him to be awake and active long after the sun had set, and so, despite the lateness of the hour, Goronwy ab Ednyved was not surprised to find Llewelyn in Aber's great hall, sharing a flagon of wine with his kinsmen, Tegwared and Einion.

They seemed to be celebrating. Llewelyn had tilted his chair back, was resting his feet on the table edge, in a rare moment of repose, and it was obvious the wine had been flowing freely. At sight of his Seneschal, Llewelyn grinned. "Goronwy! We did not expect you back till week's end. But your timing could not be better, for we've reason for rejoicing. Come, join us, and hear the news from England."

Goronwy was not accustomed to thinking of Llewelyn as vulnerable, yet looking at the younger man now, he found the words suddenly catching in his throat. But it was best done quick and clean, like an amputation. "Your news can wait," he said brusquely. "Mine cannot. Davydd has allied himself with Edward, has risen up in rebellion against you."

Llewelyn froze, and then very slowly lowered his chair back to the floor. "No," he said, "that cannot be." Goronwy did not contradict him, allowing him a few merciful moments of disbelief. But there'd been no conviction in Llewelyn's denial. Beneath the surface shock, on another level of awareness, lay an instinctive understanding, that if loving Davydd was easy, trusting him was folly.

Shoving the chair back, Llewelyn got to his feet. Neither Einion nor Tegwared could meet his eyes; they, too, had laughed at Davydd's irreverent humor, admired his courage, responded to his charm. Llewelyn moved away from the lamplight, into the sheltering shadows. Should he have seen this coming? He'd had his share of quarrels with Davydd, but even now, none that seemed serious in retrospect. So many hours spent discussing the prospects of their people, the future of Wales. Had Davydd ever shared his dream? Or had he been deluding himself all along?

It was uncommonly warm for late April, and the fire had been allowed to burn out. Llewelyn found himself standing before a smoldering hearth, staring down at the dying embers, flickering weakly amidst the charred, powdery ashes. His friends did not approach; they waited.

"Goronwy."

The older man untangled his legs, pushed away from the table. "What can I tell you?"

"Rhodri . . . is he, too, rebelling?"

"As far as I know, he seems to be holding aloof."

Llewelyn could take some consolation in that, but not much. "Rhodri's loyalties are to Davydd, not to me," he said. "We'd best keep him close, lest temptation beckon."

His voice was quite even. Goronwy looked intently into his face, was satisfied with what he saw. "We'll keep Rhodri under watch, discreetly done, of course," he said approvingly. "What of Davydd?"

"I could have forgiven Davydd much, but not an alliance with the English Crown. He might as well have invited the English army into Wales, as our mother did. It was not just his own future he was willing to risk, it was the sovereignty of Wales. And that," Llewelyn said, still in deceptively dispassionate tones, "I am not likely to forget."

"I think most of our people will hold fast for you. But Davydd will attract followers—malcontents, self-seekers, and those who feel Owain has been wronged. There are more of them than you wish to admit, Llewelyn. We must move quickly, therefore, to cut Davydd off from his would-be allies. I would suggest we lead an army into his lands, lay waste to the Dyffryn Clwyd—"

"It will not come to that, Goronwy. I think it is time you heard my news. Davydd was shrewd enough to realize he'd have no chance to overthrow me without English aid. But he is about to learn an important lesson in English reliability. You see, come the morrow his English ally will be departing Deganwy with all haste. Henry has urgently summoned Edward back to England."

Goronwy gave an audible gasp, then roared with laughter. "I think I'd barter my birthright to see the look on Davydd's face once he knows!" That thought sent him into another paroxysm of laughter, but he soon sobered. "Llewelyn, this makes no sense. Even for Henry, this is a remarkably bone-headed blunder. Surely he must know that, by recalling Edward, he is crippling Edward's ambitions for Wales?"

"He knows, Goronwy. But though Henry sees me as a threat, he is now facing a greater one. On Wednesday last, Simon de Montfort landed at Dover."

THEY had ridden all night, by dawn were approaching the English border. But there was no trace of sun; the sky was swathed in a wet, grey mist. By now they were only a few miles from Cheshire. Eleri felt no surprise, though, when Davydd suddenly signaled for a halt. It was true that England meant safety. It also meant exile.

A short distance from the road, a narrow stream wound its way through the damp grass. Davydd slackened the reins, allowed his mount to drink. A few of the men took advantage of this respite and dismounted, stretching and yawning. Eleri followed Davydd to the stream.

"There is still time," she said softly. "Return to Aber, beloved, seek Llewelyn's pardon."

"By all means," he snapped. "Owain is right lonely, after all. I daresay he'd be delighted to share his quarters at Dolbadarn with me."

"Llewelyn loves Owain not. You he loves well. He'd forgive you, Davydd. Mayhap not at once, but in time—"

"No!"

Eleri reached over, touched his arm. She was only twenty to his twenty and four, but at that moment, she felt much the older of the two. "I know how painful it would be to humble your pride, but Davydd, think! Would you truly rather rely upon Edward's charity than Llewelyn's mercy?"

He jerked free. "It is not charity! Edward will make me welcome, and not out of Christian kindness. If I had to depend upon his benevolence, I'd end up begging my bread by the roadside. But he needs me, Eleri. Our first attempt to overthrow Llewelyn was thwarted by fate, Simon de Montfort, and Edward's half-witted father. But our chance will come again, and when it does, Edward can have no better weapon at hand than Llewelyn's brother."

This was said with a certain degree of bravado, for Davydd was not as sure of his prospects at the English court as he'd have Eleri believe. But she did not seem impressed by his argument. She was looking at him somberly, and when he stopped speaking, she urged her horse closer.

"Kiss me, Davydd," she said, and he leaned toward her. When his fingers touched her cheek, he found her skin wet, but whether she wept or not, he couldn't tell, for a light, warming rain had begun to fall.

"I leave you here," she said. "Go with God, my love."

"What? But you're coming with me!"

"No," she said, "I am not."

Davydd sucked in his breath; that was a defection he'd not expected. Pride prevailed, though. "I see," he said cuttingly. "I suppose I ought to have foreseen as much. After all, you only promised to love me unto death and beyond. Not a word was ever said about exile!"

"I do love you, Davydd. I loved you enough to share your bed without a priest's blessing."

"If you love me, why will you not come with me?"

"I should think the answer to that would be obvious. I was willing to play the whore for you, with no regrets. But I will not play the fool. I speak no English, no French. I know not a single soul in all of England. What would befall me, my love, once you tired of me?"

"What makes you think I would tire of you?" he demanded, and she smiled sadly.

"You tired of all the others, Davydd," she said, and pulled up the hood of her mantle. "Farewell."

"Eleri!" But she was already turning her mare. The rain was coming down heavily now. "Go then," Davydd said. "If you have so little faith in me, go and be damned! And tell Llewelyn this for me, tell him I'll be back!"

27

Tower of London

June 1263

SIMON and his supporters met at Oxford in May, vowed to treat as enemies those who would not uphold the Provisions, saving only the King and his family. But Henry held his ground, and the long-simmering discontent soon flared into violence. The Earl of

Derby, wild and lawless and true only unto himself, sacked the town of Worcester and burned the Jewry. The young Earl of Gloucester led an army west, and seized the Bishop of Hereford, most hated of Henry's foreign advisers, casting him into prison and laying siege to the royal castle at Gloucester. Simon then assumed command, and they marched north to besiege Bridgnorth. The attack was coordinated with Llewelyn of Wales, and the town and castle soon surrendered. Simon then swung south, toward London, and a panicked Henry took refuge within the Tower.

EDWARD reached London in late June, at once sought out his father. As he crossed the Tower's inner bailey, he came upon his uncle Richard, and together they made their way toward the royal apartments.

"I hope the sight of you gladdens Henry's eyes. In truth, lad, you'll find him sorely distraught. He has been greatly disheartened by the ease of Simon's victories, and—"

Edward spat out a virulent oath. "I am heartily sick of hearing Simon de Montfort lauded as another Caesar. I for one do not fear to face him on the battlefield. Indeed, the sooner the reckoning comes, the better for England, for us all."

Richard did not agree. His was a lonely, unorthodox conviction that war was man's ultimate failure. But that was not a view he would ever share, much less seek to proselytize, for so foreign a philosophy would win him no converts, only scorn.

They'd passed through the great hall, had now reached the stairs leading to Henry's private chamber in the Blundeville Tower. Richard reached out, put his hand on his nephew's arm. "Wait," he said. "Ere we go up, I would speak with you about Bristol. The accounts we heard were garbled, confused. What is the truth of it?"

Edward shrugged. "Briefly put, some of my soldiers ran afoul of the townsfolk. Most likely, one of them got too familiar with a citizen's wife or daughter. Mayhap it took no more than their Flemish accents; never have I seen so much suspicion of foreigners. But whatever sparked the fire, in no time the city was ablaze. It got so ugly that we had to retreat into the castle, and soon found ourselves under siege!" Edward shook his head in remembered astonishment. "Fishmongers and tanners and peddlers—Jesú alone knows where they found the courage! We were in a deep hole, in truth, for the castle larders were poorly victualed. Fortunately, the Bishop of Worcester was within a day's ride of Bristol. He came, at my urging, and managed to placate the townspeople, in return for my pledge to make peace with de Montfort and the other rebel barons."

"A pledge you had no intention of honoring," Richard said quietly, and Edward gave him a surprised smile.

"Of course not, Uncle. Have you forgotten who Worcester is? He's de Montfort's pawn!"

"No, Edward, he is not. He is a man of conscience, deserves better than he got from you. But my concern is not for Worcester, it is for you. There are two things no man can hope to outrun in this life—his shadow and a reputation for duplicity and double-dealing. You give your word too lightly, lad. A king who cannot be trusted—"

"Uncle, enough. I know you mean well, but I need no lecture upon the sacred worth of a man's sworn oath. That sounds suspiciously like the gospel preached by my uncle Simon." Edward put his foot on the stairs, then paused. "Tell me," he said, "have you had word from Hal?"

Richard slowly shook his head; his eldest son's defection to Simon de Montfort was a constant ache. "Hal has been caught up in the fervor for reform," he said. "As a lad, he was always bedazzled by tales of Camelot. But in time he'll realize that this is a false quest."

His apologetic defense would have found no favor with Henry, who saw Hal's apostasy as a particularly reprehensible form of treason, but Edward was more indulgent; he, too, wanted to believe that Hal was a victim of Simon's sorcery, that the spell could be broken. "Sooner or later, we'll have a chance to talk, Uncle, and Hal will heed me. He always does."

Henry's chamber was a magnificent octagon, gleaming in white and gold, lit by four soaring bay windows; there was even a small, private oratory, hidden behind an elaborately carved screen. But the room was empty, Henry nowhere in sight. Puzzled, Edward moved forward. "Papa?"

"Edward?" Henry poked his head around the screen. "Edward, thank Christ!" He stumbled on the oratory step, flung his arms around his son's neck. He was five inches shorter than Edward, forty pounds lighter, but never had he seemed so frail, so slight; his very bones were as hollow and brittle as a bird's, Edward thought, shocked. He put his arm around his father's shoulders, catching the smell of sweat, the heavily sugared wine Henry so liked. "Disheartened," his uncle Richard had said, "distraught." Nay, this was far worse; this was defeat.

"I was praying," Henry confided. "But . . . but sometimes I fear that the Lord no longer listens. If I have not offended Him, why has He forsaken me in my time of trial? I am alone amongst my enemies, Edward, and I know not whom I can trust."

"Papa, that is not so. You have me and Uncle Richard, the support of the French King and His Holiness the Pope. Even here in London, you are not friendless. The rabble and their renegade Mayor may have

been beguiled by de Montfort, but the citizens of substance, the aldermen, still hold fast for the Crown."

"Do they? Do they indeed?" Henry laughed shrilly. "Tell me this,
then. If the aldermen and merchants are so loyal, why have they refused
to lend me any more money? My coffers are well-nigh empty, Edward,
and they know my need, yet they will not extend me another farthing
of credit! I threatened and cajoled by turns, even beseeched, to no avail.
What will we do now, lad? How can we fight a war without money?
Your Flemish mercenaries will desert you in droves if you cannot pay
them, and—"

"Papa, this serves for naught. What of the Templars? Did they, too,
refuse you credit?" Henry nodded mournfully, and Edward swore, began
to pace. "You must not fret, Papa. Leave this to me; I'll not let you
down."

Henry's shoulders slumped; he mumbled an indistinct "Gratia Dei,"
moved to the table and poured more wine. To Richard, there was something pathetic about his instant relief, his utter trust. How many people,
he wondered, realized that Edward was, at the untried age of twenty-
four, the uncrowned King of England? This talk of money gave him
more than a twinge of guilt, for he had vast resources at his disposal;
shrewd business dealings had made him one of the richest men in
England. But he had never been a prodigal spender, and Henry was
already deeply in his debt, money never to be repaid. He watched
Edward stride about the chamber, while Henry settled himself into a
cushioned window-seat; he seemed much calmer now that the burden
had been shifted onto Edward, asked no awkward questions. It was
Richard who finally said, "Just what do you have in mind, lad?"

Edward flung himself into Henry's chair of state, swung a long leg
over the lacquered arm-rest. "What would you do if the drawbridge
were closed to you, Uncle? You'd look for a postern gate, no? Well, so
shall I."

THE New Temple of the Knights Templar lay beyond the city walls,
between Fleet Street and the River Thames. The Templars, "soldiers of
Christ," were the most martial of the religious orders, and the wealthiest,
for although they had originally been founded to fight the infidel, they
had in time become the financiers of Europe, money-lenders and bankers
for the Crown, the Church, prosperous merchants, the trade guilds.
Their London preceptory looked at first glance like a small city in and
of itself, but a city without denizens, for the knights retired at Compline.
Edward had known this; he and his men passed through the gateway

into a world of cloistered silence and deepening summer shadows, a world of deceptive, timeless peace.

"I am Brother Raymond." The warden was irked at being roused from bed, for he would have to rise in just a few hours for Matins. "How may I be of service, my lord?"

"I regret intruding upon you at such an hour, Brother Raymond, but I am here at the behest of my mother, the Queen. A few months past, she gave up some of her jewels as security for a loan, and the recent unrest in the city has made her fear for their safety." Edward smiled at the Templar, man to man, and shrugged. "Foolishness, I know. But she'll not rest easy until I have seen for myself that her qualms are for naught."

The warden was not surprised that Eleanor should be behaving so capriciously; he held Henry's willful Queen in no high esteem. "So be it," he said reluctantly. "If Your Grace will accompany me, I shall take you to the treasure-house. I would ask that your men maintain silence, though, for the knights' hall lies above it, and my brothers are abed."

The undercroft of the hall was as dark and damp as a crypt, just as foreboding. Following the feeble glow of their lanterns, Edward's men advanced cautiously, weaving their way amidst the heavy coffers. The warden glanced back, saw that Edward had stopped. "Ah, no, my lord, those are the treasuries of the city guilds. The Queen's caskets are over here."

He was never to be sure exactly what happened next. He thought he heard Edward say, "But this is what I've come for, Brother Raymond." Bewildered, he started to retrace his steps. If Edward signaled, he never saw it. But someone shoved him forward, causing him to stumble, and then a hand was clapped roughly over his mouth. He struggled, to no avail, within moments was overpowered. Bound and gagged, he lay helplessly on the floor, watching in appalled rage as the men produced hammers from beneath their mantles, muffled them in burlap, and set about smashing the locks on the guild coffers.

They were very efficient, moving systematically from coffer to coffer, emptying the contents into large woven sacks. "Enough," Edward said at last. "We can carry no more." As they began lugging their booty toward the door, he bent over the warden, set a lantern on the closest coffer. "You'll pass an uncomfortable night, I fear. It cannot be helped, though." There was sympathy in his voice, but no trace of shame. Although his face was in shadow, the Templar would later swear he was smiling.

❧

EDWARD'S raid on the New Temple netted him a thousand pounds. He prudently did not linger in London, made a hasty withdrawal to Windsor Castle. It was a wise move, for as word spread of the theft, outraged Londoners spilled into the streets. Within hours, the city was in turmoil. Enraged mobs roamed about, setting fire to the houses of prominent royalists, assaulting foreigners. When the tumult did not subside, John Mansel and the Queen's uncle, the Archbishop of Canterbury, fled to Dover, where they took ship for France. To the reformers, Mansel was Henry's evil genius, and Richard's son Hal brashly sailed in pursuit. Much to Richard's dismay, Hal was captured in Boulogne by a French lord rumored to be acting at the English Queen's behest. Richard withdrew to his castle at Berkhamsted, where he labored to bring about his son's release and attempted to stave off civil war, imploring Simon to meet with him at Twyford Bridge.

But Simon was not yet ready to negotiate. He swung east, avoiding London, and was given an enthusiastic welcome in the towns of the Cinque Ports. The Bishops of London, Lincoln, and Chester were dispatched to Henry, bearing Simon's terms for peace: that Hal be set free at once, that Henry again swear to uphold the Oxford Provisions, that he expel his foreign mercenaries and surrender Dover and other castles of strategic importance to the barons. Simon then assumed control of the port of Dover, thus severing all communications with the continent. Trapped in the Tower, Henry was forced to face the most bitter of facts, that it had taken Simon just six weeks to reduce England's King to utter impotence.

"ARE you certain you know where the man lives, John?"

John de Gisors glanced back at his companions. "Somewhere along Bishopsgate Street, not far from St Helen's nunnery." Reining in his horse, he beckoned to a passing youth. "You there! Where will we find the house of Mayor Fitz Thomas?"

De Gisors was known on sight to most Londoners; he'd been a city alderman for nigh on thirty years, three times Mayor. The boy hastily doffed his cap, offered to act as guide, and after escorting them through the wide, wooden gateway of the Fitz Thomas manor, he was not disappointed. De Gisors was that rarity, a wealthy merchant who spent freely; he flipped the lad a silver half-penny.

De Gisors's nephew hastened to help him dismount, for his uncle was no longer young and his girth, as much as his fine woolen tunic, proclaimed him a man of means. "Thank you, Clement," he said, heaving himself from the saddle. A servant came from the stables, and as he led their horses across the courtyard, Clement looked about with considerable interest.

"Fitz Thomas might pander to the rabble, Uncle, but he stints himself little. A baron would not scorn to shelter here," he said admiringly, and de Gisors grunted.

"Fitz Thomas does not lack for money. He's a draper by trade, deals in only the finest wools and silks. He comes from one of London's most distinguished families, Clement, is nephew to a former Mayor . . . which makes his behavior all the more despicable, for he is betraying his own."

They were admitted by a young serving maid. Within moments, a woman was crossing the hall toward them. She was neatly dressed in a bright blue gown and snowy white wimple, but her hands and apron were streaked with flour. Unselfconscious, she smiled, explaining, "We've a new cook; I was showing him my favorite eel pasty recipe."

"Dame Cecilia." De Gisors bowed over a slim, flour-dusted hand. "I believe you know Augustine de Hadestok. This gentleman is Richard Picard, like myself a court vintner, and this is my nephew, Clement, newly come to London."

"I'll send a servant to see to your comfort whilst I inform my husband that you are here. He may not be able to see you at once, for he is meeting in the solar with Sir Thomas Puleston."

Clement had a sharp eye, caught the expressions of distaste that flickered across the faces of his companions. As soon as they were alone, he queried, "Who is this Puleston? I gather you like him not, Uncle."

"Indeed not." De Gisors lowered himself onto a cushioned bench. "Puleston is not one of us, even though he did marry into one of London's better families. He comes of Shropshire gentry, is a royal justice . . . and a born conniver. He and de Montfort are two of a kind, arrows shot from the same bow. He's the Earl's sworn man, cares not who knows it. He—"

Cutting himself off abruptly, he got stiffly to his feet. Clement turned in time to see a figure emerging from the corner stairwell. While it was obvious that this dapper, youthful man was their host, he so little resembled de Gisors's lurid characterization that Clement could only stare, mouth ajar. As Fitz Thomas drew near, he saw that the Mayor was not as young as he first appeared, but he could still more easily have been taken for an Oxford student than a merchant in his mid-forties. Of slight build, with fine, flaxen hair, Norse-blue eyes, and a friendly, ingratiating smile, he seemed so innocuous to Clement that he found himself doubting his uncle's judgment, wondering how they could possibly see this mild-mannered draper as Lucifer's henchman.

Thomas Fitz Thomas greeted them affably, as if they were friends, not political rivals, bade them be seated, and promised to be with them shortly. Clement held his tongue until Fitz Thomas disappeared into the stairwell, and then blurted out, "That is the firebrand Mayor? Jesú, Uncle, he looks like a clerk!"

De Hadestok gave a derisive snort, and de Gisors said grimly, "Appearances can mislead, lad. To look at the magpie, you'd not think a bird with such beautiful plumage would be a thief, a scavenger that feeds upon other birds' eggs. Fitz Thomas may indeed look like a church deacon, but he has the soul of a pirate. He has a diabolical ability to stir up a crowd, has turned the Folkmoot into a dangerous weapon and learned to unleash the London rabble at his will."

"The Folkmoot? Is that not a public meeting of London freemen? I thought it had fallen into disuse, was little heeded nowadays."

De Gisors nodded. "That is what makes Fitz Thomas so formidable a threat, Clement. He has resurrected the Folkmoot, made of it his own creature, serving his ends. Had you but seen him yesterday noon—" He broke off, shaking his head. "The Folkmoot met, as always, at Paul's Cross, but never have I seen such a gathering. So many men turned out that there was not a foot to spare in all of the churchyard, and they cheered lustily as Fitz Thomas preached them a fire-and-brimstone sermon. To hear him tell it, the Oxford Provisions were like Holy Writ, and when he finally put it to a vote, asking if they supported Simon de Montfort and the Provisions, the simple fools shouted their 'yeas' to the heavens, as if they'd been asked to acclaim Christ the Redeemer!"

"John . . ." Augustine de Hadestok gave a warning cough, and de Gisors spun around. If Fitz Thomas had heard the last of this harangue, it did not show on his face; his smile did not waver. Another man had followed him out of the shadows of the stairwell. Clement knew this dark, saturnine stranger must be the hated knight Puleston. Unlike Fitz Thomas, the wolf in sheepskin, Puleston at least looked the part; he could have been the reincarnation of every pilgrim's fears, the wicked brigand lurking in every dark woods, around the bend of every lonely road. Puleston had a rakish, sardonic grin and penetrating black eyes; Clement had a sudden irrational conviction that they could see into his very soul, and he flushed, looked hastily away.

After an exchange of ice-edged greetings, Puleston made an unhurried departure. Fitz Thomas wandered over to the trestle table littered with sealing wax, pens, letters, and parchment scrolls. They were in disorder, for Augustine de Hadestok had been riffling through them, and when Fitz Thomas glanced up at his guests, his smile was knowing, ironic. "What may I do for you, gentlemen?"

"Do you still mean to go to the King, demand that he accept the Provisions?"

"Demand, no. Urge him, yes. He must realize that support for the Provisions runs deep in London. Our last Folkmoot—"

"—was a farce," de Hadestok said indignantly. "You've given a voice to the lowest elements in the city, whilst utterly ignoring the views of men of consequence, men of property. And when we sought to rebut you, we were shouted down!"

Fitz Thomas shrugged. "It is unfortunate," he said, "but not surprising, that rudeness ofttimes follows apace of revolution."

De Gisors gasped. "You admit, then, that you seek to foment a revolution?"

Fitz Thomas looked at them. "Do you not know, Master de Gisors," he said softly, almost gently, "that you are even now living through one?"

Richard Picard, hitherto silent, now blistered the air with an embittered oath. "I told you we were wasting our time, John. Let's be gone from here."

"Not yet." De Gisors moved toward the Mayor. "You are no fool. You must realize the danger in what you are doing. In courting the rabble, you imperil the entire social order. Why are you doing this? What do you seek to gain?"

" 'The rabble'?" Fitz Thomas echoed, no longer amused. "I suppose by that you mean the men of the craft guilds. I'll grant you that the fishmongers, the cordwainers, and potters do not enjoy the same stature as the trade guilds—the shipping magnates like you, Master de Hadestok, or the vintners like you, Master de Gisors. But the members of the craft guilds are decent, hard-working men, men entitled to a say in the government of their city, and that you have denied them."

De Gisors was shaking his head. "Nay, you wrong me. We may have been often at odds with upstart craftsmen, but I would not call them 'rabble.' It is not their influence I fear. It is the journeymen, those who work for wages, the riffraff, the baseborn. Can you deny that such men are fickle, untrustworthy, ever on the edge of violence?"

Fitz Thomas leaned back against the table. "During my term as sheriff," he said, "I often attended inquests. The verdicts were varied, ranging from murder in a street brawl to death by mischance to the most common cause, river drowning. But when it came to the disposition of the dead man's property, again and again the finding was the same: 'Goods and chattels had he none.' When men have nothing to lose, gentlemen, when they are given no stake in what you call the 'social order,' is it truly so surprising that they do not share your belief in the sanctity of the law?"

"If I wanted to hear a sermon on the plight of Christ's poor, I would

be at Mass," de Hadestok jeered, and Picard chimed in, no less mockingly. De Gisors and his nephew were silent, the former looking tired
and troubled, the latter intrigued in spite of himself. Clement no longer
wondered why so much controversy swirled around Fitz Thomas; the
man's passion was contagious.

"What do you hope to accomplish?" he asked, not to bait the Mayor
but because he truly wanted to know. They all sensed his sincerity; he
earned himself glowering looks from his companions and an honest
answer from Fitz Thomas.

"On more than ten separate occasions, King Henry has seized control of the city's government. I want to make sure that never happens
again. In the past, aldermen have abused their office, getting special tax
exemptions, brazenly favoring their friends and family. That, too, I would
stop. I would protect our city's rights against the encroachments of the
abbey at Westminster. I would gain recognition for the craft guilds."

He paused, his eyes flicking from face to face, and then burst out
laughing. "What did you expect me to say—that I meant to sell my soul
to the Devil, my city to the Saracens? That I yearned to be a kingmaker?
My aims are more modest than that. I want to protect the welfare of my
city. I want to see the Oxford Provisions accepted by all men, its reforms
carried out. If I would also like to become London's most memorable
Mayor, what harm in that? I said my aims were modest. By the grace
of God Almighty and the Earl of Leicester, they are attainable, too." He
smiled suddenly. "I think, gentlemen, that is what frightens you so
much."

"I was wrong," de Gisors snapped. "You are indeed a fool. All this
talk of the common people, the craftsmen, apprentices, beggars. What
do they mean to a lord like Leicester? He will make use of you as long
as it serves his purposes, but he'll never see you as an ally, an equal.
He'll—" He paused, for Fitz Thomas was laughing again.

"Of course the Earl of Leicester believes in the supremacy of blood;
what lord does not? You are right when you say the Earl does not see
me as his equal. If one of my sons sought to wed his daughter, I daresay
he'd be greatly affronted." He moved forward, stopped in front of de
Gisors.

"Leicester might deny my son a highborn bride, but he would not
deny him justice. You asked why he would care about the fate of a
fishmonger, a tanner? Because even the lowest wretch is deserving of
God's mercy, the protection of the King's laws. He believes that, you
see. I've never known another lord who did, but Simon de Montfort
truly does. I'll not deny that self-interest colors his views; what of it?
Only a saint is deaf to that voice. But the Earl has a heartfelt vision of

the way the world should be. I like his vision, Master de Gisors, I like it well. So do the citizens of London."

"Come away, John," Richard Picard urged, and this time de Gisors heeded him. He turned, followed the others across the hall. But at the door, he stopped, glanced back at the Mayor.

"You do not understand," he said tautly, "do not realize what is at stake. There'll be no going back. England will never be the same!"

Fitz Thomas nodded. "God willing," he said, "indeed it will not."

ON July 13, Henry capitulated, sent Simon de Montfort word that he would abide by the barons' terms. But his belated recognition of reality was not shared by his outraged Queen. Telling Henry that if he lacked the backbone to resist these rebels, she did not, Eleanor announced her intention of joining their eldest son, Edward, at Windsor Castle. Henry, his nerves raw and bleeding, angrily bade her go, and within the hour, her bargemen were rowing away from the Tower, heading upstream.

Her ladies were obviously ill at ease as the Queen's barge struggled against the current, for Beatrice and Auda would bear the brunt of Eleanor's temper on the twenty-mile journey to Windsor. Moreover, both women were fearful of river travel, and Eleanor's anger had propelled them out onto the Thames less than an hour after the cresting of high water. They sat stiffly upright, clutching the edge of their seats, dreading the moment when their barge would have to shoot the bridge. If Eleanor shared their misgivings, it didn't show. In high dudgeon, she was railing indiscriminately, heaping verbal abuse upon her husband, Simon de Montfort, the Earl of Gloucester, Londoners in general and Mayor Fitz Thomas in particular. When she began to berate their boatmen for their clumsy piloting, her ladies exchanged glumly resigned glances; this was going to be a very long trip.

The Queen's barge soon attracted the attention of youngsters fishing along the river bank. One, bolder than his companions, shouted, "Go back to France!" The others took up the taunt. Eleanor was incensed enough to demand that they be punished, but her knights quickly pointed out that the boys would vault a fence, disappear into an alley long before their barge could reach the shore. Eleanor could not refute their logic and subsided, still fuming.

Such displays of antagonism had become all too common of late. The most unpopular Queen since the Conquest, Eleanor was attacked for her extravagant spending, her foreign birth, her multitude of acquisitive relatives, even for Henry's foibles, and—unfairly—for the crimes of Henry's de Lusignan kin, whom she detested. But nowhere was she more hated than in London, where she'd alienated the citizens by taxing all boats using the Queenhithe wharf, by claiming a payment of "queen's gold." Much of the time, she was indifferent to the hostility of her subjects, but her anger had made her vulnerable, and as she listened now to the gibes of these London youngsters, she found herself remembering the exuberant welcome Londoners had accorded her upon her first entry into their city, so many years ago.

So caught up was she in these regretful reveries that she did not at once notice their barge was losing ground, beginning to drift. The oarsmen were no longer rowing. When she rebuked them, they pointed. "Madame, look!" Turning, she was unable to stifle a gasp. Ahead lay the bridge. It was always a formidable obstacle to river traffic, but never had it presented so daunting a barrier, for it was thronged with an angry crowd, men, women, even children. They filled every available space, leaning recklessly over the railing, blocking the narrow pathway, trapping carts and pack mules, even hanging out of the windows of the houses lining the bridge. As Eleanor stared, disbelieving, a hoarse shout went up: "She comes! The bitch comes!"

"Madame." The captain of her guards half-rose, causing the barge to rock. "We'd best return to the Tower. We can resume our journey once that rabble has been dispersed."

"Indeed not!" Eleanor raised her chin. "I'll not be affrighted by common churls. We continue on to Windsor." She gestured to the oarsmen. "Row!"

Reluctantly, they obeyed; the barge lurched forward. The cries of the crowd grew louder, more strident. Eleanor sat still, head high, staring straight ahead. They could hear the roar of the river now, pounding against the piers. The tide was quickening, waves slapping the sides of the barge; they were soon drenched in spray. The oarsmen steered toward the widest arch, in mid-bridge. Above it rose the small chapel of St Thomas à Becket; it, too, had been invaded, angry, contorted faces showing at the open windows. The first missile to strike the barge was a raw egg. It landed beside Beatrice, splattered the Queen's seat cushions. Beatrice screamed and a second egg flew through the air, thudded onto the floor of the barge.

There was a sudden silence, and then an exultant shout, a collective cry of triumph. Within moments the air was alive with invective. "Drown the bitch!" The cry rose from a hundred throats; mud and garbage rained down upon the barge. Eleanor's ladies were screaming. In fending off the barrage, one of the boatmen lost his oar; the barge spun in a circle, caught by the current. Eleanor was knocked to the bottom of the boat. As it smashed against the pilings, she, too, began to scream.

The arch loomed ahead; it would later haunt Eleanor's dreams, a gateway to Hell. She was sure they were going to drown, gabbled an incoherent plea to the Blessed Virgin. Auda was mute, too terrified for speech, Beatrice sobbing, and the knights appealing to St Mildred, begging her to spare them on her day. Only the boatmen kept their heads. Rowing like fiends, they fought the river, until, sweating and cursing, they broke free from the surging current, began to pull clear of the bridge.

But those on board had no time to rejoice in their reprieve, for some in the crowd now resorted to a more lethal bombardment. No longer were they throwing rotten apples and raw eggs; rocks began to splash into the water around the barge. A knight cried out as one ricocheted off an oarlock and struck his leg. The men grunted, pulling on the oars, but they were still within range, and when a large rock crashed into the stern, an oarsman gasped, "Sweet Jesus, we've sprung a leak!"

They were not that far from shore; the wharf at Botolph Lane was less than twenty feet away. But as they rowed toward the bank, the crowd began to surge from the bridge, racing them to the wharf. Knowing they'd never make it to the Southwark shore, the boatmen continued to row for all they were worth. They reached the wharf before the mob, scrambled to safety just as the first of their pursuers rushed onto the pier. The knights fumbled for their swords, but the men had come to an uncertain halt. There were few among them who truly had murder in mind; they resorted, instead, to a more familiar weapon, the only one available to the powerless—ridicule.

Encircled by her knights, clinging to her terrified women, Eleanor heard herself mocked as the "foreign witch," as harlot and spendthrift, a French-born Circe. Hatred for her ran deep. Men who drank enough of that draught might well have gotten intoxicated on it; the spectre of violence still overhung the wharf. But something was happening in Botolph Lane. People were beginning to shout, pushing and shoving, retreating. Men on horseback had come into view. The city sheriffs were known to many, but Londoners had never been over-awed by authority. What broke up the crowd was a name—Fitz Thomas.

With the realization that their Mayor was in their midst, their ranks parted as if by magic, and he passed through, rode onto the wharf. As he reined in his mount before his Queen, Eleanor knew she was now safe, as safe as if she were still at the Tower. "God's mercy," she whispered, and then, "Jesú, my coffers!" Whirling, she stared in horror at her barge, already half-submerged. "My jewels," she wailed. "My gowns, all at the bottom of the Thames!"

To be rescued by a man she so detested was a great humiliation for Eleanor, but she found it all the more galling that she could fault neither his behavior nor his manners. Although Fitz Thomas refused to make the arrests she demanded, he made his refusal sound perfectly reasonable, explaining that the culprits had long since fled. When she would not allow him to take her back to the Tower, insisting she must have her own mare, her own escort, he dispatched a man to fetch horses and men, and he was able to disperse the crowd with impressive ease, requiring no more than good-natured banter.

It infuriated Eleanor that this man, a mere draper, should wield more influence with Londoners than she, the Queen, did. Moreover, she doubted that he was truly sorry she'd been subjected to such an ordeal. He said he was, offered apologies on behalf of his city, but when one of the sheriffs burst into laughter at sight of her, Fitz Thomas quickly came to the man's defense.

"You are usually so elegant, Madame," he said tactfully. "It did but take him by surprise to see you looking so . . . so bedraggled." And as Eleanor gazed down at her sodden skirts, her egg-splattered bodice, he added, "And you do have that daub of mud on your nose . . ." He sounded solicitous, but the corner of his mouth twitched, and she suspected he was fighting back a grin.

"Admit it, this amuses you," she accused. "Lowborn rabble, the dregs of your city, tried to murder me, their Queen, and you care naught!"

"I regret, Madame, that you were so ill-treated. I do not make excuses for them. But I will not pretend that I was surprised by what happened. If horses are kept on too short a tether, they're like to run wild when at last set free. So, too, are men."

"How dare you! You make it sound as if this were somehow my fault!"

"You have courage, Madame. I would that you also had . . ." He left the thought unfinished, but before she could pursue it further, he was turning away. She recognized the man approaching, the one Fitz Thomas had sent to the Tower, and she frowned. What ailed the lackwit? Why had he not brought back horses, knights of her household? She watched impatiently as he conferred briefly with Fitz Thomas, saw the latter shoot her a startled look, and moving forward, caught his sleeve.

"What is it? Why did this idiot return alone? What is wrong?"

"Madame . . ." It was the first time she'd seen the imperturbable Fitz Thomas at a loss. "It seems a crowd has gathered at the Tower, word having spread of your . . . mishap. My man says the mood is ugly, and the King . . . well, he is loath to open the gates as long as they remain without. He sent word that I should escort you, instead, to the Bishop of London's palace."

He saw the color crimson her cheeks, and found himself feeling an emotion he'd have sworn the Queen did not deserve—pity. "I daresay, Madame, that he had your safety in mind, not wanting to expose you to their insults and abuse," he said, knowing that might well be true, but knowing, too, that a woman as proud as Eleanor would be shamed, nonetheless, for prudent though Henry's action might be, heroic it was not. He could hear his men laughing, knew the jests they would soon be swapping, all at Henry's expense, and he said quietly, "I fear, Madame, that you must accept my offer of assistance, after all."

"I'd sooner walk barefoot through hot coals!" she spat, but she did not need the timid reproaches of her women to know she did not have the luxury of refusal; what other choice had she? "Help me mount your horse," she commanded, and as Fitz Thomas obeyed, she said, "This I swear to you upon all I hold sacred, that I shall never forget this day . . . never!"

Fitz Thomas's eyes narrowed, taking in every detail of his Queen's muddied, disheveled appearance—the gown soaked with river water, smeared with dirt and egg stains, the wimple tilted askew, the hair tumbling untidily down her back. "Indeed, Madame," he said, "this is a day I shall never forget, either," and this time he did not trouble to hide his grin.

APPROACHING from Dover, the barons would normally have entered the city through Aldgate, but the Mayor had requested that they come in from the north. They knew, therefore, that some sort of welcome was planned. None of them, however, were prepared for what awaited them as they rode through Cripplegate.

What struck them first was the noise. Bells were so much a part of their world that most men had long ago developed selective hearing, blocking out the constant chiming—for Matins, Prime, None, Vespers, Compline, Lent, for festivals, births, marriages, funerals, for city elections, pageants, processions, coronations, military victories—bells proclaimed virtually every aspect of daily life. But they had heard nothing like this wild cacophony; the very air seemed to vibrate with the pealing of so many church chimes.

Simon had never seen London look so festive. Banners were hung from the windows of upper stories, stretched across the narrow street above their heads. In place of the customary bundle of leaves signaling the presence of an ale-house, the ale-stakes were draped with flowers, and doors were festooned with hawthorn and green birch. Some householders even had bonfires burning, as if it were the vigil of St John the Baptist. Most amazing of all, the streets were reasonably clean; the rakyers must have been working since first light, for much of the debris was gone. Even the usual stray pigs and dogs were not roaming at will;

only a large grey goose was in sight, hissing and flapping its wings when foolhardy children ventured too near.

"Papa!" Harry spurred his mount forward, until they rode side by side. "Listen to them," he marveled, gesturing toward the people thronging both sides of the street. "I would that I had a shilling for every cheer you're getting!"

"Mayhap you could pass around an alms-cup," Simon said dryly, but his nonchalance was feigned. He was both taken aback and touched by the response of the London crowds. They had turned out in large numbers to witness the barons' triumphant entry into the city, and clapped loudly as the men rode by, surging out into the road to offer food and flowers, sharing wineskins with the delighted soldiers. But for Simon they reserved their most fervent cheers, for Simon they saved their heartfelt acclaim.

Joyful shouts of "Leicester!" echoed on the summer air, competing with the pealing bells, heralding his progress down Wood Street. Simon had never experienced such an outpouring of emotion. It was disconcerting at first, but exhilarating, too. Gazing upon this sea of friendly faces, he felt a shock of recognition. These people—bakers and carpenters and skinners, men of humble trades—they were his true allies. They understood his commitment to the Provisions, shared it as men of his own rank did not.

Most of Simon's supporters were young, and they were thoroughly enjoying their sudden celebrity status. Harry in particular won the crowd's favor, for he was quick to bandy quips, to accept proffered wineskins, to flirt with pretty girls. A woman had run out into the street, draped a garland of honeysuckle around his stallion's neck, and he was amusing the spectators by flinging flowers to lasses who'd caught his eye, even leaning recklessly from the saddle to claim a kiss from a buxom redhead. This delighted those watching, save only the young Earl of Gloucester, who yearned to see Harry lose his balance, fall flat on his face. But Harry had been blessed with an athlete's grace; he straightened up, his cheek smeared with the girl's lip rouge, and acknowledged the crowd's cheers with a jaunty wave.

"If there was any justice, he'd have broken his neck," Gloucester muttered, earning a speculative glance from his brother. Thomas had not been sharing in the general rejoicing. Once it had come to war, he'd had no choice but to support his elder brother; he was not altogether happy about it, though, for in being loyal to Gilbert, he was forced to be disloyal to Edward, his friend and future King. He'd noticed Gilbert's displeasure, wondered what had soured his brother's mood, for this should have been a day of triumph for him; Thomas knew that Gilbert genuinely believed in the Provisions, in the need for reforms. Now as he studied his brother's scowling profile, a glimmer of comprehension came to him.

"Does it vex you so much, Gilbert, that the cheers are for 'Leicester,' not for 'Gloucester'?" he asked, saw his brother's fair skin stain with color.

"No, of course not," Gloucester snapped. "Why should I stoop to court the commons? I leave that to Leicester. But the fact is, Tom, that I was the one who captured the Bishop of Hereford, not Leicester. We're equal partners in this enterprise, and it ill behooves him to claim all the credit."

"I doubt that is his intent," Thomas said mildly. "But whether he wills it or not, the Earl of Leicester is a magnet for all eyes. That, too, is a fact, Gilbert, one you'd best learn to live with, for any man who is linked with Leicester is bound to find himself standing in the Earl's shadow."

"Must I learn to live with his whelp, too?" Gloucester said, gesturing toward Harry. "Look at that fool!"

At first glance, the timber-framed house opposite St Peter's Church looked no different from its neighbors. But no soldier passed it without craning his neck, staring up at the woman framed in a window of the overhanging upper story. Theirs was a society in which fairness was idealized, and she had been graced with a remarkable shade of silver-blonde hair; it hung loose down her back, shimmered as the sun struck it, a gossamer cascade of light. Harry stopped his stallion so abruptly that the animal reared, pawing the air. Harry's hat was off in a gallant sweep; snatching the honeysuckle garland from his horse's neck, he held it aloft, and then sent it spiraling up through the window, into her outstretched hands.

The spectators applauded; the woman leaned out, crying, "Wait, my lord!" A moment later, she tossed an object from the window, something wrapped in homespun. Harry caught it deftly, grinned, and—to the disappointment of the crowd—tucked it away in his tunic before anyone could see the contents.

Bran at once spurred to his side; Gloucester and Thomas, no less curious, followed. Under their badgering, Harry laughed, gave them a glimpse of a large metal key. "Lord God," he said, casting his eyes skyward, "if I remember naught else in this life, let it be the location of that house!"

Bran and Thomas laughed, too; Gilbert de Clare did not. "This is a day of consequence," he said, "a day to herald the triumph of the Provisions, our victory over the King. It is bad enough that you demean it by chasing after whores without blaspheming, too."

Harry was enjoying himself enormously, too much so to take offense. He contented himself with a mock grimace. "Gilbert, how sour the grapes!"

Bran was shaking his head sorrowfully. "He is right, Harry. Your whoring is shameful." He glanced back at Gloucester, smiling. "But you must bear in mind, Gilbert, that not every man has been blessed with a wife like yours."

Most people would have taken Bran's comment as a pleasantry, indeed, as a compliment. To those in the know, it was a knife thrust under the ribs. Gloucester had been wed at the age of ten to one of Henry's de Lusignan nieces, and their mutual animosity was so pronounced, so notorious, that when the court learned of Alice de Clare's pregnancy, it was greeted with disbelief, hilarity, and a predictable spate of ribald jokes. Now Gloucester lost color so fast that his freckles seemed to take fire. Thomas kneed his mount, moving between his brother and Bran, not drawing an easy breath until Simon's sons passed on, quickening pace to catch up with their father.

Harry's expression was quizzical. "You do go for the vitals, lad. That barb of yours drew blood."

"I meant it to," Bran said. "Tom is a good sort, but Gilbert is an ass. I could stomach his hypocrisy if he were not also such a hothead."

"Yes," Harry agreed, "a pity he does not have your saintly temperament." He looked over at his brother, blue eyes agleam. "Alas, though, I thought you were defending my honor!"

"I do, Harry, all the time. You know I could never resist a lost cause," Bran said, and laughing, they spurred their horses, churning up clouds of thick, red dust, overtaking their father just as he turned into Cheapside.

Taking note of the rouge smearing Harry's cheek, Simon said, "I see you decided to ask for alms, after all."

Harry grinned, unabashed, then gave an exclamation of awe. Ahead of them waited half the city, or so it first seemed. Never had Harry seen so many people gathered in one place. Cheapside had so much open ground that jousts were held here; now the entire area was overflowing with exuberant Londoners. Staid merchants and matrons, cocky apprentices, ragged beggars, parish priests, garishly dressed prostitutes, nuns from St Helen's, minstrels and jugglers, shrieking children, pickpockets on the prowl, beaming craftsmen, Franciscan friars, coquettish young girls—all quarters of the city had turned out for his father. The scene—so colorful, congested, and tumultuous—put Harry in mind of paintings he'd seen of Judgment Day, when all should be summoned before God's Throne. Only the Jews were absent; in that vast crowd, there was not to be found even one of the white badges that Henry had decreed for every Jew above the age of seven. Although the Jewry lay just north of Cheapside, none of the inhabitants had been tempted by the victory procession. They knew better; in good times or bad, there was danger in being a Jew.

"Leicester, Leicester!" It was a rhythmic, pulsing chant, rising above the clamor of the bells, a wave that had been gaining momentum as they rode down Wood Street, cresting now in Cheapside, engulfing them in raw, surging sound. "My God, Papa," Bran gasped, "they'd make you King of London if they only could!"

Simon smiled, then shook his head. "No, lad. If London has an uncrowned King, there's the man." And he gestured toward the steps of St Mary-le-Bow, where a euphoric Thomas Fitz Thomas awaited them.

As Simon reined in his stallion, Fitz Thomas moved forward eagerly. "Had there only been time, my lord, we'd have been able to give you a truly memorable welcome. We'd have had pageants and white doves and conduits running with wine. But as I look about us, I can see that my Londoners have given you a gift of far greater value—their hearts."

"I'd heard that you had a way with words. I think we are fortunate, indeed, to have your eloquence harnessed on behalf of our cause. From here, we go to the Tower, to the King. This was your victory, too, Master Fitz Thomas. Have you a horse at hand?"

"By some strange chance . . ." Thomas Puleston was grinning broadly, leading forth two well-groomed palfreys, and Simon laughed.

"I ought to have known, Tom, that you'd never be caught unawares! Now . . . the King awaits us."

Fitz Thomas and Puleston quickly mounted, but the latter then said, "My lord," while giving the Mayor a nod, jerking his head toward the pillory across the road.

Fitz Thomas understood what the silent message meant, but still he hesitated. The men in the pillory looked utterly miserable. Bent forward from the waist, heads and hands locked into the wooden frame, they must be suffering, for not only was the position an acutely uncomfortable one, the weather had conspired to add to their woes; it was a particularly hot and humid afternoon. It was Fitz Thomas's hope that Simon would order them freed, for that was just the sort of dramatic, generous gesture sure to appeal to his Londoners. But he did not want anything to mar the mood of this day, and he suspected that Simon was not a man to muster much sympathy for lawbreakers. Puleston had insisted, however, that Simon would free the men, and gambling now on his friend's greater familiarity with the Earl, Fitz Thomas said loudly, "Those poor wretches! Think you, my lord, that they might be deserving of mercy on such a day?"

Simon glanced toward the pillory, then back at the Mayor. "On such a day, Master Fitz Thomas, all men deserve mercy," he said, setting

off another burst of cheering, for the urbane, cynical Londoners were
also capable of the most mawkish sentimentality.

Fitz Thomas paced his mount to Simon's stallion, experiencing a
moment such as few men were ever granted, one of pure and perfect
happiness. A soldier the Earl might be, the best in England he'd wager,
but he was not utterly lacking in political instincts. De Gisors was wrong;
they *were* allies in truth and in deed, together would make a new England. "This is how Adam must have felt," he said, "in the days ere
man's fall from grace, when there were no boundaries, only penny-
bright possibilities."

Simon gave him a sideways smile. "You'd best bear in mind," he
said, "that there are snakes in our Eden, too, Master Fitz Thomas."

Fitz Thomas laughed, not in the least deceived by Simon's skepticism, for as their eyes met, he was swept with certainty, an instinctive
awareness beyond refuting, that the Earl of Leicester shared his dreams
for England, that Simon, too, saw this day as a new beginning.

ARRIVING at the Tower, they found Henry awaiting them in the great
hall. Flanked by his Queen and brother Richard, he looked haggard,
even unwell. As Simon and the Earl of Gloucester knelt before him,
Simon was startled by how much Henry had aged in the months since
their last encounter. In stark contrast to the wan, dispirited Henry, his
Queen glowed with vivid, defiant color. Her cheeks flamed, her throat
glittered with jewels, and her gown was a deliberately dramatic crimson,
as red as blood. When Simon kissed her hand, those elegant, ringed
fingers twitched, clenched involuntarily. She would, he thought, nail
her flag to the mast ere she'd run it down.

"My liege," he said. "There is much for us to discuss: the justi-
ciarship, the appointment of guardians of the peace, the removal of
foreign garrisons from royal castles, and your son Edward's refusal to
yield Windsor Castle. Will it be convenient for Your Grace to meet with
us on the morrow?"

"And if it is not?" But Henry's flare of temper was fleeting; it lacked
fire, even conviction. "On the morrow," he agreed listlessly. "Now I
am tired, my lords. I wish to retire to my private chambers."

Eleanor gave Simon a look that all but scorched the air. "I trust that
meets with your approval, my lord of Leicester?"

Simon deflected the sarcasm with silence, and Eleanor took her husband's arm. They turned away, rather pointedly snubbing the Mayor, who
seemed to shrug off their rudeness with equanimity. Gloucester shouted
after them, "We'll also be discussing my estates. I'm sure Your Grace

has reconsidered, that you're now willing to give me seisin of my lands!"

Richard had not accompanied his brother. Moving toward Simon, he said quietly, "I should like to thank you for all your efforts on my son's behalf."

"I was glad that I could be of assistance. It is my understanding that, due to the French King's intercession, Hal is soon to be freed?"

Richard nodded. "God be praised," he said, and then, "Simon, it ought never to have come to this."

"Your brother gave me no choice," Simon said coolly.

"I'll not deny that Henry made mistakes, more than his share. But I doubt that you are as blameless as you seem to think."

Simon said nothing, and Richard turned, slowly followed after Henry. With the departure of the King and Queen, the atmosphere in the hall changed dramatically, the mood becoming festive. Wine began to flow freely; there was much bantering and raucous horseplay among the younger knights. Simon let them have their fun, uncharacteristically indulgent, while he shared a flagon of malmsey with Peter de Montfort and Hugh le Despenser, who'd served as Justiciar in those heady days following the adoption of the Provisions, only to be dismissed by Henry as soon as the opportunity arose.

"You did it, Simon," Hugh exulted. "By God, you did it!"

"So it seems," Simon agreed, somewhat absently, for his attention was focused across the hall, upon the boisterous Marcher lords. "I would that I could truly trust them," he confessed, "but they are a faithless breed. I keep remembering Roger de Mortimer, who swore with such passion to uphold the Provisions—until the Crown made it worth his while to switch sides."

Neither Peter nor Hugh disputed him; the Marcher lords had never been known for constancy. "What think you of Gloucester, Simon?"

"I think he's of finer mettle than the Marchers, Peter, but Christ, he's green, badly in need of seasoning." Simon frowned, for the Earl of Derby was now sprawled in Henry's chair of state, a needless provocation. But this was a day for rejoicing, not rebukes. Catching a servant's eyes, Simon ordered writing materials, then beckoned to one of his squires.

"Ranulf, find me a courier, a man I can trust. He is to leave within the hour for Kenilworth. Tell him the letter is to be given only into the hands of my Countess. Tell him, too, not to tarry."

Peter and Hugh having tactfully withdrawn, Simon sat for a time looking upon the jubilant pandemonium that rocked the hall. His sons were in the very midst of it, celebrating noisily. As he watched, Harry and Bran began to toss a wineskin back and forth, as if it were a pig's bladder football, shouting with laughter when the inevitable happened and it sprayed all within range. Simon smiled in spite of himself, then picked up a quill pen.

"To my dearest wife, greetings." He was already envisioning Nell's response. She'd impatiently break the seal, scan the letter rapidly for the heart of the message, and only then would she go back to the beginning, study it with care—if the news was good. It was the way she always read letters; he knew her habits as well as he did his own. How she would have enjoyed this day, even the noise and confusion and crowding. She so loved pageantry and spectacles, would have reveled in it all. He paused, then put the pen again to the parchment.

"Beloved," he wrote, "we have won."

28

London, England

October 1263

Hal had not removed his mantle; as he spoke, his hands kept fiddling with the clasp. So tense was he that when the pin pricked his thumb, he did not even notice the trickle of blood. Those who knew Hal best sometimes joked that he must be a foundling, so lacking was he in the volatile Plantagenet temperament. He was by nature placid, eager to please, and now his distress was genuine. There was entreaty in the look he directed toward the silent witnesses: his aunt Nell, his de Montfort cousins, the Bishop of Worcester, Peter de Montfort, the Mayor of London. He encountered no understanding, though, only mute accusations.

"Uncle Simon . . ." For it was Simon whose approval mattered, Simon who could reward with a smile, sear with a glance, Simon whose eyes had taken on the color of smoke, the glaze of ice.

"I thought you truly believed in the need for reform, Hal."

Hal flinched; his uncle's voice was low, yet crackled with intensity, with barely suppressed outrage. He was suddenly very grateful that his cousin Ned had offered to come with him. "I do, Uncle," he said plaintively, "I do! But this estrangement is breaking my father's heart!"

If he'd hoped to gain Simon's sympathy, he should have known better. Simon's eyes moved past him dismissively, focusing instead upon the man leaning against the door.

"You're becoming quite adroit at fishing in troubled waters, Edward. Lest it go to your head, you might do well to remember that some fish will snap at any hook, take any bait."

Edward smiled coolly, saying nothing, but color flooded Hal's face. "Uncle, that is unfair! Ned did not buy my support!"

Simon's smile was no less sardonic than Edward's. It was Bran who said, with high indignation, "And what of Tickhill? Ned's manor, now yours!"

"I admit Ned gave me Tickhill, but that is not why I heeded him . . ." Hal faltered, for he could find on their faces nothing but disbelief. Mustering what dignity he could, he said, "I cannot forsake my father, but this I promise you, Uncle, that I'll not bear arms against you."

"How very reassuring," Simon said, so sarcastically that Hal flushed anew. Too hurt to hide it, he turned on his heel, bumping into Edward in his haste to escape the chamber.

"God keep you, Aunt Nell." Edward included Harry and Bran in his farewell, while pointedly ignoring Guy. Opening the door to follow Hal, he paused. "I have some advice for you," he said, in an altogether different tone, one overlaid with unmistakable menace. But the warning was not directed at Simon; he was staring at Thomas Fitz Thomas. "Do not stand again for Mayor. Even if you win, it will avail you naught, for my lord father will dispatch a royal writ to the Exchequer, forbidding them to admit you to office."

Fitz Thomas had heard that Edward now harbored an embittered grudge against Londoners, blaming the innocent and guilty alike for what had befallen his mother at the bridge. But Fitz Thomas had not known that he was to bear the brunt of Edward's hostility. It was a sobering thought, the realization that he must count the King's son as his enemy.

"Does Henry plan to issue a writ forbidding the winter snows, too?" Simon inquired, and Edward swung around, Fitz Thomas forgotten.

"My father is England's King, whilst you, Uncle, are but a failed rebel. It is over for you, Simon; do you not know that yet? You had your moment in the sun—your entry into London—but your support has begun to bleed away. By Christmas, you'll stand alone, utterly alone."

"The Earl of Leicester holds London, my lord," Fitz Thomas said, and Edward laughed.

"You have just proved my point, Master Fitz Thomas. These are the only allies you have left, Simon—lowborn fishmongers and blacksmiths and beggars. But mayhap you can convert a few Jews." Still laughing, he turned, sauntered without haste from the chamber.

No sooner had he gone than Simon's sons exchanged glances, moved with conspicuous nonchalance toward the door. Nell tensed, but then she saw Peter rise, too, slip silently after them. Fitz Thomas was bending over her hand, taking his leave; she gave him the smile meant for Peter.

"Master Fitz Thomas." The Mayor stopped, glanced back over his shoulder, and Simon said, "Do you plan to stand for reelection?"

"Of course," Fitz Thomas said, closing the door quietly behind him.

Simon's tenuous control of his temper lasted until Fitz Thomas's departure, but not a moment more. "Christ Jesus," he exploded, "never have I known men so fickle, men whose words mean so little! Hal's betrayal ought not to have surprised me, for I've lost count of the Marcher lords who've been bought by Edward. So much for allies of high birth! Look at your cousin, Nell, look at de Warenne. He boasts the best blood in England, yet he swings like a weathercock in a high wind, first supporting the de Lusignans, then endorsing the Provisions, and now . . . Damn him if he's not let Edward befool him again, just like Hal!"

"I know, love," Nell commiserated, no less indignant than Simon. "Hal's ingratitude is unforgivable. He'd still be languishing in French captivity if not for you!"

The Bishop of Worcester had yet to move. Cloaked in shadow, he sat, unobtrusive, observant, for he had a gift for stillness that even a cat might envy, a heavy-lidded gaze that missed little. He was living, breathing proof of the deceptiveness of outer packaging, for he was squat, barrel-chested, jowled and florid, looking like the very reincarnation of the merry, wine-swilling monk of popular folklore. But his appearance could not have been more misleading. He was in reality an ascetic and an intellectual, austerely pious yet intensely ambitious, one who adhered to a rigid code of honor, a man either blessed or cursed with an analytical eye, a distaste for sentiment. He had never learned to value humor, or he might have appreciated the irony inherent in his friendship with Simon, Simon who was impulsive and outspoken and often reckless, all traits the Bishop earnestly deplored.

He waited, rather impatiently, for Simon's anger to run its course, and then said, "There was some truth to Edward's boasting. Simon, your position is more perilous than you seem willing to admit."

"Simon does not lack for support! It is not just the Londoners who have rallied to him. The other towns, the Oxford students, the Franciscans, even the parish priests—"

"What you say is correct, Madame. Your husband is held in great esteem by those you've just named. Unfortunately for him, for us all, that is not true for the men of his own class . . . and therein lies the danger. When the Provisions were first adopted, the barons were united in opposition to Henry. Now . . . now that is no longer so. They still resent Henry's follies, scorn his weaknesses, but they are not following us down this road. You've scared them, Simon. Your peers do not share your zeal for reform. They never did."

"I do not believe that," Simon said sharply, and the Bishop shook his head.

"You do not want to believe it. The fact is, Simon, most men prefer the devil they know . . . even feckless, hapless Henry. The King, God save him."

"He is my King, too, Walter. I do not seek to depose him!"

"No . . . but you would rein him in, curb his more lunatic whims, by force if need be, make him answerable to his council. You'd even hold parliament without him. Ah, Simon, do you not see? You'd take us down a road dark and unfamiliar, with no map, no lanterns, no known landmarks. Little wonder men balk! For such a journey as that, you'll need every ally you can get. The support of Londoners and university students will not be enough. You'll need men of high birth, men of wealth and renown."

"You mean Gloucester."

"Yes . . . Gloucester. He is the linchpin of our cause, for without his backing, the Provisions are bound to fail. But already he is shying away, and you do nothing to hold him fast. To the contrary, you—"

"What would you have me do? He lacks seasoning, bristles if any man even looks at him askance. Is it my fault that he takes offense at shadows?"

"I grant you he is no easy ally: too thin-skinned, too prideful, and so jealous of you that he's like to sicken on it. But he does believe in the Provisions, Simon. If you would but play to his pride, take him into your confidence . . . and put an end to his foolish feuding with your sons. There's bad blood between them, and when you seized John Mansel's lands, gave them over to Bran—"

"What of it? Why should I not make provisions for Bran?"

Nell was no less quick to chime in. "Have you forgotten that Bran is a second son? Simon's title and the bulk of our estates will pass to Harry. But Bran and his brothers must be taken care of, too."

They stared defiantly at Bishop Walter, in this utterly united, as they were in most things, and he knew it was useless to argue propriety or political acumen. With Simon and Nell, discretion would never take precedence over the protective passion of parent for child. "I tell you only that it would have been better had you bestowed the lands elsewhere; at the least, you ought to have consulted Gloucester ere you made the grant. If you would but indulge Gloucester's crotchets, seek to gain his good will—"

"I am his ally, not his wet-nurse, Walter. Your young lordling has passed twenty winters, is old enough to know his own mind. If he believes in the Provisions, he will defend them. If he does not, all the pampering under God's sky will not avail."

The Bishop rose from the shadows, made a strategic withdrawal, knowing full well that Simon would balk if pushed. Simon had risen, too. Nell watched as he paced the chamber, to the window, back to the hearth, to the window again. She could take pleasure—even at such a moment—in his quick, sure step. She had never known a man so at ease in his own body; even on those rare occasions when he'd had too much wine, he was not clumsy, never awkward in his movements. It was Nell's private conviction that Simon had been singularly blessed, and not just with a cat's grace. In the twenty-five years that they'd been married, only twice had he been laid low with a raging fever; so infrequently did he suffer from headaches or hacking coughs or even the inevitable winter colds that Nell sometimes resented his apparent immunity to the disagreeable afflictions that vexed the rest of mankind. And now he seemed no less impervious to aging.

He would be fifty-five in December, but his energy still burned at full flame; he could outride men half his age, and, to Nell's secret satisfaction, he looked years younger than either of her brothers. Unlike Richard, whose hairline had begun to recede while he was in his forties, or Henry, whose bald spot perfectly resembled a monk's tonsure, Simon's hair was still thick and luxuriant, if no longer the color of ink. Even before he'd reached fifty, it had begun to whiten, was now the purest shade of snow, much to Nell's delight. On those days when he was not infuriating her with his obstinacy, she counted herself very lucky, indeed, that her husband was still so pleasing to her eyes. But if there was an erotic shading to her thoughts, there was also an underlying sense of unease.

"Simon . . . have you given any thought to returning to France?"

"Yes," he said, surprising her by how readily he made that admission. "Of course I have. But it would be confessing defeat, Nell, would be an acknowledgment that Henry had won. The moment my ship raised anchor, he'd revoke the Provisions; we both know that. If I leave England, we lose any chance for reform, and place all we have in jeopardy. As soon as he dared, Henry would declare our lands forfeit. If war does come, I would rather we fought over the Provisions than over Kenilworth."

"Is that what you see ahead of us, Simon . . . war?"

"All too often," he conceded. He was back at the window; it was set with costly glass panes, for the Bishop of Durham did not believe man must mortify the flesh to find salvation. An early October dusk was settling over the city; lantern lights flickered like floating fireflies as river boats passed the Bishop's dock. Simon watched in silence for a time. " 'Fishmongers and blacksmiths and beggars,' was that what Edward called them? They may be men of low birth, of humble trades, but they do not lack for courage. Their support for the Provisions—for me— could cost them dear. I cannot forsake them, Nell." He turned as she reached his side, saying, "Can you understand?"

She nodded, and he slid his arm around her waist. "I've always been so sure," he said, "so certain of tomorrow. I always felt confident that I knew what God wanted of me. But now . . ."

She'd often teased him about that very certainty, pointing out that his will and God's Will seemed to coincide more often than not. But she could find no humor in this unexpected confession of doubt. "Hold me close," she said. "I feel so cold of a sudden."

THE October parliament broke up in rancorous disarray, hopelessly dead-locked over the issue of whether Henry should have the sole right to appoint officers of his household. As the Londoners rashly defied the King by re-electing Thomas Fitz Thomas by acclamation, Henry and Edward withdrew to Windsor, Simon to Kenilworth, and a tentative truce was worked out. But it lasted only until December, when Henry suddenly marched on Dover Castle. He was denied entry by the con-stable, and Simon hastened south with a small force. Reaching London by the first week of Advent, he encamped with his men across the river at Southwark and dispatched scouts to track the whereabouts of the royal army. A disquieting lull followed, what all knew to be a counterfeit peace.

THE weather had been rainy and unseasonably mild, but the temperature plunged suddenly on the night of December 10, and Londoners awoke in the morning to a world of frozen, foreboding beauty. Icicles adorned the eaves of every roof, festooned the branches of barren trees, sheathed ale-stakes and shop signs, spangling the city in a shimmering, trans-lucent glaze. The streets glittered in the greying dawn, powdered with snow, ice-encrusted. The air was crystalline, too, the sky the color of polished pearl, streaked with light wherever the sun sought to break through. It was a day for awe, not for travel; under cover of darkness, nature had contrived a dazzling December panorama, but man ventured into this frigid tableau at his own risk.

And yet John de Gisors, a man accustomed to sleeping late, a man whose age and wealth demanded self-indulgence, now stood shivering on a wind-whipped street within sight of the bridge. It was dubious consolation that his companions looked no less discomfited; like him, they were finding the suspense as penetrating as the cold. Augustine de Hadestok had lost his bluster. Richard Picard seemed uncommonly subdued, too. Only Stephen de Chelmsford's smile was spontaneous, for he burned with a young man's passion, undimmed by the chill, the early hour, any belated doubts.

John de Gisors was not plagued with last-minute regrets, for he was convinced that his own interests, his city's future, and his King's welfare could best be served by the death of Simon de Montfort. Yet it was unnerving, nonetheless, to be so close to fruition, poised as they were between planning and performance. At last he saw Adam running toward them. If he had a surname, de Gisors never knew it; what he did know was that this Adam was a seasoned soldier, a man willing to take great risks for the right price, a man as capable as he was cocky, to judge by his triumphant grin.

"It's done," Adam announced, only a little out of breath. "The guards were sleeping. Taking the bridge was almost too easy, no fun at all!" He held up a large metal key. "This opens the gatehouse. Without it, no man can lower the drawbridge." He balanced the key tantalizingly for a moment, then flipped it through the air. John de Gisors nearly fumbled the catch, clutching the key awkwardly to his chest as Augustine de Hadestok demanded edgily:

"But others have keys to the gatehouse; the Mayor for certes, the sheriffs, mayhap that whoreson Puleston now that he's been elected constable—"

"Make yourself easy, friend." There was genuine amusement in Adam's smile, and affable contempt. "We're a half-mile ahead of you. The door of the gatehouse has been chained shut and locked . . . with this," he said, producing a second key.

"I'll take that," John de Gisors said swiftly, thinking it advisable to reassert their authority over this insolent hireling. "Are you sure your men can hold the bridge?"

"You'd best hope so," Adam drawled, the sound of his laughter floating back to them as he began to retrace his steps, moving at a provocatively leisured pace.

They watched him go in silence, as if stunned by their own success. De Gisors gave an audible sigh, echoing Adam's boastful "It's done," but with far more fervor. "Even as we speak," he assured his accomplices, "the King is leading an army from Croydon, whilst the Lord Edward approaches from Merton. By the time de Montfort realizes his peril, it will be too late. With the bridge closed to him, he'll be trapped between the river and the royal army. God willing, this shall be a day we'll long remember—Thomas Fitz Thomas most of all!"

SIMON had chosen to quarter his men in Southwark partly for safety's sake, London offering a handy retreat should the need arise, and partly for convenience, Southwark having enough open space to accommodate an army encampment. But Simon had not taken into account the tempting proximity of the Southwark stews. Few soldiers could resist the lure of the bankside bordellos, and Simon suspected that most of his men had been sampling the hospitality of the Southwark whores. For certes neither of his sons had abstained; on his way to Mass at St Mary Overie, Simon had encountered Bran and Guy, just returning to camp, bleary-eyed and disheveled.

Simon could summon up no sympathy for their morning-after malaise, never having suffered a hangover himself. During Mass, a time when his thoughts should be turning only to God, he could not help brooding about their constant carousing. As impatient as he was with his own weaknesses, the foibles of other men, he'd always found a wealth of forbearance for the shortcomings of his sons. So proud was he of their courage, their high spirits, their impassioned loyalty, that it had been easy to indulge them, to overlook their lack of prudence, to excuse their skylarking, their tempers. Even their whoring and hell-raising could be shrugged off as the inevitable folly of youth—at first.

But Simon's tolerance was beginning to wear thin. They were no longer raw striplings; Harry was twenty-five, Bran twenty-three, and Guy twenty-one, men grown by any standard, even a permissive parent's. Just how reliable were they? A question not even love could deflect, a question he could deny but not—in all honesty—answer.

"My lord." Simon's anger at being interrupted at prayer died away as soon as he recognized the intruder. He rose without a word; so did his companions. Under the curious eyes of the congregation, they followed Simon's scout from the church.

Their squires had anticipated trouble; the horses were waiting. Turning to face Simon, the scout blurted out his news in one gulped breath. "My lord, you are in grave danger. I kept watch on the Lord Edward's camp at Merton, as you ordered, and early this morn he bestirred his men, took the road north—toward London. Once I realized his intent, I did not spare my mount, but he is not that far behind me, and Merton is eight . . . nine miles away at most."

Simon did not bother to ask if Edward's army outnumbered his own, taking that as a given, for he had less than a hundred men, and only twenty or so were knights; he'd been awaiting reinforcements. "You've done well," he said, with a smile that brought a pleased flush to the youth's face, then swung up into the saddle. While he was not particularly alarmed, there was no time to tarry.

Upon their return to their bankside encampment, they found a scene of considerable commotion. Even the most drink-sodden of the soldiers were no longer abed. The tents stood empty, while men mulled about in loud, quarrelsome confusion. At sight of Simon, they surged toward him in obvious relief, all talking at once. Simon finally got a coherent account from Guy and the young Earl of Derby. The latter looked even worse than Simon's sons, greensick from too much ale, not enough sleep, but he was wide awake now, and once Simon heard his news, he understood why; he could think of no greater stimulant than an approaching army.

This latest warning came not from one of Simon's scouts, but from a farmer sympathetic to Simon's cause. He swore that Henry had left Croydon at dawn, leading a goodly sized force up the London road.

Simon's smile was wry. "Passing strange, for it seems that Edward also plans to come calling on us. A pity they shall ride all this way in vain, but of a sudden I have a great desire to spend the day in London!"

The men laughed, and without waiting for orders, scattered toward their tents, snatching up what belongings they could. The atmosphere in the camp had dramatically altered; an air of edgy excitement prevailed, the satisfaction of a fox about to outwit the hounds.

Simon's jesting had set their mood, but Simon himself did not share in it, for he knew at once that this ambush was Edward's doing. It was too well coordinated for Henry to have devised; Henry couldn't spring a mouse-trap without catching his own fingers. No, God curse him, this was Edward's snare. But would he rely so utterly on surprise? For certes, he must have realized that, given the least warning, they'd seek safety in London. Or had he found a way to thwart their escape?

As unsettling as that suspicion was, in consequence, Simon alone felt no surprise when they reached the bridge; he was already half-braced for disaster. A crowd had gathered before the stone gateway: baffled pedestrians, curious passers-by, and frustrated tradesmen. Seeing an armor-clad knight on horseback, a man shouted to Simon, "My lord, can you help? Those misbegotten guards must be drunk, for it's well past dawn and they've yet to lower the drawbridge!"

Peter de Montfort rode at Simon's side; he clearly heard Peter's gasp, the sound a man might make if suddenly hit in the pit of his stomach. Urging his stallion forward, Simon forced his way through the crowd, under the stone gateway, onto the bridge. The drawbridge gate rose above the seventh arch, barricaded, beyond reach. Once Adam's gatehouse guards recognized Simon, they began to call down taunts, but he never heard them. As his stallion moved restively, Simon sat motionless, staring at the gap in the bridge, at that expanse of turbulent, grey water. And then he turned the horse, rode back to his men.

They were close enough to see the church spire of St Mary Overie; the priory was a quarter-mile to the west, and it was there that Simon led them. When he drew rein in a snow-sheltered grove, he found himself looking, not at the encircling ashen faces, but at the glazed December sky, as brittle a blue as he'd ever seen, a color fired on a potter's wheel. The sun had scattered the last lingering clouds. Although it had yet to warm the frigid morning air, it rendered the snow iridescent; the glistening field looked as if it had been paved with moonstones. So quiet had it become that Simon could hear an occasional snap, as icicles began to break away from swaying tree branches, to shatter upon the frozen earth below. So great was his sense of disbelief that it blocked all fear. Even knowing as he did that there could be but one outcome to such a one-sided battle, he found it impossible to conclude that God had been leading him to this moment. How could it be his destiny to die here, in these snow-clogged Southwark streets? How could the Almighty forsake him, when the Provisions could not survive him?

"Gather close so all might hear." His breath froze as soon as it reached the air, interspersing his words with wisps of white smoke. "We cannot hope to assault the bridge. Nor can we retreat in time. By now Edward's army must be within a few miles of Southwark, and the King's army cannot be far behind. But some of you can still save yourselves. With luck, a man alone may elude pursuit. For those of you who would attempt an escape, go now and godspeed. For those of you who choose to fight, I will not lie to you; we are greatly outnumbered. I can say to you only what the Almighty said to Joshua: 'Be not afraid, neither be thou dismayed, for the Lord thy God is with thee.' "

Mingling with his men were black-clad canons from the priory and frightened citizens of Southwark. With the realization that they were about to face the wrath of Edward's army, they panicked and began to stream away in all directions, intent upon hiding themselves, their loved ones, and their possessions. But Simon's soldiers heard him out in a dazed silence. Some, avoiding the eyes of their fellows, began to back away. Others closed ranks. None seemed to feel the need for words; flee or fight, it was done in eerie quiet.

Simon had risen in his stirrups so his voice might carry. Now he settled back in the saddle, but as he drew air into his lungs, he felt as if its chill had penetrated to the very marrow of his bones, for his eyes

had come to rest upon the white, stunned faces of his sons. Fear congealed his brain, his blood. Dismounting so hastily that his horse shied
sideways, he grasped Bran by the arm.

"I want you both gone from here. Now, whilst there is still time!"

"No!" Bran was shaking his head vehemently. "No, Papa. Not
without you."

"I cannot," Simon said, "I cannot," and his sons nodded slowly,
having expected no other answer.

"Neither can we, Papa."

Simon's protest died aborning. How could he deny them the right
to die with honor? It was a man's choice to make. He looked from one
to the other, feeling such pride in them, such fear for them, that words
failed him. He wanted nothing so much as to embrace them both, to
hold them close. But he'd never been demonstrative; a lifetime of constraint froze him where he was, unable to take that first step. Harry
would have taken it; he alone of Simon's sons was joyously, almost
defiantly, expressive in his affections. But Bran and Guy had learned
too well to reflect their father's reticence; when speaking the language
of emotion, they were mute.

Unable to act upon their need, it was almost with relief that they
heard Simon's name being shouted. A rider had entered the priory
grounds, reining in his mount a safe distance away. "I seek the Earl of
Leicester!" As Simon stepped forward, he declared loudly, "I come at
the behest of the Lord Edward, the King's son. He accuses you of treason, demands that you make an immediate and outright surrender."

"No."

Edward's messenger waited for Simon to elaborate upon that terse
refusal. When he realized that Simon had said all he meant to say, he
colored angrily, as if Simon's curt dismissal somehow reflected upon
him. "I hope you are ready to die, then, for you'll get no second chance
from my lord. None of you will." He raised his voice. "You fools! You're
dead men, all of you!"

Bran had been gripping his sword hilt so tightly that his fingers
were numbed. He noticed now that the courier flaunted the badge of
William de Lusignan, Henry's most hated half-brother, his family's blood-
enemy. The realization that de Lusignan might be in on his father's
death sent the blood thudding into Bran's face. Spinning around, he
scooped up a handful of snow. The snowball made a surprisingly effective missile; crusted with ice, it slammed into the man's open mouth.
He choked, reeling backward in the saddle, and Bran felt a hot rush of
pleasure to see the sudden spurt of red.

"You whoreson, you knocked out a tooth!" But he had time only
for one outraged sputter, for others were now scrabbling in the snow,

too. Within seconds, the air was thick with flying snowballs. The besieged rider struggled desperately to control his terrified mount, but the horse had the bit between its teeth. It bolted across the field, the courier clinging for dear life, leaving behind his hat, his wineskin, and a trail of garbled curses.

The sight was ludicrous enough to bring a smile to Simon's face. All around him, men were gesturing, grinning, as if they'd won a victory of sorts. He gave them a moment more, then raised his hand for silence. "This is God's acre, no fit site for a battle. We'd best withdraw, lest we bring bloodshed into the priory. But ere we do, I would urge all who mean to fight to take the cross. We know Our Lord Jesus looks with favor upon those who offer up their lives for the holy city of Jerusalem. To die for England's weal is no less hallowed a quest."

The Church might have questioned Simon's theology; his men did not. It was as if he had made them a personal promise of salvation, and they made haste to follow his example. Bran, too, knelt in the snow, marveling at his father's sangfroid. None of this seemed real to him. He had a hole in the sole of his boot, and his toes were growing numb. How could he be fretting over a frozen foot when his life's breath was ebbing away on the icy December air? He shivered, and seeing that the others were rising, he rose, too. What if they did die this Tuesday? What would become of Mama and Ellen? Harry was safe at Kenilworth—Guy always said he was the lucky one—but could he fulfill Papa's legacy? Could any man? No, this was madness! Papa could not lose to Ned. God would not allow it.

It occurred to Bran that it might be prudent to offer up a prayer to the saint whose good will mattered most on the 11th of December, but he was unable to remember whose saint's day this was. He looked around for Guy. "Today's saint—who is it?"

Guy shook his head. "Who cares? Listen, Bran, listen!"

Bran heard it, too, now, the distant pealing of bells. For the echoes to carry so clearly across the river, every church bell in London must be chiming wildly. "What does it mean?" he asked, and Guy grinned.

"Salvation, I think! Papa, the bells!"

Never had Simon heard a sweeter sound. His hesitation lasted only the length of an indrawn breath. If he guessed wrong, he'd be sacrificing their last shards of hope, for if they were trapped in the close confines of the bridge, they'd be hacked to death with appalling ease. But if he guessed right . . . The command was already forming on his lips. "Back to the bridge!"

The street was deserted; it was as if Southwark had suddenly become a plague town. But a handful of intrepid youths were clustered at the stone gate. Several ran toward Simon, gesturing. "The bridge is under attack! We can hear the screaming, saw one man pushed into the river!"

Simon spurred his stallion onto the bridge. He, too, could now hear the sounds of strife, too familiar to mistake. The Earl of Derby and Peter de Montfort had followed. They drew rein, staring up at the drawbridge gate in wonder. "Fitz Thomas?" Peter ventured, and Simon nodded.

"Or mayhap Puleston. But for the life of me, Peter, I cannot see how they assembled a force so fast!"

There was another splash, as a second man plunged from the bridge railing. The shouting had changed, taking on a rhythmic tempo, one that carried echoes of triumph. Above the cheering a new sound intruded, a metallic clanging. Simon knew it at once for what it was. In his mind's eye, he could see the axe smashing into the rope of chains, each blow ringing in his ears with such a lilting resonance that he gave a sudden, shaken laugh. "When men talk of the silver-toned harps of Heaven, Peter, I can say in all truth that I've heard them already—on the Southwark side of London's bridge!"

Behind him, Simon heard his men give a jubilant shout. He tilted his head back, watching as the drawbridge started its slow descent. There was a brief, frozen pause after it touched down, a second or so of silence. And then, utter madness. As Londoners spilled out onto the drawbridge, Simon's soldiers sprinted toward safety, and he was engulfed in a surging mob. His stallion panicked and for a few hectic moments, he was in peril from his would-be rescuers. Hurriedly dismounting, he found himself overwhelmed by well-wishers, surrounded by strangers who welcomed him as joyously as if they were all blood-kin, and Simon, a man accustomed to keeping others at arm's length, gave himself up readily to this tumultuous tide of raw emotion, to the simple and heartfelt happiness of deliverance.

All around him was chaos. Men were embracing, pounding one another on the back, voices spiraling skyward in a discordant babel of English and French. Soldiers, Londoners, and Southwark refugees mingled as one in a crowd interspersed with a surprising number of women and children, eager spectators to the storming of the bridge. There was a growing contingent of prostitutes, those young women feeling shrewdly certain that they'd find a hot demand for their services among men so recently reprieved from death. It was, Simon thought, like every fair he'd ever attended, every pageant he'd ever witnessed, as exultant as Christmas Christ-Child plays, as raucous as Southwark tavern brawls and Smithfield bear baitings—all magnified a hundredfold.

"I hope someone remembered to raise the drawbridge," Simon said, and as those around him laughed, he saw a familiar figure shoving his way toward him. Thomas Fitz Thomas wore a borrowed mantle, no hat, and the world's widest grin. But when Simon said, "We owe you our lives," he shook his head.

"Nay, my lord. I'd claim the credit if I could, but this was not my doing. Oh, there was a witness with the mother-wit to fetch me, and I at once sent for Thomas Puleston and the sheriffs, then made haste for the bridge." He grinned again, gesturing toward the cloak that trailed almost to the ground. "I even forgot my own mantle! But by the time I got here, it was already happening. As word spread of your peril, men took to the streets, emptying churches, ale-houses, city shops. Your foes never bargained for that, my lord. So many men responded to the hue and cry that those defending the drawbridge were overwhelmed by sheer numbers. Their leader was taken alive, readily offered up the names of his patrons—merchants of good repute, I regret to say. At least I am attracting a better class of enemies these days!"

"And I am attracting a better class of allies," Simon said with a smile. "Let's get off this accursed bridge. I want to speak to your citizens."

Fitz Thomas nodded approvingly, following Simon toward the Fish Street entrance. Heading for a nearby wagon, Simon used a wheel spoke as a step, swinging up onto the seat with an agility that the younger Fitz Thomas envied. Scrambling up, he said, "Shall I act as your interpreter, my lord?"

"No need, Tom," Simon said, pleasing the Mayor by this first use of his Christian name. "If I had not learned some of your language after thirty years in England, I'd have to be half-witted, in truth!"

"King Henry speaks no English," Fitz Thomas pointed out, with a malicious flash of lèse majesté that Simon felt fully warranted under the circumstances. He laughed, then raised his voice in a plea for silence. He was soon heeded; the crowd had followed him off the bridge, thronging around the wagon, eager to hear. "You saved my life," Simon declared, "and the lives of my sons, the lives of my men. But you did more than that this day. You performed a service for all of England, for you redeemed the Provisions." He paused until the cheering died down, then began to repeat himself for the English speakers. It mattered not at all to those listening that he had a pronounced French accent; they cheered even more loudly.

There was a stir on the fringes of the crowd; heads were turning. As people recognized Thomas Puleston, the realization spread that the men being herded forward by the militia were those responsible for blockading the bridge. Puleston's prisoners found themselves jeered and jostled, elbowed and shoved, spat upon and cursed. When a jokester voiced the opinion that they should be hanged from the drawbridge, his gallows humor was greeted with morbid relish, sardonic laughter.

But some took the sarcasm seriously enough to put the prisoners in sudden peril. After one hothead produced a rope, Thomas Fitz Thomas took alarm, and started to jump off the wagon. Simon was even quicker. "Bring them here!"

John de Gisors and his accomplices were dragged forward. Falling to his knees before the wagon, he grasped a wheel spoke, pulled himself upright. Although very frightened, he was determined to hold on to his dignity. He thought he could detect pity in the Mayor's face, but as he gazed up at Simon, he realized just how far Edward had led him astray. Simon had been willing to die for principle—or for pride; he wasn't sure which. He did not doubt that Edward, too, would have faced death with equal fortitude. They were a different breed than he, capable of a doomed gallantry that he could not hope to understand, much less emulate. He was not meant to play a paladin's role; why had he not seen that? The praises of the King suddenly seemed cheap payment, a fool's lure. But pleading would be a waste of breath. He remembered too well those stories of Simon's Gascony command; not even Simon's most fervent admirers ever claimed mercy to be the cornerstone of his character. His eyes were very grey, very clear, and so penetrating that de Gisors could not suppress an involuntary shiver.

"So this is the King's cat's-paw. A well-fed cat, in truth, one not likely to have ever missed a meal." Simon was studying de Gisors, but speaking to the spectators. As laughter rippled through the crowd, he continued his insulting appraisal of the portly merchant. "So what do we have? A hero who pays other men to bleed on his behalf, who wants to reap the benefits without the risk. I grant you that Sir Stoutheart would make a truly superior corpse. But he'd make an even better hostage."

His blending of practicality and poetic justice appealed to the Londoners. So did Fitz Thomas's subsequent suggestion that de Gisors and the others be forced to contribute a princely sum toward the city's defenses. No one made serious objections as the militia led the prisoners away. But neither did anyone move to disperse. There was a dawning awareness that what had happened here this day was of historic significance, and people were reluctant to return to interrupted chores, to resume ordinary activities, to relinquish the star-dusted satisfaction of the moment.

Simon, too, was loath to break the spell. Standing on the wagon, he looked out over the upturned faces, men whose names he'd never know, and he felt certain that God's Will had prevailed. A sudden swirl of scarlet and silver attracted his attention. He turned in time to see Bran flourishing the de Montfort banner aloft.

"Guy and I are going to fly it from the drawbridge gatehouse," Bran called out. "Let this be the first sight Ned sees!"

Taking the wind, the banner unfurled, streaming out behind Bran in a rippling surge of eye-catching color. As Simon watched, he began to laugh. "I was just wondering," he said to Fitz Thomas, "what Edward thinks of my 'lowborn' London allies now!"

29

Northamptonshire, England

December 1263

O N the very day that Edward failed to entrap Simon on the banks of the Thames, French envoys were landing at Dover, bearing a significant message from the King of France. When the October parliament had broken up in turmoil, Henry and Simon had sought to end the deadlock by appealing to Louis, urging him to arbitrate between them, to reconcile those unresolved differences that threatened to poison the peace of the realm. Louis now agreed to mediate, requesting that Henry and Simon meet him at Amiens on January 8, and promising that he would render his decision by Whitsunday, five months hence. On December 13, Simon and his supporters agreed to abide by the French King's findings. Three days later, Henry and Edward did the same. Both sides then prepared to depart for Amiens.

THEY left Kenilworth Castle at dawn the day after Christmas. The roads were hidden under drifts of ice-glazed snow, the sun barricaded behind wind-blown clouds, and their progress was slow. It was a tribute to Simon's determination that by dusk they had managed to cover almost twenty miles. His companions were fatigued, hungry, and chilled to the bone, eager for the shelter to be found within the market town of Daventry. But when Simon decided to press ahead, detouring three miles to the Cistercian nunnery at Catesby, no one dared to object, not even Nell.

Throughout the day, Simon's temper had been honed to a razor's edge, but Nell did not blame him for his wrathful mood; she shared it. The night before their departure, a courier had arrived with bleak tidings; Edward's Marcher ally, Roger de Mortimer, had seized three of Nell's new Herefordshire manors. It was not a propitious happening on the eve of a peace conference, and Simon's sons wondered why he was persevering in so dubious a quest.

Bran maneuvered his mount until he came abreast of Simon's sorrel stallion. "If the French King does not plan to make his decision until the summer, does that mean we'll stay in France till then?"

"That will depend upon Henry. If he remains at the French court, so shall we. If he returns to England, we will, too. Given the good faith he's so far shown, the only way I'd trust him out of my sight would be if he were entombed in the nave of that abbey he's building at Westminster."

Bran grinned, then realized that his father's bitter humor was not humor at all. "Papa, I do not understand why you ever agreed to arbitration. Do you truly expect Louis to find against his own brother by marriage?"

"Probably not."

"Why, then, did you consent?" Bran demanded, and Simon turned in the saddle, gave him a level look.

"Because," he said, "it is our last chance to stave off war."

Bran started to speak, stopped. Would war be such a calamity? Papa could not help but win; Henry was an even more pitiful soldier than he was a king. Why was Papa so loath to fight him, when fighting was what Papa knew best? But those were questions that went unanswered; Bran sensed that his father was in no mood for philosophical discourse, and easing the reins, he dropped back beside his mother.

"Is it that Henry is your brother?" he asked quietly. He could not see her face, hidden by the hood of her mantle, and had to strain to catch her words.

"Only in part. To take up arms against one's king, to resort to rebellion, even for the most worthy cause—Jesú! Simon!"

They would later speculate that a small animal—a rabbit or weasel—must have darted from the snow-shrouded thickets at the edge of the woods. Whatever the cause, Simon's horse suddenly swerved from the road. As its rear hooves hit a patch of ice, it skidded wildly, its legs entangling. As quick as Simon's reflexes were, he was not quick enough to save himself, had time only for a startled cry before the stallion dragged him down into the deep snow.

The stallion's fall spooked the other horses, and for a few chaotic moments, they were all in jeopardy. Nell dismounted with such reckless haste that she stumbled, fell to her knees. By the time she regained her feet, her sons had reached Simon, were struggling to drag him from beneath his thrashing horse. It was no easy task, for the animal was panicked and Simon stunned. So profusely was he bleeding that when Nell first flung herself down beside him, she feared he might be dead.

"Simon?" Jerking off her veil and wimple, she wiped the blood from his face, fashioned a makeshift bandage for his most obvious wound, a deep gash that angled from eyelid to temple. Her hands were shaking so badly that she kept dropping the bloodied veil into the snow, but she saw his lashes were flickering, his chest rising and falling, and gradually her fingers steadied.

Her sons had been the first to react. They, more than any of the men present, were responsible for freeing Simon. In a gesture of foolhardy gallantry, Bran had even stripped off his own mantle, wadding it under Simon's head. But now they seemed utterly at a loss, seemed no less stunned than Simon, unable to believe he could lie bleeding and helpless at their feet. It was left to Nell to take charge.

"Harry, get to Catesby. Alert the Prioress, bring back a horse litter and blankets. Bran, you and the other men go into the woods, break off some branches. Look for fir; we'll need a wood soft enough to make a splint." She swallowed, her eyes riveted upon the awkward, unnatural angle of Simon's left leg. "But first fetch our saddle blankets, and for the love of God, Bran, take back your mantle ere you catch your death!"

Cradling Simon's head in her lap, Nell sought to staunch his bleeding, so intent upon his injuries that she did not yet feel the snow soaking through her skirts. His lashes were flickering again; opening his eyes, he said in a stranger's voice, faint and faraway, "I caught my boot in the stirrup, could not jump clear . . ."

"I know, beloved, I know." She leaned over, kissed the corner of his mouth, resolutely refusing to think of all the men who died in falls from horses. "Simon, I must find out the extent of your injury. I'll try not to hurt you . . ." He said nothing and she moved her fingers gingerly up his leg; his muscles were constricted, almost in spasm. But it was not until she touched his thigh that he gasped, bit his lip until it bled.

One of Simon's squires had been kneeling by the flailing stallion. When he rose, the dagger in his hand dripped blood into the snow. "I am sorry, my lord," he said. "I know how you fancied the sorrel. But there was naught to be done; he broke a leg."

Simon's mouth twisted. "So did I."

❧

"THERE, my lord." Stepping back from the bed, the doctor essayed a tentative smile. "Some of my brethren would have unwrapped the leg after just twenty-five days, but I thought it best to wait another week, and the results bear me out. The bone seems to be healing well, and there are no signs of inflammation. Now I am ready to replace the bandages. You may have noticed that this time I've not soaked them in egg whites; instead, I've been steeping them in hot wine. But first I must pack more crushed comfrey around the break."

He was talking too much, but could not help himself; he had never tended a patient as self-willed, as intimidating as Simon. His unease made his fingers clumsy, and it took him an inordinate amount of time to rewrap Simon's bandages, then to replace the splints, to make sure that the injured leg was securely positioned in its cloth cradle.

"I know you find it frustrating to be hobbled like this, my lord," he said apologetically, fumbling with the ropes that immobilized Simon's leg. "But it could be worse, believe me. There are physicians who would have bound your leg to heavy boards, from hip to ankle. But I've found that causes the patient too much discomfort. This rope works better, believe me."

By now thoroughly unnerved by Simon's continuing silence, he straightened up, began to back away from the bed. "I must caution you again, my lord. A thigh injury is not easy to heal, and if you hope to avoid a limp, you must keep the leg perfectly still—no matter how difficult that may be."

"So you've told me . . . and told me," Simon muttered, unable to endure any more of the other man's garrulous anxiety. "Ere you depart, Master Arnaud, I'd have you fetch me that basket, the one holding my correspondence."

The doctor disapproved, but dared not object. Entering a few moments later, Nell showed no such diffidence. "Simon, you ought to be resting! And look at that tray; you've scarce touched your meal."

"I was not hungry. But I do need more candles. And I want you to find my scribe, send him up to me."

"Indeed, I will not. I'm not going anywhere until you eat some of this rice-and-lentils dish. It may not be your favorite food, but the doctor says it will help your bones to knit, will—"

"And if I balk, what do you mean to do—spoon-feed me? I said I wanted none of it. Now cease your infernal hovering and fetch my scribe."

"No!"

"Nell, you'll do as I say! Take this slop away—now!" Simon dramatized his demand with a peremptory gesture, but he miscalculated his reach, and his arm struck the edge of the table. It rocked, flipping the tray into the floor rushes. Simon was about to offer a grudging apology when Nell exploded.

"Very well done, my lord! No . . . do not say a word, hear me out! For the past month, I have been at your beck and call. I have been putting up with your foul tempers and catering to your whims, sleeping on that wretched trundle bed so I could tend to your needs myself, no matter the hour of the night. But no more. You do not want to eat? So be it. You can lie up here until you starve for all I care!"

The door was a massive, oaken structure, hinged and barred with heavy metal, but Nell still managed to slam it resoundingly behind her. Simon was the one who usually stalked out after a quarrel; now he could do nothing but fume.

He had chosen to recuperate in Kenilworth's keep rather than in the great chamber he shared with Nell, for when the door was open, he could hear Mass being said in the adjoining chapel. But his convalescence chamber did have drawbacks; he was isolated from the rest of the household. Until his squires returned, he would have to make do without his scribe, and he dumped his letters onto the bed, began impatiently to sort through them.

The first one had an incendiary effect upon an already inflamed temper. He read it, reread it, and swore savagely, futilely, for it was a ransom demand from Roger de Mortimer. In his December raid upon Nell's Herefordshire manors, de Mortimer had seized one of Simon's bailiffs, and he was refusing to release the man unless he was given the sum of two hundred marks. And he would have to be paid, for there could be no retribution while the negotiations were proceeding at Amiens.

The next letter contained more welcome news. Although the aging Earl of Hereford supported the King, his eldest son did not. Humphrey de Bohun wrote to reaffirm his support for Simon and the Provisions, and to announce his upcoming marriage to the Earl of Winchester's niece. Simon put the letter aside. So Elen's daughter was to wed. Which one? Anne had chosen the nunnery. Most likely it was Joanna, the second lass. She'd be what . . . eighteen? Could it truly be ten years since Elen died and six since Rob's death?

Simon lay back against the pillow, staring up at a cobweb glistening in a corner of the bed canopy. Rob had been thrown from his horse whilst taking part in a tournament at Blyth. His injuries had not healed as they ought; he'd lingered more than a year, bedridden, yearning for death. A sorry end for a decent man. Simon closed his eyes, said a brief prayer for his dead, and tried to push the fear away, the fear that his injury might fester, too.

Picking up another letter, he read his son's account of their arrival at Amiens. How hard this was, being dependent upon second-hand reports, upon others to act for him. Christ Jesus, why had he to break a leg, now of all times? Peter was a good man; he and Harry would do their best to make the French King understand. But he ought to have been there himself. Why did the Almighty not want him there?

He shifted, looking in vain for a comfortable position, and knocked most of the letters onto the floor. God's wrath, now what? No matter how he stretched, his fingers fell just short of the parchment sheets. A sharp stab of pain warned him of his danger; he sank back, defeated. But it was several minutes before he could bring himself to reach for the bell, to ask for help.

No one came. He waited, rang again, and again, and again. By the time he finally heard footsteps, he was seething. "Bleeding Hell, where have—" He swallowed the rest of the profanity as the door swung open, for it was not his tardy squire who entered, it was his eleven-year-old daughter.

Simon drew a calming breath. "I'm sorry, lass. I thought you were Giles."

"He's probably hiding, Papa. Everyone always does after you quarrel with Mama. We all know, you see, for she comes back to the great hall in a tearing rage, snaps at anyone who looks at her twice."

"So . . . Giles has gone to earth," Simon said, and Ellen grinned. "Just like a fox, Papa!"

He watched as she retrieved his letters, then beckoned her to sit beside him on the bed. Her hair had once been as blonde as Nell's, but it had slowly begun to darken, was now a burnished red-gold. He reached out, entwined one of her long, bright braids around his finger. "It sounds as if they all fear to face me. But not you?"

She had eyes like her brother Amaury, a tawny hazel flecked with green. They were alight now with laughter, hers the serene self-confidence of a cherished only daughter in a family of sons. "Afraid of you, Papa? I am terrified," she said, and giggled when Simon pulled her braid.

"No jokes, lass. I want the truth. Have I been as bad a patient as that?"

She nodded. "You've been just dreadful, Papa," she confided.

Simon was taken aback. "Well, then, I suppose I shall have to mend my ways. I'd best begin by making peace with your mother, but I shall need your help. See that coffer in the corner? If you could fetch my sword—" He smiled, for she was already half-way across the room. "Leave it in the scabbard, Ellen, and take care, for it's heavy. I want you to bring it to the great hall, present it to Nell."

"I'll go right now, Papa!" Holding his sword as if it were a divining rod, Ellen looked so incongruous and yet so appealing that Simon had to laugh, for the first time in weeks.

He was surprised when Nell failed to appear within the following quarter-hour, for as quick as she was to flare up, she was even quicker to laugh. As time passed, his initial puzzlement gave way to concern; it was not like her to hold a grudge. He kept listening for her, unable to concentrate upon his correspondence. Although he was growing sleepy again, he was loath to give in to it. It alarmed him that he tired so easily since his accident; it was his secret, unconfessed fear that he might not recover his full strength. Eventually he dozed, awakening an hour later at the sound of familiar footsteps.

"You're a hard woman to impress. That was the first time I've ever made an unconditional surrender, and yet— Nell? What is it?"

Nell was ashen, her eyes dark and dazed, so dilated were her pupils. Leaning back against the door, she said, "Harry and Peter have returned from France."

Simon frowned. "So soon? But they were to remain until Louis rendered his decision."

"He did, Simon. On Wednesday last, he issued the Mise of Amiens."

"What! In just a fortnight, he reached a decision that was not expected till June?" Simon sat up too abruptly, winced. "You'd not look so grim were the news good. Louis has found in Henry's favor, then? How bad is it? Has he given Henry the sole right to appoint members of his council?"

"Simon . . ." Nell came forward, unexpectedly knelt by the bed, and reached for her husband's hand. "Simon, the French King has annulled the Provisions. He has declared them to be invalid, and absolved Henry of his past promises to adhere to them."

"No . . . no! He could not do that. He had not the right!"

"I know. But he did it, nonetheless. Peter says that even Henry seemed shocked by the extent of his victory. Louis found for Henry on all counts. He held that all the royal strongholds must be restored to Henry at once, that Henry alone has the right to appoint the ministers and officers of his realm. He even denied us the right to expel those of alien birth. He . . . Oh, God, Simon, it has all been for naught!"

"I thought," he said bitterly, "that Louis was a man of honor. How could he rule upon the validity of the Provisions? We would never have agreed to arbitration had that been at issue. For five years, I've fought to safeguard the Provisions, fought for reform. Why would I allow Louis to pass judgment upon what we've already won?"

"We were betrayed," Nell said, no less bitterly. "When Harry and Peter reached London, they encountered the Earl of Gloucester. Upon

hearing their news, he insisted upon accompanying them on to Kenilworth. So, too, did Mayor Fitz Thomas. He says the Londoners are
sorely distraught, implores you to see him. What shall I tell them? Shall
I bid them wait?"

"No," he said. "I'll see them."

Harry and Peter were disheveled and travel-stained, looked weary
in body and soul. At sight of his father, Harry blurted out, "Christ,
Papa, I'm so sorry!" as if the Mise of Amiens was somehow his fault.

The young Earl of Gloucester was uncomfortable and it showed.
His relationship with Simon had chilled since the summer. This was
their first encounter in several months, and Gloucester seemed ill at ease
in the intimacy of Simon's sickroom. The Mayor of London, too, appeared inhibited by his surroundings. He made an unobtrusive entrance,
hung back as the others approached the bed.

"Do you have it?" Simon asked abruptly, and Peter nodded, silently
handing over a parchment scroll. Simon rapidly unrolled the document.
"Quash and annul the aforesaid Provisions." The words seemed to leap
off the page, as if written in blood. He read swiftly, betraying his emotions with an occasional indrawn breath. Once he quoted aloud, incredulously, " 'The said King shall be at liberty to call aliens to his
counsel,' " and then, " 'The said King shall have full power and free
rule within his realm—' "

Harry could restrain himself no longer. "Henry bribed the bastard,"
he interrupted indignantly. "How else explain it?"

"I do not agree," Peter objected mildly. "I think Louis reacted as a
king, not a judge, I think he felt threatened by any limitations upon the
powers of kingship—"

"He's Henry's brother by marriage and he's French. If you're looking for explanations, you need go no further than that," Gloucester said
tautly, forgetting for the moment that Simon, too, was French.

Harry bristled, but Simon was still intent upon the French King's
verdict. "Listen to this. 'We further are unwilling, nor by this present
ordinance do we intend, in any way to derogate from the royal privileges,
charters, liberties, statutes, or praiseworthy customs, of the realm of
England.' He affirms the Runnymede Charter, and then disavows the
Oxford Provisions! Sheer madness; one might as well chop down a tree
whilst continuing to water the roots. The Provisions are the natural
corollary of the Charter!"

He crumpled the parchment in his fist, flung it contemptuously to
the floor, then looked up at the other men. "I cannot accept this. I have
sworn to uphold the Provisions with my honor, with my life. Even if
all forsake me, my sons and I will not abandon the Provisions, or those
who put their faith in me."

"You will not stand alone, my lord," Fitz Thomas said quietly. "My Londoners will fight for the Provisions if need be."

"So will I." Gloucester startled them all by jerking his sword from its scabbard. "That I swear by the holy relics within this hilt."

It was a dramatic gesture, enthusiastically emulated by Simon's three sons. "Men will flock to your banners, Papa." Bran spread his arms wide, as if to embrace hordes of unseen supporters. "The Earl of Derby and Humphrey de Bohun and Hugh le Despenser and Baldwin Wake and John Fitz John and—"

"And you can count upon Llewelyn ap Gruffydd, Papa. He'll throw his lot in with us for certes," Harry exclaimed, as Fitz Thomas chimed in with his own assurances about the loyalties of the citizenry, the Cinque Ports, towns like Oxford and Northampton, all of which would follow London's lead.

Simon heard them out in silence, and gradually they fell silent, too. Becoming aware of his obvious exhaustion, Simon's sons exchanged uneasy glances. These sudden glimpses of their father's vulnerability unnerved them in a way that sheer physical danger did not.

"We will have time to discuss our plans upon the morrow," Simon said. "Now I would be alone with my wife."

They had forgotten Nell, forgotten that their enemies were her brothers. Casting chagrined looks over their shoulders, they were relieved to withdraw, for not even Nell's sons knew what to say to her.

Dusk was fast falling; the last of the candles had guttered out and only a hearth fire now held the dark at bay. "Shall I send for a cresset lamp?" Nell asked, and Simon shook his head, held out his hand. She came slowly from the shadows, sat beside him on the bed. Taking her hand, he brought it to his lips, pressed a kiss into her palm. After a time, he said:

"Henry may be God's greatest fool, but he is still your brother. And Richard . . . he will likely oppose us, too, Nell."

"I know," she said softly. She'd never truly thought it would ever come to this, never thought the day might dawn when her husband and sons would face her brothers and nephews across a battlefield. She shared Simon's confidence, but not his darker moods. Hers was a world of sunrises, not sunsets, a world in which hope flourished and faith was rewarded, and she clung to that comforting certainty all the more now that her need was so great.

"I trust in you, Simon," she said, "and I trust in God. Whatever happens, it will be for the best, for us and for England."

30

Gloucester, England

March 1264

TRAPPED in Gloucester Castle by his de Montfort cousins, Edward offered to talk. Emerging unarmed, as a show of good faith, he and Hal were escorted through St Mary's Gate into the precincts of the Benedictine abbey of St Peter, on to the Chapter House, where they were awaited by Harry and Bran, the Bishop of Worcester, and the Earl of Derby.

The meeting got off to an awkward start when Bran pointedly reminded Hal of his past promise not to bear arms against Simon, but Edward stepped smoothly into the breach. "Rumor has it that you got into the town with a variation of the Trojan Horse trick. Any truth to that?"

Harry and Bran exchanged grins. "We disguised two knights as wool merchants. Once they were admitted, they seized the gatehouse keys."

Edward laughed approvingly. "Right clever, if I say it who should not!"

"At the risk of sounding overly suspicious, Ned, I've never known you to be such a gracious loser."

Edward's smile didn't waver. "I'm not here to surrender, Harry. I want to arrange a truce."

Bran burst out laughing. "I daresay you do! Tell me, Ned, do you also have a swaybacked, spavined nag you hope to pass off as a pureblooded destrier? Any marshland to sell? We have you well and truly trapped, my lad. Why should we agree to uncork the bottle?"

"No reason at all . . . if you truly want war." Edward rose from his chair, began to pace. "My father does not. Nor does my uncle Richard. I was the one who argued against compromise. But now that it has come to this, to facing the two of you across a battlefield . . . Christ Jesus, I do not want that! We've shared too much . . ." He stopped, shrugged self-consciously. "There must be another way. Let me find it. If you agree to a week's truce, until the thirteenth, there's a chance I can get my father to offer more generous terms than those of the French King."

There was a prolonged silence, and then Bran slowly and deliberately began to clap. "Well said. Who could resist such a heartfelt appeal? I could. No offense, Cousin, but I'd sooner wager upon the true color of a chameleon than upon your honor."

"I fear I must agree," the Bishop of Worcester said coolly. "That was an eloquent plea for peace, but you spoke no less persuasively to me when you found yourself besieged by the citizens of Bristol, only to disavow all your promises once you were safe."

Edward flushed. "That was different!"

"How?" Harry asked, and Edward strode toward him, reached out and grasped his wrist.

"Because," he said, "I'd be swearing to you. To you, Harry. Do you truly think I'd give you my sworn word and then break it?"

Harry looked intently into his cousin's face. "No," he said. "No, I do not believe you'd lie, not to me. All right, Ned, you have your truce."

The Earl of Derby had been listening in silence, amused by the back-and-forth banter. Now he was on his feet, face red with rage. "Have you gone mad?"

Bran was no less shocked. "Harry, you cannot do this! Think you that I want to see Ned come to grief? Jesú, he's my kinsman, too! But he cannot be trusted, not anymore."

"I think he can. And the decision, like the command, is mine. If he can make peace between our fathers, it's well worth the risk." Ignoring their outraged protests, Harry held out his hand to Edward. "Do not prove me wrong, Ned," he said, and smiled. "You know how insufferable Bran can be when he gets to say 'I told you so'!"

Neither Edward nor Hal spoke as they emerged into the cloister walkway. The inner garth was still powdered with the unsightly residue of the last storm; the once-white snow was now a dingy, begrimed grey. Hal reached down and scooped up a handful. There was awe in the glance he gave Edward, but there was unease, too, for at the moment he felt no less sullied and defiled than this fistful of dirty snow. Slowly he opened his fingers, let it trickle away as if he were scattering ashes to the wind.

"You know them full well," he mumbled. "They each reacted just as you said they would." He and Edward had even joked about it beforehand, quips that came back to haunt him now, that left a soured taste in his mouth. "Ned, I have to say this. I do not like what we did in there."

He tensed, expecting a sharp stab of anger, or worse, a derisive gibe. But for once his cousin offered no mocking rejoinder, no taunts about his sentimentality, his naïveté. Edward stopped abruptly, turned to face him.

"Do you think that I liked it?" he demanded. "Harry is closer to me than my own brother. But there is too much at stake for scruples."

BY the time Harry and Bran dismounted in front of Kenilworth's great hall, their sister had reached the bottom of the stairs. "I've missed you so much!" Ellen cried, flinging herself into Harry's arms. Then it was Bran's turn. He swung her up off the ground, whirled her around until she squealed with laughter. "What took you so long? And what did you bring me?"

Her brothers looked at each other in dismay. From Ellen's earliest childhood years, they'd delighted in indulging her whims; this was the first time within memory that they'd forgotten to pick up some small trinket for her.

"Well, kitten, if you check Bran's saddlebag, you might just find some green silk hair ribbons," Harry suggested, earning himself a sunlit smile and another hug.

Watching as Ellen dashed toward the stables, Bran gave his brother a playful shove. "Good going, Harry. I promised Cassandra a keepsake. What do I tell her now?"

"You'll think of something. Now we'd best— Amaury! When did you get back from France?"

"A fortnight ago." Amaury fended off his brother's exuberant welcome as best he could, being some inches the shorter of the two. Disentangling himself from Harry's bear hug, he said accusingly, "Where in blazes have you two been?"

Bran cocked a quizzical brow. "You may be studying for the priesthood, lad, but you're not my confessor!"

"A pity, for you've never been more in need of absolution." They turned at the sound of this new voice, saw Guy leaning against the door, regarding them with an odd smile, one that managed to be both sardonic and sympathetic. As their eyes met, Bran felt a vague, uneasy premonition. Although Guy was always there if needed, he sometimes suspected that Guy took a perverse satisfaction in seeing their sins catch up with them. Harry, less observant, greeted his brother blithely, moved on into the hall. Bran followed, more warily. But there he forgot his qualms, so pleased was he at the sight that met their eyes.

"Papa! You're up and about!" Harry hastened toward the fire, detouring briefly to give Nell a quick kiss. "This is the best news we could have gotten! Did you make a sacrificial bonfire to burn your splints? We have good news, too. First of all, we settled your debt with that whore-son de Mortimer. With some help from Llewelyn ap Gruffydd, we laid waste to Mortimer's lordship of Radnor, seized his manors at—"

Simon held up a hand for silence. "I would speak with my sons alone," he said, and the hall rapidly emptied; only Nell remained, stand-ing just behind Simon's chair. As the door closed after the last of their servants, Simon turned glittering grey eyes upon his sons. "Now," he said, "tell me what happened at Gloucester."

"You know about Gloucester?" Harry asked in surprise. "You mean the news beat us back to Kenilworth? Well . . . I suppose I'd best begin at the beginning. The town gates were barred to us, but two of our knights pretended—"

"I was told that you had Edward trapped within the castle. True?"

Harry nodded slowly, and Simon reached for a crutch, maneuvered himself upright, brushing aside their efforts to help. "With Edward in our hands, the war would have begun and ended there at Gloucester. And you let him go?"

Bran froze, then gave his brother a look of appalled pity. But Harry did not yet understand. "We agreed to a truce, Papa," he said calmly. "Ned promised to do all he could to stave off war, to persuade his father—"

"And you believed him?" Simon interrupted incredulously, and Harry nodded again.

"Yes," he said. "He gave me his sworn word. He—"

"He played you both for fools. He kept your truce only as long as your army was within sight of Gloucester. Then he seized the town, imposed harsh fines and penalties upon the citizens, and rode straight for the royal encampment at Oxford—no doubt laughing all the way!"

Bran made an involuntary gesture, his hand brushing his brother's sleeve. Harry jerked away from the touch. Darkness lurked in the corners of the hall, beyond the reach of rush-light, and Harry turned instinctively toward the shadows, plunged into their depths as if seeking sanctuary. But there he paused. "Bran is not to blame," he said, his voice muffled, all but inaudible. "He tried to warn me, but I would not listen. I failed you, Papa, not Bran."

At Simon's silent query, Bran nodded, before blurting out, "There are worse mistakes, Papa, than one made from the heart."

"Bran is right, Simon," Nell said softly, keeping her eyes all the while upon her eldest son. "You taught our sons that a man's life counts for naught without honor. Mayhap Harry learned that lesson too well, but my love, he learned it from you."

Simon's anger still burned at white heat, but as he looked upon that solitary figure deep in shadow, he found his fury changing focus, away from Harry and onto the man who'd so cruelly duped him. Shifting his crutch, he limped toward his son.

"Harry." The younger man turned, reluctantly; Simon thought he caught a glimmer of tears beneath Harry's lashes. "I'll not lie to you, not deny that you disappointed me. But you did not shame me, Harry. The shame is Edward's, not yours. Now we'll say no more on this. You made a mistake, lad. Just be sure you learn from it."

"I will," Harry said tautly. "As God is my witness, I will."

THE prospect of English civil war dismayed the French King, who opposed on principle all strife between Christians. He hastily dispatched an envoy, who prevailed upon Henry and Simon to make one final attempt at negotiation. A truce was declared on March 18, and Simon and his supporters offered to accept the Mise of Amiens if Henry agreed to banish aliens from his service. Henry refused.

When war did come, though, the fire was kindled by neither Henry nor Simon, but by the Londoners. On March 31, they rioted, burning the town houses of the hated William de Lusignan and a prominent royalist baron, Philip Basset. Then the mob turned its fury upon the Westminster mansion of Henry's brother Richard. Not content with that, they marched the seven miles to Isleworth. There they demolished Richard's cherished fish ponds, destroyed his orchards, reduced his favorite manor to a charred ruin.

Richard was outraged. Overnight, he was transformed from a man arguing for moderation to one hellbent upon vengeance. He, too, now echoed Edward's insistence upon a battlefield resolution, and Henry heeded them. On Thursday, April 3, the King raised his red dragon standard and the royal host headed for Northampton, where Simon's army was quartered.

They reached Northampton at dusk the following day. Arriving a few hours later, William de Lusignan and Roger de Mortimer were escorted to Edward's command tent, where a strategy session was in progress. Those within offered by their very presence poignant testimony to the divisive, internecine nature of this war, for Henry, Richard, and Edward were not the only ones estranged from their own kinsmen. Philip Basset's son-in-law was Hugh le Despenser, Simon's Justiciar. The Earl of Hereford's son still held fast for Simon. And Hugh Bigod, the Earl of Norfolk's brother, had a stepson, Baldwin Wake, awaiting their assault on the other side of the city walls.

But de Lusignan and de Mortimer were not men to dwell upon vain regrets, or missed chances for peace. The thought of impending war troubled them not at all. What did was the sight of Davydd ap Gruffydd so at ease in Edward's circle. It was to be expected that they would harbor suspicions of the Welsh, for theirs were Marcher lands. But their dislike of Davydd was as personal as it was political, for exile had not tempered his bravado. He was no less cynical, no less self-assured at Edward's court than he had been at Llewelyn's, and as he was one of the few men not intimidated by William de Lusignan's kinship to the King, he and de Lusignan had crossed verbal swords more than once. Now, however, he was too absorbed to pay the other man any mind; hunched over the table, he was sketching a plan of Northampton's streets.

"Our first attack was driven off," Edward informed his uncle. "But that was just to get the lay of the land. On the morrow the siege begins in earnest."

William de Lusignan appropriated a coffer seat. "Who has their command?"

Philip Basset glanced up from the map. "Leicester's son and Peter de Montfort. They prudently refused our challenge; only fools would fight a pitched battle when so greatly outnumbered. No, they mean to hold the town and castle until Simon de Montfort can come to their rescue."

"But that," Edward said, "shall not be. It's a full three days' ride from London to Northampton. Even if Simon spurred his horse till it foundered, there's no way he could reach them in time. I know Northampton well; its defenses will crumble in a day, two at most."

He sounded so sure, so blessedly free of doubts that Henry felt a pang of envy. He got slowly to his feet, stiff from a day in the saddle. "I am going to bed," he said, all too aware that his presence was not needed.

Edward gave him a brief, preoccupied smile. "We fight our first battle at dawn," he predicted, "and our last. By this time tomorrow, our war will be won."

"It's ready," Davydd announced, laying down his pen. "And not badly done, if I do say so. Luckily it's been just a month since I was in Northampton."

Edward came over to look, nodded approval. "We will attack at the South Gate. And whilst we keep them busy there, Philip will lead an assault along the northwest priory wall. If the Prior spoke true, we'll be into the town ere they even realize what's happening."

"The Prior?" William de Lusignan echoed, frowning. "What do you mean?"

Edward grinned. "We're playing the game with loaded dice, Will. Unlike most of the townspeople, the Prior of St Andrew's is loyal to the Crown. He sent us word that he'd secretly undermined the priory wall, then put in temporary supports. Tomorrow he knocks them out, and we breach the wall as easy as this!" With a sudden snap of his fingers.

De Lusignan reached for a wine cup, held it aloft. "To your obliging Prior! How is it that your luck never fails?"

Edward reached over, claimed his uncle's cup. "I have something better than luck, Will. I have God's favor."

BRAN was exhausted. Although it was not yet mid-morning, he'd been up for hours. The first attack had come at dawn, and he'd been in the thick of it. They'd beaten the invaders back, managed to keep them off the town walls, but their victory was a fleeting one. He knew they'd be back. In the meantime, though, he meant to take full advantage of this lull in the fighting. Turning his stallion onto Gold Street, he headed for the castle.

An eerie quiet prevailed. Saturday was market day in Northampton. But now the streets lay deserted. The men of the town were up on the walls, most willingly, some impressed into service. Their women were barricaded behind shuttered windows, barred doors. God pity Northampton should it fall to Ned's army. Bran at once disavowed the thought. His father would come in time. They had only to hold out for a few days.

Approaching the horse market, Bran spotted a friend. He shouted, and Baldwin Wake reined in his mount. "Where do you go? To the castle?"

Bran nodded. "I thought to have some of the garrison relieve the men at the South Gate. And then raid the kitchens; I had a mouthful of bread this morn, and nothing since. Damnation, Baldwin, but I hate this! I'd much rather be on the attack—"

"My lord, look!" His squire was pointing. A lone rider was galloping toward them. Recognizing Peter de Montfort's youngest son, Bran and Baldwin spurred their mounts to meet him.

Robert de Montfort yanked on the reins so abruptly that his lathered stallion went back on its haunches. "Bran, thank God! They've breached the walls at St Andrew's Priory! We cannot hope to hold them—"

"Baldwin, get reinforcements from the castle! Rob, your father is at the South Gate; warn him!" Bran's last words were carried back by the wind. He was already passing the Dominican friary, his stallion lengthening stride, needing no urging, flying.

At the Marehold, he encountered a small band of Oxford students; when Henry ordered the university shut down, some of the youths had chosen to fight for the Provisions at Northampton. They had been a welcome addition to the rebel army, proving themselves surprisingly adept with crossbows and slings, and they responded readily to Bran's shouted appeal, streaming after him into the priory grounds.

There all was chaos. Monks mingled with disheartened defenders, ready to run. Livestock milled about, untended, bleating goats and barking dogs adding immeasurably to the confusion. Women and children who'd seen the priory as a safe refuge now fled in panic, leaving behind them a trail of discarded and dropped belongings. They scattered as Bran galloped through the gateway, too terrified to distinguish friend from foe.

There was a large gaping hole in the priory's garden wall; men were already scrambling through. Within moments, though, they were diving for safety as Bran's stallion plunged toward them.

Bran gave his horse its head, and the roan soared over the rubble. Landing as gracefully as any cat, it easily overtook the retreating soldiers. Bran's sword was soon bloody to the hilt. He fended off an upthrust halberd, swung the stallion about, and slashed a path to the scaling ladders propped against the wall.

Climbing a siege ladder was always a perilous undertaking, but never more so than now. With each thrust of his sword, Bran sheathed it in flesh, while his stallion raked its teeth into exposed backs and legs, trampled those unfortunates who tumbled underfoot.

"My lord, come back!" Only his squire had dared to follow Bran beyond the wall. To his vast relief, Bran heeded him, raced the roan back into the priory. His reckless charge had dazzled the students. They eagerly did his bidding, made ready to repel the next rush.

The enemy regrouped with surprising speed, and this time they succeeded in making another break in the wall. Bran's courage, never in doubt, now verged upon the suicidal. Again he sent his stallion into the breach, managed by sheer audacity to slow their momentum, to check their onslaught.

But as more and more soldiers rallied to the attack, Bran pressed his luck once too often. The third time that he ventured beyond the priory walls, he found himself surrounded. His stallion reared, screaming defiance, and Bran lashed out with his sword. His blade sliced into the nearest shoulder, and as the man fell, he spurred his horse forward. The stallion slammed into the encircling men, broke free, and bolted across the field. Bran jerked on the reins, but the animal had the bit between its teeth. He heard his squire's voice, shrieking his name, with each stride was being carried deeper into enemy territory. Desperately he sought to turn the runaway roan, and as its breakneck speed slowed, he began to hope that he might yet manage to make it back to the priory. But by then they were upon the ditch.

It was too late to swerve. The stallion made a gallant attempt to hurdle the trench. But its hind legs struck the embankment. As it tumbled backward into the ditch, Bran was fortunate enough to be thrown clear. He landed hard, though, striking his head against the side of his helm, and all went dark. When he came to, he was bruised, breathless, half-blinded by his own blood, and there was a sword leveled at his throat.

He'd lost his own sword in the fall. Now they claimed his dagger, dragged him roughly up the side of the ditch. But when one of the soldiers pulled off his helm, the atmosphere changed dramatically. At sight of that thatch of raven hair, those narrow grey eyes, the man gave an elated shout. "Jesus wept, you're Leicester's son!"

Astounded by their good fortune, they crowded around, all talking at once. Bran found himself suddenly surrounded by smiles. One of the men, a burly youth with scarred face and black eye patch, even stripped a dirty bandage from his own arm. "Here," he said. "We cannot have you bleeding to death, not when your blood is as good as gold!"

Bran took the bandage; although his head wound seemed superficial, it was still bleeding copiously. "Was my stallion hurt?"

"By rights the both of you ought to have broken your necks after a tumble like that! Damned if I can explain it, for he's not even limping."

Glancing back to make sure the soldier wasn't lying, Bran was shocked to see how far his horse had taken him; they were more than a quarter mile from the priory. "You've breached the walls," he said dully.

"Your capture took the heart out of their defense. But it— Hellfire!"

Bran swung about, at once saw the cause of the soldier's outburst. As several armor-clad riders swerved in their direction, Bran's captors clustered protectively around him, fearful of losing their prize.

"Did I not tell you, Will? It's de Montfort's whelp!"

Bran's breath caught in his throat. Staring up at Roger de Mortimer and William de Lusignan, he felt a sudden rush of fear, far greater than any battlefield dread.

Roger de Mortimer ignored the soldiers, fixed Bran with a malevolent stare, and between them rose the spectre of his smoldering Radnorshire manors. But it was William de Lusignan who held Bran's eyes, whose smile sent a chill along his spine.

"You're the one they call Bran. Tell us . . . how fares your father? We hear he lies crippled in London, unable to play a man's part. It must be true if he's sending his striplings to fight for him."

"What would you know of playing a man's part?"

From the corner of his eye, Bran saw his captors grinning; their dislike of de Lusignan was heartening. He watched warily as the older man dismounted, still smiling.

"How old are you, lad?"

"Twenty and three, why? You want to know my birthdate, too? My favorite wine?"

"You're de Montfort's son for certes. You have his black Saracen coloring, his brazen insolence. But there is one great difference between you."

"And just what is that?"

"Your father has been blessed with a long life," de Lusignan said and then laughed, for he was close enough to hear Bran's ragged intake of breath. "Of course it need not be. It's true you're de Montfort's spawn, but you're also my sister's son. I'd not want it said that I lacked all family feeling. I'm willing to spare your life—if you beg for it."

Bran's fist clenched around his bloodied bandage. "Rot in Hell!"

De Lusignan had at last lost his smile; his hand dropped to the hilt of his sword. Stepping back, he said, "Seize him."

The soldiers did, unwilling but not daring to disobey the King's brother. There was a suspenseful pause as de Lusignan studied his struggling nephew, and then he said, "Kill him."

Part of it may have been their loathing for de Lusignan. Or their involuntary admiration for Bran's doomed gesture of defiance. Much of it most certainly was the loss of a large ransom. But at that, the soldiers rebelled. "He's our prisoner, my lord," the one-eyed soldier shouted, and the others chimed in angrily.

De Lusignan ignored their protests. He raised his hand and three of his men dismounted, drawing their swords. The soldiers released Bran, grudgingly gave ground. Only the one-eyed youth seemed on the verge of mutiny, fingering his dagger as if he wanted to throw it to Bran.

Bran began to back away as the men closed in, fanning out with purposeful intent. There was an unreality about the entire scene, as if he were watching someone else trapped between the ditch and the advancing soldiers. Even the shouting now seemed to be coming from a great distance. The men were almost upon him when an armed knight galloped into their midst.

He was young and vaguely familiar to Bran, with the greenest eyes he'd ever seen, eyes astonishingly, incongruously agleam with laughter. "Do not let me spoil the fun," he said. "Four heads for the price of one is a rare bargain."

"This is none of your concern, Welshman!"

Davydd smiled over his shoulder at the King's outraged brother. "I thought it only fair, my lord Earl, that your men should know what reward to expect for this service they do you. What will you give them for slaying de Montfort—a half shilling apiece? No offense, but you're not known for your generosity, are you? Now the Lord Edward on the other hand will likely offer them a decent burial, mayhap even a Requiem Mass."

"Damn you, what are you babbling about?"

"You did not know?" Davydd queried, in mock surprise. "The Lord Edward gave express orders that his de Montfort cousin was not to be harmed. So I suspect he might well take it amiss that you had the lad murdered."

"And how do I know you're not lying?"

"You do not, of course," Davydd agreed cheerfully. "Mayhap I am. But what if I'm not? Are you willing to risk it?"

Much to his chagrin, de Lusignan realized he was not, for he was gradually coming to comprehend the vast and dangerous differences between Henry and his firstborn son. "Sheathe your swords. We'll take him into custody, deliver him to the King."

At that, Bran found his voice. "Like bloody Hell you will!"

Davydd grinned. "I think young de Montfort suspects he might suffer an unfortunate mishap on the way—trying to escape."

None of them had noticed Philip Basset's approach. "What in Christ's Passion is happening here? Have you all forgotten that there is a battle going on in the town?" His eyes flicked toward Bran, widened in recognition. "I see. You soldiers there, escort the King's nephew to Lord Edward's command tent. The rest of you men get back onto the field." Adding pointedly, "My lords? You are coming, too, I trust?"

The command was his; he had his way. Within moments, Bran found himself alone with his original captors. "Christ's pity," he said softly, then heard Davydd laugh.

He had reined in his stallion a few feet away. "Well put. Right about now you must feel like a bone thrown to a pack of hungry dogs!"

Bran nodded slowly. "I'll not argue that." And then, "Now I know who you are. You're Llewelyn's brother!"

"Always," Davydd said dryly. Shifting his gaze to the downcast soldiers, he said, "Cheer up, lads. It was inevitable that he'd be claimed by the King. But all is not lost. Edward is likely to reward you for keeping him safe." He started to follow after the others, then swung about, reaching for a wine flask at his belt.

"Here, Cousin," he said, flipping the flask at Bran's feet. "I daresay you need this more than I do!"

THE next twenty-four hours were the most wretched of Bran's life. His guards were friendly, influenced, perhaps, by accounts of his confrontation with William de Lusignan, and they kept him informed of the siege progress. The town fell that same afternoon, and Peter de Montfort and his men took refuge within the castle. But Bran knew the lamentable state of its defenses; its west wall was near collapse. Peter could not hope to hold out until his father's arrival. Heartsick, helpless, Bran feared that his father's dream was dying in the narrow, muddy streets of North-ampton.

It was not until Compline the next evening that he was summoned to Edward's tent. "Sit down," Edward invited, waving away the guards. Busying himself with several flagons of wine, he announced, quite mat-ter-of-factly, "It's over. Peter de Montfort and the castle garrison sur-rendered just after Vespers."

"If you expect me to drink to your victory, you can damned well choke!"

Unfazed, Edward continued to pour. "Since when do you turn down good wine? This batch comes from Bordeaux; you'll not even have to spit out the sediment!"

Sloshing a cup into Bran's hand, he said, "You're the talk of the camp, Cousin. Your exploits at the priory were—"

Bran jumped to his feet. "Go ahead, Ned, gloat, but I swear—"

Edward looked surprised. "Bran, I'm serious! Those devil-be-damned charges of yours were the stuff of which legends are made. Then there was the way you defied our de Lusignan uncle. Death before dishonor," Edward joked, but his eyes were shining. Taking a seat across from Bran, he said, "You did yourself proud, lad. Although I should be the last man to be lauding you like this. After all, I'm the one who took the town, only to have you end up as the hero of the hour!"

His praise was balm to Bran's mangled pride. He took a deep swal-low of Edward's wine, deciding that if ever there was a night to get thoroughly drunk, now was the time. "I've a favor to ask, Ned. If you can find out what became of my stallion, I'd like Davydd ap Gruffydd to have him. I daresay he was more interested in vexing de Lusignan than in saving me. But never had I been in greater need of a guardian angel; I just did not expect my angel to be Welsh!"

Edward laughed. "A man could go mad trying to unravel Davydd's motives. He's about as trustworthy as a wolf on the prowl, but having him at our court is like having a lance aimed at Llewelyn's heart. So it's well worth indulging his fancies, overlooking his flaws. And he can be right likable—when he wants to be. But whatever his reasons, I confess I'm glad he chose to meddle when he did."

Bran set his wine cup down, gave Edward a level, searching look. "Why did you do it, Ned? Why order my life spared?"

Edward shrugged. "It should be obvious. You must owe me at least a hundred pounds, mayhap more. And I've never yet known a man who paid back a debt from the grave. Besides, I expect you'd have done the same for me."

"No," Bran said, "I would not," and Edward, rising for more wine, spun around to stare at him.

"I might have," Bran said, "a month ago," and Edward relaxed.

"I see," he said. "You bear a grudge for Gloucester Castle."

"No," Bran said. "For Harry."

"That was a shabby trick, I know," Edward conceded. "I expect it'll take some time ere he can forgive me."

"Not in this lifetime," Bran warned, saw that his cousin didn't believe him. Edward was crossing the tent, where he spoke briefly with a servant before sauntering back with another flagon of wine.

"They'll be bringing in our supper. I thought I owed you one good meal ere you depart for Windsor Castle; you leave at dawn."

Bran had known there'd be no question of ransom. "You think it's over? You're wrong, Ned, dead wrong. You may have outwitted Harry and outfought me, but you've not yet faced my father."

Vengeful in defeat, Edward could be magnanimous in victory. Forbearing to take offense, he poured a generous amount into Bran's cup. "What shall we drink to—better days?"

It occurred to Bran that, whatever happened now, their lives would never be the same. "No," he said, reaching for his wine cup. "To yesterdays."

WHILE a lone rider might cover forty or more miles a day, an army was lucky to make half that distance. Although Simon left London at dawn, it was full dark before they came within sight of the walls of St Albans Abbey. Two more days lay ahead of them, two more days trapped within a swaying horse litter, two more days of suspense, envisioning a town under siege, begrudging every mile, every minute that stretched between Northampton and deliverance.

Roger de Norton, the Abbot of St Albans, was awaiting them inside the north gateway, an honor more properly accorded a king than a rebel earl; Simon was surprised and heartened by the warmth of his welcome.

The guest house had been made ready for him. A hearth fire took the chill off the April air, and a table was laden with uncommonly rich Lenten fare: a roast pike in aspic, gingered carp, sugared pancakes. Yet the Abbot's demeanor was not that of a bountiful host. Enveloped in Benedictine black, he paced at Simon's side like a somber, disquieted shadow, intent upon private griefs, secret sorrows. Simon's fatigue had dulled his perception; he did not even notice the Abbot's distraction. Nor did his companions. Humphrey de Bohun and Guy were regarding the food with relish, while Harry trailed behind, so quiet, so remote he might have been a stranger to them all. Harry, the abiding optimist, born to sunlight and daydreams and cheer, now found his every breath poisoned, his peace haunted, so great was his fear for his brother.

"My lord . . ." The Abbot stopped suddenly, in the center of the room. "I'd meant to wait till you had eaten, rested. But that seems dishonest, somehow, even with the best intent. Less than an hour ago a man arrived at the abbey, seeking you. He was at Northampton, my lord, and he says . . . he says the town has fallen to the King's army."

"No!" Harry darted forward, grabbed the Abbot's arm. "That's a lie!"

Simon reached out, released his son's grip. "Bring him to me."

He still held fast to hope; a mistake, a lie. But then the door opened. Nicholas Segrave had served under his command in Gascony. Simon stood quite still, watching the other man walk toward him. He moved very slowly, his steps leaden, as uneven as Simon's own. There was dried blood on his hauberk, his hair, even his boots, and as he looked at Simon, the dirt on his face streaked with tears.

Simon swallowed. "My son?"

"Alive, my lord. God was that merciful. But all is lost."

"Tell me," Simon said.

"They took the town Saturday, we think by treachery. Your son was captured trying to stave off their attack on the priory. Twice he ventured alone beyond the walls, then his horse bolted and threw him. And once they were in the town, we could not hope to hold out. Yesterday Peter de Montfort yielded the castle, and Edward then turned the town over to his soldiers for their sport. They took more than eighty barons and knights prisoner, gutted your army . . ."

There was a strained quiet, and then a slamming door, as Harry fled the chamber. The others didn't move, watched Simon. The Abbot was taken aback by his utter stillness. He knew of Simon's temper, had expected him to rave and swear, to rage like a lion deprived of its whelp. As frightening as his violence would have been, Simon's frozen silence was no less unnerving. He waited for Guy or Humphrey to speak, to act. When neither did, he said, "My lord, what can I do for you? Mayhap if you were to go to the church . . ."

Simon turned. Yes, the church. Alone in the dark, alone with God. "I thank you," he said. "But not yet. First I have need of pen and parchment." How cold he was of a sudden, how tired. He could feel tremors shooting up his bad leg, an ache that burned into the bone. "I would be alone," he said, "so I may write to my wife."

"MY lord of Leicester, I thank you for sparing me these moments. The other innkeepers have chosen me to speak for them. I hope you'll not think me presumptuous for coming to you like this, but we did not know what else to do. Your eldest son . . . he's been frequenting the ale-houses in the town, where he's been drinking himself sodden. He . . . he seems very distraught, my lord, and his temper is raw. Last night he got into a nasty brawl, and witnesses say he provoked it. My lord, it is not for us to chastise an Earl's son; if you could but talk to him . . ."

Running out of words, he waited anxiously to see if he'd offended. His relief was vast, indeed, when Simon said tersely, "I'll see to it."

As the door closed behind the grateful innkeeper, Simon glanced toward the young man slouched in the shadows of the window-seat. "Why did I have to hear about this from strangers?"

Guy sat up abruptly. "How could I be the one to tell you, Papa? Harry would never forgive me!"

"No, I suppose not," Simon conceded. "I know the demon that torments him—guilt. He blames himself for Bran's capture, for our loss at Northampton."

Guy shrugged. "Well, it is hard to argue with that. If he'd not let Ned go—"

" 'What if' and 'if only' are games for fools, Guy. What if the French King had not betrayed our trust? If Henry's honor were not such a tattered flag? If only his brother Richard had been the firstborn . . . Where do you stop?"

"Papa . . . how much longer do you mean to tarry here at the abbey? I'm not good at waiting."

"You think I am?" Simon asked dryly. "But we've no choice. Until our scouts get back to St Albans, we've no way of knowing where Edward intends to strike next. It could be London, the Cinque Ports. Or he might choose to head north. The Midlands hold fast for me; he'd find tempting targets in Leicester, Nottingham, mayhap even Kenilworth."

Guy gasped, but after a moment, common sense mercifully reasserted itself. Kenilworth was the most impregnable stronghold in the realm; his father had seen to that. It could never be taken by force, could only be starved into submission. But thinking of his mother in the midst of a siege brought home to him, as Bran's plight had not, just how precarious was his family's future.

Getting to his feet, Simon walked over to the table. Guy had noticed that he favored his bad leg more obviously as the evening advanced. "How does the leg, Papa—truly? Is there much pain?"

"Some," Simon admitted. "It seems worse when it rains, or if I've been on it too long. I care naught about the pain, but it's likely to be weeks ere I can ride. Of all the times to take a fall!"

"If only—a game for fools, Papa," Guy murmured, and Simon gave him an intent look, and then a crooked smile.

There was a soft knock; the Abbot and the hosteller entered, followed by a young man in a sweat-stained, muddied mantle. "My lord, Brother Raymond and I were coming to invite you to dine with us on the morrow. But instead, I again find myself the bearer of bad tidings."

Simon looked past the Abbot. "I've seen you," he said, "in the Fitz Thomas household," and the youth nodded.

"Indeed, my lord. I am the Mayor's clerk. He bade me come to you, entreat you to return to London with all haste."

"Edward?" Simon said sharply, and the man shook his head.

"Nay, my lord, it is our own fear that threatens us. When word reached us yesterday of Northampton's surrender, the people panicked. All know what evils can befall a captured town; at Northampton, not even the churches were spared. Rumors took fire, and soon the entire city was ablaze with suspicion and dread. Men swapped fears in the streets, the ale-houses, and no tale was too outlandish to be believed. There was talk of treachery in Northampton, and people remembered how John de Gisors had plotted with the Lord Edward to trap you in Southwark. By day's end, rumors were rife of a conspiracy to betray the city to the King."

"Was there truth to these rumors?"

"In all honesty, my lord, we do not know. But this morning, the townsmen sought to root out the Judas in our midst. First they burned some of the houses of those known to be King's men. And then word spread that the Jews were in league with Lord Edward, that they'd made duplicate keys to the city gates, that they were hoarding Greek fire. A large crowd gathered in Cheapside, and from there they surged into the Jewry. The Mayor did what he could to stop the killing, but in truth, my lord, our city is out of control. Scores are dead, and as I rode out of Aldersgate, the sky was black with smoke from the Jewry."

"Does the Mayor give credence to these rumors about the Jews?"

"Nay, my lord, he does not. But he can find few to heed him. He believes that only your presence can quell the panic."

"Guy, go find your brother. You, come with me." Simon was halfway to the door before he remembered the Abbot. "I thank you for your hospitality, Abbot Roger, but there's much to be done and little time. We depart at dawn for London."

The Abbot made the sign of the cross. "Go with God," he said, and then, "My lord, is there anything that we can do for you?"

Simon paused, his hand on the door latch. "Yes," he said at last, "there is. You can pray for my son, for my men taken at Northampton."

As the door closed behind him, a sudden gust of wind rattled the shutters, tore one free. Brother Raymond hastened over to refasten it, while the Abbot stood where he was, staring after Simon.

"He is the one in need of our prayers," he said. "He lost more than his son at Northampton. He may well have lost his war, too."

THAT Wednesday, April 9, in God's year 1264, was a day of bloodshed and horror, would be a blight upon the memory of a great city. Fear found a natural mate in bigotry; the resulting union brought death and misery to the most defenseless and vulnerable members of the community. As mobs roamed the Jewry, looting and burning, forcing Jews to convert at knife-point, Mayor Fitz Thomas and the Justiciar, Hugh le Despenser, sought to end the slaughter. By offering refuge within the Tower of London, they were able to save some lives. But hundreds died in the madness that convulsed the city on that Wednesday in Holy Week, just ten days before the most sacred of Christian celebrations, the advent of Easter.

31

London, England
May 1264

FROM Northampton, Henry's army took Leicester and Nottingham, while Edward raided the lands of the Earl of Derby. Having reassured himself that London was in no immediate danger, Simon and the Earl of Gloucester launched an attack on Rochester Castle, which controlled the London–Dover road. The town fell that same day, and they laid siege to the castle. But upon getting word that Edward was approaching London, Simon hastened back to defend it again. The royal army was not yet ready to assault the capital, though. Instead, Henry and Edward circled around London, and raised Simon's siege at Rochester. So bitter had the war become that those of Simon's men unlucky enough to be captured were cruelly mutilated, their hands and feet chopped off. Henry and Edward then marched to the coast, hoping to secure ships for a naval assault upon London. But Dover Castle still held fast for Simon, and the sailors of the Cinque Ports put out to sea rather than obey the King's command. Thwarted, Edward captured the Earl of Gloucester's castle at Tonbridge. Simon still controlled London, but the circle was closing.

May was always a favorite month for the English, the most festive season of the year. Now it was a time of fear and uncertainty, and a chronicler wrote: "There was no peace in the realm. Everything was destroyed by slaughter, fire, rapine, and plunder. Everywhere there was clamor and trembling and woe."

ON this first Sunday in May, it was a rare sight to see a Jew on the streets of London. As soon as they left the illusory shelter of the Jewry, Jacob ben Judah and his son found themselves to be the cynosure of all eyes. The hostility they encountered was predictable, but muted. Like drunkards awakening after a lost weekend, Londoners were reluctant to remember, to face the consequences of their orgy of blood-hate. The infirm, aged rabbi and his newly scarred son reminded them of what had been done in the Lord's Name, and many were ashamed of their city, while wishing that Jacob and Benedict would discreetly disappear back into the Jewry where they belonged.

Jacob ben Judah sometimes envisioned his life as an hour-glass, one in which the grains of sand had dwindled down to the merest handful, for he was approaching his biblical three-score years and ten. Three English Kings had reigned within his memory span, and under each, his people had suffered. It had not always been so. In the time of the present King's grandfather, the Jews had thrived. But the coronation of the crusader-King, Lion-Heart, had been an anointing in Jewish blood. Survival was easier under Richard's brother John; he claimed their gold, not their lives. But life was hardest of all under the pious Henry, for in these years, the Church felt itself under siege, threatened by heretics, by internal schisms, above all, by the Jews who dwelt so precariously and conspicuously in their midst.

Approaching the Cheapside Cross, they recognized a man Jacob knew well, an apothecary who had often sold him herbs and ointments. Rabbis received no salary from their congregations, and Jacob eked out a living as a physician, a profession not as profitable as men supposed, for the Jewish community was a small one and his few Christian patients came to him surreptitiously, risking the damnation of their souls for the sake of their bodies. In the past, the apothecary had always greeted Jacob as a colleague, according him the respectful title of "Master." Now, face flushed, eyes averted, he passed Jacob and Benedict by in silence, as if twenty years of good will had never been.

Jacob said nothing, sorrowing over the frailty of decent men, the many who were so easily intimidated by the few. But Benedict's mouth twisted down. "The coward," he muttered, and Jacob's heart was flooded with pain.

It had been just twenty-five days since Benedict had been cornered in an alley near their Milk Street home, and his wounds had yet to heal. The blood-color crimson of his sling drew all eyes; upon it, he had defiantly pinned his badge, the dangerous, degrading symbol forced upon all Jews by order of the King. But if the people they encountered looked first at his badge, it was the ugly, inflamed welt above Benedict's eye that drew their stares. So raw and reddened was it that it elicited an involuntary wince from all but the most callous passer-by, and each time that Jacob looked upon it, as a father, not a physician, he was sickened. He knew full well that had he not chosen to visit kindred in Oxford, he would likely have died in the ruins of his ransacked house, for it was Benedict's youth that had saved him, enabling him to wrest a club from one of his tormentors, to fight his way free. Yet Jacob found himself wishing fervently that Benedict, not he, had been in Oxford on that April eve.

He could not keep his eyes from his son's wound, and when Benedict at last caught him at it, he sighed, said, "I fear, lad, that you'll have a nasty scar."

The young man's eyes blazed. "I hope to God I do," he said. "I'll bear it proudly to the end of my days!"

Jacob had nothing to say to that, no comfort to offer. He could not even assure Benedict that the horror of his memories would fade with time, for he knew better. He at least could recall days of comparative peace, days when their world had not seemed so dark, so fraught with peril. Benedict had no such consolation; the brief years of his life had been passed in a vortex. Born in the year that the Pope ordered the burning of their Talmud, coming to manhood amidst Christian accusations of ritual murder and coin clipping and usury, Benedict had never known a time in which Jews were not treated as heretics, looked upon as the enemies of Christ.

Benedict stopped so abruptly that Jacob stumbled against him. "Son? What is—" By then his eyes had tracked the path of Benedict's gaze. A young woman stood framed at an open window, brush in hand, and as the sun struck her free-flowing hair, it enveloped her in a halo of fire, bright enough to blind. Jacob drew a constricted breath. Miriam's hair had been that same shade of red copper. Miriam, child of light, quick-tongued, freckled, an angelic imp on the verge of womanhood; Jacob had been awaiting the day when he'd send the matchmaker to her father, seek her for his son. Now as he gazed up at the young woman in the window-seat, tears filled his eyes. He still did not know how Miriam had died. Benedict had said only, "I saw her body." No more than that.

"My son," he said softly, but at his touch, Benedict pulled away.

"Do not, Papa." His tone was fierce, his eyes imploring. "Do not speak of her," he said, and they walked on in silence. Ahead lay their destination; the towering spire of St Paul's Cathedral stabbed the sky, pierced a passing cloud. It was a daunting sight, for they were forbidden entry by both their own laws and those of the Christian faith. Benedict suddenly spun around, barring the way.

"Papa, there is still time to abandon this mad quest. Not only is it foolhardy; it is futile. What makes you think Leicester will listen to you? It's well known that he has no liking for Jews." Adding scathingly, "He is a devout Christian, is he not?"

"I'll not deny he's shown little sympathy for our plight. Yet if what men say of him is true, he is not like the others of his class, does not believe that justice is but a privilege of the highborn. He may not heed me; at least I shall try. If I do not, this man Fitz John will have murdered with impunity."

" 'This man Fitz John,' " Benedict echoed grimly. "Better say it as it is, Papa—this lord. Even if he were not, what matter? What Gentile was ever punished for killing a Jew? But if you must reach for the moon, why not also seek the sun? Why not beseech Leicester to take measures against the Earl of Gloucester, too? Is his guilt any less than Fitz John's? After the London massacre, he let his men loose on the Canterbury Jews; is he never to answer for it?"

"Gloucester may be too great a lord to do earthly penance. But he will answer to God," Jacob said solemnly. "Never doubt that, Benedict."

His son was not so sure; he'd not been blessed with Jacob's sublime faith. The gateway loomed before them; as they passed through into the churchyard, Benedict hunched his shoulders, bracing for the worst. As he feared, their appearance created a stir; they'd not even reached Paul's Cross before they were accosted by a well-dressed man of middle years, flushed with indignation.

"You profane our Holy Day by your presence here," he said curtly. "You'd like it not if Christians were to invade your temple—"

"But you do." Benedict's smile was bitter. "Your Dominican friars often force their way into our synagogue, compel us to interrupt our prayers whilst they preach."

The man's mouth dropped open. It may have been sheer shock at being rebuffed by a Jew. It may have been instinct. But there was something about this dark, intense youth that alarmed him. The ugly slash on Benedict's forehead seemed to sear like a brand; the man found himself mesmerized by it, unable to tear his gaze away. The tension of the moment slowly ebbed. Turning abruptly on his heel, he strode off.

Jacob expelled an uneven breath. As he looked at his son, all he could see was a coiled bow, a hempen bowstring drawn back to the breaking point. He ought never to have allowed the lad to come, never. And yet how could he have prevented it?

"We'd best wait on the south side of the churchyard, Papa. Leicester will enter at the west door." Benedict had often surprised his father by the stray bits of miscellaneous information he managed to garner, and it seemed natural to Jacob that his son should somehow know the chief entrance of the cathedral. He followed, praying that his hunch was right, that amidst the preparations for war, Simon de Montfort would still find time to attend a Requiem Mass for the dead of Northampton.

The ensuing wait was a stressful one, and when Simon finally did arrive, they almost missed him, for they had been watching for his horse litter. It was the talk of London, so unusual was its design, a box-like structure suspended on long poles, custom-made to cushion a healing leg. They did not notice the men on horseback, therefore did not recognize Simon until the crowd surged forward.

Simon was known on sight to both Jacob and his son; over the years, they'd often watched him ride through London's streets. Jacob was startled now to see how suddenly Simon seemed to have aged. The darkly circled eyes, the tautly set mouth, the lack of spring in his step: to Jacob, they spoke of sleepless nights, troubled days. How fearful he must be for his family, Jacob thought, so familiar an emotion that he could not repress an instant of identification with the highborn Earl, even a flicker of unwelcome pity. For time was running out, the shadows cast by Northampton lengthening. And Jacob's faith began to waver; how could he expect a fair hearing from a man with his back to the wall?

Benedict, too, was staring at Simon. But for him it was simpler. He saw an English lord, a crusader knight, an enemy.

As soon as he dismounted, Simon found himself surrounded. People pressed in on all sides, hands outstretched. But they sought neither alms nor banter, just the reassurance of his presence in their midst. A strange hush had fallen over the churchyard. In recent days Simon had only to venture out onto the street for these subdued, anxious crowds to gather. It had chilled him to the bone once he understood. Theirs was the courage of despair. They knew what horrors had befallen the citizens of Northampton, of Leicester, Nottingham, knew what vengeance Edward would exact from them. And yet they held fast, attempted no deals, no eleventh-hour surrenders, trusting in Simon to conjure up a miracle, to save their city. It was a terrible burden, their trust.

Simon frowned at sight of the Jews, that they should stand so boldly in the very shadow of God's House. But he made no effort to learn the reason for their unseemly presence here; he had greater cares. He was both surprised and annoyed when Jacob stepped into his path.

"My lord, it is most urgent that I speak with you. If you could but give me a few moments after the Mass . . ."

All day long, men asked favors of him, sought to lay small claims to dwindling hours. This at least was an easy request to refuse. Simon shook his head, said brusquely, "I have no time to spare." But as he moved past the rabbi, Jacob's next words halted him in his tracks.

"The Bishop of Lincoln would have found the time, my lord," he said, and Simon swung around to stare at him.

"The Bishop of Lincoln was very dear to me. I would not have his name bandied about by disbelievers."

Jacob was of a sudden assailed by dreadful doubts; could he have been wrong about this man? "I knew His Grace," he said, adding automatically the blessing his brethren accorded their dead, "May peace be upon him."

"Where did you know him?" Simon demanded, so suspiciously that Jacob was thankful he could give an honest answer, that he had truth on his side.

"In Oxford. I was born there, made it my home for many years. During the lord Bishop's tenure as Chancellor of the university, he desired to learn Hebrew, sent into the Jewry for a tutor. I was the one summoned."

"He did mention such a tutor," Simon conceded, still wary. "That was you?"

Jacob nodded. "I do not think, my lord, that he would have been offended to hear his name in my mouth."

Simon was still frowning. "In less than two days, I lead an army out of London. If this matter of yours was so pressing, why did you not seek me out ere this?"

"I did, my lord. But your servants always turned me away."

The church bells had begun to toll. Simon glanced toward the cathedral, back toward Jacob. "Come to the Tower after Compline. I will try to find time for you then."

Benedict had never expected that Simon might actually agree to see his father, and he was appalled at the thought of returning to the Tower, so recently his own refuge. "Papa, you must not do this," he cried, pulling his father aside. "This man is not to be trusted. You'd imperil yourself for naught!"

"I know well the risk," Jacob admitted. "But if we do not speak for our dead, who will?"

IT had been a very long day for Simon. After knighting several of his young supporters, he met with the Earls of Gloucester and Oxford, the Bishops of Chichester, London, and Worcester, and the city's Mayor. It was a council of war that resolved upon one last plea for peace. On the morrow the Bishops were to depart for Sussex, to put before Henry an offer to negotiate, even to pay reparations.

But none of the men gathered in the Tower that evening truly expected that the Bishops would prevail, Simon least of all. He suspected that even if he were to renounce the Provisions, it would not be enough. Edward wanted blood. So, too, did Richard, still aggrieved over the sacking of his Isleworth manor. And theirs were voices Henry would heed, if indeed he needed prodding. Simon was well aware just how much his brother-in-law now hated him.

Reaching for a wine cup at his elbow, he found himself wondering if it was all foreordained. He could not compromise. Henry could not keep faith. Mayhap this was meant to be, even as far back as his first days at the English court. But if a battlefield confrontation was inevitable, he was by no means ready to concede that it was lost, no matter the odds, and he said abruptly:

"We must hope for the best, whilst making ready for the worst. We have to assume that Henry will spurn our offer. If so, we shall be facing the King's army within the week."

The Earl of Gloucester shifted in his seat. His belief in the Provisions had not faltered, but sometimes he could not understand how it had ever come to this, that he should be a ringleader in rebellion against his King, while still four months shy of his twenty-first birthday. Nor did he share the others' almost mystical faith in Simon's battle lore. "I am not sure that we'd be wise to force a confrontation," he confessed. "Our scouts say the King's army numbers nigh on ten thousand, twice the size of ours. Why seek the King out when we'll be at such a decided disadvantage?"

"What would we gain by delay? We lost the heart of our army at Northampton, can expect no reinforcements. But that is not true for the King. His Queen has hired enough Flemish mercenaries to overrun half the country. Would you have us await their arrival on English shores? Do you want to find yourself trapped in London? In my life, I've been both the besieged and the besieger, and I know damned well which I prefer!"

At that moment, Simon happened to catch the Bishop of Worcester's admonitory eye, and he made a half-hearted attempt to curb his impatience. "We cannot allow Henry to regain control of the coastal ports. If I were he, I'd be laying siege to Dover even as we speak. Instead, he seems to be heading for the Earl of Surrey's castle at Lewes, for reasons that totally escape me. The men of the Weald hold fast for us—and if Christendom boasts better bowmen, they're to be found only in Wales. No, Henry has blundered into hostile territory, and we'd be fools not to take full advantage of it."

"What of the Londoners, Simon?" The query came from Hugh le Despenser, but it was in every man's mind. War, as they knew it, made no provisions for volunteers. Men rode to battle because they were bound by oaths of fealty, or because they were paid to fight. But the Londoners were neither knights nor mercenaries. Townsmen unskilled in the ways of war, they were drilling daily in Cheapside, determined to prove themselves, undaunted by Edward's oft-quoted jeer that not a one of them would know a halberd from a hayrick in the dark. Observers could not help but be impressed by their resolve. If few of the battle-wise knights believed that zeal could offset experience, those were doubts they kept to themselves. For as green and raw as these London recruits were, they were needed, each and every one.

"I've decided to put the Londoners under Nicholas Segrave's command," Simon said, earning widespread mutterings of approval, for Segrave was a seasoned soldier, respected by all. Nor was there competition for that command; too many feared the Londoners might break under their first taste of battle.

Humphrey de Bohun smothered a yawn; sleep was a stranger to them all these days. "Has there been any word from the Earl of Derby?"

Simon shook his head. "Not since Edward seized his castle at Tutbury. But if he meant to fight with us, he'd be here."

Derby's defection was a bitter disappointment, if not altogether unexpected; the young Earl was one for looking to his own interests. But Gloucester could not keep from suggesting sourly, "Mayhap he'd still be with us if Harry de Montfort had not antagonized him so needlessly at Gloucester. Derby is known to have been outraged when de Montfort let Edward go, and who can blame him?"

Harry flushed, half rose from his seat. But Guy was quicker. "What would you know of it? Whilst my brothers were fighting de Mortimer and his Marcher allies, you were holed up in Tonbridge. The only action you saw all spring was when you attacked the Canterbury Jews." Adding with a sneer, "I daresay they resisted fiercely!"

Gloucester was on his feet, face mottled with rage. "The Canterbury Jewry was rife with treachery; you ought to be thankful I rooted it out in time. As for being 'holed up' in Tonbridge, I was keeping watch upon the coast! I then moved on Rochester, took the town, and—"

"The Devil you did!" Harry cut in hotly. "I was there, remember? It was my father who captured Rochester, by sending that burning barge against the bridge pilings—"

"Enough!" Simon could outshout anyone when he chose. "I cannot believe that you'd be fools enough to fight on a cliff's edge. Are the odds facing us not daunting enough without shedding our own blood?"

His sons at once subsided. So, too, did Gloucester, mollified that Simon's anger had been so indiscriminately aimed. It was the Mayor who tactfully dispelled the tension by changing the subject. Simon was coming to rely more and more upon the finesse of his London ally, a draper with all the instincts of a born diplomat. Gloucester rose, headed for the privy chamber tucked away into the north wall, and with his departure, the atmosphere lightened still further. A break was in order. As men relaxed, Simon rose stiffly, moved toward the hearth. His leg had begun to throb, a sure sign of fatigue; it was with a dull sense of surprise that he realized it was nigh on seventeen hours since he'd last seen a bed.

He was pleased when he was joined by Thomas Fitz Thomas; as unlike as the two men were, a genuine bond was developing between them. It occurred to Simon now that Fitz Thomas might be loath to relinquish command of his Londoners to Nicholas Segrave. But with his first words, the Mayor began to laugh.

"I nurse no delusions of grandeur, my lord, am no soldier. Just tell me what you would have me do."

After dealing with unpredictable, thin-skinned personalities like Gloucester and Derby, Simon found Fitz Thomas to be a veritable godsend, and he gave the younger man a grateful grin. "Bless your good nature, Tom! But it is no easy task I ask of you. I want you to remain in London, to hold the city for us. If any man can keep the people from panicking again, you're the one."

"I hope to God you're right, my lord." Fitz Thomas was no longer smiling, for he knew the fear that seethed just beneath the surface of his city. If Simon lost . . . But there were fates too dire to contemplate. He was secretly relieved by Simon's request. London was the lodestar of his life; come what may, he wanted to be with his city. "My Cecilia has kin in St Albans," he confided quietly, "but she refuses to leave London, insists that her place is with me."

Simon's smile was wry. "Passing strange," he said, "that you should say that. After Northampton fell, I wrote to my wife, told her I thought it best that she travel to Dover, take ship for France and there wait out the war, as Henry's Queen is doing. I gave Nell no choice in the matter . . . and where is she now? Paris? Montfort l'Amaury? No . . . Kenilworth."

Fitz Thomas laughed. He would have imagined that Simon de Montfort, of all men, was master of his own household—had he not once met Simon's headstrong lady. They were, he thought, like twin comets, blazing across the heavens in flaming harmony, and some of his unease began to ebb. If ever a man was born to win, to triumph over all adversity, it was this man. How could he lose to the inept, feckless Henry? "My lord . . . have you had any word about your son?"

Simon shook his head. "All we know is that Bran is being held at Windsor Castle. But beyond that, we—"

"Beg pardon, my lord Leicester." The guard had not ventured far from the door, instead, raised his voice, and in consequence, turned all heads his way. "There's an old Jew at the land-gate, seeking entry. We'd have chased him off, but he insisted that you're expecting him."

"Damnation!" Simon had forgotten entirely about his morning encounter at St Paul's. But when the Constable of the Tower impatiently ordered the guard to "send the Jew away," Simon reluctantly countermanded him. "No . . . I did agree to see the man. Send him up."

Under different circumstances, Benedict would have welcomed this opportunity to inspect the uppermost chamber of the White Tower, for London legend held that twenty years past, a highborn Welsh prisoner had plunged to his death from one of these windows. Now, however, it took an enormous effort of will just to cross the threshold, so overt was the hostility within.

"I feel like Daniel entering the lion's den," he whispered, "or one of those Christian martyrs in a Roman amphitheater." That was too flippant for his father's taste, though. Jacob gave him a burning glance, a silent warning to guard his tongue as if his life depended upon it, for well it might. Chastened—the last thing he'd wanted was to add to Jacob's anxiety—Benedict followed his father into the chamber.

Benedict truly did feel as if he'd run straight into a stone wall, so oppressive was the atmosphere in the room. His father had once made a grim jest, that a Jew in England was caught between the twin perils of Scylla and Charybdis. But to Benedict, the Church was always a greater enemy than the King, for it was the Church that taught its sons and daughters to hate Jews as an act of faith, it was the Church that branded them as Antichrists and heretics. It frightened him to recognize the white tunic and black cloak of a Dominican Prior, for if the Templars were the knights of Christ, the friars were His foot-soldiers, and of all the orders, the Black Friars were the most zealous. Glancing nervously about the chamber, his eyes were drawn to a large, carved crucifix high on the wall above their heads. Idolators. *Gods of silver or gods of gold, ye shall not make unto you.* He shivered suddenly. What had ever possessed Papa to come here?

"Master Jacob, is it not?" As the speaker came out of the shadows, Benedict felt a jolt of recognition. His was an embittered conviction, that there was not a Gentile alive whom a Jew dared trust—with the possible exception of this man. He owed Thomas Fitz Thomas his life, for it was the Mayor's men who had gotten him to safety in the Tower. Fitz Thomas had gone into the Jewry himself, seeking to end the slaughter, and now the sight of him took Benedict's breath, conjuring up a memory of disturbing vividness—Fitz Thomas's fair hair in disarray, his face the color of chalk under the harsh glare of torch-light, mouth contorted with rage, with an emotion Benedict had not expected a Christian to feel—horror.

Simon was looking at the Mayor in surprise. "You know this man, Tom?"

"Yes, my lord, I do. I've dealt with him in the past, when problems arose in the Jewry," Fitz Thomas said, and smiled at Jacob and his son, as if offering courtesy to a Jew was too commonplace to warrant comment. It was, Benedict thought, a brave thing to do under the eyes of three Bishops. But he seemed to detect a faint thawing in the chill, eloquent testimony to Fitz Thomas's standing with his highborn allies. Simon moved forward, and after glancing at Jacob's cane, gestured for a servant to bring forth a stool.

It was at that moment that the Earl of Gloucester emerged from the privy chamber. "God's wrath! Why are these Jews here?"

Benedict was no less shocked than Gloucester. His greatest fear had been that Fitz John, the man his father meant to accuse, might be present at this meeting. He'd never given a thought to Gloucester. Now, confronted with the young Earl, he felt blood surging into his face, roaring in his ears, and as Gloucester strode toward them, he stepped protectively in front of his father.

"How dare you come amongst us like this, after what you've done?" Gloucester demanded, and Benedict began to tremble with a killing rage.

"What we've done?" he echoed. "The massacre was of your doing, not ours!"

"Whatever happened, you brought it upon yourselves. Had you not been plotting to betray the city to the King—"

"That is not so! We knew nothing of a plot! Why would we conspire with the King? Why would we risk our lives for a man who bleeds us white?"

"Why do you Jews do anything—for money, of course! You'd like nothing better than to stir up dissension between Christians, for no evil is beneath you. You befoul our very air with your infidel breaths, you poison England with your vile, foreign ways, you blaspheme and—"

"We are not infidels! We believe in one God as you do, the God of Israel. And we are not foreigners." From a great distance, Benedict could hear a voice strangely like his own, slurred with fury, impossible to silence. "We came to England at the behest of William the Bastard—just as your people did. We have lived here for nigh on two hundred years. We speak Norman-French as you do. My family does not call me by my Hebrew name, Berechiah, they call me Benedict. England is our home, too!"

"Your home, by rights, should be in Hell! But we are not deceived by your guile. You are servants of Satan, dwelling in our very midst. Yet the day is coming when we shall no longer tolerate your presence amongst us, for you mock Christ's Passion, you profane the Eucharist, you crucify Christian children in your accursed rituals—"

"Lies and more lies!" Benedict was vaguely aware of someone pulling at his sleeve. But he could not stop himself. A red haze swam before his eyes. Blood of the innocents—the shade of Gloucester's hair. Miriam's hair. "Those are tales told to frighten the simple, the gullible. No men of sense give them credence," he said scornfully, "only fools!"

Gloucester gave an audible gasp. As if in slow motion, Benedict saw his fist clench, his arm swing back. But the blow never connected. Simon was suddenly between them, catching Gloucester's wrist in mid-air.

"Would you shame me by striking a guest at my hearth?"

Gloucester wrenched free, with such force that he stumbled backward. So easy was it to transfer his fury from Benedict to Simon that the two men blurred in his mind, the French-born Earl and the foreign Jew he sought to protect. Why? What true Christian would take a Jew's part? And as he stared at Simon, Gloucester felt a rush of fear—what if Leicester were in league with the Jews? God's truth, but the Earl was as glib as any Jew, preached the Provisions like Holy Writ. Had he been too quick to heed Leicester's beguilements? What if he'd allowed his passion for the Provisions to imperil his soul?

There was such a wild look on his face that Simon's anger gave way to alarm. "Gilbert? Are you ill?"

Gloucester blinked, and his panic receded. Leicester was French, he was foreign, he was not to be trusted. But he was no heretic. "You do shame yourself, my lord," he said unsteadily, "by consorting with these alien disbelievers, these . . . these agents of evil. God sees—and judges. You'd best bear that in mind. As for me, I'll not stay in the company of Jews. I value too highly my immortal soul." He did not wait for Simon's response. Convinced that the last word had been his, he stalked from the chamber.

Jacob slowly unclenched his fingers from his son's arm. "Thank you, my lord," he said huskily, convinced that Simon's intervention might well have saved Benedict's life. Simon turned toward him, and he saw how little his gratitude meant to the other man; Simon was furious.

"If Edward and Henry had but one wish," he snapped, "I daresay it would be for this—a falling-out with Gloucester on the eve of battle!" His eyes fastened coldly on Benedict. "If you'd come here with evil intent, you could not have done more damage to our cause."

The mere suggestion was enough to chill Jacob, for he knew that even if Simon himself did not suspect their motives, there were men in the room who would. So accustomed was he to dealing with religious bias that he'd rarely given much thought to the political dimensions of their danger. Now he was suddenly seeing his people from Simon de Montfort's perspective—as the King's accomplices—and the implications were darkly disturbing.

"I can understand why you would view us with suspicion, my lord. We are a significant source of revenue for the King. I'll not deny that the tallages levied upon England's Jews help him to make war upon you. But my lord of Leicester, the fault does not lie with us. We are not partners in crime, we are the King's chattels. I believe the exact legal concept is called 'servi camerae,' but that does not matter. What does is that my people are totally dependent upon the King's will, the King's whims. If we keep his coffers filled, it is not by choice. In all the wars and rebellions that have torn England asunder—King Stephen versus the Empress Maud, King John and his barons, King Henry and you, my lord—never have the Jews interfered. We have no vested interest in the King's victory. We do but obey—to save our lives."

Simon's mouth twitched. "If I did not know that Jews were barred from universities, I could believe you were a lawyer."

Jacob's relief was considerable. Simon's response had been sardonic but not hostile, and he dared hope that he had planted a seed. His belief that the Earl of Leicester was an honorable man, one amenable to reason, once more seemed plausible, worth pursuing. But it was then that his son's bitterness burst forth again.

"Papa, do not waste your breath. How can you expect this man to heed your appeal? One of his first acts as Earl of Leicester was to banish all the Jews from his domains!"

Jacob was appalled, but as he turned back toward Simon, he saw no anger in the other man's face, only surprise. "Indeed, I did expel the Jews from Leicester," he said, so matter-of-factly that Jacob suddenly understood why Simon had taken no offense; he did not see his action as one that needed defending. "But it was not done to punish the Jews. My intent was to protect my Christian brethren, to keep them from being sucked dry by Jewish money-lenders. Holy Church imposes responsibilities upon those who wield power, and one of them is to combat the evils of usury."

The other men had been listening in silence, with varying degrees of interest or amusement or resentment. At that, though, murmurs of approval rose from numerous throats. The Bishop of Worcester was quick to confirm Simon's concept of Christian lordship, in clipped, dispassionate tones that could not disguise a visceral antipathy, nuances of distaste not lost upon Jacob or his son. But Humphrey de Bohun's antagonism was not cloaked in even the thinnest veneer of civility; he was known to be deeply in debt to Hereford money-lenders.

"You speak right eloquently of the poor, persecuted Jews. But what have you to say of their money-lending? Are you one of that accursed breed? Do you prey upon a man's need, lead him on till he's hopelessly entangled in your web?"

Fitz Thomas's voice came calmly from the shadows. "Master Jacob is a physician, I believe."

"I have been charged interest rates as high as sixty percent of the debt!" But Humphrey's indignation was no longer dangerously directed at Jacob; Fitz Thomas's interruption had been adroitly timed for maximum effect.

Jacob prudently kept silent; money-lending was about as risky a topic as there could be between Jew and Gentile. It was his son who rushed heedlessly ahead, his son who had always spoken of money-lenders with disdain. "They charge such high interest rates," Benedict said, "because they have so little chance of ever collecting the debt. The King can cancel it at any time, and often does, a magnanimous gesture that costs him nothing and earns the debtor's gratitude. A most successful business transaction, for only the Jew suffers. Nor is that his only risk. The King levies tallages whenever he is short of funds, and if a Jew cannot scrape up the money demanded, he'll find himself rotting in gaol whilst his family and friends beggar themselves on his behalf."

"How truly heart-rending!" The speaker was obviously a de Montfort son; Benedict just wasn't sure which one. As he leaned forward, the candles reflected glints in eyes as dark and opaque as wood-smoke, and Benedict decided this must be Guy. They were very close in age, very alike in coloring, and yet they could have been born in different centuries, so alien were their worlds. Guy was smiling, without amusement. "Those do sound like occupational hazards to me," he said challengingly, "hardly grounds for condolences."

Jacob did not like the intensity of his gaze. It alarmed him that one of these young lords should single his son out for special notice, and he sought hastily to draw attention back to himself. "You would be right, Sir Guy—if money-lending was an occupation of choice. But that is not so. For most of my brethren, it is the only livelihood open to them. We are barred from the craft and trade guilds. We are not permitted to sell our goods in your market places. Your Church forbids us to work for Christians, or even to employ them. Because we cannot take your oaths of homage, we cannot hold land. Your universities are closed to us. So, too, are your courts, since we cannot swear upon your holy relics. So how are we to live?"

He paused for breath, trying to gauge the impact of his words. While none had yet to interrupt, only a few seemed to be truly listening; he was heartened, though, that Simon was one of them. He hesitated, and then concluded quietly, "Your society barricades all roads but one. Is it fair, then, to scorn us for taking the only path possible?"

His question found no favor with his listeners, save only Benedict, who felt a surge of pride. But of all those affronted by Jacob's presence there, none were as irate as the Prior of London's Dominican friary. "What do you expect from us—that we pity your plight? It is God's Will that you suffer for your sins. Your punishment for the crucifixion of Our Lord Christ was the destruction of your temple. From that day, you were condemned to wander the world, outcasts and Ishmaels, bearing the curse of Cain."

The exhaustion came upon Jacob without warning, sapping his strength, and he looked yearningly at a nearby footstool. But in the confusion following Gloucester's return, Simon had forgotten to give him permission to sit. He leaned heavily upon his cane, not realizing how much his fatigue had dulled his caution until he heard his own voice, saying with rash candor, "Your Scriptures may speak of our suffering, but they also decree, 'Slay them not.' Your Book of Psalms, I believe?"

"How would you have such knowledge of our Holy Writ?"

The question seemed innocuous; Jacob knew better. No answer he gave would satisfy the Prior, and equivocation would only inflame his suspicions all the more, for the Dominicans were quick to detect the scent of sulphur. He temporized, and then deliverance came from an entirely unexpected quarter.

"In all honesty, I see nothing sinister in his familiarity with Scriptures," Simon interrupted, with obvious impatience. "He tutored my lord Bishop of Lincoln in Hebrew for years. I'd wager some of that time was spent in theological debate." A faint smile touched the corner of his mouth. "The Bishop," he said, "was a fisherman. But what he angled for was souls."

Jacob nodded gravely. "The Bishop of Lincoln was a renowned scholar," he said. "I came to have great respect for him."

"So did I." Simon's eyes fell upon the stool and he gestured, freeing Jacob to sit. Leaning back against the table, for he'd become adept at inconspicuously favoring his weakened leg, he said, "Now . . . tell me what you want from me."

Jacob sank down gratefully on the stool. "I want justice, my lord. You were not there to see the horror with your own eyes, and I do not think you realize the full extent of the bloodshed. Men were slain at evening prayers, bled to death in their own homes. Our women were not spared, not even our children . . . Our synagogue was burned, our houses were looted, our cemetery in Wood Street desecrated. My lord, it was a slaughter of innocents. We—"

Fitz Thomas could bear to hear no more. "It was an abomination unto the Lord, and it shames me that it should have happened in my city. If only I—"

"Nay, you've no cause to reproach yourself. You did your best to stop the carnage." Jacob glanced toward Hugh le Despenser. "As did the Justiciar. But there is a madness that comes over men at such times, a . . . a lust for blood."

Simon nodded. "And for gold," he said grimly.

"Indeed, my lord. Not all of them had killing in mind. Some must have seen the rioting as a rare chance for ill-gotten gains. Men kill for many reasons, they steal for but one—greed." Jacob drew a bracing breath. "There were your men amongst that mob, my lord."

Simon didn't deny it. "Yes," he said, "it's likely there were. You would think that if a man embraced a noble cause, he would not be capable of such base crimes, and yet that is not so. I confess I've long been baffled by the contradictions in man's nature. How is it that Edward can have so much courage and so little honor? Men say King John was cruel, vengeful, and faithless. How is it, then, that he cared more for the weal of his subjects than Henry does?"

Moving away from the table, Simon stood for a moment before Jacob, eyes searching the aged rabbi's face. "On the eighteenth of April, I captured the town of Rochester, laid siege to the castle. Whenever I take a town, I give orders that my men are not to commit sacrilege, that there's to be no raping or looting. I've hanged men for disobeying those commands. Moreover, this was Good Friday, one of the most sacred days of the year. And yet some of the soldiers still plundered the priory of St Andrew, stole holy relics, and stabled their horses in the cloisters, even in the nave of the church."

Jacob's fatigue was miraculously gone, alleviated by this sudden infusion of hope. He felt certain that this was the first genuine conversation Simon de Montfort had ever had with a Jew, for a man of his rank would not deal himself with money-lenders, would leave that for his steward to do. This tenuous accord, however tentative, however unlikely, was, God willing, a beginning.

"I agree with you, my lord. I would that I could understand man's cruelty to man, for we are all brothers in Adam. It must be that they lose their identity in a crowd, become nameless, faceless, and free to sin . . . I do know how difficult it is to punish them, even to identify them." He saw that Simon was listening intently, and he got to his feet, no longer choosing his words with care, letting them spill out spontaneously, from the heart.

"But there is one man, my lord, who cannot deny his guilt. There are witnesses, for his arrogance was such that he cared not at all who saw him. When that maddened mob surged into the Jewry, he was in the forefront of the attack. He did his share of looting and burning, and then he led men to the house of Isaac, son of Aaron, a wealthy money-lender. They emptied Isaac's coffers, stripped the embroidered hangings from his walls, stole his candle-sticks and plate, took all that could be carried out. And then they torched the house. But ere they did, this man ran Isaac through with his sword. My lord of Leicester, he must be punished for this despicable crime. You alone have the power, I entreat you to use it. Call him to account for his sins."

Simon was frowning. "Who is this man?"

"His name, my lord, is John Fitz John."

There was a second or so of silence, and then pandemonium. "Who?" If Simon sounded incredulous, the other voices were hotly indignant.

"Do you not know who he is? Fitz John is Gloucester's cousin!"

"And my friend!" Harry jumped to his feet so hastily that he jarred the table, tipping over several wine cups, which, in turn, set off a wave of startled oaths. Harry paid them no heed, so single-minded was he in defense of Fitz John, a favorite carousing companion. "I'll not have his name slandered!"

Hugh le Despenser was on his feet, too. "John and I are kinsmen; our wives are sisters. I did what I could to stop the killing in the Jewry, and I would see the offenders punished. But you cannot treat a man of John's rank as if he were a common churl!"

"Your timing is deplorable, old man!" Guy alone of the speakers did not sound in the least offended. Making no attempt to hide his amusement, he said, "My lord father knighted Fitz John this very noon!"

Jacob had not been disheartened by the uproar; he'd expected no less. But at that, he took a quick step toward Simon, unable to hide his dismay. "My lord, is that true?"

Simon nodded. "Do you have any idea what you ask of me?"

"Yes, my lord, I do. I know this man is of good birth, but that did not keep you from serving justice in Gascony. You protected the Gascon people, townsmen and farmers who were being cheated and robbed by the lords of their province. You called them bandits and cast them into prison. Why can you not do the same for Fitz John?"

"I was right," Simon said. "You do not understand in the least. It is not Fitz John's blood that concerns me, it is the life blood of England. Have you paid so little heed to our plight? In a matter of days, we'll be facing the King across a battlefield, and the odds are not in our favor. Not only is my army badly outnumbered, a good portion of my men are green London lads who've never drawn blood. But I cannot spare even one of them. And you'd have me lose one of my best commanders? Not to mention the knights and men-at-arms who owe allegiance to Fitz John! I have risked all for the Provisions; not even my family has been spared. You must be mad if you think I would sacrifice our only chance of victory for your vengeance!"

Benedict was not surprised, and therefore, not disappointed. He found he actually preferred such a pragmatic refusal, for he'd been expecting an exoneration based upon birth. But it was different for Jacob. For him, Simon's refusal was shattering.

"How can you be so indifferent to our suffering? Do you care nothing for the fact that the blood of my people is on your hands?"

"How dare you make such an accusation? The killing in the Jewry was none of my doing, and well you know it!"

"Oh, I know you took no part in the killing. And I believe you disapproved of it, mayhap even deplored it. But my lord, that is not enough. Where is your outrage?"

"What in blazes are you talking about?"

"This man felt it!" Pointing toward Fitz Thomas. "He was appalled by the slaughter. Why were you not equally appalled, my lord? I know what is said of you, that you feel bound to protect the weak and the poor. It must be true, else these Londoners would not be so willing to die for you. Again and again you've shown a surprising sympathy for the downtrodden, the defenseless, and it does you great credit. But what people are more oppressed than mine? Why do you harden your heart against us? Why have you no pity to spare for the Jews?"

"Because you deny Our Lord Christ!"

There was such passion in his voice that Jacob took an instinctive step backward, dropping his cane. But with Simon's next words, he realized that Simon's emotion was not anger.

"I was taught that over every Jew, God holds His breath, waiting to see if he will decide for Christ. How can you give Our Lord such grief? How can you reject salvation?" Simon reached out, grasped Jacob's arm. "It took courage for you to come here. Yours is a soul worth saving! Why will you not admit that Christ is the Messiah? Do you not fear damnation?"

It was utterly still. Benedict had moved to his father's side, and he now waited wordlessly for Jacob's answer. The rabbi met Simon's eyes without flinching. "I think I can best answer you, my lord, by posing a question. I know you took the cross in your youth, passed some months in the Holy Land. Many of your fellow crusaders were taken prisoner by the Saracens. If that had happened to you, and you were given a choice between abjuring your Christian faith and death, which would you have chosen?"

"Death," Simon said simply, with no bravado, and Jacob nodded.

"Just so, my lord," he said softly.

As the implications of his answer sank in, Simon's disappointment was as sharp as any sword. So intense had his desire been to bring Jacob from darkness to light that he'd convinced himself he would prevail, that this time God would not hold His breath in vain. He stepped back, released Jacob's arm. "I'll not deny," he said bleakly, "that your people are willing to die for your beliefs. But that proves nothing. Not even martyrdom can sanctify a false faith."

Jacob bent down, slowly retrieved his cane. "I've had my say. We'll take up no more of your time, my lord."

Benedict took his arm, expecting at any moment to hear a summons to stop, not yet convinced they could escape this particular lion's den unscathed. But Simon watched them in silence, and after an endless trek, they reached safety, the enveloping dark of the stairwell.

A PALL had settled over the room. Most of the men felt uncomfortable, without knowing exactly why. Nerves were on edge, tempers frayed, and when Guy made a dubious joke about John Fitz John and the money he suddenly had to spend, Harry almost hit him. Simon silenced them with a look, which stung more than words could have done. He now knew where Fitz John had gotten the funds he'd so generously put at their disposal. But he did not regret his refusal to punish the man. That was an easy decision to make, a soldier's decision, the only decision. What disturbed him was his failure with Jacob.

"It was like watching a candle," he said suddenly. "It flickered, seemed about to catch fire, and then guttered out."

The Bishop of Worcester slid a wine cup along the length of the table. "You ought not to have seen those Jews, Simon. You've cares enough at the moment, need not take on any more."

"I'm sorry I did," Simon admitted. Picking up the cup, he then set it down untasted. "But after what happened in the Jewry, I suppose I owed them that much."

"Nay, my lord, do you not see the danger in such thinking?" The Dominican Prior startled them all, so loudly did he speak, for all the world as if he were preaching a fire-and-brimstone sermon at Paul's Cross. "You see now how insidiously they insinuate themselves, how beguiling they can be. They would take shameless advantage of our pity, if we let them."

While the Bishop of Worcester agreed with the sentiments, he disapproved of the extravagant delivery; in his experience, the friars always indulged in unnecessary theatrics, and it irked him that they had such success in swaying the people. "It is sadly true," he said, "what Seneca so long ago concluded, that no enemy is more capable of inflicting injury than a familiar one. I regret the killings, of course. Jews bear witness on our behalf that we have not forged the prophecies about Our Lord Christ. They are not to be harmed; they must be converted to the True Faith, to save their souls and to hasten the Second Coming. But until then, they must be strictly segregated, lest their heresies infect unwary Christians."

To Simon, that sounded like an oblique rebuke. Had he indeed let his guard down too much? "I well know we must be wary of them," he said, but still his disquiet lingered, and he moved restlessly to the window.

Fitz Thomas, sensing his mood, followed with a cup of wine. So did a contrite Harry, and Simon allowed his son to prop cushions under his leg, too tired to deny his discomfort. He leaned back in the window-seat, watching them both, and after a long silence, said, "When I was just a lad, about eight or so, my lady mother summoned before her all the Jews in the French city of Toulouse. She demanded that they renounce Judaism, accept the Christian faith. When they refused, she had them imprisoned, and gave their children to local families, to be raised as Christians. But even then, most of them still held fast. Only forty-seven would agree." A look of surprise crossed his face. "Strange, that I should remember the exact number, after so many years . . ."

This was a story Harry had not heard before. Simon had told his sons how he'd been trapped in a siege at the age of seven, and he'd related how, when his father once needed reinforcements, his mother had led them herself. But this he'd never shared. "What happened to the Jews, Papa?"

"When my father returned to Toulouse, he did not approve. Oh, he hated Jews, hated all heretics. Indeed, when he suppressed the French Cathars at the Pope's behest, he showed so little mercy that the Cathars learned to fear him more than Satan himself. Thirty years later, when I came to govern Gascony for the King, there were men who hated me for my name alone, because I was his son, so long and so bitter were their memories."

Fitz Thomas silently held out the wine cup. Simon took it, drank slowly. "But if he would slay a heretic without qualms, he did not believe in knife-point conversions. So he set the Jews free, saying that was a poor way to bring a man to God."

It was with a start that Simon realized they were all listening, not just Harry and Fitz Thomas. Setting the wine cup down, he got to his feet, making a conscious effort not to limp.

"What of the children, my lord? The ones taken from the Jews? Do you remember their fate?"

"Yes, Tom, I remember. The Cardinal Legate refused to return them to their parents, saying the salvation of their souls mattered more than kinship of blood."

"My lord Leicester?" Slouching by the door, the guard straightened up hastily at Simon's approach.

Simon glanced back at the Bishops of Worcester and London, knowing neither they nor the Dominican friar would approve of what he was about to do. As an Earl, a knight, a soldier, he was indifferent to the approval of his peers, following his own instincts, his own concept of honor. But as a Christian, he was obliged to heed other voices, to be guided by the ethics of his Church. He paused, then beckoned to the guard. "Those Jews that were here," he said. "See that they get safely back to the Jewry."

IT was a long walk from the Tower to the Jewry, and much of it had been passed in silence. Jacob was oblivious to his son's clumsy attempts at consolation. Benedict's assurances that he'd done his best mattered little against the reality of Simon de Montfort's refusal. After a time, Benedict, too, lapsed into silence, for by then he was aware of the men trailing them. They were not conspicuous, stayed a consistent twenty feet behind, but Benedict's every instinct was alerting him to danger.

Curfew had rung, and the streets were all but deserted. As they moved up Fenchurch, they encountered few passers-by. They had not lost their shadowy pursuers. Benedict's mouth was dry. Although Jews had been forbidden by the Assize of 1181 to bear arms, Benedict had a contraband dagger concealed in his sling, for he'd vowed never to be defenseless again. He fingered it surreptitiously, while studying Jacob's cane; if need be, it could serve as a weapon. If only he'd been alone! He knew the narrow, twisting streets of the city well enough to out-distance any pursuit. But his father was too frail to run, too infirm to fight.

From time to time, he risked a glance back over his shoulder. The men had gained ground, for Jacob's pace was flagging. They were close enough now for Benedict to notice the moonlit badges that adorned their sleeves. The badge was familiar—a crimson cinquefoil. Benedict had seen it that very night, worn by retainers of the Earl of Leicester. His thoughts whirling, he sought desperately to make sense of it. If they'd incensed Leicester as much as that, why had he not ordered their arrest there in the Tower? But what reason could his men have for following them, save evil intent?

They'd almost reached the end of Lombard Street; ahead lay Cheapside. "Papa, I do not want to alarm you, but—" Benedict's warn-ing went no further, for at that moment they were hailed by the City Watch.

"You do know that curfew has rung?" The voice was polite, for both Benedict and Jacob were respectably dressed. But as soon as the man's lantern light struck their white badges, all deference vanished. "Why are you out on the streets at such an hour?" The tone suspicious, verging upon belligerence.

"We're on our way home," Benedict said swiftly. "We know it's late, but my father was meeting tonight with the Earl of Leicester, and curfew rang whilst we were still at the Tower."

"The Earl of Leicester?" The man nudged his companion. "Was that before or after you supped with the Pope?"

Benedict waited until his voice betrayed no anger; he'd pushed his luck enough for one night. "We were with the Earl. I am not lying."

"I say you are! Why would the Earl waste time on Jews?"

"You'd best ask the Earl that." The speaker, a lean youth with the sharp eyes of a huntsman and a voice brimming with lazy good humor, sauntered toward them, saying cheerfully, "Unlikely it might be, but true it is, too. Not only did our lord meet with them, he dispatched us to escort them back to the Jewry."

The men of the Watch looked skeptical, but those cinquefoil badges were impeccable credentials. Saving face with a gruff admonition to be "off with you, then," the Watch departed. Benedict was half-relieved, half-sorry to see them go, for it was not easy to put his trust in men who were strangers, Gentiles, and loyal to Simon de Montfort. "I thank you," he said awkwardly, "but we're safe now. There's no need to accompany us any further."

"I can see you've had few dealings with the Earl," the young soldier said with a grin. "If our lord tells a man to perform a task, he'd damned well better do it! He entrusted your safety to us, and that means we'd trail you to the back of beyond if need be."

They made an improbable quartet: the silent rabbi, his wary son, and the high-spirited, young de Montfort retainers. But as they approached Old Jewry Street, the soldiers proved as good as their word, disappearing into the darkness with a jaunty farewell wave. Benedict felt no shame at having so misread Leicester's intent; suspicion was a survival skill. "Do you want to rest awhile, Papa?" he asked, and Jacob shook his head. They were almost upon the alley that offered a shortcut to their Milk Street house, but Jacob passed it by, and after one curious look, Benedict fell into step beside him. He had a good idea as to his father's destination.

Their synagogue occupied the northwest corner of Old Jewry and Catte streets. It had been badly damaged in the rioting, partially burned, and although the surviving Jews had made what repairs they could, it still bore visible scars of the April attack. Like me, Benedict thought, raising his hand to his forehead. The moonlight cast ghostly shadows, here revealing a broken window, there a cinder-smudged stain. The smell of smoke seemed to linger on the air, and he wondered if his senses were playing him false. By night, the synagogue looked more like an abandoned temple than a living House of God, like the ancient ruins of a bygone people, a long-dead past. That was a frightening thought, and he tugged on his father's sleeve with sudden urgency. "Papa . . . let's go home."

"Home?" Jacob turned at his touch, but there was in his voice a tone Benedict had never heard before, an echo of utter despair. "Home," he repeated. "And where is that, lad? Where is our home?"

32

Lewes, England

May 1264

THE sun was at its zenith when they reached the hamlet of Offham. Jordan de Sackville, a Sussexman who'd thrown in his lot with Simon, gestured to their left. "That is the road to Lewes, my lord."

"And risk being caught between the hills and the river? I think not," Simon said dryly, marveling that he should have to point out so obvious a pitfall. "What I am looking for is a way up Offham Hill, bringing us out onto the Downs."

De Sackville grinned. "Scriptures say that he who seeketh, findeth. Follow me, my lords." And he led them west toward a hollow known to locals as the Coombe, where they ascended a winding trackway, emerging at last onto a broad, treeless upland. Simon saw before him an emerald carpet of new spring grass, strewn with the sunlit saffron of gorse and primrose, and below, the town of Lewes, ensconced within a bend of the River Ouse. Leaving their horses in order to elude any of Henry's sentries, they continued on foot. The plateau was four hundred feet high, ideal for reconnaissance. The castle of Henry's de Warenne cousin, the town's narrow main street, the walled priory of St Pancras— all lay open to Simon's appraising eye.

At first sight, Lewes put Simon in mind of Shrewsbury, for both had formidable natural moats. The River Ouse snaked its way along the east flank of the town, then swung in a circle, toward the priory. According to de Sackville, the river was tidal, rendering impassable any approach from the south. With the castle rising to the north, the town's defenses were impressive, indeed. But as Simon studied the river's width, those muddy marshlands to the south, a shadowy smile hovered around the corner of his mouth. There was one fatal flaw in Lewes's defensive shield—it was open to attack from the west. Should an army descend from these heights, sweep from the Downs into the valley, the town's defenders would have no way to retreat. Under a surprise assault, Lewes might well become a death trap.

"We can go," he said. "I've seen enough."

BY the time they returned to Fletching, the small village where Simon had encamped his army, the sun was low in the western sky and random clouds were reflecting the blood-red of a Sussex sunset. The day before, the Bishop of Chichester had attempted—in vain—to persuade Henry to negotiate. Although he had no expectations of success, Simon had that morning dispatched the Bishops of Worcester and London with one final appeal, but they had yet to return. Night fires were already burning; his battle captains had gathered before his tent, where a harried cook was stirring salted beef in a huge, iron cauldron. The meal forgotten, they crowded around Simon as soon as he dismounted. He sensed, even in these battle-seasoned soldiers, some of the same unease that had infected the Londoners; they, too, seemed to take an obscure comfort in his physical presence. But he did not fault them for their fear; only a fool would face such daunting odds with equanimity.

"My news is good," he said, as his squire brought forth a stool; although Simon's injury was much improved, he knew better than to sprawl cross-legged in the grass as his sons, and younger men like Hugh and Gloucester and Fitz John, were doing. "Jordan de Sackville's spies say that last night every tavern in the town was overflowing with Henry's soldiers. So confident is he of victory that he allows his men to celebrate in advance of the event. He's quartered in the priory rather than in the castle with Edward, ever a one for his own comfort, and even there men caroused till dawn, drunken knights sleeping off their excesses in the church itself." Simon's mouth was tightly drawn. As a moralist, he found such antics distasteful; as a battle commander, sheer madness.

Shaking his head, he said, "As amazing as it sounds, they have taken no measures to discover our whereabouts, have sent out no scouts. We saw but one outpost all day, on the Downs overlooking Lewes, and the men were dicing and arguing amongst themselves, never noted our passing. Whilst they know, of course, that we are in the Weald, they have no idea that we are but nine miles from Lewes."

One of his squires was holding out a bowl and spoon. Simon accepted without enthusiasm; all his life, he'd eaten and drunk sparingly, and even though this might well be his last meal, he could summon up no appetite for the heavily spiced stew. "We are in agreement," he said, "that Nicholas Segrave and the Londoners will form our left battle," a decision too obvious to merit discussion, for the left wing was the position of least importance. Simon paused, his eyes searching out Thomas

Puleston and the other Londoners within hearing range. "In saying this, I do not mean to impugn the courage of the Londoners. Some of these men fought with me at the siege of Rochester last month and acquitted themselves well. But most are green lads, poorly armed. It would be no disgrace should they break ranks before a charge of mounted knights. There may be a way, however, that we can lessen this risk. If the Londoners could outflank the castle, they'd have a better chance in the streets than out on open ground."

The circle was suddenly lit with smiles, for Simon's strategy offered a welcome spark of hope. There were murmurs of relief, and Nicholas Segrave rose with characteristic dispatch, went off in search of his raw recruits. Gloucester took his place, having gone back for a second helping of stew. Squatting there in the grass, he looked very young, his nose peeling, for the sun was no friend to redheads, a grease smear on his chin, carrot-colored hair wildly askew. But the blue eyes were coolly fastened upon Simon's dark face, eyes that challenged even as he asked, with affected nonchalance, "And who is to command the vanguard—you, my lord?"

"No . . . the command is to go to my sons, Harry and Guy," Simon said, triggering an exultant yell from Harry and an indignant, disbelieving sputter from Gloucester. Before the young Earl could launch into a diatribe of protest, Simon added, with poorly concealed impatience, "Sometimes, Gilbert, you jump ere you're stung. I want you to have the center command."

Deflated, Gloucester sat back in the grass. Guy was openly laughing at him, and for a moment he wavered between resentment and delight, but the latter won, for Simon had indeed conferred upon him a signal honor. Glancing about to see if it was one the other men begrudged, he saw on their faces perplexity. And only then did the full impact of Simon's words penetrate. "But what of you, my lord?" he blurted out. "If I take the center and your sons the right wing, what command have you?"

"I mean to keep a force in reserve, the knights of my household and some of the Londoners. They shall be under my personal command," Simon said, a statement that produced no enlightenment, only puzzlement. Even war-wise veterans like Fitz John and Humphrey de Bohun looked baffled.

Hugh le Despenser had enough self-confidence to admit ignorance. "I confess this is a tactic I've never heard of, Simon. We are already outnumbered by two to one. Do you truly think it wise to reduce our forces even more?"

"That we are outnumbered makes our need for a reserve all the greater." Simon saw that he'd not convinced them, but their doubts did not trouble him, for he trusted his battle instincts implicitly, did not need the confirmation of others. "Unless the Bishops of Worcester and London have wrought a miracle in Lewes, we fight on the morrow," he said, and more than one man released a breath soft as a sigh. So soon! "Ere the battle," Simon continued, his gaze coming to rest upon Gloucester and the equally young Earl of Oxford, "I shall knight you both."

"Indeed?" For the moment, his defenses down, Gloucester exchanged grins with Oxford. "What of Tom?" he prodded, and as Simon nodded, he jumped to his feet, calling out his brother's name. He was often a trial to them all, but now their smiles were indulgent, each man able to identify with his excitement, remembering his own initiation into knighthood. Harry alone did not want to remember, for it was on an October day three years past that he and Bran had been knighted by their cousin, the man he would face tomorrow across a battlefield.

Humphrey de Bohun set his supper bowl down in the grass, where it was promptly snatched up by one of their canine camp-followers. Unperturbed by the ensuing laughter, he got unhurriedly to his feet. "Sunrise comes about four or so. If we expect to get much sleep tonight, we'd best get busy now."

"Sleep," Simon commented, "will be in short supply. I have no intention of waiting for sunrise. Come dawn, I want us within striking distance of the Downs."

He saw that once again he'd startled them. A night march was no less an innovation than a reserve force, and warfare as they knew it was essentially a conservative science, mistrustful of change. But as before, no one challenged him. "Humphrey, you'll fight with my lads. Hugh, I'd like you with me. You, too, Tom," he said, and an enormously flattered Thomas Puleston quickly nodded assent. Simon looked thoughtfully at the others. Fitz John he assigned to Gloucester's command, the experienced John Giffard to their weakest link, the Londoners under Segrave. "I know," he said, "that some of you are dubious of a night march. I grant you it is an uncommon tactic. But tomorrow we need all the gains we can get. In failing to keep us under surveillance, Henry has been criminally careless, and I mean to take full advantage of it. Surprise is—" He got no further; the sudden stirring throughout the camp heralded the return of their peace envoys.

The grim faces of the Bishops of Worcester and London conveyed their message with no need of words. Their last hope had failed them, their one chance of avoiding war with their sovereign, and the men watched in sobered silence as the Bishops dismounted, delivered two parchment scrolls. "The King spurned your appeal, Simon, saying there could be no peace as long as you insisted that he uphold the Oxford Provisions."

"You told him we would be willing to pay thirty thousand pounds, as reparations for damages done by our supporters?"

The Bishop of Worcester nodded tiredly. "It counted for naught. Henry's brother, King of the Romans"—never had Richard's title been given such sardonic stress—"insisted that all of the thirty thousand pounds be paid to him alone, to indemnify him for the loss of his Isleworth and Westminster manors."

There was an astonished silence, and then, a burst of derisive laughter. Richard had never been popular with his brother's subjects, for his were virtues—intelligence, pragmatism, business acumen, a lack of rancor—that found little favor with a populace that judged a great lord by reckless courage and open-handed generosity and prowess on the field. Now, none were surprised, only scornful, that Richard should put property above principle.

Simon broke the seal on Henry's letter, moved closer to the fire, and read it aloud. Formally phrased, the gist of Henry's message came in the last sentence: "We . . . do defy you." Without comment, he reached for the second letter, rapidly scanned the contents, and looked up with a twisted smile. "I need read no further than the salutation: 'Richard, by the Grace of God, King of the Romans, ever august, and Edward, of the illustrious King of England the firstborn, to Simon de Montfort, Gilbert de Clare, and all the accomplices of their perfidy.' "

The Bishop of London, known as a mild-mannered man of placid temper, now startled them with an outburst of unwonted bitterness. "They crave blood! Lord Edward's exact words to me were 'They shall have no peace, unless they put halters around their necks and surrender themselves for us to hang them up or drag them down, as we please.' "

Such provocative words acted like flint to tinder; men began to mutter angrily, defiantly. Simon took the letters, deliberately fed them into the fire. "So be it," he said tonelessly, and unsheathed his sword, holding it aloft so that the shining blade reflected red flickers of flame. "I, Simon de Montfort, Earl of Leicester, do hereby renounce all allegiance to Henry Plantagenet, no longer acknowledge him as my King and liege lord."

It was a solemn moment, and it showed on their faces. Men stared at Simon's naked sword, and more than a few wondered how it had ever come to this, for Scriptures said that rebellion was as the sin of witchcraft. Then the Earl of Gloucester stepped forward. Whatever his failings of judgment, he had never lacked for courage, and drawing his own sword, he said in a loud, carrying voice, "I, Gilbert de Clare, Earl of Gloucester, do also renounce . . ."

As Simon watched, one by one they followed his example, disavowed their oaths of homage. He looked at the tense, firelit faces: Humphrey, who'd be facing his own father; Hugh, who'd once seemed too light of heart, too fickle of purpose; John Giffard, to whose safekeeping he'd entrusted Nell and Kenilworth; John Fitz John, whose courage was unquestioned, but whose honor was tarnished, stained with Jewish blood; Nicholas Segrave, comrade of the Welsh wars, his Gascony command; Thomas Puleston, a Shropshireman by birth, a Londoner by choice; Gloucester and Oxford, rebels with the most to lose; the sons Nell and God had given him, whose blood was precious to him beyond measure. And he found himself thinking of the men who weren't here. Peter, for thirty years his friend, his mainstay, caged at Windsor. Bran, his second-born. Thomas Fitz Thomas, who had pledged his life and his city in the cause of reforming the realm. The prisoners and dead of Northampton. Those he'd loved, those he'd trusted. Will of Salisbury, who'd found a martyr's crown at Mansourah. Rob de Quincy, whose death had been a mercy. The Bishop of Lincoln and Adam Marsh, long dead, but not forgotten, never forgotten. Would they have understood?

The Bishop of Worcester was standing just a few feet away, and Simon moved toward him, touched the sleeve of his cassock. "Will you hear my confession?" he asked quietly.

THE dark was fading at they came within sight of Offham Hill. There they left their baggage train, along with three disaffected Londoners— Augustine de Hadestok, Richard Picard, and Stephen de Chelmsford, Edward's collaborators in the abortive Southwark ambush; only John de Gisors, elderly and ailing, had been judged safe enough to leave behind in London. After chaining the hostages within Simon's custom-made horse litter, the army took Jordan de Sackville's roundabout route, began their slow, cautious climb up onto the Downs. The grass was wet, the air cool, for it was only the 14th of May, all around them the first stirrings of a springtime dawn. They heard linnets trilling from the shelter of gorse bushes, the warning chatter of jay and jackdaw, alerting the Downs inhabitants that man had invaded their domain, the sudden, piercing shriek of the swift—aptly named the Devil bird—a sound eerie enough to cause some of the town-bred Londoners to grope for crucifix or rosary. But for every magpie to break cover in a flash of iridescent blue, there were hedge sparrows that remained unseen, birds that stilled their song as men passed by, ebony-eyed foxes that monitored their approach, sentries invisible and ever-vigilant.

The furred and feathered denizens of the Downs were better sentinels than their human counterparts. Reaching the top of the hill, Simon's scouts discovered a solitary sentry, sound asleep under a gorse bush. He had a rude awakening, and when Simon began to put questions to him, he needed no prompting, eager to buy his life with what information he had to offer.

"The King is to command the center battle, his brother the left wing, and Lord Edward the vanguard. They mustered about ten thousand men, including a fair number of Scots, sent by the King's son-in-law, the Scots King. What else can I tell you? In the castle with Lord Edward are his de Lusignan uncles and his cousins, the Lord Hal of Almayne and John de Warenne. Also Hugh Bigod and a renegade Welsh Prince, Davydd ap . . . something."

"Why were you keeping watch by yourself?"

"No one came up to relieve us, my lord. The others decided to return to Lewes for food and drink. We drew lots and I lost . . ." He trailed off, disconsolately. "Bad luck twice-over for me. But we could see no harm in it, for you were said to be miles away, and not likely to force a battle, what with having lost half your army at Northampton. Also, the King thinks you are still crippled from your fall, not yet able to sit a horse. By God, he's going to get a right nasty shock!"

"That," Simon said, "is what we are counting upon." He gave the soldier a final glance, one of dismissal. "In truth, you are luckier than you deserve. Had you been one of my sentries and I found you asleep on duty, I'd have hanged you." He never heard the sentry's stammered thanks, was already turning away, for he'd spied a familiar face amidst the London contingent. Beckoning to the young man who'd sought him out at St Albans with news of the London rioting, he said, "Does Mayor Fitz Thomas know that his clerk has gone off to war?"

"Yes, my lord." Prompted by his comrades, the youth stepped forward shyly. "I am Martin of Aldgate, my lord, am honored that you remember me."

"I always remember a bearer of bad tidings," Simon said wryly, pleased to see that Martin at least was properly outfitted with hauberk and sword, the Mayor's doing, no doubt. Too many of the Londoners had only the meagre protection of leather gambesons, had only slings and makeshift weapons. It took courage to ride to war so ill-armed. "Good luck to you, lad," he said, thus making of Martin an instant celebrity, able to secure an enviable position in the front ranks as Simon began to address his army.

"We are about to fight a man anointed by the Almighty as England's King. I took an oath to him. But I also took an oath to reform the state of the realm. I fought in the Holy Land for the faith of Christ, would gladly have given my life for the glory of God Eternal. This day we fight for justice, for Christ's poor, for the weal of England, for the promises broken and the trust betrayed. Our cause is just, our quarrel good. Let us now pray to the King of all that if He be pleased with our undertaking, He may grant us victory. To Him Whose we are, let us commend ourselves, body and soul."

Swinging from the saddle, he knelt, and then lay prone in the grass. His men did the same, stretching out their arms, raising their voices to Heaven. They had sewn white crosses upon their surcoats, breast and back, to identify and inspire. To the Bishop of Worcester, there was a painful poignancy about the sight, row after row of white crosses catching the sun, burial markers for graves not yet dug. But as the men rose, he saw upon their faces the fervent faith of crusaders.

Simon had remounted his stallion, reining in a few feet away. "Will you be safe here?" he asked, and the Bishop nodded.

"You've given them a great gift," he said, "the belief that even if they die, it will be in a holy quest." A faint smile flitted across his lips. "I think it fortunate, Simon, that you use your talents for good, not evil, for I could not help thinking that these men would follow you even unto Hell."

Simon did not return the smile. "They *are* following me to Hell. They just do not know it yet," he said, and the Bishop saw that his eyes were fixed upon the Londoners.

"My lord!" The shout came from the crest of the hill. Simon urged his stallion forward, at once saw the cause of the alarm. Grooms had ventured out onto the meadows north of the castle, seeking forage for their equine charges, only to run into the advance guard of Simon's scouts. After a brief skirmish, the surviving grooms were in flight back toward the town, where they'd soon be raising a panicked hue and cry. Dawn's light seemed to be chasing them across the valley; the horizon was aglow. From the Downs, Simon's men could see the shadows in retreat, could make out bodies crumpled in the grass, bright splotches of color amidst a sea of green. "First blood," Simon said, with grim satisfaction. The battle of Lewes had begun.

THE Londoners had hoped to reach the town before the royalist army could react; there was sure to be utter chaos as men scrambled to dress, to array themselves for battle. But Edward had been more prudent than his father, had stationed lookouts in the north tower of the castle. As dawn broke over the Downs, a horrified sentry was stumbling into the tower stairwell, shouting for the King's son. While Henry was just rolling out of bed, bleary-eyed and bewildered, Edward was already arming himself, alerting his battle captains. He had the advantage, as well, of geography, for the castle was a half-mile closer to the Downs than the low-lying priory. In consequence, the Londoners had only reached the bottom of Offham Hill when Edward's cavalry sallied forth to intercept them.

Nicholas Segrave and his knights spurred forward to meet the charge, the Londoners struggling to keep pace. They came together with shattering impact, with a splintering of lances and a clash of swords. Martin had never seen anything like it; he slowed, stared open-mouthed as horses were flung back on their haunches, as men traded blows and curses, as Segrave's knights were overwhelmed by sheer numbers. It happened so suddenly that there was no time for fear. One moment there was a writhing, thrashing line, there was dust rising and stallions screaming and blood spurting. And then the line was giving way, there were riderless horses shearing off from the fighting, there were men down in the grass, and Edward's knights were upon them.

Martin brought his sword up, braced his feet, and swung as a horseman came within range. His sword glanced off the knight's shield, and he staggered backward, a numbing pain shooting down his arm. Shocked, he dropped the sword; he'd not even seen the blow coming. The Mayor's hauberk had saved his life, though, for the metal links had not broken under the thrusting blade. But the men around him were not so fortunate. Swords were slashing through their leather gambesons, rending flesh, smashing bones. Another knight was bearing down upon him, and Martin snatched up his sword. At the last moment, the knight swerved toward closer prey. The man stumbled, and, as Martin watched in horror, fell beneath the destrier's flailing hooves.

"Martin, look out!" Wat, journeyman to a currier in the Shambles, shouted his warning just in time. Martin dived sideways as a chained mace sliced the air above his head, only to trip over a body sprawled at his feet. Rising to his knees, clutching his sword in a death-grip, he glanced down and his stomach lurched, for the dead man had a bloody, gaping gash where his face should have been.

He made no conscious decision to run. It was made for him. All around him, men were in flight, and he was swept along with them, a twig helplessly adrift on a surging flood-tide of fear, a torrent that engulfed the field, carrying all before it. Some of the Londoners followed Segrave's retreating knights toward the river. Most, Martin among them, fled back up the hillside.

But Edward's cavalry did not slacken pursuit. The north slope of Offham Hill was well wooded, yet even after the Londoners reached the sheltering trees, the slaughter continued unabated. Their headlong flight began to resemble a grisly roundup; the knights harried them like wolves stalking a flock of sheep, putting stragglers to the sword, herding them toward clearings where there was more space for killing.

Martin's breath was coming in ragged gasps; his injured arm was throbbing; he was scratched and sore from falls into the brambles and hawthorn, and through his dazed mind kept running one bewildered refrain: Why do they not stop? His battle lore might be second-hand, but he'd read enough tales of knights-errant to know that soldiers did not pursue defeated men like this—more than two miles from the field.

He had no idea what had become of Wat, or Ralph, the weaver's son, or Andrew, the goldsmith's apprentice. His friends were gone, either dead on the field or running for their lives. Looking over his shoulder, he saw a knight strike down a man he knew well, William Gratefig. "Blessed Lady, Holy Mother . . . " He had not breath enough for prayer. If Gratefig—an important man, a former city sheriff—could be run through like a pig on a spit, what chance had he?

Risking another backward glance, he stumbled over an exposed tree root. It was a bruising fall; the metal rim of his kettle helmet slammed into his temple. His vision blurring, his head spinning, he lay still until the dizziness passed. A huge oak towered above him, dwarfing the other trees in the clearing. Sunlight filtered through a cloud of leaves, casting soft shadows, warming his face. The sounds of the hunt were fading. Almost, he could believe he was alone in a woodland world of enchanted calm, centuries removed from the horrors of Offham Hill. And then he noticed the corpse. The body was of a young man, lacking even a leather gambeson. His tunic was soaked with dark, clotted blood; so was the grass, for he'd taken a sword thrust in the abdomen. His face was contorted, and to Martin, mercifully unfamiliar. He struggled upright, made the sign of the cross.

"I tell you, Davydd, I saw some of them go this way."

Martin froze. "So? Has Your Grace not slain enough Londoners for one day? Jesú, from the way you've gone at it, I'd think someone must be paying a bounty on them!" This second speaker spoke accented French; he sounded oddly detached, as if this carnage had naught to do with him.

Martin peered through an opening in the thickets. A handful of riders had reined in not twenty feet from where he lay, but he saw only the knight upon a huge, white destrier. His hauberk caught the sun's rays, shone like silver; the sword resting upon the pommel of his saddle was three feet long, the blade well smeared with blood. Martin's mouth went dry. He knew he was looking upon the Lord Edward, knew now why their pursuit had been so relentless, so implacable. He and his comrades were paying for a July day at London Bridge, paying for every rotten egg that landed in Queen Eleanor's barge, for every shout of "Drown the bitch," for every promise sworn to Simon de Montfort. He sank lower in the grass, staring at the King's son, astride that lathered, restive stallion. *And I looked, and behold a pale horse, and his name that sat on him was Death.* They were coming this way, coming straight toward him. He slumped down on the ground next to the corpse, daubed some of the dead man's blood on his face, and made himself go limp. His cheek pressed into the grass, his heartbeat drowning out every other sound, he held his breath.

FROM the heights of the Downs, the men of Simon's army had watched in stunned disbelief. That the Londoners should break and run was no great surprise. But no one had envisioned a catastrophe of this magnitude. Not even the most experienced soldiers had ever seen a rout occur with such shocking speed. In what seemed to be the blink of an eye, it was over, their battle lost before it truly began.

Simon had ridden his stallion to the very edge of the bluff, staring down at the battlefield below. It was strewn with bodies, abandoned weapons, the wounded and the dying. The high grass was trampled and torn, bloodied. Loose horses galloped aimlessly, the scene one of utter desolation.

"Simon?" Hugh le Despenser and a sheet-white Thomas Puleston reined in beside him. "What do we do?" The question was rhetorical, for to Hugh, there could be but one answer. Use the reserve—thank God for Simon's foresight—to fill in the gap on their left flank, then await Henry's army from the defensive heights of the Downs . . . and pray as they'd never prayed before. "Shall I order the reserve to align themselves along the left battle?"

Simon glanced toward him, revealing a face as ashen as Puleston's. "No. Hold the reserve. Sound the advance."

"You would take the offensive? Christ's pity, man, why? How high can a bird fly if its wing be broken? Edward just crippled us, Simon. You saw it!"

"They saw it, too. Give them time to think about it and they'll lose all stomach for battle. We attack and we attack now, ere Edward returns to the field and whilst Henry's men are still in total confusion." Simon gestured toward the distant army of the King. They were hastening to array for battle, but the best proof possible of the disorder and turmoil in the enemy camp was that Henry's great dragon banner was to be found leading the left battle, not the center.

Hugh said something about too great a risk, but Simon was no longer listening. With his left wing destroyed, he could not afford the luxury of caution. He'd always been willing to take chances other men spurned; now, that willingness was all he had. He raised his arm, let it fall sharply. Their trumpets blared. The banners of Gloucester and de

Montfort caught the wind, and the center and vanguard began their descent from the Downs.

"What would you have us do, my lord?" Puleston had been badly shaken by the slaughter of his fellow Londoners, but his voice was level; he had himself in hand.

"When Edward comes back to the field, he'll cut open Gloucester's flank. Unless we can stop him."

Theirs was a small band for so great a task. Hugh and Puleston exchanged bleak looks, then turned their eyes toward the field below. Both the center and vanguard were now engaged, and the fighting looked savage, the fierce hand-to-hand combat of men with little to lose. Simon, too, was watching intently. They were still outnumbered, but as long as Edward stayed off the field, the disparity was not as lethal. Moreover, his sons and Gloucester seemed to be acquitting themselves well, pressing the attack with enough verve to have gained a slight edge. Neither Henry nor Richard had ever shown a flair for command. But where in bloody Hell was Edward?

Simon swung away from the battlefield, turning to stare at the wooded heights of Offham Hill. A suspicion was stirring, one so improbable that only now was it infiltrating his conscious awareness. "Where *is* Edward?" He did not even realize that he'd spoken the question aloud. Supposition was crystallizing into certainty. "The fool!" He whirled his stallion about. "Hugh, do you not see?" he demanded, eyes ablaze with sudden light, with a wild, surging hope. "I can scarce believe it, but Edward has left the field! If he were regrouping his men, he'd have been back by now. He's still in pursuit of the Londoners!"

They gazed at him in wonderment. But after a moment, Hugh shook off Simon's spell. "Simon . . . Simon, what if you're wrong?"

"I'm not." Simon was smiling. "As God is my witness, Hugh, I'm not!"

His household knights and the surviving Londoners had gathered around him, but not too close, giving his stallion plenty of respectful room, for destriers were notorious—in fact, prized—for their fiery temperament. Simon had found this particular mount in France, the buy of a lifetime. His color was an unfashionable black, and he was not as big-boned as others of his breed. But most destriers could not sustain their speed, their natural gait a jarring trot, and Simon's black stallion could fly like the wind. He was said to be half-Arab, and Simon often thought that one day he must experiment with such cross-breeding. He'd named the destrier Sirocco, after the hot Saracen windstorms, in tribute to the animal's blazing speed, and now, feeling Sirocco quiver under his thighs, feeling the stallion's eagerness to run, he thanked the Almighty for giving him the best horse of his life in this, his time of greatest need.

His squire was holding up his great helm. He took it with reluctance; while the eye-sights were wide enough to provide adequate vision, helms were heavy, often weighing twenty-five pounds, and so uncomfortable that no knight ever donned one until the last possible moment. Cradling it in the crook of his arm, Simon looked out over the assembled men. When he spoke, it was to the Londoners. "Your brothers died for us. You could not save them. But you can avenge them. If the shepherd is taken, the sheep will scatter. So . . . we ride against the King!"

SIMON'S surprise attack upon Henry's left flank was even more successful than he dared hope. He had to hold Sirocco in check, lest he outdistance his own knights, but they were not far behind; his confidence was contagious and the odds suddenly in their favor. Gathering speed as they charged down the hill, they were upon Henry's men before they even realized their peril.

From the corner of his eye, Simon caught movement. He didn't recognize the coat of arms on the knight's shield, but that mattered for naught; what was relevant was the lance leveled at his chest. Simon braced himself, took the thrust dead center upon his shield. The lance shattered, rocking him back against the saddle cantle, but he retained his seat, and when the knight circled, sword drawn, Simon got the better of the exchange.

He had no time to relish his triumph, though, found himself threatened by two of Henry's borrowed Scotsmen. As one of them grabbed recklessly for Sirocco's reins, his partner thrust upward with a halberd. It was a bold maneuver, deserving of success. But Simon had faced it before; for nearly forty of his fifty-five years, he'd studied the arts of war. He was not sure that experience was a fair trade-off for the loss of youth, but at least he was beyond surprising. He made use of his spurs, and Sirocco reared up wildly, dragging the Scots soldier off his feet. Simon struck him in the face with his shield, then swung the stallion around to deal with the halberdsman. But the man was gone, letting the tide of battle flow between them.

That tide was changing; Simon could sense it. The vanguard was attacking with renewed zeal, scenting victory, while Henry's soldiers were demoralized, on the defensive. A man was defeated as soon as he believed it, and Simon could see that belief on the faces of the King's men. By the time he'd crossed swords with one of Hereford's knights, the line was unraveling. The knight realized it, too, suddenly spurred out of range; why die for a cause already lost?

When it happened, it was with stunning speed, almost as fast as the collapse of the Londoners' left wing, for no contagion spread like fear. All around him, Simon now saw men in flight, saw the field swept by his army's white crusader crosses. But he could no longer find the King's great dragon banner.

A knight on a chestnut destrier drew up alongside him; even before he saw the emblazoned shield, he recognized the stallion as Hugh's. "Take some of our knights," he commanded, "and cut off any retreat into the castle!"

THE prelude to the battle had begun in nightmarish chaos for Henry. He and his men had from the first been at a distinct disadvantage, thrust from sleep into the shock of mortal combat. Henry was never at his best in the mornings, and he found himself fretting unduly that he'd ended up commanding the left wing, the position of least honor. He was coming to realize, too, just how ill-advised had been his choice of the priory for his command headquarters, for the town was on higher ground and thus blocked his view of the castle and Downs; he went into battle not yet knowing that his son had taken the field against the Londoners.

But worse was to come. Henry, for all his martial pretensions, was not that familiar with hand-to-hand combat, for he'd fought in very few pitched battles. Castle sieges, the debacle at Saintes, an occasional foray against Gascon rebels, several disastrous campaigns against the Welsh— that was the extent of his actual battlefield experience. Now, in his fifty-seventh year, he found himself fighting not only for his crown, but for his life.

Henry did not lack for physical courage; his was a moral cowardice. But his survival skills were rusty. Within the first half hour of fighting, he suffered numerous small cuts and bruises, a sprained wrist, and a wrenched knee. He was truly shocked that his own subjects should be trying to kill him. He could accept the hostility of Welshmen and Gascons, but how could good Englishmen fight against their King? The wind shifted and he caught his first glimpse of the enemy banner—the crimson and silver of de Montfort. It could not be Simon; even he could not lead a charge from his horse litter. It must be Harry and Guy, then. He was facing his blood-kin, fighting his own nephews! God curse her, this was his sister's fault. If she'd not been hot to have Simon in her bed, he'd have been spared all this grief! Well, he would indulge her no more. When the battle was done and de Montfort dead, she could plead in vain. Why should he pity Simon de Montfort's widow?

He was slow to realize the extent of his danger, so sure was he that the Almighty would favor a consecrated King. Another commander would have known they were giving ground; Henry needed to be told, and there were none at hand to tell him. He was vastly relieved when one of his couriers found him; at least now he'd learn what was happening on the rest of the field. His bodyguards and knights of his household formed a protective circle, and he could not help wishing he might shelter there indefinitely. But a king's lot was a hard one. "How does my brother?" he demanded, was stunned by the reply.

"Poorly, Your Grace. He's being hard-pressed by Gloucester, barely holding his own. But it's Lord Edward you ought to be worrying about. Sire, he has gone off after those Londoners, has left the field altogether!"

"I do not understand. What are you saying?"

The courier never got a chance to answer. Something was happening; something was very wrong. Henry turned a bewildered face toward the source of this new turmoil. Men were looking toward the west, pointing and shouting. And then they were running.

Henry spurred his horse forward, crying, "Do not run! Hold fast!" His attempt to rally his men came to naught; no one seemed to be paying him any mind. As he glanced again toward the west, he thought he saw a second de Montfort banner. But he had no time to puzzle it out. His stallion shied suddenly, shuddered violently, and went down. Henry kicked his feet from the stirrups, scrambled free. It was only then that he saw the blood gushing from the animal's belly, saw the soldier with sword poised to strike again. Cornered, he surprised even himself. Straddling his dying horse, he fought off his assailant with a gritty resolve he'd never shown before, and would never find again. After what seemed to be an endless exchange of blows, the other man backed away, and he let his sword arm go limp. The man had not even possessed a hauberk, doubtless one of de Montfort's lowborn Londoners. That a common churl had almost killed a King! Where were his bodyguards?

"Sire!" A knight was galloping toward him. His shield was split and his surcoat so blood-stained that his coat of arms was impossible to decipher. "Here, take my horse," he insisted, sliding from the saddle and holding out the reins.

By now, Henry had recognized the voice of Philip Basset. A gallant gesture, he thought approvingly, reaching gratefully for the reins. "What has hap—"

"There's no time to talk! Make haste and mount, ride for the castle. I'll do what I can to hold our men here till you can—"

"Run away? No!"

"My liege, the battle is lost! De Montfort has launched an attack upon our flank, and our men are fleeing for their lives. Look for yourself. The day is his!"

"No! No, that cannot be! I am England's King, how could I lose?

Where is Edward?" Henry shook his head, repeating plaintively, "Where is my son?"

EDWARD had pursued the fleeing Londoners for a full four miles. By the time he felt his mother had been properly avenged, the sun was high overhead. But even after he realized how long he'd been gone from the battlefield, he was not unduly perturbed. Like his father, Edward could not conceive of defeat. Collecting as many of his men as he could find, he started back toward Lewes. They were approaching Offham Hill when they ran into one of William de Lusignan's knights, and he had news to gladden Edward's heart. On the lower slope of the Downs, less than a half mile to the west, lay the enemy baggage train. With his own eyes, he'd seen Simon de Montfort's standard, seen his personal horse litter. Edward needed to hear no more. With a gleeful shout, the cry of a hunter closing in on his quarry, he spurred his stallion into action.

MARTIN was still very frightened. He'd seen sights this day he could never forget, his dreams would be haunted for years to come, and his nightmare visions would be real. He felt no shame for running. Under the circumstances, that was common sense, not cowardice. His true test of manhood came later, when he determined to return to the battle. It was the last thing he wanted to do. Never had life seemed so sweet; dizzy with the dazzling joy of reprieve, he could easily have gotten drunk on the sounds and scents of spring alone. But he owed it to the two men whose approval meant all, Mayor Fitz Thomas and Earl Simon. Clutching his resolve to his breast like a life-saving shield, he began a slow retracing of his earlier panicked path. As he reached the hamlet of Offham, he came upon a weeping girl, whose torn bodice and bloodied skirt told a familiar story. Soldier's prey, she stirred quick pity, but at sight of him, she screamed, fled into the woods. Offham's few cottages had been plundered, stripped of what little they had. Martin looked at the broken crockery strewn about, the bedding wantonly destroyed, a dog's body in an open doorway, and he wondered how he could ever have thought there was glory in war.

Near Offham Church, he encountered a fellow fugitive, a youngster of seventeen or so. The boy was pathetically grateful for the company, and quite voluble. Within moments, Martin learned that his name was Godwin, that he had worked as a stable boy in a Southwark inn, that his employer had forbidden him to go off with the army, and he fretted that he'd lost his job. He babbled on about London ale-houses and a girl named Aldith, even the Smithfield horse fair, about everything but the battle. Martin glanced at Godwin's tunic, at the telltale rip where his white cross had been torn away, and the boy, following his eyes, blushed. "Nay, lad, you mistake me," Martin said hastily. "I meant no reproach. But I must tell you, Godwin, that I am on my way back to the battle."

Godwin stared down at the ground, scuffed his shoe in the grass, his fingers plucking nervously at those loose tunic threads. "I'll come with you," he mumbled.

"Good lad! Here is my idea. Earl Simon left a brave knight, Sir William le Blound, to guard the hostages and the baggage train. We'll seek him out, ask him what to do."

Godwin brightened considerably, for it seemed as likely as not that le Blound would tell them to stay with the baggage, and he fell in step beside Martin as they trudged toward Coombe's Hollow. Martin was only now discovering how very tired he was, and he let himself be lulled by the boy's compulsive, inane chatter. He did not hear the sounds of battle, therefore, until it was almost too late.

"And Aldith, she told me—"

"Be still!" Godwin subsided, hurt, but when Martin took shelter in the bushes beside the path, he made haste to follow. They crept forward, by now close enough to see Simon's standard, unfurled to full length against the bright, cloudless sky. William le Blound and his men were offering a valiant defense, but they were outnumbered, and as Martin and Godwin watched, they began to die.

"Do they think Earl Simon is in the horse litter?" Godwin whispered, eyes wide and wondering.

"I do not know." Martin gasped, quickly crossed himself as William le Blound slumped over his horse's neck, slid slowly to the ground. His death took the heart out of his men. Those who could, fled, and Edward's knights turned their efforts upon the horse litter. The door was chained shut, but a few blows with a battle axe freed the hostages. Augustine de Hadestok and his co-conspirators were dragged out, babbling avowals of loyalty that no one heeded. Their panicked protests gave way to screams. Swords flashed; within moments, the hapless merchants were hacked to death.

Martin looked away, sickened. In a day of horrors, somehow this seemed the most obscene horror of all, that Augustine de Hadestok, Stephen de Chelmsford, and Richard Picard should have been slain by their own allies. Godwin was tugging at his sleeve, urging him to flee, and indeed now was the time, while Edward's soldiers were ransacking the baggage. But they'd only covered a few yards before they encountered an armed knight.

He appeared to have been watching them for some time, at ease astride a bright chestnut destrier, his sword unsheathed and bloodied, but pointing downward. Rather than a great helm, he wore an old-fashioned kettle helmet with nose-guard, and the face turned toward them was young, sun-browned, surprisingly benign. But they were too frightened to notice his lack of rancor.

Davydd had no particular liking for Londoners; they too often acted as if the Welsh had tails. But he could see no sport in killing these bedraggled, scared youngsters. Poor fools, if they had any sense they'd not be here at all; what did it really matter to them whether Edward or de Montfort prevailed? At that, he gave a low laugh; what did it matter to him, either? "Go on," he said abruptly, "be off with you." They gave him an incredulous look, then bolted. Davydd watched until they were out of sight, then urged his stallion into an easy canter, toward Simon's ravaged encampment.

Edward had removed his helm, was drinking deeply from a leather wineskin. "Here," he said. "Take your first victory drink of the day."

Davydd accepted the wineskin with alacrity. "Did you truly expect to find de Montfort in that horse litter?"

Edward's smile was faintly self-conscious. "I suppose I let my hope run away with me. I ought to have known better. Even if he had to be tied to the saddle, Simon would be on the field."

Davydd wiped his mouth with the back of his gauntlet. He'd never learned to feel at home in England, either as hostage or fugitive, but rarely had he felt as alienated, as solitary as he did today; taking part in this embittered English civil war was like being a stranger at a particularly unpleasant family reunion. "Who are they?" he asked, glancing with mild curiosity toward the bloodied bodies of the hostages.

Edward shrugged. "Who knows?" Raising a hand, he shielded his eyes, looked appraisingly up at the sun. "It's past noon. We've tarried here long enough."

They drew rein on the crest of the hill, where their first glimpse of the battlefield seemed to confirm Edward's every expectation. The battle was over, part of the town in flames. Bodies beyond counting lay sprawled in the sun, some already stripped by looters. Men were searching the field for friends or gain, others tending to the wounded, still others chasing loose horses. Only to the south, beyond the priory, did sporadic fighting continue, and that flurry of action degenerated, even as they watched, into a rout.

Edward laughed. "The dolts, they're going to blunder right into the mudflats! Simon will lose even more men in that marsh than he did in the river."

"Do you think he still lives, Ned?" Hal asked hesitantly, for he could not imagine Simon dead, any more than he could the sun plummeting from the sky.

"No," Edward said flatly. "He's not a man to be taken alive." Turning in the saddle, he raised his voice. "We'll give our horses a brief rest; they've been roughly used this day. But the sooner we get back to the castle, the sooner we can begin celebrating!"

Some of them were ready to celebrate then and there, and wineskins were soon passing back and forth. It was left to Davydd, the outsider, to stumble onto the truth. Moving to the edge of the bluff, he gazed down at the battlefield. So many widows, so many orphans made this day. And not all the tears shed for de Montfort would be English. Llewelyn had suffered a defeat, too, lost an ally worth his weight in gold. His eyes shifted from the trampled meadows to the town. Blood of Christ! For a long moment, he sat motionless in the saddle, scarcely breathing. Could it be that he'd wagered once again on the wrong horse?

His sudden shout drew all eyes. Edward was moving toward him, though without haste. Davydd spurred his stallion away from the bluff. "If we won the battle," he said tautly, "why is the castle under siege?"

His words started a stampede. Within moments, the bluff was lined with shocked, silent men. But if most of them needed time to assimilate what they were seeing, Edward did not. One swift, disbelieving glance to substantiate Davydd's claim, and he was running for his horse. Swinging up into the saddle, he paused only long enough to replace his helm. "What are you whoresons waiting for?"

They obeyed, but with no great enthusiasm. Davydd noted how slow some were to mount; experienced riders were unaccountably having difficulty with their horses. Others, like William de Lusignan, Davydd's particular bête noire, and his equally detestable brother Guy, had yet to don their helms, a sure sign that they had no intention of resuming the fight. None of this surprised Davydd in the least. Edward might well be distraught enough to throw his life away in a grand gesture of defiance, but he'd find few willing to travel that lonely road with him. The battle was lost; they knew it even if Edward did not.

A rider was coming from the priory, coming fast. He was angling toward the west when he looked up, saw Edward's banner at the top of the hill. Swerving sharply in their direction, he met them half-way down the slope. "Go back, my lord, save yourself whilst you still can!"

"Coward! How dare you abandon your King like this?"

"The battle is over! My liege lord is Roger de Mortimer, and he's long since fled the field. Simon de Montfort has triumphed, has won a victory beyond imagining."

"No!" Edward's face was hidden by his helm, but his voice betrayed him. "I do not believe you! God would never favor him over us!"

De Mortimer's knight prudently said nothing. But by then, Hal had reached them. "What of my father?"

"I do not know. The King sought refuge in the priory when he was cut off from the castle, but I've heard nothing of your lord father." The knight glanced uneasily toward the King's son. "After . . . after you left the field, my lord, de Montfort attacked the King's left flank. God knows where he got the men, but of a sudden he was there, and we were trapped between his knights and their vanguard. And once our line broke, he threw his men against our center. It was over so fast, I can still scarce believe it . . ."

"Cousin, we'd best make haste." John de Warenne maneuvered his mount alongside Edward. "Pevensey Castle is less than twenty miles away. From there, we can take ship for France—"

"You'd run away? What of my father, your King?"

"What would you have us do, Ned?" William de Lusignan demanded impatiently. "Why sacrifice ourselves for a battle already lost? I say we retreat whilst we still can. There'll be other days, other battles— but not if we fall into de Montfort's hands."

"Listen to him, Ned," de Warenne entreated. "De Montfort may have won the battle, but he need not win the war."

"I'll not abandon my father!"

The passion in Edward's cry silenced them, but only for a moment. William de Lusignan glanced toward his brother, then nodded slowly. "So be it, then. As for me, I'm riding for Pevensey. De Montfort would barter his soul to catch me here, alive. You think he does not bear a grudge for Northampton? I could count myself lucky if he did not turn me over to that whelp of his, wrapped in a red ribbon!"

"Damn you, then, go! But I'll not forget your craven flight, and you'll find I make a more dangerous enemy than de Montfort!"

De Lusignan was not impressed. "Good luck; you'll need it." And then, to the others: "If we circle around the castle, we ought to be able to reach the bridge." He waited no longer, rode off without a backward look, and with him went his brother Guy, their de Warenne cousin, Hugh Bigod, and more than three hundred knights. Edward was left alone on the field with his cousin Hal and the men of his own household.

There was an unobserved witness to this scene. Davydd had discreetly slipped away amidst all the turmoil. While he was in utter agreement—for probably the first and last time—with William de Lusignan, he had known better than to argue the point with Edward. A man just realizing the fatal extent of his own folly was not likely to be all that rational. But Davydd was not about to risk death to keep Edward content, and he had no intention, either, of risking capture. De Montfort would gladly wrap him in a red ribbon, too, a belated birthday present for his good friend and ally, Llewelyn of Wales.

And now what? He'd sooner take refuge in a lazar-house than Pevensey, preferring the company of lepers to de Lusignans. If he could make his way north to Guildford, he knew a lass there who'd take him in. After that, who could say? But something would turn up. It always did. Sheathing his sword, he left the battlefield behind. Like de Lusignan, he did not look back.

AFTER leaving the priory, Simon made a circuit of the battlefield. Pursuit continued to the south, where Henry's men were mired down in the river marshes. The castle garrison still held out, but surrender was inevitable. Now there were prisoners to be taken and wounded to be retrieved and dead to be claimed. Once he'd satisfied himself that these tasks were being carried out, Simon headed back toward the castle. He was still half a mile from the town when he came upon Humphrey de Bohun. He at once signaled his men to halt. "Were you wounded?"

Humphrey had been sitting in the grass, tended by a young squire. Dismounting, Simon waved him back as he struggled to rise. "I took a blow on the elbow, think I broke a bone." Reaching with his free hand for Simon's wineskin, he looked up intently into the other man's face. "My father . . . he lives?"

"You've no need to fear. He survived the battle unhurt, is now in custody." Simon had already removed his helm; now he jerked back his coif, ran his hand through tousled, sweat-drenched hair. "I'm getting too old for this, Humphrey. Even my eyelashes ache."

Humphrey managed a smile that was part grin, part grimace. "Not for long; there's no restorative like victory. Is it true that Henry fled to the priory?"

Simon nodded. "But he'll not be leaving; we have it well ringed with men. He has no choice but to surrender—" He paused, having noticed a band of approaching horsemen. One of them spurred ahead at sight of him. Sliding from the saddle even before his stallion had come to a complete halt, Harry flung his arms around his father, nearly staggering Simon by his impetuous rush.

"You did it, Papa! For years to come, men will be talking of this day, of your victory! Not Charlemagne, not Richard Lion-Heart, not even Caesar—"

"You're too sparing with your praise, lad," Simon said gravely, and then the laughter in his eyes spilled over, and he returned the hug. He had always found it easier to show affection to this son, not because he was favored over his brothers, but simply because his own emotions were so open, so unguarded; Harry's exuberance was usually catching. "I'm proud of you, Harry. You and Guy brought honor to our House this day."

Harry looked as if he'd been awarded an earldom. "I bear welcome tidings, Papa." He gestured toward the riders now drawing near. "Gloucester is bringing you a right valuable pawn—my uncle Richard!"

Simon was delighted, both that Richard was alive and that he was taken. "Gloucester captured him?"

"Not exactly." Harry's grin had more mischief in it than malice, for he was fond of Richard, in an absent-minded sort of way. "When the center broke, Uncle Richard, his lad Edmund, and a handful of men took refuge in yonder windmill. They even barricaded the door with sacks of flour! But some of Gloucester's men soon surrounded the mill, shouting, 'Come out, King of the millers!' Uncle Richard will never live this down!" After a moment, though, Harry's smile faded. "What of Ned, Papa?"

"I've men on watch. If he wants to resume the battle, we'll be ready." Gloucester was only a few yards off. If not for that familiar thatch of fiery hair, Simon could have been looking at a stranger. So accustomed was he to Gloucester's dourness, his inevitable and infuriating suspicions, that he suddenly realized he'd never seen Gloucester laughing before. But for the moment, the young Earl was brimming over with good will; he did not even seem to resent Harry for appropriating his news, for being the one to tell Simon of Richard's capture. "Behold," he cried, "the King of the millers!"

By now that was a stale joke, but his men chuckled dutifully. Richard stared straight ahead, stony-faced. He was not bound, but neither was he foolish enough to make a hopeless break for freedom; he cherished his dignity far too much to lose what little he had left. At sight of his brother-in-law, Simon bit back a grin. He'd seen hundreds of blood-soaked bodies this day, had also seen men well smeared with river mud. But Richard was the first one to be covered with flour.

At Richard's left stirrup rode his younger son Edmund, a wide-eyed, flustered youngster of fourteen, and on his other side, a flushed, fair-haired youth only a few years older, who scrambled hastily from the saddle when Gloucester beckoned. "John, come meet the Earl of Leicester," Gloucester said expansively. "This is the lad who accepted the royal surrender."

"Who are you, lad?" Simon asked, and the boy, dazzled by all this attention, mumbled something none could catch.

Gloucester laughed again. "This is John Befs of Tewkesbury, squire to John Giffard."

Simon glanced toward Richard's frozen profile. A squire! No wonder Richard looked so sour. "Kneel," he said, and the boy did, bewildered, not comprehending until Simon unsheathed his sword. "Be thou a knight," Simon said, bringing the flat edge of the blade down upon the squire's shoulder. The boy got slowly to his feet, his face aglow. Simon was equally pleased; in a day of bloody necessity, there was enormous satisfaction in this one act of pure, innocent chivalry.

"Thank you," Richard said stiffly. At least now he had yielded his sword to a knight. Simon read his thoughts without difficulty, shook his head.

"I did not do it for you," he said. "I did it for the lad."

Richard raised a hand, swiped ineffectually at his flour-streaked face. "We ought to have known better than to have held you so cheaply," he said bitterly. "One thing you've always excelled at is killing."

Simon was not offended. Under the circumstances, he was willing to give Richard a certain leeway, if only for Nell's sake. Harry was not. "And what do you excel at, Uncle? I've often wondered," he snapped. Simon looked at his son in faint surprise, for a barb like that was more Guy's or Bran's style than Harry's. But then, Harry had not been himself for some weeks, not since Bran's imprisonment. Well, mayhap now he could stop blaming himself, Simon thought, at last having time to appreciate the dramatic dimensions of his victory. Bran would be freed, and Peter, all the prisoners taken at Northampton. The Londoners would be spared further suffering. The Provisions would be the law of the land, no less honored than the Runnymede Charter. What an England they would fashion now!

He looked toward Gloucester; it was only fair to give credit where due. "You fought well this day, Gilbert, showed a talent for command."

"Yes, I did," Gloucester agreed, unwilling to admit how much the compliment pleased him. But he was happy enough to share the glory, and added generously, "We all did ourselves proud. All but the Londoners, that is."

"They did the best they could." Simon's voice was suddenly cool.

"I do not doubt it." Gloucester could not resist the sarcasm, but there was no venom in it; in his present frame of mind, he was willing to overlook much. "I think," he began, and then stopped, turning as they all did, toward the direction of the town.

"My lords!" The rider was coming at a dead run, his mount kicking up great clods of grass and dirt. "My lord Fitz John sent me to find you, to tell you Lord Edward came back onto the field!" He reined in, panting. "But when they realized the battle was lost, the other lords balked. They headed for the bridge near the Franciscan friary. There was fighting, and some drowned when they rushed the bridge. But the de Lusignans and de Warenne got across. I'm sorry, my lord. We all know you wanted them taken."

"What of Edward? Did he flee, too?"

"No, my lord, he did not. With less than a score of men, he fought his way into the priory, joined his father the King."

JOHN Fitz John's first attack upon the priory had been repulsed by the desperate men sheltering within. He was about to launch a second assault when Simon galloped up. Thick, black smoke overhung the priory; orange flames, fanned by the wind, flared from the windows of the frater, licked at the roof of the church. Soon after Simon stopped the onslaught, a flag of truce was waved from the great gate, and then a gaunt, smoke-smudged figure was emerging onto the dusty, blood-stained street.

"I am William de Neville, Prior of St Pancras," he began, but to his dismay, John Fitz John interrupted curtly, demanding to know if he was not formerly the Prior of St Andrew's in Northampton. Fitz John did not remind those listening that it was a monk of St Andrew's who had betrayed the town to Edward; he did not have to. But the Prior did not have the luxury of denial. "Yes, I was," he acknowledged reluctantly. His eyes swept the circle of men, hastily sought out Simon. "My lord Leicester, I beg you to halt your assault whilst my monks fight the fire. Your arrows have set our church aflame!"

"A grievous mistake." Simon slanted a flinty look toward Fitz John. "I would not deliberately burn a House of God."

"Thank you, my lord." The Prior sighed. "You'll allow us, then, to put out the flames?"

"I think it time, Prior William, to put out all the flames. Go back and fight your fire. And deliver a message to the King. Tell him I am offering a truce, from this hour until sunset tomorrow. Choose from amongst your monks two to speak for the King. I will send into the priory two of the Franciscan friars to act on my behalf—our behalf," he amended, remembering Gloucester just in time. "We are all reasonable men," he said, with enough irony to amuse his soldiers. "I am sure that we can come to terms."

Fitz John watched, frowning, as William de Neville hastened back into the priory. "Why a truce? Give me just two hours and I'll give you the King."

"He is not a fox you've run to earth, Sir John. He is the King of England, and we can spare his dignity." Simon's smile was suddenly grim. "What else does he have?"

33

Lewes, England

May 1264

THEY met in the priory Chapter House. Neither
Henry nor Edward appeared to have slept, theirs the dazed, hollow-
eyed look of men suffering the greatest of all possible bereavements,
the loss of God's favor. At sight of Simon, Henry began to tremble with
impotent rage, with a visceral fear that was immune to common sense,
impervious to Edward's repeated reassurances. "I yield my sword to
you, my lord of Gloucester," he cried, "and only to you!"

Simon stepped back, watching without comment as Gloucester accepted Henry's sword. But Henry's next act could not be as easily shrugged
off. Glaring at Simon, he said in a loud, belligerent voice, "Need I remind
you that I have another son, safe in France with my Queen? Should any
evil befall me or Edward, Edmund would be the rightful heir!"

Edward winced; he thought he'd managed to allay that particular
fear. Simon and Gloucester looked equally outraged. Gloucester dropped
Henry's sword into the rushes, with the grimace of a man coming upon
something unclean. No one was touchier about his honor than Gloucester—with the possible exception of Simon, who said icily, "You, my
liege, are England's King. No one challenges that." Adding, with a sudden glint of steel, "From now on, however, you will be governing as a
king ought."

Henry gasped, but Richard forestalled him, falling back, out of habit,
into his role of peacemaker, a role he was regretting more and more
ever having abandoned. The loss of every manor in Christendom would
not justify yesterday's battle; why had he not seen that sooner? "Did
you know that Philip Basset was sorely hurt?" he asked hastily, and
Henry shook his head, made mute by a remorseful memory—riding off
to safety on Philip Basset's horse. Moving toward the table, Richard
picked up the document awaiting their seals. He read rapidly, and when
he raised his eyes to Simon's face, they held a gleam of reluctant respect.
"You never fail to surprise me, Simon. You've just won one of Chris-

tendom's great victories, and yet your terms are exactly the same as they were ere the battle began!"

Simon's pride still bled. "Sometimes," he said coldly, "I suspect the lot of you must be deaf. For as far back as I can remember, I talk and you listen not. I fought for the Provisions, no more, no less. How often do you have to hear it to believe it?"

"I think you're beginning to get our attention." But Edward's sarcasm was lame. As his eyes locked with Simon's, defensive color flooded his face. "Go on, say it! I know what you're thinking—that I played the fool yesterday, lost the battle for my father."

They'd rarely seen his nerves so raw, but he elicited little sympathy from either Simon or Gloucester. The latter's smile was a dazzle of deadly mockery. "You're too modest, Ned, in tallying up your sins. You lost the battle on the field, but then, by scorning flight, you lost the war as well!"

Edward glanced toward his father. "I did what I had to do," he said roughly, surprised when Simon nodded agreement.

"It may have been a foolhardy gesture," he said, "but it was also a gallant one." Some of Edward's high color began to ebb. For just a moment, he looked young and vulnerable, flustered. Unlike his father, he was capable of learning from his mistakes; Simon had seen evidence of that. But what lesson, he wondered, would Edward draw from the battle of Lewes?

Edward stepped forward, formally handed Simon his sword. "Hal and I shall surrender ourselves on the morrow, as agreed upon. What happens then?"

"You shall be placed in the custody of my son Harry, taken to Dover Castle."

Edward's mouth twitched. "And to think, Uncle, that your enemies accuse you of lacking a sense of humor!" For the first time, he looked directly at Harry, standing in the shadows near the door, and then he grinned. "Dover would not have been my choice of residence, but at least I'll have no complaints about the company—Cousin."

The olive branch fell short. Harry gave him the cool, appraising look of a stranger. "I'd not wager upon that if I were you—Cousin," he said, and not even waiting for Edward's response, turned and walked out.

Edward watched him go, then summoned up an exaggerated shrug, a display of amused indifference that none found convincing. Sensing their skepticism, he abruptly began to query Simon about the battle casualties. Two thousand, seven hundred known dead, Simon said somberly, and more who drowned in the river and marshes, whose bodies might never be found.

Those were sobering figures; death had claimed nearly one out of every five men. If theirs was a society that glorified battlefield prowess while deploring battlefield deaths, it was because none could honestly reconcile their Church's "Thou shalt not kill" with the seductive allure of a chivalric brotherhood based upon the sword. Even the comforting concept of a "just war" was not applicable when Christian fought Christian, and a respectful silence fell, the not entirely hypocritical honor the living accorded the dead.

Henry alone felt no compunction that so many had died. The numbers did not even register with him. Like one staring too long at the sun, he was blinded to all but his helpless hatred for Simon. It acted upon him like a sickness, set his heart to pounding, his pulse to racing, leaving him weak and debilitated, dizzy with the sheer intensity of the emotion, one frightening in its unfamiliarity, for his was not a violent nature. Now, however, he felt himself unforgivably wronged. "Why do we waste so much time?" he demanded suddenly. "We are here to affix our seals to that accursed Mise. Let's do it, then, so we can end this . . . this wretched farce!"

There was an awkward silence. All eyes turned instinctively to Simon for guidance. And only then did Henry fully comprehend the consequences of the battle of Lewes. The crown was still his, the command Simon's.

UNDER the Mise of Lewes the Oxford Provisions were recognized as the law of the land. An arbitration commission was to be set up to deal with specific disputes, but under no circumstances would Henry be allowed to appoint foreigners to his council. He would also be required to curb his extravagant spending, to live modestly until his debts could be satisfied. A full amnesty was proclaimed for Simon de Montfort, the Earl of Gloucester, and all their followers. There were to be no ransom demands for men captured at Lewes; they were to be freed, as were the prisoners taken at Northampton. And Edward and Hal surrendered themselves as hostages, as pledges for their fathers' good faith.

FROM Lewes, Henry and Simon moved on to Battle, and then to Canterbury, so that Simon could check coast defenses. In consequence, a fortnight passed before they had their entry into London. Once again the Londoners turned out in large numbers to welcome Simon into their city, but it had been—for them—a bitter-sweet victory, and the procession was muted. London resembled a brilliant, vividly colored painting—bordered in black. Simon found himself cheered by women whose faces were wet with tears, by men who'd staked their very lives upon his triumph, by those fresh from ale-houses and others coming from funerals, by the reprieved and the newly widowed, the joyful and the bereaved. It was a celebration stained with blood.

After seeing that Henry was comfortably—and securely—lodged at the Bishop of London's palace, Simon continued on to the Tower, where Richard was installed in Henry's lavish Blundeville chamber. Only then did Simon finally have time for private conversation with the man who'd proved such a steadfast ally. They were sitting around a table in the upper chamber of the keep, Simon and Thomas Fitz Thomas and Harry and Peter de Montfort, newly freed from Windsor Castle. Peter seemed little marked by his captivity, answering Fitz Thomas's queries with composure, saying that, Yes, he'd been well treated, and No, he'd never doubted that Simon would prevail, and Yes, young Bran had been released with him, but the lad had headed first for Kenilworth, wanting to check upon his mother and little sister.

"We expect him to join us here within the next day or so," Simon interjected. "And so will my wife, once the roads seem safe again."

Fitz Thomas needed no elaboration upon that last remark, for Londoners had grim, first-hand knowledge of the dangers of the road. Henry had, at Simon's behest, ordered all his castle garrisons to lay down their arms. But the garrison in Gloucester's captured castle at Tonbridge had refused to obey, and at Croydon had ambushed a group of Londoners returning home from the battle.

Simon's thoughts mirrored Fitz Thomas's own. "Those responsible for the Croydon killings have fled to Bristol, barricaded themselves within Edward's castle there. But I'll do my best to see them brought to justice."

"It seemed particularly cruel to me," Fitz Thomas confessed, "that men should have survived the battle, only to be struck down so close to home. That ambush stirred up much fear in the city. As if we did not have suspicions enough after the fire!"

"Were you able to catch the man who set the blaze?"

"Yes . . . a draper, I'm sorry to say! A man named Richard de Ware, an accomplice of the hostages slain at Lewes. Fortunately, we were able to contain the fire, but not before many houses in Milk and Bread streets burned to the ground." Fitz Thomas frowned, remembering. "It was a bad time for us, my lord, not knowing yet that you'd won the battle . . . especially bad for the poor Jews. Whenever men are fearful, they seek scapegoats, and there was another outbreak of violence and looting in the Jewry. This time we were able to establish order right quickly, but coming so soon after the slaughter in April . . . And then, by sheer evil luck, many of the Jews' houses were burned in the fire. Well, it is little wonder that the Jews panicked. They took refuge here in the Tower, refuse to leave, and in truth, who can blame them?"

Simon, too, was frowning. "Do you remember, Tom, that elderly Jew who sought me out just ere I left London? Jacob ben Judah, I believe he was called. Is he here, too? Good, for I wish to speak with him. Can you send a man to fetch him?"

Fitz Thomas hid his surprise. "I will see to it at once, my lord." As he moved toward the door, Simon cast a speculative look in his son's direction. Harry had joined them two days ago at Rochester, having delivered Edward and Hal safely to Dover Castle. He'd been unusually subdued since his return, was obviously troubled, for Harry's face was never meant for subterfuge, betrayed in equal measure his joy and his pain.

"You've said very little about your journey to Dover. No problems with Edward?"

"No . . . although I think Ned expected softer treatment than he got. I kept him on a tight rein, treated him as a prisoner, not a Prince, and he liked it not." Harry was staring down at a wax spill on the table; Simon could see only the sweep of surprisingly long lashes. "I thought . . . I thought that if I could make him pay for his treachery, I'd feel better. But the worse I treated him, the worse I felt . . ."

Simon had suspected as much. "You have every reason to be angry with Edward. But if you need to make your peace with him, there's no shame in it. In all honesty, I doubt that I could forgive such a betrayal, but if you can, then do so. The bond between you began in the cradle, not an easy one to sunder. But bear this ever in mind, Harry. Edward might deserve your friendship. He does not deserve your trust."

"You need not worry, Papa. What is it that Scriptures say, the serpent is more subtle than any beast of the field? Well, when it comes to guile, Ned could put that serpent to shame in the blink of an eye. Like a spider, he can spin a web even in his sleep."

As an assessment of Edward, Simon found it right on target. The door opened, and Fitz Thomas entered, just in time to hear Peter say pensively, "Think you that there's any truth to that? Do spiders spin in their sleep?" Harry insisted it was so, that he'd read it in a bestiary, and he and Peter were soon swapping stories of arcane animal lore. Did Harry believe crocodiles wept over their prey? Did Peter believe that the hyena could change its sex at will? What of the griffin, said to have the head of an eagle, the body of a lion? Had Harry ever met a man who'd actually seen one?

Fitz Thomas listened, amused, until he noticed that Simon was not listening at all. He was gazing into the closest candle flame, as intently as if it were a soothsayer's lamp, looking up with a startled smile at the sound of Fitz Thomas's voice. "What did you say, Tom?"

"I was but wondering, my lord, if what I heard was true, that you are asking two French Bishops to assist in the arbitration. Might I ask why?"

"To help Henry save face. I think he might find our medicine easier to swallow if the French King wields the spoon."

That made sense to Fitz Thomas. He knew that there were some Londoners who felt Simon's triumph had been bought with their blood, Londoners who wanted vengeance with their victory. Simon's peace terms had been too moderate for their liking; Fitz Thomas had even heard a bitter quip making the rounds of ale-house and tavern, that Simon fought a sight better than he bargained. But as a politician, he'd long ago learned the necessity of governing by consensus, and was in full agreement with Simon's cautious approach. "Will the French King consent?"

"How can he not . . . now? We submitted to trial by combat, would not have won if our cause were not just. I do not see how the French King or the Pope can continue to oppose the Provisions, not if they be men of any honor."

"What happens next?"

"We're calling a parliament for next month, shall put before them our plans for reform—three electors, who will then nominate a council of nine to advise the King in the governance of the realm."

"Will you summon knights to the parliament, as you sought to do three years ago?" To Fitz.Thomas, that had been a remarkable innovation. He hoped that Simon would not recant now that he was in a position to put his political theories into actual practice.

"Yes, we will. I know what my enemies say, that I take my allies where I can find them. And there's some truth in that, for most of my support does come from the knights and shire gentry. But if the King holds power by a covenant with his people," Simon said matter-of-factly, although that was a hypothesis most would reject out-of-hand as alarmingly radical, "it only makes sense that their voices should be heard. The knights speak for an important element of the community, ought to have some say in how it is governed." He paused, his eyes coming to rest thoughtfully upon the Mayor's face. "And if the knights should be included, then logic demands that so should the towns. When parliament meets again in January, I hope to be able to summon citizens from London, mayhap even from some of the other cities."

He smiled suddenly. "If I so surprise you of all men, I can well imagine what others will say, none of it likely to gladden my wife, who takes criticism of me very much to heart!"

But Fitz Thomas was too astounded and too excited to joke in kind. "Do you truly think you can do this?"

"I do not know," Simon admitted. "In all honesty, I have no surety at all as to what the future holds—save that danger lurks behind every bend in the road. Henry is no willing partner in this strange union of ours, and he does not lack for allies. His Queen and John Mansel are said to be raising an army in Flanders. The de Lusignans, de Warenne, and Hugh Bigod have gotten safely to France. The Pope is hostile to us, the French King suspicious, the Scots King Henry's son-by-marriage. The Marcher lords are not to be trusted." Simon smiled again, this time without humor. "If enemies are riches, Tom, I am richer than Croesus, far richer than I care to be!"

"And yet you won before against all odds—at Lewes."

Simon nodded slowly. "Yes, I did. But winning that detestable battle was easy, compared to what lies ahead."

JACOB ben Judah and his fiercely protective shadow followed a servant across the inner bailey, up into the Tower keep. Once they'd reached the stairwell, Jacob's hand closed upon his son's sleeve. "Why do you think he has summoned us?" he asked softly.

"I have no idea, Papa," Benedict lied. So alarming were his suspicions that he wanted to spare his father, if he could, until the final moment of revelation. One of Simon de Montfort's first acts as Earl of Leicester had been to banish all Jews from his domains. Now that he was King in fact, if not in name, why should he not seek to banish the Jews from the very realm of England?

They hesitated before the chamber door, neither one wanting to cross that threshold again. But at least tonight they faced only an audience of four: Simon and his firstborn and the Mayor and a grey-haired man neither recognized. After an exchange of wary greetings, Simon gestured for them to sit. "I want you to persuade the other Jews to leave the Tower," he began. To his surprise, all color drained from Jacob's face.

"My lord, this is our last refuge! If you turn us out of the Tower, we will be defenseless, utterly at the mercy of our enemies!"

"You mistake my intent. The Tower is always available as a shelter in times of travail. I am not denying you refuge. I want your people to return to their homes, to resume their daily lives."

Jacob and Benedict exchanged astonished glances. "My lord, I, too, want that," the older man said cautiously. "More than anything. But I do not think it possible after what has happened. My brethren are sore afraid—and with good cause."

"Would it ease their fears if public proclamations were made, forbidding all subjects of the King to harass or threaten them?"

Jacob did not answer at once. "My lord, I do not mean to give offense. But in the past, kings have taken the Jews under their protection, just as your popes have from time to time ordered that we not be harmed. These decrees did not save us in times of trouble. Words do not deflect swords. Why should those who hate Jews pay any heed to these proclamations?"

"Because," Simon said, "when the King offers you his protection, men will know he speaks for me. They know, too, that my word is good, and that I warn but once."

Jacob was studying Simon intently; it was not easy to trust after so bloody a spring. "What you say is true," he said at last. "Even your enemies admit you're a man of your word. It might well be that your protection would count for more than the King's. I can promise nothing, my lord, but I will speak to my people, will urge them to heed what you say."

"Good. Tell them we will send letters patent to all the towns where there have been recent outbreaks of violence. In each place, twenty-four respected citizens will be chosen to act as guarantors for the safety of the Jews in their community. I will also—"

Benedict could keep silent no longer. "Why?" he blurted out, too amazed for discretion. "Why are you doing this?"

"You Jews contribute to the royal coffers, do you not? As your father himself pointed out in this very chamber, Jewish revenues are important to the Exchequer. Now that the economy of the realm is my concern, naturally I want to restore order as quickly as possible."

It was a blunt, pragmatic answer, no less straightforward than Benedict's question, one he could accept. But it was a half-truth. Simon suddenly pushed away from the table, got to his feet. Startled, Jacob and Benedict did, too.

"The King's powers are not absolute. The Lord God gives him a sacred trust, and in return for the obedience and loyalty of his subjects, he must provide protection and justice—even unto the least of them. If I am to exercise rights of kingship on Henry's behalf, the responsibilities, too, must be mine. It becomes a debt of honor owed to all of Henry's subjects."

Jacob was speechless. He well knew that the chivalric code was more fable than fact, as honored in the breach as in the observance. Moreover, it was an ethics system for the aristocracy. Thus a knight could rape a peasant girl or cheat a serf, and feel no shame, for they were not covered by the tenets of chivalry. But Simon de Montfort had his own version of their code. If his could include the weak and needy, could it not in time come to include the Jews, too? Jacob tried to hold his hopes in check, before they ran away with him altogether. At least, this was a beginning, a blessed beginning.

"I thank you, my lord," he said. "Your protection will enable my people to pick up the broken threads of their lives, to put some of the horror behind them."

Simon frowned, but Jacob knew why; no Christian crusader could be truly comfortable, cast as a defender of infidels. "We are in agreement, then," Simon said tersely. "If you—"

The door opened with enough force to startle them all. Jacob and Benedict tensed at sight of Guy de Montfort. There were some men who had only to walk into a room to cause others to scent danger; Guy had impressed both Jacob and Benedict as such a one. Now, however, he barely glanced their way. "I've been scouring the city for you, Papa. There is a repentant sinner here, in need of absolution!" He laughed, and shoving the door back, with a nice flair for the dramatic, he revealed his brother.

Bran grinned self-consciously, but whatever he might have said was lost in the turmoil. Harry whooped, vaulted across the table to embrace their lost sheep. Simon, too, was hastening forward, with Peter only a step behind.

A son's homecoming was a private moment, not to be shared with strangers. Jacob and Benedict offered polite excuses, eliciting from Simon only the vaguest of responses in return; he was smiling at his second-born, all else forgotten.

"Come, I'll see you out," Fitz Thomas said; he, too, felt out of place in a family circle so tightly drawn. The laughter of the de Montforts followed them as they entered the stairwell, cut off suddenly by the closing door. So dark was it that Fitz Thomas was only a sensed presence, a cheerful voice. "When you speak to the other Jews," he said, "I'll go with you." He brushed aside Jacob's thanks as if his gesture were of no moment; he sounded as if he was smiling. "You'll not regret it, Master Jacob. If there is one man in Christendom who can be trusted with no reservations, Earl Simon is that man."

Jacob, still caught up in his visionary dreams of a new England, murmured agreement. Benedict said nothing, but his silence challenged, and Fitz Thomas reached out unerringly in the dark, touched his arm. "You can trust him, lad," he said. "You'll see."

It was an eerie conversation, disembodied voices in a black void. Benedict would later remember and marvel, both at the oddness and the unguarded honesty of his answer. "I cannot trust him," he confessed, "however much I might want to. But—but I think I do trust you. And if you have such faith in him, well . . . mayhap that is enough."

AS word spread that Simon was at the Tower, he found himself besieged by petitioners: aldermen eager to curry favor; relatives frantic for word of missing loved ones; friends of John de Gisors, seeking pardon for the elderly merchant. Simon's sons soon found excuses to disappear; even Peter defected, only Fitz Thomas holding fast till the end. It was very late by the time Simon finally left the Tower, and almost midnight when he reached Durham House. Dismissing his escort, he entered the great hall. It was dark, silent, the household asleep. To Simon's surprise, though, Bran was waiting up for him.

"Where have you been, Papa? We expected you back hours ago!"

"I had trouble making my escape. But I'd have thought you'd be out celebrating with your brothers." Simon paused, gave his son a quizzical smile. "Why," he asked, "are we whispering like this?"

Bran quickly gestured for silence. "So we do not wake Mama."

"Since Kenilworth is nigh on ninety— Here? Where? My bedchamber?"

Bran grinned, beckoned Simon toward the hearth. Simon stood for a moment by the settle, gazing down at his sleeping wife. When he glanced up at his son, Bran shrugged.

"I could not tell you, Papa. She swore me to silence, for she was bound and determined to surprise you. I tried to convince her she ought to wait, but she wanted to come to London straightaway, and you know Mama once she makes up her mind! You'd best be forewarned, though. She's right vexed with you, for she had a special supper planned."

He raised his candle, revealing to Simon the elaborate table setting: silver candlesticks and polished plate and scarlet roses on a linen tablecloth as immaculate as new snow. Looking back at Nell, Simon saw that she had taken equal pains with her appearance. Sometime during her long, frustrating vigil, she'd discarded her veil and wimple, but her gown was a vivid shade of turquoise silk, and she wore at her throat the pearls he had bought for her in Paris. Leaning over, he caught a seductive hint of jasmine. She sighed and her lashes fluttered as he lifted her in his arms, but she didn't wake, pillowing her head on his shoulder as if she were asleep in her own bed.

Nell had not neglected their bedchamber. Strategically placed candles gave off muted, flickering light, and the air was perfumed with her favorite sandalwood incense; she'd put out wine and wafers, even scattered rose petals over the turned-back sheets. She murmured wordlessly as he laid her down upon the bed, but her breathing stayed slow, even.

Her hair caught the candle sheen, stray wisps curling softly at her temples, against her cheek. Simon sat beside her on the bed, content for a time just to watch her. He was a fitful sleeper, easily roused, often wakeful, utterly unlike Nell, whose sleep was usually peaceful, deep and dream-filled. Now she looked serene, slightly disheveled, and, to Simon, irresistible. He found it impossible to believe more than twenty-six years stretched between this night and that October eve at Odiham Castle, when he'd bedded her for the first time. Bending over, he touched his mouth to hers. She sighed again, her lips parting, responding with drowsy desire, not yet fully awake.

"Nell . . ." He pressed his lips to the hollow of her throat, and her eyes opened, sleep-shadowed, the color of a harvest sky at twilight; he'd always regretted that of all their children, only Harry had her eyes.

"I knew," she said. "I knew you'd win. I never doubted, beloved, never . . ."

"Liar," he said tenderly. Her mouth clung to his, tasted of wine. He slid his hand into the bodice of her gown, and she wrapped her arms around his neck, kissed him again, hungrily. And then she pushed suddenly against his chest, struggled to sit up.

"Simon, where in blazes were you? You ruined my surprise, not to mention the meal!"

He argued his case with kisses, and she was soon laughing softly. "I confess," she said, "that I did not really race all the way from Kenilworth just to have supper with my husband. I was hoping that I might get to sleep with the victor of Lewes."

"I think," he said, "it can be arranged." Her breath was hot against his ear, her hair coming loose about her shoulders. He removed the remaining pins, and she shook it free, a cloud of gold faintly threaded with silver.

"You're still so fair," he said wonderingly. "Few men have my luck. For of all the women in Christendom, I have the only one I want, right here in my own bed."

"Simon, it's been two full months. I thought I'd go mad, in truth. No more, my love. No more separations; I can bear anything but being apart. No more battles; you've fought your share. Promise you'll keep me close from now on. Promise me . . ."

Once before she'd sought to bind him with such a vow. But it was different now. He was no longer young, had indeed fought his share of battles. "I will," he said, his mouth seeking hers, for in the quiet, fragrant dark of their marriage-bed, it was an easy promise to make, even to believe.

34

Wallingford, England

November 1264

Simon's promise to his wife was as short-lived as their hopes for peace. By July, the army of Flemish mercenaries hired by Henry's Queen and John Mansel was preparing to set sail from Damme. Simon issued an urgent call to arms, and the English responded in heartening numbers, flocking from the towns and villages to Barham Downs in Kent. As the sailors of the Cinque Ports patrolled the Channel, Simon forbade the import of Flemish cloth and woolens, and Flanders abruptly lost interest in harboring enemies of England's new government. Simon's fledgling revolution benefited, too, from the notorious caprices of the Channel weather; its treacherous tides were made even more dangerous by high winds and heavy swells. Eleanor's invasion failed to materialize; her fleet never sailed.

Peace remained elusive, though. Roger de Mortimer and his fellow Marchers, nothing daunted by their defeat at Lewes, reverted to defiance as soon as they were safely back in their own border fortresses. They refused to yield either the royal castles in their keeping or the prisoners they'd taken at Northampton, and in late July, Simon and the Earl of Gloucester led a punitive expedition into the Marches. Joining forces with Llewelyn, they captured the castles of Hereford, Hay, and Ludlow, and brought the rebels to submission in less than a month.

When circumstances demanded a swift military strike, Simon had few peers. But he needed, as well, the skills of a master diplomat and the patience of Job. He could defeat his enemies, but he had little success in winning them over, either in England or abroad.

The French King opposed on principle any limitations upon the God-given powers of a king, even so incompetent a King as Henry. But he was not overtly hostile, his disapproval tempered by his innate sense of fairness and a genuine respect for Simon the man, whatever his suspicions of Simon the reformer. Simon's most dangerous and most implacable foe was to be found, not at the French court, but in the Holy See.

The Pope had never forgiven Henry's lords for thwarting his grandiose plans for the kingdom of Sicily, and he'd long nurtured a grudge against Simon as the most vocal and persuasive of the English King's critics. Now that Simon had added rebellion to his sins, the Pope's enmity was unrelenting. His legate, the Archbishop of Narbonne, ordered the English to renounce the Provisions of Oxford, and when his demand was rejected, he summoned the Bishops of London, Worcester, and Winchester to Boulogne. In their unhappy presence, he excommunicated Simon and his sons, the Earl of Gloucester, Hugh le Despenser, Mayor Fitz Thomas, and many of their supporters, even the Earl of Norfolk, whose only crime was cooperating with Simon's government.

Once back in England, however, the Bishops refused to publish the sentence of anathema. The papal documents were shredded, cast into the sea. Raging at the effrontery of "this pestilent man," the Archbishop of Narbonne took matters into his own hands, formally laid England under Interdict on October 21. But church bells continued to resound in London, Masses continued to be said throughout the land, and the English clergy continued to support the excommunicate Earl—as if the papal damnation had never been.

FROM Dover, Edward had been moved to his uncle Richard's castle at Wallingford, then briefly to Kenilworth. On this foggy Thursday in Martinmas week, he was back at Wallingford. Although his confinement was more rigorous than that of his cousin Hal, who'd been entrusted with a diplomatic mission to the French court in September, Edward was still accorded the courtesies of kingship, one of which was the right to receive visitors. The man escorted that morning into Edward's chamber had been admitted without challenge, for Ancel de Bassingbourn's cousin Humphrey was a stout supporter of Simon de Montfort. What only Edward knew was that Ancel's loyalties lay not with Humphrey but with Humphrey's father, Warin de Bassingbourn, one of the knights defiantly holding out at Bristol Castle.

Ancel brought welcome news of the world beyond Wallingford. "Leicester is no longer at Dover," he reported, "is now at Windsor with the King. The Archbishop of Narbonne has been summoned back to Rome by the sudden death of the Pope, and rumor has it he might well be chosen as Urban's successor. You must," he urged, "pray to the Almighty that it should come to pass, for Narbonne, unlike his fellow French Bishops, is no friend to de Montfort.

"My lords will be pleased to hear that de Montfort's troubles are breeding like rabbits. In their zeal to protect the coast, the sailors of the

Cinque Ports have been seizing all shipping, and with imports cut off, prices are soaring; a pound of pepper that sold for sixpence now costs three whole shillings, and wine prices have more than doubled. But strange to say, the shortages have not yet soured the common people on de Montfort's outlaw government. Some of them," Ancel admitted, "are even wearing garments of white wool instead of cloth brightly dyed in Flanders, flaunting the plain English homespun as proof of their unity, their unshaken adherence to their 'common enterprise.' "

Ancel paused to gulp down some wine before volunteering that Simon's second son, Bran, had been besieging Pevensey Castle since September, to no avail. "He has managed, though, to mortally offend the Earl of Gloucester, admittedly no great feat! But the bad blood betwixt Gloucester and the young de Montforts has now spilled over to Gloucester's brother Tom; a one-time friend of my lord, no?" Edward nodded thoughtfully, and gestured for Ancel to continue. This he did with relish, relating several public brawls between Gloucester and one or another of Simon's sons. "They do," he concluded gleefully, "but rub salt into a raw wound, for he's already greensick with jealousy. He never was one for hiding his feelings, and only a blind man could fail to see the rancor he harbors toward de Montfort."

Edward nodded again. "That was inevitable. Three electors—Gloucester, the Bishop of Chichester, and de Montfort, all equal—in a pig's eye! Chichester is a saintly soul who thinks Simon can verily walk on water. And Gloucester could no more outwit Simon than he could sprout wings. That so-called trinity of theirs does but mask the truth—that Simon de Montfort rules England at his pleasure."

"I doubt he gets much pleasure from it these days, my lord. Gloucester's envy and de Montfort's arrogance make for a right queasy mix! You do know of the honors de Montfort has bestowed upon his sons? He entrusted the custody of Dover Castle and the Cinque Ports to Harry, named him warden of Kent, and Bran warden of Sussex and Surrey. And when Gloucester complained, de Montfort brushed his objections aside. In truth, my lord, they make most peculiar bedfellows! Gloucester is one who wants tender handling, yet de Montfort is the least likely man to indulge him. After Gloucester insisted he had the right of ransom over your uncle, the King of the Romans, a claim de Montfort rejected out of hand, he was later heard to say that dealing with Gloucester was verily like stroking a hedgehog!"

Ancel grinned at that; so did Edward. But Hal was indignant. "It was agreed there were to be no ransoms levied. Gloucester always was a grasping bastard. Is it not enough for him that he's gotten the lands of our de Lusignan uncle and Peter de Savoy? And that in addition to the bulk of the de Warenne estates!"

Edward shrugged; he had more important matters on his mind than Gloucester's greed. "What of the Londoners, Ancel? Did they reelect that misbegotten Mayor of theirs?"

Ancel nodded, bracing for a bitter outburst, for he knew how much Edward detested Fitz Thomas. When it didn't come, he could not hide his surprise. "You seem so . . . so composed, my lord. I must confess that I'd expected to find you pacing and raging like a caged lion!"

Edward's smile was thin, mirthless. "For once I can afford to be patient, Ancel. For all the courtesy and deference shown my father, he remains a captive King, Simon's puppet monarch, and that is not a sight to give men comfort. Gloucester will not long be alone in suspecting Simon's intent, for he is exercising a king's authority, without a king's right. He cannot legitimize his power—but he dare not relinquish it, either. And each day that passes only deepens his dilemma. Time is my ally, his enemy."

This was the moment Ancel had been awaiting. "More than you know, my lord."

Hal didn't comprehend, but Edward did. He leaned forward, suddenly tense, expectant. "When?"

Ancel smiled. "On the morrow," he said, "at dawn."

EDWARD was beginning to regret having confided in his uncle. He wanted to savor the excitement of their impending rescue, but Richard was too inherently cautious, too conservative to relish risk-taking. For the past quarter-hour, he had been conscientiously pointing out all the ways such an escape attempt could go wrong.

Aware that he was losing his audience—Hal had wandered to the window and Edward's eyes were glazing over—Richard drew a sharp, aggrieved breath. "I think you ought to pay heed to what I say. Who knows Wallingford's defenses better than I? It will not be easy to take. And if the assault fails, have you considered the consequences? Ours is a right comfortable confinement, Edward, for which we can thank my sister. There are those of Simon's supporters who would see us more closely held, but Nell has argued against it, and Simon has so far heeded her. Not a week goes by that she does not send us sweetmeats, fresh venison, wine. How many men have so gentle a gaoler, lad? My sister loves us well, but if you force her to choose between us and de Montfort, we'll be the ones to regret it. She's still besotted with the man, even after twenty-odd years, and worse, he's managed to infect her with his political heresies . . ."

Edward was no longer even making a pretense of listening. He rose, swallowing a yawn, as Hal swung away from the window in sudden panic. "Je—Jesus God," he stuttered, "we've been betrayed! Guy de Montfort just rode into the inner bailey!"

Edward's nerves were steadier; after a daunting second or so, he shook his head. "How could Guy know? It's mere chance that brought him here, and glad I am of it!"

"Glad?" Hal looked so dumbfounded that Edward began to laugh.

"Yes, by God, glad! Use your head, Hal. If Guy is killed in the assault, small loss. But if he survives, he'll make a right valuable hostage."

Hal was easy to reassure; wanting to believe was always enough for him. Richard remained skeptical, but Edward had ample confidence for them all, and he awaited the coming of day with edgy anticipation.

ANCEL's cousin, Warin de Bassingbourn, had undertaken, at the Queen's urging, to rescue her son. Making a daring dash from Bristol Castle to Wallingford, he began his assault just before dawn on the second Friday in November, and before the surprised garrison could rally to the defense, he and his men managed to breach the outer curtain wall, to take possession of the outer bailey.

As the first sounds of combat reached the castle keep, Edward unshuttered the window of the chamber he shared with Hal, tied a strip of scarlet cloth to the latch. The sun had not yet burned away the autumn haze drifting off the Thames, and men running across the bailey disappeared into sudden patches of billowing, ghostly mist. Wallingford's mangonels were now being manned, sending huge rocks over the walls, blind assaults followed sometimes by silence, sometimes by muffled screams. Edward could see the defenders crouched on the wall walkway, loosing arrows and curses at random into the fog. When a de Montfort knight took an incoming arrow in the throat, toppled backward into the inner moat, he felt a surge of savage elation; a pity it wasn't Guy!

Soon after the attack began, harried, grim-faced guards flung open the door of their chamber, ushered in Richard and his younger son, Edmund. They joined Edward and Hal at the window, riveted by the chaotic activity below in the bailey. Each time one of the castle defenders fell, Edward and his cousins cheered lustily. Even Richard, knowing as he did that a deep, double moat and curtain wall still stood between them and their rescuers, found himself, nonetheless, getting caught up in the excitement.

There was a sudden lull, and then a man's voice echoed over the wall. "I have a message for your castellan! Tell him that Sir Warin de Bassingbourn demands that he send out to us the Lord Edward and his royal kinsmen. Should you be foolish enough to refuse, we'll show no mercy when we take the castle, will put all within to the sword."

Edward and Hal pounded each other on the back, traded playful punches, intoxicated by the ease of their victory. Edward was vowing to find a barony for de Bassingbourn when the door was once more thrust open. "Not the others, my lord, just you," the captain said brusquely, and Edward paused in the doorway, looking back with a rakish grin. "Whilst I'm gone," he quipped, "start packing," and moved jauntily into the stairwell, to the accompaniment of his cousins' laughter.

He was not surprised to be taken up to the roof battlements; what better post for overseeing the castle defenses? Simon had entrusted Wallingford to Richard de Havering, a phlegmatic, colorless individual who had, nonetheless, managed to antagonize Edward, so unwavering was his loyalty to Simon and the Provisions. He and Guy were leaning over the embrasure, gesturing down into the bailey. They turned at Edward's approach, and de Havering said stolidly, "We want you to tell de Bassingbourn to call off the attack."

Edward's laughter was not feigned for effect; his amusement was genuine. "And I want a long life and God's blessings. What of it?"

De Havering remained impassive, but Guy betrayed impatience. "Show him," he said tersely to the castellan.

"Show me what?" Following de Havering to the embrasure, Edward watched, uncomprehending and not a little suspicious, as the castellan signaled to the men below. They at once set about winching the mangonel beam back, loading a large boulder. That done, they released the skein, and the beam snapped upright, thudding into the crossbar with awesome force, catapulting the boulder in a wide arc across the bailey. Edward's eyes locked onto its flight, but as soon as it soared over the wall, he shrugged. "So? I've seen more mangonels than I can count. Why should one more matter to me?"

"Ah, but this is no ordinary siege weapon." Guy's smile was sudden, unsettling. "Unless you agree to call off the attack, we will indeed do as your friends demand and send you out to them—by way of that mangonel."

Edward prided himself upon his aplomb, but for once, words failed him; he could only stare at Guy in disbelief. Rallying—too late—he mustered up a fairly convincing burst of scorn. "You're bluffing. You'd never dare do that!"

Guy stepped closer. "You tell me, Ned," he said coolly. "Am I bluffing?"

For a long moment, Edward searched the depths of his cousin's eyes, a chilling, fathomless sea-grey. "Damn you . . ." Little more than a whisper, throbbing with intense, impotent fury, a hatred beyond assuaging. Swinging around, he strode toward the embrasure, shouted for de Bassingbourn. "Pull your men back if you value my life!"

THAT November trouble flared up again in the Marches. Roger de Mortimer and Roger Clifford suddenly seized the royal castles of Gloucester and Bridgnorth. When Simon hastily mustered a force and headed west, the Marcher lords burned the bridges over the River Severn. But they had overlooked Simon's Welsh ally. Llewelyn ap Gruffydd attacked from the rear, kept them hard-pressed until Simon reached the border. Once again he triumphed; the recalcitrant barons surrendered to him at Worcester on December 12. But after two Marcher rebellions in three months, Simon was not disposed to be lenient. De Mortimer and Clifford and their confederates were ordered to abjure the realm, exiled to Ireland for a year and a day. Simon then compelled Edward to yield to him the earldom of Chester, in exchange for twelve de Montfort manors of comparable value in Leicestershire. After nearly thirty years, Gwynedd and Cheshire were once again allies, as in the days of Llewelyn Fawr.

Writs were then issued to the January parliament. Only five Earls and eighteen barons were summoned, evidence of Simon's lack of support among the nobility. But eleven Bishops, sixty-five Abbots, thirty-six Priors, and five Deans were expected to attend. So, too, were two knights from each shire, and—for the first time—two citizens from each city and borough of the realm.

CHRISTMAS Eve festivities at Kenilworth were lavish enough to stir up suspicions among Simon's detractors, ever on the alert for symptoms of regal aspirations. But Simon was, as always, disdainfully indifferent to appearance, and the huge, lakeside castle was soon echoing to the music of harp and gittern and pipe, ablaze with torches and cresset lights, thronged with bedazzled guests, royal hostages, knights, men-at-arms, and servants. The great hall was abundantly adorned with evergreen; holly and laurel and mistletoe "kissing bushes" dangled above doorways and window-seat alcoves, festooned over-hanging candelabras. A mammoth yule log had been ceremoniously lit, to burn until Epiphany. The popular Shepherds' play had been performed after a multi-course supper, and pages now circulated with traditional Christmas drinks—elderberry and pear wine; hot possets of milk, ale, egg, and nutmeg; even gariofiliac, a brew of gillyflower petals and claret, which Henry was known to favor.

Simon's minstrels were providing entertainment: haunting ballads, lively carols, bawdy lays. But many in the hall were finding the interaction between the guests to be equally diverting. Henry could not conceal his antipathy; from his seat on the dais, his eyes tracked Simon with baleful intent. The Earl of Gloucester was also in a foul temper; he'd already quarreled publicly with his wife, clashed briefly with Guy, and his eyes, too, kept seeking out Simon. To some, it seemed as if a morality play was being enacted in their midst: the sullen, captive King, the overbearing Earl, and his discontented, unpredictable ally, all sharing a stage meant for one, with Henry's dangerous son and the volatile young de Montforts waiting impatiently in the wings.

Had he been aware of these sentiments, Edward might have concurred, for he did feel like an actor, one giving a difficult performance. He was determined, though, that none should suspect the depths of his rage; that same day, he'd been compelled to order his Cheshire tenants to serve Simon as they'd once served him, and he feared that Simon's ploy might well hinder further rebellion in the Marches. His mood was not improved any as he looked about the hall, for he soon spied a surprising face. It infuriated him that London's Mayor and his wife should be present at these Christmas Eve revelries, but he hid his indignation; no stranger to guile, he was learning discipline, too.

Spotting Bran by the open hearth, Edward moved to join him, motivated by sheer mischief. Bran didn't notice his approach, so absorbed was he in his female companion. Edward had never seen Bran so smitten, but he was not at all surprised, for the Lady Isabella de Fortibus was an undeniable matrimonial prize, dowager Countess of Aumâle, Countess of Devon in her own right. Moreover, this wealthy young widow had attractions quite separate and apart from fertile lands and filled coffers—smoky dark eyes, a languidly seductive smile, a voluptuous body.

But as tempted as he was to intrude upon his cousin's courtship, Edward detoured sharply at sight of another familiar face. "I've been looking for you, Tom," he said, and Thomas de Clare spun around, flushing darkly. This was the first time he'd seen Edward since family loyalties had driven him to desert his King, his Prince, and he waited wretchedly for Edward's stinging rebuke.

To his astonishment, Edward was smiling. "I have asked my uncle of Leicester if I might have some companionship during my stay here at Kenilworth. We decided upon my cousin Harry and you. Is that agreeable to you?"

"I would be honored, my lord!" Thomas was not such an innocent as to take Edward's forgiveness at face value, but he was too relieved to worry overmuch about ulterior motives. Beckoning to a passing servant, he was reaching for two wine cups when a sudden clamor erupted behind them. Thomas whirled in dismay, for he'd recognized one of the angry voices as his brother's. With Edward cheerfully keeping pace, he hastened to the rescue.

Gloucester's face was reddening rapidly. "Talking to either of you is but a waste of breath," he charged, glaring first at Harry and then Guy. "Your father could blaspheme against Our Lord Christ Himself and you'd still defend him. You find fault with nothing he does, not when he usurps authority or ignores the opinions of men of good faith, not even when he protected the Jews and their satanic practices!"

Harry and Guy exchanged glances. They were puzzled themselves by Simon's changed attitude toward the English Jews, for they found it hard to reconcile with their Church's exhortations against infidels and heretics. Nothing on God's earth could have induced either of them to admit that to Gloucester, though, and they responded with one voice, shot through with mockery, intended to enrage.

"It seems to me," Harry drawled, "that poor Gilbert is becoming unnaturally obsessed with the Jews. That is all he talks about these days, Guy, rather pitiful . . ."

"Indeed," Guy agreed, heaving a theatrical sigh of regret. "I can see the day coming when he'll begin to blame them for failing crops, bad weather, mayhap even wretched marriages."

Guy had enough finesse not to underscore the insult by looking toward Gloucester's wife as he spoke, content to let Gloucester's suspicions take root on their own. They did; Gloucester took a threatening step forward, his right hand groping instinctively for a sword that wasn't there.

Simon was on the far side of the hall, deep in conversation with the Bishops of Worcester and London, had not yet heard the raised voices. Nell was closer, however, and started hastily in their direction. So did Peter de Montfort. Thomas and Edward were converging upon them, too, albeit with differing aims. But it was to be a child who defused the danger of confrontation.

"There you are, Guy. You promised to dance with me, remember?" Ellen suddenly materialized between her brothers, and, as if oblivious to the tensions, slipped her arm through Guy's. This was her first adult fête; she smiled demurely at her audience, then tugged impatiently on Guy's sleeve. Not in the least taken in by her wide-eyed innocence, Guy grinned, allowed her to lead him out to join in the carol.

Gloucester seethed, yet he could hardly have permitted his anger to spill over onto a twelve-year-old girl. But if one target of his rage had escaped him, that still left Harry, and he was about to renew the quarrel when Thomas and Edward reached them.

Thomas put a placating hand on his brother's arm, while trying to invent a plausible excuse for luring Gilbert away. It was Edward who quite inadvertently solved his dilemma. Smiling benevolently upon them, ignoring the strained silence, Edward blandly observed that it was a most impressive Christmas revelry, was it not? "My uncle Simon has outdone himself, offering us a fête worthy of a king."

But that was too heavy-handed, even for Gloucester. He gave Edward an irate look, snapped that if Edward yearned to be a puppeteer, he'd best learn to pull the strings with greater skill, and then stalked off, with Thomas in concerned pursuit.

"You're losing your touch, Ned," Harry gibed, and Edward nodded ruefully. But as his cousin started to turn away, he reached out, caught Harry's sleeve.

"Harry, wait. I have something to say. You know me, know how apologies stick in my throat. But if I owe one to any man, it is surely due to you. I wronged you, Harry, and I am indeed sorry."

Harry's eyes flicked to his face, then away. "But you'd do it again."

Edward hesitated. "Yes," he admitted, "probably I would."

"Leave it to you," Harry said at last, "to be honest about your hypocrisy," but despite the flippancy, he made no move to depart, and after some moments, unexpectedly asked if Edward missed his wife and babe.

Eleanora had sailed for France soon after the battle of Lewes, taking with her Edward's infant daughter, his first child. She and the baby were now residing with Queen Eleanor at the French court. Edward nodded, and after another silence, Harry blurted out, "She can return at any time, Ned. My father would issue a safe-conduct tomorrow if that be your wish."

Edward's mouth softened. But then he shook his head. "Better she should stay in France until the . . . the dust settles."

"You mean until you can figure out a way to outwit my father," Harry said, but without rancor. "A pity, lad, that you always have to learn things the hard way."

Edward experienced a sudden rush of emotion, regret and rage at the fates that put him so at odds with this cousin, of all men. "If only—" he began, and then caught himself. "Tell me, Harry . . . the truth now. Would Guy really have launched me from that accursed mangonel?"

"Only Guy can answer that. But you were probably wise not to have wagered your life on my brother's good will. He likes you not," Harry said dryly, and Edward grinned.

"I assure you there's no love lost on my part, either. But enough of Guy. What say you we seek out Bran, bedevil him and his lady love?"

Laughing, they bore down upon Bran and his Countess. But their prey was wary; grasping Isabella's hand, Bran ducked into the privacy of a window alcove, one that was conveniently bedecked with mistletoe.

Having evaded his rambunctious kinsmen, Bran took the lady in his arms, took full advantage of the overhanging kissing bush. But he was not as unobserved as he thought; his retreat had caught his mother's attention.

The light was subdued where Nell stood, but it seemed to Richard that sudden shadows hovered like moths about her mouth, under her eyes, never quite alighting. "The prospect does not please you?" he queried, surprised. "Most women would take joy in such a daughter-in-law, both landed and lovely. I thought, too, that Isabella was your friend."

"She is," Nell acknowledged. "She is worldly and witty, and indeed I enjoy her company. But I suspect, Richard, that Isabella is a friend for the good times, not the bad. Not that my qualms will matter much if she'll have Bran. That lad of mine is not one to seek a mother's permission to go a-wooing."

Linking her arm in Richard's, Nell drew him farther into the shadows. "It may seem presumptuous that I should dare to ask a favor of you, but—"

"Nay, you have every right, Sister. I in no way blame you for my predicament. What would you ask of me?"

"That you talk to Edward. Henry is beyond hope, but Edward is no fool. Surely he can be made to see that Simon cares only for England's weal. The Oxford Provisions are neither radical nor extreme, are merely the natural corollary of the Runnymede Charter."

Richard's smile was wry. "Lass, you forget that the Runnymede Charter was forced upon our father. Henry and Edward would gladly disavow it if they could, so that argument will find little favor with our nephew."

"But he must be won over, Richard! Not even Simon can spur a hobbled stallion forward, and that is the state of the government as long as Henry and Edward remain obdurate."

"Nell, I honestly would help if I could. I agree that the Provisions in and of themselves are not so objectionable. In the same way, I can see Simon's logic in permitting the towns to participate in parliament. More than most lords, I appreciate the importance of commerce in the scheme of things; much of my income derives from trade, after all. But were I King of England, I daresay I'd have a different outlook. No king would willingly acquiesce in the lessening of his authority."

"Mayhap not, but a king ought to be far-sighted enough to realize that if reforms are inevitable, better he be the one to carry them out."

Neither Nell nor Richard had heard Simon's footsteps. He smiled at Nell, then finished the thought. "You'd be doing us all, including Edward, a service if you could convince him of that, Richard. I suspect he's laboring under a dangerous delusion, that if only I were to be stricken down by the Almighty or mayhap the Marcher lords, all would be well. Tell him for me it's not so. The seeds have already been sown, and I need not be the one to harvest the crop. Tell him that, Richard."

"He's not likely to heed me."

"A pity," Simon said laconically, then held out his hand to his wife. "It's nigh on midnight, but we've time for one more dance ere the Mass begins."

Nell entwined her fingers in his, followed him out onto the floor. In vain, the Church fulminated against the carol as sinful; it remained the most popular of dances, as much a pleasure for spectators as for the participants. The dancers swung to the left, chanting the chorus: "Pride is out, and pride is in, and pride is the root of every sin." Colors swirled like bright banners as they circled, a kaleidoscope of vivid, ever-shifting images illuminated by the swaying, overhead candelabras. Richard watched as Simon and Nell passed from light to shadow, back to light again, and it came to him that the spinning circle of the carol bore an uncanny resemblance to Fortune's Wheel. It was, for Richard, an usually fanciful thought; he shrugged it off, and then noticed that, across the hall, Edward, too, was watching the dancers, watching Simon all the while.

35

Odiham, England

March 1265

Sɪᴍᴏɴ's parliament was in session from January until mid-March. Its major accomplishment was the formal recognition of peace terms, but the moment men would most remember was the bitter, public clash between Simon and the Earl of Gloucester.

Gloucester's grievances were numerous. He was outraged that Simon had forbidden an upcoming tournament at Dunstable, for he had been eager to face Simon's sons across the length of a lance. He was resentful of Simon's unilateral decision to appoint his son Amaury as treasurer of York, that post having become vacant by the January death of John Mansel. He was still vexed that Simon had spurned his demand for ransoms, and he was alarmed by the arrest of the Earl of Derby. Derby had been plundering his neighbors, taking advantage of the country's civil strife to indulge in outright extortion and robbery, and few pitied his plight. Yet when Simon cast him into the Tower of London, Derby's fellow barons were genuinely shocked. While a lord might expect to pay for political transgressions, it was unheard of to punish one for criminal offenses, and by imprisoning Derby, Simon seemed to be setting a dangerous precedent. But above all, Gloucester begrudged Simon his supremacy, castigating the French-born Earl as "an alien interloper who deprives Englishmen of their due rights and keeps England's King in servitude."

Simon's response was predictable: withering sarcasm that evoked laughter throughout Westminster's great hall. He had a grievance, too, for Gloucester was harboring the Marcher lords, in defiance of his own government's expulsion edict. Gloucester struck back with the hyperbolic rage of one in an untenable legal position; unable to offer a valid defense for sheltering men ordered to abjure the realm, he chose, instead, to withdraw to his estates in the Marches.

Parliament then took up the question of Edward's continuing captivity, and it was agreed that he should be freed in return for his solemn oath to adhere to the peace terms. No one, least of all Edward, expected this freedom to be more than an illusion. But although still under Simon's surveillance, he did gain a small measure of autonomy, and Edward was not about to scorn any advantage, however slight. Like many in England in that spring of 1265, the King's son was playing a waiting game.

NELL was exhausted, for the normal routine of Odiham had been thrown into turmoil. Just two days ago, Harry, Edward, and Hal had arrived, accompanied by a sizable escort, and that very afternoon Simon had ridden in with an even larger retinue. As delighted as Nell was to see her husband, she knew Odiham's larders would be hard-pressed to accommodate these new arrivals. The stables now held three hundred thirty-four horses, instead of the usual forty-four. And the men would be no less hungry than their mounts. Nell's cooks normally baked one hundred thirty loaves of bread a day; by dark this Thursday eve, more than eight hundred loaves had been devoured, and consumption of wine soared from ten to seventy-four gallons. Simon had missed dinner, and supper was, in consequence, an elaborate affair, as Nell's cooks labored to produce a tempting Lenten menu: seventeen hundred herrings alone, so much pike and mackerel that Odiham's fish ponds would soon be emptied. On the morrow she'd have to send some of her servants to fish the stews at neighboring manors.

Supper may have been a culinary triumph, but it had not been a festive occasion, even though all the de Montforts were gathered under one roof; Bran alone was missing, off besieging Pevensey Castle again. Family reunion notwithstanding, the tension at the table had been thick enough to slice and serve up on trenchers. Harry and Guy were sulking; they'd been as hot as Gloucester to hold that Dunstable tournament, and they resented their father's interference, agreeing among themselves that he too often treated them like green striplings with no sense. Edward was also in a surly temper; his leash was proving to have less slack than he'd hoped. Thomas de Clare was obviously ill at ease, caught off balance by his brother's latest tantrum. Even the younger de Montforts—Amaury, Richard, and Ellen—were unusually subdued, ever a barometer for their father's moods. Simon had been withdrawn and silent throughout the meal, distracted by thoughts that seemed none too pleasant; moreover, he looked so tired that Nell's heart ached for him.

Nell's ladies, Christiana and Hawisa, had assisted her in undressing, then discreetly disappeared, leaving her alone to wait for her husband. But Simon had lingered in the hall, giving Hal additional instructions; their nephew was to be dispatched again as an emissary to the French court, in consequence of which he alone had been in cheerful spirits that night. Nell was drifting drowsily toward sleep when she finally heard Simon's footsteps on the stairs, a low murmur of voices. Reaching for the bed hangings, she was surprised to find that Simon was accompanied not by a squire, but by Colin, their farrier.

Simon crossed to the table, searched for pen and parchment as the blacksmith watched anxiously, twisting his cap in huge, hammer-scarred hands. "There you are, Colin," Simon said. "I've written: 'Let it be known, lest sinister suspicions arise hereafter, that the right ear of Colin the farrier of Odiham, son of Elias the farrier, was torn off in an alehouse brawl.' Keep it in a pouch around your neck, and show it the next time someone thinks you might be a runaway serf or a maimed felon." He waited until Colin backed out, stammering his thanks, then sank down in the nearest chair.

Nell grabbed for her bedrobe. "Could that not have waited till the morrow?" she chided. "And where are your squires? You look half-asleep on your feet."

"I sent the lads off to bed. No, stay there, Nell; you'll catch cold."

Nell ignored him, swung her legs over the side of the bed. "It could not be any more chilled up here than it was down in the hall tonight. I've rarely seen Edward so sullen. Is he still brooding about the cancellation of the Dunstable tournament?"

"I daresay our idiot sons are," Simon said, so acidly that Nell's eyes opened wide. "But I expect Edward has weightier matters on his mind; last week he had to surrender six royal castles. They were too strategic to leave in untrustworthy hands: Dover for certes, Nottingham, Corfe, amongst others. We had Henry turn them over to Edward, and he then yielded them to our control for a period of five years. It was all I could think to do, Nell, that would safeguard the government whilst still preserving Edward's titles and rights to them. But I cannot blame Edward for being disgruntled about it."

Nell leaned over his chair, began to massage his neck and shoulders. "I want to ask you about an unlikely story Harry told me, that when Mayor Fitz Thomas swore fealty to Henry, he dared to lecture Henry about a king's duties! Did that truly happen, or was I taken in by another of Harry's infernal jests?"

Simon's sudden grin belied his fatigue. "No, by God, Fitz Thomas did indeed do that. After pledging his fealty to Henry, he added, 'My liege, so long as unto us you will be a good lord and King, we will be faithful unto you.' The way Henry choked, I thought he was going to swallow his tongue!"

"Where does Fitz Thomas find his courage?" Nell marveled. "So meek and mild he looks—until he opens his mouth!" Leaning over still farther, she kissed his cheek. "Simon, I've seen drawn bowstrings less taut than you are. For pity's sake, love, come to bed."

He nodded, got stiffly to his feet, and began to extinguish the candles; it was the first time in many months that she'd seen him limp. She shed her robe, climbed, shivering, into bed, and rolled over to make room for him. "I hate sleeping alone," she confessed. "The bed feels so empty when . . ." She paused, frowning, for as her fingers slid along his chest, they'd encountered a patch of chafed skin. "Simon, why did you not tell me you had a rash? I've some orris root salve in my coffer—"

"You need not bother," he said, and when she would have risen, he reached up, caught her arm. "Nell, let it lie."

He expected her to argue. Instead, she grasped the sheet, jerked it back. He might have quenched all the candles, but the hearth fire still burned. Her eyes moved slowly, searchingly, over his body. His chest hair was soft and springy, easy to entwine around her fingers, faintly shadowed with silver as it slanted down toward his groin. Her fingers hovered, from habit, above his ribs, where an old scar traced a sword's jagged passing. But she saw only the telltale red blotches.

"I'd wondered why you suddenly wanted to undress in the dark," she said. "You did not want me to know you were wearing a hair shirt." He confirmed her suspicion with silence, and she bent down, impulsively put her lips to the abraded, scraped skin. "But Simon, why? You have God's favor, need not offer proof of your faith. Wearing a hair shirt is a gesture of truly admirable piety, but it is also a penance, and beloved, you have nothing to atone for!"

"I am not so sure of that, Nell, not any more. I no longer know what the Almighty wants of me, fear that I am failing Him. In truth, much of the time I feel like a man clinging to a rope that's dangling over a sheer cliff. I can neither go up nor down, can only hope to hold on."

"I've never heard you sound so disheartened. Is it Gloucester? Surely you do not think his envy would spur him to out-and-out rebellion?"

"No," he said, without hesitation. "He truly does believe in the Provisions, in the need for reform. No matter how much he hates me, how could he betray his own conscience? He'll not abandon the Provisions, but it will not be easy to coax him back into the fold. I sometimes think he's more trouble as an ally than he would be as an avowed enemy!"

He slid his arm around Nell's waist, drew her into an embrace comforting in its very familiarity. Pillowing her head in the crook of his arm, she was silent for a time. "Simon . . . why are you still so angry with our lads? I grant you that their idea of a tournament was sheer lunacy. Ere it was over, blood would have been flowing in earnest. But I'm sure they did not think—"

"Ah, Nell, it is not just the tournament. They never seem to consider the consequences of what they do. They bait Gloucester at every chance, race blindly ahead, churning up great clouds of dust and giving nary a thought for what lies around the next bend in the road. Did you know that men now call Harry 'the wool merchant'? When I entrusted him with enforcing the prohibition against exporting wool, he took the charge too much to heart, auctioned off the wool he seized and kept the proceeds. He meant well, used the money to pay his men-at-arms, but he ought to have seen the folly of it. And Bran has been even more reckless. As soon as I appointed him as Constable of Portchester, he set his sailors to patrolling the coast, where they were soon preying upon Channel shipping. I had to intervene personally on behalf of a Bayonne merchant, order Bran to release his ship!"

"The young make mistakes, Simon. You're right, of course; they chase after danger the way they do whores, and at times they can be foolhardy beyond belief. But they are good lads at heart, and they love you well, as few fathers are ever loved."

"I know," he said. "I know, too, that much of the blame is mine.

If I had reined them in as I ought, if I'd not turned such a blind eye to their hell-raising, mayhap they'd not now be balking at the first prick of the spurs."

"You're overly tired," she said. "That's why you're so dispirited. But this, too, shall pass, my love. You'll be able to smooth Gloucester's ruffled feathers, and—"

"And then what?" he asked, and there was something chilling in the very quietness of the question. "I patch up an uneasy peace with Gloucester, succeed in exiling the Marcher lords, and mayhap even manage to bring our sons to their senses. Yet nothing will have truly changed. How long can I hold Henry hostage? How long ere Edward breaks loose? We'd best face it, Nell. I'm fighting a war that cannot be won."

"That's not so, Simon! Once Edward can be made to see the need for the Provisions—"

"That would take nothing less than a miracle."

Nell was not put off by his sarcasm. "I've been told that God is good at miracles," she shot back, and coaxed from her husband a reluctant smile. She was not surprised that he'd failed to mention the most obvious option open to him. If he'd truly despaired of winning, why not withdraw to France? Other men would; she knew that. But she knew, too, that he could not, knew he'd see flight as a betrayal of those who'd come to believe in him, who'd made his cause their own.

"Simon, there is a question I must ask of you. Have you lost faith in the Provisions, in—"

"Jesú, no!"

"One more question, then. If you had it to do over again, would you still have sailed from France last spring?"

"I've thought on that—long and hard—and each time the conclusion is the same. I'd do it no differently. If it be God's Will that the Provisions prevail—and I do believe that—how could I refuse to fight for them?"

"Then, my love, you've no reason to despair. You've done what you had to do, have no cause for regrets. Our Lord may test you, but this I do know—He would never forsake you, never!"

"Nor would you, my heart," he said, and although his face was in shadow, she knew he was smiling. "Of all the manifold mercies that the Almighty has seen fit to bestow upon me, I am most grateful for you. You've done me a great service tonight, for you've made me see that I was in danger of doubting the Lord's intent. The answer is so simple, Nell; Thy Will be done."

Nell's relief was beyond expressing, so thankful was she that she had found balm for her husband's troubled spirit. "Thy Will be done," she echoed gratefully, and would have sworn that she meant every word of that softly breathed prayer. But such was her faith in Simon that it colored her faith in God; unable to conceive of defeat, she never doubted that the Lord, too, willed Simon to win, and falling asleep in Simon's arms, she did not dread the morrow, so secure was she in the strength of her yesterdays.

SIMON parted from Nell on April 2; in the company of his sons, Henry, and Edward, he reached Gloucester at the end of April, soon moved on to Hereford, where he learned that William de Lusignan and John de Warenne had landed in South Wales. But he was able to "patch up a peace" with the Earl of Gloucester. On May 12, the young Earl came to Hereford, renewed his homage to Henry, and on the 20th, a proclamation was issued, declaring that the Earls of Leicester and Gloucester were now "of one mind and harmonious in everything."

THE Benedictine priory was chiming Vespers. A silvery, melodic sound, it echoed above the strident clamor of Hereford's narrow, noisy streets, floated on the wind as far as the meadows where Harry and Edward were squabbling amiably. They cocked their heads, listening to the bells, but made no move to start back to the castle; there were at least two hours of daylight remaining. While there were always watchful eyes upon him, Edward was no longer denied the recreational pastimes of a prince; he and Harry frequently went riding or hunting in the woods known as the Hay, albeit under escort. On this mild Thursday in late May, they had been racing their horses on the level ground north of the town walls. Edward had been given a flashy chestnut stallion a few days past, and he'd been eager to try his new mount's speed. Much to the amusement of his companions, all his boasting came to naught. The stallion had pulled up, lame, in the first trial, and he'd been compelled to borrow mounts from his guards in order to continue racing against Harry and Robert de Ros, a young baron who had distinguished himself at Lewes, enough to be entrusted with the custody of the King's son.

They were making quite a commotion, cheering their horses on, exchanging barbed banter and boisterous jokes, and they soon attracted an audience of bored townsmen. Money changed hands, wineskins were passed back and forth, rows broke out, and by the time Thomas de Clare reached the meadow, the scene was as raucous and rowdy as any fair or market-day gathering.

Thomas drew rein, watching as Harry's lathered roan nosed out a rangy gelding Edward had coaxed from Rob de Ros's squire. Harry was laughing; he'd lost few wagers so far, for his stallion was the class of the lot. Edward was laughing, too, uncommonly good-natured in defeat. He accepted a wineskin, was raising his arm to blot sweat from his brow when he spotted Thomas. Their eyes linked above the heads of the crowd, and Thomas nodded slowly. He would never forget the look on Edward's face, an unguarded instant of blazing, white-hot triumph.

Thomas wished he could share in it, but he had too squeamish a conscience. Not that he faulted Ned for seeking any means of escape. It was his brother's deception he could not stomach. In truth, he'd never been all that enamored of the Provisions. But Gilbert had been a true believer. So how could he cast them aside like so much rubbish? And how could he give his sworn word, profane holy relics with a knowing lie? Men were damned for less.

Edward took his time in beckoning to him. Never had Thomas so envied the King's son his icy nerves than as he watched Edward trade affable insults with Harry and Rob de Ros, for all the world as if nothing more was at stake than a carelessly laid wager.

Thomas sighed, sought to rouse himself for what lay ahead. This was no time to dwell upon Gilbert's dishonor. That was between Gilbert and God. All that mattered now was Ned's escape. For if they failed, Ned would never have another chance and he'd be lucky to see the sun again.

"Come take a look at my horse, Tom," Edward called out. "He seems to have gotten some gravel embedded under his shoe." Thomas hastened toward him, and as they bent over to inspect the chestnut's foreleg, he whispered that all was set. Roger de Mortimer had men concealed in a wood on the Tillington road, ready to escort them the twenty-three miles to Wigmore Castle. They need only await the signal.

It was not long in coming. A horseman appeared on a distant hill, waved his hat twice. Thomas quickly remounted; Edward was already in the saddle. "Harry!" As his cousin turned, he swept off his hat in a mocking farewell salute, then spurred his stallion forward. The chestnut had been chafing at the bit. Given its head at last, it bolted, went thundering across the field at a dead run.

There were cries of astonishment from the spectators, slow to comprehend what they were seeing. Not so Harry and Rob de Ros. Within seconds, they were running for their own mounts, shouting for their men.

So swiftly had Harry reacted that Edward and Thomas did not have that much of a head start. By the time they reached the road, their pursuers were only a few lengths behind. But there they hung, unable to close the gap.

"Do not be a fool, Ned! You cannot hope to escape!"

Edward looked over his shoulder. "What'll you wager, Harry? That heaving, staggering nag you're riding?"

Thomas risked a backward glance, saw that the roan stallion was indeed laboring. Heart alone had taken it this far; despite Harry's frantic urgings, it was shortening stride. So were the other horses; their best speed lay back on that grassy meadow. Slowly, inexorably, Edward's chestnut and Thomas's unraced bay began to draw away.

Roger de Mortimer was—for once—as good as his word. As they raced through the hamlet of Tillington, a large body of horsemen came galloping out of the woods. Harry's companions hastily yanked on their reins, flung their horses back upon their haunches. Harry alone charged ahead, ignoring de Ros's dismayed shout: "Harry, no! You're not wearing mail!"

"We did it, Ned!" Turning to share his wonder, Thomas was horrified to find that Edward had checked his stallion. Paying no heed to Thomas, he watched until he saw his cousin extricate himself, pull back to safety. Only then did he urge his horse to catch up with Thomas, giving his thwarted pursuers one final glimpse of his chestnut's streaming, golden tail before disappearing into the distance.

EMERGING from Simon's chamber, Peter de Montfort paused at the sight of their tragic, young faces. He'd never seen two souls so wretched as Robert de Ros and Harry, and beneath his anger, pity stirred. Guy was not so charitable. From a shadowed window-seat, he stabbed his brother and de Ros with eyes of implacable ice. "Idiots!" he snarled, loud enough to be heard, meaning to be heard. Rob de Ros would normally have bristled; now he merely glanced at Guy, his the indifference only unmitigated misery can engender. Harry never even looked Guy's way, unable to tear his gaze from that closed, oaken door.

"Does he know?" he asked, very low, and Peter nodded.

"His rage must have been terrible," Rob de Ros ventured, almost inaudibly. But this time Peter shook his head.

"No . . . ," he said, still sounding somewhat bemused. "He heard me out in silence, utter and absolute silence. In truth, this is a side of him that I've never seen before. Not only did he not seem outraged, I do not even think he was surprised!"

Harry flinched. "I have to see him," he said, and Rob gave him a look of awed admiration, for Simon de Montfort was the last man on God's earth he'd have wanted to face at that moment. Peter shrugged, stepped away from the door, and Harry raised his head, squared his shoulders, then reached for the latch.

Twilight had descended upon the vale of the Wye, blurring and softening the outlines of the world beyond the window. The sky was still too pale for night, too dark for day. It was an hour Simon had never liked, a time of transition, of ambiguous boundaries and hazy silhouettes. A few stars glimmered through the dusk, and below, the river washed against the south curtain wall, winding about the castle like a mourning ribbon, black and lusterless, flowing from the Welsh heartland toward the mouth of the Severn. Wales. He said it aloud. Wales and Llewelyn ap Gruffydd. Why not? What did he have to lose?

He hadn't heard the door opening. When he didn't turn from the window, Harry froze where he was. "I do not blame you for not wanting to look upon my face," he said huskily. "How you must hate me now!"

"I do not blame you, Harry. How could I? I was the one who taught you to trust a man's word."

"He played me for a fool, Papa! How can you forgive that?"

"And Gloucester played me for one. He came to Hereford for one reason only—to gain the time he needed to plot Edward's escape."

Remorse can be a selfish emotion; Harry had been focusing only upon his own part in the debacle. "You think Gloucester is behind it?" he asked, somewhat dubiously. "The men we saw wore de Mortimer's colors . . ."

Simon discovered that patience—always perverse—came more easily once a man reached the outer limits of exhaustion. "If Gloucester's was not the guiding hand, why did his brother flee with Edward? No, it has to be Gloucester, and I should have suspected . . . But I did not believe he would betray the Provisions. Nor did I think he would besmirch his honor with a false oath. More fool I . . ." He looked back at his son, for the first time noticed the blood staining Harry's sleeve. "Peter told me you'd crossed swords with de Mortimer's men, but not that you'd been hurt. Why did you not let the castle leech—"

"Christ, Papa, do you think I care about that? I do not understand you. How can you be so calm, so . . . so stoic? I let Ned escape! Why do you not rage, curse me as I deserve?"

"Harry, unless I'd kept Edward in chains, this was bound to happen sooner or later."

For Harry, that was absolution come too cheaply. "But do you not see what this means? Now that Ned has his freedom, you'll have to fight another war!"

"Yes, I know. And mayhap that, too, was bound to happen. Mayhap Our Lord seeks a resolution."

Unsheathing his dagger, Simon slit Harry's blood-soaked sleeve, pulled his reluctant son toward the table. Sponging water onto Harry's gashed arm, he said quietly, "Do not torment yourself so, lad. I defeated Edward once before, did I not? God willing, I expect to win this next battle, too."

36

Pipton, Wales

June 1265

"I'VE been told that in exchange for aiding Edward's escape, the Earl of Gloucester demanded that Edward agree to abide by the ancient laws of England and ban all aliens from the King's council. Is that true?"

Simon nodded. "The irony of it, Llewelyn, is that I would once have been content with those very terms myself. But Edward and Henry balked at conceding even that much."

"Is Gloucester fool enough to think Edward will honor that pledge?"

Simon shrugged. "In truth, I have not given it much thought. I have enough troubles of my own without taking on Gloucester's, too."

Llewelyn's smile was wryly sympathetic. "I suppose you have had better springs."

"I have had one setback after another," Simon admitted. "After Edward escaped, I summoned our levies to assemble at Worcester. But Edward cut them off, took the town a fortnight ago. They've burned all the bridges across the Severn, destroyed the fords. I'd dispatched Robert de Ros to hold Gloucester Castle, but Edward has had it under siege for six days now, and if the castle falls, we'll be stranded on the wrong side of the Severn, unable to get back into England, to join forces with my son Bran."

Llewelyn had his share of spies and superior scouts; most of what Simon had said was already known to him. He was very impressed, though, by Simon's candor. His past experience had taught him that men invariably sought to put a high gloss upon the nakedness of their need. Favors were usually solicited in the oblique language of dissimulation, appeals made by indirection, rarely broached so boldly.

Simon seemed to read his mind, saying abruptly, "I've no time for game-playing. I need your help, Llewelyn. We both know it, so what point is there in pretense?"

"I admire your honesty, owe you as much in return. I do not find it easy to trust Englishmen. But I do trust you, Simon, and our past alliance has been to our mutual benefit. I am quite willing to aid you in your struggle against the King's son."

Llewelyn paused, signaled for wine. Simon had first thought Pipton an odd choice for a conference; it was a sleepy little hamlet deep in the hills of Powys. But upon his arrival, he'd found Llewelyn comfortably ensconced in a fortified house overlooking the River Wye, De Treveley Manor, home of the hereditary lords of Pipton. They were sitting crosslegged on cushions, Welsh-style, but the chamber was well-lit, and as soon as Llewelyn beckoned, a servant moved unobtrusively to refill their cups, vanished just as inconspicuously. Simon shifted impatiently, and now it was Llewelyn's turn to demonstrate how well attuned the two men were to each other's thoughts.

"I know," he said dryly, "words are cheap. You want to know the particulars. Fair enough. I will pledge to support your government against our common enemies. I will renew homage to Henry as my liege lord. I will put thirty thousand marks at the disposal of the royal treasury, paying three thousand marks every Michaelmas. Lastly, I am prepared to provide you with the services of my Welshmen—five thousand spearmen and bowmen."

Simon felt no relief, not yet. "And what do you want in return?"

Llewelyn thought it best to make his greatest demand first. "I want the English Crown to recognize me as Prince of Wales, to acknowledge that the other Welsh lords owe fealty to me as their liege lord." He waited, but Simon was silent. "I want you to recognize my rights to Painscastle, Hawarden, and Ellesmere, all of which I now hold. And I want the Crown to assist me in recovering those castles and lands which were unjustly taken from my uncle, Davydd ap Llewelyn."

Those were hard terms, and would find no favor in England; even his London supporters would regard any concession to the Welsh as a deal with the Devil. But Simon had known Llewelyn would take full advantage of this God-given opportunity, demand as much as he could for Wales. He was too astute a politician, too ambitious a Prince, to confuse friendship with statecraft.

"Henry will likely have a seizure when I tell him. But in all honesty, I do not find it so peculiar a notion, that a Welshman should rule Wales. I agree to your terms, Llewelyn, accept on behalf of the English government."

Llewelyn grinned, clinked his cup playfully against Simon's. "What next, Simon? Where do you go from here?"

"South . . . into Gwent. I cannot risk a pitched battle yet, cannot take on Edward, Gloucester, and all the Marchers, too, not until Bran brings up our reinforcements. My main concern is to find a way to cross the Severn. If I can take Newport, I can then send word to Bristol, ask them to dispatch ships for us. Edward's garrison holds the castle there, but the townsmen are on my side, and I know I can count upon them for help."

Llewelyn nodded approvingly. "A clever move, one that ought to break you free of their snare. I'll do what I can, too. Gloucester is Lord of Glamorgan, and has castles in Gwent. Let's see how many we can put to the torch."

"That," Simon said, "is a prospect I find right pleasing. But what happens then, Llewelyn? Will you take the field with me in England?"

"No," Llewelyn said, "I will not. I'll fight with you here in Wales and in the Marches, but once you cross the Severn, you're on your own."

Simon's eyes never left his face, eyes dark and riveting. "Why?"

"Because," Llewelyn said, without hesitation, "I cannot be sure you'll win." When Simon would have risen, he reached over, grasped his arm. "You are more to me than an ally, Simon. You are a friend. I want you to win your war, for your sake as well as mine. And indeed, I think you will. But as I said, I cannot be sure, and whilst I would willingly risk my life, I cannot risk the sovereignty of Wales. If, God forbid, you do fail, Edward will then turn upon Wales. If I were dead, too, how easy it would be for him . . ."

His words seemed to echo in the silence that followed. Few men could accept a truth so unpalatable, but he was wagering that Simon would prefer honesty to equivocation or evasion.

Simon was still studying him, his face inscrutable, and Llewelyn began to wonder if he'd misjudged the other man, after all. But then Simon settled himself back upon the cushions. "I cannot fault your logic," he conceded, with a grim smile. "But I wonder if you've thought this through. We both know that this treaty would not long survive me, that you'd never again gain such favorable terms from the English Crown. You've as much at stake as I do, Llewelyn, for this chance will not come again for Wales. I agree that a prince can ill afford to be reckless, but too much caution can cripple, too. There are times when you have to risk all upon one throw of the dice."

Llewelyn was smiling, too. "Ours is a land famed for its eloquent speakers, but you'd hold your own with the best of them. Poor tongue-tied Henry; he never had a chance!" Setting down his wine cup, he suggested, "Shall we join the others in the hall? My Welsh allies will be chafing at the bit."

Simon had not really expected to prevail. "There is something I want to say first. I, too, think of you as a friend, Llewelyn. Yours are the attributes I would have looked for in a son—courage tempered by common sense. We are already kinsmen of sorts, for your grandfather was wed to my wife's sister. But I would see us more closely bound. You have no wife as yet. I would remedy that by offering you my daughter."

"No wonder you've fared so well on the battlefield. You're devilishly good at surprises! This is Ellen? You have but the one lass, no?"

Simon nodded. "We've cherished her all the more for that. Because of her youth—she'll not be thirteen till October—Nell and I would insist upon a plight-troth now, with the marriage to take place once she passes her fourteenth birthday. I would, of course, provide her with a generous marriage portion. And although I realize that, as Ellen's father, I am hardly an objective judge, I truly do think she has the makings of a beauty."

"The Lady Nell's daughter? That I can well believe." Llewelyn laughed suddenly. "I was just thinking," he said, "that we'd be closing the circle. Llewelyn Fawr's grandson and the Lady Joanna's niece. I think such a marriage would have pleased them. I can say for certes that it pleases me. I would be proud, Simon, to wed your daughter."

ELLEN de Montfort was not happy at Dover Castle. She felt dwarfed by its vastness, overwhelmed by its massive walls and sinister-looking siege weapons. She missed the comfortable dimensions of Odiham, the familiar routine of daily life in a castle that was first and foremost a home, not a fortress. Above all, she missed Odiham's glorious gardens, hedged in hawthorn for privacy, ablaze with iris and marigolds and lilies. Odiham's gardens had roses climbing over trellised turf seats, a flowery mead carpet of daisies and periwinkles. Dover had no gardens at all. When she wanted to take their dogs for a walk, she had to confine them to the open space beyond the kitchen, taking care they did not dig in the small herb plot or splash in the fish stews.

She had four of them with her on this afternoon in early July: Blanchette and Sable, her mother's sleek greyhounds; Roland, her brother Harry's favorite alaunt; Avalon, her own cherished briard, a New Year's gift from her father. The briard was said to be descended from an ancient breed of sheep dog favored by Charlemagne, and Ellen loved it dearly, despite her brothers' claims that it looked like a bush with feet. She loved animals in general, even those not considered pets, like cats, but she was particularly drawn to dogs, upon which she bestowed fanciful names culled from minstrels' tales and chivalric myths. Her brothers grumbled, but humored her, as usual; Guy alone balked, insisting he was not about to own a "Tristan" or a "Lancelot."

Whistling for Avalon—she was inordinately proud of the fact that Harry had taught her to whistle like a boy, with two fingers—Ellen wandered over to a wooden bench. This was a strange summer, unlike any she'd ever known. She'd been frightened only at first, when her mother had gotten word of Cousin Ned's escape from Hereford. They'd departed Odiham in great haste, galloped through the night toward Portchester. She'd stopped being afraid then, for Bran was there, and he'd personally escorted them to Dover. While she didn't much like Dover, she did feel safe here.

But she was so bored, and so lonely. Amaury and Richard were always off running errands for Mama, and she was like a veritable whirlwind, so busy was she. Arranging to send horses to Bran and spices and sweets to Uncle Richard back at Kenilworth, ordering additional mangonels for Dover's defense, seeing that their fourteen highborn prisoners were well treated and yet well guarded, dispatching letters to Papa, to Bran, to London's Mayor, the French King, entertaining two of Louis's ambassadors and the townsmen of Sandwich and Dover and Winchelsea, doing whatever she could to win new converts to Papa's cause.

"Ellen!" She jumped guiltily to her feet, for she was supposed to be laboring over her lessons. But there was no reproach in Nell's voice. "Sit down, darling." Taking her daughter's hand, she drew her back to the bench. "A courier just rode in with a letter from your father."

"What does he say, Mama? Can I read it?"

"Yes . . . later. First we need to talk. Ere your father departed Odiham, he thought we ought to tell you then, but I said to wait; if it had fallen through, there'd be no need for you to know."

Ellen could contain herself no longer. "Know what, Mama?"

"I do not mean to keep you in suspense, for I am sure you'll be pleased. Ellen, your father and I have arranged a brilliant marriage for you."

Ellen had always expected to hear those words, but not so soon. "Is . . . is he English, Mama?" When Nell shook her head, she bit her lip, struggling to hide her dismay. While she trusted her parents to pick a worthy husband for her, she was loath to live abroad, far from the people she most loved; her Aunt Isabella's fate was uppermost in her mind, the Emperor Frederick's neglected consort, dying in lonely isolation in a distant, alien land.

"Ellen, do you not want to know your husband's name? You shall have a crown, for we have betrothed you to Llewelyn ap Gruffydd, Prince of Wales."

"Wales," Ellen breathed, and closed her eyes for a moment, dazzled by the sudden brightness of the sun. "Truly, Mama? Like Aunt Joanna?"

"Yes, Ellen, like Joanna," Nell said softly, and then Ellen was in her arms, clinging tightly, whispering over and over again:

"I'm so glad, Mama, so glad . . ."

"I'd hoped you would be, darling." Nell's eyes misted. From earliest childhood, her daughter had been enthralled by tales of great romance, by tragic heroines like Iseult and Guinevere. But no love story had so beguiled her as that of her own aunt, who'd found her destiny in the alpine heights of Eryri, in the arms of a gallant Welsh Prince, a man who'd loved her enough even to forgive adultery. Nell had been reasonably certain that her starry-eyed Ellen would be eager to follow in Joanna's hallowed footsteps, but there was relief in confirmation; she'd not have wanted to see the child wed against her will.

"How old is he, Mama—my Welsh Prince? Is he like Joanna's Llewelyn?"

"Well, he is thirty-six or thirty-seven, I believe. And he's dark, tall for a Welshman, and pleasing to the eye." Nell laughed. "I took a liking to him from the very first, do not think you'll be disappointed. Now— is he like Llewelyn Fawr? In some ways, yes—for certes, he shares his grandfather's ambition, his ability, his dream for Wales. But your Prince is more intense, more earnest than Joanna's Llewelyn. I often suspected that he regarded the world as something of a perverse joke, man most of all. Your Llewelyn is more serious-minded, more like your father."

"Then he must be a very good man," Ellen concluded, with utter confidence; she could envision no greater compliment than a comparison with her father. "Will he come into England to meet me ere the wedding?"

"Yes, of course. But not for a while, not until . . ."

"Not until Papa has fought Cousin Ned."

Nell nodded reluctantly, and Ellen groped for her hand. "What else did Papa say in his letter? Was his other news bad?"

"Some of it, yes. Gloucester Castle fell to Edward on the twenty-ninth. But you need not fret, Ellen. Your father is a man well able to take care of himself. He has captured the Earl of Gloucester's castles at Monmouth, Usk, and Newport, is now awaiting ships from the good men of Bristol. And Bran is hastening west with a large force. He ought to be able to link up with Simon within the next fortnight, mayhap sooner. Once he does, the danger is over."

Ellen nodded somberly. She liked her cousin Ned, was sorry that he'd been led astray by evil advice. She did not doubt that when the inevitable battlefield confrontation came, her father would prevail. But men would die, die for naught. "It's so sad, Mama," she said, "so sad . . ."

NIGHT had fallen over Newport, but the darkness was flame-lit. Out in the harbor, the last of Simon's Bristol ships were burning down toward the water-line, and wind-driven cinders swirled high above the castle, blown from the smoldering bridge that had spanned the River Usk.

Simon stood on the castle walkway, watching as the harbor fires were quenched, one by one, by the black icy waters of the Severn estuary. So much had happened so fast that he'd lost all sense of time; it seemed like days instead of hours since the Bristol transport ships had appeared on the horizon, their long-delayed deliverance. But as they approached the harbor, disaster struck. They were intercepted by three fast-moving galleys, lurking in ambush for the clumsy flatboats, from their mastheads flaunting the banners of the King's son. As Simon and his men watched in horror from the shore, Edward's galleys swooped down upon the Bristol ships like hawks upon pigeons. The fight was brief, savage, and one-sided. By the time it was over, eleven of the Bristol ships were afire, and as they floundered, began to sink, they dragged down with them Simon's last hope for crossing the Severn.

And worse was to follow. While Simon's men were mesmerized by the catastrophe taking place out in the harbor, a large enemy force was landing upriver. They were almost upon the town before Simon's sentries sounded the alarm. Soon two battles were being fought, one on the heaving decks of the Bristol ships, another on the muddied banks of the Severn. Edward's men had the advantage of surprise and numerical superiority; Simon's soldiers had to give ground. As they retreated back into the town, for a time Newport's fate hung in the balance. Simon finally managed to stave off utter defeat by setting fire to the wooden bridge that arched over Newport's second river. He would later see the irony in that: one river his nemesis, the other his salvation.

Unable to cross the Usk, the attacking force withdrew, and darkness soon concealed the ugly evidence of the day's carnage. Bodies were mercifully shrouded in shadows, bloodied ground camouflaged until the morrow. Only the fires still burned.

The wind was hot upon their skin; Simon's face stung from exposure to flying embers and ashes. He'd ventured himself onto the bridge, and his hair was singed, so blackened by smoke and soot that he seemed to have miraculously shed decades, regained the raven hair of lost youth. He was flanked by two equally dark heads, Harry and Guy, gazing out across the harbor in stunned silence. Peter and Hugh le Despenser, too, were mute. What was there to say?

"Simon!" Humphrey de Bohun was hastening along the wall walk. "I did as you ordered," he reported, in a voice hoarse with fatigue. "We've posted sentries at every approach to the town." Seized by a sudden coughing fit, he spat over the wall, leaning upon the merlon for support. "My throat feels like I've been swilling sawdust; does any- one have a wineskin? That whoreson Edward is getting too good at this game! You think he'll move in on the morrow?"

"Yes . . . which is why we pull back tonight. What defenses does Newport offer? No town walls, just an earthen bank and outer ditch— how long ere they breach that? We've no choice but to withdraw into the Welsh uplands. Llewelyn controls the upper Usk valley. At least there we will be safe from pursuit."

They could take meagre comfort in that; there'd be considerable hardship in a retreat into Wales. During this past month, they'd soon sickened on the unfamiliar Welsh fare, yearning for bread and ale, nei- ther of which was a staple of the Welsh diet. But no one objected. How could they? They were doomed if they stayed where they were, and all knew it.

Out in the harbor, the last flaming wreck disappeared beneath the waters of the Severn. Simon turned away from the wall. "We'd best make haste," he said. "We're running out of time." For a moment, his eyes lingered on their smoke-smudged, haggard faces. "Jesú, the lot of you look like men on the way to the gallows! The prospect of eating Welsh food cannot be that disheartening, can it? I'll not deny that this day was a disaster. But there'll be other days. By now Bran will have gotten my last summons, alerting him to the urgency of our plight, to the need for speed. All we can do is retreat beyond the Usk, then wait for him to reach us."

Simon paused, rubbing his hand wearily over his eyes; they were bloodshot, smoke-sensitive, swollen from lack of sleep. "The rest," he said, "is up to Bran."

37

Kenilworth Castle, England

July 1265

SIR John d'Eyvill and his Yorkshiremen reached Kenilworth in mid-morning on the last day of July. As they rode down High Street, past the priory of St Mary the Virgin, toward the red sandstone walls of the de Montfort fortress, John experienced first surprise, followed by awe, and then dismay.

He was surprised to learn that Bran had arrived at Kenilworth only yesterday, for that meant he'd covered no more than nine miles a day, a slow pace even for an army. He was awed by his first sight of Kenilworth. The castle was situated at the junction of two streams, which Simon had dammed to flood the valley. Surrounded by a vast man-made lake, said to extend more than a mile, Kenilworth could be entered only by a fortified drawbridge at the end of a long, walled causeway. John had never seen such formidable defenses; there was even a sluice-gate to control the flow of water. He was impressed, too, by the size of Bran's army; it numbered well into the thousands. John's initial elation soon gave way to dismay, though, for this vast multitude of men was encamped out in the open, clogging the streets of the village, spilling out of the priory, sprawling in the sun by the lake's grassy shore.

He found Bran's command tent in a shady grove of oaks, within a stone's throw of the lake. It was a stifling, humid day, the sky bleached white, the air heavy and still, and his soldiers looked yearningly at that beguiling expanse of bright blue water, churned up by hundreds of splashing, cavorting men. As John dismounted, he heard his name called, and turned as Baldwin Wake emerged, dripping, from the shallows. "You look half-broiled, Johnny. Why not wash off all that trail dust?"

"First things first. Bran's summons to me was dated at Winchester on the seventeenth, fully a fortnight ago. What took you so long to reach Kenilworth?"

"You're a hard man to please, Johnny. If we gave you a blooded stallion, I daresay you'd be too busy counting its teeth to say 'Thank you.' So we tarried on the way; is the result not worth it?" Baldwin waved an expansive arm about the crowded encampment. "With your arrival, we have twenty banneret knights in our ranks!"

Taking a towel from his squire, he rubbed himself vigorously before tucking it about his waist. "The response has been right heartening, Johnny. In fact, that's what slowed us down. After Winchester, Bran sought men in Oxford and Northampton. He's been casting his nets as wide as possible, rallying support wherever he can find it—amongst de Montfort retainers, knights of neighboring shires, the towns, even some of Gloucester's tenants. Believe me, we've not been idle. Bran is bound and determined that this time he'll not fail his father; he means to bring Earl Simon an army too vast to count!"

John joined Baldwin on the grass. " 'This time'?" he echoed.

"Did you not know? Bran is in Simon's bad graces these days. Simon thought he'd been over-zealous in seizing Channel shipping. Then there was that trouble over the tournament; Simon was sorely vexed with Bran about that. Nor was he pleased by Bran's lack of progress at Pevensey. He seems to think Bran might have had greater success had he spent more time laying siege to the castle and less time laying siege to Isabella de Fortibus!"

John grinned; Bran's friends took merciless delight in teasing him about the coquettish yet elusive Countess of Devon. "I know Pevensey Castle is still holding out. What about the lady?"

"Oh, she might take Bran eventually—but not until she's sure Simon will prevail. In the meantime, she keeps our lad on the hook, with just enough slack on the line, but ready to reel him in—if and when."

This jaded prediction came from the Earl of Oxford; he'd waded ashore in time to catch the end of their conversation. Choosing to let the sun dry him off, he stretched out beside them in the grass while his squires retrieved his clothes. "If we be tallying up Bran's sins, you'd best add Winchester to the list. He says his father will be in a tearing rage when he hears, although—"

"What happened at Winchester?"

"It's one of the few towns holding fast for the King, and we'd probably have done better to pass it by. But we did not, and they denied us entry."

"They did more than that," Baldwin chimed in indignantly. "They took our messenger up onto the city walls, murdered him before our very eyes!"

"Jesú!" John sat bolt upright in the grass. "I trust you made them pay for that insolence."

"Of course we did! We assaulted the town, took it with some help from the monks of St Swithun's, who let us into the priory. It was the best sort of retribution, both swift and profitable!"

"And Bran thinks Simon will be angry about that? Why?"

"Well . . . some of our men plundered and burned the Jewry, too."
To John, that was an anti-climactic answer. "So?"

"It does not make sense to me either, Johnny," Oxford confessed.
"But Bran swears that Simon will be wroth with us, what with the Jews
having been taken under the protection of the Crown. As sore beset as
we've been this summer, I'm not about to fret over some slain Jews.
But Simon does put great store by his word, and if Bran wants to make
amends by bringing him twice the men he expected, well, mayhap that's
for the best. I've no more desire to face down Simon in a fury than Bran
has!"

"Few men have, Rob," John said dryly. "I'm sure Simon will be
pleased by your diligence. But in all honesty, he might well fault you
for your speed. It has been a month, has it not, since he sent Bran that
summons?"

"Why should another week or two matter? You do not truly think
he's in such danger—Earl Simon?" Oxford and Baldwin laughed in
unison at so preposterous a notion. "The Earl is the best battle commander in Christendom; did he not prove that at Lewes?"

John was touched by their faith in Simon; he was also chilled by it.
They were not novices to battle, but they seemed remarkably innocent
to him in their readiness to confer divinity upon Simon. He deferred to
none in his admiration for de Montfort's martial skills, but any man
born of woman was vulnerable to mischance, to errors of judgment, to
the vagaries of fate. He would have told them that, had he thought
they'd heed him. He was only thirty, three years older than Baldwin,
five years senior to Bran and Oxford, not a great gap in age. Yet he
found himself marveling at their raw youth, and it occurred to him that
such eager disciples would only have reinforced Bran's deep-rooted
belief in his father's invincibility. Well, he was here now; mayhap he
could instill a sense of urgency into their enterprise.

"Whether or not there was a need for haste," he said bluntly, "there
can be no excuse for the laxness here at Kenilworth. Whatever was Bran
thinking of, to let his army encamp outside the castle walls? Look about
you: men sleeping in the sun like overfed cats, taking baths in the lake,
dicing, chaffering with harlots. I expect to find some whores with an
army, but outnumbering the soldiers? What did you do, empty the
Southwark stews? This camp is a disgrace. All you lack is a company
of players, complete with jesters, monkeys, and mayhap a dwarf or
two!"

"They're due in tonight," Baldwin said, straight-faced, to the
amusement of those within earshot. "If I did not know better, I'd swear
you were a fugitive from a Franciscan friary! It's hot as Hades; we'd fry

in the castle. After eating dust for days, Bran thought our men were entitled to a little ease, some time to scrub off the grime of the road. As for the women—God help the commander who'd begrudge his men a chance to spill their seed ere the battle begins!"

"If I were planning a drunken revelry, I'd for certes invite the lot of you," John said coldly. "But I doubt if that is what Edward has in mind."

Oxford decided this was an opportune time to intervene. "Truce! Johnny, what you're saying makes sense. But Baldwin is right, too; there's not room enough for us all in the castle. And Edward is more than thirty miles away, at Worcester. He is not about to launch an attack upon a castle like Kenilworth; whatever his other failings, he is not crazed!"

"I can see one small flaw in that argument; you're not sheltered behind Kenilworth's walls!"

"But how would he know that? Second sight?" Baldwin pointed out triumphantly, and John conceded defeat. Mayhap he'd have better luck with Bran.

"Is he in his tent?" he queried, and they nodded, watching expectantly as he stalked purposefully across the grass. Lifting the canvas flap, he ducked inside, but a moment later, backed out hastily, red-faced. "Why did you bastards not tell me he was with a whore?"

They were laughing too hard to answer. John was turning away in disgust when a tousled dark head poked through the tent flap. "Johnny? I thought that was you! We need to talk. Can you come back in a quarter hour?" The flap opened wider, giving the men a glimpse of a flyaway mane of tawny hair, a glimpse of skin much paler than Bran's. Quite unfazed by her nudity, the woman raised up on tiptoe, whispered in Bran's ear. He grinned. "Make that a half hour, Johnny," he said, and dropped the tent flap.

THEY were awaiting Edward in the Chapter House of the Benedictine priory at Worcester. But even that vast stone cavern could not stave off the oppressive heat, and the men were soon sweating, snapping at one another.

Thomas de Clare truly believed in the rightness of Ned's cause, but it occurred to him that he had no liking for most of his confederates in this quest of theirs. His eyes swept the chamber, narrowing in critical appraisal. Few could abide William de Lusignan, save mayhap his wife. He had no quarrel with de Warenne, but he found the Marcher lords to be a thoroughly bad lot. Roger de Mortimer, in particular, roused all his suspicions. De Mortimer was half-Welsh, for his mother, the Lady

Gwladys, had been a daughter of Llewelyn Fawr, and Thomas wondered now if that tainted blood could explain his savage temper, his puffed-up pride. Nor did he hold John Giffard and William de Mautravers in any great esteem. Like him, they had fought for Simon de Montfort at Lewes, like him, had then switched sides. Thomas saw his own defection as a return to his true loyalties; if not for his brother, he'd never have forsworn Ned. But Giffard and de Mautravers had been swayed by greed, by fear of losing ill-gotten gains, having fallen out with de Montfort over a refused ransom and lands they'd unlawfully seized after Lewes. They'd so far shown great fervor in their newfound loyalty to Ned, but Thomas was not impressed; a converted Jew, he thought, is the first to eat bacon, to flaunt his crucifix.

Voices rose sharply, a brief, ill-natured exchange between the Marcher de Mortimer and the Earl of Gloucester. Thomas watched his brother warily; Gilbert was already complaining to him about de Mortimer, with the rancor he'd previously reserved for Simon de Montfort and his sons. It takes little to set tempers ablaze in weather like this; if Ned does not come soon, we'll all be at each other's throats.

Only one man present seemed at ease. Stretched out on a monk's bench, Davydd ap Llewelyn appeared to be dozing, equally impervious to the heat and the squabbling. God rot him, Thomas thought resentfully, why does he not sweat like the rest of us? What a motley crew we make: a renegade Welsh Prince; a pack of Marcher cut-throats; that French whoreson, de Lusignan; a couple of self-serving turncoats; Gilbert, who collects grudges like a beggar collects alms; and me, dragged along—will I, nill I—in his wake. God help him, Ned deserves better.

At that moment, Edward entered the chamber, trailed by a disheveled youth in a travel-stained tunic. Edward strode toward the central pillar, came right to the point. "I have just learned that my cousin Bran arrived at Kenilworth Castle yesterday eve. We cannot permit him to join forces with his father. If we leave Worcester by late afternoon, we can reach Kenilworth by dawn on the morrow, can fall upon Bran's men whilst they still sleep."

There were murmurings at that, but no outpourings of enthusiasm. Edward knew why; despite his impressive successes in the Severn valley, he'd yet to live down that rash charge at Lewes. It seemed, he thought sourly, that one headstrong act, one heedless mistake, could haunt a man till the end of his days. The looks he was getting now were distinctly skeptical. Roger de Mortimer, never one to tread lightly, blurted out boldly, "I see no logic in that. Why strike at the whelp instead of the sire?"

"When you're facing two foes," Edward said coolly, "it makes more sense to deal first with the lesser threat."

"But I thought the son's army is far larger than Simon's!"

"Think you that numbers alone assure victory? Did you learn nothing from Lewes? I know my cousin well; the Brans of this world are born to be battlefield heroes, not battle commanders. Simon is penned up in Hereford, his supplies running low, his horses and men wasted and bone-weary after a month in Wales, but even so, he is the dangerous one."

"It still sounds daft to me," de Mortimer protested, undaunted. "Kenilworth is thirty-four miles from here. How could we possibly get there by dawn? That's a seventeen- or eighteen-hour march!"

"We'll make it in less than fifteen," Edward said, and they all looked at him as if he'd taken leave of his senses. Davydd stirred and stretched, before favoring the English King's son with a lazily mocking smile.

"So whilst we lay siege to Kenilworth, Simon de Montfort awaits our coming at Hereford, and dies of old age . . . is that the plan?" he drawled, evoking laughter even from avowed enemies like de Mortimer and de Lusignan. Edward alone was not amused.

"Do you truly think me so foolish as that?" he asked, in a dangerously soft voice, and the laughter stilled. "I agree that Kenilworth Castle could likely hold out for years. But it so happens that we need not besiege it. You see, my cousin Bran has obligingly encamped his men in the town." He saw their disbelief and beckoned to the youth in the shadows. "My lords, I should like to present my best spy."

Thus summoned, his agent stepped forward into the light. He was a thin youngster, slightly built, too nondescript to attract notice, ideal camouflage for one plying such a hazardous trade. He did not seem intimidated by his highborn audience, saying composedly, "Lord Edward speaks true. I saw his cousin's folly with my own eyes. They pitched their tents by the shore of the lake, sent out no scouts, and posted but few guards. When I rode out of Kenilworth, they were drinking and carousing and bathing in the lake. Never have I seen a better opportunity for ambush."

They were at last listening intently. Davydd won his way back into Edward's good graces by asking an eminently sensible question, one that showed how seriously he was now taking this venture. "We know Bran means to join forces with Simon. How do we know he'll still be at Kenilworth on the morrow? Mayhap he'll be well along the road toward Hereford."

The young spy shook his head, revealing an unexpectedly impish smile. "God has indeed favored us, my lords. Earl Simon's son is expecting a supply train tomorrow. How likely is it that he'd set out ere its arrival?"

Edward's audience still looked dubious; a forced night march was too novel a tactic for their liking. *As it was done since the memory of man runneth not to the contrary, so must it always be done.* The words, sardonic, impatient, familiar, echoed suddenly in Edward's ears, so vividly that he almost spun around to look for Simon. "Now you know my intent," he said abruptly. "So why, then, are we tarrying here with so much still to do? Need I remind you that we cannot afford to squander even a single hour?"

They rose, filed out. But as Thomas passed Edward, the latter signaled for him to stay. Soon they stood alone in the circular, vaulted splendor of the Chapter House, Edward and Thomas and the mud-splattered would-be instrument of Bran's downfall. "Seek out my steward," Edward said with a smile. "He'll see that you are well rewarded." The youth knelt, turned to go. But as he reached the door, he paused to adjust his cap, and Thomas's jaw dropped. Unable to credit what he'd just seen—two neatly pinned-up brown braids—he gasped:

"God in Heaven, a lass!"

Edward and his accomplice exchanged amused grins. "I'd as soon you kept that to yourself, Tom. They had enough trouble trusting in the word of a green stripling. Jesú forfend that they ever learn my spy was a wench!"

The girl departed, with the same insouciance that had enabled her to penetrate an enemy encampment. Thomas chuckled, but as he turned back, he saw that she'd taken Edward's good humor with her. He looked suddenly tense, somber. "So much can go wrong, Tom," he said, "so much . . ."

Thomas was amazed; he'd never heard Edward admit to doubts before. "I think your plan is inspired, Ned," he said earnestly. "I truly do."

"Inspired?" Edward smiled then, a smile so bleak, so bitter, that Thomas caught his breath. "I am but taking a page from my godfather's book, Tom. A night march and a surprise attack worked very well for Simon at Lewes, did it not? God willing, it will work as well for me at Kenilworth."

Thomas was silent, not knowing what to say. He'd forgotten that, just as Harry de Montfort was King Henry's godson, so Edward was Simon's.

BRAN awoke with a start, unable to breathe. Opening his eyes, he discovered why; he'd inhaled some of his bedmate's tangled swirl of hair. He spat it out, sat up on the pallet. Reaching for his braies, he pulled the drawers up over his hips, tightening the drawstring. He didn't bother with his chausses or tunic, started to hunt for his shoes. In the midst of the search, a pair of arms entwined themselves around his neck, a pair of breasts pressed against his back. "My lord . . . ?" Yawning. "You want me now?"

"No, it's too hot, lass." It was, too; where their skin touched, it clung, sticky with sweat. Standing up, he fumbled for a wineskin, drank and passed it to the girl. She was so dazzled by his good manners that she actually found herself regretting that he did not want to couple with her again, and when he reached for the tent flap, she could not keep from crying out:

"Where do you go, my lord?"

"I'm just going out to take a piss. It's sweltering in here; mayhap I'll take another dip in the lake."

"Again?" She was accustomed to humoring the quirks of her customers, but never had she encountered one so bizarre. In truth, the man was besotted with bathing, even insisting that she take a bath herself ere he'd bed her! Were all lords so daft about soap and water?

She looked so dumbfounded that Bran grinned. "Go back to sleep," he said, not unkindly. Guy always swore that a man could not go wrong by treating a slut like a lady and a lady like a slut. For certes, it seemed to work with harlots; they were pitifully grateful for any scrap of courtesy. Mayhap he ought to have tried it on Isabella, a thought so outrageous that he burst out laughing.

The lake shimmered invitingly, silvered by the last glimmerings of starlight. A welcome breeze wafted off the water, dried the sweat trickling down his chest. Not yet dawn and already ungodly hot. Poor Johnny; the castle must be like a veritable oven. Several of the blanket-clad forms stirred sleepily as he passed. A few early risers were relieving themselves by the edge of the lake. A dog's howling floated over the castle walls, cut off by a spate of cursing, inventive enough to make Bran grin. But the cursing soon faded and quiet once more reigned throughout their camp, lulling the dozing men back into a deeper sleep.

Bran loved the stillness of summer, loved this tranquil, turquoise hour just before the dawn. He quickened his pace until he reached the lake, stripped off his braies, kicked off his shoes, and plunged in. He was a strong swimmer, a relatively rare accomplishment, and he swam well out into the lake, sending up diamond droplets of crystalline water in his wake. Wading back to shore, he discovered that he'd forgotten a towel, but a freckle-faced youngster gladly offered his. Others drifted over, their accents telling Bran that he'd wandered into the midst of his London volunteers. He was quite willing to linger; he liked these cheeky, cheerful, sharp-witted townsmen, so quick to rally round in his father's time of need.

They were arguing the merits of Southwark ale-houses when the dogs began to bark. A man shouted from the castle battlements; another took it up. The Londoners would have ignored the noise had Bran not interrupted himself in mid-sentence. "It must be your supply wagons, my lord," the freckled youth ventured. "Right on time, too—"

"No . . ." Bran sounded so strange that he drew all eyes. As they watched, uncomprehending, one of their wineskins slipped from his fingers, spilled into the grass. "Christ Jesus . . ." Almost a whisper, as intense as any prayer. "God help us, we're under attack!"

They gaped at him, disbelieving. But then the screams started. Bran shouldered them roughly aside, running for his tent. He didn't make it. An armed knight, seeming to appear from nowhere, bore down upon him. The Londoners shouted a futile warning, as Bran dodged a death-dealing blow from a spiked mace. But as the stallion galloped past, it brushed him with its heaving hindquarters. He was flung sideways, into the smoldering embers of a dying campfire. The Londoners reached him just as he rolled clear. His face was bloodied, his eyes dazed. "My sword . . ."

"You'll never make it, my lord!" They gestured, and he saw that the camp was already overrun with mounted knights, ripping open the sides of tents, chasing after fleeing, naked men, trampling the slow and the clumsy underfoot. Women were shrieking, men shouting, fire arrows spearing the sky above their heads. Bran could no longer find the de Montfort banner; they were surrounded by the streaming gold and scarlet lions of his cousin Ned.

"My lord, what should we do?"

The question acted as a catalyst, enabling Bran to focus his thoughts. His head was gashed, his forearm burned, but he didn't feel the pain, not yet. "We've got to get into the castle. There's a boat tied up in the rushes . . ." His eyes sought their only salvation—a fortified sanctuary, an island citadel, his father's castle of Kenilworth, an awesome silhouette against the brightening sky, its massive sandstone walls blood-red in the first light of dawn. Why had he not heeded Johnny's warning? Christ forgive him, why had he not listened?

In less than an hour, it was over. Edward's victory was total. Some of Bran's men managed to escape into the castle. Others fled, naked, across the fields to safety. More died in their beds, bled to death in the debris of their own tents. The Earl of Oxford and fifteen banneret knights were taken prisoner. Bran's supply train was seized on the outskirts of town, and so many horses were captured that Edward could now provide an unheard-of luxury, a mount for every man in his army.

"We'll rest here today," Edward announced, "and return to Worcester on the morrow."

Gloucester frowned. Their triumph had been tarnished for him upon discovering that Bran had escaped. "I think we ought to lay siege to the castle," he said, his yearning for vengeance momentarily overcoming his common sense. His suggestion reaped only ridicule, and for a few tense moments, it looked as if the two greatest Marcher lords, Gloucester and Roger de Mortimer, were about to cross swords.

Edward made haste to intervene, dispatching de Mortimer to take charge of their highborn captives. "I understand your disappointment, Gilbert. I want to take Kenilworth as much as you do, for not only is Bran sheltered within those walls, so is my uncle Richard. But we could besiege the castle from now till Judgment Day and it would avail us naught. Simon has made it well nigh invincible. That is why we must make sure he never reaches it."

Glancing around, he beckoned to a nearby knight. "Philip, fetch me the de Montfort banner. Get Oxford's, too, and as many others as you can find."

Gloucester grinned. "I never knew you were one for collecting trophies!"

Edward's smile was indulgent. "Not trophies," he said. "Bait."

EDWARD'S triumph at Kenilworth was such a resounding success that he dared to hope he had at last vanquished memories of his blunder at Lewes. He had, after all, done precisely what he'd set out to do; he'd even managed to reach Kenilworth in an amazing fourteen hours. As they returned to Worcester—at a more moderate pace—Edward felt complacently confident that his August 1 exploit was likely to pass into legend.

They reached Worcester very late on Sunday, the 2nd, in remarkably high spirits for men whose war was not yet won. The shock was all the greater, therefore. As they'd made their way back along the hilly Worcestershire roads, Simon had seized his opportunity, and that same day ferried his army across the Severn at Kempsey, just four miles south of Worcester.

Edward exploded in a rage spectacular even when measured against the formidable furies of his Plantagenet forebears. Why had they not sent him word at once? Did they think de Montfort's movements were of such little interest to him? Did they not realize what could happen now that Simon had broken free? London lay open to him. So did Kenilworth. Short-sighted, simple-minded fools!

No one was so rash as to dispute him; they prudently let his anger burn itself out. When he finally stormed off in the direction of the priory cathedral, his lords took hasty counsel among themselves, much alarmed. They could not possibly attack de Montfort on the morrow, as Edward was vowing to do. Christ on the Cross, their men had covered a staggering sixty-eight miles in little more than two days, and fought a battle between marches!

Listening to them hold forth upon the folly of Edward's intent, it occurred to Thomas de Clare that not one of them was willing to confront Ned—not his brother Gilbert, not de Warenne, not the swaggering de Lusignan, not even the fiery, reckless Roger de Mortimer. Secretly amused by their sudden skittishness, he wondered if Ned knew that they were learning to fear him. Caught up in this intriguing line of thought, he was taken aback, therefore, when Gloucester said:

"So we agree, then? My brother Tom is to be the one to talk to him, to make him see reason. Tom? What are you waiting for? Go after him!"

Thomas found Edward in the nave of the cathedral, standing before the marble tomb of his grandfather. Turning at the sound of footsteps, Edward said in a conversational tone of voice, one that held no echoes of his earlier rage, "King John of evil fame; how often have I heard him called that! Think you, Tom, that he was as black-hearted as men say?"

"I . . . I do not know," Thomas stammered, caught off balance by this sudden shift in mood, and Edward shot him a searching look. Light from a recessed wall torch spilled over onto the tomb, onto the brilliantly colored effigy of a long-dead King. Edward's eyes caught the light, too; they held an amused blue gleam.

"How did you get to be the lucky one, Tom? Did they draw lots? Well, you need not fret. You can go back and tell them that you've bedazzled me with your nimble wit, your irrefutable logic."

"Then you'll not march on Kempsey tomorrow?" Thomas asked, much relieved when Edward shook his head.

"How can I expect our men to fight another battle without even pausing for breath? I knew they could not, even as I swore upon all the saints that we would." Moving away from his grandfather's tomb, he gave Thomas a wry smile. "I lost my head, so desperate am I to bring Simon to bay. I was afraid, Tom, afraid that he'd fade away on the morrow, slip right through our net. But to force a fight ere we're ready would be madness. Once before, impatience was my undoing. I'll not travel down that road again."

"So what will you do, then?"

"I've already done it—put myself in Simon's place. By all accounts, they had a rough time of it in Wales. His men sickened on the Welsh food; how many Englishmen could long abide a diet of milk and mutton? They're bound to be disheartened, too, for I've thwarted Simon's every move for nigh on two months. Now he has taken advantage of my absence, succeeded in crossing the Severn. But he well knows his danger. By now he knows, too, that Bran has finally reached Kenilworth.

What he does not know is that his reinforcements are never coming. As urgent as is his need to put distance between his army and mine, he's been crippled, knows that neither his men nor his horses are capable of making a mad dash for Kenilworth. So what does he do? What can he do but seek to make the best of a bad bargain? He sends scouts to keep vigil on Worcester, to warn him should I venture toward Kempsey. Tomorrow he gives his army a much needed day of rest. And at dusk, he pulls out, thus escaping both the heat of the day and prying enemy eyes."

Edward paused. "I grant you that he could strike out for London. But I am gambling on Kenilworth. There are two roads he can take—and I mean to cover them both, to cut him off ere he can reach Kenilworth and safety. Tom? Why do you look at me like that? You do not agree with my reasoning?"

"I think," Thomas said slowly, "that you have read Simon de Montfort's mind, and it scares me some—how easily you did it. Have you any idea, Ned, just how much this past year has changed you?"

Edward considered that in silence for several moments. "Mayhap you're right. If so, I do owe a debt to my uncle Simon. As you know, I do not always repay my debts. This one, though, I will repay—but in the coin of my choosing."

38

Evesham, England

August 1265

Wᴵᴛʜ the coming of August, Simon's luck at last changed for the better. Bran sent word of his long-awaited arrival at Kenilworth, and Simon's scouts discovered an unguarded ford across the Severn. His army crossed the river on Sunday, August 2, passed the night and the following day at the Bishop of Worcester's manor at Kempsey. Once sunset had flamed over the rolling Worcestershire hills, they were on the move again, heading east under cover of night. By dawn on Tuesday, they were within sight of the sweeping curve of the River Avon, could see the distant limestone walls of Evesham Abbey.

To Henry, Evesham rose up out of the gloom like a vision of salvation. Spotting his nephew not far ahead, he cried out, "Harry! I need you!"

Harry's companions grimaced, for Henry had long since exhausted their reserves of patience, and only Simon's formidable will kept his men from treating their King with the contempt they felt he so richly deserved.

It had begun with Edward's escape. What should have heartened Henry seemed instead to have plunged him into a bottomless pit of self-pity and despair. He no longer made any pretense of enduring with fortitude. His complaints were constant, vociferous, quarrelsome, and often petty: unseasoned cold food, hard beds, blisters, saddle sores, cramps, stomach colics. Henry's forced sojourn in Wales was an undeniably unpleasant experience for one accustomed to the luxuries of Westminster and Windsor. But theirs was a world in which men were expected to shrug off suffering, to make light of battle wounds and broken bones. Henry's peevish harangues won him scant sympathy from Simon's swaggering young knights. Their concept of kingship was, consciously or not, cast in Simon's image, and they felt betrayed by these disillusioning glimpses of a too-mortal monarch, one who bewailed the lack of a soft pillow and whined about belly aches in the midst of a life-and-death struggle for England's soul.

Harry alone seemed willing to humor his unhappy uncle, and when the others now muttered of wet-nurses, he came good-naturedly to Henry's defense. "You're a hard-hearted bunch of bastards, in truth. He's an old man, deserves some pity."

"Let Papa hear you say that and you'll be the one in need of pity," Guy warned. "Lest you forget, he's but a year younger than Henry!"

"And are you comparing the two of them? That would be like matching a wolfhound against a lady's lap spaniel," Harry said with a grin, and checked his stallion in answer to Henry's summons.

"Is that Evesham? We are going to stop at the abbey, are we not?" Henry asked eagerly, and his distress was acute when Harry shook his head.

"I doubt it, Uncle. Whilst you look at Evesham and see the abbey, my father will see only a potential trap. Look how the river curves around the town—like a horseshoe—and with but one bridge. Should an army come down upon Evesham from the north, it'd be like corking a bottle." Good intentions aside, Harry was unable to resist a small jab. "Just as it was at Lewes."

Henry scowled, then suddenly kicked his mount forward, taking his escort by surprise. Alarmed, they spurred after him, but Henry was already reining in his stallion, having caught up with Simon.

"Harry says we'll not be stopping at the abbey. I'm telling you here and now that I'm not going another foot beyond it. I've been in the saddle all night, am bone-weary and half-starved."

"Alcester is but another ten miles or so. We can dine there," Simon said dispassionately. Since taking Henry hostage, he'd invariably treated him with icily correct courtesy—subject to sovereign—falling back upon all the prescribed formalities to distance himself from the distasteful reality of their mutual plight: that he was in fact holding his King against his will.

"That's three more hours, mayhap even four!"

"It cannot be helped, my liege. Evesham is in too perilous a—"

"Harry spouted the same nonsense, babbling about a battle commander not wanting to fight with a river at his back. But I know better, Simon, for I know you expect to meet Bran today on the Kenilworth road. So the danger is past, for you'll then have an army twice the size of my son's. If you refuse, it can only be because you take pleasure in taunting me, in mocking my impotence!"

"That is not so. It was never my intent to humble your pride, and I have truly tried to make your predicament as tolerable as I could."

"How? By dragging me into that accursed Welsh wasteland, by forcing me to make that odious treaty with Llewelyn ap Gruffydd? You know how wretched I was in Wales, how I sickened, but did you care? And now when all I ask is a decent meal and a chance to hear Mass, you'd begrudge me even that meagre consolation! How can you claim to be my liegeman when you would deny me God's Word?"

The Bishop of Worcester was an intent witness to this tense exchange, to their continuing war of wills. He'd finally concluded that Henry was avenging himself the only way he could, by seeking to crack Simon's shield, to goad him into a rage that would give the lie to his show of deference. Worcester very much doubted that Henry would succeed, no matter the provocation, for Simon was equally determined to accord Henry the trappings of kingship.

The Bishop had an astute eye for the foibles of his fellow men, and he'd soon realized why Simon was so loath to surrender this particular fiction. It validated the central core of his claim: that his was not an insurrection against his King, but only against the King's unscrupulous advisers. To abandon that premise would be to brand himself as a rebel, and the Bishop knew Simon could never accept that. His position was ambiguous enough as it was: a man whose natural instincts were for command arguing for a government of compromise and consensus, a prideful, highborn lord drawing much of his support from the commons, a Frenchman leading a movement hostile to aliens. Worcester had eventually decided that the enigma of Simon de Montfort could be explained only in terms of Simon's very personal vision of chivalry, in a code of ethics that somehow managed to mingle the partisan passion of the zealot with the poetic gallantry of the knight-errant. He felt no surprise, therefore, when Simon—his fabled temper notwithstanding—yielded to Henry's extortion.

"Oliver!" He beckoned to a young knight. "Send word ahead to St Mary's. Tell them we shall be stopping there so the King may hear Mass," Simon said, so grimly obliging that his forbearance was in itself an insult, a peace offering to a wayward child.

THE Benedictine monks of St Mary's welcomed Simon's army with heartfelt enthusiasm, and as word spread of their arrival, the townspeople began to trickle into the abbey precincts, bringing freshly baked bread, wineskins, sacks of apples and wild plums. Simon had found familiar solace in the shadowed, incense-scented church, in the sonorous Latin liturgy of the Blessed Eucharist. Now, watching his young soldiers flirt with pretty village lasses, he no longer regretted having given in to Henry's tantrum.

The monks had set a bountiful breakfast for Henry, but as he followed them into the abbey frater, he looked more like a man unjustly deprived of a grievance than one savoring a victory. While the King dined, Simon made ready to depart. These preparations were interrupted, however, by the arrival of one of his scouts, bearing triumphant tidings—the approach of an army from the north, flying Simon's forktailed lion and the Earl of Oxford's silver star.

Simon had earlier sent a sharp-eyed lookout up into the church's central tower, and when he now yelled down a confirmation of the scout's report, a common sigh of relief swept the ranks of Simon's army. For weeks they had dwelt too intimately with danger, outnumbered and outmaneuvered by an enemy who seemed to foreshadow their every move. For weeks they'd subsisted on half-rations and hope, balked by Edward and a muddy river, baffled by Bran's laggard response to his father's need. Only their faith in Simon had kept them from despairing, and now, with that faith justified, with deliverance at hand, they laughed and joked with the exuberant intensity peculiar to the newly reprieved. Their hardships suddenly took on the sheen of high adventure, and the abbey garth was soon a scene of cheerful bedlam. Wineskins went soaring up into the leaden sky, cheers rattled windows and spooked horses, competing with the distant echoes of summer thunder.

Simon was willing, for once, to indulge their tomfoolery. They were good lads, were entitled to kick over the traces—for the moment. He was tightening Sirocco's girth when he sensed a presence, turned to find a young monk hovering nearby. The youngster colored, then shyly thrust toward Simon a large, red apple.

"For your horse, my lord," he blurted out, and glowed with pleasure as Simon fed his offering to the stallion. A lover of horses, he'd never been this close to one of such high caliber, and his eyes lingered on Sirocco's sleek lines, caressed that glossy ebony coat. Only belatedly did he remember his manners. "I am Brother Damian, my lord. We are right honored to have you at our abbey. We in Evesham believe in the reforms, believe in you. We give no credence to the lies put about by your enemies, know you do not seek to rule as a king—" He broke off in dismay, fearing his tongue had once again run away with him.

"Is that what my enemies say—that I would be a dictator?" The boy nodded, appalled to think he might have offended. "Do you know what I think, Brother Damian? That St Luke was right: 'Woe unto you when all men should speak well of you.' " Simon had spoken so seriously that it was a full moment before Damian caught the amused glint in the depths of those unsettling grey eyes.

"Can you not stay longer at the abbey, my lord? There is a storm coming for certes," he pointed out hopefully. But Simon was shaking his head.

"No, lad, as soon as my son—"

"My lord Earl!" A horseman came racing through the gateway, scattering men in all directions. He paid no heed to their startled curses, spurred his stallion across the garth and reined in before Simon. The animal came to a heaving halt, frothing at the mouth, caked with lather. The rider—one of Simon's best scouts—was in no better shape, soaked with sweat, bleeding, an arrow shaft protruding from beneath his rib cage. "A trick," he panted, "a foul trick . . . They fly your son's banners, but the army is Edward's!"

THE wind was rising. It tore leaves from shuddering trees, flattened the marsh grass, and hurled dark clouds toward the fleeing sun. By the time Simon reached the north window in the church tower, the storm was nigh. He could see it sweeping across the vale, bearing down upon them from the north, shadowing the army of the King's son. Edward had taken up position on the crest of Green Hill, closing off the loop of the River Avon with a line of steel. A mile lay between their thousands and Evesham, no more. Simon needed but one glance to know that he and his men were doomed.

He sucked in his breath, jolted by a surge of purely physical fear, the body's instinctive reaction to peril. But he'd faced death too often, had long ago learned how to make fear serve him; self-preservation was a powerful motivating force in and of itself. The fright bred into bone and muscle was a familiar foe, one he knew he could vanquish. But what followed it was far more terrifying, a fear born of the brain, one that offered him a haunting glimpse of the future, a lightning-lit landscape of desolation and lost faith. Was their dream to die with them, too? Had it all been for naught?

No. No, it could not be. They would not be abandoned in their time of need, for their cause was just and would prevail. He would not fail his trial of faith, would not disavow a single yesterday. Death came to all men, but defeat only to those who doubted. *Fear not, I am thy shield, trust in me and be not afraid.* He unclenched his fist, eased his desperate grip upon the shutter latch, and then turned to face those who'd followed him up into the tower, followed wherever he led, his sons, his friends.

"We must commend our souls to God," he said, "for our bodies are theirs."

They looked at him, stunned, still caught up in the struggle he'd just won, groping for faith in the face of calamity. Harry swallowed, found his voice. "Is Bran dead?"

Simon hesitated only briefly; they had time for naught but truth. "Yes, most likely he is," he said, conjuring up without warning a phantom grief in the guise of memory: a ghost with ink-black hair and cocky grin, passionate and reckless—and bloodied. He blinked and the apparition vanished, leaving only Harry and Guy, not yet understanding, clinging to hope. Sweet Christ, how young they were! How could it be God's Will that they, too, should die this day? "Edward would be upon us ere we could all retreat across the bridge. But there is still time for you to save yourselves." He tore his eyes from his sons. "You, too, Peter . . . Hugh. I'd not see you sacrifice your lives like this. For the love of God," he said huskily, "go and go now, with my blessing!"

They would not. Even as he made the plea, Simon realized it was in vain; they'd never agree. His sons would stand by him till the last. So would Peter, no friend more faithful. And Hugh, who had a son, too, a child of three, never now to know his father. Humphrey, who'd seen his own family torn asunder by his belief in the Provisions. The young men below in the abbey garth, who'd fought with him at Lewes, only to die with him at Evesham. He could save none of them.

"Papa, you must listen to me!" Harry reached out, grasped Simon by the arm. "Do not throw away your life for naught, take what men you can and cross the bridge. I'll hold Ned here, give you the time you need to retreat. Let me do this for you, Papa, I beg you!"

Simon's eyes misted. "You know I cannot, lad," he said softly, and suddenly there was nothing more to be said. They looked at one another, recognizing the moment for what it was—one of farewell. Harry made it easy for them. Stepping forward, he embraced his father, thus freeing the other men to do the same.

"Papa . . ." Guy seemed to have shed years in a matter of minutes; Simon had rarely seen him look so vulnerable. "What will happen to Mama and Ellen?"

That was the question Simon had been most dreading. "Edward will not make war on women, not his own blood-kin. He and Richard will speak for your mother and sister, Guy, will not see them suffer for sins not theirs."

Harry's eyes—so like Nell's—were riveted upon his face. "You truly do believe that, Papa?" Simon nodded; he had to believe that.

"Come," he said. "We must give our men a chance to flee if they so choose. Some of them can still escape over the bridge if—"

"Mother of God!" Simon's lookout spun around, pointing. "It is too late," he gasped. "We're all dead men!" The tower offered commanding views of the abbey and town. They could see quite clearly now the blue-and-white banners of Roger de Mortimer, flapping wildly in the wind as his men moved in from the east, blocking the bridge, cutting off all escape from Evesham.

THEY crowded into the churchyard just east of the bell tower, pressing in so they might hear Simon speak. A hush slowly fell as he reined in his stallion before them, looked out upon their upturned, ashen faces.

"Scriptures say that man born of woman is of few days and full of trouble. That you know right well. You know, too, that death comes to us all, to the king in his palace and the crofter in his hut. All a man can do is hope to face it with courage and a measure of grace. Most of us shall die this day, for we meet a foe twice our numbers, and there will be no quarter given. But we do not die in vain, that I can promise you."

Simon paused, drawing a steadying breath as lightning seared the sky above their heads. "You've every right to ask why it must be. I would that I had an answer for you. But the ways of the Almighty are not for mortal man to fathom. The Holy Land is soaked with the blood of true believers, those who died for Christ before the walls of Jerusalem. Because they died, does that mean their Faith was false? So, too, is our cause just, and it will triumph. The men of England will cherish their liberties all the more, knowing that we died for them." Again thunder sounded, drowning out his next words. He waited for the echoes to abate, and then concluded quietly:

"I am proud to fight with men such as you. Go into battle with good heart, knowing we have right on our side, and knowing, too, that whosoever believeth in Our Lord Christ shall not abide in darkness, but shall have life everlasting."

There was no sound now but that of the coming storm. Simon turned his horse toward the base of the bell tower, where his captains awaited him. But before he could dismount, Henry rushed forward, into the stallion's path. Sirocco reared up, as Simon swore and Humphrey de Bohun snatched Henry from harm's way. He seemed oblivious to his peril, intent upon Simon and only Simon. "This is madness," he cried, "sheer madness! Surrender whilst you still can, Simon. You cannot hope to win, so why ride out to certain death?"

Simon said nothing, thinking of all the good men who'd died because this inept, faithless fool had been born a King's son. "I pity a man who has nothing in his life worth dying for," he said, so scathingly that Henry recoiled. Swinging from the saddle, he beckoned his captains closer, with the point of his sword drew Edward's battle formation in the dirt at their feet. The men moved in, Henry forgotten.

"As every hunter knows, bringing his quarry to bay is but half the hunt. He still has to make the kill . . . if he can. There is a chance, a tattered rag of a chance, that we might be able to break free of this snare. Edward has posted his men between the branches of the river, but that is a fair piece of ground to cover, about a mile, so he's bound to have stretched the line thin in places. If we hit them between their vanguard and their center . . ." He demonstrated with his sword, drew a slash in the dirt.

"I am going to propose a novel battle plan. Envision a battering ram with our knights as the iron-rimmed head, the men-at-arms as the oaken beam . . . and the Welsh at the tail, for I think them likely to run. I watched their faces whilst I was speaking to the men, and I do not think," Simon said dryly, "that they are enthralled at the prospect of dying for English liberties. In truth, I cannot blame them, for this is not their war and I am not their Prince."

He'd just offered them a precious gift, a glimmer of hope, however slight, and when he gave the command to array their men, they obeyed with alacrity. Henry had been listening in dawning horror, slowly coming to comprehend what Simon's battle plan would mean for him, and he reached out, plucked frantically at the sleeve of Simon's surcoat. "You cannot take me with you!"

"We have no choice. We have to have you with us if we break through—"

"But you will not! You're all going to die, and if you take me out onto the field with you, I'm likely to die, too! What would that prove?"

"That the Almighty has a sense of humor," Guy snapped, piercing

Henry with a look of such venom that his mouth went dry. He was surrounded by hatred, could see it on all their faces. They blamed him for their plight, would see him dragged down to Hell with them. "You cannot do this, Simon," he pleaded. "It . . . it is not just!"

Simon had been reaching for Sirocco's reins. He paused, his eyes glittering, his contempt at last breaking free. "We are all in God's Hands," he said tautly, "even you."

Sirocco was skittish, unnerved by the storm, eager to run. Simon reined the stallion in with difficulty, stopping within a few feet of the Bishop of Worcester. They regarded each other in a silence that expressed more than words could have done. "I shall pray for you, Simon," the Bishop said at last, and Simon found a flickering smile.

"I know of no man whose prayers are more likely to be heeded than yours. But there is something else you can do for me." Stripping off a gauntlet, he pulled a sapphire ring from his finger, dropped it into the Bishop's palm. "I would ask that you give this to my wife," he said, and the Bishop nodded, throat suddenly too tight for speech.

The monks and townspeople had clustered by the gateway, and as Simon led his army out of the abbey grounds, more than a few watched with tears trickling down their faces. Feeling a wetness on his own skin, the Bishop thought dully, So the rain has begun. But when he raised a hand to his cheek, he found that he, too, wept.

THE ground slanted up sharply toward the north. As Simon's army reached the crest of the ridge, they could see the enemy spread out above them, row after row of armed knights. Less than six hundred yards separated the two armies. Only then did Edward give the signal to advance. Slowly, at first, they began to move down the hill.

"They come on well," Simon said to Peter. "But then, they learned that from me. I'd wondered, Peter, just what lesson Edward would draw from Lewes. Now I know."

Peter did not reply. He was flanked by his sons, just as Simon's two sons hovered at his stirrups. Their faces were shielded by their helms, although it was not difficult to guess their thoughts. Simon raised his arm. "Advance banners! For Almighty God and England!"

His knights spurred forward, collided head-on with Gloucester's line. The sounds of battle began to rival the rumblings of thunder. Simon's men had nothing to lose, and they pressed onward with such reckless abandon, such crazed courage, that Gloucester's troops began to give way. Simon's men pushed them back as far as the Worcester road, and some dared to hope that they would break free, after all.

But it was not to be. Edward had positioned cavalry on his and

Gloucester's flanks, and they now wheeled inward, entered the fray. They hit Simon's men on both sides. His Welsh had faded away even before the battle began, and the sheer superiority of numbers soon told in Edward's favor. Simon's army was beaten back from the road, out-flanked, and then surrounded.

Henry was never to forget the horror that followed. Once it became clear that there'd be no escape, his guards lost all interest in him, were soon fighting for their lives. Henry found himself forsaken in the midst of mayhem. He feared the thunder and lightning as much as he did his son's men; never had he seen a storm like this, one to herald the end of the world. He jerked half-heartedly at his helm, before deciding that protection mattered more than recognition. Whenever anyone came too close, he shrieked, "Do not harm me! I am your King!" And it seemed to work; more than one attacker sheered off at the last moment. But then he took an arrow in the shoulder. It was a fluke, for crossbowmen were to play no great part in the battle, and it did no real damage, embedding itself in a link of his hauberk, only scratching the skin. For Henry, though, it was one affliction too many. He gave way to panic, was in a state bordering on hysteria when the Marcher lord Roger de Leyburn finally found him.

De Leyburn reined in his mount alongside Henry's without fear, for Henry had never even drawn his sword. "My liege?"

"Yes," Henry sobbed, "yes!" And then, no longer forgotten, he was surrounded by men who would protect him with their lives if need be. De Leyburn reached out, took his reins. As they led him to safety, Henry glanced back only once at the carnage continuing on the field. Simon's banner still flew, but he could no longer find Simon's raging, black stallion, and in the butchery the battle had become, he could no longer find Simon.

When Sirocco went down, Edward's men closed in for the kill. But Simon was able to fight his way free. The field was strewn with the bodies of men and horses, with discarded weapons, and it was becoming dangerously slippery, so much blood was there. Most of Simon's men were dead. Peter lay sprawled almost at his feet. For a time, Simon and Harry had fought back to back, but then the tide of battle had torn them apart. Now he stood at bay by the edge of a muddy spring, as men pressed in on all sides, jostling one another in their eagerness to strike at the Lord Edward's great enemy. So far Simon was holding them off, but for every two blows he deflected, a third got through his defenses. He was bleeding from half a dozen wounds, rocked by blows he never felt. There was neither pain nor fear, no thoughts at all. Just the lightning blazing overhead and the clash of swords, the lunge and cut and parry learned a lifetime ago, as a boy at his father's French castle of Montfort l'Amaury.

Lightning seared the air, struck a tree on the crest of the hill, and for a moment, the bloody landscape was bathed in an eerie, unearthly light. They were moving in upon Simon again; again he fought them off. But this time they managed to get between him and the spring. He could no longer protect his back, and as he crossed swords with one of de Leyburn's knights, another man darted forward, plunged a dagger into the base of his spine. The force of the blow knocked Simon to his knees, and he found he could not rise, the last of his strength bleeding away into the trampled grass, into the reddening waters of the spring.

"God's grace . . . ," Simon gasped, stretching out his hand, but his sword was beyond reach. With his last conscious act, he fumbled weakly for his dagger, waiting for them to fall upon him. But they did not. It was the night that closed in—hours ere its time, swirling, blinding, shielding—and Simon stopped struggling, gave himself up willingly to the dark.

The men would never be able to explain what had halted them, why they found themselves unable to act, to draw their weapons upon the dying man. It may have been the awesome fury of the storm; they would later agree, with superstitious dread, that the tempest seemed to intensify just as de Montfort fell. It may even have been Simon himself, for so long a legendary figure even to his enemies. Whatever the reason, they hesitated, crowding in closer to see, but not yet ready to kill.

It was then that William de Mautravers found them. Shoving his way into the circle, he glared about him in disgusted disbelief. "What are you faint-hearted milksops waiting for? Since when are we so tender with traitors?" Striding forward, he raised his sword, snarling, "Beg, you bastard!" But he was too late. Simon's eyes were already glazing over; he never saw the sword start on its downward swing, was dead by the time it plunged into his chest. De Mautravers jerked the blade free, and, as if to wreak vengeance upon the body for the escape of the soul, he struck again and again. Some of the more squeamish soldiers backed away, those who did not believe in mutilating the dead. De Mautravers was soon splattered with Simon's blood, and the little spring turned crimson. The rain was coming down in torrents now; the storm had broken at last.

THEY had never seen a storm of such ferocity. Much against Bran's will, for he was half-crazed by his desire for speed, they had to shelter for a time in Alcester. Bran fumed in vain; there was nothing to be done but wait out the squall. As soon as the rain slackened, though, he propelled them out into it, for nothing mattered more than reaching his father with the remnants of his Kenilworth army.

As soon as Edward had withdrawn, they'd set about retrieving their broken fortunes. Some of Bran's men had gotten away, and they came back once the enemy retreated, gamely volunteering for another try at Edward. But horses were even scarcer now than soldiers, and it had taken Bran and John d'Eyvill all Monday to scrounge up mounts for their pitifully reduced force. A messenger from Simon had arrived in the midst of their horse-hunt. Upon learning that his father had crossed the Severn, Bran became frantic, would have moved Heaven and earth itself to keep his rendezvous with Simon on the Kenilworth road. He managed a minor miracle, and they marched out of Kenilworth Castle shortly after dawn on this rain-darkened Tuesday.

John d'Eyvill was impressed by Bran's sudden, frenzied industry, but he could not help wondering why it had taken such a disastrous defeat to rouse Bran to the responsibilities of manhood. Well, better late than never, he supposed. He was in cheerful spirits himself; he was always invigorated by action. "Poor Baldwin," he said. "Captured first at Northampton, now at Kenilworth. Not only did he miss Lewes, he's like to miss the next battle, too. Bad luck, indeed—or good, depending upon the way you look at it!"

Bran merely grunted, never taking his eyes from the muddy road ahead. He'd shared nothing of his inner turmoil these three days past, and John could only speculate, but he suspected there was more to Bran's urgency than mere remorse. It was as if his own misfortune had stripped blinders from Bran's eyes, and he suddenly saw other men— even his father—in a new and vulnerable light. Had he belatedly realized the dangers his father had faced in Wales? John thought that was indeed the case. Why else would he be in such a tearing hurry to reach Simon, knowing that Simon would not likely forgive his criminal carelessness at Kenilworth?

"Johnny!" Bran's sudden shout tore John from this reverie, but he did not at once see what had occasioned Bran's alarm. Bran had the keener eye; when he pointed, John, too, saw the rider emerging from the mists of wind-driven rain. He was gesturing frantically, close enough now for them to recognize him—the scout they'd sent in search of Simon. John got a sudden sick feeling in the pit of his stomach. Bran was already galloping toward the man.

"Go back, my lords! We're too late! Dead, they're all dead!"

"You're lying!"

"God's truth, my lord, I am not! There was a battle fought at Evesham! Your father is dead, he's—"

Bran's hand dropped to the hilt of his sword, and for a moment, it truly looked as if he meant to draw it upon the scout. But then he spurred his stallion, went off down the road in a wild shower of mud. His two squires cried out in alarm, started after him. The scout had half-turned his mount, almost as if he, too, meant to follow. But by then, John had reached him.

"Tell me now, and quickly, what you know. You say there was a battle?"

"Not a battle, my lord—a slaughter. I saw the bodies . . . saw . . ." The man shuddered, crossed himself.

"Why are you so sure that Earl Simon is dead?" John saw the scout hesitate, and said roughly, "What are you not telling me? What are you so loath to say?"

The man looked John full in the face for the first time. "I saw de Mortimer's men and they had . . . they had Earl Simon's head on a pike."

"Bleeding Christ! And you let Bran go—"

"How could I stop him?" the scout protested, but John was no longer listening. He swung back toward their men, saw on their faces his own horror. "Quentin, hold them here! If you are threatened or I do not return, lead them back to Kenilworth!" With that, he gave his stallion its head, set off in pursuit of Simon's son.

John d'Eyvill was not in the least sentimental, as tough and indomitable as the Yorkshire moors that bred him. But as he rode, he found himself praying that Bran would somehow miss de Mortimer's men, that he'd not see their grisly trophy. Misbegotten Marcher savages, they could put the Welsh to shame! Damn them all, and damn Edward, too, for allowing it! The lad had enough griefs to bear, enough guilt for a lifetime and more. At least he could be spared this.

But when he finally did overtake them, he saw at once that he was too late. They were halted on the crest of the hill; below them lay the vale of Evesham. One of Bran's squires had stumbled into the bushes, was vomiting weakly into the muddied grass. The other boy seemed bereft of all powers of speech; he looked dumbly up at John, tears cascading down his face. A few yards away, Bran sat his horse in the middle of the road. He neither moved nor spoke as John drew up alongside him, did not turn even when John reached over, grasped his arm.

"Bran? Bran, look at me!"

He might have been speaking to one stone-deaf; there was no response, not even the flicker of an eyelash. Bran continued to gaze blindly into some private vista of his own. John felt tears prick his eyes; he knew all too well what the younger man was seeing, what he'd be seeing for the rest of his days.

"Come on back, lad," he said quietly. "We can do nothing for him now. It's over."

BY 10:00 A.M., the battle of Evesham had ended, but the killing was to continue throughout the day. With victory assured, the Marcher lords began to hunt down the fugitive Welsh. They showed no mercy; to the horror of the monks, some of the Welsh were slain within the church itself.

A dazed, disheveled Henry was reunited with his son, but for all the talk of restoring the King, it was soon apparent to the monks that England's true King was uncrowned. It was Edward who gave the orders, issued commands, took charge of town and abbey, and it was Edward who gave the monks permission to bury the dead.

THE church was darkened, still. When a candle sputtered into life, it revealed a heart-rending sight to the elderly monk: row upon row of bodies. All afternoon his brothers had been retrieving them from the field, laying them out in the church until they'd run out of room. Brother Abel was an old man, but never had he seen death on such a dreadful scale. He limped among them, sickened.

He paused before a particularly pitiful victim: no more than sixteen, just a squire. He bowed his head, began a prayer for the boy's soul as the north transept door swung open. Brother Abel held up his candle. "Who goes there? Ah, it's you, Damian. Have you another body, then?"

They paid him no heed, moving with measured steps toward the High Altar. For all that the burden they carried rested upon a rickety ladder, draped with a muddied cloak, they bore it with somber dignity. Brother Abel followed, puzzled, watching as they carefully set the ladder down upon the tiles. Brother Damian stood for a moment staring at the torn, dirt-smeared cloak, and then spun around, strode to the altar. Before they realized what he meant to do, he'd snatched up the altar cloth. Kneeling, he gently tucked it about the body, smoothing out the wrinkles with painstaking care. "There," he said, " 'tis more fitting," and at last Brother Abel understood.

"Earl Simon?" he said softly, and Brother Damian gave a jerky nod. "What is left of him. Those whoresons threw him to the dogs!"

Brother Abel winced, not for the Earl, who was beyond pain, but for his stricken young colleague, for all those who'd loved or believed in Simon de Montfort. Slowly, stiffly, he knelt by the body. "Blessed are they which are persecuted for righteousness' sake, for theirs is the kingdom of Heaven. May—" He got no further. A door opened; there was a sudden flare of light.

They'd learned caution this day. Brother Damian leaned over, breathed upon the candle, for he was not at all sure if Edward's permission to bury the dead would be a grace extended to Simon. They could hear footsteps now in the nave, a murmur of voices. "Shall I accompany you, my lord?" "No." A one-word reply, but it was enough to send a chill along Brother Damian's spine. Recognizing the voice as Edward's, he hastily drew the others back with him into the shadows.

They crouched in the corner, following the progress of that flickering light. So far Edward had not looked their way. He was walking among the bodies, moving up one row and down another until he found the one he sought. The lantern spilled light in a wavering circle; Edward's hand seemed suddenly unsteady. He set it upon the floor, made the sign of the cross. "I swear to Christ, Harry, that I'd have saved you if I could," he said, and the monks exchanged wondering looks as the victor of Evesham knelt by the body of an enemy and wept.

THEY reached Kenilworth at dusk, after a nightmare retreat that none would ever forget. Many of them had lost family or friends at Evesham, and all feared the future, feared the King's vengeance now that Simon was dead, their dream destroyed. Kenilworth, the most impregnable stronghold of the realm, suddenly seemed a frail refuge against a world gone mad.

John d'Eyvill sighed with relief at sight of those formidable castle walls. "We made it," he said, not surprised when Bran gave no response, for he'd not spoken for hours, had said less than half a dozen words since they began their desperate dash back to Kenilworth Castle. John knew that people handled grief in many different ways, but Bran's way alarmed him. He was riding at John's stirrup, almost close enough to touch, but John could not help thinking that he was not really there at all.

As they rode across the causeway, they could see troubled faces peering through the embrasures of the outer curtain wall. By the time they were admitted into the inner bailey, the entire garrison was awaiting them, eager to learn the explanation for their unexpected return—and yet dreading it, too.

"My lord, why are you back? Why did you not join forces with Earl Simon?"

The question was directed at Bran, but John knew it would be for him to answer; command had fallen to him by default. He hesitated, searching for the right words, knowing there were none, and one of his men, grieving for a brother and cousin, forestalled him.

"The Earl is dead. They're all dead, every one of them. They slaughtered our men like sheep, sparing none, and then they hacked Lord Simon to pieces, struck his head on a pike for their ungodly pleasure."

Somehow, his revelation was even more appalling for the flat, toneless way in which it was delivered. John heard gasps, muffled cries of disbelief and horror and pain. He swung about, just in time to see Bran's face twitch, as if he'd taken a blow.

They were looking to John for confirmation, and he nodded bleakly. "Raymond speaks true. The Earl of Leicester and his men died this morn at Evesham."

Kenilworth had been Simon's pride and joy, and he'd chosen its castle garrison with the utmost care. These men were his unto death, fiercely loyal, sublimely sure that he could not fail. As they grieved now for Simon, for their kinsmen and neighbors, they grieved, too, for their loss of faith, the annihilation of hope. It was no safe place for the King's brother, but that never occurred to Richard. His initial surge of joy had been swiftly tempered at sight of his nephew's bloodless face. As glad as he was for Henry, for himself, he could still mourn for Nell's sake, could even spare pity for her sons, and, with his own son, fifteen-year-old Edmund, in tow, he started down the steps of the great hall, ready to offer Bran what small solace he could.

It was an act as ill-advised as it was well-intentioned. To men struggling to accept the unthinkable, he was the enemy, the only one within reach. The castle blacksmith's son had died at Evesham, and as the stricken father's eyes lit upon Richard, his pain spilled out of control. "By God, you'll not be gloating over my poor lad's body!" he shouted, and flung himself at Richard's throat. His startled victim staggered under the onslaught, lost his balance, and fell down the steps.

Before Richard could regain his footing, the blacksmith was upon him again, and now others joined in the attack, for these anguished, angry men wanted nothing so much as a target for their rage, a target suddenly provided in person of the King's blood-kin. They could strike at Richard—pompous, prudent, little liked—as they could not at Henry, could punish him for Edward's sins, for their suffering, and as Richard struggled to rise, he was kicked and cursed, beaten back onto the ground.

Dazed, bleeding, Richard sought to protect himself as best he could, bringing his arms up over his head, his knees up to his chest. From what seemed like a great distance, he could hear his son screaming, the sound muffled by the blood thudding in his ears. It came to him, more with a sense of astonishment than fear, that he was going to die here in the dirt of Kenilworth's inner bailey, that these grief-crazed men were going to beat him to death.

But then the shouting changed, no longer the collective cry of a mob bent mindlessly on murder; the lethal circle seemed to be breaking apart. Through a swollen eye, Richard caught a glimpse of a stallion's thrashing forelegs, pawing the air above his head. His assailants were scattering, retreating before the horse's flailing hooves. Richard rolled over to find his nephew standing astride him, sword drawn.

Bran's face was contorted, streaked with tears. "Get back! I'll not let you whoresons dishonor my father like this!"

His fury was frightening, for it was not that far from madness, and the men sensed it. It was suddenly very quiet. John d'Eyvill pushed his way through to Bran's side. "He is right," he said loudly. "We will avenge Lord Simon, that I swear to you. But not like this. Is there a one of you who can say the Earl would have wanted this?"

No one could. The men began to back away, some shame-faced, others numbed. The killing fever had broken, would not flare up again. Realizing that the danger was past, Richard tried to sit up, and John reached down, helped him to his feet. Bran flung his sword into the dirt, turned and stalked away.

"Papa!" Edmund threw himself into his father's arms, sobbing, and Richard wobbled anew, clutching at John's arm to steady himself.

"I'm all right, lad," he said, and discovered, somewhat to his surprise, that he was. His bruises would fade, his cuts would heal; only the memory would linger.

"Bran!" His cry went unheeded. Bran was already half-way across the bailey. Richard limped after him, calling out his name until Bran at last stopped, turned slowly to face him.

"You saved my life. I'll not forget, that I promise you. I'll do whatever I can for Nell, for you, too, lad."

Bran said nothing, but at mention of his mother's name, he seemed to flinch. Richard found himself unable to continue, so great was his pity for his sister's son. He reached out, put a hand on Bran's arm, half-expecting him to pull away. He did not, seemed to be focusing upon Richard for the first time. But Richard was never to know what his response might have been, for just then Edmund joined them.

Edmund was still trembling. It had all happened too fast; now shock had set in and he felt suddenly queasy. "Thank you for saving my father," he said, giving Bran a look of shy sympathy. Although he'd prayed earnestly for his cousin Ned to triumph, he'd long harbored a secret admiration for his dashing de Montfort cousins. Harry, in particular, had sought to lighten his confinement, and remembering now Harry's casual kindness, his gallantry, and his good-humored pranks, Edmund could not keep from voicing his concern. "Harry . . . he is not dead, too?"

He saw at once that he'd made a grievous mistake, would have called the question back if only he could. Bran wrenched free of Richard's grip, whirled, and plunged through the doorway of the keep forebuilding. They could hear the clatter of his spurs upon the stairs, and then, a slamming door, a bolt being thrown back. It was too much for Edmund; to his dismay, he burst into tears again. "Papa, I did not mean . . ."

Richard gathered him into a comforting embrace; Edmund, at least, he could console. "I know, lad, I know."

Edmund wiped his face with his sleeve. "If Cousin Bran had not come to your aid . . ." He could not repress a shiver. "What can we do for him, Papa?"

"We can pray for him, Edmund, pray for God to heal his hurt."

Neither was aware of John d'Eyvill's approach, not realizing he was within earshot until they heard him say, "I doubt that even God could help Bran now."

That was a statement cynical enough to distress Edmund and to anger Richard, who said coldly, "Take care, Sir John, lest you commit blasphemy."

John merely shrugged. "Blasphemy? Nay, that is but the Gospel according to Evesham. Bran's father and brothers died for his mistake. He arrived at the battle not in time to save them, but in time to see Earl Simon's head on a Marcher pike. You tell me, my lord King of the Romans, just what prayers can exorcise a memory like that."

FROM the chronicle of the thirteenth-century monk Robert of Gloucester:

"Such was the murder of Evesham,
For battle it was none."

39

Dover Castle, England

August 1265

MONDAY, August 10, was typical of Nell's over-burdened afternoons; her responsibilities seemed to multiply in direct proportion to the day's diminishing hours. For some moments now, she'd been laboring to reassure one of her ladies in waiting; Hawisa's brother was with Simon's army, and the waiting was shredding her nerves raw. While Nell sought to dispel Hawisa's qualms, her steward,

Richard Gobion, hovered close at hand, as did her patient scribe, pen poised to do his lady's bidding.

Having convinced Hawisa that she need not read sinister significance into the silence echoing from the west, Nell beckoned to her steward. "Richard, did you arrange to send those barrels of herring to St Mary's Hospital? Very good. I looked over your inventory, agree that we'll need additional supplies of firewood. More corn, too, enough to get us through until harvest-time. You'd best send some men to Wickham on the morrow. As for the wine, let's buy it again from Master Augustine, the vintner at Sandwich."

Gobion was the epitome of efficiency, would carry out her orders with dispatch, and Nell at last felt free to turn her attention back to her scribe. "Mauger, are you ready? Write as follows: 'To my dear husband, the Earl of Leicester, greetings. We are all well, although I will admit to some unease of mind, for I have not heard from you for almost a fortnight. I assume that by now you have been able to reach Kenilworth, so I have instructed Picard to go there first. Now for my news. I have sent our youngest lad to Winchelsea to engage men-at-arms. I'm sure you remember the raw pride of sixteen, Simon; so set was he upon playing a man's part that I had to let him—' God's wrath!"

Mauger and Hawisa were equally startled. When the screaming came again, Nell paled, for this time she recognized the voice. "Jesú, my daughter!" Mauger darted for the door, jerked it open just as Richard Gobion stumbled back into the bedchamber. "Madame," he cried, "hurry!"

Nell found herself assailed by noise, by a rising babble of distraught voices that broke and swirled about her in a surging current of tumultuous sound. The great chamber was in utter chaos; the scent of fear was in the air. All eyes were turning toward Nell, hands plucking at her sleeve as she moved unflinchingly into the very midst of this maelstrom. But she was intent only upon reaching her weeping daughter. "Ellen? My God, child, what's wrong?"

"Oh, Mama!" Ellen sobbed, flung herself into Nell's arms. "He . . . he said . . ." She could not get the words out, choked on her tears. Nell could make out only "Papa" and "dead."

Grasping Ellen by the shoulders, Nell shook her until the child's hair whipped wildly about her face. "Ellen, get hold of yourself! Your father is not dead. Who told you that he was?"

"Wat . . . Wat did," Ellen gasped, pointing an accusing finger toward a red-faced youngster who suddenly found himself alone in a crowd, naked to Nell's wrath. He was a huge, hulking youth, a good-natured, slow-witted lad who could, nevertheless, work wonders with horses. He towered over Nell, but he'd begun to tremble even before she drew her arm back, slapped him across the mouth.

"How dare you terrify my daughter and disrupt my household with your vile gossip? Look at you, stinking with ale! Instead of the stables, you were in the town, at the Mermaid's Tail, I'd wager! Dare you deny it? No, I thought not. Get your belongings together; I want you gone from here within the hour."

Ignoring the young groom's horrified sputter of protest, Nell swung around to face the others. "You'd best take this fool's fate to heart, all of you, for I will dismiss any man who brings ale-house babble into my household—no matter how long he's been in my service. Is that understood?"

"My lady!" Wat fell to his knees. "It was not ale-house gossip, I swear by my very soul! There was a man coming up the hill to the castle, and I stopped, for his horse had gone lame . . . He told me, my lady, he told me! If I ought not to have believed him, I'm most heartily sorry! If you'll but give me another chance—" The rest of his plea was drowned out by a sudden resurgence of sound; people were turning toward the door. Not daring to abandon his supplicant's pose, he glanced over his shoulder, then gave a stutter of excitement. "Th—that's him! The stranger I met on the road!"

But he was no stranger to Nell, this haggard, begrimed man limping toward her, bearing her husband's badge upon his arm and grief beyond measure upon his face. Nell tried to swallow and failed. She stood very still as he passed through the suddenly silent crowd, treading upon the floor rushes as if his boots were lined with lead, so heavy was his step. It took him a long time to reach her, this man who had loved Simon well, who'd served him for twenty faithful years. Nell swayed slightly, dug her nails into the palm of her hand, watching wordlessly as he slowly sank to his knees before her.

"I'd rather cut out my tongue than bring you news like this, my lady," he said, his voice thickening as his eyes met hers. Reaching into his tunic, he drew forth a wax-sealed parchment.

Nell did not take it, looked upon her brother Richard's signet without recognition. "Tell me," she said, very low, and his eyes filled with tears.

"There was a battle, my lady. On Tuesday last, near the abbey of Evesham. The day . . . it went against your lord husband. He and your sons died on the field. They are dead, my lady, they are all dead."

NELL's memory was no longer functioning as it should; her recollections were fragmented, marred by strange gaps and sudden blanks. There were moments she could recall with merciless clarity, hours she could not remember at all.

She remembered standing in the great chamber, her ears echoing with the words "They are dead." She remembered struggling to quell the ensuing panic. And she remembered trying to allay her daughter's hysterics. Ellen's grieving was so frenzied, so intense, that she'd finally resorted to a sleeping draught of henbane and black poppy. Nell remembered every one of Ellen's screams. But once she'd been able to withdraw into her own bedchamber, she remembered nothing beyond the sound of the bolt sliding into place against the door.

She'd lost hours, more than a few, for the chamber was dark, unlit by candles or cresset lamps. The only illumination came from two unshuttered windows. She reached for the edge of the bed, pulled herself to a sitting position in the floor rushes. Her movement disturbed the dog huddled at her feet. It whined, licked her hand, and Nell leaned over, rested her cheek against the greyhound's silky head, its fur silvered by faint shimmerings of moonlight. Her eyes stung, swollen to slits, and her skin felt hot to the touch. Could the soul be stricken by fevers, too? She was forty-nine and her health was good. Yet now she got to her feet with difficulty, and as she moved toward the door, it was with the faltering, slow step of a very old woman.

Men had spread their bedding out along the walls of the great chamber, as if this were a night like any other. And some were, indeed, sleeping. But more were slumped in the shadows, seeking comfort from wineskins, staring dully into space. Nell's second greyhound had been keeping lonely vigil by her door; it greeted her now with joyful wriggles and blissful tail wagging. Nell patted it unthinkingly. Then she saw the other dog, the black alaunt, for so many years Harry's devoted shadow.

The pain was savage enough to restore portions of her blocked memory. So had it been during those anguished hours alone upon the floor of her bedchamber. The grieving had come in waves—Simon, Harry, Guy, then Simon again—with no time to catch her breath. No sooner would she fight her way free of one memory when another would engulf her. A birthday, a night of lovemaking, a glimpse of cherished ghosts, haunting the lost country of childhood, sturdy, boisterous boys of her flesh, Simon's blood. Pranks and playful bedlam. Simon's return from the Holy Land, on the beach at Brindisi. Harry's laugh and Guy's swagger. The familiar look upon Simon's face when he had a problem to solve, so stubbornly single-minded, so intense—and then the sudden flash of a quicksilver smile. Nell had no defenses against memories like that, memories that would drag her down to drowning depths—if she did not blot them out, save her sanity with denial.

There was a chair a few feet away. Nell stumbled toward it, caught the wooden back for support. When a solicitous voice offered assistance, she shook her head. "Let me be." Only a whisper, but so fiercely uttered that her samaritan prudently withdrew. When she at last pushed away from the chair, her greyhounds and Harry's alaunt loyally trailed her across the chamber, into the great hall that filled the entire east side of the keep. Only when she entered the narrow, shadowed passage that led to the sacristy and chapel did the dogs hesitate, abandon their escort.

The sacristy was dark; so was the nave. Not until Nell reached the chancel did she find a flicker of light, two tall candles on either side of the altar. Kneeling in the circle cast by their feeble glow, she made the sign of the cross. "I beseech Thee, Lord God Almighty, all powerful and everlasting Father . . ." But she got no further, the words lodging in her throat. She could not complete the prayer. She could not seek solace from a God Who allowed such evil, a God Who had turned His face away whilst her husband and sons died in His Name.

It came as a shock, the recognition of this dangerous, unholy rage. But the flame was too hot to be disavowed. She could not deny that her grieving was inextricably entwined with a bitter sense of betrayal. How could the Almighty have abandoned Simon in his hour of need? No, she would not pray to such a God. She would find it easier to follow the example of the wife cited in Scriptures, the one who had counseled her suffering husband to "curse God and die."

But she could not even do that, dare not crave blessed oblivion, an end to her pain, lest this one perverse prayer be answered. If she died, what would befall her children? If Richard's letter was to be believed, Bran was half-crazed with grief and guilt. Amaury was just nineteen, trained in naught but the theology of the Church. The younger children were even more vulnerable, dazed and defenseless amidst the wreckage of the only world they'd ever known. They had no one now—no one but a mother who lacked even the will to live.

"I am not strong enough. I cannot do what must be done, Simon. You must not forsake me now. Give me a sign that you're still with me, that I'm not alone . . ."

Her words trailed off into a despairing silence. She sat on the floor by the altar for a long time, not sure if she was indeed waiting for a response. If so, it did not come. Never had she felt so alone as she did then, there in the dark of a deserted chapel, crying out to a dead man.

DOVER'S keep was a masterwork of defense, thick enough to accommodate a number of mural chambers within the width of its walls. Standing before the door of her daughter's chamber, Nell at last forced herself to reach for the latch.

Ellen's nurse slept on a pallet by the foot of the bed. So did Nell's own damsels, Christiana and Hawisa. Amaury was the surprise, slouched in a chair by the window, keeping vigil at his sister's bedside just as Nell's greyhound had kept one for her. He did not look as if he'd slept any. At sight of his mother, he jumped to his feet. Nell put her finger to her lips. "Did the sleeping draught work?" she whispered.

He nodded. "Yes, but she wept in her sleep."

Nell reached for his hand, led him back to the bed. Ellen stirred as they bent over her, whimpered softly. Nell sat down beside her daughter, gathered the sleeping child into her arms. Ellen whimpered again, opened eyes dark and drugged. "Mama?" Her lashes flickered; she was fighting her return to reality.

"I'm here, Ellen," Nell said softly. "I'm here."

THE monk from Evesham Abbey arrived in mid-afternoon. It was a Sunday, the 16th of August, the day after the Feast of the Assumption of the Blessed Virgin Mary. But to Nell, it was simply Day Twelve, for the familiar calendar was forgotten, and she now calculated all time as of the day of her husband's death.

The monk had been uncertain of his reception; as young as he was, he knew how easily missions of mercy could go astray. But he need not have worried. The word "Evesham" was an instant passport into the presence of Simon's Countess and her children, and within moments, he'd been escorted from the great hall into the privacy of Nell's bedchamber.

Nell was flanked by two young men, whom she introduced as her sons, Amaury and Richard. "And this is my daughter, Ellen," she said, slipping a protective arm around the waist of a pale, pretty child with great, tragic eyes. "You are Brother . . . ?"

"Damian, my lady." He'd rehearsed this speech so often, but he found himself suddenly tongue-tied, at a loss for words. "We've not had an abbot for two years now. My brothers and I . . . we decided on our own that one of us should come to you, tell you of the battle, of the Earl's last hours . . ."

"We want to hear," Nell said, "to hear it all. But you can do even more for us, Brother Damian. You can end our suspense—one way or the other. You see, two days past I heard from—Well, the name does not matter. Suffice to say he was one who believed in my husband. He sent us word that my son Guy did not die on the battlefield. We've been afraid to believe him. But you were there, you tended the wounded, you buried the dead. If any man knows the truth, you must. Brother Damian, does my son still live?"

Damian hesitated. "Yes, he does, but . . . but Madame, I would not give you false hope. Sir Guy was one of the few found alive after the battle. We treated him in our infirmary, and he was later taken— despite our protests—by horse litter to Windsor Castle. His wounds are most grievous, my lady, and in all honesty, he may not survive."

Nell's arms tightened around her daughter. After a long pause, she said, "False hope, Brother Damian, is better than none."

Damian saw that he need not have fretted about misleading the Countess; this woman would never again err on the side of optimism. But her sons still clung to the innocent faith that was their birthright, looked much more relieved than he knew his news warranted. He wondered whether he ought to try again to stress the gravity of Guy's injuries, but decided that would be a needless cruelty to the Countess— and to her daughter, for he sensed that for Ellen, too, hope had died at Evesham with Simon and Harry de Montfort.

"You said there were others found alive, too?"

"Yes, my lady, but pitifully few, most of them close to death . . . like Sir Humphrey de Bohun. It is a miracle that he survived this long, but a cruel one; those who love him can only pray that God soon frees him from his pain." He saw Nell's mouth tighten, remembered, too late, that Humphrey was a friend. "But my news is not all dismal, Madame. Peter de Montfort's sons survived the battle, and I think their wounds will heal in time. So, too, will Sir Henry de Hastings, Sir Nicholas Segrave, and Sir John Fitz John recover."

"And that is all?" Amaury sounded bewildered. "Why so few?"

"Evesham was not like other battles. Even after your father's men fell, their enemies kept hacking at them. Sir Guy Baliol, your lord father's standard bearer, was so mangled that we could not even strip off his armor, had to bury him in his bloodied, broken chain-mail."

Damian fumbled within the scrip at his belt, drawing out a crumpled scrap of parchment. "We kept count of the bodies, my lady. With your lord husband died one hundred eighty knights, two hundred twenty young squires, and two thousand men-at-arms. And then there were the Welsh. They fled the field at the onset of the battle, but that did not save them. Large numbers drowned trying to cross the Avon; local folk have begun to call one ford 'Dead Man's Ait,' so many bodies were found there. And those who got across the river still had to escape Roger de Mortimer's men, for he hunted them down without mercy. We cannot ever be sure how many died, but we think several thousand Welsh perished ere that bloody day was done, mayhap even more."

Ellen broke her silence at that, with a soft sound, almost like a whimper, quickly stifled. Damian wondered why the Welsh deaths should so distress her; his heart went out to this troubled child, and he was racking his brain for some comfort to offer when Nell said, "Tell us of the battle."

He did, haltingly at first. Simon's arrival at the abbey. The coming storm. The false banners. Reliving it in the retelling, he tore open an unhealed wound, and when he at last concluded, tears were running freely down his face. "Men will not forget how Earl Simon died. They will not forget his courage, and they will not forget his faith."

"Faith," Nell said slowly. "Do you think that my husband's faith faltered once he realized he was doomed?"

"Oh, no, my lady! I know it did not, for I heard him speak to his men ere the battle began. Their cause was just, he said, and would prevail. Indeed, never did his faith burn so brightly as in the last hour of his life!"

Nell turned away abruptly, moved to the window. "He was lucky, then," she said, and if there was irony in that, there was also envy. Ah, Simon, how did you do it? How could you hold fast in the face of certain defeat? You should have taught me how, my love, should . . . She was perilously close to tears, but she would not give in to them. What good would tears do now? "My husband and son . . . where are they buried, Brother Damian? At the abbey?"

She heard him gasp, a sound so full of pain that she spun around, caught upon his face a look of sheer horror. "My lady, I . . . I thought you knew!"

"Knew what? Tell me!"

"I . . . I cannot," he stammered, "not before the little lass . . ."

Ellen's eyes darkened, pupils dilating in sudden fright. But she said resolutely, "If it concerns my father, I have a right to know!"

"What are you keeping from us?" Amaury reached Damian first, with Richard just a step behind, and the young monk gave way before the intensity of the onslaught.

"I will tell you," he agreed wretchedly, knowing no other way, for obedience was as essential to his calling as it was inbred in his soul. "Lord Simon's body was shamefully abused after his death. A man called Mautravers chopped off his head, impaled it upon a pike, and then—"

Ellen's cry would long echo in his ears. Clasping a hand to her mouth, she whirled, fled the chamber. Nell followed at once, and Damian sank down weakly upon a nearby stool, fervently thanking God for his reprieve; his was not a tale for female ears. Amaury and Richard looked as if they, too, yearned to flee the chamber, but pride was a powerful snare. They would not fail their father, would not shirk a man's burden, and they waited mutely for Damian to tell them what they dreaded to know.

He tried, clumsily, to soften the impact, but without much success. He was only half-way through his grisly narrative when Richard blanched, choked, and bolted for the privy tucked away in the south chamber wall. Amaury, looking scarcely less sickened himself, hastened after his brother, leaving a guilt-stricken Damian in sole possession of the chamber.

He could hear sounds of retching, Amaury's murmurings of comfort. Never had his throat felt so parched, and he looked wistfully at a wine flagon on Nell's bedside table, but he was not about to drink—unbidden—the Countess of Leicester's wine. He was earnestly wishing himself a thousand miles away from Dover Castle, from the havoc he'd so innocently wrought, when the door opened, and Nell reentered the chamber. He saw her eyebrows shoot upward, and said miserably, "Your younger lad . . . he took sick."

Nell glanced toward the privy, back at Damian. As the implications of his words sank in, she lost color as rapidly as Richard had. "You told them, then," she said. "Now you may tell me."

"My lady . . . you do not want to know," he entreated, to no avail. She regarded him steadily, and he found that he was no more capable of defying her than he would have been of gainsaying Simon.

"After they beheaded him, my lady, they hacked off his arms, his legs, his . . . his private male parts." Damian swallowed with difficulty. No matter what, he'd not tell her of the vile acts committed upon the Earl's body; nor would he tell her about the dogs. "I was told that the Marcher lords sent the Earl's severed limbs to various towns in the realm. I do know for a fact that Roger de Mortimer sent Lord Simon's head to Wigmore Castle, as a . . . a gift to his wife!"

He wasn't sure what reaction he'd been expecting, mayhap that she would weep or faint, what he imagined to be woman's natural response to man's cruelty. He found her utter silence far more unnerving than screams or tears. Only once did she make any sound at all, a hissed intake of breath when he told her of Maude de Mortimer's ghastly trophy. Her eyes had narrowed upon his face, too hot to hold tears, a blue-white blaze of such fury that he shrank back, remembering all the stories he'd heard of Plantagenet rages, tales that carried the scent of sulphur and smoke. His life had been a sheltered one; until now he'd never known that a woman, too, could burn with a killing fever.

Nell was trembling. She brushed past Damian as if he were not there, crossed to her bedside table. The flagon was fashioned of fine Venetian glass; hers had been a life of luxury and privilege, for was she not the King's sister? Beside the flagon lay a psalter, bound in Spanish leather, engraved with a Latin cross. She reached first for the psalter. As Damian watched, uncomprehending, she flung it from her, into the ashes of the hearth. Damian gave a scandalized cry, was bending to retrieve the prayer book when Nell sent the flagon crashing into the hearthstones above his head. It shattered in a spray of glass; flying splinters shivered the air. Damian cried out as one cut into his neck. He scrambled to safety just as Amaury and Richard came rushing out of the privy.

Nell seemed as oblivious of her sons as she was of Damian. She was staring blindly at the wine staining the white-washed wall of her bedchamber. Her cheek was bleeding, but she was no longer trembling. The psalter lay, half-opened, in the ashes, and Amaury snatched it up. Nell continued to watch the wine drip down the hearthstones. "I suppose," she said, "that I should count myself lucky. After all, they could have sent his head to me!"

Damian flinched, surreptitiously crossed himself. Nell saw and laughed, a laugh to haunt his dreams no less than her daughter's tears. Richard looked at the frightened monk, at his brother, kneeling by the hearth, clutching the psalter to his chest, and then at this white-faced stranger who was his mother. "Mama?" he said, and the fear in his voice reached her. Nell turned, caught him to her in an embrace both fierce and tender, not letting him go until they both were breathless and the blood from her cheek smeared his, too.

"Madame . . ." Damian hovered by the door, afraid to stay, unwilling to go. "God forgive me, for in seeking to comfort, I brought only pain. At least I can offer this small measure of solace. We claimed your husband's body, mangled and maimed as it was. We dared not give him the funeral he deserved, but we buried him before the High Altar in our church, sent his soul on to Paradise on the wings of our prayers." Even so simple an interment had not satisfied Simon's enemies. Damian had heard talk of exhuming his body, had heard the Marcher lords arguing that a man dying excommunicate was not entitled to lie in consecrated ground. But nothing could have compelled him to share this new threat with Simon's widow.

"What of my son?"

"He received an honorable burial, my lady . . . at the behest of the Lord Edward."

At mention of Edward's name, Simon's sons froze. Richard's hand closed convulsively about the hilt of his dagger, and Amaury spat out a most unpriestly oath. Only Nell did not react. Exhaustion was now claiming her. She felt suddenly weak in the knees, sat down on the edge of the bed, and Damian was overcome by remorse. She looked ravaged, and he'd done his part, wittingly or not.

"My lady, if only I could have brought you something of your husband's! But those scavengers stripped him of his armor, stole his crucifix, his rings. We did retrieve a few scraps of his clothing, and part of his hair shirt, but then they disappeared." Stumbling across the chamber, he dropped to his knees before Nell. "I've done naught but fail yóu, my lady. I should have realized how much men would crave such relics, but I was not thinking clearly. Had I only hid them away as I ought—"

"What are you talking about? What relics?"

"Lord Simon's bloodied hair shirt, my lady! I only hope the thief was moved by piety, not greed, for in truth, he could easily sell bits of it to those coming to pray at Lord Simon's grave—"

" 'Pray at Lord Simon's grave?' " Nell echoed, and Damian nodded eagerly. She did not know! His mission was not in vain, after all; he was to be the one to tell her.

"People began coming to the church within a day or two of the battle, my lady. It took no longer than that for word to spread that we'd buried him there. Afterwards, they'd slip away to the battlefield. Your lord husband died beside a small spring, and people have been coming to it every day since the battle. They pray, and then they take away a vial of the water. When the Lord Edward learned of this, he was enraged, posted a guard. So now they come at night. Not just from Evesham, either, but from neighboring villages, some even as far away as Gloucester."

"But why?"

The monk looked at her solemnly. "He died for them, my lady, just like St Thomas à Becket. Already I have heard of miraculous cures. There was a village lass burning with fever, sure to die, until her mother bathed her in water from the Earl's spring. And then there was—my lady? You look at me so strangely. Have I offended you in some way?"

"No, you have not offended me," Nell said wearily, not knowing whether she wanted to laugh or cry. "My husband was an honorable man, mayhap even a great one. But he was a man, Brother Damian, not a saint. He was very much a man." The young face upturned to hers reflected disappointment, but not doubt, and Nell realized that Brother Damian, too, was a believer. Well, Jesus had His disciples; why not Simon? The thought was so blasphemous that she shivered, appalled by her own irreverence. But in a world gone mad, why should she be the only one still of sound mind?

A FIRE had been lit in the hearth, and the shards of broken glass swept up. But the wall had not been scrubbed clean; Nell had said to let it be. They gathered together now by firelight, a circle broken beyond repair. The thought was Nell's, one she did not share with her children. Reaching out, she brushed the hair back from Ellen's face. "We need to talk of the future," she said. "Amaury, I am making arrangements to send you and your brother to France as soon as—"

Both youths broke into heated protests, Amaury insisting that he'd not leave her and Ellen, and Richard vowing that he would go only to Kenilworth Castle to fight with Bran.

"Fight? We've nothing left to fight for!" Nell caught herself, said more calmly, "We can do naught for the dead. It is the living who must concern me. We are not entirely without resources, hold the two most formidable castles in England, Kenilworth and Dover. I mean to make use of them, to strike the best bargain I can. But first I must see to your safety. My life is not in danger; nor is Ellen's. For you, though—"

"Mama, all know I study to be a priest, and Richard is but sixteen," Amaury interrupted, giving his brother an apologetic look. "Why should we be in danger?"

"And would you trust your lives to men who would so dishonor the dead?"

That silenced them both. They looked away, unable to meet their mother's eyes. Nell had been warned that Henry had ordered ships to patrol the Channel, with the specific intent of stopping her from sailing for France. Now she leaned forward, began to explain her plan for smuggling them out of England. But within moments, they were interrupted by Richard Gobion.

His message was one she'd been expecting for some days: a knight was seeking admittance—on the Lord Edward's behalf. Nell rose to her feet. "I will see him."

Edward had chosen a spokesman with some sensitivity. There was no swagger in the man's bearing, and as he knelt to kiss Nell's hand, she saw in his eyes a flicker of genuine pity; it was not his fault that was the one emotion she could never abide.

"My lady, Lord Edward bade me give you this letter. He bade me also to reassure you that you are not in danger. He said that your womanly fears, however natural, are for naught; he does not wish you or your children ill. You are his kinswoman, and he does not blame you for Simon de Montfort's crimes. You need only put yourself in his hands, and he will see that you suffer no harm. But you must, of course, surrender Dover Castle forthwith."

Nell reached for Edward's letter, but did not break the seal. "I think not," she said, and the knight blinked, looking so startled that she almost smiled. "You may tell the Lord Edward," she said, "that the Countess of Leicester says no."

40

Dolwyddelan, North Wales

August 1265

Iᴛ was a splendid summer's eve, that fleeting breath between day and dusk. The heavens had taken on the distinctive deep turquoise of a Welsh twilight, and although no stars yet shone, drifting clouds still retained sunset tints of lavender and lilac. But the men within Dolwyddelan's great keep were blind to the beauty beyond the window. They saw neither the evensong sky nor the sylvan heights of Eryri, saw nothing but a lightning-seared, bloody field by Evesham Abbey.

Silence reigned, for the language of outrage was soon exhausted, even more so that of grief. Goronwy and Einion exchanged troubled looks. For nigh on an hour, they'd watched as Llewelyn stalked aimlessly about the chamber, a man driven by demons they understood all too well. Not that he'd shared so much as a word of his regrets. Nor would he if left to his own devices, for he'd never learned that wounds of the spirit should be lanced like those of the flesh, exposed to the healing, open air.

Goronwy at last decided to confront his suspicions head-on. "You are not to blame, you know . . . or do you?"

Llewelyn gave him a brief, guarded glance, and then a shrug. "If any man is to blame," he said, "I suppose it is Bran de Montfort."

Goronwy was not taken in by that apparent indifference. "You were right to refuse to fight on English soil, Llewelyn."

"I thought so at the time. Now . . . now I am not so sure. Mayhap if I had agreed to take up arms with Simon, he'd not have been at Evesham that day."

"Mayhap not," Goronwy agreed. "And mayhap you'd have died there on the field with him. Can you deny that, too, is a possibility— even a likelihood?"

Llewelyn could not. He moved restlessly to the window, watched as shadows laid claim to the valley. The sounds of a woman's sobbing echoed across the bailey; he wondered for whom she grieved amongst the dead of Evesham, a husband? A son? Goronwy could absolve him of blame for Simon de Montfort's death, but what of the Welshmen who'd died, too, on that Tuesday morn? Welshmen run down like rabbits by Roger de Mortimer, murdered long after the battle was done, with ice-blooded deliberation, for which there could be no forgiveness. There might be naught he could do for Simon now, but he could avenge his dead. He could teach his Marcher kinsman that there was not always so much sport in hunting Welshmen.

The woman's weeping was audible to the others now. Einion flinched away from the raw, wrenching sound of a stranger's grief, aching for that unknown mourner, aching for all the dead of Evesham, Welsh and English alike. "So many sorrowing women," he said sadly, "so many heart-stricken children. I shall pray for the widows of Evesham, and I shall pray first for de Montfort's lady, as I know you've long had a fondness for her, Llewelyn. In truth, though, I do not see how she can bear up under such a blow; what woman could?"

"You're wrong, Einion. Nell de Montfort is Eleanor of Aquitaine's granddaughter; blood like that tells. And she was far more than Simon's bedmate, was for nigh on thirty years his soulmate, too, his partner, his confidante, and his consort. Did you know he even named her as sole executrix of his will, advised his sons to be bound by her counsel? That is a rare honor, for theirs is a world in which noblewomen are customarily denied the wardship of their own children. No, a woman like that will not break. Nell de Montfort will find the strength to endure, to survive her loss. I am not so sure, though, if her daughter can."

That earned him a sharp look from Goronwy. If Llewelyn the Prince was a canny pragmatist, he knew that Llewelyn the man was a secret romantic, his heart constantly at war with his head. While the politician invariably prevailed over the clandestine counsel of the idealist, Goronwy was always on the alert for slippage. He had a deep distrust for passion, and sensed that Llewelyn's cool exterior was but camouflage, leaves strewn across pitfalls of impulse and deep emotion. It had occurred to him that Ellen de Montfort's plight was all too likely to tug at Llewelyn's heartstrings, and he sought now to cure any fevers of misguided gallantry with a dose of unsentimental reality, saying swiftly, "When you write to the Countess of Leicester, convey my condolences. A pity there is so little we can do for her. I trust she'll understand that naturally there can be no question now of honoring the plight troth?"

"Naturally," Llewelyn said, so dryly that Goronwy flushed, disconcerted that Llewelyn should have read his mind so easily. "Nell de Montfort is no cloistered nun, Goronwy. She is worldly wise enough to expect me to disavow the plight troth. But what of the little lass? How could she understand?"

"I'm sure the Lady Nell will explain it to her," Goronwy said warily, still not completely convinced that Llewelyn was going to heed his common sense and not his conscience.

Einion chose that moment to add his voice to Goronwy's. "You're too hard on yourself, Llewelyn. The girl is not your responsibility. Pity is an indulgence you cannot afford, not when it comes to making a marriage of state. You might as well be crazed enough to marry for love!"

That was so preposterous a proposition that both Llewelyn and Goronwy had to smile. "I know I cannot marry the lass now," Llewelyn admitted, "for that would indeed be madness. But there is a bond between us, and I cannot utterly forsake her in her time of trouble. I shall write to Nell that my alliance with Simon holds good for his sons, too. I shall offer them refuge in Wales if any of them so wish. And I suspect that I'll find my peace haunted in days to come by a child I've never even met."

Llewelyn turned away from the window; the last of the light was gone. "I keep thinking of a verse from Scriptures, something about darkness over the land. That is indeed true for England after Evesham, although I think Edward will discover that Simon de Montfort casts a long shadow. In my life, I have been privileged to know two extraordinary men, one of whom was my grandfather, the other my ally. As far back as I can remember, I've been striving to prove worthy of Llewelyn Fawr's legacy. I cannot help wondering what Simon's legacy will be. For now, I fear, naught but suffering . . ."

"It is never easy to lose a husband, a father—"

"No, Einion, I was not thinking of the de Montforts. As deeply as they grieve, time and God's Grace will heal some of their pain. And they are far from friendless. Remember, for all that he seems destined to become an English saint, Simon de Montfort was French-born, his bloodlines amongst France's finest. I do not doubt that his kinsmen will rally to his wife and children. Moreover, I speak from experience when I say that Nell de Montfort is a woman of considerable charm—and the French King has a soft heart for grieving widows." Llewelyn smiled faintly. "I'll wager that Nell finds at the French court enough sympathy to send Brother Henry into spasms!"

Servants were moving about the chamber, lighting candles one by one. Llewelyn watched the flames flare into life, then said somberly, "I have great sympathy for Simon's family. But it is the Londoners I truly pity. God help them, for no one else will."

THE first Friday in October was cool and overcast; at midday, it might have been dusk, so leaden was the sky. London's streets were strangely

stilled, shops tightly shuttered, houses barred and bolted and forlorn—
or so they seemed to Cecilia Fitz Thomas as she trudged up Bishopsgate
Street. Never had she seen her city so deserted. The cocky street urchins
had vanished as if by alchemy; so, too, had the beggars, the vendors,
the ale-house patrons, the nosy neighbors, all the usual eyewitnesses
to the raucous, highly visible currents of London life. The few people
Cecilia did encounter passed her by in preoccupied, funereal silence,
shoulders hunched against the wind, heads down. Even the dogs were
gone, save for an occasional stray, scurrying for shelter. They carried
fear like fleas, Cecilia thought; they, too, scented blood. Leaves swirled
around her ankles, clung to her skirts, blowing about the road in desolate
disarray; somewhere a loose shutter banged. Like a town besieged from
within, London lay open to its enemies, immobilized by suspense, awaiting the King's verdict. Cecilia shivered, quickened her step.

She was passing through the gateway into the courtyard of the Fitz
Thomas manor just as two men exited the hall, started down the outer
steps. She recognized them without difficulty, for Jacob ben Judah had
conferred often with her husband in the past year, seeking together to
ensure the safety of Jacob's Jewish brethren. It was a source of pride to
Fitz Thomas that he had indeed succeeded in drawing off some of the
anti-Semitic poison from his city. Even in the panicked aftermath of
Evesham, there'd been no killing of Jews, no terrified, drunken mobs
surging into the Jewry—impressive tribute to the moral authority that
Fitz Thomas still wielded in these last doomed days of his mayoralty.

"Good morrow, Master Jacob. This is your son, is he not? I hope—
What? Something has happened; I can see it in your faces. For God's
sake, tell me!"

"I fear the news is bad, Mistress Fitz Thomas," Jacob said gravely.
"Whilst we were meeting with your husband, it came—the summons
from the King."

He got no further. Cecilia gasped, then gathered up her skirts, began
to run. Jacob's face was grey, his breathing so uneven that Benedict put
a supportive hand on his elbow. His father seemed to have aged years
in the weeks since Evesham, become as brittle as glass, as faded as sun-
dried flax. "Do you want to go back inside, Papa?"

"Nay . . . to yonder horse block. I need to catch my breath . . ."
Sinking down upon the weathered mounting stone, Jacob found himself
panting as if he'd been laboring under a hot sun. So unfair that the
body should wear out ere the soul did. But there was very little of fairness
in the world as he'd known it; that was a privilege not often extended
to Jews. "I know we are at odds over Simon de Montfort, Benedict. But
whatever else he was, he was a fair man, and he tried in his way to be

fair to us, too, after Lewes. Now . . . if it's true that the old King has become somewhat addled, the Lord Edward will keep his hand on the reins, and I fear him, lad, I fear him sorely. He is a man utterly sure of his own righteousness, and he has no liking for Jews."

Benedict could not help himself. "Neither did de Montfort." Try as he might, he could not share his father's sorrow for a Christian lord, a crusader knight. "I agree with you, Papa, that under Edward we'll be like sheep in the midst of wolves. But then, so were the Jews in Winchester!"

"And would you want to be held accountable for another man's crime? Lord Simon's son bears the guilt for the Winchester bloodshed—and grievously has he answered for it. 'God is not mocked; whatsoever a man soweth, that shall he also reap.' "

If so, then why had the murderous John Fitz John—of all men—been one of the few to survive the carnage of Evesham? But that was not a question Benedict would ever put to his father; his doubts, like his fears, he kept to himself. "Papa . . . I do not want to quarrel. I do not deny that Simon de Montfort did change toward us in the year that he exercised power in the King's name. But though he sought to protect us, he was never our friend—as that man was and is." He swung around to point at the silent Fitz Thomas manor. "I never thought I could learn to trust a Gentile, never thought a Christian was capable of treating Jews like men—no more, no less. I regret de Montfort's death, but I grieve for Thomas Fitz Thomas, a good, decent man who does not deserve the evil about to befall him."

And in that, they were in full accord. Jacob took his son's hand, struggled to his feet, and together they began their slow trek back to London's Jewry.

THE great hall was empty, but at the sound of Cecilia's footsteps, a tearful maid servant emerged from the kitchen. "He's above-stairs, in the solar. Oh, my lady, what will happen to us now?"

Cecilia didn't answer; she didn't know. Letting her mantle slip unheeded to the floor, she started for the stairs. The solar was in semi-darkness, shuttered, lit by a single tallow candle. "Tom?" she whispered, and one of the shadows moved.

"It has come," he said, no more than that. But there was no need to say more. Two days earlier, Roger de Leyburn had taken their surrender to Henry at Windsor, London's abject and inevitable submission to the King's will. Fitz Thomas shoved his chair back. "Roger de Leyburn sent word that we are to meet him tonight at Vespers in the church of

All Hallows Barking. Then on the morrow, Thomas Puleston and I, amongst others, are to accompany de Leyburn under safe-conduct to Windsor, where the King and the Lord Edward await us."

Cecilia choked on a sob. "Edward's safe-conduct is as worthless as his word!"

"I know," he admitted, and she darted forward, knelt by his chair.

"I asked you once before to flee with me. Now I beg you, Tom, whilst there's still time! Please . . . we can sail tonight with our sons, be beyond Edward's grasp ere he learns of your escape. Alexander le Ferrun chose exile, a better fate than awaits you at Windsor—"

But he was shaking his head. "I cannot, Cecilia. Flight would cheapen the cause for which we fought. If they could dismiss me as a self-server, a man who cared only for saving his own skin, so, too, could they dismiss our aspirations."

He got to his feet, drew her up with him. "You must try to understand, my dearest one. It was not treason, was but a dream bred before its time, that the King should not be accountable only to God. No mortal man ought to be entrusted with power such as that, for any king's son may be born a fool." His mouth twisted. "Who would know that better than Henry's hapless subjects? I was right to seek a voice for my Londoners. I was right to pledge my hopes to Simon de Montfort's quest. I can disavow none of it, Cecilia."

She clung in despair, no longer arguing. "I am so afraid, Tom. Are you not afraid, too?"

"Of course I am afraid," he confessed, kissing her upturned face, her trembling mouth. "But Lord Simon would not run from his fate, and I'll not run from mine."

THE royal safe-conduct proved to be as false a coin as Cecilia Fitz Thomas feared. Upon their arrival at Windsor, Thomas Fitz Thomas, Thomas Puleston, and three fellow Londoners were turned over to Edward, cast into a dungeon in the castle keep. Henry then made a triumphant entry into his capital city, where he evicted more than sixty families from their homes, bestowing the seized houses upon supporters of the Crown. Numerous hostages were taken, scores arrested. But royal vengeance was indiscriminately meted out. Of the five men chosen as hostages for the entire city, three of them had been loyal to Henry, and of those despoiled of their property, more than a third had been royalists. Civil liberties were suspended, the city's government taken over by a bailiff hand-picked by Henry. London Bridge was given to Henry's Queen. A staggering fine of twenty thousand marks was imposed upon the city, one that would take fully thirty-five years to pay. And in the records of

Henry's reign there began to appear the words "Offense—a Londoner."

The Londoners were not the only ones to suffer from royal reprisals; Henry had fifteen months of humiliation to exorcise. Summoning parliament, he pushed through a controversial edict for the seizure of the lands of any man deemed an "accomplice" of Simon de Montfort. The term itself was not defined, no advance finding of guilt was required, and as the forfeited estates were to be granted to Crown partisans, the potential for abuse was enormous. Richard argued vehemently against such sweeping, dubious confiscations. Edward, too, counseled moderation, for he was clear-sighted enough to see the danger in dealing too harshly with rebels or rebel sympathizers; if a man was to be stripped of all he owned, what incentive, then, had he to lay down his arms? But Henry was too bitter to heed any voice but the one crying out for revenge, and he found support for his wavering will in the relentless vengefulness of the Marcher lords. If, like the Romans, he must make a desert and call it peace, so be it.

At Richard's urging, a half-hearted attempt had been made to come to terms with Bran, but it was doomed to failure; Simon's enemies had no sympathy to spare for his son. As September yielded to October, a defiant de Montfort banner continued to fly from the battlements of Kenilworth Castle, and to that formidable refuge flocked those who would not forsake Simon's "common enterprise." Others rallied to John d'Eyvill, hid themselves in the Fenlands, in the dark forests of Sherwood and Rutland, and here might well be found the genesis of the Robin Hood legends, those firelit tales of outlaw exploits, for they were reckless and sometimes gallant, these men known as "the Disinherited," as "the Faithful."

Nell had succeeded in getting her two youngest sons to safety in France, along with eleven thousand marks. Dover Castle still held out, though, for Nell's letters to her brother and to parliament had gone unanswered, and she was determined to cling to the only leverage she had left. But in mid-October, her highborn prisoners bribed two of their guards, overpowered the others, and seized control of Dover's great keep; Nell herself narrowly missed being taken, too. Her men laid siege to the keep, but this was a God-given opportunity for Edward, and he made the most of it, leading a lightning assault upon the beleaguered stronghold. Caught between Edward's besieging army and the rebelling prisoners within the great tower, Dover's garrison could not hope to prevail. On October 18, Nell agreed to surrender the castle to her nephew.

EDWARD was taken aback at sight of his aunt. Nell was not a tall woman, only of average height, but her bearing was such that few ever realized it; even surrounded by her towering de Montfort brood, she'd not been overshadowed, more than held her own. This was the first time that Edward had seen her without that deceptive aura of vivacity. It may have been the heightened perception born of pity. It may have been the stark black, the coarse russet of widowhood. Or that she'd obviously lost weight; he'd been told she ate virtually nothing at mealtimes. But never had she seemed to him so vulnerable, so delicate and fragile and defenseless, an impression that lasted only until she raised her lashes and he found himself looking into the eyes of an unforgiving enemy.

"My lord," she said, dipping down in a curtsy that was as correct, as controlled, and as chilled as her voice, "the castle is yours."

She was flanked protectively by Richard Gobion, her steward, and John de la Haye, Dover's constable. They watched him warily, men resigned to their fate but unrepentant. Edward was not disturbed by their demeanor, one of stolid, reluctant compliance. He had only contempt for men who groveled in defeat, although he was equally irked by men who refused to admit they'd been bested, men who faced ruin with a sneer, a swagger. Not vengeful in victory unless he bore a personal grudge against the foe he'd vanquished—like the luckless Thomas Fitz Thomas—Edward was willing now to allow these diehard de Montfort loyalists their pride. For his aunt, he was willing to do far more, and taking the gatehouse keys from Nell's outstretched hand, he said, "Is there somewhere we can talk alone?"

Edward had hoped that privacy might ease the tension between them, but the atmosphere in Nell's bedchamber seemed alive with echoes, with all she dared not say. He was holding out a leather pouch. "The Bishop of Worcester asked me to deliver this into your hands, as he's not in a position to do so himself."

Nell noted that the Bishop's seal was intact, bore no signs of tampering. She felt no surprise; Edward's were not petty vices. "What shall happen to him?" she asked, dropping the pouch onto her bedside table.

"It seemed best to leave his punishment to the Church. The Pope's new legate intends to suspend Worcester and the Bishops of Winchester, London, and Chichester, summoning them to Rome to account for their sins."

"And what sins are those?" Nell asked tonelessly, but Edward refused the bait.

"That is between the Bishops and His Holiness the Pope." He took a step toward her. "Aunt Nell, I have news of Guy. The doctor at Windsor has written to me that he seems likely to live, after all." Hers was an expressive face; he realized half-way through his revelation that she already knew. So even at his father's favorite castle, de Montfort tendrils had taken root. Unless it was a natural sympathy for a grieving mother? "Guy must have a great will to live," he said, "for his wounds were grave, indeed. But I am glad he'll survive—for your sake and for Bran's."

"I should like to see Guy ere I sail for France." Nell had resolved to put her pride aside, to beg if need be, but she saw at once that she'd be humbling herself for naught. "You'd truly deny me even that?" she demanded incredulously. "A last farewell with my wounded son?"

"No, I would not!" Shaken out of his poise by her scorn, Edward looked surprisingly young; he was, she remembered, just twenty-six, a year younger than Harry, Harry who would be forever twenty-seven. Her eyes misted, but the tears didn't fall. In these past two months, her grief had frozen; she sometimes felt as if her heart were encased in ice. Ice and fire, anguish and rage, the only emotions she seemed able to summon up.

Edward had moved toward her. Reaching out, he grasped her by both arms, oblivious to her recoil. "Aunt Nell, if it were up to me, I'd take you to Guy tomorrow. But my father forbade it, and he . . . he is the King."

"Yes," Nell echoed, "he is the King."

He let her go, stepped back. "Uncle Richard and I argued against sending you into exile, but my father would not listen. He has hardened his heart against you, Aunt Nell. He was furious when you managed to get your younger lads to France. He even wrote to the French King, urging Louis to seize the money you'd entrusted to them."

"He must have been most disappointed when Louis refused," Nell murmured, and he saw that this, too, she'd known.

"He was," he admitted. "I could understand why he hated Simon, but I do not understand why he should hate you—and yet I fear he does. They do not even refer to you in the patent rolls as the 'King's sister' anymore; it is always as the 'Countess of Leicester.' "

"Henry's hatred does not surprise me. What does is his resolve. It seems he has hardened his backbone as well as his heart."

From Edward's earliest years, ambivalence had characterized his relationship with Henry, love for a devoted father vying with chagrin for an incompetent King. He was not offended now by his aunt's lethal sarcasm, for he had long ago learned that to remain loyal to so foolish yet so loving a father, he had to distance himself from Henry's foibles— while swearing upon his very soul that he would be a King no man would dare to mock.

"The Marcher lords spur my father on," he said. "So, too, does Gloucester. Surprisingly, he has been arguing for clemency; mayhap he feels guilty for having forsaken the Provisions. But he has not a shred of pity for anyone who bears the de Montfort name, and he's done his share to salt my father's wounds, he and de Mortimer."

De Mortimer. Edward's good friend and carousing companion. Nell swung away from him, locking her eyes onto the patch of sky visible from the window. It was a vivid shade of blue, a harvest sky; her color, Simon always claimed.

"Aunt Nell . . ." She turned, reluctantly, to find Edward regarding her with unsettling sympathy, unsettling for it seemed sincere. "Aunt Nell," he said, "I am not your enemy."

"I am glad to hear you say that," she said, as evenly as she could manage. "For it would not be easy to ask an enemy's aid."

"What can I do for you? You need only name it," he said, before caution compelled him to add, "provided that it is in my power to do so."

She'd placed the parchment upon the table, awaiting just this moment. Handing it to him, she said, "That is a list of the twenty-two men and women of my household. I ask you to allow them to remain in England. I ask you to spare them exile from their homeland and their families."

He glanced but briefly at the list, hesitating only at the name of John de la Haye, her constable. "I shall write to the Chancellor, informing him that I have taken them under my protection, and I shall instruct him to order the shire sheriffs to make sure they retain seisin of their lands."

She'd not expected it to be so easy, had been afraid to let herself hope. She closed her eyes for a moment; at least she could do this for her people, for those who'd served her so faithfully. At least their worlds, too, need not be wrecked. "Thank you."

"Where will you go?"

"There is a Dominican convent at Montargis, south of Paris. I shall—"

"A convent! You do not mean to take vows?"

"No, I shall not take vows," she said, smiling for the first time; he wondered why the smile held such bitter amusement. "The convent was founded by my husband's elder sister; his mother is buried there. When I sought to think where my daughter and I could go, it was Montargis that came first to mind."

"Ellen," he said softly, not noticing how the sound of her daughter's name in his mouth affected Nell. "She has been in my thoughts, for I know how much she loved Simon . . . and Harry. I suppose she'd not want to see me?"

"No, she would not. Can you blame her?"

He shook his head; this time he'd caught it, a glimpse of the flame burning just beneath the surface. He was quiet for some moments, and then said slowly, "Harry never blamed me for upholding my father's rights, no more than I blamed him for heeding Simon. He understood that I was doing what I had to do. I'd hoped, Aunt Nell, that you would understand, too."

It may have been the way he claimed Harry—her son, her first-born—as his ally. It may have been the hint of reproach, as if it were unsporting of her to hold a grudge. It may simply have been inevitable from the first, no matter what her vows of self-control. But it all fell apart in the time it took her to draw a constricted breath, her composure and pragmatism and common sense fragmenting as thoroughly as the glass flagon she'd once flung into this hearth. "Yes, Harry understood loyalty," she said. "But do you think he'd also have understood the butchering of his father's body? Look me in the eye, Edward, and tell me he'd have understood that!"

This was an accusation he'd obviously been braced for; he showed no emotion, although he could not keep color from rising in his face. "That was not my doing," he said impassively. "I can understand your anger, but it is not fair to blame me for what de Mautravers and de Mortimer—"

Nell interrupted with one of Simon's favorite oaths. "If that is to be your defense, spare me any more of it. I am the daughter and sister of English Kings, was wife to two Earls. Power is no foreign tongue to me; I speak it as well as any man. No soldier under my husband's command would ever have dared to maim a fallen foe, for all knew that Simon would never have countenanced it. Just as all knew you would!"

"You are wrong," he said, not quite so calmly this time. "I am not responsible for what was done to your husband's body."

"No? I suppose you are not responsible, either, for desecrating his burial place? I suppose you know naught about that? Simon's body—what was left of it—was dug up and reburied in unhallowed ground, all done, of course, without your knowledge or consent! Go ahead, make that claim—if you dare!"

She saw his eyes flicker; that he hadn't been expecting. "I am sorry you learned of that," he said, after a very long pause. "I'd hoped you would not. It is passing strange, but Simon's enemies seem to hate him all the more now that he is dead, as if he somehow cheated them of their vengeance. De Mortimer and Gloucester raised such a hue and cry about his burial in consecrated ground that we agreed to their demand, and his body was removed from the church, laid to rest in a secluded corner of the abbey grounds. I cannot speak for Gloucester or de Mortimer or even my father, but I can tell you why I agreed: not to bring further shame upon Simon, and for certes not to give greater grief to those who loved him. It was a political decision, Aunt Nell. His grave was becoming a shrine of sorts, attracting too many malcontents and even some misguided pilgrims. It seemed wise to stop this foolishness ere it got out of hand. I'd have no objections to his reburial in the church at a later date, once all this absurd talk of martyrs and saints has ceased."

"You'll have a long wait," Nell snapped. "Time is no longer your ally; now it is Simon's. You may have defeated the man, but I wonder how you'll fare against the legend. You should have stopped them, Edward. Your Marcher friends did you no service, for when they hacked Simon's body to pieces, they tarnished your great victory, turned it into something base and mean-spirited. And the irony is that, in seeking to dishonor Simon, they did but dishonor themselves. All the blood in Christendom will not dim the luster of my husband's memory. For men will remember Simon de Montfort!"

Edward's mouth was tautly drawn, and the flush along his cheekbones was very noticeable now. But there was grudging honesty in the answer he gave her. "Yes," he conceded, "Simon will be remembered." Reaching for her hand, he brought it to his lips in a very formal farewell. As he turned to go, his gaze fell upon her list, where it had fallen, unnoticed, to the floor. Nell saw it, too, and stiffened. For an endless, suspenseful moment, Edward's eyes held hers, and then he reached down, retrieved the list and tucked it away in a pouch at his belt. At the door, he paused, glanced back over his shoulder. "But I shall be remembered, too," he said.

As soon as the door closed, Nell sat down abruptly upon the bed, utterly unnerved by the magnitude of the risk she'd just taken. What a fool she'd been, for she'd never have forgiven herself if she'd destroyed her household's hopes of reprieve. And yet she could not have kept silent, no matter the cost. There was nothing rational about her rage; it was a physical force, no more within her ability to control than any storm of nature, any tempest of God. There were times when it frightened her, this anger that seemed to have burned into the very depths of her brain, this anger that spared so few, not even Simon.

As she'd once counted her rosary beads, now she counted her enemies, all who'd wronged her children. First and foremost, her accursed weakling of a brother. Edward. Gloucester. Roger de Mortimer and his wife, she who so liked battlefield keepsakes. A man whom she'd never heard of ere Evesham, and now would never forget—William de Mautravers. And as she lay awake at night, thinking what the future might hold for Ellen, who was to have been a Princess, for Amaury and Richard, for Guy, mewed up behind Windsor's walls like a crippled hawk, some of her anger would spill over onto Bran, Edward's unwitting pawn, and onto Simon, who'd died with honor intact but his family's future in ruins, and lastly, onto herself, for believing so blindly.

It was awhile before she remembered the Bishop of Worcester's message. Breaking the seal, she shook out a small object wrapped in cloth and a letter tied with ribbon. She opened the letter first, but without any expectations of solace. The Bishop of Lincoln and Adam Marsh had been as much her friends as Simon's, but not so Worcester. She suspected that he suffered from a malady all too common to churchmen, a basic distrust of women. She knew for a certainty that he'd often disapproved of her, for once, years ago, he'd made the mistake of lecturing her about her failings as a wife, admonishing her to be more submissive to her lord husband. When she had related that to Simon, he'd roared with laughter, but Nell had not been amused, and her relationship with Worcester had never fully recovered from that rocky beginning.

With admirable restraint, the Bishop made no mention of his own jeopardy, offered his condolences in language as pedantic as it was elegiac. But then he'd written: "I came across something in Scriptures that could well serve as Simon's epitaph, hope it will comfort you as it did me. 'I have fought a good fight, I have finished my course, I have kept the faith.' "

Nell's hand jerked; the words blurred. "He's right," she said aloud, in a voice suddenly husky. "He's right, Simon. That was written for you. I know that. So why am I finding it so hard to let you go?"

After a pause, almost as if she'd expected an answer, she resumed reading. "I want to tell you, Madame, of a conversation I had with Simon. It was a night in late July; that day we'd sought again to cross the Severn, had again been driven back. It was probably the bleakest moment of a bleak campaign, for we'd not yet heard from your son, our supplies were running low, and our men were understandably distraught. It was very late, we were alone, and for the first time, we talked about the likelihood of defeat."

Nell put the letter down, only to pick it up again almost at once, afraid to read further, afraid of what she might discover, and yet afraid not to read it, too. Had Simon's last days been poisoned by despair? If he'd lost hope, she did not think she could bear to know. Holding the letter up to the light, she read:

"I asked Simon if he'd ever feared that all our struggles, all our suffering might be in vain. Not a priest's question, and he shamed me by his answer, by the shining certainty of his faith. He said no, my lady, and then he told me of a cave he'd found whilst in the Holy Land. It was said to have magical powers; a man could shout and long after it had died away, it echoed back as if from the very bowels of the earth. Simon had so marveled at it that he'd never forgotten it. And that night in Hereford Castle, he said that whilst it might seem as if we were but shouting into the wind, our echoes, too, would come back in time, echoes to hearten the godly and haunt kings. He laughed then, but he believed it, my lady, and I found I believed, too."

Nell did not realize she was crying until tears splashed onto the parchment, bled into the ink. "It was then that Simon said, 'My fears are not for England. My fear is that because I could not fail my God, I might well fail my wife.' "

Nell's throat closed up. "Simon, you knew . . ." The letter fluttered from her fingers, and she wept as she'd not wept since that first night of her widowhood. She lay prone upon the bed, clutching a pillow as if it alone could keep her afloat, for she truly did feel as if she were drowning, strangling on her own sobs. And yet this hot, surging tide was somehow easier to bear than the ice-encrusted desolation that had so blighted her heart, her soul. When the spasms finally eased, she was panting, trembling, drenched in sweat. Sitting up, she wiped her face with the sheet, then groped in the floor rushes for the letter.

"I would that I could remember all we said that night, my lady. Alas, I cannot. I do recall that Simon talked about your children, in particular, your little lass; I think he saw her as more vulnerable than your lads. And then he truly surprised me. He'd moved to the window, for as you know, he was never one for sitting still. I always thought it a minor miracle that you ever kept him immobile long enough for that broken leg to heal. It was quiet; neither of us had spoken for a time, when he said softly, 'All men fear for their families; in that I am no different from any soldier asleep out in the hall. But I am luckier than most, for I have a wife able to cope with Armageddon itself. As I entrusted Nell with the defense of Dover Castle, so, too, could I entrust her with our children's future, should it ever come to that.'

"I must confess, my lady, that I'd never taken your true measure, and I could not keep from voicing my doubts, for that seemed too onerous a burden for the frail shoulders of a wife. I feared I might have offended him, but Simon was amused, instead. He said, with that sudden smile of his, 'If there is but one woman in Christendom capable of matching wits with Edward, that woman is mine.' "

Nell could read no more; she began to fumble with the cloth, jerking until a ring tumbled out into her lap. She recognized it at once, a sapphire cut into the shape of a cross, set in heavy gold. It was Simon's favorite ring, given him by the Patriarch of Jerusalem and never off his finger since his long-ago return from the Holy Land. Nell touched her lips to the cerulean gemstone. "Relics from the saint of Evesham fetch a pretty price, my love. If worst comes to worst, we can always pawn it."

She was astonished by her own words; for the first time, the bitterness had been diluted with a hint of humor. Unfastening her crucifix chain, she looped it through Simon's sapphire ring, dropped it down between her breasts; it felt warm against her skin, a tangible talisman to ward off the dark, to ward off demons, mayhap even hers.

"You did not fail me, beloved. And I will not fail you. I swear to you, Simon—and to God—that no matter what lies ahead, I shall not lose faith."

ON October 26, Henry invested his younger son, Edmund, with the earldom of Leicester. Two days later, Nell and her daughter sailed for France.

41

Kenilworth Castle, England

January 1266

ENGLAND in the fiftieth year of Henry's reign was an unquiet, troubled land. There was no peace, for Henry's terms had been too harsh; there were too many men with nothing left to lose. Banding together, they joined John d'Eyvill on the Isle of Axholme, in the marshes of the River Trent. There Baldwin Wake came, upon escaping confinement. And there, too, Bran had come, bringing with him some of the Kenilworth garrison.

But in December, it was Edward who led troops to Axholme, and it was Edward who had the victory. A Christmas surrender took place on Bycarrs Dyke. Bran and his companions were compelled to place themselves "at the King's award and ordinance, saving life and limb and prison," and Bran accompanied Edward under safe-conduct to Henry's Christmas court at Northampton. There Richard pleaded eloquently on his behalf. Edward, too, argued for clemency, and for a time Henry vacillated, pitying his nephew in spite of himself. But in the end, it was Roger de Mortimer and the Earl of Gloucester whom he heeded. Bran's claims to the Leicester lands and titles were declared forfeit. Henry agreed to grant him five hundred pounds a year; in return, he was to abjure the realm, never to return to England.

But before he sailed, there was one final service he must do for the Crown. It was bitterly cold. Snow had been falling since dawn and by the time they reached Kenilworth, they were half-frozen. Ice glazed the surface of the lake, thick enough to still the water's surge but not to bear a man's weight, and the castle's formidable walls were almost obscured by the swirling snow. Bran drew rein, glanced back at Edward. "You want me to ask for entry?"

"No . . . you might find so warm a welcome within that you'd decide to stay," Edward said dryly, and Bran shrugged. He was doing what they demanded of him, seeking Kenilworth's surrender, but Edward knew he did not care whether he succeeded or not. No more than he'd cared whether he came to terms with his uncle the King. Or that he was now moving within arrow range of the Kenilworth garrison. Edward had never before realized what a redoubtable shield indifference could be. He watched intently as Bran rode toward the Brayes Tower, called out for Henry de Hastings.

Edward and Thomas de Clare exchanged startled looks. Henry de Hastings was one of the few survivors of Evesham, and had contrived to escape custody once his wound had healed. But until now Edward had not known his whereabouts. Bran was continuing to advance, utterly undaunted by the sight of crossbows protruding from the tower embrasures. "I am Simon de Montfort," he shouted. "Tell Henry de Hastings I would talk with him."

The words, no more than what Bran could have been expected to say, nonetheless gave Edward a peculiar jolt. After a moment, he realized why. This was the first time that he could remember Bran ever using his given name. The wait seemed endless; it had begun to sleet. After an interminable time, a horseman emerged from the gatehouse, started down the causeway. Another ice-encased delay, and then a voice echoed mockingly from the battlements of the Brayes Tower.

"Is that truly you, Bran? I cannot say much for the company you're keeping these days!"

Bran disregarded the sarcasm. "I bear a message from the King. He promises that if you yield the castle now to the Lord Edward, he will seek no reprisals against you."

Again, the words were right; could he be faulted if they sounded as if he were parroting foreign phrases, quoting from an alien tongue?

Edward felt an unwelcome stab of pity. Kicking his stallion, he moved closer, heedless of his men's cautionary cries.

They had their answer almost at once; obviously it had been well rehearsed. "Tell the King," Henry de Hastings shouted down, "that we will surrender Kenilworth at the command of but one person—our lord's lady. We'll yield the castle to the Countess of Leicester and no other!"

Behind him, Edward heard exclamations of anger and dismay. For himself, he was not surprised. "Bran?" He nudged his stallion forward, ignoring the prickling at his neck as he ventured into the sights of a dozen bowmen. "Bran?"

Sitting his horse before his father's castle, blinded by blowing snow and sleet, Bran was laughing. Peal after breathless peal, laughter choked and jagged and defiant, a sound that scraped along Edward's spine like the point of a knife.

AFTER failing to effect the surrender of Kenilworth, Bran was taken back to London, where he was kept under such close surveillance that he began to suspect treachery. On February 10, he succeeded in eluding his warders and fled to Winchelsea, where the men of the Cinque Ports were still in rebellion. Edward followed, won yet another decisive victory, and then shrewdly offered the defeated men a full pardon. But Bran managed to evade capture and escaped to France.

UPON her arrival at Montargis, Nell had been warmly received by the nuns, who'd gladly rented her one of their guest houses on the priory grounds. Their new home was far less luxurious than the accommodations to which they were accustomed, containing only a hall, a kitchen, and a small bedchamber for Nell and her daughter; moreover, the ship carrying Nell's household goods had been captured by Channel pirates. But Nell's regrets were not for castles, her sorrowing not for manors or jewels.

It was now spring, a verdant, lush May. During her six months at Montargis, Nell's life had regained a measure of stability. She had won for herself powerful partisans in the French King and his Queen. To Henry and Eleanor's dismay, Louis and Marguerite not only made Nell and her sons welcome at the French court, they urged Henry repeatedly to make peace with his sister, to restore her dower rights in the Pembroke estates. Henry so far remained obdurate, but it was a comfort to Nell to know that she was not friendless, that in France and in England there were still those willing to speak out on her family's behalf.

Nell had never been a worrier—until Evesham. Now she spent long, sleepless nights, brooding over what the future held for her children. Her two younger sons seemed to be adjusting to their loss. She'd sent Richard to the court of Simon's kinsman, the Count of Bigorre, and the reports she'd been getting were encouraging; with the resiliency of youth, Richard was applying himself to the lessons of knighthood. Amaury, too, appeared to be adapting himself to their changed fortunes. He was living in Paris, and planned to enter the University of Padua once Nell was able to arrange for his expenses.

But Nell could take no consolation in the plight of her other sons. For them she could do little, for she could not provide what they most needed: freedom for Guy, absolution for Bran. Nor had she been successful in easing her daughter's pain. Ellen was a stranger to her now. Gone was the blithe, carefree chatterbox, the affectionate imp who'd been her father's pet, her family's spoiled, cherished darling. The Ellen after Evesham was a silent, shadowy wraith, looking out upon the world with huge, haunted eyes, as if awaiting yet more grief. Nell feared for Ellen's future most of all. Without a proper marriage portion, what sort of husband could she hope to find? No man of rank would take a wife without lands, a wife who might bring down upon him the enmity of the English Crown. They were not penniless, would be able to provide a marriage portion to tempt a knight. But to Nell, a King's daughter, that was an unthinkable comedown for her child. How could she expect Ellen to be content with a mere knight, when she ought to have had a Prince?

It was in hopes of cheering her daughter's spirits that Nell had sent her to Paris for a fortnight's stay with Amaury. Ellen had returned that afternoon, but it was obvious the visit had not been a success. She'd been very subdued, shrugging off Nell's attempts to draw her out. Nell had no better luck later in a circumspect interrogation of Juliana, the young Frenchwoman she'd engaged to act as Ellen's maid. The two girls had taken an instant liking to each other, had become quite close in these months at Montargis. But Juliana could tell Nell little, other than what she already knew, that Ellen had not enjoyed herself at the French court.

Vespers were sounding when Nell heard the music echoing from their bedchamber. The harp had been a betrothal gift from Llewelyn, and Ellen had practiced so diligently that she was now quite proficient. The door was ajar and Nell paused before it, listening to the melody. But then Ellen began to sing softly: " 'May thy prayers from Heaven aid us, Thou whose bitter death hath laid us, now defenseless and forlorn.' "

Nell stiffened, for the words were familiar to her; it was one of the many songs written about the battle of Evesham. She waited until the music died, and then pushed the door all the way open. Ellen was sitting on the bed, with her ever-present briard stretched out beside her. She looked up as Nell entered, hastily ordered the dog onto the floor. "Whilst I was at the French court, I learned a new song about Papa, called 'Lament for Earl Simon.' Do you want to hear it, Mama?"

Nell shook her head, but Ellen was already reaching for the harp. " 'But by his death, Earl Simon hath in sooth the victory won. Like Canterbury's martyr, he there to the death was done—' "

"Ellen, enough!" Nell drew a deep breath. "I did not mean to speak so sharply, lass, but in truth, I care not for such songs. Move over so I may sit beside you. I am indeed sorry that you found so little pleasure in your visit. Were you not well received at court? Louis and Marguerite have—"

"No, it was not that. The French King and Queen were very kind. People were friendly, but . . . but they stared at me so, Mama!"

"You must get used to that, darling. Pretty girls always attract stares. But they also stare at you because you are Simon de Montfort's daughter. And that, too, you must learn to accept."

Ellen was silent, twisting a loose strand of hair around her finger, a new nervous habit Nell had been laboring in vain to break. "Mama . . . Amaury told me that the Countess of Devon is now insisting that she was always loyal to the King. And she even claims that she never welcomed Bran's advances, that he forced them upon her! How can she lie like that?"

"Very easily, it seems," Nell said acidly. "Is that what upset you so?"

"I was angered by her lies. But no, Mama, it was not the Countess of Devon. It was Amaury. He says . . . he says he is going to Italy!"

"I know. He wants to study religion and medicine at the University of Padua. Ellen, do not look so forlorn! Italy is not Cathay; he'll be back."

"But Mama, Italy is so far away. I feel as if we're being blown about by the wind, that we'll never be together again. Guy is in England, Richard in Bigorre, and Bran . . ."

She stopped, and Nell finished for her. "And Bran is in Normandy, seeking to raise troops to relieve Kenilworth Castle. You know that, lass, read his letter—"

"I know what he wrote, Mama, but I still do not understand why he has not come to see us, not once!"

"Ellen, I've told you that your brother blames himself for what happened at Evesham. He is not yet ready to face us—"

"But we've forgiven him and he knows that!"

"Yes, we've forgiven him. But he has not been able to forgive himself, and until he does . . ." She paused, for Ellen was no longer listening. Rolling over, she buried her face in a pillow. Nell sighed, softly stroked her hair. She suspected that every family had its own alliances, its shifting coalitions dictated by age or need or affinity. In their family, it had always been Harry and Bran, Bran and Harry. Brothers in blood, twins in spirit, so closely attuned that they could finish each other's sentences, so habitually together that to see Bran was to look about for Harry. It had been an exclusive intimacy, though, by its very nature excluding their brothers. Only Ellen had been admitted into that charmed circle, an indulged if unequal member of a very select society, one more casualty of Evesham.

"It is not fair, Mama, not fair . . ." Ellen's voice was muffled by the pillow, and Nell had to shove the briard back, for the big dog was determined to jump upon the bed and comfort its young mistress. "Was it not enough that I lost Papa and Harry? Must I lose Bran, too?"

Nell reached over, slipped an arm around her daughter's shoulders. "You've not lost Bran, but you must be patient with him, Ellen. Sit up now, and I shall brush your hair and share some news with you. Whilst you were gone, I had a letter from your cousin Joanna." Ellen looked blank, and Nell added, "Joanna de Quincy, lass, Elen's daughter, remember?"

Ellen nodded, with no real interest. "Humphrey de Bohun's widow," she said, and Nell frowned; must the child identify everything in terms of death?

"Yes," she said briskly, "Humphrey's widow. You must never think, Ellen, that all people are as faithless as Isabella de Fortibus. The Londoners could give the lady Countess of Devon a sharp lesson in loyalty. Joanna wrote that there was a riot in London on the sixth of May, that men burst into the guildhall, crying their continuing support for Thomas Fitz Thomas, demanding that he be released from prison. It availed them naught, of course; they were dispersed by force. But I am sure it comforts Fitz Thomas to know that the Londoners would risk so much on his behalf. Just as it comforts us that men still hold your father in such esteem."

Nell hesitated then, for while her next bit of news was sure to hearten Ellen, there was a risk in imparting it. As always, she chose to gamble. "Joanna also had most welcome news from Wales. Llewelyn has won a great victory over the most detestable of the Marcher lords. On Whitsun Eve, he defeated the army of Roger de Mortimer at Bry-, cheiniog. Whilst de Mortimer lamentably escaped with his life, he was one of the few who did, fled the field with his ambitions and his honor— such as it is—in tatters."

The mere mention of Llewelyn's name had been enough to dry Ellen's tears. "Oh, Mama, what wonderful news! I knew Llewelyn would avenge his dead, I knew it! Will he write and tell us of his triumph?"

"Yes, Ellen, I am sure he will," Nell said slowly, all the while thinking that it might be better for her daughter if Llewelyn did not.

COMPLINE had ended; the church was hushed and dark, lit only by a single torch in the choir. This was Nell's favorite hour, the only time she had to be alone with her God and her husband. Carrying a horn lantern, a wine flagon, and an embroidered prayer cushion, she moved from the nave into the choir, then on into the Lady Chapel. Kneeling before the altar, she sought to empty her mind of rancor, to open her soul to God's healing. For a long time, her prayers had been forced, recited by rote, devoid of comfort. But as winter thawed, so, too, had her faith. If her prayers were not as heartfelt, as ingenuous as they'd been before Evesham, that was a secret she shared with no one, not even God. She had not lost belief, and it seemed to her that the Almighty could ask no more than that, for if she now paid her debt of devotion with a devalued coin, the debt itself was no longer free from doubt—not after Evesham.

Now she prayed for her husband's soul, the souls of the daughter dead in Bordeaux and the son dead at Evesham. She prayed for the parents she'd never truly known, and for those she'd loved—Elen and Rob de Quincy, Joanna and Llewelyn, the Bishop of Lincoln, her sisters, her cousin Will, who'd died at Mansourah. And lastly, she prayed for the dead of Evesham, for Peter and Hugh and Humphrey and all the men who'd ridden out to die with Simon.

When her prayers were done, Nell moved the cushion, wine flagon, and lantern to the other side of the chapel, and settled herself comfortably before the memorial stone she'd obtained for her husband. "I am worried about Ellen," she confessed. "I fear, Simon, that she is deluding herself, clinging to false hopes. I have explained why the Welsh Prince disavowed the plight-troth, and she says she understands. Yet I wonder if that's truly so. She makes music with his name, just as she does with his harp, and with the least encouragement, she'll dwell upon his exploits by the hour. I can see why she'd be loath to lose Llewelyn, too, after losing so much. But it makes me most uneasy, my love. If she is harboring fantasies, envisioning Llewelyn as her rescuer, as the gallant hero of a chivalric romance, she's going to be dreadfully hurt. I've always been fond of Llewelyn, but he is no Lancelot, no Tristan, if such men ever—"

She stopped, head cocked toward the choir. But the footsteps soon receded, and she relaxed, picked up the flagon. "Last week one of the nuns overheard me talking to you, and now all the sisters are convinced that I, too, pray to the saint of Evesham. Only a nun could be such an innocent. Any other woman would have laughed, knowing no wife could ever see her husband as a saint!"

Nell laughed, too, but then she set the flagon down, untasted. "Scriptures say that blessed are they that mourn, for they shall be comforted. But when? Simon, I miss you so much. Some days are better than others, and some are bad beyond belief. Your birthday, our wedding date. April first was the worst, I think, for that was the last night we spent together. And I expect that August fourth shall be the hardest day of all. But as much as I dread it, I sometimes wonder if the pain will lessen after that. Now I torment myself by thinking that this was your last Christmas, your last spring. Mayhap if I can say it's been a year since Evesham, mayhap then . . ."

Nell reached out, traced with her fingers the name engraved upon the stone. There were times when she felt Simon's presence so strongly that she could almost believe he was about to walk through the door; occasionally she even imagined she heard his footsteps. But there were other times, like tonight, when she felt very much alone, when memories were a poor substitute for the flesh-and-blood embraces of a man she'd loved for more than half her life.

"Elen de Quincy once told me about something Llewelyn Fawr did after my sister Joanna died. Elen said he had trouble sleeping—until he began to use Joanna's pillow. So I found one of your old mantles—the dark green wool—and I spread it across my bed at night. It sounds mad, I know, but Llewelyn was a clever one, beloved, for it does help—a little."

Usually she took comfort from these quiet conversations with Simon, but tonight there was none. She made no move to go, though, for only an empty bed awaited her. She was reaching for the flagon when a door slammed, footsteps sounded in the nave. Too heavy a tread for a nun; Father André? Nell got wearily to her feet. But the shadow cast upon the choir wall was too tall for the priest. She raised the lantern, suddenly cautious. "Who goes there?"

"It's me, Mama."

The voice, so familiar and yet the last one she'd have expected to hear, froze her in mid-step. "Guy?" she whispered, disbelieving until he moved into the light. "Dear God!"

"No . . . Guy," he said, redeeming a lame joke with a truly dazzling smile. And then she was in his arms, and they were both laughing through tears, holding fast.

Still trying to catch her breath, Nell reluctantly stepped back, studying his face with hungry eyes. "I cannot believe you're here! Why did Edward not write me that you were to be freed?"

He smiled again, this time with a glint of malice. "It came as a surprise to Ned, too."

"You escaped?"

He nodded proudly. "The fools moved me from Windsor to Dover— Dover! They might as well have chosen Kenilworth. Papa's support was always greatest amongst the men of the Cinque Ports, and Evesham has not quenched their fervor. It was easy to find a friendly guard, so easy it took all the fun out of my escape! We picked a cloudy night, the Thursday after Easter, and by dawn, we were out of the castle, out of the town, aboard a fishing boat bound for France. By the time I was missed, we were under sail."

"The Thursday after Easter," Nell echoed. "That was April twenty-second, nigh on a month ago. Where have you been all this time? Why did you not come to us at once?"

"What I had to do could not wait. I went to Normandy," Guy said, suddenly grim, "to look for Bran."

Nell's hand tightened on his arm. "Did you find him?"

He nodded. "In Rouen." He'd moved out of reach, had begun to pace. Whether by heredity or emulation, Simon's sons shared his restless habits, his inability to be still for very long. "During those long weeks at Windsor, when I was lying bedridden, weak as a mewing kitten, with no company but my own thoughts, I would sometimes pass the hours, Mama, by imagining what it would be like—that confrontation with my right beloved brother. And I entertained myself by arguing the reasons— pro and con—for killing him."

He heard Nell's indrawn breath, and swung back toward her, at once contrite. "Ah, Mama, I did not mean it, no matter how often I sought to convince myself I did. But my bitterness was real enough— and justified, by God!"

"What happened, Guy, in Rouen?"

"Bran . . . Bran offered no excuses. He faced my rage without flinching. In truth, I think he'd not have defended himself even if I'd drawn my sword. And I saw then that Bran and I had both been wounded at Evesham. But my injuries healed, and his have not."

"Is Bran still in Rouen?" At least now they'd know where to write, Nell thought, but Guy was shaking his head.

"No, Mama, he's here . . . at Montargis. I convinced him it was time to face you, no easy task, I'll admit. He's waiting for you out in the church." Nell whirled; she'd only taken two quick steps, though, before Guy blocked her path. "Mama . . ."

Nell's smile was both wry and understanding. "You need not fret, lad. If I could forgive Almighty God, how could I not forgive my own son?"

The nave was dark, and Nell felt an anxious pang; had he gone? But then he moved away from the door, into the moonlight, and she could not stifle a gasp. Of all her sons, Bran most resembled his father, for unlike his brothers, he, too, was clean-shaven, and he looked so like the Simon of her lost youth that Nell found herself unable to speak. Misreading her silence, he took a backward step, and she cried out his name, held out her arms.

He came, hesitantly, as if he no longer had the right. "Mama, I—"

"Hush, love," she said, "hush," and then they were clinging tightly, in an embrace both anguished and yet exultant, too, a survivor's embrace. When they finally moved apart, Nell raised her hand, wiped tears from her face, and then, from Bran's. By now, Guy had reached them, and she turned toward him, too, saying huskily, "Come. It's time we awakened Ellen."

"It's late, Mama. Ought we not—"

"No, Guy, this is no night for sleeping. This is a night for talking, for remembering, for grieving, and for rejoicing, a night for calling up our ghosts." For a moment, her eyes lingered upon Bran's face. "Yes," she said, "when we speak of Simon and Harry, it will hurt, and we'll weep. But we'll laugh, too."

"MAMA?" Ellen sounded sleepy, bewildered. "It's so late," she yawned. "What is amiss?"

"Nothing is wrong, love. Here, put on your chemise; we have visitors."

Ellen obeyed, struggling to get her arms into the sleeves of the garment. "I do not understand," she said, and then, "Mama, wait!"

Nell ignored the protest. "For these guests, Ellen, a chemise will do," she said with a grin, and pulled the bed-hangings back.

"Mama, my hair is not even combed! I—Bran!"

"It's me, kitten," he said softly, and Ellen burst into tears. He bent over the bed, and she flung her arms around his neck, sobbed into his shoulder.

Nell watched, fighting tears, too, as Ellen embraced Bran, then Guy, then Bran again. Juliana and Nell's own maid, Emma, had been awakened by the commotion, were grabbing for their bedrobes, and, beckoning Emma aside, Nell said quietly, "I want you to go into the hall, awaken our cook, for my sons have not eaten. Tell him to kill one of the chickens and take a pike from the fish pond. I'd also like a subtlety, with eggs and almonds. Tell him not to rush, but tell him, too, not to stint his efforts, to make enough for the entire household. And I shall want him to break open the wine sent to us by the French King, the tun from his Pierrefitte vineyards."

Emma swallowed a yawn, quite willing to be awakened for a feast. "In other words, my lady, spare no expense?"

To Nell, those innocuous words seemed to echo from another lifetime. "Exactly, Emma," she said, "spare no expense. For too long, the de Montforts have had nothing to celebrate. But tonight we have reason, and we shall do it in style; we shall do Simon proud."

42

Montgomery, Wales

September 1267

THE siege of Kenilworth had begun in earnest in June of 1266. Edward assailed the castle from one side, his younger brother, Edmund, led an assault upon a second side, Henry upon a third, and Roger de Mortimer upon the fourth. But their vaunted siege weapons proved ineffectual against Simon's formidable water defenses. The garrison remained defiant, cutting off the hand of one royal messenger, sallying forth for daring attacks upon the enemy camp, even leaving the gatehouse open during daylight hours, so sure were they that the lake was an obstacle no army could overcome. When the papal legate, Ottobuono Fieschi, solemnly excommunicated them all, the unrepentant rebels paraded the castle surgeon upon the walls, dressed in a mock bishop's cope, where he proceeded to "excommunicate" the King and the legate. There were more than twelve hundred men sheltered behind Kenilworth's massive walls, and as the siege dragged on through the summer into the autumn, Henry began to fear that his Exchequer would be the only casualty of the campaign.

It was the threat of bankruptcy, then, that finally ended Henry's dependency upon the vengeance-hungry Marcher lords. He was at last willing to heed those who counseled moderation. The result was the Dictum de Kenilworth, which offered rebels the opportunity to buy back their forfeit lands, at rates ranging from two to seven times their annual value. The Dictum's terms were harsh ones, but still preferable to outright confiscation, and many men grasped at this frail reed, made their peace with their King.

But some rebels scorned the Dictum. John d'Eyvill still held out on the isle of Ely, and the de Montfort banner continued to fly over Kenilworth, although the castle was now besieged by a new, more dangerous foe—hunger. As supplies dwindled and men sickened, the garrison agreed to yield if Bran could not relieve them within forty days. But as sympathetic as the French King was to Simon's family, he was not willing to permit an invasion of his brother-in-law's realm; he would not allow Bran's recruits and mercenaries to sail from French ports. And so it was that after defying the Crown for more than sixteen months, Kenilworth Castle surrendered to Edward on December 14, 1266.

The French King's action had doomed Kenilworth. Guy de Montfort found that easier to accept than Bran did, for Guy was already looking toward Italy, where the French King's brother Charles was seeking to claim the much-disputed crown of Naples and Sicily. Guy was shrewd enough to see that where ambition ran rampant, opportunity, too, flourished. Joining Charles's campaign, he soon demonstrated some of Simon's flair for command, and his star rose rapidly, as he earned for himself not only a powerful royal patron, but the sort of renown that his world reserved for battlefield gallantry. But Bran remained in France, haunted by Kenilworth's fall, by yet another failure.

Kenilworth's surrender had not brought peace to Henry's realm. John d'Eyvill continued in rebellion. An even greater threat, though, was posed by the discontent of the Earl of Gloucester, for he was now badly at odds with his erstwhile allies. He and Roger de Mortimer had almost gone to war over the lands of the late Humphrey de Bohun, and Gloucester had even accused de Mortimer of plotting his death. His relationship with Edward was deteriorating, too. Gloucester's had been one of the few voices arguing for clemency—for all but the de Montforts—and he was embittered that his advice was taken so lightly. He'd been hoarding grievances for months, and in the spring of 1267, his resentment spilled over, sweeping him into an act of startling, dangerous defiance. In April, he seized the city of London.

It should not have come as such a shock, for the straws had been in the wind for some time. Gloucester had made no secret of his unhappiness, and he'd found two unlikely allies in Llewelyn ap Gruffydd and John d'Eyvill. The truce with Llewelyn was only surprising on the surface; Llewelyn would cheerfully have dealt with the Devil if he thought it would benefit Wales. The pact with John d'Eyvill was more astonishing. But d'Eyvill was a pragmatist, and he could even take a very grim amusement in this turn of events, that the man most responsible for Simon de Montfort's downfall should now be helping him to advance Simon's aims. Nor were these alliances of expediency unknown to the Crown. Gloucester's disgruntled wife had seen to that, warning her uncle the King that her husband planned to move on London. Unfortunately for Henry, it was a warning he'd not taken seriously, dismissing it as a woman's spite. By the time he reconsidered, it was too late. Gloucester and John d'Eyvill held London.

A tense stalemate developed, which was to last for fully two months. But no one truly wanted another bloody Evesham. Henry's brother Richard offered to mediate; so did the papal legate, trapped within the Tower. Gloucester agreed to yield the city, provided that amnesty was extended to all his followers, and in turn, Henry promised to abide by the Dictum, to consider restoring some of the Londoners' rights and liberties. Edward was not easily reconciled to Gloucester, but Richard and his son Hal eventually prevailed, and on June 18, Henry entered his capital in triumph.

That left only Llewelyn ap Gruffydd in rebellion against the King. He was braced for the worst, a full-scale military campaign, no quarter given. What he got, instead, was a peace offer. He sent his uncle, Einion ap Caradog, to negotiate with the papal legate at Shrewsbury, and on September 25, they came to terms, terms Llewelyn could not have hoped to better.

Llewelyn had gained some impressive concessions from Simon de Montfort at Pipton; he now gained concessions of equal magnitude from the English Crown. Henry agreed to recognize Llewelyn as Prince of Wales, as liege lord to the other Welsh Princes; not even Llewelyn Fawr had soared so high. His conquests were recognized; no Welsh prince ever wielded the power he now did, from the upper waters of the River Taff to the northern shores of the isle of Môn.

If Llewelyn was the winner, the great losers were Edward and Roger de Mortimer. Edward agreed to relinquish all claims to those oft-disputed Welsh cantrefs known as the Perfeddwlad. Roger de Mortimer's losses were even more sweeping: Gwerthrynion and his claims to Brycheiniog, Ceri, Cydewain, and possibly Maelienydd, for while the treaty permitted him to build a castle there, it also stipulated that if Llewelyn could establish his claim to it, the cantref would be his.

Roger de Mortimer had complained loudly and bitterly—and in vain. What interested Llewelyn, though, was why Edward had agreed to this treaty. He knew England was war-weary, yearning for peace after so much bloodshed. And the siege of Kenilworth had been an exorbitant drain upon the royal treasury; Henry was in dire need of the money Llewelyn was willing to pledge for peace on his terms. The papal legate and Richard had argued persuasively for conciliation; Henry, as usual, wavered. But it was Edward who'd tipped the scales—why?

Edward was too intelligent not to realize what a bloody, drawn-out campaign awaited them in Wales, not to recognize that his men had no stomach for a life-and-death fight with Welsh will-o'-the-wisps who excelled at ambush and were harder to track down than morning mist. Llewelyn was sure, too, that Edward trusted Gloucester not at all. The Earl shifted allegiances with the wind, and the danger that he might again ally with Llewelyn was not to be dismissed out of hand. Moreover, Llewelyn knew that Edward was eager to take the cross, to join the French King's crusade; Jerusalem beckoned far more seductively than did Aber. And even the loss of the Perfeddwlad was a sacrifice greater on parchment than in practice; Edward might lay claim to those four cantrefs, but the troops patrolling them were Llewelyn's.

Such were Llewelyn's speculations about the motivations of the King's son. The result, though, was not in doubt; he took away from Shrews-bury a victory greater than any he could have won on the field. He in turn agreed to pay twenty-five thousand marks into Henry's depleted coffers, and to reconcile with his brother, restoring to Davydd those lands he'd held prior to his defection four years earlier.

ON Michaelmas, the 29th of September in God's year 1267, Llewelyn ap Gruffydd came to the town the Welsh called Trefaldwyn and the English Montgomery. There he did homage to the English King, and the Treaty of Montgomery was formally ratified.

Llewelyn had not seen Henry for a number of years, and he was genuinely shocked by the man he found at Montgomery. Time had not been kind to Henry. Llewelyn knew his age—just shy of sixty—but if he had not, he'd have sworn that Henry had passed his biblical three-score years and ten. Gone was the elegance, the good-hearted naïveté of the King Llewelyn had first met at Shrewsbury so long ago. The man to whom he knelt in the great hall at Montgomery Castle was a frail, stooped stranger, who presided over the ceremony with a vague, faintly anxious air, like an actor worrying that he might forget his lines. Llewelyn thought it rather pathetic, the way he kept glancing toward Edward, as if waiting for cues.

He'd not expected to pity any English king, but he'd not expected that any English king could be so impotent—so irrelevant. Even a brain seizure had not robbed his grandfather of his wits or his will; as long as he drew breath, all knew who ruled Gwynedd. But Henry seemed to cast no shadow at all. Even when he flared up at a clumsy servant, there was more petulance than anger in his rebuke, and he clung to his grievance with unseemly stubbornness, grumbling and fussing to all within earshot, not subsiding until Edward discreetly signaled for the offending servant to disappear. And as he watched, Llewelyn was torn between regret that any man should face his twilight years with so little dignity, and disgust that he should have to swear fealty to such a liege lord.

Ah, Simon, he thought suddenly, you were doomed to failure. No matter how you tried, you'd never have taught Henry to be a king, no more than you could have taught him to fly. His eyes were roaming the hall, finding many familiar faces. The papal legate, a peacemaker justly glorying now in his success. Gloucester, voice pitched too loud, underscoring his argument with wide sweeps of his arm. His audience, Henry's son Edmund, nodding politely, noncommittally. Edmund was just twenty-two, well-spoken and well-mannered. In their brief acquaintance, Llewelyn found him to be pleasant enough, but he could not get past the title. Earl of Leicester—for him, there'd be but one.

Across the hall, Roger de Mortimer was glowering at Gloucester, at Llewelyn himself, at the world at large, his outrage a source of heartfelt satisfaction to Llewelyn. His gaze returned to the dais, lingering upon the man standing behind Henry. For a moment, their eyes caught, held— for a moment. Llewelyn could read nothing in Davydd's expression, and he hoped that his own face was no less impassive. Not for the surety of his soul would he have betrayed himself before these English eyewitnesses.

Edward was approaching, beckoning him toward the privacy of a window-seat. Llewelyn was sure that the Englishman had more in mind than an idle exchange of social courtesies, but he was willing to play the game until Edward revealed his true intent, and accepting a wine cup from a passing servant, he said politely, "I believe I heard that you had a son born last year?"

Edward smiled. "John, my first lad. And my wife is with child again."

Llewelyn offered congratulations, all the while thinking how fitting it was that Edward should have named his firstborn son after his grandfather, for he was cast far more in John's mold than in Henry's.

Edward wasted no time in maneuvering their conversation toward the direction in which he wanted it to go. "In view of your alliance with Simon de Montfort and his sons, I expect that you've remained in contact with my aunt, the Countess of Leicester."

And what did he want to know about the de Montforts? Llewelyn nodded, deciding to try various types of bait, see which one lured Edward from cover. "As a matter of fact," he said, "I had a letter very recently from the Lady Nell. It seems Bran is thinking of joining his brother in Italy. You have heard, I daresay, that Guy now stands high in the favor of Sicily's new King. Especially after he took Florence at Easter."

Edward grunted. "I know. Whilst I like it not, I cannot say that Guy's success surprises me, for I often suspected that he had the makings of a good commander. Unlike Harry and Bran, who never showed a lick of sense on a battlefield, just the sort of crazed courage that gets men killed. But for all that, the wrong brother died at Evesham. Harry was worth a dozen of Guy."

Having triggered so interesting a response with Guy's name, Llewelyn decided to see what effect he'd get with another de Montfort brother. "In her letter, the Lady Nell mentioned that the Bishop of Rouen is giving Amaury permission to be ordained as a priest. No surprise there, for the Bishop was a good friend of Simon's. But the Pope for certes was not, and yet Amaury seems to have found a friendly ear at the papal court. You do know that he petitioned the Pope on his father's behalf, claiming that Simon had received absolution ere he died and was thus entitled to lie in consecrated ground? If the Pope finds in Amaury's favor, I expect it will be rather awkward for the English Crown, having to rebury Simon in Evesham Abbey."

Llewelyn was unable to deny himself this last gibe, for he'd thought it barbaric to deny Simon a Christian burial. "Although I understand that removing Simon's body from the abbey did little to discourage the faithful. I've been told that pilgrims still flock to Evesham, to the church and spring where he died."

"Some still come," Edward conceded reluctantly, "but not in numbers of any significance."

Llewelyn drank to hide a smile. If Simon's cult was of so little consequence, why, then, had the English Crown felt the need to deal with it in the Dictum de Kenilworth? For the eighth article of the Dictum forbade Englishmen to think of Simon as a saint and prohibited any talk of the "vain or fictitious" miracles attributed to him. Llewelyn was enormously amused by it all; if Simon seemed an unlikely candidate for sainthood, it was a truly diabolic form of vengeance. After all, how does one discredit a saint?

Edward's thoughts seemed to be mirroring his own—minus the amusement—for he said abruptly, "It is easy enough to sanctify a dead man. His virtues take on such legendary proportions that all his flaws are forgotten. Simon de Montfort could be as prideful and overbearing a bastard as ever drew breath, but who remembers that now?"

Llewelyn almost laughed aloud. Ah, Simon, he thought gleefully, you're proving to be a right lively ghost. May you haunt Edward till his dying day. It occurred to him now that this might be an opportunity to do Nell a good turn. "Whilst we are speaking of the de Montforts, Your Grace, I have a query regarding the Countess. She'd informed me that your lord father yielded this spring to the urgings of the French King, and agreed to restore her dower rights in the Pembroke estates, five hundred pounds a year. And it was my understanding that Bran was to be allowed to claim his father's lands, with the provision that he must sell them to you or the King should you so demand. But that was four months ago. May I ask why the terms have not been fulfilled?''

Edward shrugged. ''If de Montfort's friends have not forgotten him, neither have his enemies,'' he said, his eyes focusing for a moment upon the Earl of Gloucester, still holding Edmund captive with an impassioned monologue. ''And the Exchequer is a dry well these days. Then, too, Bran seems loath to trust my father's word. But it is my hope that we will be able to resume payments to my aunt ere too much time goes by.''

If not in this lifetime, the next, Llewelyn thought skeptically. ''The Lady Nell has met with greater success at the French court. Within the past fortnight, the French parlement found in her favor, ordered her half-brother, Hugh de Lusignan, Count of La Marche, to pay her four thousand livres a year, as her rightful share of her lady mother's Angoulême inheritance.''

He had at last startled Edward with news he'd not yet heard. He blinked, and then grinned. ''Did they, by God? Good for Nell!''

Llewelyn was taken aback by Edward's enthusiasm, so obviously unfeigned. It showed briefly on his face, and Edward's smile turned quizzical. ''Why look so surprised? I never wanted to see my aunt beggared, am right glad that she has bested my de Lusignan uncle, although it'll be no small feat to squeeze so much as a sou from that one's clenched fist.'' He paused, studying Llewelyn over the rim of his cup. ''I am very fond of my aunt,'' he said, slowly and deliberately, ''and of my cousin Ellen. Their well-being matters to me.''

So he'd finally come to it, and it was not the sons at all; it was Ellen.

''Ellen is a sweet lass. Whilst I was being held at Kenilworth, she often wrote to me, seeking to raise my spirits. I regret that she had to suffer for her father's sins, and now that she is of an age for marriage— she turns fifteen next month—I've been thinking of the need to find a proper husband for her.''

''Have you, indeed?'' Llewelyn said coolly. ''I rather doubt that the de Montforts would welcome your interest.''

''The fact remains that Ellen's marriage is bound to be of concern to the Crown. Her position is an awkward one, as I'm sure you'll agree. Her value upon the English marriage market has been tainted by her father's treason. I would not want to see her make a match of desperation, to demean herself by wedding beneath her rank. But neither would I have wanted to see her as Princess of Wales. I am glad, my lord Llewelyn, that you were prudent enough to realize how unwise such a marriage would have been.''

Llewelyn's rage rendered him speechless—fortunately—for it was his father's blood surging in his veins, it was Gruffydd's white-hot hatred that seared to the very bone, heedless of consequence. By what right did this Englishman dare to tell a Welsh Prince whom he could or could not marry? But his heritage was not only Gruffydd's passion; it was Llewelyn Fawr's common sense, too, and he fought back his fury, the urge to fling his wine cup in Edward's face.

Edward was watching him intently. Llewelyn forced himself to meet the younger man's gaze, to finish his wine, waiting until he was sure that his anger had iced over, that his voice would reveal nothing of his inner turmoil.

"I am glad we had this chance to talk, for I've a question to put to you. I was hoping that you could clarify for me a peculiar disparity in your English justice—or so it seems to Welsh eyes. On the one hand, you have the Earl of Gloucester, who fought against the Crown at Lewes, and subsequently dared to defy the King—and you, my lord—by seizing London. His punishment was a full pardon. Then there are men like John d'Eyvill and Baldwin Wake, who fought for Simon de Montfort, and after surrendering to you at Bycarrs Dyke four months after Evesham, they renounced their allegiance again as soon as they were free. Nicholas Segrave was another who fought at Evesham, survived, and rebelled once his wounds healed. Yet all these men have been pardoned, given full seisin of their lands, no?"

Edward nodded. "Sometimes clemency is not only an act of Christian piety," he said dryly, "but also one of policy."

"But it is an exclusive privilege, your English clemency . . . no? How else explain that these men have been restored to favor whilst the Mayor of London, who neither went back on his word nor took up arms against you, still languishes in a Windsor dungeon?"

Llewelyn saw at once that his thrust had hit home. Edward's jaw muscles tensed, his fair skin darkening; his eyes of a sudden reflected the wintry, bleached blue of a December sky. Llewelyn had seen other men look at him as Edward did now, battlefield foes who'd just crossed swords, taken his measure as an opponent, returning to the fight with a greater wariness.

"You are more like de Montfort than I realized," Edward said, with a tight smile. They were both on their feet now, and Edward turned as if to go, then struck back, still with a smile. "Whilst you are pondering the mysteries of our laws, my lord Llewelyn, you might think on this. It was English justice that restored your brother Davydd to his rightful place."

DUSK was smudging the contours of the distant mountains, but Llewelyn could still see the walls of Montgomery, spreading out to the south of the castle. It was not a sight to give him pleasure, for Montgomery was an English town on Welsh soil, chartered by Henry forty years earlier.

After returning to his chamber to prepare for the evening's entertainment, Llewelyn had given Einion and Goronwy ab Ednyved an account of his midday conversation with Edward, sparking in his uncle and Seneschal an outrage to equal his own. Having finally exhausted all the abusive possibilities he could conjure up to describe Edward, Goronwy rose, but at the door he paused to deliver a final, cautionary verdict upon the English King's son. "Do not let your guard down with him, Llewelyn. It sounds to me as if his comments were intended as more than a condescending pat on the head. I think they were also meant as a warning."

"I do not doubt it," Llewelyn agreed. "You need not worry, Goronwy. Edward Plantagenet is no man to hold cheaply. Far better to take him at his own inflated estimation!"

Goronwy exited, laughing, and Einion rose to pour mead for Llewelyn and himself. "Edward will not be easy to outwit, lad—not like Henry."

"I'm not worried about outwitting Edward, but about outfighting him. Any man who could outmaneuver Simon de Montfort—"

When the knock sounded, they both assumed that Goronwy had returned. "I wonder what he forgot," Einion said, starting for the door. As he reached for the latch, Llewelyn had a sudden premonition, and he swung away from the window just in time to see his brother framed in the doorway.

Davydd sauntered into the chamber with his usual aplomb. He was, they now saw, trailed by a castle page, a youngster bearing a tray piled with fragrant wafers. "Set it down there, lad," he said, and flipped the boy an English coin before turning toward Einion with a cajoling smile. "I'd gladly ask you to join us, Uncle, but there are three things best done in privacy: laying with a wench, confessing to a priest, and bloodletting between brothers."

The corner of Einion's mouth quirked in spite of himself. But it was to Llewelyn that he looked for confirmation, not withdrawing until the latter nodded.

"Thank God, you've got mead! They drink naught but noxious ales and sugared wines in England, as backward a country as I've ever encountered." Appropriating Einion's cup, Davydd slid the platter across the table. "Help yourself. The castle cook is Welsh, and he gave me the angel's-bread baked for Henry. You do not want any?" Straddling a chair, he tilted it at a precarious angle to study his silent brother.

"I missed you, Llewelyn. Did you not miss me—not even a little? No, I see not. So much for my fabled charm! And yet you must admit that I can be good company, for I have a cheerful nature, an inexhaustible supply of bawdy stories, and more sources for gossip than I can begin to count. I do not mean stale gossip, either. For example, I'm sure you know that Gloucester is pressing a lawsuit against his own mother. But do you also know that his estranged wife is sharing her bed with Edward?"

Davydd paused for breath, took several deep swallows of mead, watching Llewelyn all the while. "I cannot keep this up forever. For Christ's pity, Llewelyn, say something—anything!"

"Is Edward truly coupling with Gloucester's wife?" Llewelyn asked, and Davydd laughed in relief.

"God's truth! Oh, he's being discreet about it. He always is, for he seems fond of his wife, does not flaunt his concubines at court. But he has even more reason for caution this time. Although it would take an act of God to get Gloucester into Alice's bed again, I'd wager that he expects her to live as chastely as a nun till the end of her days, and if he ever found out . . . well, that's something to think about, is it not?"

Reaching for a wafer, Davydd tilted the chair back even farther. "Ere I forget to ask, how is my daughter doing?"

Llewelyn slowly shook his head. Even after three years, the memory retained the vivid clarity of utter astonishment. The arrival of Davydd's messenger was in itself not so great a surprise. Davydd's fortunes had plummeted after Lewes, and although Llewelyn didn't expect it, it was not inconceivable that Davydd might swallow his pride, seek a reconciliation. But when the messenger was ushered into Aber's great hall, it was not an olive branch he bore, but a green-eyed baby girl.

"Only you," he said, "would have had the gall to send your bastard offspring to the brother you'd betrayed."

Davydd shrugged. "What else could I do? Mary—her mother—had died in childbirth, and Mary's kin took her in . . . as long as I made it worth their while. But after Lewes, I could not be so free-spending, and they would no longer keep her. What could I do with a babe? I was on the run, remember! I was not going to abandon her, for she's of my blood—our blood. Would you have had me deposit her at de Montfort's door? You were the only one I could think of, Llewelyn."

He leaned forward. "Tell me . . . how fares she? Did you find a family to take her? Or did you keep her at court?"

"I kept her at court," Llewelyn admitted, and Davydd laughed again. "I knew you would!"

Davydd's laughter had always been contagious. It came as a shock to Llewelyn, though, to hear himself laughing, too, as if there were no shadows between them. He stopped abruptly, reached across the table, and grasped Davydd's wrist. "Do you truly think I'd ever be able to trust you again?"

The question was more than challenging; it was insulting—deliberately so. But Davydd seemed quite unfazed. "No," he conceded, almost cheerfully, "probably not. Hellfire, Llewelyn, I doubt if I'd trust me, either!"

By now, Llewelyn was well aware that his brother's smile was a weapon in and of itself, dangerously disarming. But even so, he was not as immune to its effects as he would have wished. Releasing the younger man's arm, he said with sudden bitterness, "I would to God I knew when you were being serious—if you ever are."

Davydd no longer looked amused. "For what it's worth," he said, "it was not personal. I never wished you harm, Llewelyn. I wanted only to free Owain and claim my fair share of Gwynedd."

"Understandable aims; some might even say laudable ones. But you were not very squeamish about how you achieved them, were you?"

"Because I turned to the English for help?" Davydd set his chair back upon the floor, with a thud. "Jesú, Llewelyn, if the ends do not justify the means, what on God's earth does?"

"Honesty at last!"

"I wish you did not sound so surprised. The truth is not an utterly alien tongue to me, even if I do not get much practice with it." Davydd splashed more mead into his cup, did the same for Llewelyn. "I must say that you're taking the return of the Prodigal Brother rather well . . . why?"

"It is not as if you were sprung upon me at the eleventh hour. I expected Edward to make use of you. Few men are as skilled as he at sowing seeds of dissension, and with you, Little Brother, he has a ready-made Trojan Horse, does he not?"

"He thinks he does," Davydd said. "So . . . what happens now?"

Llewelyn did not respond at once. "If I had a month to prepare myself for your return, I had four years to think about your departure, about what you did—and why. Would it surprise you if I said that I could understand?"

"Yes—exceedingly."

"Well, I can. There is some justice in your claims, Davydd . . . and they are well grounded in Welsh law. I am the one who is in violation of it, not you. Under the old ways, you and Owain and Rhodri have an equal right to the governance of Gwynedd."

"Somehow I doubt that you're about to recant, to offer to divide your crown into four equal portions."

Llewelyn's smile was grim. "You're right; a crown cannot be divided without destroying it. And that is true, as well, for a country. Wales must be kept whole, or England will swallow it all. If that means transgressing the old laws, so be it. I value Welsh sovereignty higher than Welsh tradition."

"A nicely turned phrase, but where are we going with this conversation? I'm gratified that you can see my side of things, but it does not sound as if you're offering anything more tangible than sympathy. So what you're saying, then, is that we go back to the way it was ere I rebelled, except, of course, that I'll now be kept on a much tighter leash."

"No, I'm not saying that. If it did not work four years ago, why should it work now? Our grandfather faced this very same dilemma; he could not resolve it, either, could find no way to reconcile the claims of his two sons. Our father died because of that failure. There has to be another way. I do not want to kill you, Davydd, or to see you shut away from the sun and sky—like Owain. But neither do I want to spend my days wondering how long you'll be loyal this time."

Davydd was watching him warily. "And have you a solution? If so, you've gone Merlin one better!"

"Not a solution—not yet. A possibility. Very simply put, I need an heir. Owain could no more govern Gwynedd than he could walk on water. But you, Davydd, you could. God knows, you're clever enough; too clever by half. No one has ever questioned your courage. All you seem to lack is scruples . . . and that never excluded any claimants for the English crown. Prove to me that you can be trusted, and I'll consider naming you as my heir."

"I thought you might dangle a carrot in front of my nose to keep me in harness. But I never expected such a gilded one. I need a moment to think on this. Why should you not wed and beget a son? You're only thirty-nine; time is still your ally."

This next was not easy to admit, but it had to be said, for it alone could give legitimacy to his offer. "I ought to have had sons by now," Llewelyn said reluctantly. "In these past twenty years, I've taken my share of women into my bed, but not a one has ever gotten with child. It may happen yet; I've known men who fathered children after giving up hope. But if it does not, I would be willing to give you serious consideration."

"But no promises?"

"None whatsoever. If it be God's Will that I have a son, I shall. But it is not God's Will that shall determine your future; it is mine."

"That's honest enough, and more than I expected, I admit. We have a pact, Llewelyn, and you, my lord Prince and brother, have a newly loyal liege man. I shall seek earnestly to mend my ways, not the first to be seduced by the golden glimmer of a crown." But beneath the surface sarcasm, there were unmistakable undertones of excitement. Davydd was raising his cup in a mock salute. "To trust, an admirable virtue I shall be taking very much to heart. Now . . . what say you that we give Edward a scare by entering the hall arm in arm, the very image of brotherly devotion?"

Llewelyn burst out laughing. "Damn you, Davydd, but I did miss you." And Davydd's startled smile would long linger in his memory, for it was utterly free of mockery, a smile of unguarded and genuine delight.

THE chapel was small, but starkly elegant, its white-washed walls and marble altar silvered by moonlight, splashed by rose tints filtering through windows of stained scarlet glass. Llewelyn paused before a stoup of holy water to bless himself, then raised his lantern and moved into the chancel, with Davydd following a few steps behind.

Kneeling before the altar, Llewelyn offered up a winged prayer for the soul of the man he'd most loved, the man who'd entrusted him with a vision, one that had never burned so brightly as it did in this twilit border church. Rising, he used his lantern to light a candle for Llewelyn Fawr.

"Who is the candle for—your grandfather?"

Llewelyn nodded. "Our grandfather. I wish you'd known him, Davydd. Llewelyn Fawr—he well deserved such praise, deserved the title, too. He was in truth the first Prince of Wales."

Davydd was surprised by the emotion that now surfaced, one closely akin to envy. For a moment, he wondered what different roads he might have taken if he—like Llewelyn—had been following the map bequeathed by Llewelyn Fawr. And then he shrugged, said flippantly, "If you mean to abdicate, Llewelyn, I'd as soon you did it in my favor, not a dead man's."

Llewelyn laughed, not taking his eyes from the candle's shimmering, luminous light. "Ambition alone is dangerous, Davydd, if not coupled with a vision."

"I'd say it is dreams that are dangerous," Davydd objected, only half in jest. "It was a dream that led to Evesham, was it not?"

Llewelyn turned, dark eyes capturing the candle's glow. "Yes," he said. "But it was also a dream that led here, to the Treaty of Montgomery." Picking up his grandfather's taper, he sought to kindle a second candle. The wick sputtered, but then caught fire, shot upward in a clear white flame.

"In Nomine Dei Patris et Filii et Spiritus Sancti," Llewelyn said softly. "May you rest in peace, Simon."

Afterword

Walter de Cantilupe, Bishop of Worcester, died on February 4, 1266. The other prelates who had supported Simon de Montfort—the Bishops of London, Lincoln, Winchester, and Chichester—were suspended by the Pope, and three of the four endured years of exile, one dying in Italy, two not returning to England until King Henry was dead.

The recalcitrant rebels, John d'Eyvill, Nicholas Segrave, and Baldwin Wake, received royal pardons. Baldwin Wake wed Hawise de Quincy, Elen and Rob de Quincy's youngest daughter, before February 1268; their great-granddaughter, Joan, the Fair Maid of Kent, wed Edward Plantagenet, the Black Prince, and her son ascended the English throne as Richard II.

Thomas Fitz Thomas, London's memorable Mayor, was kept in prison until April 1269, when he was finally able to gain his freedom upon payment of five hundred pounds. But his properties had been confiscated, and his sons were burdened with debt. Fitz Thomas's health suffered during his long imprisonment; he was dead by 1276. His widow, Cecilia, later married John de Stepney, a prosperous London fishmonger. Fitz Thomas's colleague, Thomas Puleston, was not released from prison until 1275; he died within two years.

The subsequent histories of Eleanor (Nell) de Montfort, her children, Edward Plantagenet, and Llewelyn and Davydd ap Gruffydd will be related in my next novel.

POPULAR veneration of Simon de Montfort continued into the early years of the fourteenth century. So strong was public sentiment in Simon's favor, so many miracles were alleged to have occurred, that it is conceivable he might eventually have been canonized by the Roman Catholic Church had it not been for the unrelenting hostility of the English Crown. Simon's son Amaury succeeded in winning the Pope's support, and Simon's body was reinterred before the High Altar in the abbey of Evesham. The abbey was demolished in the sixteenth century by Henry VIII, but in 1965—the seven hundredth anniversary of Simon's death—a memorial was erected upon the site of his grave, dedicated by the Speaker of the House of Commons and the Archbishop of Canterbury. The stone, brought from Simon's birthplace, Montfort l'Amaury, was engraved with the words: "Here were buried the remains of Simon de Montfort, Earl of Leicester, pioneer of representative government . . ."

Author's Note

FALLS THE SHADOW was originally intended to be the shared story of two men, Simon de Montfort and Llewelyn ap Gruffydd. But I soon discovered that I'd set myself an impossible task, for the scope and breadth of their lives could not be compressed into one volume. My solution was to yield *Shadow* to Simon, and to devote my next book, *The Reckoning*, to Llewelyn.

The very least that can be said of Simon de Montfort's life is that it was eventful, often improbable, so much so that I feel I should attest to a few of the more unlikely occurrences. Simon truly did remind Henry that an addled French King had been confined for his own good, an insult Henry never forgave, for twenty years later he could recount Simon's words almost verbatim. Some of their heated exchanges in the course of Simon's Gascony trial come straight from the pages of medieval chroniclers; Simon did indeed dare to warn Henry that, were he not a King, it would have been "an evil hour" for him. Henry actually did accuse Simon of seducing Nell, a charge made before Henry's entire court. Simon's contemporaries reported that he wore a hair shirt, a gesture of piety as natural to the medieval mind as it is alien to ours. The wild thunderstorm that broke over Evesham field during the battle was not a novelist's dramatic indulgence. So violent a storm was it that men invested it with a superstitious significance out of all proportion to an act of nature; one chronicler even compared it to the tempest that raged over Calvary as Jesus Christ was crucified. And Simon's son Bran did arrive at the battlefield in time to see his father's head upon a pike.

Although *Shadow* is my third book, I still find myself torn between two faiths. The novelist's need for an untrammeled, free-flowing imagination is always at war with the historian's pure passion for verity. I do try to keep fact-tampering to a minimum, but it occasionally is necessary in order to advance the story line. The Welsh Princes met at Ystrad Fflur Abbey in October of 1238; I changed the date by several weeks to accommodate the birth of Simon and Nell's son Harry. For the sake of convenience, I referred to Henry's "Painted Chamber," although that term did not come into use until some years later. And I chose to call Henry's half-brother, the Earl of Pembroke, by his family name, William de Lusignan, rather than by the name by which he is generally known to history—de Valence—that of his birthplace. As in my novel *Here Be Dragons*, I used Welsh spellings and place-names wherever possible, although I chose the slightly Anglicized "Llewelyn" over the pure Welsh of "Llywelyn," and I used the medieval v for phonetic reasons, as in Davydd and Ednyved.

It is not easy to resurrect a time so far removed from ours. Wales, in particular, remains uncharted terrain, for medieval sources were often incomplete, ambiguous, occasionally in conflict. In dramatizing Davydd ap Llewelyn's capture of his half-brother, Gruffydd, I have followed the chronology of the English monk Matthew Paris, rather than that of the Welsh chroniclers, for the reasons so persuasively set forth by Gwyn A. Williams in "The Succession to Gwynedd, 1238–47."

History has not been kind to Henry. The consensus is that he was one of England's most incompetent kings. He did leave a legacy, though, that many a more capable monarch might well envy—Westminster Abbey. And however wretched a sovereign, he was a loving father. His devotion to his deaf-mute daughter, Katherine, was atypical for his age, utterly at odds with the bias personified by Matthew Paris, who dismissed Katherine as "pretty but useless."

This was the first of my books in which I had to deal with the ugly underside of medieval society—the anti-Semitism that was so pervasive, so poisonous a part of daily life. I sought to explain how and why people were infected, making no excuses, but attempting to root this evil in the context of the thirteenth century.

Lastly, I would like to say a few words about Simon de Montfort. A French-born English hero, lordly champion of the commons, an honorable adventurer, he continues to be as controversial and enigmatic and paradoxical a figure in our time as he was in his own. Men have been arguing about the man, his motivations, and his legacy for the past seven hundred years. To an admiring Winston Churchill, "de Montfort had lighted a fire never to be quenched in English history." But the historian Sir F. M. Powicke, while grudgingly according Simon a certain "murky greatness," also saw him as a "dark force." Victorian historians in particular tended to overestimate Simon's contribution to constitutional government, lauding him as "the father of the English parliament," ascribing to him sentiments and aspirations no medieval man could have harbored. Simon's admirers and his critics do find some common meeting ground, all agreeing that Simon was able, arrogant, courageous, hot-tempered, and charismatic. Opinions then begin to diverge widely. A saint he most surely was not. For myself, I saw in him glimmerings of a Shakespearean tragic hero, one doomed by his own flaws. History's judgment upon Simon de Montfort has been fluid, fluctuating over the centuries in accordance with prevailing political winds, for each age interprets the past in the light of its own biases. But the verdict that lingers in the imagination is that of Simon's contemporaries, the medieval villagers who flocked to his grave, the steadfast Londoners, the poor and the powerless who believed in him, who did not forget him.

S.K.P.
November 1987

Acknowledgments

I WOULD like to thank the following people, without whose support *Shadow* might still be that, a shadowy idea, a might-have-been book. First and foremost, my parents, William and Terry Penman. My American editor, Marian Wood of Henry Holt and Company. My American agent, Molly Friedrich of the Aaron M. Priest Literary Agency. My British editor, Susan Watt of Michael Joseph Ltd. My

British agent, Mic Cheetham of Anthony Sheil Associates, Ltd. Valerie LaMont and Joan Stora, who were brave enough to read a manuscript piecemeal. Cris Reay, my own "fail-safe system" for verifying historical facts, no matter how obscure. Geoffrey Arnott, Britain's best battlefield guide. Dr. Edwin McKnight, who generously acted as my "medical consultant" for Llewelyn Fawr's cerebrovascular accident. Linda Miller, for all the artistic inspiration. Dave O'Shea, whose evocative photographs of North Wales have gotten me through more bouts of writer's block than I care to count. And lastly, I would like to thank the staffs of the National Library of Wales, the British Library, the University College of North Wales Library, the research libraries of Evesham, Shrewsbury, and Bordeaux, the University of Pennsylvania Library, and a special expression of appreciation to the staff of the Caernarfon Archives for helping me to pinpoint the site of the battle fought near Bwlch Mawr in 1255.

HERE BE DRAGONS
introduced a world of darkness

FALLS THE SHADOW lit the way . . .

And then came **THE RECKONING**

*Don't miss Sharon Kay Penman's
dramatic Medieval trilogy*

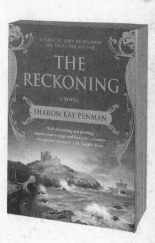

"Penman's characters are so shrewdly
imagined, so full of resonant human feeling
that they seem to breathe on the page."
— *SAN FRANCISCO CHRONICLE*

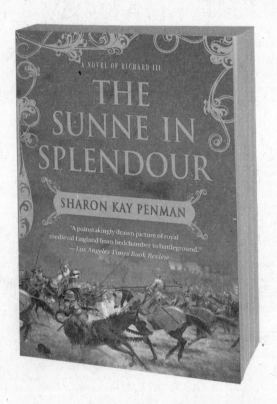